THE DYING SUN

L.J. Stanton

THE DYING SUN

BY L.J. STANTON

SWORD & BOARD LLC.

ISBN: 978-1-7347279-0-6 (Epub)
ISBN: 978-1-7347279-1-3 (Hardcover)
ISBN: 978-1-7347279-2-0 (Paperback)

Library of Congress Control Number: 2020907899

Front cover image by Nele Diel, https://www.artstation.com/nelediel
Book design by Larissa and Robert Stanton

Printed by IngramSpark, Inc. in the United States of America

First Printing, 2020

Sword and Board, LLC.
ljstanton@swordandboard.gg

Visit https://www.swordandboard.gg

To my long-suffering husband, Rob, and to Kiraiko, Kero, and Inwe.

L.J. Stanton

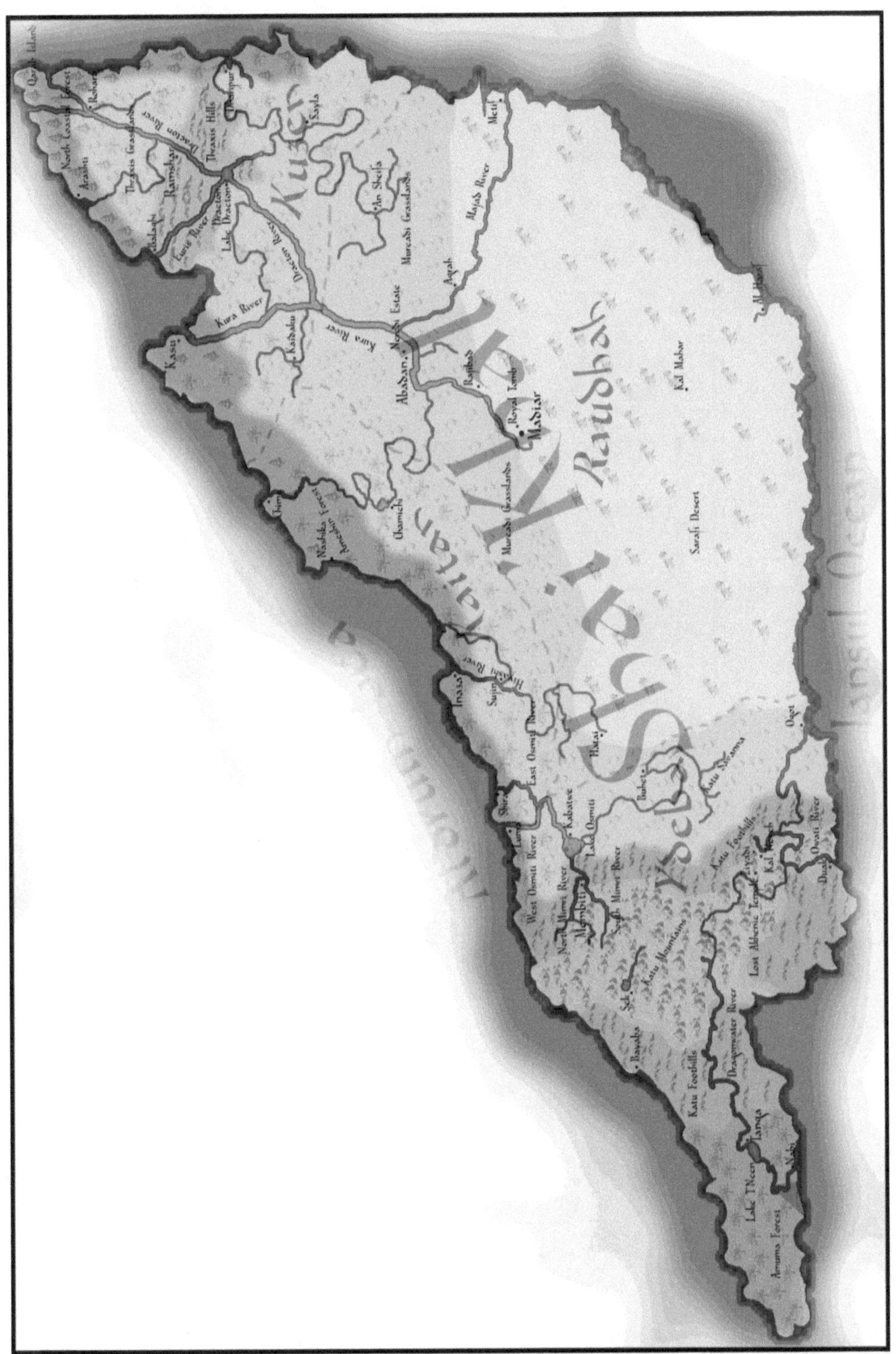

THE DYING SUN

PROLOGUE

Breathe, Ruya told herself. She clutched a thick tome to her chest and shut her eyes. Eerie silence washed over her. The room was rank with the familiar scent of decay. She'd sat at the deathbeds of hundreds, if not thousands, of people at this point in her life. A necessary duty of the high priestess of death.

But she'd never seen anything like this before. Bodies were sprawled all over the catacombs, easily a hundred people all piled haphazardly atop each other. She tried not to look at their faces as she walked over and around them. They weren't the first casualties of this war.

They wouldn't be the last.

She hesitated before she entered the last room in the catacombs. In the center was a large sandstone ossuary. The flickering light of a single torch sent shadows dancing across the pale walls. Ruya approached and pushed the stone lid halfway off. She placed the tome inside reverently. The lid slid shut with a final, echoing thud. Pale-green necrotic fog began to slip out of the crack between the lid and the ossuary itself.

"Was this really necessary?" Ruya asked herself.

"Yes."

The voice came from the shadows, and Ruya jumped. A tall creature emerged, human in all appearances but decidedly not. Ruya sighed in relief, then shivered. Her now-empty hands rubbed her arms from the cold.

"Kyran, I knew them. All of them." Ruya gestured toward the archway where a few of the corpses were visible. She didn't look. She didn't want to see their empty faces looking back at her. Ruya didn't trust her legs to support her if she did.

"Their sacrifice will be remembered." Kyran wiped blood off his pale hands onto his salwar. He approached Ruya and wrapped his arm around her with uncharacteristic warmth. Ruya took to it, leaning on him.

"Where is Tsillah?" Ruya asked, craning her neck behind him to see if she could make out the devata anywhere.

"She's exploring her new home," Kyran said. "We should leave." He glanced to the walls. The white stone was beginning to sprout black necrotic rot that grew rapidly outward like vines.

Ruya nodded. She had no desire to be here any longer. The curse would spread quickly and leave this place unsafe for anyone other than Tsillah. Kyran took Ruya's hand, leading her away from the ossuary. She carefully tiptoed around the bodies, following in Kyran's footsteps toward the light of the High Temple.

Back to the world of the living.

Back to the war.

CHAPTER 1

3RD OF DU'ITH, MONSOON SEASON, 902 UNIFIED AGE
KASU, KUZEN PROVINCE

The rain pounded on the goat-hair tent. A few drops leaked through thin patches in the canvas onto the ground. A Yahidah man hunched over his bedroll as he folded it methodically. Adrian was well accustomed to travel. His road-worn clothes covered him head to toe, and his kufiyah hid his curly black hair. The only attire that wasn't thinning from weeks of rough treatment was the black kameez Adrian had pulled on especially for today. Stitched on its breast was a silver scorpion. It would have attracted too much attention on the road, but today he hoped it would gain him unquestioned passage into Kasu.

"You ready, Maj?" Adrian turned and asked the gelding.

The horse ignored him, preferring to frantically pull out the last of the feed from the net. Yahidah tents were always large enough to house horses when the weather turned ill like this. Adrian tacked up Majdy quickly, leaving the feed net as the second-to-last item Adrian packed and tied behind the gelding's saddle. The last was the messenger satchel, its contents the reason for his journey. Adrian felt a lump form in his throat as he picked it up. He'd only felt this much dread over one other message. Last time, the fate of the Rising Sun Throne had hung in the balance. Now, Adrian worried there were even higher stakes. He couldn't imagine there was a good way for today to end. Hopefully the duqa's desmoterion would at least be out of the rain.

Adrian tossed the messenger satchel over the horn on Majdy's saddle, then led the gelding out into the rain. He turned around, raising a gloved hand as he did so. Adrian focused on the tent, ignoring the cold raindrops that slid through every nook and cranny onto his skin. Magic flowed from his fingertips, and the tent shuddered. Long poles bent, fabric folded, and the tent began to pack itself. A slight headache throbbed behind Adrian's eyes—the price to pay for even a small piece of magic. Once the tent lay on the ground in the mud, Adrian tied it to drag behind Majdy.

He left a cover over the saddle and began walking alongside the horse toward the road.

The rain didn't lessen throughout the day. By the afternoon, Adrian had swapped walking for riding. Creaking saddle leather punctuated every step closer to Kasu. The road was busy with small carts and wagons pulled by little Tsukarai ponies bringing wares to and from the port city.

All travelers gave Adrian a wide berth. A lone Yahidah normally raised suspicion along the coast, but it was the silver scorpion that earned mistrust and deference. The road turned, and the thick trees cleared to show the city's main gate. A crescendo of noise spilled over the gray stone walls. From the ramparts hung the banners of House Himoto, white with a black crab in the center. Guards at the gate wore black haoris over black-and-white hakamas. Two held long naginatas, while the others had thin katanas tied to their belts. They let most travelers slip through the city gates with little more than a scrutinizing glance. As Adrian approached, the naginatas were lowered. Water dripped from the bladed poles that now blocked the gate.

"What's your business in Kasu?" one guard asked. He walked up to Majdy and placed a hand on the gelding's bit.

Adrian pointed to the scorpion on his chest before digging into the messenger satchel. Carefully, so as to not soak the rest of the contents, he pulled out a small leather letter case. Stamped into the leather was a crown inside a sun, twin rearing horses on either side of it. The Madiaran House royal crest.

"The Shah sent me to deliver this to the duqa," Adrian explained. He made sure the guard could see the crest but held the leather letter case just out of reach. Even so, Adrian was quick to return it to the saddlebag. The guard frowned before he let go of Majdy's bit and gestured to the naginata-wielding guards. They rested their weapons, the Kasu gate open for passage once more.

Kasu was one of the largest trading ports along the Aldruin Sea. The smell of fish, ambergris, musk, spices, and wet wool filled the air. Adrian's trailing tent earned him glares as he rode through the main bazaar. In spite of the rain, the city bustled. Men pulled rickshaws quickly through the streets. Commoners hid under rain shades and navigated around puddles. Bamboo chimes rattled in the storm, adding an eerie undertone to the loud haggling of merchants.

As he approached the auction stage, he could see a crowd had gathered. Nearby merchants were silent. Majdy slowed, the gelding carefully picking his way through the people. Adrian looked to the auction stage. His lips turned downward in a grim frown. Swan-necked horses like Majdy were tied behind the stage, their riders standing atop the wooden structure. Not merchants, nor Kasu guards. Royal Guards. Their red achkans were dark from water and blood. Adrian had narrowly missed the worst of the scene. The executions were over; the guards had nailed the criminals to crossbeams.

The bodies wore the same uniforms as the Royal Guards, but their coats and salwar were open to reveal bloody stumps where their manhoods had been. Signs hung from their necks with their crimes: rape, murder, and extortion.

Adrian looked away and focused on the road. Five years ago, such crimes within the Royal Guard were commonplace. Corruption had been synonymous with the red achkan. But after Mansur's murder and Merikh's ascendance to the Rising Sun Throne, one of the first issues tackled by the young shah had been corruption within the royal court, the Akhenic Temple, and the Royal Guard. Merikh had simple expectations of those who wore Madiaran crimson: follow the laws they were meant to enforce. Punishments were swift and cruel when a guard failed to do so.

Adrian passed the stage quickly, riding under the red wooden archway into the garden of the Temple District. The Akhenic Temple had once controlled the district, but now Adrian saw small shrines alongside the road with strange statues he didn't recognize. Statues of men and women, always with animals. Devatas, the favored pets and spies of the Pantheon gods. Pantheon heresy had always held sway on the coastline within cities like Kasu and Inaza. The thick mists of the Aldruin were rife with myths and legends, steeped in ancient tales that the rest of Shai'Khal dismissed as children's stories. Djinnic temptations that the Faithful knew better than to truly indulge.

But three years ago, whispers of Pantheon priestesses had started. Women who could do truly remarkable feats of magic. One, a swordswoman with inhuman speed and strength. The other, a necromancer who could perform miracles. *Impossible* miracles, beyond what even the greatest sorcerers were capable of. The rumors were out of control, fueling the already tenuous situation within the Akhenic Temple. Most priests condemned the Pantheon cultists as heretics and apostates. Few seemed to agree on the correct course of action to deal with them. The Priest Council would have sent out and enforced a unified response—*if* they hadn't been gutted by the Shah's corruption crusade.

The Himoto Manor gate was guarded by three men and two large dogs with thick coats and curled tails. Matagi dogs, built for hunting boar and bears, were favored by the Tsukarai nobility for guarding their estates. The scorpion emblem on Adrian's chest was enough to get past them without issue. Servants dressed in subdued gray kimonos waited for him on the other side and quickly showed him to the barns. Out of the rain, Majdy let out a satisfied blow and shook the water off his coat. As Adrian dismounted, a groom immediately tried to shoo him away from Majdy.

"The duqa is expecting you," a servant explained without looking at him.

Adrian hesitated. In Madiar, it was unheard of to not look after one's own horse. Even the Shah tended to his mare after a long ride. The Tsukarai nobles didn't seem to indulge in the same custom. Adrian rubbed the gelding's neck. It would do more harm to keep the duqa waiting than to let someone else handle Majdy. He reached for the satchel and pulled the Shah's letters from it, clutching the leather case close to his chest as he moved to follow the servant.

Gravel crunched under his feet as they walked through the stone garden. A copse of cherry trees, a small creek, and a pond brought the well-groomed garden to life. They walked up a steep wooden bridge over the creek before reaching the main entrance of the manor. The door slid open, and a servant ushered Adrian inside and toward the tearoom. He followed quietly, wishing now that the duqa had been in less of a hurry to see him. Clean, *dry* clothes would have helped wick the chill from his bones.

The servant crouched down beside the tearoom door and slid it open gently. As he did so, a disconcerting wave of nausea crashed over Adrian, and he stumbled into the room. He bowed deeply, trying to hide his sudden clumsiness, but he'd been caught off guard. There were three women sitting lazily on the tatami-mat floor around a sunken hearth. Adrian recognized the duqa, who sat directly across from the door. He had seen her when she'd come to Madiar to swear fealty to Merikh five years ago.

Her reserved expression was helped by the white paint on her skin. A hookah hose rested against her black-and-white kimono, the hookah bubbling off to her left. The other two women, Adrian assumed, were the priestesses and the source of the nausea. He'd felt strong magic before, and at first, Adrian dismissed his reaction as road weariness. After all, he had adjusted years ago to cope with the overbearing pressure of the Shah's aura. A necromancer and an ice sorcerer, Merikh was the first sorcerer in centuries known to have more than one magic affinity, and his aura was deafening to the unadjusted.

But *this* was worse. It sent a shudder down Adrian's spine, disquieted his stomach, and left him with the uneasy feeling that he'd left something important unattended and forgotten.

The woman to the duqa's right was a Tsukarai like the duqa. She had no paint on her face and was dressed plainly in a gray kimono, like a servant. Her black hair hung loose around her narrow shoulders. Adrian shifted his focus to the other woman, whose brown eyes pierced him with a scrutinizing stare. Adrian barely gave the look a second thought, instead entranced by her hair—he'd never seen hair that red before. It was bright and vibrant, without the telltale stain of ocher. Her skin was even paler than the high priest's. The rumors were true—one of the priestesses was an Aegalian.

The Shah won't be pleased, Adrian thought. Duqa Sachiko's association with the priestesses was cause for concern in Madiar. Adding "foreigner" to the list of detractors of this priestess wouldn't help the situation. The duqa gestured for him to join them. He took a few steps toward the hearth but remained at a respectful distance. When he bowed his head, water dripped down from his kufiyah onto the bamboo.

"To what do I owe the pleasure of hosting the Shah's steward?" Duqa Sachiko asked softly. She picked up the metal teapot from the hearth and poured him a steaming cup. Jasmine mixed with the hookah's anise vapor, causing Adrian to forget her question. He hadn't had a cup of good tea in weeks.

"Sachiko, he's exhausted," the Tsukarai priestess said gently. "Let the poor boy have a moment to enjoy the tea a little."

Adrian shook his head. "Apologies, Duqa Sachiko, but who are these women?" Adrian asked, glancing between the priestesses innocently. It was always better to ask questions he already had the answers to when talking with nobles.

"I'm Ruya, high priestess of Ikharon, the god of death," the Tsukarai priestess said, introducing herself cheerfully. "The one glaring at you is Sarka, the champion of Livinja, the goddess of war."

"For gods' sake, Ruya, I'm not glaring," Sarka muttered before taking a sip of her tea.

Adrian cleared his throat and looked back to Duqa Sachiko. "Duqa, the Shahanshah sends his regards." Adrian put the leather letter case in front of him and untied the straps around it. There were two letters inside, one for the duqa and one for the priestesses. He wiped his gloves on the tatami mat in an effort to dry them a little before he carefully pried the letters apart. The first letter Adrian extended to the duqa. She cracked the seal carefully and unfolded the paper. As she read it, Adrian turned a little to face Ruya. He extended the second letter toward her.

"If you're the...priestess of death, then this is for you."

Unlike the letter to the duqa, this one looked old. The crisp paper was faded and browned. Black glyphs covered the edges. Ruya smiled warmly at him as she leaned forward to take the letter. Her dark eyes held his gaze.

"Ruya, be careful—" Sarka warned too late.

As Ruya's fingertips brushed the parchment, the letter exploded in necrotic fog.

CHAPTER 2

He expected corpses. Adrian had seen the Shah's magic at work before. The necrotic fog ate away at the body, aging it rapidly before decay set in. It was a painful, awful way to die. Adrian glanced down at his gloved hand—he still bore the scar from his first encounter with this curse. It had faded, but even after nine years, some of the age spots still looked as harsh as they had when Adrian first received them.

"The letter. Bring it here," Mansur ordered with a cavalier wave of his hand.

Adrian bowed his head, finished pouring the coffee, and placed the carafe on the coffee table. To his dismay, when he crossed the room to the desk, he found it covered in letters.

"Quickly now, boy. You should know better than to keep your shah waiting."

"He's never going to find the one you want," Merikh said tersely. The Shahzade's tone made Adrian determined to be correct on the first try. One letter looked well-traveled, its edges rough and browned. Adrian picked it up enthusiastically, assuming this was the letter the Shah wanted to show his son. A letter, perhaps, from one of the far-reaching provinces. That would explain the yellowing paper.

It exploded into pale-green fog. The pain was unbearable, shooting through his arm. Adrian's vision blurred, every joint in his body screaming in pain. He could hear shouting, but he couldn't focus on it through the pain. A hand clamped down on Adrian's shoulder.

"Akhenios, it hurts!" Adrian cried.

"Of course it does. You're dying." The Shahzade's tone was kinder now, although still laced with irritation. The fog disappeared, the pain lessened, and

when Adrian looked at his hands, he was astounded to see livered age spots and saggy skin reverting to what it had been before almost perfectly.

"Thank you! Great Prophet bless you, thank you!"

His adulation was met with a scoff. "The Great Prophet wouldn't have to bless me if the Shah would be more careful with my curses. Akhenios's sake, what if I hadn't been here?"

Adrian kept his eyes down to avoid the Shah's wrath. He flinched as he heard Mansur's fist slam into the Shahzade's face, and again as he heard Merikh retch. Adrian then picked Merikh's bloody teeth off the carpet and hurried after the Shahzade to the infirmary. The heir to the empire bore a blackening eye and a broken jaw. It was an exceedingly uncomfortable experience to watch the healers put the Shahzade's teeth back in and set his jaw.

"How charming! Your shah is stronger than I thought possible with Ikharon in exile."

The fog cleared as suddenly as it had appeared. A bright smile greeted Adrian. There was no decay in Ruya's lips, her skin unmarred by age. A quick glance at the other women proved the same to be true. Adrian's jaw nearly hit the floor.

How is that possible? He felt light-headed and reached for his tea. Adrian's fingers closed on air as he was knocked back onto the ground. The wind was gone from his lungs as he stared up at the pale ceiling. Sarka's foot was planted firmly on his chest. He felt a chill on his left breast and quickly put his hand over the scorpion emblem. Ice had begun to rise off the stitching, the protection enchantment coming to life, until Adrian forced it down. He didn't think his life was in danger. Not yet, at least.

"Charming? The Shah tried to *kill* us, Ruya!"

"Tried and failed. No harm done—except perhaps to that poor man's ribs! For mercy's sake, let him up!" Ruya waved off the other woman's comment as she examined the letter.

"Who are you?" Sarka demanded instead, relenting the pressure on his chest a little bit.

"Adrian Charmichi," he told her, coughing as he tried to get his breath back. "Ajir steward to the shah."

"Ajir?" Sarka shot the duqa a questioning look.

"The Shah's closest puppets," Duqa Sachiko answered. "They have long strings and ask no questions. Just do as they're ordered, regardless of the cost."

"I usually fetch coffee and deliver *normal* letters," Adrian admitted pointedly as he craned his neck to look at the duqa.

Sarka took her foot off his chest and sat back down. Ruya leaned over and helped Adrian sit up. He adjusted his kufiyah back in place, a few black curls of hair straying from behind the scarf. Adrian then gingerly touched his ribs, relieved when they didn't smart under his fingers.

"Well..." Ruya cleared her throat. "...by surviving this little test, we've earned an assumption of innocence."

"Innocence?" Sarka asked warily.

Ruya handed the letter to her.

"Someone tried to kill the Shah," the duqa clarified, "and laid the blame at our doorstep."

It had been a poor attempt. Adrian wasn't entirely convinced that the Shah had even been the intended victim. Anyone in Madiar worth their salt knew at least a few of the Shah's eccentricities. A decent assassin would have known Merikh didn't drink alcohol. But the poisoned wine *did* kill a vizier.

"The man claimed to do it to benefit the Pantheon, to remove a descendant of the Great Prophet from the throne," Adrian offered.

"Blame us, force the Shah to 'deal' with the Pantheon. Sounds like a gift to the high priest," Sarka scoffed as she crumpled the letter in her hand. It burst into flame, and Sarka brushed the ashes off into the inset stone hearth between them.

Ruya laughed. "Well, I suppose it was terribly rude of us not to die, then. Would have made life much easier for Merikh."

Sarka nodded, a twitch of a smile breaking her serious expression. Adrian picked the small porcelain teacup up off the bamboo mat. The tea no longer steamed. He cupped his hand under the bottom of the teacup and focused on his magic. A small flame appeared, hovering in the gap between the cup and his hand. As steam began to rise, the flame disappeared. The duqa fidgeted with her letter from the Shah, unfolding it and then folding it closed again.

"Sachiko?" Ruya asked.

"There's been an increase of Royal Guards in Kasu. Fresh guards from Madiar. I've seen them replacing the old ones—or purging them. Amir Navin insists the Shah is simply increasing patrols throughout Shai'Khal, but my legate in Madiar claims otherwise." The duqa took a deep breath from her hookah. The vapor that followed hung in the air, gently wafting and turning over in the warm air above the hearth.

"I assure—" Adrian started.

"Your assurances are worth less than smoke, Ajir. The Shah had every intention for that curse to kill me too, not just the priestesses, didn't he?"

Adrian downed the last of his tea. So much for a comfortable place to sleep. It seemed as though a visit to the duqa's desmoterion might be in order after all. He tried to choose his next words carefully.

"If the three of you had died, then justice would be done. It would have proved your heresies false and given more credence to the claims from the would-be assassin. But you're not dead." Adrian shrugged. "The Shah requests the priestesses come with me to Madiar. You are free to return to your business, Duqa Sachiko, with the full faith, confidence, and support of the Shah."

"How *dare* he!" Duqa Sachiko snapped, twisting the letter in her hand. It crinkled loudly. "My family has always been loyal! We were among the first to throw our support behind Shah Merikh after Mansur's murder!"

Her indignation was met with silence. Adrian bit his lip and looked down at the tatami. Nothing she said was untrue. House Himoto was an ancient ally of House Madiaran. But her support of the Pantheon cult had forced the Shah's hand. Backing these women had given them access and support that had spread their religious views throughout Kuzen. Sachiko was the reason these women had gone from an annoyance for the amir to a thorn in the Shah's side. The duqa had brought this upon herself.

"What if we refuse your shah's invitation?" Sarka asked, crossing her arms.

"I wouldn't recommend it," Adrian said flatly. *Akhenios be kind, don't make this difficult.* If they refused, Adrian was certain that the Shah would personally see to Kasu's siege and the prolonged death of these women. A gentle hand on his shoulder pulled Adrian from his prayer. Ruya smiled at him. Her hand felt warm through his wet clothes.

"Sachiko has seen to a room for you. I'd like speak with Sarka alone."

Ruya's suggestion left no room for protest. The weary ache in his bones made Adrian more than happy to comply. The tatami rasped under his feet as he stood and walked from the room. A servant on the other side of the door led him down the hallway to a small guest room.

The room was sparsely furnished. A low Tsukarai-style bed sat beside the outer wall. A silk privacy screen was set not far from it, shielding a stack of enchanted heated stones. Hung above the stones were the rest of his wet clothes, as his bags had been unpacked for him. A clean gray kimono hung from the privacy screen, compliments of the duqa.

"Thank you," Adrian said, dismissing his escort.

The door slid shut behind Adrian, and he began to peel off his wet clothes. The silk kimono took him a few attempts to tie. Adrian was certain he hadn't done it correctly by the time it was good enough to stay in place. While the bed called to him, Adrian crossed the room to his saddlebags instead.

Within was another leather pouch. Adrian carefully untied it. He pulled a clean, dry piece of paper, an inkwell, and a quill from it. The Shah would want a report. Adrian dipped the quill in ink, then smoothed the paper on the floor.

Adrian hesitated. Where to begin? He rubbed his chest, his ribs still sore. *Champion of war. Well, she plays the part,* Adrian thought. They both did. He'd never seen magic like that. Nothing that strong. Ruya hadn't even appeared fatigued, whereas after the Shah had set the curse on the letter, Adrian had helped him to bed. No one should have been able to undo that curse. That had been the point. Ruya's magic simply wasn't possible.

Is he going to thank me for telling him so? Is he even going to believe me? Adrian put the quill down. No, the Shah probably wouldn't believe him. He would read the report and assume Adrian was road weary and hyperbolic at best. At worst, that Adrian was compromised and spewing Pantheon propaganda. Adrian rubbed his eyes. He *was* tired, and he still didn't have an answer from the priestesses as to whether they'd be coming to Madiar, willingly or not.

The letter could wait.

Morning fog from the Aldruin had yet to clear when Adrian roused himself from Himoto Manor. The gate clacked shut behind him as Adrian left. The guards gave him free rein of the city, though Adrian had no intention of wandering past the Temple District.

It was eerily quiet. Even the sound of his riding boots on the gravel seemed muted. The Tsukarai believed the mists carried monsters, good and evil creatures that could affect the fortunes of those who crossed their paths. Any self-respecting Yahidah threw such superstitious talk aside. The Akhenic Temple categorically dismissed such creatures as myths, pure and simple. The mist was simply mist. There was nothing to fear from it.

The red-and-black Akhenic Temple slowly took form. It was a looming, impressive monument to Akhenios. As he approached, Adrian could see it had seen better days. Scorch marks scarred the wooden columns. Slander and blasphemies were carved into the paint. The steps were broken and the door hung ajar. Adrian put his hand on it gently, pushing it the rest of the way open.

Inside the temple didn't fare any better. It had been abandoned; Adrian could see the cobwebs between columns and over the broken remains of Akhenios's statues. He carefully picked a path between pieces of rubble toward a smaller statue. It had been knocked over, the hawk on Akhenios's shoulder smashed to pieces on the ground. Adrian reverently lifted the statue back onto its stand.

Why do you allow this? Adrian wanted to ask. Not that Akhenios answered his prayers. The god didn't seem to interfere in the affairs of mortals. Akhenios kept His hand out of the course of the world. He'd given the Akhenic Scrolls to the Great Prophet, and now it was up to His people to follow them. Adrian didn't expect exceptions to be made for him.

Adrian turned away from the statue and sat down on one of the few remaining benches that hadn't been burned or smashed. The hatred and anger that had been brewing for decades toward the Akhenic Temple was now fully unleashed. The last high priest, Idowu, and Mansur had both been corrupt representatives of Akhenios, enough to sour the faith for many citizens of Shai'Khal.

"Are you always greeted so warmly wherever you go? Or are you simply disliked in Kasu?"

Adrian jumped to his feet and turned to the door. Ruya was silhouetted by what little morning light had burned through the mists. She stepped carefully through the rubble, the sound of her wooden sandals echoing off the stone walls. The long sleeves of her brown kimono gathered dust from the rubble. She hardly looked like a priestess, but she no longer looked like a servant. Ruya gestured back to the bench, and Adrian sat down. She followed suit.

"Sarka has a great many things to say about you and your shah. A great many worries about the sort of reception we'll receive in Madiar." Ruya didn't look at him as she spoke. Instead her eyes wandered over the temple.

"You'll come, then?" Adrian asked, relief crashing over him.

"Of course! Who are we to refuse the summons of the *Shahanshah*?" Ruya asked, not bothering to hide her amusement.

"What are you?" Adrian blurted out and immediately winced in regret. He had better manners than that.

Ruya laughed kindly. "We are simply servants of forgotten gods and goddesses who are ready to return to the world."

"Why now? Why not a hundred years ago? Or five hundred from now? How am I supposed to believe you're anything more than a sorceress?" Adrian demanded earnestly.

He didn't believe her, not one word. Ruya and her companion might be deluded into thinking they were the priestesses of gods, but Adrian didn't see it. The fact that she had repelled the Shah's magic was impressive—and horrifying—but it wasn't divine. Piety and magic could make for grand delusions. These women were simply buying into their own propaganda.

"Sarka and I have a plan, one I'd prefer not to deviate from, if possible. And why not now?" Ruya asked with a coy smile.

"That doesn't answer my question at all," Adrian pointed out. He was used to his superiors using double-talk and maneuvering around questions. Nobles were incapable of answering anything plainly.

"You never answered mine either. I come here every morning. Normally I have a long line of dying seeking comforting words and a candle or two lit to Ikharon. Today, only you. I can't blame that entirely on the mist."

Adrian tapped the scorpion embroidered on his breast. "Common people fear the Ajir. I don't blame them—if you see one of us away from the Shah, there's probably bad news following. And as far as the duqa…" Adrian shrugged. "I'm common born, and the Shah trusts me. That rubs people the wrong way. Well, that and the poison letters." Adrian returned Ruya's infectious smile.

The woman shook her head. "I would argue it's a smart leader who raises an adviser from the lowest born to a seat at his table. Helps to keep him in touch with the common people."

Adrian's smile began to fade. "I don't think I do much to ground him, bayan. But it's a comforting idea, isn't it?"

"That's what I'm here for," Ruya said, waving her hand in a vague gesture to the temple around them.

Adrian frowned. "It's not just me keeping the people at bay. They think some monster is going to snatch them out of the mists if they leave the safety of their homes. Destroying the bastion of faith hardly helps those rumors."

Adrian watched Ruya's smile slowly disappear.

"We had no part of this, I assure you," Ruya said.

"Didn't you? They're your followers."

Ruya's smile flickered back to life. "See? You must do a better job of keeping Merikh aware of the fragility of his position than you think."

More games. Adrian shook his head.

"Tell me, Adrian, what sort of reception will we receive in Madiar?" Ruya asked. "That letter wasn't the warmest summons we've ever received. Not the coldest either, sadly."

Adrian scoffed. "It won't get any warmer. There won't be a parade. If anything, it'll be as plain a welcome as possible until you're within the palace complex. Then…" Adrian hesitated. Who knew? "The Shah won't be pleased to know how easily you shrugged off that curse."

Ruya laughed. "Mortal men and their delicate egos. I mastered that curse over a thousand years ago. Perhaps Merikh will let me teach him a thing or two."

"Perhaps." It wouldn't be the first time a defeat had been turned into a chance for discovery.

"I hear your master isn't an ardent follower of Akhenios." Ruya's tone was a little more careful now, more measured as she tread into territory she'd undoubtedly heard plenty of rumors about.

"The Shah is the head of government and enforcer of law and order," Adrian said. "He leaves religion to the Temple. As far as his personal beliefs, I'm hardly at liberty to pass them along."

"Ah. So no, he's not a champion of the faith. Heartening. That would have made this much harder."

"What do you want from him?"

"We need his help." Her answer was quick and earnest.

Adrian shook his head. "Help with that plan you don't want to deviate from?"

"Exactly."

"A plan you won't be enlightening me on at any point?"

Ruya smiled and shook her head. They sat in silence; the heavy atmosphere of the Temple held a somber tone.

"I think I'll speak with Sachiko about restoring this place," Ruya said as she stood. "You're right. It's a shame what's happened here."

The casual way she referred to the duqa spurred a thought in Adrian. "A word of advice, bayan?" Adrian offered. "You'll have to remember to call him the Shahanshah. He is the master of an empire, after all."

Ruya shrugged. "Perhaps. But I like the way 'Merikh' falls off the tongue," she said with a playful wink.

Adrian bit his lip and said nothing. He watched Ruya retreat from the temple and leave him alone once again.

Great Prophet, guide me, Adrian prayed. Ruya didn't seem to grasp the seriousness or tenuousness of her situation. He could only pray that by the time they reached Madiar, her tone would change.

CHAPTER 3

5th of Amanith, Monsoon Season, 902 Unified Age
Madiar, Raudhah Province

The monsoon rains parted with the morning sun, leaving Madiar deceptively clean in its warm glow. Minarets and towers capped in bronze and gold reflected the sunlight, a rare sight in this season. Clouds had already formed to the north, and the wind carried the sharp scent of rain. The city would have only a few hours of reprieve. Merikh intended to put those hours to proper use.

Horses pawed impatiently at their stall doors, nickering at the stablehands as the men and women meticulously portioned out the animals' breakfasts. The hands ignored Merikh, as he stuck to the far edge of the aisle, out of their way. Outside of the barns, he was their shah. Inside, head trainer Sumiya was god, and even Merikh was subject to the ornery seventy-year-old woman's wrath. At the end of the aisle was a tall enchanted slate board that had the day's schedule written on it with riders' assigned horses and turnout schedules. Only here did Merikh pull rank. He took three horses for himself: Zahira, Iksandar, and Remahdi.

"Shahanshah?" One of Sumiya's trainers approached, bowing his head briefly. "Sumiya is cranky about the footing. She's asked for you to take care of it."

"Asked?" Merikh sounded skeptical, and the trainer appeared flustered for a moment. Merikh waved him off. Sumiya hadn't asked. She'd probably grumbled for the last half hour about how little she could get done until Merikh deigned to show his face and fix the problem.

The arenas were flooded from the rain. The sand was dark and slick with puddles in the few hoofprints that hadn't washed away. Merikh stood outside the main arena, centered his magic, and focused on the water. The temperature fell. Water rose out of the sand in each of the half dozen riding arenas. The water collided in the air, creating massive orbs of ice above the arenas. When the sand was dry, the orbs broke into small pieces and scattered into the nearby water troughs and wells. Merikh stifled a yawn with his hand before returning to the barn to fetch his first horse.

Remahdi was a dainty mare and looked almost comically small with Merikh. Long limbed and tall, Merikh could almost wrap his legs around her barrel. She'd never cut it as one of his regular mounts, but the mare had twice as much heart as Iksandar and more attitude than Zahira. She put Merikh through his paces without fail, and he'd eaten more sand from her than any other horse.

But today she behaved surprisingly well, despite the wind picking up. By the time she tired, her coat was dark and slick with sweat. Somehow she still managed to find the energy to spook at a training flag at the opposite end of the arena.

Merikh brought Remahdi to the arena's center. He set himself deeper into the saddle, and the mare stopped firmly. As much as he tried to keep the barn a retreat from politics, it never failed to follow him here. Merikh glanced toward the gate and gestured for the bald elderly man on the other side to enter.

Grand Vizier Nikias dressed plainly, a simple brown kaftan only a few shades darker than his Yahidah skin. He barely dressed better than the servants, although no one would mistake him for one. Like Sumiya, Nikias was among the eldest of the palace staff and had served under Merikh's father. He knew more secrets about the palace, Madiar, and Shai'Khal than anyone else. He was a man not to be underestimated, even in his plainness.

"What is it?" Merikh asked as Nikias approached and stood by the mare's shoulder.

"I just received word from the city guards, Shahanshah. There's a large caravan from the northern camel road. Considering Adrian's letter yesterday..."

"Our *dear* guests have arrived." Merikh looked back down at the mare with a small frown. Working Zahira and Iksandar would have to wait.

Nikias took a step away from the mare as Merikh dismounted. Merikh gave Remahdi a rub on the neck before quickly untacking her. The moment the bit left her lips, she tossed her head, trotted a few feet away, and dropped into the sand with a happy groan. He smiled and shook his head. There were few things less dignified and more awkward than a horse rolling.

While Remahdi rolled, a small block of ice formed in Merikh's free hand. As it melted, he cleaned the slobber and pieces of hay that had stuck to the bit. Merikh dried it on his white kameez, the shirt already covered in dirt from the mare, then collected the saddle and blanket. Nikias walked beside him as he carried the tack from the arena. The shorter vizier struggled to keep pace in the deep sand. With a glance from Merikh, the gate opened ahead of them and shut behind them.

"Go. Make sure the guards are fully prepared," Merikh said, dismissing Nikias.

The old man bowed and headed back through the barn to the white marble stairs leading up to the palace. Without the grand vizier at his side, it would have been easy to mistake Merikh for one of the grooms. He dressed plainly and practically for the barn. The signet ring on his hand and his gold eyes were the only hints at his station.

When Merikh returned to the arena, the mare was waiting patiently at the gate. Sand covered her body and wicked off the sweat. Remahdi looked quite pleased with herself. As he haltered her, Merikh heard the groan of the palace gates. A moment later, grooms were jogging horses to ties. Their pale-yellow blankets all bore the same sigil—a diamond with a sun inside. The Akhenic Sun, which meant High Priest Alcaeus had just arrived and was being ushered into the palace. Undoubtedly the Temple guards, the Order of the Onyx Swords, had spotted the caravan from the temple minarets and had guessed their purpose.

Merikh walked Remahdi the long way around to the barn. He checked her chest occasionally to make sure she had cooled down before they made their way back to her paddock turnout. With the thin halter hung in place, Merikh went back into the palace through the barracks. His presence was largely ignored by the officers; they gave short salutes and then simply went on their way.

The barracks gave way to the arched corridors of the palace proper. Merikh turned to the wall beside him. It appeared, at first glance, the same as any. White marble covered with intricate vine-like calligraphic designs in shimmering hues. But as Merikh approached, the wall opened ahead of him to reveal the servant corridor that would eventually connect to the royal suite. Just because Alcaeus was here didn't mean Merikh had any desire to see him promptly. These hidden paths ensured Merikh never ran into any priest or noble he was unprepared to speak to. He wanted time alone with these cult leaders before Alcaeus was given an audience—*if* the high priest was given one at all. Merikh had let Alcaeus abuse enough of his time since coronation. The man wrote an insufferable number of essays and letters, hoping for a close working relationship with the Crown. Today, the man would wait.

Once inside the royal suite, Merikh changed out of his riding clothes into something a bit more fitting of the meeting to come. The red achkan coat over the black salwar kameez looked similar to his dress uniform, though it lacked the lavish accoutrements. Merikh splashed water on his face and scrubbed off the dust and dirt from the barns. He'd shaved earlier in the morning, and he was ever grateful he hadn't inherited his father's propensity for a quick-growing beard. Anything to look less like Mansur. His father had always kept a well-groomed beard and short cropped hair. Naturally, Merikh was clean shaven, and his hair was just long enough to require tying back when he trained with the swordmaster.

As Merikh finished cleaning up, he felt someone approaching the door. Growing up, sensing the souls of those around him had been deafening. When his necromancy had first manifested itself, the overwhelming pressure had forced Merikh into seclusion for weeks, until a tutor could be found. Well, the pressure *and* the ghosts. Mansur had simply thought him insane—six years old and mad. Necromancy was rare and taboo. For it to manifest in the Shahzade…well, insanity had been preferable for Mansur. It had been one of Merikh's many unforgivable disappointments.

Merikh glanced at the door and focused on the handle, and it opened quickly ahead of the soul. A guard stood on the other side and bowed.

"Shahanshah, the high—"

"Alcaeus is here," Merikh interrupted. "See him to the Oleander Pavilion and have the grand vizier speak with him to keep him busy."

"Yes, sire. There's another ma—"

"There's a caravan of cultists with Adrian and the priestesses. Have the cultists housed somewhere in the Hock District, and have Adrian and the priestesses brought here."

"As you command," the guard said, bowing his head and turning to leave.

"Under no circumstances is Alcaeus permitted to have any contact with them," Merikh added.

The guard nodded. As the door shut, Merikh crossed the room to his desk. Nikias had left a stack of paperwork on it earlier. Treasury accounts, crime reports, petitions—Merikh preferred a hands-on approach to his empire. Mansur had dumped these responsibilities on Merikh as a teenager, and he had no desire to pawn them off now. It made for long days, short nights, and more headaches than perhaps previous shahs had ever cared to deal with. At the end of his reign, Merikh wanted the satisfaction of knowing he had personally reshaped Shai'Khal in his image. There would be nothing left of Mansur's hedonistic corruption, nor his grandfather Kurush's despotic bloodshed.

A chill shuddered down Merikh's spine, surprising him. He had never felt magic like that before. No auras had ever pressed so strongly against his own, especially at such a distance! The only souls Merikh could feel were the guards at the end of the corridor—men who had been standing there for some time. It was several minutes before Merikh grew used to the uncomfortable pressure. A few minutes more before the sources appeared.

Merikh glanced at the door. It opened ahead of the Ajir steward. Adrian stepped inside the royal suite and bowed deeply. The two women behind him merely bowed their heads. The redheaded woman's gesture was stiff and forced. A Tsukarai and an Aegalian woman. Merikh kept his disappointment hidden. A half-Aegalian bastard leading the Akhenic Temple was bad enough. A full-blooded Aegalian champion of war was an ill omen.

"Shahanshah, may I present Ruya, high priestess of Ikharon, and Sarka, champion of Livinja," Adrian said as he gestured to each woman. For having spent two months on the road, Adrian looked remarkably well. Despite the Ajir steward's faith, traveling with these cultists did not appear to have drained him.

"Fetch some coffee, Adrian, then retire. I'm sure there's a young man excited to hear of your return," Merikh ordered.

A tired smile grew on Adrian's face before he bowed and quickly left. Abandoning the paperwork, Merikh gestured to the low coffee table in the center of the room. Ruya grinned brightly and promptly sat down across from Merikh. Sarka remained standing. He could see her gaze darting about the room, counting exits and looking for probable hidden doors. Healthy paranoia for a self-proclaimed champion of war.

When Sarka deigned to join them, the three sat in silence. Their magic was no less overwhelming in person. It had been a long time since Merikh had felt so distracted by other sorcerers. By adulthood, Merikh's aura had surpassed that of even his tutors. He was impressed despite feeling threatened.

"Your letter was intriguing," Ruya said, breaking the silence as she clasped her hands together and rested them on her lap.

"'Intriguing' is a gross overstatement, I'm sure," Merikh said, "but it did the job."

Did the job? Sarka scoffed. "You sent a cursed letter in response to the *implication* we tried to have you killed. Now you invite us to your...private residence." She gestured to the room around them. "No viziers, no nobles, no servants. Only two guards, what, fifty feet down the hall? You're taking an exceptional risk meeting us this way. Why?"

"Calculated risks are a necessity, wouldn't you agree? I am now quite confident that if either of you wished to end my life, you would do so regardless of any obstacles put in your way. I prefer not to use the Ajir as senseless fodder."

Truthfully, Merikh refused to give these women a public audience. Too many ears hearing a message he didn't know if he approved of yet. Was that part of what offended her so?

"You might note we *haven't* tried to kill you," Sarka told him bluntly. "A courtesy *you* didn't extend."

"Sarka, please," Ruya said through gritted teeth, shooting a steely glare at her companion. "We've been out of the world far too long. All we're looking to achieve is a means to stay and bring our masters out of exile."

"You mean gods," Merikh corrected, his tone disbelieving.

Ruya smiled. "Yes."

Her voice was genuine, almost childlike. Merikh held back a scoff and merely glanced to the door. He could feel Adrian's soul approaching. The door opened, and Adrian entered carrying a tray with a gold-plated carafe and matching cups. The room quieted as the Ajir steward poured the coffee. Adrian tried to hand Merikh a cup, but Merikh gestured to the table.

"I don't want anything," Sarka muttered.

Merikh wondered if she was simply paranoid or discourteous. Ruya, on the other hand, smiled and graciously took the coffee from Adrian. She thanked him quietly before Adrian bowed and left. Ikharon's priestess took a long sip from her cup. She smiled, shut her eyes, and leaned into the plush back of her seat. Merikh hid his amusement behind a stoic mask. It was good coffee, naturally, but he'd never seen it get that reaction before. Plying someone with coffee was far cheaper than doing so with good wine or araq. He'd keep it in mind for future dealings with the priestess.

"I don't think I've ever had this before," Ruya commented excitedly once she opened her eyes and came back to the world. She offered her cup to Sarka, but the other woman waved it off. Ruya shook her head and put the coffee down on the table before she looked back to Merikh.

"I do understand how impossible what we preach sounds. Gods trapped on islands in the Aldruin mist for nearly a thousand years. But surely you've been to your own coastline? You know that mist isn't natural. It never leaves. What weather is unchanging with the seasons?" Ruya asked. "A necromancer such as yourself can no doubt feel there is an unnatural block in the way of your magic. Akhenios keeps the gods away from Aljemel, locks it away from the living completely. You will never reach your full potential while Ikharon is trapped. Magic itself will remain stunted until the gods are free."

Her words rang with uncomfortable truths. The mists weren't natural. Merikh had felt that during his year-long patrol with the Royal Guard as the Shahzade. The mists were unnerving, confounding, with a strong magical aura all their own. His tutors had explained the mists away as simply a natural well of magic, although the fact no one had ever found a way to tap into it made Merikh skeptical.

As far as Alhanem and Aljemel were concerned, again, Merikh saw truth in her words. Breaking the barrier into Alhanem was difficult. It was a dangerous necessity for necromancy, the ability to break into the prison for eternally condemned souls and the home of djinns. Aljemel, on the other hand, the eternal utopia, was completely off limits and unattainable.

Merikh reached for his coffee, buying time to think, when Ruya grabbed his wrist. His head exploded in pain, white hot and blinding. Just as suddenly as it came, it left, and Merikh could see again.

But the world had changed.

He was alone. Alabaster stone columns supported a domed ceiling. An altar sat across from him.

The High Temple, Merikh realized. Banners hung from the columns, dozens of sigils alongside the Akhenic Sun. In front of each sigil were tall statues of men, women, and creatures not quite human or monster. The Pantheon.

Merikh stepped up to the altar, an impulse disturbingly not his own. Behind it was a door and he— No, not a him. These hands were small, delicate, far paler than his.

Ruya's hands, Merikh thought. These were her memories. The door opened beneath her touch, leading to a stairwell. In her other hand was a large black leather tome.

Nausea crashed over Merikh. The world blurred and changed. A shred of worry pushed through from Ruya's own thoughts. She hadn't meant for him to see so much. Now she took him somewhere else, somewhere wholly unfamiliar to him. Fog overwhelmed the scene, pale gray and piercingly cold. He'd never felt cold like this. As an ice sorcerer, he was almost immune to a chill. But this cold clung to him, soaked into his bones, and stayed. Black volcanic rocks pierced the mist, and the longer Merikh looked, the more he could see.

An old man towered over him. His piercing blue eyes and cold features matched a statue in the temple. The overwhelming pressure of the man's aura left little doubt in Merikh's mind that the man beside him was no mortal. Merikh had only felt this sort of power once before in his life, when his necromancy tutor had accidentally summoned a djinn. Merikh was suddenly confident of Ruya's ability to tear his soul from his body with a look. He was equally confident that whatever this creature who claimed godhood was, it could do the same to Ruya with even less effort.

Ikharon. The thought came from Ruya intrusively, and Merikh didn't doubt it.

There was movement in the mists. The valley below them was full of creatures of myth, impossible creatures from the stories Nikias had told Merikh as a child. Pale dogs the size of ponies, hairless and covered in spines, snarled at the shambling corpses of mortohas. Red-eyed leopards disappeared into the mists and reappeared on the opposite side of the valley whenever they wished. Within the center, regarded warily by the rest of the creatures, were creatures of unnatural beauty. Rakshasas. Undead blood drinkers that could hide in humanoid form.

The world blurred again, but when it came back into focus, they hadn't gone anywhere. Ikharon was no longer beside him. The valley below was nearly empty, save for a few driftwood shelters built by the rakshasas. The creatures were barely recognizable. Their features were drawn, and their skin had taken on a sick translucent quality. Long fangs had destroyed their lips, leaving a perpetual snarl on mangled faces. All were thin and feral. The nausea began to subside, replaced by a strong ache of homesickness from Ruya. Merikh latched on to the vulnerability and pushed back. In myth, Ikharon had carried a grimoire of untold power. If that was true...

Shadows replaced fog. They were in the catacombs underneath the High Temple. Ruya pushed the lid from an ossuary in front of them and placed the black tome within. Surprise and fear replaced Ruya's homesickness. She'd underestimated Merikh.

A splitting headache hit him. The world went black. He could feel Ruya's panic. And then the warmth of her hand on his wrist grew cold.

He could smell blood.

A whip cracked.

Ruya pulled Merikh from the memory. The royal suite snapped into focus. Merikh looked down at his arm when she let go of it. Ruya tapped her hand on the table, thudding it once. The sound surprised Merikh, still reeling from the assault on his senses. His hand went to his belt, and moments later, his khanjar dagger plunged through her hand, the curved blade hooking into the table. Merikh let go of the dagger as Ruya shrieked in pain. Ice wrapped in necrotic fog formed in the palms of his hands as he stood.

Sarka's sword was at his neck.

CHAPTER 4

Merikh's pulse raced. It pounded in his ears. He hadn't been this out of control in years. The cold from Sarka's blade brought clarity. He hadn't even seen her *move*. She'd been seated on the other side of the table. Now she stood at his side. The ice disappeared from his hand as the chill began to recede from the air.

"Sarka...let's...just take a step back," Ruya muttered through gritted teeth. "Can you...get me a bandage?" She inhaled sharply.

Sarka sheathed her blade, glaring daggers at Merikh as she did so. She hurried around to the other side of the table and began digging through the pack she'd brought with her. Merikh sat down and took a deep, unsteady breath. His mind was still reeling as he got his bearings. He was back in the royal suite. The blood and the whip were long gone. Merikh's mind was his own again.

Once Sarka had the bandage ready, Merikh pulled the dagger out of Ruya's hand. The high priestess hissed through her teeth as the blade moved, and Sarka wrapped Ruya's hand deftly. The white bandage quickly turned red. Merikh glanced at the wall by the door. There was a row of bells with strings that led into the wall. Each bell had a name, and with a look, Merikh rang the one labeled infirmary.

"Thank you," Ruya said, cradling her hand and sighing. "I didn't mean to startle you, Merikh."

"If you do that again, I'll cut you apart," Merikh promised. Even if he couldn't kill her, she could bleed, and she felt pain. That was enough. He still felt unsteady, the chill from her memory clinging to his bones.

"What makes you think you'd get another chance?" Sarka's hand was near her hilt again, but Ruya shook her head and gestured for Sarka to sit down.

"I'll never need to do that again," Ruya said. "Now you know the truth."

Merikh finally managed a sip of his coffee. The warmth helped balm him, though his heart was still racing. The ease with which she'd broken through his barriers shouldn't have been possible. She'd made him feel like a *child* again. A sorcerer required mental discipline to master any strong magic, and protecting one's mind from outside influence was among the first things a young sorcerer had to master. Without it, they'd never have enough self-control to work magic within their limits. To have Ruya force her way into his mind as easily as if he'd opened the door and invited her in? The violation left him reeling. But it wasn't all for naught.

Ruya had been honest with her memory. She was whole-heartedly convinced that she was the high priestess of Ikharon and over nine hundred years old. That she had been trapped on an island for centuries with her god.

"What exactly do you need?" Merikh asked carefully as he put the coffee down.

"Akhenios's strength is waning," Ruya told him. "That's the only reason we were able to leave Aldruin in the first place. Our mission is to convert any we can, but more importantly, find and destroy the Akhenic Key, the device Akhenios is using to imprison our gods."

Souls approached from down the hallway, and Merikh opened the door ahead of them. A healer walked in with a servant. Merikh gestured to Ruya's hand. Silence overtook the room as the servant laid out supplies for the healer, and the woman proceeded to carefully unwrap the bloody bandage. As the healer worked, Merikh mulled over what Ruya's request would entail.

Request. As if I have a choice, Merikh thought. There was unrest brewing throughout Shai'Khal because of these women. Pantheon cultists and Akhenic Faithful were already devolving into violence in some cities. In others, Akhenic temples had been vandalized and overrun by cultists. The mission these women were on would not simply stop if Merikh declined their proposition. Now he saw assassins he couldn't beat sitting across from him. They would place another puppet on the throne if he refused them. Merikh could feel the efforts of the past few years unraveling before him. He'd attempted to repair the damage his father's neglect had done, the disunity it had sown between the provinces. Merikh had managed to avoid all-out war when he'd taken the throne. Now the only way before him was paved in blood.

Once Ruya's hand was cared for and the healer gone, Merikh continued.

"You're asking for my support to paint Akhenios as the villain in the Unification War."

"He *is*," Sarka said forcefully. "He took everything for himself and imprisoned the rest of the gods. His own sister is among them!"

"Is that the story you've used to build up your following on the coast?" Merikh asked coldly.

"No," Ruya answered. "Akhenios was undeniably greedy. But it can't have gone according to plan since he no longer appears to walk among you. We do not seek to put an end to the Akhenic Temple. Akhenios is a god. I want ours to be recognized alongside him. For the people to be allowed to worship them. For all of us to finally be *free*."

"You want to rewrite the foundations that this empire—*my* empire— was built upon," Merikh corrected her. Shai'Khal had once been split into four countries, and the Great Prophet of Akhenios had brought them all to heel. If it weren't for the Great Prophet, the Yahidah would still be nomadic horsemen skirmishing with Umbeah at the Ydeban border, the Tsukarai providing weapons and supplies to both sides as long as neither stepped foot in their territories. To paint the Great Prophet as anything *but* the Unifier of Shai'Khal would give fodder to secessionist movements.

"I don't want to rewrite history, Merikh," Ruya corrected with a gentle smile, "I want to augment it and make it correct. We don't want to destroy everything achieved in the past nine hundred years; Shai'Khal has become so much more than what it was."

"Do you understand why? We stopped waiting at the feet of so-called 'gods' to fix our problems. We wiped superstition away with truth. The Scrolls call your gods djinns."

"Did Ikharon *feel* like a djinn?" Ruya asked.

Merikh frowned. No, the man in her memory had not oozed with the pervading corruption of djinnic magic. He was a powerful creature. Perhaps a djinn that had found some way to mask itself? Or perhaps, yes, a god. But he wasn't the only god in the Pantheon. He hadn't been the only creature on the island either. What all would be set free?

Sarka folded her arms across her chest and cleared her throat.

"There will be war, otherwise Livinja wouldn't have sent me. It's unavoidable. We *will* destroy the Akhenic Key, with or without your help. My goddess wants Akhenios to pay for what he's done, and she's not the only one. If Ruya and I fail, other priests and champions will come in our place. I'm confident you don't want the champion of chaos to follow in our footsteps.

"Now, I can either lead men bearing your standard, or they'll bear Livinja's. But if we have your support, you'll be the shah who heralded in a new age for Shai'Khal. The Pantheon Prophet, the mere mortal to whom all the gods owe their freedom. *If* you can manage to keep your head on your shoulders. Isn't *that* worth the risk?" Sarka's tone wasn't careful; it was a strange mix of excitement and disgust. For a champion of war, she seemed to dislike profiteering from it.

An idealist. How quaint, Merikh thought. Her threat was unpleasant yet honest. Nothing less than Merikh expected. She'd have an army. Merikh could think of at least three other houses who would happily claim the throne if given half the chance. But these women had thrown their weight around enough for one morning. He needed time to think.

"You've had a long journey. Rooms have been arranged for the both of you. I've taken enough of your time. Go rest. I'll summon you in the morning," Merikh said abruptly as he stood and focused on the door. It opened, and the guards on the other side stood a little straighter.

"They will escort you. It would be in your best interests to stay within your rooms until you're called for," Merikh instructed, loud enough for the guards to hear.

The women stood, and Ruya smiled brightly. The coffee had hit her.

"Thank you, Merikh," Ruya said.

Her repeated informality was insulting, but he wouldn't give her the satisfaction of seeing it get under his skin. Not when he had no recourse. Merikh watched as the guards escorted them down the hallway. Once they were out of sight, Merikh rang the summons bell for a servant and sat back down. In the silence of the royal suite, he could hear the sounds of the returned monsoon outside the tall glass windows. When the servant arrived a few minutes later, she knocked on the doorframe and bowed.

"Fetch the grand vizier," Merikh ordered.

"Of course, Shahanshah. He's with the high priest," the servant offered, undoubtedly attempting to be helpful, but Merikh had run out of patience for the day.

"I didn't *ask* where he was," Merikh snapped.

The servant woman flinched and bowed deeply, then backed away from the door. With a glance from Merikh, it shut. He stood, took another sip of coffee, and headed to the balcony. The doors opened ahead of him, allowing the crash of rain to overwhelm the room. Merikh leaned against the doorframe. The awning above kept Merikh dry while the water dripping from it froze into icicles. Puddles turned to ice the longer Merikh lingered in his mood.

He disliked being dictated to. He'd put off this problem long enough for the course to be set before him without his input. Akhenic priests had always treated Merikh with suspicion. Necromancy marked him as a danger, as someone tainted. Such views had left Merikh and the Temple with a mutual distrust. Purging the Priest Council of criminals, of men and women who had conspired with the last high priest and shah to murder mage children before their magic could manifest fully, had not helped that distrust.

Merikh had allowed the Pantheon problem to fester as a wound in Alcaeus's side. Now that petty act had drawn Merikh into a position he didn't wish to be in. But the common people viewed him as their young, progressive shah. He would find a way forward.

His way forward.

Knuckles rapped on the suite door, and with a thought, it opened and closed firmly. The grand vizier waited by the door. Merikh collected his thoughts before he turned back to the room. The balcony doors shut out the rain, and the ice melted.

"You sent Alcaeus away?" Merikh asked.

"Yes, Shahanshah. He's livid," Nikias said. He stood near the coffee table, and Merikh gestured for him to sit. Nikias did so while Merikh remained standing. He couldn't sit now, so he paced instead.

"Your meeting went poorly?" Nikias asked finally.

Merikh laughed bitterly. "In the course of a day, I've become a puppet. Either for Alcaeus or for these women."

"No hope of staying out of this, then?" Nikias asked, his brow furrowed as he began to work through scenarios in his mind. He absentmindedly ran a hand over his bald head in thought.

"No. Unless you see a different option?" Merikh asked as he stopped pacing.

Nikias sighed and leaned back in his chair. His fingers danced on the armrest.

"Your army is loyal to you. You're liked well enough by your nobles, enough for them to follow your lead down a moderate path. None of them will want to alienate you fully yet. And you still have a title to auction off," Nikias pointed out.

Merikh scoffed and rolled his eyes. *This again,* he thought. The grand vizier brought up the subject almost weekly now. Four years on the throne, and Merikh had yet to marry a khanum and produce an heir—an oversight that Merikh was certain kept Nikias up at night.

"Merikh," Nikias said, his voice softening, "it'll solidify your position, whichever you choose. Put another piece on the table, one you'll control. One that *owes* you."

Merikh sighed in irritation and sat down on the divan. "You know quite well that title is already taken. Mansur made sure of it."

Nikias shook his head. "Duq Alaziz has wanted his daughter free of that contract since it was signed. You can either continue to ransom the duq's support with her, or you can ingratiate yourself to him by absolving the contract. Then you have Duq Alaziz's gratitude and the opportunity to tie yourself to another household. Amir Xolani has a daughter, so does Duqa Enitan—"

"A *child*, not even thirteen." Merikh's lip curled in disgust. "Don't play games with me, Nikias." He had no desire to deal with the impetuousness of a child khanum, nor the stomach to take one to bed. Nikias knew it. Merikh knew the only reason Nikias threw that option at him was to make the others more palatable.

"Then your best options are Duqa Adanna or Sayida Loralee," Nikias said.

Not much in the way of options, Merikh thought but kept it to himself. The Great Prophet of Akhenios had been Umbeah, but after the first Yahidah khanum, the Madiaran line had carefully married only to Yahidah. Merikh bore no resemblance to his Umbeahan ancestry, and he could practically feel the wrath of his ancestors if he mixed Yahidah blood again with an Umbeah like Duqa Adanna.

Sayida Loralee, on the other hand, was from a family of unpredictable loyalties. The Neredis had been on both royalist and rebel sides of wars during the empire's history. Merikh's father hadn't trusted Duq Alaziz in the slightest. Who knew if the sayida would prove more loyal than the last khanum?

"What do you think is best for this country, Shahanshah?" Nikias asked after a long moment.

Merikh ran a hand over his head, pulling his black hair away from his golden eyes.

"The Akhenic Temple is corrupt. Alcaeus might not be, but a healthy head is worth very little on a diseased body. Ruya showed me memories...if these women are killed, *if* they can be killed, and *then* the creatures they represent arrive on our shores... Well, I'll be dead, and who can know what happens after that?"

"The country tears itself apart with religious war and noble feuding. The lack of a khanum and shahzade to ensure succession are among your many failings, Shahanshah," Nikias teased with a lopsided smile.

"You're insufferable when you're correct, old man." Merikh stared off at the wall. "Arrange a meeting tomorrow with Alcaeus, Ruya, and Sarka."

"What are you going to do?" Nikias asked.

Merikh shrugged. "If I'm going to be a puppet, I expect to be well paid. I have Ruya's offer. It's only fair to give Alcaeus the opportunity to counter. And I ought to look the man in the eyes if I'm to inform him that his world is about to crumble."

A bidding war never hurt anyone, though Alcaeus would need to make a hefty offer to counter Ruya and Sarka's. After all, to be owed by *gods* was tempting. It opened possibilities Merikh hadn't dared to dream of. Having the gods owe him a favor was the first truly intriguing possibility to tempt him in years, even if such a favor would need to be carefully arranged. Merikh remembered well the myths and fables Nikias had told him as a child, of mortals making deals with gods and djinn. They rarely turned out well. When all was said and done, Merikh had no intention of being turned into a goat over a technicality.

"And about the khanum problem?" Nikias asked again.

The room chilled, and frost spread over the water pitcher on the table.

Nikias continued, unfazed. "You can't keep putting it off. If nothing else, it creates a happy distraction for the people."

"Regardless of my decision tomorrow, a noble Quorum must be arranged. I will need their guidance," Merikh said, his irritation plain. "But not in Madiar, where Alcaeus, Ruya, and Sarka may influence talks. You will remain here to manage them."

He mulled over his options for a moment, and Nikias let him. The grand vizier knew when to push and when to wait.

Merikh decided after a moment. "Write to Amir Olumide. Rajibad will do. The city can handle the influx."

"Are you sure you want to spend that much time around Duq Rashad?" Nikias asked, raising a brow skeptically.

"Akhenios be kind, maybe he'll give me an excuse to be rid of him finally," Merikh said, ignoring the glare from Nikias.

"And you'll deal with the khanum—"

"*Yes,* Nikias, I will deal with it there."

Nikias raised his hands in submission but did nothing to hide his amused smile. The man wanted a child in the palace again, Merikh was certain of it, for more than simply succession. The grand vizier missed doting on one.

"What were they like, Ruya and Sarka?" Nikias asked, changing the subject to a slightly less sour conversation.

Merikh shrugged. "Sarka is ill-tempered but looks the part of Livinja's fire champion. Ruya is...much shorter than I imagined."

Nikias smiled and shook his head. "Well, some details were lost to time, I see."

"It's…strange to meet women from childhood stories," Merikh said. "Tareq—you remember him, my first necromancy tutor—he would have been a stammering fool if he'd lived long enough to see this. To meet the 'greatest necromancer in history.'"

"You don't believe she's that woman?" Nikias asked.

Merikh shook his head a little. "I don't know."

"Would you if your pride were out of the way?"

"Careful, Vizier." The temperature dropped a little and proved Nikias's point.

"Apologies, Shahanshah."

"If she is," Merikh continued, "it doesn't really matter what Alcaeus says tomorrow."

Nikias nodded slowly. Merikh glanced to the door, and when it opened, Nikias stood.

"I'll bring the letters for your signature and seal before midafternoon," Nikias said as he bowed.

Merikh nodded, and the grand vizier left. It would be a few hours before Nikias returned, time Merikh intended to put to good use in the palace archives. If that book in Ruya's memories was in fact Ikharon's grimoire, Merikh needed to know.

CHAPTER 5

5TH OF AMANITH, MONSOON SEASON 902, UNIFIED AGE
MADIAR, RAUDHAH PROVINCE

"What do you mean, the Shah won't see me?" Alcaeus demanded, leaning forward and placing his coffee back on the table.

The servant jumped a little at Alcaeus's question. He didn't mean to yell, but between the rain and the surprise, he hadn't been able to measure his tone.

"I'm sorry, he's only asked for the grand vizier," the woman apologized, looking at the stone near Alcaeus's feet.

"You informed him I'm here?" Alcaeus asked, looking to Nikias.

The grand vizier nodded. Nikias sat nearby on a stone bench, the table between them covered in platters of honeyed fruits.

"He knows."

"Then—"

"Mawla, I regret to inform you the Shah will not see you today." Nikias stood, his tone final. "He has quite the busy schedule, and without an appointment, it can be impossible to fit someone in. I will speak with him on your behalf and find an agreeable time in the future for the two of you to speak."

Alcaeus bit the inside of his lip. "That's unacceptable. Nikias, don't toy with me! I *know* who he meets with right now! They certainly had no *appointment!* The mere fact he's met with them is disgraceful. I don't interfere with monarchal matters; he has no right interfering with theological ones!"

"I'm sure I don't know who or what you're alluding to, Mawla," Nikias said, "but I'll pass along your displeasure when I speak with the Shah next. Enjoy your coffee and fruits, compliments of the Shah." He then left the garden pavilion.

The innocent look on Nikias's face made Alcaeus's blood boil, but this time he held his tongue. It had never done him any good to argue with the grand vizier. The man simply became stone-faced and pled ignorance. It was infuriating, and Alcaeus didn't want to take his frustration out on the wrong person.

And I thought Mansur was difficult. Alcaeus ran his hand over his face. When his predecessor, Idowu, had died, and Alcaeus had taken up his mantle, he'd been given the daunting task of keeping Mansur in line. To be the moral compass of a man utterly lacking in most virtues had been no small task. But at least Mansur had felt a healthy respect for the Akhenic Temple and fear of damnation in Alhanem. Merikh seemed to lack what little sense his father had possessed, as strange a thought as it was.

"Mawla, is there anything I can do for you?" the servant asked, still standing near the table.

Alcaeus took a deep breath and let it out slowly. "Make your master a god-fearing man? Is that possible?" he asked, trying to find a touch of humor to apologize for yelling earlier.

The woman smiled a little in spite of herself before she bowed.

"Actually, there is one thing. Duqa Enitan's legate, Rabb..." He snapped his fingers, trying to remember the man's name.

"Rabb Khamisi Saqqaf?" she offered, and Alcaeus nodded.

"Rabb Khamisi! Yes. Is he in Madiar presently?"

"I believe so. Would you like me to send for him?" she offered.

"Yes. Thank you."

She bowed and stepped down the stairs to exit the pavilion through the sheltered path. The high priest grabbed his coffee and leaned back in the chair, listening to the downpour. It had been four years since he'd been in this garden. On that day, the invitation had come to the temple with the gift of an enormous enchanted icebox.

At least that's still useful, Alcaeus thought. The gift had been unnecessary, though appreciated. One didn't simply turn down an invitation from the heir to the throne. Particularly one so overdue. Alcaeus had offered a supportive ear to Merikh after Khanum Aliyah had been brutally executed. In the years that followed, Merikh hadn't once taken Alcaeus up on the offer. But his invitation hadn't come as a complete surprise.

The icebox had come on the heels of an unforgivable act. Mansur had beaten Merikh to within an inch of his life, and though the Shahzade had recovered, only a fool thought there would be no retribution. Whatever insane lesson Mansur had hoped to teach, it had been bound to fail. The empire had held its breath throughout Merikh's recovery. The icebox had arrived mere days after Merikh's first public appearance. Alcaeus had been certain of what Merikh wanted to discuss with him that day, but until arriving in the garden, he hadn't been sure what advice he'd provide.

Ice had surrounded this pavilion then, creating the same privacy the monsoon rains gave Alcaeus now. Merikh had been waiting for him, sitting on a chair that had been since removed from the garden. As high priest, he had outranked Merikh, and the then-Shahzade had stood when Alcaeus approached. He'd used a cane, and Alcaeus could still remember the blood that leaked through the bandages and stained the chair. Alcaeus had no doubt the display of weakness had been the grand vizier's idea. Merikh was far too proud a person to try and garner sympathy. Still, it worked. The shock of crimson blood had unbalanced Alcaeus. He hadn't seen the dangerous necromancer in front of him that day. No, he'd seen the young boy from thirteen years prior, grown into a man who bore the brunt of his father's drunken wrath.

"The Shah is losing his grip on reality. I fear I will not be long for this world if the thought should catch his fancy—or his mistress's..."

Alcaeus remembered how quickly he'd interrupted Merikh, assuring the Shahzade that he understood. What sort of monster would he have been if he'd said anything else? Alcaeus had reassured Merikh that Mansur's death would be neither murder nor treason. After all, there was precedent for it. Most of Merikh's ancestors had taken the throne that way. Mansur killed Kurush for the throne, and Kurush murdered not just his father but almost his entire family. No one expected Mansur to die of old age.

Naïvely, Alcaeus had assumed Merikh's worries were for his soul. That the young necromancer was keenly aware of what happened to the damned and didn't want to spend eternity in Alhanem for patricide. The politics of succession hadn't figured into Alcaeus's mind; that if Merikh rushed the high priest of Akhenios to crown him, no one else would have the chance to claim the title for themselves. No, Alcaeus's mind had been purely on saving Merikh's rotten soul. It was a mistake he'd never make again.

"High Priest?"

Alcaeus smiled and gestured for the tall Umbeah nobleman to approach and sit down. Rabb Khamisi was an imposing man built like an ox, dressed in an elaborate purple-and-silver khalat with a turban covering his shaved head.

"I admit, Mawla, I was waiting for your summons, but I didn't expect to meet here." Khamisi gestured to the Oleander Pavilion.

"Nikias implored me to enjoy the remaining coffee and fruit, a consolation for not meeting with the Shah. Meals shouldn't be had alone." Alcaeus pushed one of the platters closer to Khamisi, and the legate made a show of picking up a date to humor Alcaeus.

"Rumors say the Shah meets with cultists."

"I fear they're true."

Khamisi shook his head. "Between you and I, this shah should have taken his last breaths when his necromancy manifested. Mansur would never have entertained such guests."

"Talk like that has lost many men their heads, Rabb, and it's not a sentiment I share," Alcaeus chided. "Besides, they're women. Mansur *would* have seen them."

"Apologies," Khamisi said, frowning.

"Duqa Enitan. How is her health? And her daughter, Sayida Munashe?" Alcaeus asked.

Khamisi shrugged. "It's been months since I was in Tanga. Last letter I received indicated they are well."

"Has she planned her pilgrimage to the High Temple yet?"

Khamisi shook his head. "No, Mawla, not that I am aware."

"Can I rely on her unfailing support?"

"Is the situation that dire?" Khamisi leaned forward, resting his elbows on his knees and clasping his hands.

"Hopefully not, but the Shah is a difficult man to read. I'd rather prepare for the worst than be surprised."

"The country is faithful. Shai'Khal won't tolerate a cultist shah." Khamisi leaned back against his seat and offered a dismissive wave.

"I fear I lack your faith, Rabb," Alcaeus admitted. Duqa Sachiko Himoto was the most outspoken Pantheon supporter, but she certainly wasn't the only one. Without a strong Priest Council, it had been difficult to provide a uniform response to the cult. There were rogue factions within the Temple that made combating their insidious cultist message even harder. After all, they didn't deny Akhenios as *a* god, simply denied him as *the* God. There were other factions within the Akhenic Temple itself that spouted equally extravagant-sounding heresies.

Alcaeus's words were met with a good-natured laugh.

"Well, you're only human after all, High Priest. The duqa is Faithful. The Umbeah would never abandon Akhenios. If the need should arise for an army, my mistress will raise one."

"Thank you. I may need you on short notice within the next few days—"

"I am yours to command, Mawla," Khamisi interrupted. "You need only ask."

The next morning, Alcaeus prayed alone in the inner sanctum of the High Temple. Alcaeus's troubled soul had kept him awake most of the night. After a messenger arrived early from the palace, he'd headed straight for the inner sanctum to pray.

Unlike some of the previous high priests, Alcaeus kept residence in the High Temple. After all, crises of faith were prone to dark hours. Acolytes had come in an hour ago to light candles and burn incense, but they'd done their duties quickly and left the high priest alone. He knelt on a prayer mat in front of the towering statue of Akhenios. A great hawk rested on Akhenios's outstretched arm, a ram lay at his feet, and a spear was held close to his chest in his right hand. The tip almost reached the dome ceiling.

"Mawla?" an acolyte called quietly from the door.

Great Prophet, lend me your strength. Alcaeus cleared his throat. "What can I do for you?" he asked.

"There is a Royal Guard here to escort you to the palace, and the Onyx Swords are prepared to ride with you."

"Thank you. Will you send word ahead to the palace for Rabb Khamisi to join me?" Alcaeus requested.

"Of course, Mawla."

Alcaeus lingered on his prayer mat. He pressed his forehead back down on the ground between his hands. *Great Prophet, give me the words to bring your son back to the light.*

Alcaeus straightened, grabbed his sandals, and left the inner sanctum. The soldiers were waiting for him outside in the portcullis. When Alcaeus emerged, the Onyx Swords bowed. The Royal Guard merely bowed her head before she stepped toward him. To Alcaeus's surprise, there was a silver scorpion embroidered on her left breast.

An Ajir? Why was Merikh sending one of his elite personal guards on a simple escort?

"High Priest, I am Ajir Farhana. The Shahanshah requests the pleasure of your company this morning."

"So I've heard," Alcaeus said. "How is the Shah's mood?"

Farhana shrugged one shoulder. "It's cold today." She gestured toward the rain clouds above. "It's cold in the palace too. I blame the rain more than the Shah. Shall we?" Farhana gestured toward their horses.

The ride to the palace was short, the hour early enough that the Prophet's Way wasn't overflowing with merchants or travelers. Rain fell more gently than yesterday; the aqueducts weren't overflowing their bounds. The air smelled of wet sandstone, the scent earthy and rich. The morning felt calm and helped steady Alcaeus's mood.

Once inside the palace, Alcaeus was led to a small council room. The long table and chairs took up most of the space. What little sunlight made it through the monsoon clouds came in through small arched windows that gave the room a cramped feeling.

The servant left Alcaeus alone to wait, and he did so by the window. It overlooked part of the palace garden. Alcaeus smirked bitterly at the realization. The garden below was the same one he'd met Merikh in four years ago; the same one where he'd waited with Nikias yesterday. Alcaeus doubted the view was mere coincidence. It was a reminder that Alcaeus had put everyone in this position by crowning Merikh. Perhaps meant as a reminder of why Alcaeus had helped Merikh in the first place. He was better than the alternative—and there were no trueborn alternatives.

"High Priest?" Khamisi knocked on the doorframe.

Alcaeus gestured for him to come in and sit. The rabb did so, and a comfortable silence fell over the room. Alcaeus felt no need to waste breath before Merikh arrived, and unlike yesterday, he didn't have to wait long.

Merikh was flanked by Nikias and two women when he entered the room. He wore a look of slight irritation and distaste. Merikh was nearly ten years younger than Alcaeus, though no one would have guessed it. The Shah was an old soul and carried himself with self-assuredness and lacked the cocky self-deception most young men had. He could have been charismatic like his father, but Merikh had never put forth the effort. A small blessing. Merikh's irritation contrasted sharply with the small Tsukarai woman at his side. She smiled brightly, having the appearance of being the only person who truly wanted to be there.

The Shah gestured to the seats around the table, and everyone took their place except Nikias. The grand vizier remained by the door, a handheld scribe desk in his hands and a quill readied.

"I do not recall sending a summons for you, Rabb Khamisi," Merikh said, his tone cool.

"I asked him to be here," Alcaeus answered, gesturing for Khamisi to remain seated. "Is that a problem?"

"Not at all," the Tsukarai woman said, glancing at Merikh.

If he's had to deal with that all morning, that explains the irritation.

"Who are they?" Alcaeus asked, suspecting the answer already as Nikias introduced Ruya and Sarka.

Khamisi shifted uncomfortably in his seat as they were introduced, while Alcaeus found himself staring at Sarka. He'd never met another Aegalian. Even if he was only half, no one let him forget it. Alcaeus hid his pale-brown hair under a black ghutrah, but he couldn't hide his blue eyes any more than she could hide her freckles or milk-white skin.

"With respect, you two simply *can't* be the champion of Livinja or the high priestess of Ikharon. *If* they exist, they're djinns." Alcaeus then glanced to Merikh. "Shahanshah, a man of your education surely isn't humoring such things. Your family line is proof enough of Akhenios and the Great Prophet."

"Livinja and Ikharon exist, just as Akhenios does," Sarka answered instead. "I've played cards with your Great Prophet. Doesn't change the fact that Akhenios is a power-hungry, backstabbing, traitorous *worm* of a god."

"Sarka, that was unkind," Ruya chided her gently.

Alcaeus barely heard her, as Khamisi stood abruptly.

"How *dare—*"

"Sit down, Rabb Khamisi. You are welcome here only so long as you are seen and not heard," Merikh ordered.

Khamisi's jaw clenched. He relented and sat back down.

"Shahanshah, these women are rabble-rousing blasphemers," Alcaeus said. "I fail to understand why you've taken such a keen interest in a theological matter."

"Your Faithful masses are abandoning the Temple to riot, High Priest," Merikh answered carefully. "The Kasu temple is in shambles, Duqa Sachiko openly worships Pantheon gods, and rumors say she isn't the only one. You don't believe these matters are concerning?"

"On the contrary, I do. My Onyx Swords should be given leave to take back the Kasu temple and try the duqa for apostasy. Let me try *these* women for apostasy!" Alcaeus gestured to Ruya and Sarka.

"Your Swords are for temple protection only. They lost the Kasu temple, and it is the duqa's prerogative to aid them in retaking it, should she decide to. As far as trying the duqa for alleged apostasy, what would you do with her when found guilty? Execute her?"

"There is only one god, and it's Akhenios." Alcaeus shot Sarka a pointed look before continuing. "To believe differently undermines the very reason you inherited the crown, Shahanshah. You would be a horse breeder, nothing more, without the Great Prophet's blood in your veins. Shai'Khal would be merely a continent, not a grand empire. Would I execute the duqa?" Alcaeus hesitated only for a moment. "Yes. I would see her die, along with these women. They are apostates and blasphemers. Their faith makes them traitors."

"We don't deny Akhenios or his prophet," Ruya interjected quickly, clearly worried Alcaeus's words might hold sway with Merikh. "The gains made by uniting Shai'Khal are impressive, and no one seeks to undo them. I remember what Shai'Khal was like before—I have no desire to see it return to such disorder and chaos. There is no need for anyone to die, Alcaeus. We don't want to see your faith abandoned! Your scrolls aren't wrong, not entirely, just misguided. We can amend the scrolls to be true, and with your help, find out why Akhenios has abandoned you. Why hasn't there been a high priest who that *speaks* with Akhenios since your Great Prophet? There is no reason we can't work together to find answers."

Khamisi's hand slammed onto the table, and the Umbeah man stood.

"*Everything* that comes from her mouth is an affront to Akhenios! If your father were alive, her tongue would be cut from her head!" Khamisi shouted, gesturing wildly.

The room grew cold, and the closed door flew open with a loud bang, silencing Khamisi. Alcaeus shivered.

"Out, legate, before you lose *your* tongue," Merikh ordered, his tone as cold as the room.

"If *they*—" Khamisi started.

"Clear the room, Nikias. The priest and I have a great deal to discuss."

No one moved. Sarka and Ruya glanced to one another, worry written in Ruya's frown. Nikias left his post at the door and began quickly ushering Khamisi and the cultists from the room. Khamisi planted himself firmly until Alcaeus gestured to the door. The legate reluctantly followed the others out, but Alcaeus didn't think he'd go far. Undoubtedly, there was an audience on the other side of the now-shut door.

The temperature in the room rose again, and Merikh leaned back a little in his chair. He looked almost comfortable, as if he'd let down a few of his walls. Alcaeus didn't trust it. Mansur had always appeared quite friendly, even as he broke necks.

"Duqa Enitan holds many views blasphemous to the Madiar temple," Merikh said. "Yet you keep her legate in confidence and would hang Duqa Sachiko."

"Worshiping Akhenios over so-called 'dragon bones' is harmless," Alcaeus said frankly. "Worshiping an alleged *goddess of war* is an entirely different matter. They seek to divide our country. I won't be the only deposed leader at the end of such an experiment."

"You would have me execute Duqa Sachiko, her family, and every cultist following the Pantheon within Shai'Khal?"

"I...I would. You took decisive action against the Priest Council when you found criminals among them. Why hesitate to do so when there are traitors in yours?"

"The duqa isn't a traitor if I worship Ikharon."

Alcaeus gaped at him for a moment. It was as if the Shah were speaking a different language. Alcaeus managed to collect himself quickly.

"You *believe* these women? You'd...you'd ask me to amend the Scrolls, to bring the Pantheon into our temples?" Alcaeus stammered.

"Believe them? That they speak for gods?" Merikh shook his head. "No, not particularly. But I don't believe in Akhenios or that *you* speak for him either. The Scrolls are full of vague parables and stories. A few more with additional characters will hardly ruin them. The fundamentals of your faith, the rules and scripture, the most important of these, hardly require faith in a god to find validity. Your priests would have been damned for killing children, regardless of worshiping Ikharon or Akhenios."

Alcaeus couldn't speak for a moment, dumbfounded by Merikh's words. He'd known the Shah had no love for the Temple—the man hadn't stepped foot in one since Mansur died and he was no longer dragged to it—but this? Alcaeus clenched his fist under the table and tried to keep his temper in check.

"Whether you believe in Akhenios or not is your business, Shahanshah. But your *people* shouldn't pay for your heresies or your poor judgment. I don't know what promises those women have made to you, but they are *false*. I always thought you had better judgment than to be so easily swayed by charlatans!"

"You are out of line, priest," Merikh admonished.

"O-out of line?" Alcaeus stammered. "Perhaps, but nevertheless, I am right. I must stand firm to protect the Temple and the Faithful. I won't allow the Scrolls to be amended. Not by them, not by you. Think about the consequences! Do you believe your nobles will support you without the Temple? I put that crown on your head!"

"You believe you can remove it as easily?" Merikh asked, his tone once again measured and impossible to read.

"I have no desire to," Alcaeus said quickly. "Don't put me in a position where we have to find out. If you accept these women, accept their gods, I cannot support you. Not as our shah."

"High Priest, take time to reconsider your position. In my few years as shah, have I led our country astray yet? Or brought her back to purpose? Can you name another who could possibly do better?"

Alcaeus frowned. Objectively, Merikh had been good for Shai'Khal. The rampant corruption that had plagued Shai'Khal's nobility, priesthood, and Royal Guard were all becoming manageable. Laws had been put in place that aided the common people, and taxes had been reallocated to maintaining Shai'Khal instead of royal appetites. They were grand enough improvements to convince people to ignore the rumors of undead roaming the darkest reaches under the palace. To ignore the whispers that the Shah himself partook regularly in torturing criminals for his necromancy experiments. But he'd only been shah for a few years. His record wasn't good enough to support heresy.

"Go. Pray if that will help," Merikh said as he glanced over his shoulder. The door opened with the look. Alcaeus took the cue to leave, glad to do so. He needed air.

Khamisi, the cultists, and Nikias sat on benches in the hallway in uncomfortable silence. When Alcaeus left, Nikias entered. The door shut before the women could enter. Alcaeus said nothing to them, and Khamisi followed him down the white hall until they were out of earshot.

"What happened?" Khamisi asked quickly.

Alcaeus stopped. His hands were shaking. "I think we'll need your mistress's allies and army before long."

He's gone mad. Absolutely mad. So much for the Great Prophet's divine blood and purity. He's lost his mind, Alcaeus thought. Something those women had whispered in the Shah's ear had twisted his mind. It would lead to

Shai'Khal's destruction if they went down this road—the Temple's too. Alcaeus refused to sit idly by.

Whatever it took to save the Akhenic faith, he'd do it.

CHAPTER 6

6TH OF AMANITH, MONSOON SEASON, 902 UNIFIED AGE
MADIAR, RAUDHAH PROVINCE

Adrian lay on his bed, trying to coax his body to move. The day after a long journey always hit him hard, but bringing Ruya and Sarka to Madiar had been especially draining. That, and sometime during the quiet hours of the night, Mahmud had snuck into his room.

The other man had left to grab breakfast from the kitchens, and Adrian would have been sleeping still if it weren't for the bronze bell near the door. The summons had rung once. The Shah awaited. Adrian had left all his notes for the Shah with Nikias yesterday. By now, Adrian assumed Merikh had gone over them and expected clarification.

Great Prophet, where do I start? Feet on the floor helped. Adrian swung his legs over the bed, stretched his back, and then froze.

The bell rang again. It *never* rang twice. The Shah wasn't a man to be kept waiting, nor a man who let his impatience show quite so obviously. Panic spurred Adrian on. His boots abandoned by the bed, Adrian pulled a long kaftan over himself to hide his nightclothes, then he hurried from the room. The door slammed shut behind him as he took off toward the servant corridors. He didn't notice the worried looks, nor did he hear the rumors. He barely paid attention to those around him until he reached the correct door. Adrian stumbled out into the hall before the royal suite. The guards didn't acknowledge him as he approached the ice-covered door. The magic disappeared, and the door swung open.

"Shahanshah?" Adrian asked, shutting the door behind him. The room was cool, and the sound of rain was muffled by puddles turning to ice outside the balcony. From across the room, Adrian recognized his road-worn reports

49

strewn haphazardly across the Shah's desk. The Shah barely glanced at Adrian before speaking.

"I need *everything* you left out of your report, even the slightest unimportant details. Anything you can recall." There was an urgency hidden in Merikh's tone, one Adrian only knew to look for because of the bells.

"Of course, Shahanshah. What happened?" Adrian asked quickly. It'd been *years* since he'd seen Merikh like this.

The Shah cleared his throat. "I may have made a small mistake when speaking with the high priest this morning."

"You spoke with the high priest?"

Merikh stopped reading and looked at Adrian in surprise. "You must be the only one in the palace not to know."

"Apologies, Shahanshah, but I was sleeping," Adrian confessed.

"Gods forbid I interrupt your rest, steward."

Adrian bit his lip and stared at his bare feet. He'd stepped in something sticky in the servant hallway that had discolored his brown skin.

"It won't happen again," he promised.

The gesture earned him an exasperated breath. "Of course it will. I have other men to lie to me, Adrian. Now sit down and give me truth."

The chair wasn't the most comfortable by design. *Easier to get rid of people that way,* Adrian had overhead Mansur explaining once to no one in particular. The last shah had had few sober moments, and in his drunken ones he enjoyed talking at anyone who would listen, usually while pawing at his mistress. Adrian bit his lip, unsure of where to start, and Merikh offered him no direction. "Truth" was a vague and loaded word. He'd left thorough reports. Adrian had written notes for himself every evening at the campfire. Normally, Adrian wasn't subjected to Merikh's doubt. That was Nikias's domain. It left him floundering.

"I tried to give a thorough report, Shahanshah. The Pantheon has a great deal of support on the coast among the Tsukarai. It plays into their superstitions surrounding the mists, validates their blasphemies. Sarka is more reserved, but Ruya...I've never met a necromancer who lives life to its utmost fullest like she does. She drinks men under the table and beds anyone willing. She tries anything, legal or less so. That attitude has made her rather popular in

Kuzen, compared to the uptight Akhenic priests. I think the merchants hope Pantheon acceptance will open the market to their more lucrative trades. Your self-restraint and the anti-corruption policies within the Royal Guard have hurt the north. I think they're hoping Ruya will fix that."

"You mentioned..." Merikh paused, searching through the reports until finding one in particular. "...that the Akhenic Temple in Kasu has been abandoned by the priests, and that many of the Akhenic temples in the surrounding areas have already been converted to Pantheon usage?"

"Yes, Shahanshah."

Merikh nodded once, then gestured for Adrian to continue. Adrian cleared his throat, unsure what to continue with.

"I, um...you may need to write a letter to the duqa to calm her. She was rather livid at the attempt on her life."

"Indeed? How *unexpected.*" The words dripped with sarcasm, and Adrian flinched.

"Apologies." Adrian cleared his throat again and tried to get more comfortable in the chair. "If I may...you're going to have enemies within your government no matter what you choose. The north will go to arms if you try to crush the Pantheon, and both those priestesses are stronger than you are. I don't know if you *can* go against them now that they're here. If you side with them, Ydeba and the Akhenic Faithful will fight you. The high priest probably can't kill you as easily." He knew he was out of line before the room chilled even more.

"I put myself in this position. You did attempt to warn me, after all," Merikh said as he lifted up one of Adrian's reports. The Shah put it down and drummed his fingers thoughtfully on the wooden desk. "You worship Akhenios, do you not?"

"You know I do," Adrian said reluctantly, uncomfortable with the direction this question would inevitably arrive at. "Ruya and Sarka preach that Akhenios is part of the Pantheon. Maybe He is, and history wrote the rest out. You've written your father out of history as much as possible, so I don't take history as guaranteed truth. Does it matter if Akhenios is the only god or one of many? The Scrolls mean the same, don't they?" He scrambled for words and was relieved when Merikh leaned back comfortably in his tall-backed chair.

"The high priest doesn't agree. I do. Moderation is important. Nikias is not a man of much faith. In fact, I think my magic might have destroyed whatever faith he had in his youth. With the priestesses here, and my slip of the tongue earlier, Alcaeus will propagate that I worship Ikharon and djinn—"

"*That's* the 'small mistake'?" Adrian blurted out incredulously, his eyes wide.

Merikh shot him a look and continued. "You, on the other hand, are common born and Akhenic Faithful. As long as it's *safe* for you to do so, I want you to be seen worshiping in the temple. In uniform, as the Ajir steward. A representative of the Shah humbling himself before Akhenios will help considerably."

Adrian fidgeted uncomfortably in his chair for a moment. His faith had always been private before, and he preferred it that way.

"Adrian?"

To Adrian's relief, Merikh's tone had softened. Its edge of formality lost, no longer a shah speaking to his steward. No, the tone was familiar and set Adrian at ease. A tone that honored the decade-long friendship between the two men.

"May I say no?" Adrian asked, biting his lip.

"There are others in the Ajir who may be more comfortable with such a display. But I hesitate to send a soldier into the temple. I don't need them to antagonize the Onyx Swords. You're unoffensive."

Adrian couldn't help but laugh. "Thanks."

The ice was melting outside the balcony doors. Whatever worries had plagued Merikh before were waning.

"Are you up to this task?" Merikh asked.

"I won't be disingenuous, Shahanshah. I won't parade around like a peacock. But I'll pray in uniform, and I'll make sure people know the Shah isn't going to burn down their temples or force new beliefs upon them."

"Good. Then you should go now—midday prayers should be soon." The Shah returned to the reports on his desk.

Adrian stood and bowed his head before walking toward the door.

"Before you go," the Shah said quickly. "Did the priestesses mention a book at any time? Or a key?"

Adrian shook his head. "No, Shahanshah. Ruya alluded to a plan going forward, but no specifics. I think she wanted to talk to you first."

The Shah nodded before glancing at the door. It opened ahead of Adrian and shut behind him.

Go be a puppet, Adrian thought with a heavy sigh. He could have said no; he knew that. But it didn't really matter in the end, did it? Not unless he stopped praying at the High Temple. In Madiar, he was well enough known as the Ajir steward that even without his uniform, he'd be recognized and his presence politicized. At least Merikh had given him the agency to own it.

Midday prayers had already begun when Adrian approached the Temple District. He'd stopped back at his quarters to dress and scarf down a small portion of the breakfast Mahmud had left him. The black kameez with the silver scorpion embroidery made him no friends as he passed through the gates and walked down the Prophet's Shade. The walkway was named for the ancient olive trees planted by the Great Prophet, which created a canopy above the path. The planting had been a peace offering to the people of Madiar after the Great Prophet had conquered the Yahidah.

A Kujaree priest recited passages from the Scrolls from one of the temple's minarets, calling the last stragglers to prayers. Adrian bowed his head and followed a small group of men and women inside the temple. It was much colder inside. The temple had few windows, designed to keep the building cool during the Dry Season. The domed ceiling above was painted with dozens of murals.

One in particular caught Adrian's eye. The golden dragon of the Great Prophet was coiled around a white-faced djinn with flaming red hair. The djinn appeared to be dying, crushed by the dragon and torn by its claws. But the djinn's sword impaled the dragon's mouth, piercing its skull. A victory and a loss for the Great Prophet. It was a cautionary tale against the power of djinn. A story about the importance of strong faith in the face of great evil. Adrian grimaced.

Today of all days, he thought.

Adrian's attendance brought whispers. Normally he would have hung back. He would have prayed from the last row and left. But today he made a show of washing his hands and feet at the ablution fountain before putting his boots aside. He approached the altar, kneeled, and placed his palms on the prayer mat before shutting his eyes. The gesture made Adrian all the more aware of the burning stares shooting his way, but he tried to push them away.

Akhenios, benevolent Creator, Master of Aljemel, Protector of Men and Destroyer of Djinns, Your servant implores You to soften the hearts of the Faithful and open their minds; and guide Merikh down the righteous path.

It felt like an eternity before Adrian felt comfortable rising from the mat. When he did so, he was relieved to see most of the room had cleared. The high priest remained, and acolytes were snuffing out candles.

"One of the homeless stole your boots," Alcaeus said when he noticed Adrian rising. "I thought he might need them more than you."

"Probably." Adrian sighed in exasperation. It would make walking back to the palace decidedly harder, which undoubtedly the point.

"Must you return to your master so quickly? Or can the Shah spare you long enough for some chai?" Alcaeus gestured toward a hallway away from the main chamber.

Adrian reluctantly followed the high priest. The other man wasn't much taller than Adrian; his strides were much easier to keep up with than the Shah's. Or perhaps the priest was more practiced walking alongside men than ahead of them.

"Have you spoken with the Shah since this morning?"

"I have."

"Yet you came to pray anyway?" Alcaeus cast Adrian a sidelong glance before pushing open the door at the end of the hallway. It opened to a small atrium. There were two benches side by side in front of a large fountain. The bubbling water was harder to appreciate when the monsoons still broke over the walls outside. The fountain was quite plain, a simple geometric design and blue painted lines over the marble.

"The Shah respects—" Adrian stopped short after his words earned a disbelieving snort from the high priest.

"I'm sorry. Perhaps he does. You're...his steward, correct? That makes you..."

"Adrian Charmichi."

"Adrian is a rather Aegalian name. How did your father pick it?" Alcaeus studied Adrian's face, undoubtedly looking for traces of shared heritage. He'd find none, for while Adrian wasn't full-blooded Yahidah, there was only a small smattering of Tsukarai blood muddying it. Nothing Aegalian as far as he knew.

"My mother did. My father died before I was born. She thought it sounded nice, I suppose."

"How did you become the Ajir steward? I had many meetings with your predecessor. If you'll forgive me for my impudence, you're quite young, and Charmichi isn't exactly a family of note."

"Imtiyaz took his life instead of swearing fealty to the Shah after succession," Adrian said, unsure of how much the high priest actually knew about the goings-on in the palace. "As far as my accession, Imtiyaz took pity on my mother before I was born and gave her work in the palace. I was one of the few children around when the Shah was young. I think the Shah took pity on me and appreciated the company. As far as promotion to steward...I can manage the household just as well as men twice my age. Better, if those men believe in terrorizing the staff the way Imtiyaz did."

"I see. A new age of mercy within the palace brought on by our Faithful steward. How long can we expect to still see a Faithful man at the Shah's side? How long will the Ajir still worship within the temple?"

"I think that's up to you and your Onyx Swords. As long as I'm allowed to enter, I'll be here."

"You believe that?"

"Wholeheartedly," Adrian said as he met the priest's gaze. "I've been given no reason not to."

"Do you really believe you can serve your master and your god?"

Adrian hesitated, and the high priest nodded knowingly.

"Adrian, I can only imagine how difficult the road ahead will be for you. No one becomes Ajir without...well, some sort of bond with their shah. You may see him as a brother, and maybe you think you can steer him back to the light given time. But listen to me: there are men who dwell in shadows, and then there are men who *are* shadows."

"And you think the Shah is the latter." *Maybe he's right.* The thought surprised Adrian. Even Mansur had been god-fearing, but fear was not an expression Adrian associated with Merikh. Even when he'd been close to death, Merikh hadn't looked afraid. Frustrated and angry, but never afraid.

"The man has lived through a great deal and never sought Akhenios through any of it," Alcaeus said. "His magic has left him open to djinnic influences, and now the corruption spreads. I hope and pray that I'm wrong. That the Shah isn't..."

Adrian shook his head. "Mawla, he's not a djinn worshiper."

"No? Then he's worse—completely faithless. Your master said as much this morning. That scares me more than djinn worship. A sorcerer and a shah who holds himself accountable to no one?" The high priest frowned.

"He's accountable to the people."

"But only those who think like him. Not the Faithful, as we're being ignored and pushed aside for the Pantheon."

Adrian sighed and ran a hand over his face. "You can't make everyone happy, but you can try to keep everyone safe. Nobody wants war."

"And yet he sits with the self-proclaimed champion of war at his side."

"Well, Sarka is perhaps a poor choice of companions, but even she doesn't want to go to a needless war."

"You all speak as if *I'm* the one pushing for it." The high priest looked frustrated. "No one *wants* war. But if Amir Xolani and Amira Jin walked into the palace and told the Shah they were claiming sovereignty over their provinces, do you think he'd take it lying down? Share power and have no issue with it simply because neither one took his particular crown? No! Merikh would *destroy* them for the mere thought that they could carve their own little country out of his empire, and no one would fault him for it! That's only land and lives. I contend with *souls*, the eternal condemnation or salvation of our empire! I'm supposed to sit back and invite usurpers in and sign off on damnation? What sort of high priest would I be if I allowed that?"

Adrian didn't have an answer or an argument to counter with. He wasn't a grand debater, certainly not against a theologian. His silence was enough. The high priest straightened his black ghutrah.

"We're all accountable for the choices we make. For the orders we follow. Be mindful of your soul before you follow your master into the shadows. Alhanem is a cold, dark, and permanent place. A place your master might be comfortable in, for a time, but it's not a place for you."

The high priest stood, placed a hand on Adrian's shoulder, and squeezed tightly. "I'll see about that chai for you and if an acolyte has shoes you can borrow. Or I can send someone to the palace to fetch a replacement. I'm sure the Shah pays you enough for you to own more than one pair of boots?"

"The chai is fine. I can manage without boots or buy a pair from a cobbler. As you said, the Shah pays enough," Adrian said flatly.

Alcaeus let go of his shoulder.

"Very well. I hope to see you again tomorrow. May the Great Prophet guide your path."

The high priest retreated from the atrium. Adrian remained, staring at the fountain. *He had to know the priest would talk to me. He knew he'd sow doubts. Why send me so unprepared?* Adrian thought, running his hands over his face. A test of loyalty? Adrian dismissed the notion. Merikh had sent him here for more reasons than just to be seen as Ajir and Faithful, but the Shah wasn't prone to fickle tests of loyalty like that. Adrian was certain his bumbling had done little to reassure the high priest that Merikh would be true to his word and protect his people. But perhaps the point had merely been that Adrian had tried. *Am I meant to offer peace?*

Adrian stood from the bench, deciding against waiting for the chai. Whatever the plan, mulling it over here wasn't helping anyone. He had a long walk ahead of him through muddy streets.

CHAPTER 7

9th of Amanith, Monsoon Season, 902 Unified Age
Madiar, Raudhah Province

Ruya had spent enough time in a prison to recognize one, no matter how gilded. The palace practically shimmered, but Ruya had no intention of trading mists for marble and gold. The shared suite for Ruya and Sarka would have been comfortable if they had been granted the freedom to come and go from their rooms as they wished. Unfortunately, that singular freedom had yet to be granted, and the champion of war grew restless.

The intricately woven carpet near the window had grown threadbare from Sarka's almost nonstop pacing. Her irritation kept the temperature in the room brutally hot. No amount of fanning managed to keep Ruya comfortable, and there was only so much time she could spend in the cold, enchanted waters of their bath. It reminded her too much of the constant cling of humidity on Ikharon's island.

Ruya had tried to arrange for an audience with Merikh, but the man seemed to be enjoying flexing his muscles and reminding them they were on *his* schedule. Young mortal men were adorably quaint.

If it were simply a power play between her and Merikh, Ruya would happily wait him out and then refuse his summons. He was shah, but she represented gods. He needed to learn his place below them. Unfortunately, Sarka was likely to burn the palace down before they managed to get to that point. *That* might make converting the masses rather more difficult. Ruya would have to make her careful counterplay sooner than later. She'd already underestimated Merikh once and paid the price. It was a lesson she didn't care to repeat. Her hand was still sore, but that was of little consequence.

Merikh had found the grimoire in her memories. He shouldn't have been able to, but he'd managed it nonetheless. Ruya hoped he didn't realize what he'd seen, or that he understood how truly foolhardy its pursuit would be. Tokens of the gods were not to be trifled with, Ikharon's in particular. Necromancer or not, the grimoire would kill Merikh. He'd never survive the enchantments on it; Ruya was fairly certain of that fact.

At the end of the day, he was a boy. Twenty-four years old but a boy. Ruya had been practicing necromancy for a few hundred years before banishment, and while her power had waned, it was certainly nothing to scoff at when demonstrated—and a demonstration *was* in order. Ruya had no intention of showing off too much. Egos were delicate, and she had no desire to bruise Merikh's so terribly that he reconsidered their agreement. He simply needed a small lesson in humility and respect. It would do him well once the Pantheon was free. No god would take kindly to being dictated to by a mortal, even if he were their...

Pantheon Prophet. That's what Sarka called him. Ruya couldn't help but smile at the thought.

"Please tell me you're smiling because you have a plan," Sarka said, interrupting her thoughts. She was pacing a deeper groove into the carpet.

"Of course I have a plan. I need your help for it, just to make sure nothing goes wrong," Ruya said as she reclined on the divan and gestured for Sarka to come over.

"How does *napping* help?" Sarka asked, her frustration apparent as she approached and stood over Ruya.

"Rest always does the body good, but I'm not napping. My body is going to go limp when I spirit-walk, and I'd rather be limp lying down than sitting up. Fewer odd cramps and spasms when I come back."

"Are you sure that's safe?"

Ruya shrugged a little and closed her eyes. Potentially not. It left her soul quite vulnerable to outside influence. If Merikh decided to betray them now, she was giving him the perfect opportunity to do so.

"What do you need me to do?" Sarka asked.

Ruya heard the rustle of cloth and leather as Sarka sat down on the ground beside her.

"If I'm gone for a long time—let's say an hour—I want you to bring me back to my body. You do that with pain," Ruya explained. "Excruciating, sharp pain would be preferred, something to remind my soul it belongs to a still-living body."

She heard Sarka scoff and mutter something. Sure, it wasn't a great plan—Ruya didn't much care for the idea of Sarka having to torture her back to her body—but Ruya doubted that it would be necessary. She hadn't needed help returning to her own body since after the first time she'd tried spirit walking. That had been over a thousand years ago.

"How will I know you're gone?"

Ruya smiled mischievously and peeked at Sarka. "You'll know."

She shut her eyes again. Three deep breaths, and she focused on separating her soul from her body. From her toes through her feet, up her legs to her core, fingertips to wrist, through her arms, until she felt a weight on her chest. There was a moment of excruciating pain, a breathtaking whiteness, and then back to the faded black of closed eyes. She heard the champion jump.

"Vindaram's breath, that's not natural," Sarka muttered.

Ruya sat up, aware that her body wasn't moving. The first time she'd done this, the moment she'd realized she wasn't part of her body, she'd free-fallen through the floor into the ground. *That* had been unpleasant. Ikharon had snapped her soul back up quickly. Ghosts rarely experienced such problems, their perception of the world clouded by their denial or anger. Abandoning one's own body willingly was always a small shock. Ruya opened her eyes and glanced down. Her soul, given form in her pale-green necromancy magic, peeled off of her body as she stood and walked away from the couch.

"Perfectly natural." Ruya's words were barely more than a whisper. Trying to command language without lungs to breathe from was exceptionally hard.

Sarka stood up, shaking her head in worry and agitation as she warily eyed Ruya's soul. "Hardly. Are you sure this is a good idea? What if he—"

"Everything will work out just fine. I'm going to have someone bring you a calming chai. You worry too much," Ruya said before crossing the room and walking into the wall.

Every soul had its own unique feeling. Distinguishing one particular soul from a sea of them at a distance took more skill than Ruya had. But she didn't need to try very hard with Merikh. Sorcerer auras lit up like beacons.

There were a handful of minor sorcerers within the palace, but only one aura screamed for attention.

Ruya carefully avoided other souls, walking within the stone of the walls themselves. After all, she didn't want to give an innocent servant or guard a fright. Merikh wasn't moving, making it easier for her to navigate a private path.

Perhaps the servants weren't lying about his schedule, Ruya thought. Merikh's soul was surrounded by six other souls. One she recognized as the grand vizier, Nikias. She'd met him a handful of times since arriving in Madiar. The other five, Ruya didn't know, and for a moment she hung back in the wall of the council chamber.

The conversation stopped, and Ruya frowned. *Well, so much for gossip.* Though she could hardly expect Merikh not to feel her soul.

"I'll speak with the rest of you later. Nikias, would you have Ruya's body brought here?" she heard Merikh say, and she held back laughter at the sounds of confusion on the other side of the wall.

"Shahanshah?"

Ruya imagined Merikh must have given them a look or gesture, as the souls filtered rather quickly out of the room. When they were gone, Ruya stepped out of the wall. The room wasn't overly large. A table and cushioned chairs took up most of the room. Water trickled from a fountain in the far wall, flowing across the room and into the gardens below the window.

"That is a rather neat trick," Merikh said. He sat at the head of the table, surrounded by stacks of letters. Each had broken wax seals of different colors. She recognized a few of the vassal house crests—particularly the crab of House Himoto, Duqa Sachiko's family.

"Isn't it?" Ruya said, her voice soft as she concentrated on sitting down at the table. Despite his rather well-adjusted manner, Ruya could see that her condition...bewildered him. Merikh had most likely never considered the most practical applications of necromancy. Ruya imagined most of what he knew was quite beneath a sorcerer of his strength, and she wondered, if he'd lived the life of a scholar instead of a shah, how much more accomplished would he be?

What a waste of magic.

"You wanted my attention. You have it until the grand vizier arrives with your body. Then I expect you to remain within the confines of your skin and suite."

Ruya smiled and shook her head. "I will happily stay within my skin, but I think you've quite made your point. This is your palace, and I am happy to remain wherever you would like me to. But both Sarka and I require a longer leash. Your ancestor kept us in a prison for nine hundred years. Sarka fares rather poorly finding herself imprisoned once again, even if both our prison and jailer are easier on the eyes than before."

Merikh's eyes narrowed ever so slightly. He didn't care for the compliment or teasing. The man was utterly stiff and uncomfortable when it came to any sort of relaxed interaction. Ruya made a note of it. As long as she could make him uncomfortable, she had the upper hand. He was clearly a proud man, which gave Ruya another mark in her favor. There was little Merikh would be able to imagine and say that could ever make her uncomfortable.

"I won't have the two of you roaming the palace or Madiar," Merikh said dismissively. "Far too dangerous for you and those around you."

"We can't die."

"I don't believe that matters if Onyx Swords manage to string you to a breaking wheel, or kill those who try to protect you."

"I suppose that's fair, in Madiar. In your palace, on the other hand, I'm sure we both could become quite safely lost within it."

"Undoubtedly," Merikh said dryly. He seemed unconvinced that her request was a good idea, and Ruya didn't blame him. She couldn't be certain of where exactly Merikh stood on matters of faith, and she didn't want to push it so soon. The paranoia and arrogance of his station seemed almost obviate to faith, or perhaps there was a history Ruya simply didn't know. But Merikh hadn't trusted the Akhenic priest, nor did he trust them.

"We're not here to undermine you. This is your country, and we make no claim to it. If there were a way to do this without your help, we would. The world becomes very messy when priests and politicians intertwine for more than a night. You know we can't do this without your help, and if you treat us as allies, you'll reap the benefits."

"Do you truly understand the position you've put me in?" Merikh asked as he leaned forward in his seat and placed his hand on the pile of letters in front of him. "You have spent years undermining me. You put me in a position where no matter the choice, peace is impossible. Then you expect me to let you wander the palace, to give you the opportunity to influence my viziers and nobles, with only the promise not to undermine me further? You couldn't make it a *week* before doing this"—he gestured at her soul—"and yet you ask for trust. Where has that trust been earned or returned? I have people to protect. Your presence makes many of the men and women who live and work here uncomfortable."

Ruya tried to take a deep breath before shaking her head a little at herself and the futility of the gesture.

"Sarka is a soldier. The grand general of the Flaming Legion. You can find tales in your library of her, and perhaps you were told stories as a boy. I'm sure some have become quite exaggerated with time. But I remember the...what do you call it, the war?"

"The Unification War."

"Of course! Unification. I *remember* the Unification War. I walked the fields alongside Kumbukani, Ayurlyse's high healer. I laid souls to rest when he couldn't fix their bodies. I remember the scorched battlefields left behind by Sarka and her soldiers. She isn't as strong as she was in our glory days, but that fire should not be left in a cage to simmer. I don't think I have to tell you she doesn't care for you, but she could be your greatest ally if you give her the chance. Let her be among her people again. She has no mind or desire for politics. Let her spend time around your soldiers. Let their opinions of you influence her. Most Royal Guards I've met seem to think fairly highly of you."

"High praise." Merikh smirked. "But that threat hardly answers my question. And what kind of choice is that? Comply with your wishes, or Sarka burns my city to the ground."

"Well, probably just the palace," Ruya teased. "I'm not trying to threaten you. I know the position we've put you in is untenable for a powerful man. Four years without answering to anyone, and now two women are dictating the future of your country to you. Anyone would rankle under such pressures. I truly wish we had come to this place under better circumstances, but here we are. If you give Sarka enough freedom to stretch her legs and speak to someone other than myself, you will reap the benefits. If nothing else, let us into your library and archives. It'll keep us busy and move us toward finding the Key faster. Perhaps we can end the war before it truly begins."

Merikh sighed and looked at the pile of letters in front of him. There was a great weight on his shoulders; Ruya could practically see it. In the silence between them, Ruya began to feel the touch of Sarka's aura. Nikias's soul approached alongside her. The champion was undoubtedly protecting Ruya's body.

Nikias knocked on the door, and it opened. The grand vizier held the door for Sarka, who walked in carefully.

Gods, I really am small. It was strange to see her body carried in the arms of the champion so easily. The grand vizier looked quite spooked by the whole encounter. Nikias tried not to stare at her soul or at her body as Sarka laid it carefully down on the table between Merikh and Ruya.

"Shahanshah, is there anything else you require?" Nikias asked, his voice strained.

Merikh patted the letters under his hand. The grand vizier gave the table and Ruya's body a wide berth before picking up the letters in his arms. Merikh whispered something to Nikias as the old man collected the paperwork, though what exactly was said, Ruya couldn't tell. She let it slide, instead focusing back on her body.

It was easier to return to her body than to leave it, though Ruya could have done without the excruciating pain. Joining her soul back to her body felt as if every inch of her skin were on fire. The desk under her felt cold, and Ruya flattened her palms against it. She couldn't feel temperature as a soul, and clearly her conversation had raised Merikh's ire more than she'd expected.

It feels wonderful to be cold, she thought before opening her eyes. Nikias had left the room, and Sarka stood by the door with her arms folded across her chest. Ruya scooted off the table and back into a chair before gesturing for Sarka to sit down. Merikh took a deep breath, visibly collecting his thoughts. The walls he hid behind had changed from merely protecting his thoughts to projecting more regal stoicism. He'd made up his mind.

"We will not be speaking like this again. You will stay within the confines of your skin, or I will give the high priest what he wants and let the Akhenic Temple try you both for heresy. Understood?"

"Of course." Ruya smiled.

"Any concerns regarding your accommodations should be brought to the Ajir steward, not to me. While it might surprise you, I do, in fact, have more important matters to handle than your comfort." Merikh gave Sarka a rather pointed look. "As far as the library, the grand vizier will draw up access papers."

"You don't allow free access to a library?" Sarka couldn't hide her surprise.

"There are fragile books and scrolls within it. You're not a scholar, therefore you need the escort of one. I won't have you ruining an ancient tome because your temper flickered."

Ruya cleared her throat. "That's more than fair." Paranoid, of course, but Ruya wasn't going to press their luck. Besides, extra eyes and hands would only help narrowing down what books might be useful to them.

"In regard to access throughout the palace, you will have a Royal Guard escort at all times. At present, you are not welcome in court."

Ruya tried to protest, but Merikh raised a hand to silence her.

"That may change in the future," he continued.

It will. Ruya had no doubt. He needed her there, swaying minds to their cause. But pragmatically, she could understand his reluctance. He needed to prove that he was still in control to his inferiors, lest they believe him simply a puppet.

"Of course," Ruya said. "What of the city? I'd like to establish a Pantheon temple, a place to pray. We have followers in the city from Kasu that I'd like to reassure that all is well."

"Name three of them, and I'll have the Ajir bring them to the palace. They are free to find a place to worship. You are not going into the city yet. The Royal Guards will keep the peace should the Akhenic Faithful take issue with your followers."

Ruya glanced at Sarka, who frowned and bit her lip. Being separate from their followers was hardly ideal, but they'd have to take what they could get for the moment.

"Thank you, Merikh. Now, what can we do to help you?" Ruya asked. The question surprised him, and Merikh shook his head.

"Do as I ask. That should be plenty." Merikh stood but gestured for Ruya to stay put. "I'll send for guards. You will remain here until your escort arrives. Then, you will return to your suite until they've been briefed on where you may go."

The door opened ahead of Merikh and shut firmly behind him. A thick wall of ice appeared, covering the door completely. Sarka scoffed and petulantly formed a tongue of flame that quickly melted the ice.

"We have what we wanted. Must you push?" Ruya scolded.

"He's hiding something."

"Probably a lot of somethings, but let's be fair, so are we."

"I don't miss this, you know." Sarka walked away from the door and sat down at the table. "Pissing contests."

"Yes, it's much easier when you simply go where you're paid to," Ruya said flippantly. The temperature rose again. "Oh, come on, you know that's not unfair of me. Payment in faith is still payment."

"It wasn't profiteering. My soldiers fought justly. *Always.*"

Ruya simply nodded, happy to let the subject drop. Livinja was a careful goddess, not as passionate as her counterparts of chaos and wrath. All the same, she was often dragged into the conflicts Skyndar and Belara would create. Sarka led those legions, and those legions were hardly defending themselves. The distinctions Sarka had were ones Ruya believed made out of guilt, but she was not going to confront Sarka about them. Whatever let the champion sleep at night.

"At least we'll have archive access now," Ruya said with a smile, trying to change the subject. "What do you plan to do once Livinja is free? The first thing once this is all over?"

"I'm going to walk old battlefields, Ruya."

Sarka's words held a weight to them that brought a long silence only broken by the door opening. Two guards entered to escort them back to their suite. It was another hour before Sarka was given separate accommodations within the barracks.

CHAPTER 8

20TH OF TAVITH, FIRST HARVEST, 902 UNIFIED AGE
RAJIBAD, RAUDHAH PROVINCE

The Rajibad river docks teemed with people. Normally it would be busy with merchants bringing in wares, but this week was different. The Rajibad guards clad in dark-blue uniforms were joined by the red-clad Royal Guards. Merchants were crammed tightly into half as many docks as usual to unload from. The rest of the docks unloaded retinues of noblemen and noblewomen. It wasn't every day the Shah summoned a Quorum; the last time had been after Mansur's assassination for Shah Merikh's coronation. Another Quorum didn't bode well. It worsened the uneasy feeling in Loralee's gut brought on by the ferry.

Normally they would have ridden from Abadan to Rajibad. It was a six-day ride, worth every minute in the saddle. But the Quorum had her father, Duq Alaziz, worried. With the arrival of Amira Jin Nakano in Abadan, they'd opted for the ferry. Three days on the river had been spent in hushed discussions, many of which Loralee's father tried to keep her from. He'd barely spoken to her outside of those meetings, and his displeasure at her presence hadn't lessened since leaving Abadan. But how could she pass up an opportunity like this?

Loralee nimbly tacked up her dapple gray mare, Amarante, while the servants unloaded the ferry. House Neredi guards tacked up their horses nearby. The pale-blue uniforms stood in stark contrast with the solid black ones of House Nakano. House Nakano guards waited patiently on foot for their amira. Her father had offered Amira Jin a horse, one she'd graciously accepted. Riding a little Tsukarai pony into Rajibad would have been beneath her. To have her riding on a Neredi horse was an honor. And it gave Loralee someone else to ride beside other than her irritated father.

Loralee glanced over her shoulder discreetly to look at him. The duq's dark eyes were narrow and his jaw clenched. How much of that was her fault, Loralee wasn't sure.

I just want you to be safe, he'd argued. Loralee and her mother had quickly trampled all over that. The Quorum would be as safe as anywhere—safer, perhaps, considering the number of guards. There were many higher-priority targets for an assassin's blade than a lowly sayida.

"Are you ready?" Jin led the little bay mare she'd been given toward Loralee. The horse had already managed to get a line of drool over the amira's cherry kimono. It was the only part of Jin's attire out of place; her black hair was tied back in a perfect bun. Jade beads hung from a hairpin and framed the amira's painted face.

"Are you sure *you* are?" Loralee asked, glancing dubiously at Jin's tack. Loralee handed her mare to Jin before double-checking the amira's saddle. The cinch tightened an inch. Loralee buckled the clip and retied the knot before taking her mare back from Jin.

"I'll never understand why a horse is preferable to a rickshaw." Jin shook her head as one of her guards gave her a leg up into the saddle.

Loralee simply shrugged and mounted her mare. "Rickshaws lack personality." Loralee rubbed her mare's neck. Amarante had been one of Loralee's first horses; they'd grown up together. The idea of riding a rickshaw was barely more repugnant than the idea of a carriage.

"*Personality,*" Jin scoffed. "Ride with me. I don't think Duq Alaziz will miss you."

Both women glanced toward Loralee's father. He nodded back at them. His expression softened a little, the edge of his mood seemingly relieved by the homey comfort of his saddle. Loralee adjusted her pale-blue sari, the gold bangles on her arms jingling quietly as she did so. She carefully checked her hijab, her dark hair hidden behind the blue-and-silver scarf. It was all gaudier than she preferred when riding, but she couldn't afford to show a slovenly first impression with their host. Nor with the other attendees.

Colorful banners from the different noble households hung over the main road toward the Rajibad palace. They were predominantly the dark blue and gold of the Attar family, the leopard crest displayed proudly, but each of the many noble houses summoned to the Quorum were represented. Loralee glimpsed the pale-blue banners with the white antelope of House Neredi, and her nerves relented a little.

I have every right to be here, in spite of Baba's worries, she reassured herself.

Jin reached out and touched Loralee's arm gently as they passed through a large sandstone archway. Their retinue joined the teeming mass of other nobles and their attendants.

"The green riders there." Jin barely nodded her head toward them, and Loralee was careful not to gawk as she turned to look. "The Afolayans."

They were an infamous noble house. Their family tree rather prolifically ruled the northern province of Kuzen, and the Shah's late mother had been the sister of Amir Navin and Rabb Mahdi. For all the influence the Afolayan family should have had, they rarely exerted it over Shai'Khal's politics. Instead, their wealth came from the poppy fields in the north. Opium, hashish. If it grew and could alter perception, then the Afolayans had a hand in the growing and selling of it.

"Is it me or does the retinue look...small?" Loralee asked.

Jin nodded. There were plenty of guards, but Loralee didn't see anyone old enough to be the amir or any of the other Afolayan city nobles.

"I don't see Amir Navin. Or... Oh, Akhenios be kind." Jin tsked and shook her head. "He sent Rabb Bilal Nagi. The little one there."

Nagi? Loralee blinked in surprise. The amir could have sent his brother instead. For the amir to send his *nephew* was a dangerous maneuver and a slap in the face to the Shah.

"If the Shah's own uncles won't come..." Loralee drifted off.

"Who else isn't here?" Jin asked. "Good question."

Thoughts of politics left Loralee as the Rajibad palace came into view. The large white marble columns and domed roof were a breathtaking sight. Loralee slowed her horse a little. Jin smiled and shook her head.

"It's a crude imitation of the Madiar palace. The architect couldn't *quite* bastardize it well. Looks like a squat toad if you ask me," Jin lamented.

Loralee's jaw dropped. "Amira!"

Jin tsked. "You'll understand when you see Madiar."

"*If,* my dear amira. If," Loralee corrected.

Jin rolled her eyes and slapped Loralee's wrist with her paper fan. "*When*, Sayida. Of that, I have no doubt and every hope."

The amira grew serious when the man and woman standing on the top steps of the palace caught her attention. The older man wore a dark-blue kaftan with elaborate golden patterns embroidered into the fabric, which caught the sunlight with a faint shimmer. The woman's abaya matched, and thick golden bands covered her sleeves and wrapped her hair.

"Amir Olumide and Duqa Emilia?" Loralee asked.

Jin nodded. "You've met them before?"

"No, never had the pleasure. They leave buying horses to Duq Hasad," Loralee said, her tone distracted as they approached the Attar barns. Duq Hasad was younger than Loralee by a few years, but he had a promising eye for horses and a straightforward honesty that her father had immediately taken to. As the younger of the two Attar sons, Duq Hasad was set to inherit nothing after his parents' death and would need a proper vocation of some kind. His brother, Duq Rashad, was hardly expected to provide for him. Loralee was certain her father was trying his best to make Hasad invaluable to the running of the Attar barns. Because of that, Loralee had never made the trip to Rajibad before. Duq Hasad came by himself when his father needed horses.

"Ah. Well, speaking of people you haven't met, there's the Shah." Jin once again carefully nodded her head. Three men had emerged from the portcullis behind the amir and duqa. She recognized Duq Hasad right away. The teenager was a touch gangly. He hadn't quite grown into his limbs yet, and his nervousness could be seen from a mile away. He had a bad habit of bouncing on his heels. The other two, Loralee assumed were Duq Rashad and Shah Merikh, but which was which, Loralee couldn't place at a distance. Unlike the amir and duqa, neither man wore their family colors. And the men bore a closer resemblance to each other than the Attars.

No wonder there're rumors, Loralee thought.

Amir Olumide had been the closest of friends and allies to Mansur and had spent much of his youth in Madiar at the palace. That hadn't changed when he married Emilia, at least, not at first. That was when the rumors all began to split off. Some believed Duqa Emilia an adulteress, having seduced Mansur.

Loralee had her doubts, as Amir Olumide and Duqa Emilia had a reputation of being far too close a couple for something like that to have happened. Surely if that had been the case, then Duqa Emilia would have been careful enough *not* to get pregnant.

No, Loralee leaned toward the other rumors—that Mansur raped Emilia, and she'd ended up carrying his child. That Amir Olumide had returned to Rajibad to protect his wife and try to quell rumors that the child wasn't his. Duqa Emilia swore that Rashad was the amir's son, but the rumors persisted. Royal bastards were few and far between, as most had been hunted down and killed by Mansur or Merikh. The fact that Duq Rashad lived proved that, if nothing else, the amir wasn't particularly bothered by the rumors or the idea of raising another man's son as his heir. And that perhaps Rashad was content to remain heir to Rajibad and become just the amir once Olumide died.

"I see," Loralee said vaguely back to Jin. Try as she might, the two men looked too similar for her to pick which one was the Shah without help. Both men were tall and long limbed, with the same sharp cheekbones. The one on the right was a little taller. His hair was cut short, and a thin, well-groomed trace of a beard lined his jaw. There was a cockiness to his posture that Loralee assumed made him royal.

The amira smiled and shook her head.

"He's the one on the left, not the one you're looking at," Jin teased.

"Of course he is. *Obviously.*" Loralee's tone mocked the amira, but Jin understood the relief in her eyes.

"It's not a mistake you'd make if we were closer," Jin said. "The eyes give it away. And the vexing aura."

"I just didn't expect him to look so plain," Loralee confessed quietly.

The man on the left was dressed in a black-and-silver salwar kameez that looked more befitting a grand vizier than a shah. Instead of brashness, the Shah's posture looked far more cautious. Not insecure, just...observant. Almost scholarly compared to the man beside him. Loralee supposed it wasn't surprising to see in a sorcerer. The Shah was clean shaven, unlike most noblemen, and his black hair fell in unkempt waves almost to his shoulders. Vanity didn't appear to be one of his vices.

The women dismounted at the barns, and Jin waited for Loralee as she untacked their horses. No self-respecting Yahidah noble let a groom handle their horse, but as a Tsukarai, Jin hardly shared that opinion. By the time Loralee finished both horses, her father had caught up and untacked his horse. Alaziz walked over to Loralee and put his hand on her shoulder gently.

"You know how I feel about you being here," Alaziz told her quietly. "*Please* be careful. Do my heart a favor and don't talk to the Shah beyond whatever is necessary. And hopefully nothing will be necessary."

Loralee put her hand over his. "You worry too much, and it shows, Baba," Loralee teased before squeezing his weathered old hand. He frowned, the worry lines thick on his face. Alaziz wasn't as old as he looked, but a lifetime outside in the sun and wind had stolen his youth and leathered his skin. Alaziz shook his head, dropped his hand off her shoulder, and then headed up the stairs behind Amira Jin. Loralee held back a sigh before following her father.

Perfunctory greetings met with deep bows were the norm. Loralee barely paid attention as Amir Olumide and Duqa Emilia greeted Jin and Alaziz. They gave the ritually demanded warm welcome to the Attar home, insisting that if anything could be done to make their stay more pleasant, to let them know. Meanwhile, their tones clearly stated that such requests would be absolutely boorish, considering Alaziz's lesser station. Not to mention, if the Shah had found no reason to complain, then surely a duq from Abadan couldn't.

Normally, Loralee would have been far more attentive to what was said. But nothing had prepared her for the disquieting feeling that hit her halfway up the stairs. It wasn't quite nauseating, but it sent a shudder down her spine, and a pit grew in her stomach. It took her a moment to place it.

Magic.

Loralee was no sorceress, but she couldn't remember ever feeling an aura so prominently. *No wonder Jin finds the Shah's presence uncomfortable,* Loralee thought.

"Duq, you've been remiss. Hasad speaks quite highly of your daughter. Is this Sayida Loralee?"

Loralee rose a little from her bow, raising her eyes from the alabaster steps. In front of her, Duq Rashad stood.

"Of course. Apologies, Duq Rashad," Alaziz said, his tone unabashedly resigned. "May I present my daughter, Sayida Loralee Neredi."

Duq Rashad extended his hand to her, and Loralee had barely taken it before the duq pulled her out of her bow and onto the same step as her father and Jin.

"I think our future khanum has done enough bowing for the day, wouldn't you agree, Sayida?" Rashad asked, his smirk widening into a disarming smile. A chill touched the air, as if the sun had gone behind a cloud, but there were none to be seen.

Loralee hesitated a moment before meeting Rashad's gaze. Should she feign ignorance or confirm his assumption?

"Duq, I believe that's up to the Shah, not me. But my back does appreciate it." Loralee smiled, glancing briefly toward the Shah. He had a sour look on his face, his golden eyes slightly narrowed. The man looked less than impressed with the topic.

"Well, future khanum or not, a beautiful woman shouldn't be hidden staring at the ground," Duq Rashad continued, letting go of Loralee's hand.

The Shah cleared his throat. "Duq Hasad, you should show your guests to their quarters. Duq Rashad, don't you have a..." The Shah hesitated, deliberately making a show of looking for a word. "...concubine or a *different* sayida somewhere who requires your attention?"

Despite the warning tone, Rashad laughed.

"Several, I'm sure. Not all of us have your *exceptional* self-restraint, Shahanshah."

"A pity, I'm sure," Duq Alaziz interrupted. He gestured to the youngest Attar son. "Come, Duq Hasad, show an old man somewhere to rest his bones."

Hasad nodded and gestured toward the arched doors through the portcullis. Jin bowed, Loralee and her father following suit, before Hasad led them inside. Duq Alaziz's posture grew irritated the moment the doors shut behind them.

"Your brother is an idiot, Hasad," Alaziz muttered.

The young man shrugged. "It's amazing what charm and good looks lets you get away with. I'm sure the Shah would have his head if Rashad wasn't so well-loved. Or prolific." Hasad tried to hide the bitterness in his voice.

There were ten years between Hasad and Rashad, and Loralee wondered if Hasad would make it to see his twenty-fifth natal anniversary if that sort of bitterness was overheard by the wrong person.

Alaziz quickly turned the subject to horses, and the two duqs became lost in conversation as Duq Hasad led them through the halls of the Attars' palace. With the men distracted, Jin touched Loralee's elbow, and the two women fell back to follow from a few feet behind.

"I thought your betrothal was a secret?" Jin whispered.

"So did I," Loralee said. "Baba never speaks of it, and it's never garnered any attention before."

Loralee herself had only become aware of her betrothal a few years ago, when Merikh ascended to the throne. When the summons had arrived for her parents, requesting the duq and duqa's presence in Madiar to pay tribute and swear fealty to their new shah, her father had been more than relieved that Loralee had not been invited. Only then had he allowed her mother to explain the bare minimum: Mansur and Alaziz had negotiated the betrothal of Loralee and Merikh over a decade ago, and she was to speak of it to no one.

Naturally, she'd kept that secret as well as any sixteen-year-old could. Loralee had told Jin, and they had kept that secret since. The thought had been exciting at first. Loralee had grown up on the same stories as everyone else. Fantastical myths with great heroic shahs and amirs, of cunning and beautiful khanums, and so of course it had colored her perception. Her excitement had died four months later, when the Royal Guard passed through Abadan and beheaded a hundred merchant rabbs and sayidas who hadn't sworn fealty to their new shah.

In the years since, Loralee had been just as content as her father to leave the matter alone. The Shah seemed to have no desire to call on her, and Loralee had begun to wonder if he even knew about the betrothal.

"I wonder if Amir Olumide knew of it when it happened, or if Duq Rashad has been digging around. And if he has, has he been looking into you or the Shah?" Jin mused.

Loralee bit the inside of her lip and said nothing. She didn't know. In that ignorance, Loralee suddenly felt woefully unprepared for their stay in Rajibad. If nothing else, that brief interaction showed exactly why her father was so worried. Perhaps his fears were not so ill-placed. If the Attars knew, others might. The blood of the future khanum was most definitely worth spilling.

"Loralee." Alaziz pulled her from her thoughts. He was standing in front of a large door, and he gestured toward it.

"Amira Jin, if I may steal you away to show you where the amirs' wing is?" Duq Hasad asked, leaving Alaziz's side. He hesitated near Loralee. "If you can find the time, sayida, I know your father will be quite busy with the Quorum, but if you could spare a moment..." Duq Hasad had little of the eloquence of his brother, and Loralee smiled.

"What would you like?"

"Well, we have many of your former horses here. I'd love to show their progress to you."

Loralee nodded before bowing her head and walking to her father.

"That one is yours. That one"—he pointed his thumb over his shoulder to across the hall—"is apparently mine."

"I'm shocked we earned separate accommodations," Loralee said as she opened the door. The room was small. It had a bed, a small writing desk, and a little sitting area. Even so, it was spacious compared to the ferry. Alaziz turned to cross the hall, and Loralee tapped his shoulder.

"Baba, may I have a word?"

"In here. I need to rest and prepare," he said, gesturing to his room. Loralee shut her door behind her and followed her father across the hall. Alaziz's accommodations weren't much grander than hers, but Loralee doubted her father would do much more than sleep there. Alaziz shut the door behind Loralee and sighed as he ran a hand over his graying beard.

"I know what you're going to ask, and the answer is still no."

"What harm could it do?" Loralee asked, trying not to raise her voice in frustration.

"Did you not hear what Duq Rashad said to you? Did you not feel the cold? I won't have you be a bone between the duq and the Shah."

"That was really the Shah?" Loralee asked, her dark eyes widening in awe. There were plenty of rumors about the Shah's magic, some more fantastical than others. The idea he could affect the weather seemed absurd, even on a small scale like that. But her question was simply met with a glare.

Alaziz crossed the room to where servants had laid out his bags. He untied them quickly and began digging out notebooks.

"Baba, I can avoid the duq and the Shah. But let me attend the Quorum. I promise I won't speak! I can sit quietly and learn. The Quorum is an invaluable opportunity, and who knows when the next one might be?"

"Possibly never, in which case, nothing here is useful. Since I became duq, I can count on one hand how many times I've met nobles like Amir Navin or...well, *any* of the Ydeban nobles. You don't need the connections here. I should never have let your mother convince me to bring you along."

"If Maman were here, you know she'd agree with me."

"If your maman had her way, you'd be having chai with the Shah this afternoon and married tomorrow. I thank the gods she isn't here, and you should too," Alaziz muttered, digging deep into his bags for a notebook buried at the bottom.

Loralee laughed. "I'll pass that along!"

Duqa Jasira, Loralee's mother, couldn't be more opposite from Alaziz. Younger and full of life, the duqa adored the political arena and rarely tired of its machinations. Whereas Alaziz worried about Loralee's potential marriage, Jasira was ecstatic. Loralee had no doubt her father wasn't far off from his estimation of events had Jasira been present. But Alaziz had insisted the duqa remain in Abadan to care for the city in his absence. In spite of their differences, the duq and duqa were a formidable couple and an impressive example of an arranged marriage working out well. Loralee hoped her own marriage, regardless of her husband, would end up at least as amiable.

"Loralee, you're not going to encounter most of these nobles again. Your presence will be nothing but disruptive. It already is, if Duq Rashad's comments are indicative of anything. I doubt Amir Xolani brought his daughter. Even if he did, Duqa Adanna won't be present in the Quorum. Neither will Duq Rashad. They're set to inherit a great deal more than you. You can help Duq Hasad with the horses. Keep an eye on the horses in other barns too, just in case there's any stock worth breeding. Leave the politics to me, and lay low."

"Baba—"

"No. Go write your mother, let her know we've arrived here safely. If you get a bird sent off today, her chastisement for me will arrive before the Quorum," Alaziz said, his serious expression cracked with a warm smile.

Fine, Loralee thought, simply bowing her head.

"As you ask," she conceded for the moment and left Alaziz alone to his work. She'd leave the subject dropped for the rest of today, but there were three more days before the Quorum started. Plenty of time, she hoped, to change her father's mind.

CHAPTER 9

23rd of Tavith, First Harvest, 902 Unified Age
Rajibad, Raudhah Province

Three days of arguing with Alaziz hadn't changed his mind. Loralee had made the mistake of mentioning that even if these were nobles she would never meet as duqa of Abadan, if she became the khanum, they were nobles she *needed* to know and be prepared to deal with. Alaziz had dug in his heels and buried his head in the sand, the discussion halted permanently.

So while Alaziz and the other nobles sat in the Quorum this morning, Loralee made her way to the Attar family barns. A Neredi guard escorted her, though she left him at the mouth of the barns and went to find Amarante's stall alone. The gray mare nickered at her gently as she approached, and Loralee slid her hands under the mare's dark mane. In the cold desert morning, her fingers welcomed the warmth. Once Loralee could feel her fingertips again, she haltered Amarante and brought the mare out of the stall.

Movement caught Loralee's attention, drawing her eye down the aisle, out to the arena at the end of the barn. A small crowd was gathered at the fence. Loralee glanced back to Amarante.

"A quiet ride might be out of the question," Loralee muttered under her breath before leading the mare down the aisle.

Once outside the barn, Loralee frowned. The Shah was putting a bay horse through her paces in the arena. A few of those watching were dressed as Attar grooms. Loralee imagined most were nobles in situations like hers—here, but unwelcome in the Quorum. Loralee shook her head. She knew her father was already seated, waiting on the Shah.

This is ridiculous, Loralee thought. She turned and took Amarante back to her stall, then returned to the arena. Away from the crowd at the arena gate, two elite Ajir guards and a young man clad in black stood. As Loralee approached, the one guard raised his hand.

"Move on, bayan."

"Has the Shah been informed the Quorum awaits? His council is ready," Loralee said.

"I'm sure he knows," the servant answered, "but we thought this ride would go a lot smoother than it has, Sayida Loralee." He raised his hand a little off the fence to point at the pair.

There was white foamy sweat on the mare's shoulders and between her legs. Her delicate nostrils were flared and her ears stiff. She looked far from impressed with the questions being asked of her by the Shah. Granted, he didn't appear particularly thrilled with her answers. There was a tension in his posture that hinted at him deliberately making her current prancing and head-tossing difficult. There was an easy answer he was trying to get her to give, only the mare wasn't seeing it.

"She doesn't take well to long trips and foreign places?" Loralee asked, trying to hide her surprise that a servant had recognized her.

The servant shook his head. "Normally she does, but sometimes she just overthinks her answers. I'm...pretty sure the Shah has been trying to just get her to walk nicely for a while now."

The young man sounded unsure. He wasn't a groom, that much was clear. Loralee folded her arms across her chest and watched in silence for a few minutes before the mare finally stopped trotting and prancing. The mare took a step at the walk, lowered her neck, and then licked her lips before letting out a deep, contented breath. The Shah stopped her and immediately dismounted. He rubbed the bay mare's neck affectionately as he stood beside her.

"Adrian." The Shah glanced over toward the gate, and it opened.

The servant stepped through it, and the gate closed behind him. Adrian trudged through the sand toward the Shah, who handed him the mare's reins.

"The Quorum waits for you, Shahanshah," Adrian informed him. "The sayida wanted to make sure you were told."

"Cool her down. *Walk* her. If she won't under saddle, then lead her," the Shah instructed, ignoring his servant's words.

Adrian moved to the mare's side and shortened the stirrup, nodding at his instructions. The Shah walked back toward the gate. It opened, and Loralee bowed her head.

"Shahanshah." Loralee kept her eyes firmly on his riding boots. It hid her surprise when the Shah leaned in to speak with her. As it had yesterday, his aura was overpowering, and Loralee fought the urge to step away from him.

"You are *not* the khanum. Do not presume to influence my schedule again, sayida. And do not pester my steward."

Loralee nodded once. "Apologies, Shahanshah. It was not my intention."

"Of course not." His tone was bored, or perhaps simply disinterested. The Shah straightened up and headed inside. One of his guards followed while the other remained at the arena gate.

Loralee let out a slow breath as she watched the Shah leave. The feeling of teetering off balance lessened as the distance between them became greater. Sorcerers of his strength were exceptionally rare. Loralee had never been around anyone anywhere nearly that strong. Powerful men didn't make her nervous as a rule. Her title protected her well enough. When it didn't, Loralee knew her way around a dagger or shamshir. But magic was a completely different animal, and she didn't trust it. Not when it would be all too easy for a man like the Shah to take her soul as a plaything.

Loralee turned back to the arena. Men and women killed for the privilege to breed their animals to royal stock. Breeding races and tournaments were not for the poorly bred nor faint of heart. To even become a groom in the royal barns took exceptional talent. Few of those grooms, as far as Loralee understood, were elite enough horsemen and women to be given the privilege of working with the best of the best horses, the private mares and stallions of the Shah.

Adrian, clearly, was not among those elite. His posture was too rigid; his seat fought against the horse. Loralee could have picked half a dozen things wrong with him. And yet...there he was, riding a mare worth more than the Neredi estate. Riding in a saddle that might as well have been the throne.

How does a servant earn the right to sit in the Shah's saddle? It was a question Loralee left unanswered as she returned to the barn. The encounter left her irritated, and Loralee pulled Amarante out into the aisle just to groom. She was in no mood to ride, not now.

Nikias would like her. If the grand vizier had come to Rajibad, it would have been him nagging Merikh about appointments this morning instead of Sayida Loralee. Perhaps "nagging" was too strong a word for it, but Merikh's tardiness, much like his choice of venue, wasn't without reason. He was more than happy to let the nobles stew for a little while, to mutter amongst themselves. It was a petty move, but anything that helped crack the carefully planned masks of the nobles was worth it.

The doors groaned open ahead of Merikh, silencing the conversation of those inside. Amir Olumide had set up benches for the nobles to sit at in a semicircle toward a throne, with more than enough room for the nobles in attendance to sit comfortably. They'd sectioned themselves into their provinces, easily recognizable from the divisiveness between the races of the old kingdoms. There were more empty spaces than Merikh had hoped, though it didn't surprise him.

Rabb Khamisi's presence at the meeting with Alcaeus hadn't boded well. Merikh was certain the rabb had immediately sent word to Duqa Enitan. Her allies had undoubtedly been told Alcaeus's side of events. Their absence at the Quorum spoke volumes about their loyalty. Of the Ydeban vassal council, four appeared to have abstained from attending. Merikh hardly recognized all of his nobles, but he was willing to bet each missing person hailed from the far side of the Katu Mountains. The farthest reaches of his empire and most rebellious to Yahidah rule, they were the Umbeah nobles who looked for any excuse to push yet again for an independent Ydeba.

The nobles rose to their feet as Merikh walked into the room, sitting down after he took his place at the throne. He held back a wince as he sat. Olumide had tried to make it comfortable, but the soft cushions offered little support and made Merikh's back ache almost instantly, and it was already sore from the jarring ride on Zahira.

All the more reason to try to keep this short, Merikh thought.

"Amir Xolani, your province has shrunk, I see," Merikh said.

The amir from Ydeba stood from his bench. The Umbeah man was tall and clean shaven, with an orange turban on his bald head. It matched the black and orange of his kaftan, the vibrant color contrasted against his dark skin. Xolani had his sleeves pushed back to his elbows, making visible the elaborate ceremonial scars on his arms. The scars told stories, drawn representations of the important events in the amir's life. It was a method of record-keeping Merikh was glad his family line had left behind. He had enough scars to last a lifetime as it was.

"Shahanshah, I spoke at length with Duqa Enitan and her sympathizers. They find your denouncement of the Akhenic faith untenable. I hope this council will give me reassurances to send them that their fears are unfounded. That their shah hasn't thrown in with cultists and djinn sympathizers." Amir Xolani bowed his head before sitting down again.

"It would have been prudent for them to bring their worries about their shah *to* their shah directly. I do appreciate your presence here." Merikh cast a pointed look toward the Kuzen provincial nobles. Duqa Sachiko sat in the most prominent seat.

Damn you, Navin. But to Merikh's surprise, it wasn't the duqa who stood. Instead, a young boy dressed in green and silver cleared his throat. He then stood from the bench and bowed.

"Shahanshah," the boy said, his voice cracking. He couldn't have been more than fourteen, if that. His cheeks still held their baby fat.

"Who are you?" Merikh asked.

The boy nodded quickly, wincing as if to chide himself for missing a cue. Merikh hazarded a guess that the boy had received barely any training before being thrown at this task.

"Rabb Bilal Nagi, Shahanshah. Duqa Aminah is my aunt. R-rather, Amir Navin is my uncle. Through marriage," the young rabb stammered, oversharing nervously.

"Thank the gods," Merikh said with a smirk. "You had me worried we shared blood."

A few laughs smattered through the Quorum. Bilal shrank back and fidgeted with his cuffs. He was a whelp among jackals. House Nagi had fallen from prominence generations ago. Now they were barely more than merchants playing at power. Hardly appropriate representatives of a governing amir. The message was quite clear: Amir Navin believed this was a small problem and none of his concern.

"Amir Navin," the boy said, "he sent this. He regrets he cannot attend but wishes to assure you of his undying loyalty." Bilal picked up a letter that had been sitting on the bench beside him and lifted it up toward Merikh.

"Do your feet work?" Merikh asked. "Approach."

"Oh, of course." Bilal nearly tripped in his haste. He bowed deeply in front of the throne and held out the letter. Merikh took it from him carefully before shooing the boy away. Merikh cracked the seal and read it quickly. It was a gross show of flattery and what Navin perceived as loyalty. In reality, it was nothing more than a reiteration that until this started affecting his coffers, Amir Navin didn't care one way or another who believed what. He had bigger problems to deal with, such as the Thief Lord.

"The entirety of House Afolayan agrees with this?" Merikh asked.

"Yes, Shahanshah."

"Nagis included? Do you know what this says?"

Bilal bit his lip and grew pale. "N-no, Shahanshah, I don't know what it says."

Merikh crumpled the paper in his hand. A small flicker of green fog surrounded it, and the paper turned to dust. He brushed it off on the throne's armrest.

"You should be more careful with what you ascribe yourself to, then," Merikh said.

Bilal was undereducated but not hopeless. Merikh could only hope the boy learned from this encounter.

"Tell my uncle that his fealty is appreciated. So much so that I look forward to his continued show of it in the form of troops and supplies."

Bilal nodded frantically. The doors groaned open again.

"Your uncle will be anxious to see you, I'm sure," Merikh said, clearly dismissing him.

Bilal tripped and stumbled out the door, and it shut behind him quickly. The boy wasn't needed at the Quorum; there was nothing he could contribute. Merikh would handle his uncle's insult at a more advantageous time than preceding a potential war.

"Duqa Sachiko, I trust you can confer with your counterparts and represent them?" Merikh asked.

She nodded.

"Good."

Merikh took a deep breath and sat a little straighter on the throne. A lightning flicker of pain spasmed across his back. A moment later, a thin layer of ice began to relieve the irritation. It would only last a few minutes, but something was better than nothing.

"Undoubtedly," he went on, "there have been concerning rumors throughout your provinces and cities about the Pantheon priestesses, the Akhenic Temple, and where your monarchy stands on the matter. My aim as shah is not to interfere in Temple matters *unless* it is in Shai'Khal's best interest for me to do so. The culling of the Priest Council was one such matter. Once again, I find myself forced into a position requiring action. Regardless of what our subjects believe, they are still citizens of Shai'Khal. Your duties, as my representatives, is to protect them from persecution and enforce *my* laws, not the suggestions of the Akhenic Temple."

"Shahanshah." Amir Xolani stood and bowed respectfully. "My legate informed me that the false priestesses presently reside within the Madiar palace."

Duqa Sachiko cleared her throat. "They're not false, Amir. You'd know that if you met them."

"Ruya and Sarka are guests in the palace for the time being, yes," Merikh said. "Whether they are false or true is not my place to determine."

"Your Highness, why not hand them over to High Priest Alcaeus for scrutiny, then?" Amira Jin spoke up quietly.

Merikh wasn't sure if she was shy or just soft-spoken. Her father had died suddenly from a bleeding fever a few years ago, making Amira Jin the youngest amira in generations and one of the few present close in age to Merikh.

"If you do that, Shahanshah, they'll be tortured and executed without being given a fair chance," Alkont Sen Kokawa interjected quickly. The alkont sat beside Duqa Sachiko. His city of Kaidaku had been along the route Adrian had taken when he brought Sarka and Ruya to Madiar. Apparently their brief influence had been enough to sway the alkont to their side. That or Duqa Sachiko had been a prolific advocate on their behalf.

"A fair chance? They don't *need* a fair chance," Kontess Rehema said loudly, her tone final. "They're cultists and should have been executed long before their poison spread." The elderly Umbeah woman from Buhet had been one of Mansur's strongest supporters. Luckily, that loyalty seemed to have rubbed off on Merikh as well, though he was unsure how far he could push it.

Merikh raised his hand, and those standing sat back down.

"Perhaps, Kontess Rehema. But they weren't, and they won't be executed. They have a large following along the coast, sympathizers and believers among the nobility. The reality of the situation is that these beliefs aren't going to disappear. It is up to us to create a new Shai'Khal prepared to deal with them, one that protects Pantheon believers as much as Akhenic."

"If a limb is dead, you cut it off, Your Majesty, not let it fester and rot the body," Kontess Rehema countered boldly.

"Forgive me, kontess, but what rot would that be?" Duq Alaziz asked firmly. "The one that murders children or the one that offers diversity?"

Merikh held back a smile at the look on the kontess's face. Her lips were pursed tight, her eyes narrowed as if the duq had just force-fed her a lemon.

"Kontess," Merikh said, clearing his throat, "I have no desire to watch our country rot. But I do not see it happening from Pantheon supporters, nor from the Akhenic Faithful." Merikh added the last words quickly as Xolani and other Faithful shot him rankled looks. "Work with me to keep our citizens safe. Then work with the high priest to *peaceably* convert the willing back to Akhenios."

The kontess hardly looked mollified.

The Quorum continued for another few hours before Merikh disbanded it for the day. Little had been accomplished, but Merikh expected nothing more for the first day. It gave him a feeling for who he could rely on, who needed to be swayed, and who would oppose him. A few would support him purely on blood, Kontess Rehema among them. Her allies would stay in line.

Merikh worried more about keeping Amir Xolani on his side. The amir's sister, Baruna Azmera Iherjirika, had kept quiet through the Quorum but had looked upset. Her city, Duak, was a key port in Ydeba on the southern coast. Without her support, it would be all too easy for her to siege her neighboring city Ogot and to whisper treason in Amir Xolani's ear.

If he could keep Amir Xolani and Kontess Rehema placated, then at least the Umbeah nobles present would side with him. The rest of the nobles were more difficult to gauge. Alaziz's support hardly came as a surprise. The man wanted his daughter out of that betrothal agreement. Now he hoped to garner enough favor to be rid of it. But there had been a reason for Mansur to have leveraged Alaziz's support, and Merikh was unwilling to simply let it go. Especially when Amir Olumide had been conspicuously silent through the proceedings thus far.

Merikh left the room escorted by his guards to ensure privacy as he headed back to his quarters. Adrian met him at the door, the young man bowing before following Merikh into the room.

"Is there a bird from Nikias?"

"Several, Shahanshah. I left the paperwork on your desk," Adrian told him. "How did the Quorum go?" The question was asked hesitantly. With the door shut behind them, Merikh ran a hand over his face.

"As well as can be expected. I want you to arrange for a dinner tonight with the amirs and amira. A private one. No husbands, wives, or children. Raid Olumide's stores for wine and araq."

"Of course, Shahanshah."

"Go." Merikh dismissed Adrian. Alone, Merikh began flipping through the paperwork on the desk sent from Nikias. Updates on the state of affairs in Madiar—blessedly quiet for the moment—and copies of papers Nikias had pulled from the palace archives from the era before Unification and the banishment of the gods. Hardly light reading, but it was still more relaxing than the Quorum.

CHAPTER 10

"There will be war, Duq Alaziz. Half of Ydeba's nobles didn't even *attend*. Perhaps four armies at least are already set against the Shah. And who can trust the Afolayans? Another three, four armies for sale?"

Kontess Yasmina leaned back, away from the low table, as she finished speaking. The Quorum had disbanded hours ago. While the amirs were stolen away for a private dinner with the Shah, Olumide had entrusted Alaziz with conferring with the rest of Raudhah's provincial nobility. Araq flowed freely at Alaziz's table as the duq listened carefully to the worries of his compatriots. Loralee sat cross-legged on a thick pillow beside him, a frown plain on her lips.

"There are at least a dozen of us who are loyal, Kontess Yasmina," Alaziz reassured her, "many of whom will abstain from any uprising in Ydeba. If you can keep your port safe, I can't imagine a war coming to Al Haraf.".

Her city rested on the southern coast, on the opposite side of the Sarafi Desert. It was nearly impossible to reach safely by land. Between the desert and Emani thieves, it was far too precarious for most to try. The Jansul Ocean was far less risky. More importantly—and Loralee knew her father was far too kind to say so—Al Haraf was unimportant in the grand scheme of Shai'Khal. It could be surrendered to any Ydeban usurpers and then taken back at leisure. Its capture wouldn't cripple Madiar's supplies. The Tsukarai cities, on the other hand...Amira Jin was devoutly Akhenic Faithful.

I hope you're being reasonable, Jin, Loralee thought. Otherwise, Loralee didn't want to think about how the meal with the Shah was faring.

As the conversation died down, Loralee finished her third glass of araq and excused herself from the room. She was drawn back down to the Attar barns for one last check on Amarante for the night. Seeing her mare would quiet Loralee's thoughts.

The stars shone brightly through the cold, cloudless sky. Enchanted lamps gave off a pale-blue glow, creating just enough light to see by comfortably without disturbing the horses. Amarante nickered gently as she stuck her nose over the stall door. When Loralee stood in front of her, the mare rubbed her nose into Loralee's chest and blew into her sky-blue kameez.

"Thanks." Loralee laughed, pushing the mare's head away before brushing the hay and snot off her chest. The mare was fine, but Loralee had trouble shaking the disquieting feeling that lingered from the dinner. No one had come out of the Quorum today with an overabundance of confidence in the situation, only certainty of the open enmity between the Shah and high priest. The last time the Crown had taken arms against the Temple had been 300 years ago, during the Mage War. That war had ended quite poorly for the Crown. Loralee could only hope this confrontation had a better outcome. Regardless of her father's dislike for the Madiaran family, his loathing of the Akhenic Temple was stronger. Betrothal or not, for better or worse, her family would ally with the Shah.

The jingling of coins and the sharp whisper of hushed voices snapped Loralee from her thoughts.

"Are you certain?"

"Completely. The whole retinue will be gone by the end of the week. The Shah's not going to linger here any longer than necessary, and the Quorum will either tear itself apart by then or have hit a wall."

"Yeah, right. Same way you were certain about the damn wine?"

Loralee carefully opened the stall door and shut it quietly behind her. She stuck to the shadows, one hand on Amarante's back to make sure the mare knew where she was. Getting kicked by her horse was the least of Loralee's concerns. The hour was late, the barns deserted. Undoubtedly these men had thought it a safe place to conduct less-than-savory business within the Attars' palace.

"How was I supposed to know he doesn't drink? All nobles drink!"

"Except the Shah."

Loralee barely breathed as two men walked down the barn aisle, passed Amarante's stall, and hesitated at the mouth of the barn.

"This should work, as long as you keep up your end of things."

When Loralee no longer heard footsteps, she tempted fate and moved to the front of the stall. The barn was empty, but she didn't dare leave until she felt confident of her solitude.

Gods, now what? Loralee shut the stall door behind her. The araq hadn't worn off. She still felt off balance, and it tired her. Her bed called rather strongly. But...a vizier was rumored to have died a few months ago. Poisoned wine. Had that been meant for the Shah? Loralee groaned. The right thing to do was to report this to the Ajir captain traveling with the Shah and warn him. Of course, no one knew she'd heard what she had. She could claim ignorance and go to bed.

Can I live with his blood on my hands if he dies? The thought was unwelcome. Loralee double-checked that she'd closed Amarante's stall properly, then headed inside to find the captain.

Loralee got lost twice in the maze of twisting corridors inside the Rajibad palace. She accidentally happened upon a well-lit hallway with an overabundance of red-clad Royal Guards. They all stood a little straighter as she approached. Before she could speak, one turned and approached her.

"Bayan." He bowed his head respectfully. "The Shah has retired for the evening, and he doesn't entertain visitors."

"I have no interest in seeing the Shah," Loralee admitted, perhaps too quickly and with a little too much relief. "I need to speak with your captain."

The guard looked reluctant, as undoubtedly the captain had also retired for the evening. He nodded after a moment and gestured for her to follow him to one of the first doors in the wing. A quiet knock was all that was required to rouse the inhabitant. A gray-haired man opened the door. His red achkan coat had been pulled on haphazardly, a semblance of formality just in case.

"What is it?" The captain glanced from Loralee to the guard.

Loralee cleared her throat. "I overhead some troubling talk regarding the Shah," Loralee said carefully.

The man stifled a yawn. "As has everyone, Sayida....?" She could see him wracking his mind for her name.

"Sayida Loralee Neredi. This talk was about poisoned wine and a more fruitful attempt next time."

That caught the captain's attention better. He ran a hand over his face as he groaned in abject frustration. The door shut for a moment, and when it opened again, the captain had his riding boots on and his achkan buttoned shut.

"The Shah is still awake, I'm sure."

"I didn't want to bother him," Loralee said, balking. Her father would have a heart attack if he heard about Loralee meeting with the Shah well after most of the nobility had retired to their rooms.

"Either we bother him now, or I bother him when we're done, and then I'll be tracking you down when he inevitably wants to hear this report from your lips. Let's cut out the middle man so I can get to bed."

The captain didn't wait for her to answer. He simply walked across the hall and knocked once on another door. It opened a crack, although no one stood on the other side. The captain pushed it the rest of the way open and bowed.

"Apologies, Shahanshah." The captain rose and gestured for Loralee to enter the room. She took a deep breath, smoothed her kameez, and followed the captain inside. To Loralee's relief, the Shah was fully dressed, still in the same red achkan and black salwar he'd been in for the morning ride. He didn't appear readied for bed at all. A lamp burned low on his desk, and a small pile of paperwork rested nearby. He looked tired, as if he'd been close to falling asleep at his desk. The look disappeared behind a well-practiced stoic mask.

"What is it?" the Shah asked, his tone unimpressed.

The captain turned to Loralee, fully expecting her to answer. Loralee bowed her head.

"It's a small matter, Shahanshah. I had no intention of intruding on your evening. I overhead talk in the barns moments ago, discussing what may be an attempt on your life. I thought it prudent for your captain to know."

"But not prudent for me?" The Shah scoffed and pushed his chair away from the desk to look at Loralee easier. "What exactly did they say?"

"They mentioned they tried to poison your wine, and they were interested in your retinue's departure in a week."

"Did you see them?"

"No, Shahanshah, I did not. I thought I recognized one of the voices, but I couldn't place him."

The Shah drummed his fingers along an armrest for a moment.

"Bashir, find the leak in the Attar household. I'll speak with you later," the Shah said, dismissing his guard.

Loralee bit the inside of her lip, trying to hide her discomfort as the door shut behind the captain. Merikh's aura was no less disquieting now than it had been before, perhaps more bothersome, thanks to the araq. The Shah did little to ease her discomfort. He remained seated and unmoving as he studied her in the half light of the lamp. She felt extremely self-conscious under his gaze, thanks to Amarante's snot stain across the chest of her kameez. Loralee hardly felt prepared for a private audience with the Shah, or any late-night meeting with a good-looking man. He might have been handsome, but his hawklike eyes and aura made it difficult to pay attention to much else.

The Shah finally broke the silence. "A rather late hour to be attending to your horse, Sayida."

"It's been a trying day, Shahanshah. I wanted to check on my mare and make sure she'd settled in well," Loralee explained. Her answer earned a slight raise of his brow, a skeptical look in his golden eyes.

"How trying a day could it be, outside the Quorum?"

"I would have attended, had I been welcome," Loralee clarified quickly. "There are many outside the Quorum who worry about what has been said within it."

"How much has the duq shared with you?" the Shah asked, his tone impossible to judge.

Loralee hesitated, and doing so earned her a smirk.

"I would see the future khanum well-informed of the affairs in Shai'Khal," the Shah said. "That is, after all, why you came to Rajibad, isn't it?"

Loralee shook her head, unconsciously leaning away from him at his question. She'd argued strongly with her father that the betrothal wasn't why she wanted to attend, and it was true. She'd agreed to try and avoid the Shah as best as possible, having no intention of bringing attention to the betrothal. But if she were completely honest, of course the betrothal had figured into her plans. It was her first chance to truly measure the man she was tied to. So far, she didn't know what to think of him, and she had no idea how to answer his question without offending him. Loralee had hoped to gather a more informed opinion of him from a respectful distance. Certainly not like this. She took a deep breath and chose her words carefully.

"Shahanshah, you've sat on the Rising Sun Throne for four years already. I assume if you had any intention of following through on the last shah's arrangement, you would have done so by now. I wish to be informed of Shai'Khal's affairs, but only as the heir to Abadan. If that's the case, a late-night dalliance between the two of us may be misconstrued. I value my reputation."

"Is that what this is?" Merikh asked with a cocky smirk. "A dalliance?"

Heat rose in Loralee's cheeks. "I—"

Merikh waved it off, the smirk waning. "The Ajir guards don't gossip, otherwise they wouldn't be Ajir. Your reputation will remain intact, unless you happen across someone else on the way back to your room tonight. I imagine the only one who might be wandering still is Duq Rashad. I'm confident he'd keep your secret if you kept his."

Loralee looked away, smiling a little and unsure what to say.

"I know little of the duq," she said finally, "and I think it's safest to keep him at arm's length."

"Heartening to hear, though surprising considering you seem close with his brother."

Loralee laughed. "Duq Hasad doesn't talk about his brother; he prefers his horses. If I can pry him away from my father for a moment, that's all he talks about."

"Ah, so that's why Duq Alaziz came. To talk horses with Duq Hasad, not because I summoned him," Merikh said, his tone more relaxed.

Loralee shook her head. "If he came for horses, then he came to get a peek at yours. Not at the Attars'. The best horses in their barns are all ours," Loralee said with more pride than she should have. The influence of the araq hadn't worn off.

"I'm glad I didn't bring my stallion. I would hate to hear of an unauthorized covering while I'm busy with the Quorum." Merikh was baiting her, and she took it without thinking.

"My family are not thieves," Loralee corrected sharply.

"Apologies, Sayida, of course not. House Neredi has a rather impressive reputation for honesty and hard work. I wouldn't *dare* impugn it." His tone was infuriatingly amused.

"There's a time and a place for deception, too much of it just makes life harder," Loralee said, brushing a wavy lock of her black hair back over her shoulder. "Besides, the horses see right through it. It's far too trying to be one person in the barns and another elsewhere."

Merikh shook his head, an amused look on his face from the lecture Loralee hadn't even realized she'd given. He said nothing for a moment, but the silence between them was more comfortable now.

"I am surprised the duqa didn't join your father here," Merikh said. "Your mother is far more politically inclined. And from what I hear, a Pantheon worshiper too, unlike your father."

"My mother worships Ayurlyse, alongside Ikharon and Livinja. My father is loyal to the Crown, not to gods. He worships his horses, Shahanshah," Loralee admitted. Growing up, Loralee had seen her mother worship Hisahti, the fertility goddess. After Jasira's miscarriage, the duqa had taken to Ayurlyse, the goddess of healing. After Ruya and Sarka's arrival, it had surprised Loralee how quickly idols of war and death had arrived on her mother's mantel.

"And who do you worship?"

"Not Akhenios," Loralee answered quickly. "I'm not a woman of much faith, Shahanshah. No gods have ever answered prayers as far as I can see, so it makes one skeptical. To whom do *you* pray?" Loralee asked.

Merikh took it in stride and shrugged. "Ikharon, of course," he said, his tone lightly patronizing. "Who else?"

"You're starting a war. Livinja would be more prudent," Loralee said flippantly.

"Do my ears deceive me, Sayida, or are you implying I'm both negligent and foolish?"

Heat rose in her cheeks again as embarrassment crashed over her. It hadn't been her intention at all to insult him. The conversation had taken a more relaxed turn, and she'd become carried away. But if he was irritated or amused, Loralee couldn't tell. Merikh had that stoic look again, the well-practiced mask all nobles had to master. She could see him scrutinizing her response, but he gave no hint for her to read him with.

"Neither, Shahanshah. I merely make a suggestion. Even if I had, it doesn't matter what I imply here as long as you can prove it untrue out there." Loralee gestured back toward the door.

Merikh smirked and shook his head. Apparently she'd given the correct answer.

"Another piece of Neredi wisdom."

Merikh stood from the desk and crossed the room to a nearby table. His steps were deliberate; every motion seemed planned and executed with great care, despite his tiredness. When the Shah picked up the pitcher of water off the table, it became covered in frost. To her surprise, the glass he poured he lifted and offered to her. Loralee couldn't tell if she'd offended him or not. Water was a dangerous gift from an ice sorcerer. Reluctantly, she approached and took the cup from him. She didn't drink anything until after the Shah poured himself a glass and drank.

"I apologize, Shahanshah, if I've offended you."

Merikh shook his head. "Of all the things that have offended me today, your conduct here is not one of them."

Loralee nodded, uncomfortably aware of his closeness. She was glad when he walked back to his desk. He looked tired once more as he sat and placed the cup down. Merikh cleared his throat and unbuttoned the top two buttons of his achkan, the high collar undoubtedly uncomfortable under his jaw after a long day.

"If you heard the man from the barn again, would you recognize him?" the Shah asked, changing the subject.

"I believe so, yes."

Loralee heard the door open behind her. The Shah was looking down at paperwork on his desk, seemingly lost in thought.

"Good night, Sayida Loralee."

"Good night, Shahanshah." Loralee bowed her head, placed the half-finished cup down on the table, and made a quick exit. She felt like she could breathe fully again as she walked down the corridor away from the Shah's suite.

Loralee made it to her quarters without encountering another soul, quite relieved to do so. The door shut behind her, her bed calling. She changed quickly and then crashed on the soft blankets.

I'm a complete fool, she thought as she bit the inside of her cheek. Reflecting on the evening's encounter made it clear the Shah had been toying with her the entire time. Poking and prodding, testing her while revealing as little about himself as possible. *I should have left with the captain. I should have protested being alone with him.*

What impression had he taken of her? Did he think she was comfortable frequenting men's quarters after sunset? *What does it matter?* Loralee tried to reassure herself. He'd made a point of avoiding answering her question about whether or not he had any intention of making her khanum, instead poking at her choice of words. He hadn't seemed particularly worried about what her visit might look like or how it would reflect on either of them.

Loralee stifled a yawn with the back of her hand. Well, even if he'd learned more about her than she had of him, she'd still learned something. The Shah's father had been a man with a notorious reputation around women. Shah Mansur hadn't been able to keep his hands to himself. More than a few women had accused him of rape—not that those accusations were ever prosecuted.

Now that Loralee was alone in her bed, she realized how thankful she was that the current shah hadn't taken after his father. Not one of his guards would have lifted a finger in her defense if Merikh had decided he wanted more than conversation. Instead, the Shah had treated her as if she were an equal. He'd let her get away with speaking candidly. He'd even offered her a drink before pouring his own.

He already treated me like the khanum. Loralee dismissed the thought as soon as she had it. No, that was ridiculous. She'd come bearing information, and he'd been appreciative. That was *all.* Loralee pulled the blankets over her body and curled up into them tightly. For the first time since leaving Abadan, she wished she were home. Well away from the Quorum's politics, from the Shah's intrigues, and from assassination plots.

CHAPTER 11

24th of Tavith, First Harvest, 902 Unified Age
Rajibad, Raudhah Province

Araq was a most useful drink. Merikh favored the effect it had on those around him, even if Merikh hadn't touched the stuff in years. The amir dinner had been borderline friendly after each of the amirs and the amira had partaken in enough of it.

Amir Xolani desperately wished to remain loyal to Merikh—that had become clear last night. He was looking for an excuse to stand up against the nobles in Ydeba who called for holy war. Xolani would be called a heretic and a race traitor if he didn't side with them. An Akhenic Faithful, Xolani had much to lose by taking this position. Merikh suspected Xolani to be a Royalist, a man devoted to the preservation of the Great Prophet's bloodline. They were a subset of the Akhenic Faithful who held strongly to the belief that there would be another Great Prophet from the royal line. Alcaeus, even as high priest, was simply some half-Aegalian bastard who was playing steward until the Prophet arrived again.

It had also become abundantly clear that Amir Xolani either knew little or nothing about the Neredi betrothal. The amir, after a few drinks, had less than subtly dropped hints that his daughter was still very much bastard free and without betrothal entanglements.

Amira Jin, on the other hand, had remained quite subdued throughout the evening. An Akhenic Faithful like Xolani, she seemed to struggle far more with the theological issues at stake. But she owed Merikh. His sweeping reforms since Mansur's death had directly led to her rather happy marriage. She would have been heirless and wifeless without him, a point Merikh wouldn't let her forget anytime soon.

Not to mention, she'd arrived in Rajibad with Duq Alaziz. The families were close. According to notes Nikias had prepared for him, Jin and Loralee had spent alternating seasons at each other's estates growing up. If Jin hadn't known about the betrothal before Rashad had opened his damn mouth, then she certainly did now. It gave the amira more to consider. Would she be willing to set her men against Neredi cavalry? Merikh doubted Jin had any desire to break those bonds so completely. Particularly if Merikh decided to elevate Loralee to khanum.

The unfortunately unpredictable element in all of this was Amir Olumide, not Amir Navin. Amir Navin could be trusted to follow whatever interests kept his skin intact and his coffers full. Olumide had been close to Mansur, almost like a brother. Yet when Merikh had sent Adrian to confirm the amir's support for Merikh's ascension to the throne, the amir had thrown his seemingly wholehearted support behind the plan to murder Mansur. Rajibad had celebrated his succession for weeks after even Madiar had stopped.

Olumide protected Rashad as his own son, when Merikh was certain Rashad wasn't. The father and son were close, and that relationship worried Merikh. If Rashad had Madiaran blood and admitted to it, Olumide could very well make a bid to put Rashad on the throne. Olumide could easily become the power behind the throne, shah in all but name until he died, or until Rashad grew a backbone. With resources stretched thin by a war in Ydeba, it would be the perfect time for an Attar army to siege Madiar and claim to be saviors of the empire.

Merikh had no idea whether the Attars were truly Akhenic Faithful or if they worshiped more gods behind closed doors. Worse, Merikh couldn't be sure the Attars were completely blameless now in the latest attempt on his life. Of course, there was a chance that Olumide was a genuine friend of House Madiaran. That his anger over the alleged rape of his beloved wife had been sated by Mansur's death, and that his soldiers would follow the red banner of Usman into battle without hesitation.

Merikh doubted his luck.

Then there had been the most unexpected visit of Sayida Loralee. Merikh had been able to smell the araq on her breath when she'd taken the water from him, earning her slipups more leeway in hindsight. She looked like her mother—though with quieter fashion tastes—but she clearly took after her father's more straightforward approach to politics. At their first encounter in the morning, Merikh hadn't been certain whether he'd simply offended her sense of fair play by being late, or if it had been a deliberate attempt to throw her weight around and test him.

Now, after the evening's enlightening "dalliance," it was clearly the former. She seemed to be a woman of strong morals, prone to equally strong convictions and positions without thinking of what sort of trouble taking those positions might create. Loralee had handled herself well enough when cornered, keeping straight to the point. Loralee could easily have tried to press the issue of their betrothal. Instead she'd seemed just as happy to let it slide as he had been. There had been plenty of other women given similar opportunities who had failed that test of ambition and modesty.

Now we'll see how well she thinks on her feet with an audience, Merikh thought.

The water hadn't been altruistic last night, even though the woman had clearly needed it. While she'd been distracted, Merikh had focused on the little golden chain on her wrist and guided it into his hand. Now the bracelet rested in the pocket of his khalat, the morning air cold enough for the longer robe to be necessary over his salwar kameez.

Merikh didn't make the Quorum wait for long today. They'd barely gathered before Merikh arrived. He'd sent Adrian ahead, the steward having arranged for coffee and chai to be served. A few nobles looked tired, a little worse for wear after last night. While Merikh doubted a warm drink would earn him any favors, it wouldn't hurt.

Merikh had barely sat down before Amira Jin spoke, catching him by surprise.

"Shahanshah, may I have the floor?"

"Of course, Amira." Merikh gestured in front of him.

Amira Jin stepped away from the bench seat to the center of the room. Merikh watched her carefully. For her to pounce at the first opportunity made him nervous.

"My thanks to you, Your Majesty, and to Amir Olumide for the generous meal last night. It gave me a great deal to consider, and I spoke at length with Kaitan's nobility afterward."

Jin took a deep breath. Merikh saw her knuckles whiten as she gripped her kimono sleeve. She was trying to hide her nerves.

"There are many in my province who support the Pantheon. Many others who support the Akhenic faith. I cannot fault either belief, but I cannot support the Pantheon in good conscience. My god is Akhenios and—apologies, Shahanshah—no sorceress can change my mind. Now this Quorum, regardless of the name, is a war council. Your Majesty, I will not see my province to war."

"My sincere hope, Amira Jin, is to avoid a war," Merikh interjected when she paused.

Her words were important, particularly the care with which she chose "sorceress" over priestess. Sarka's fire magic made few nervous—the elemental magics tended be better accepted—but Ruya's necromancy... Well, Merikh had put up with ignorant fears of his magic since he was a boy. What a terrifying concept for the god-fearing! Necromancers leading their temple and their empire.

"Of course, Shahanshah. Perhaps it is avoidable, if we all tread carefully. But I will not be involved in a military solution and have instructed the leaders of my province not to do so either."

"They swear as such?" Merikh asked, his tone deliberately difficult to read. He didn't want her parsing out his skepticism.

Jin turned back toward her seat. Alkont Rinji Mitani stood, walked over to Jin, and bowed before handing her a scroll. As he returned to his seat, the amira approached the makeshift throne. Merikh took the scroll from her and unfurled it. Sworn oaths from each of the six Kaitan noble houses to remain neutral, to enforce royal decrees in their cities, and keep their roads safe while protecting the virtues of the Akhenic faith.

"What happens, Amira Jin, if the high priest and I issue contrary decrees? Or if there is a confrontation between Akhenic Faithful and Pantheon believers?"

"Regarding the former, Shahanshah, I wish to preserve Kaitan as it stands today. The Royal Guard and Onyx Swords will be expected to maintain a peaceful coexistence within my borders. If they can't, then they'll be arrested for disturbing the peace regardless of any new decrees from either side.

"Regarding the latter…I will not sit idly by and see temples burned." Jin glanced pointedly toward Duqa Sachiko. "And such efforts will be prosecuted to the fullest extent of the law, regardless of the religious beliefs of those charged. Our temples have no obligation to make room for the Pantheon. But the Temple has no right to stop the Pantheon believers from setting up their own temples in other districts, provided they have the proper paperwork for such a thing."

Merikh rolled the scroll back up and gestured to Adrian. Unlike yesterday, the young man remained in the Quorum and stood near the door. Adrian came to Merikh's side, and Merikh handed him the scroll for safekeeping.

"I will accept this. You and your nobles should be mindful that this scroll is proof of treason if you cannot enforce neutrality. If one of your nobles fails, Amira Jin, your fate is tied to theirs."

"I am not afraid of that responsibility, Shahanshah," Jin said. "If that is agreeable, then I would like my province to be dismissed from the Quorum. We can hardly claim neutrality and then be privileged to a council without the high priest present."

"Once the Quorum has finished for the day, I will be speaking with you and your provincial nobles to outline the neutrality agreement further. You may leave." Merikh gestured to the door, and it opened. Jin bowed deeply, the jade beads hanging from the comb in her hair rustling.

"Thank you, Shahanshah." She didn't hide the relief in her voice well. Her walk to the door was slow and deliberate.

Merikh could feel her pace quickening outside in the hall, her soul making a hasty retreat, undoubtedly aware of how fickle Mansur would have been in the same situation. The last shah would have likely had her hunted down by Ajir and put on spikes in the hallway, a grim display for those within the Quorum to be forced to walk past upon exiting this evening. Fortunately for her, Amira Jin was more useful to Merikh alive.

Each of her nobles bowed respectfully before following their amira from the room. Merikh doubted their intentions were as genuine. They would support their amira openly, policing their cities and borders to prevent troops from crossing. Six armies at grass instead of moving against him made Merikh breathe a little easier. But he was under no illusion that those nobles now leaving the Quorum wouldn't be throwing their support behind their own beliefs more subtly. Particularly considering how many of them ruled port cities. Amira Jin was honorable, and it'd likely be the death of her in a year or two.

Not if I'm dead. The thought nearly made him smirk. She'd shown her allegiance lay with her god, but only so far as to leave the dirty work to others.

With the door shut behind the Kaitan nobles, Merikh quickly filled the silence. "Amir Xolani, Amir Olumide, did you confer with your nobles last night?"

"Apologies, Shahanshah, I'm not as young as I once was," Olumide said as he stood and bowed his head. "Duq Alaziz spoke with the nobles; I conferred with him afterward. I share Amira Jin's assessment. As much as you might wish to avoid war, without conceding to the high priest, it appears unavoidable. Unless Amir Xolani can give us a means to appease the rebellious fires burning in his province?"

Amir Xolani stood, joining Amir Olumide in the center of the room.

"My nobles would tolerate the Pantheon better if I could return to Membiti and assure them that their shah worships Akhenios," Amir Xolani said, "that the letter Rabb Khamisi sent stating the Shah's denouncement of Akhenios—and of High Priest Alcaeus—were misheard or misinterpreted."

Merikh wondered how often those flippant words were going to come back and bite him over the course of the next few years. He had no illusion about the length of time a war with the Akhenics might take. If they were truly unlucky, a war like this could easily be passed down to Merikh's heir.

"The high priest can concern himself with gods, true or false ones. Your nobles should worry less about where I pray and more about the men and women set to die if war should break out. My views toward the Akhenic Temple have not changed since I was the Shahzade. None of you opposed me then."

"There were no false priestesses living in the palace at that time, Shahanshah," Xolani said, bowing his head as he did so. "Many worry who will mother the next shahzade with no khanum to temper the time you spend with the priestesses."

He made a weak attempt at being respectful at least. Still, Merikh couldn't help but laugh at the absurdity. The idea of Ruya—or gods forbid, *Sarka*—in his bed was beyond ridiculous.

"Amir Xolani, will it put your mind at ease if Shai'Khal has a khanum before the season is out?" Merikh asked, carefully watching the ripple through the room. It had taken him four years to get to this point—no one had expected that proposition. It left Xolani stunned, perhaps even hopeful. In stark contrast, Duq Alaziz had stiffened in his seat, a hard look on his face.

"Shahanshah, it would. Particularly if the khanum is Akhenic Faithful." Xolani sounded measured but hopeful.

Merikh nodded ambiguously before looking to Amir Olumide. "If Duqa Enitan and her allies cannot find the agreements dictated by this Quorum amenable, where do the Raudhah nobles stand?"

"With their shah, of course. What sort of Yahidah would we be if we did anything else? Duq Rashad will lead Attar troops wherever you ask. Kontess Dalal"—Olumide gestured back toward the kontess of Metif, a port city along the Raudhah-Kuzen border—"has ships and men to offer. Rabb Ghazal and Sayida Malika have armies to offer. And Duq Alaziz offers the finest cavalry—outside of your riders, of course—in Shai'Khal for your use."

"The rest of your nobles?"

"They offer akhenits, Shahanshah. We would hate to see the royal coffers depleted to feed our troops."

The last war between the Yahidah and Umbeah had been nearly 700 years ago, but it might as well have been yesterday considering how easy it was to stir each race against the other. The Yahidah would follow him purely on blood. Once they crushed the "Umbeah rebellion," then they'd handle the religious matter. It would take careful control of the Yahidah nobles to ensure they didn't destroy the few Umbeah allies Merikh had with overzealous actions. He wasn't the only one concerned. Amir Olumide's quick throw of support clearly worried the Umbeah who had come. Amir Xolani's sister in particular, Baruna Azmera, was whispering hurriedly with Sayida Aret Okeke.

The door opened before Merikh could try to balm their worries. Ajir Captain Bashir walked in, bowing his head briefly before approaching the throne. He stood to Merikh's right, undoubtedly desiring to have a more or less unobstructed view of the chamber as he leaned in close. His words, after all, weren't meant for the Quorum.

"We have him."

Merikh nodded. He caught Adrian's eye, and with two fingers, gestured for the steward to approach. Captain Bashir made room, allowing Adrian to take his place at Merikh's side.

"Fetch Sayida Loralee."

Loralee took breakfast in the Rajibad palace garden. They were lacking compared to the lavish gardens of Abadan, but she hardly expected verdant grandeur from a desert city. Even with enchantments and aqueducts, there was little more than olive trees and scrub among the rocks.

A table had been set for her by the small pond, and the bubbling fountain and occasional birdsong kept Loralee company. The Quorum had already started, and Loralee expected to be alone for the meal. The solitude suited her fine—her tolerance for araq had never been particularly good, and while her stomach felt fine, her mind was still groggy.

When the garden gate clacked, Loralee bit back a sigh. It was only polite to offer the newcomer something off her table, but there was no one here whose company Loralee particularly wanted. At least, none who weren't occupied by the Quorum. Even Duq Hasad was more tiresome than she wanted right now. Loralee didn't have the capacity to talk training or remember which of the Attars' horses had once been theirs.

It was to Loralee's complete surprise and delight that the gravel-crunching footsteps belonged to Amira Jin. The amira walked slowly, partially hunched over so the toddler at her side could hold her hand as they walked. Loralee stood, smiling brightly.

"Is this Myeong?" Loralee asked.

The last time Loralee had visited Jin, the woman had been pregnant. Now the child was almost three. Jin nodded before sitting down at the table beside Loralee. The amira pulled her daughter into her lap. Myeong looked at Loralee with sleepy eyes before burying her face in her mother's kimono.

"Apparently she's shy today." Jin rubbed the little girl's back, her tone distracted.

"When did she arrive?" Loralee asked. Myeong hadn't been with Jin's retinue, or Loralee would have seen her on the ferry.

"Just before the Quorum started, with her uncle Rinji. Iseul doesn't handle the pressure of motherhood on top of leadership well." Jin frowned. Loralee dropped the subject. The women's private lives were hardly best discussed in a garden where Loralee couldn't guarantee privacy.

"I thought you'd be in the Quorum. What happened?" Loralee asked. "Don't tell me the Shah is at the barn again." Surely he wouldn't tarry two days in a row?

"I asked to leave," Jin said with a nervous laugh, "and it worked."

Loralee blinked in surprise. "Oh?"

"I spent half the night arguing with my nobles about whether or not magic creates divinity, what blasphemies they can and can't live with, and if any of it is worth going up against whatever army a couple of necromancers might raise."

"And here I thought you were too devout to believe in Ikharon's legion of the dead," Loralee teased, though the look on Jin's face made her frown again. "I'm sorry."

"No, it's fine. I don't believe in it, not in anything related to the Pantheon. But there are more than a few of my nobles who do. Plenty who don't. These differences haven't interfered with my province in the last three years, and I don't intend to let it start now. Kaitan will remain neutral, come what may to the rest of Shai'Khal."

"With a small preference toward the Shah, I hope," Loralee said as she reached for the ceramic teapot and poured Jin a cup. Meals were always served with extra dishes in the desert. Hospitality laws required it of the wealthy.

"Loralee..."

"I know, I know. Neutrality. I'm relieved, honestly," Loralee said, handing Jin the chai. "The idea of Neredi and Nakano soldiers meeting on a battlefield turns my stomach."

"Mine too, though I worry about the turning point Shai'Khal sits at. Those women are sorceresses, pure and simple. It's a slippery slope if all it takes to create divinity is powerful magic. Our shah won't be content to sit in their shadow."

"The women aren't divine, their gods are. The Shah already lives in the shadow of his father, his ancestors, and Akhenios. A few more gods and their priests and priestess doesn't change that."

Loralee failed to reassure the amira.

Jin shook her head. "I'm sorry. I shouldn't have said anything. I don't want to argue theology with anyone. Not you, not the Quorum, and the Shah respected that. I have his word that if I can keep Kaitan out of this war, no harm will come to my family."

"And if not?" Loralee asked quietly. She didn't get an answer right away, as Myeong unburied herself from her mother's kimono and began reaching for the grapes while Jin tried to drink her chai. Loralee reached over and picked a few grapes off the vine. She sliced them carefully before handing the tiny pieces to Myeong.

"If not," Jin said finally, "then I suppose I'll have to hope you become khanum and are willing to beg for mercy on behalf of my little one." Jin futilely smoothed a stray cowlick of black hair on Myeong's head.

"I'm not sure what the odds of that are going to be," Loralee said. "Becoming khanum, I mean. You know I'd move Aljemel itself to keep your family safe."

"You give yourself far too little credit."

"No, I really don't," Loralee said flippantly. The words had passed her lips before she could stop them or consider the ardency of her denial and how it would be received.

Jin looked at her suspiciously. "Oh? What have you heard?"

"Nothing, I just—"

"Don't *nothing* me," Jin said incredulously. "Out with it. You heard something."

Loralee felt her cheeks growing hot, and Jin's eyes went wide.

"You spoke with him."

"Jin—"

"It's fine, you don't have to tell me. Keep your secrets." The amira smiled knowingly. To Loralee's relief, Jin let the subject drop.

She had no desire to tell Jin about the conversation with the Shah the night before. Instead, the conversation went to safer topics such as Myeong and affairs in Inaza. The Migration Festival, the celebration of gigantic whales passing through Inaza's waters, was underway. Both Jin and Loralee were sad to miss it. Loralee had attended a few times growing up, and she'd never forgotten going out in a small boat on the Aldruin and seeing massive whales the length of several horses.

Loralee wasn't sure how long they were sitting together before she heard the garden gate clack shut again. A moment later, the Shah's steward approached.

"Amira Jin." He bowed and then straightened up. "Sayida Loralee, I have an order for you from the Shah."

"Do you now?" Jin shot Loralee an infuriating smile, one that earned the amira a glare in response.

"Yes?" Loralee asked, trying to ignore the impishness of her companion.

"If the amira can spare you, the Shah requires your presence in the Quorum," Adrian said, glancing to Jin.

Loralee's heart sank. There were several reasons she could think of that the Shah might wish to see her publicly. None of them were cause for elation.

Amira Jin nodded. "If the Shah desires to see the sayida, who am I to interfere?" Jin asked, her words chosen quite deliberately.

If they'd been alone, Loralee would have returned the gesture with a playful jab of her own. But the Shah's steward was not a man to be relaxed or informal around. Loralee stood and bowed her head to Jin before following Adrian from the garden. Once inside the palace, Loralee hesitated.

"Steward?" she asked, stopping.

"Yes?" Adrian stopped and turned to look at her. He was younger than her by maybe a year or two; she couldn't quite tell. His dark eyes were kind, if a little nervous looking.

"Do you know what the Shah wants?"

Adrian shook his head. "Sayida Loralee, I am a servant. The Shah gives an order, I carry it out. But..." He hesitated, concern twisting his lips in a slight frown for a moment. "Never mind."

Damn. Loralee thought better of pressing him. His reconsideration worried Loralee, but she gestured for him to lead on. *This undoubtedly has to do with last night.* A pit formed in Loralee's stomach. Had the Shah found the men she'd heard? If so, what had they said? Gods, had they incriminated her alongside them? If they had...

If nothing, she tried to convince herself, *the execution of an innocent sayida would turn the Yahidah against the Shah and radicalize Jin. He can't afford it.* Loralee hardly found her own arguments reassuring or convincing, and she shook her head. They walked the remaining distance in silence. When they approached the chamber, the doors opened by magic.

"I believe that's your cue, Sayida," Adrian told her.

Wonderful, Loralee tried to hide her nervousness. Regardless of what happened here, her father was going to be livid.

The doors opening quieted the room. Loralee felt all eyes on her, then returned to the center of the room. Kontess Maliha Zabat of Dharipur, a city in Kuzen, looked particularly irritated by the interruption. Loralee lingered near the door, unsure if she was meant to go sit by her father and wait until the Shah called her to the center or not. That moment of uncertainty allowed the kontess to resume speaking.

"As I said, our ports will—"

The Shah shook his head, his hand raised slightly off the throne's armrest. Two fingers pointed to Loralee before waving her to the center of the room.

"Thank you, Kontess Maliha. That will be all," the Shah said.

Loralee met Maliha's searing gaze for only a moment as she approached. The kontess yielded the floor unquestioningly. Loralee bowed deeply. To her dismay, the Shah stood from his throne and approached her.

That dismay turned to surprise when he stood in front of her, reached down, and took her hand. His touch was light and shockingly cold as he guided her to stand straight again. He barely held her hand, and to Loralee's renewed dismay, the Shah didn't let go of her.

"It was brought to my attention last night, then repeated this morning, that I have been *negligent* in my duties..."

Oh shit, Baba is going to kill me, Loralee thought as she tried to hide her shock. Thoughts of wrongful prosecution flew far from her mind, replaced instead by a far greater and stranger worry: marriage.

The room fell completely silent. From the corner of her eye, Loralee could see Kontess Maliha's glare. More than that, she could *feel* it. There were more than a few women pursuing the khanum's crown.

Gods, don't do it. Don't you dare.

"...and that you, my noble council, should have the utmost confidence in the safety and stability of your monarchy. My focus for the past four years has left little time to thoroughly ensure that confidence, particularly considering the events of the past few months."

Merikh took a few steps away from the center of the room, guiding Loralee with him. Loralee barely heard his words, focusing instead on his expression. He knew what this looked like; there was a satisfied touch of a smirk on his lips. But was that smirk there because he planned on finally letting his government in on the secret that he'd been betrothed since he was a small boy or for something else?

"Now, to that end..." Merikh gestured back toward the door.

Four Ajir guards walked in. Two were dragging a beaten man, barely recognizable through the blood. Loralee barely contained her relief as Merikh let go of her hand and approached the guards. Her fingers had been going numb from the cold, and she fought the urge to warm them. He gestured for Loralee to follow, allowing her to stand a few feet away from him instead of at his side. The beaten man tried to shrug off the guards.

"I am Rabb Adwin Sy, legate to Alkont Sefu Okeke. This is—"

Ice covered the man's mouth, smothering his words.

"Is this the man you heard, Sayida Loralee, admitting to poisoning wine meant for me months ago and conspiring toward a second attempt?"

Merikh asked. He already knew. Loralee could see that plain as day. He never would have put on this little charade without absolute certainty.

"He is, Shahanshah," Loralee said, more confidently than she felt. The man sounded similar to one of the voices from last night, but then again, so did half a dozen of the servants she'd spoken to this morning alone.

Merikh nodded. The Ajir guards stepped away. As soon as they did, a dozen spikes of ice shot from the ground and impaled the man. Loralee covered her mouth and looked away, the sound of ice slicing skin and organs nearly emptying her breakfast on the marble floor. She heard exclamations of shock and disgust. Someone else nearby retched on the floor.

"A warrant will be sent out to all corners of Shai'Khal. Whomever brings me the head of Sefu Okeke will inherit his estate. Amir Xolani, I look to you to find a replacement alkont for Nabi."

"He has family." Amir Xolani stood. "And an heir."

"All of whom neglected to attend the Quorum. If Sefu's son intends to inherit the alkont title, then he can send me his father's head and all will be forgiven," Merikh said before turning from the dying legate in the center of the room to look at another Umbeah noblewoman.

"Sayida Aret Okeke." The Shah's tone softened ever so slightly as he addressed the elderly Umbeah woman. "My Ajir captain would like to have a few words with you, to confirm you had nothing to do with your brother's treachery."

"Shahanshah, I would like to accompany her during this conversation," Baruna Azmera declared.

Merikh nodded, and Azmera helped the older Umbeah woman off her bench. Sayida Aret's hands were curled from age, and she walked with a pronounced limp. There was only so much healing magic could accomplish against the onslaught of age. Loralee watched the sayida leave, pointedly avoiding her father's gaze.

"Sayida Loralee," Merikh said.

Loralee bowed her head and focused on his riding boots. "Shahanshah?"

"You have my personal gratitude for bringing this matter to my attention. Such loyalty will not be forgotten. You may leave."

Loralee didn't have to be told twice. She bowed quickly, then turned to leave. Loralee barely made it to the edge of the circle before she heard fingers snap.

"Sayida, I forgot…"

Horse shit, Loralee thought. He'd forgotten nothing; his smug tone made that clear. Loralee stopped and turned around to face Merikh again and did her best to hide her surprise. Even so, she still reached for her wrist. Merikh stood in front of the throne, his hand extended, a delicate golden chain hanging from between his thin fingers.

"You dropped this last night."

"My thanks, Shahanshah. I can't imagine how it came into your possession." He'd caught her off guard, and the fact that a dying man stood between them made it hard for her to concentrate. "It had to have come off in the barns when I overheard the legate," Loralee added quickly. She knew damn well it hadn't.

The tug of a smirk and the raising of a brow made it quite clear what the Shah was thinking. *Is that the best you can do?* No, but it was all she had at the moment. Her emotions had her completely off balance. Fear of a proposal, relief from being wrong, and horror and disgust at the execution of the legate were hardly the best conditions for clever wordplay. Particularly when the realization hit her.

This show hadn't been for the Quorum. They were the secondary audience. He hadn't once looked away from her to see the reactions of those around them. No, he'd set everything up to allow for this moment between them. Loralee pushed the thought from her mind. She'd linger on it more later—others would too, undoubtedly—but all she wanted right now was *out* of the Quorum. She didn't meet the Shah's gaze as she approached and took the bracelet back. To Loralee's relief, he allowed her to leave without remembering anything else that might have slipped his mind.

The doors to the Quorum shut heavily behind her. Alone again, Loralee ran a hand over her face and leaned against the nearby wall. Her lie had been completely transparent. From the barns to the Shah? He used completely different barns than the rest of the nobles. Following that lie only led to a handful of conclusions. He had either been looking at Neredi horses with

Loralee after the amir dinner last night—in which case, why would he have needed her to listen to the legate's voice?—or he'd had other cause to be in the Neredi barns with Loralee. If the bracelet hadn't been in the barns at all, it led to the salacious conclusion. With a reputation as prudish as his, Loralee had never expected the Shah to be the one to perpetuate such rumors.

Loralee groaned and straightened up from the wall. She wanted air and time to think, but she had no idea how long the Quorum would last today. She had no intention of being caught in the barns or the gardens by one of the nobles. Particularly one such as Kontess Maliha. Loralee was certain the kontess wouldn't be the only one interested in prodding Loralee for more information, whether as a rival or out of curiosity or need.

Loralee made her way quickly to her suite, closing the door firmly behind her before crossing the room and throwing open the windows. Oppressive heat radiated inside. Right now she preferred it to the cold. She knew she needed to prepare for whatever happened next. After twice failing twice the tests that the Shah had placed in front of her, she was all the more determined not to fail a third.

CHAPTER 12

The Quorum ended earlier than Loralee expected. Its end was heralded to her by way of a thud on her door, her father's knuckles hitting the wood as he pushed it open. It was all the warning she received before the storm entered.

"What in Alhanem have you done?" Alaziz demanded as he shut the door behind him. His temper took on the quiet, brooding disappointment of a horseman. Alaziz wasn't a man who raised his voice. Loralee could count on one hand how often she'd heard him yell.

Loralee placed a thin ribbon between the pages of the book she was reading, then placed it down on the table nearby. "I went to the barn to see Amarante after dinner. I overhead the legate…" Loralee drifted off as the image of the impaled man came unbidden to her mind. A shiver ran down her spine. Alaziz let out a frustrated sigh as he crossed the room. He grabbed the nearby chair and sat down beside Loralee.

"You should have come to me. I would have handled it. You promised me you would avoid the Shah."

"I didn't want to interfere with Quorum affairs," she said. "It sounded as if you were busy after dinner conferring with Amir Olumide. I went to the Ajir captain, not the Shah. I assumed that would be the end of it. I didn't expect the captain to decide to immediately involve the Shah. If I'd gone to you instead, you would have done the same. Then the captain would have demanded I speak with the Shah anyway."

"Only I might have been present," Alaziz pointed out. "'Dropped in the barn?' Your mother made you a better liar than that." His tone was accusatory, and Loralee didn't appreciate it.

"He surprised me! I thought I took it off last night before bed. A bed I went to alone, so don't give me that look. Do you really think I slept with him?" Loralee asked, not expecting an answer but happy to shame her father into a little silence. "The Ajir captain did leave us alone, but we remained both completely dressed and separate from each other. I stayed by the door, he sat at his desk..." Realization hit her.

"Except?" Alaziz prompted.

"Except for when he rose and gave me water. The table was between us, he had me approach him to take the glass. He must have stolen the bracelet then, though whether he used magic or has quick fingers, I can't guess." Loralee sighed in frustration. "I'm sorry, Baba." He didn't have to say anything. She knew she should have been more careful.

"Between the Quorum chamber and here, I've had six nobles come to speak with me," he said. "All of them were trying to size us up. Or rather, size *you* up. They're trying to see if you're a distraction thrown at them by the Shah, if we're trying to curry favor with him between your legs, or if you're in line to be khanum and he simply hasn't announced it yet. I don't have to hear them to know rumors will already be spreading about the possibility of a Shahzade in nine months. Kontess Maliha looked ready to flay you. You stole her moment in the sun."

Loralee felt anger rising in her chest at his frank and crude assessment of the situation. She shook her head.

"There won't be a shahzade in nine months because *nothing happened* between us," Loralee reiterated, then sighed in exasperation. "This was bound to happen someday, wasn't it? You signed the betrothal, after all! Surely you thought it would benefit us?"

"At one point, it would have. It kept you from Madiar and got Mansur off my back. Now it doesn't. Now it just puts you in harm's way, and I won't have it."

Loralee furrowed her brow and leaned forward in her seat. "Baba, what are you talking about? Kept me from Madiar?"

Alaziz hesitated. Loralee was certain if there had been something strong for him to drink, he would have bought himself time by gulping it down.

"Mansur looked every bit the shining hero when he took the throne," he said. "Kurush was a tyrant. But the shine wore off quickly. You can't hide your true nature forever. Plenty of nobles had their eye on the Rising Sun

Throne, and he thought me among them." Alaziz shifted in his chair uncomfortably, then continued.

"It's the same old succession story. Until you consolidate power in some way, you worry about someone else coming in and knocking you off. So Mansur worked hard to do so. He thought I'd either make a bid for the throne or support one. Our army was twice as large back then. And maybe, if the right person had tried, I would have considered it. Kurush killed your grandfather two years before Mansur took the throne. I was young and hungry for vengeance.

"Mansur saw that and decided to ride to our home with a regiment of Royal Guards. He made himself at home. Spent a week terrorizing your mother and charming you. You were a toddler, and that sick excuse of a man had no problem sitting with you in the garden and listening to whatever story you wanted to tell him about the lizards. Or help you brush an old gelding. You adored him—though to be fair, you adored anyone who shined attention your way. At the end of that week, Mansur made up his mind that you'd be khanum. After all, if we were loyal subjects, how could we possibly object to our only daughter marrying his own son and heir?"

Alaziz stopped and bit his lip. Loralee waited, offering him a gentle smile to continue.

"He gave us the choice of either sending you to Madiar to be properly educated by the finest tutors—handpicked by Mansur—or sending half the Neredi Guard out for retraining in Madiar for your future protection. I chose to send the guards. To keep you out of any conflicts that might arise and away from a crazed lunatic. The correct choice, considering a few months later he had the Khanum executed. I don't want to think of all that went on in the palace after Aliyah's death. The fact I've never heard back from any of those men I sent to Madiar is enough to know I made the right decision, even if it will always haunt me."

Worry was written all over Alaziz's face. He'd done his best. Loralee couldn't fault him for it.

"Everyone is about to be at war; Abadan won't be much safer than Madiar," Loralee pointed out. Her words hit harder than she'd expected. Alaziz looked as if she'd just slapped him. He stood and began to pace.

"At least in Abadan I don't have to worry about you living at the mercy of the cruel son of a lunatic. I saw what his father did to women, what he tried to do to your mother in our own home! Kurush was no better. Do you really think that behavior skipped a generation purely because the Shah stole your bracelet instead of forcing himself on you? I don't want you marrying a rapist or murderer," Alaziz half yelled, hesitating only a moment in his pacing.

"Everyone knew what Mansur was," Loralee said. "But since his death, there hasn't been so much as a *rumor* of rape in the palace. Perhaps this shah is different? He purged the Priest Council of corruption. And look what's happened to the Royal Guard! Mansur let them run wild. Now any guard with his manhood where it doesn't belong loses it."

"Loses it and his life, or did you forget the crucifixions? The Shah might have a low opinion of rape, but he certainly has no aversion to murder. There's no middle ground with him. Have you already forgotten the legate in the Quorum? The Shah murdered a man mere feet away from you! And the man didn't die immediately."

Loralee bit the inside of her lip. No, she hadn't forgotten. "What do you mean?"

Alaziz shook his head and laughed bitterly. "Loralee, the ice was *necrotic*. He bound the soul to its body well past the time it should have naturally left. Rabb Adwin suffered until the Quorum was over. Only when the Shah let the ice disappear did he pass on. Maybe you're right. Maybe this shah is different from his father. Or maybe he's simply more careful." Alaziz scoffed.

"You should be more careful where you say such things."

Loralee jumped. She hadn't heard the door open. Alaziz's pacing stopped, and he looked to the door.

"This was meant to be a private conversation, Shahanshah," Alaziz said unapologetically.

"I assumed so, courtesy of the closed door and the ignored knock." Merikh straightened up from leaning against the doorframe and entered the room proper. "The amir ought to speak with sun enchanter about dampening the sound in his guest wing." He crossed the room to the small table with a pitcher of water and poured himself a glass. "I can't *imagine* why my father questioned your loyalty, Duq Alaziz."

"There is a long way between treason and not wanting my daughter married—"

"To the cruel son of a lunatic. Indeed," Merikh interrupted, his brow raised and a skeptical look in his golden eyes.

How much did he hear? Loralee wondered, frowning. A tense silence followed. Loralee cleared her throat.

"Shahanshah, to what do we owe the honor of a visit?" She didn't bother to hide her irritation. The door, after all, had been shut.

"Our betrothal, Sayida Loralee. Duq Alaziz, will you leave us?"

Alaziz shook his head. "No. If there is any discussion to be had, then I would be here for it. *I* signed it, after all."

The room chilled. Frost spread over the outside of the water pitcher.

"One man who signed that betrothal is already dead. It is no longer an agreement between children. Is your daughter incompetent or incapable of negotiating on her own behalf?"

"If she were, would that matter?"

Loralee's jaw dropped at her father's insult. She was *hardly* incapable of handling this conversation, regardless of how she'd bungled her previous interaction with the Shah. He'd had the upper hand the first time by being sober. The second time, he'd deliberately orchestrated a situation to throw her off balance. She would do better this time. He'd come to her.

"If I thought her incompetent, I wouldn't be here," Merikh said, his tone cool. It didn't faze the duq.

"Respectfully, Shahanshah, I'd rather not leave my daughter alo—"

"Duq Alaziz, you will not find a man in Shai'Khal who bears more ill will toward Mansur and the stain of his reputation than me. What possible good could come from harming your daughter?"

"Baba," Loralee interrupted, standing up from the divan, "I believe Duq Hasad had a few questions about Haji, the stallion we sent? You can be of more use in the barns. Besides, there are Neredi guards outside the door should I need them. If my feeble mind can't grasp the Shah's meaning, I'm sure one of the guards can help me."

The look Alaziz gave Loralee clearly showed he hadn't meant what he'd said. He'd dug himself into a hole he couldn't easily get out of, and now no one wanted him here. If he protested much more, it would be all too easy for the Shah to order the Ajir to remove him. Even if Loralee couldn't see any Ajir through the open door, she doubted they were far.

Alaziz let out an irritated breath, tossed his hands up, and walked toward the door. As he passed Merikh, he hesitated, as if about to say something and then thought better of it. Instead, the duq bowed his head and left. Loralee doubted he'd go far. With her father gone, Loralee moved to stand. It was rude to have sat for as long as she had with a person of higher birth present. Merikh shook his head, letting her remain seated while he made no move to step away from the water pitcher.

Good etiquette required her to wait until Merikh addressed her. The silence continued for a long moment as he simply studied her. His hawklike eyes were no less unnerving now than they had been when she was tipsy from the araq. At least now, she'd been around him enough that his aura was no longer as difficult to handle.

It was clear Merikh was perfectly content in the uncomfortable silence between them. Loralee could only imagine how many people had hung themselves with their words trying to fill the silent void. She only hoped she'd do better.

"The duq informed me that your display this morning hit its mark perfectly." Loralee raised her arm and jingled her bracelet. "Kontess Maliha wants my head. I suppose she hoped the next khanum would come from Kuzen. Why not her?"

"Her three bastards of questionable heritage—and her age—give me pause." Merikh shrugged and took a sip of water. The frost on the pitcher disappeared, and the room slowly grew warm again. He crossed the room to Loralee, stopping beside the table she'd placed her book down on. The Shah picked it up carefully, as if holding an Akhenic relic, and he read the spine. He placed the book down gently on the table before moving Alaziz's chair away from Loralee, creating a less intimate space before sitting down.

"Surely there have been other women of fewer years and fewer bastards who have been willing and able to give you an heir? I'm sure many have been vying to do so since you hit maturity. How have you managed to avoid attending to this before now?" Loralee asked earnestly. She knew it was a bold question, but she wanted an answer. After this morning and what he'd done to her reputation, he owed her one.

"Are you so eager to give up your claim?" he countered. The Shah took a sip of water before he continued. "Do you imagine cleaning up Mansur's messes has been easy? It has been an incredibly hectic four years, even without this Pantheon issue. The last thing I desired was a distraction, another drain on my already limited time. Using the khanum title as a bargaining chip, dangling the hope of it in front of great houses, has helped smooth out many issues in the past. It bought you time to mature as well. Or would you have been an eager bride at sixteen?"

Loralee looked away from him, and she saw his smirk out of the corner of her eye.

"I thought not. But with the country on the verge of war, Shai'Khal can no longer afford the khanum's role to remain unfulfilled. The Quorum demands succession secured." His honesty came as a surprise.

Loralee nodded once, deliberately appearing thoughtful.

"I see. Our great and powerful shah needs a wife and a baby to be his shield against the Akhenic Faithful," Loralee said glibly. Dangerously so, as she saw Merikh's jaw clench. She shivered, the hairs on her arms and neck standing on end.

"Negligent, foolish, and now cowardly. What a terrible first impression I've provided."

Last night, when he'd called out her unintentional insult, his tone had been difficult to read. Now, it clearly conveyed his irritation. Loralee had been given leeway last night due to the alcohol. She would receive none today.

"No, Shahanshah. My apologies for insinuating as such. It's not a cowardly man who lifts his shield when a spear threatens," Loralee said, adopting a far more respectful tone. "Our contract was signed by one man who would see it absolved, and another who's dead and clearly incapable of seeing the contract fulfilled."

"Would you see it absolved?" the Shah asked, shifting his position in the chair with a small wince. His tone was difficult to read, more neutral than the tone of moments before.

"I would see myself as more than a shield," Loralee admitted.

"And undoubtedly more than a hostage," Merikh said knowingly.

Loralee stiffened. He'd heard a great deal more than Loralee had thought if he'd heard Alaziz's explanation of Mansur's contract. Or perhaps he'd known more details of this betrothal than she had.

"If you are in need of a hostage, Shahanshah, then you have better choices. My family, regardless of my father's personal feelings toward you, supports the Pantheon. The Neredi Guard is yours regardless of whether I'm in your bed or not. Duqa Enitan's daughter would fill the role of a hostage khanum," Loralee suggested carefully.

"Children are unpredictable creatures, particularly when torn from their parents and thrown in gilded cages," Merikh countered, his tone exasperated. "I don't care to be a shah murdered by his khanum, nor do I have the stomach to take a child to bed. Amir Xolani wishes to see a shahzade within the year, but I'm not sure if the Bhengani girl is old enough to carry a child, let alone bear one."

Loralee had a feeling the Shah was tired of explaining his choices.

"Amir Xolani—"

"Has a daughter, Duqa Adanna, who is well-loved in Ydeba and would strengthen Madiar's ties to the Umbeah. I have heard much to commend her from the grand vizier, who has been quite anxious to have succession handled for some time now."

Do better. The words weren't said, but Loralee could read them in his posture. She shrugged.

"Amir Xolani will be a less antagonistic father-in-law than mine." She hazarded a smile.

"Undoubtedly." His tone warmed a little.

"Then there you have it, Shahanshah. The Quorum's demands fulfilled and a happy start to a family. Now, if I may, I had hoped to catch Duq Rashad before he retired for the evening. One of his stallions caught my eye; it's not from the usual Attar stock," Loralee said, her tone coy.

It was an obvious lie, and she expected the Shah to see through it. To follow where she led. Whether the animosity between Merikh and Rashad was purely based off a strange coincidence of looking like brothers, or whether they were both Mansur's sons, it didn't matter. The Shah had shown his distaste for

Rashad twice in her company. If he'd already played out the pros and cons of marrying Duqa Adanna, he knew how upset the Yahidah would be with bringing Umbeah blood into the line again. That the Attars and Neredis were the two strongest houses in Raudhah—and only a short march from Madiar's walls. She hadn't answered his question about whether or not she was eager to give up her claim to the khanum title. And maybe it had left him wondering whether she was willing to throw it away or whether she simply didn't wish to have him attached to it. A man she'd now insulted repeatedly and lived to tell about it.

Merikh smirked and shook his head. "You might wish to stay out of the barn in the evening for a little while. With the attention your father lavishes on Duq Hasad, he would be a significantly more suitable man to spend your time with. An arrangement easily made with a few choice words to Amir Olumide. Duq Rashad can easily be given other distractions, such as Duqa Enitan's daughter. Although I think even he has age requirements for his bed."

Loralee floundered for a moment, unsure of what to say. Merikh raised his hand a little, his expression more relaxed. Of course he won that round, but it was easy to win when the marriages of nobles all required the approval of the Shah.

"What I wonder, Sayida, is what commends you to be khanum. You've already said your family will continue its fealty toward me without you as khanum. Perhaps the duq would feel stronger fealty if I were to abandon this betrothal. Your ties to Amira Jin no longer matter, as I have her sworn to neutrality. The only reason you've given me to make you khanum is my own paranoia—a matter I can easily work around. Are you free of ambition, or have you brought up these points purely out of fear?"

"I am not afraid to be khanum, Shahanshah," Loralee said quickly. "But my father's fears are valid. Your mother wasn't the first khanum to die at the command of her shah. In fact, if my knowledge of history is correct, other than your grandmother, every recent khanum has died by their husband's hands. My ambition is less important than my desire to meet my grandchildren. Violence runs in your blood; you showed as much today. I don't want to live in perpetual fear of my husband."

"Are you afraid of me?" There was amusement in the Shah's tone.

Loralee hesitated. "Not yet."

The Shah nodded, then cleared his throat. "From what little I remember of my mother, she was poised, articulate, and beautiful. She was also unfaith—"

"So was your father," Loralee interrupted, not cowing to the cold look it earned her. It was a double standard she wouldn't abide.

"Neither understood *loyalty*. That is what killed them both in the end. I am not Mansur, regardless of what Duq Alaziz may think. I keep the vows I make. Your lack of eagerness for the khanum's title, the manner in which you've conducted yourself, and yes, the guarantee your father won't risk supporting insurrection while you're at my side are all reasons to make you khanum. Unlike Mansur, I am not in the habit of forcing a woman to stand at my side or lie in my bed."

Loralee bit the inside of her lip. "Shahanshah, where does that leave us?"

Merikh laughed mirthlessly. "Sayida, that is entirely up to you."

He eyed her carefully. Loralee, reluctant to meet his gaze, stared at the ornate rug on the ground to his right. She'd had four years to make an estimation of Merikh from a distance. She didn't know what to think of him in person. But she'd had plenty of time to consider whether she wished to be khanum, regardless of the quality of the man sitting on the throne. Would she truly be able to live with herself if she turned down the opportunity to influence the direction of the empire? To elevate her bloodline to royalty?

Loralee wiped imaginary dirt off her lehenga skirt.

"If anything were to happen to me—"

"Your father is not a man to be crossed. Amir Navin and Rabb Mahdi took my mother's death in stride. No one cared for her loss. You, on the other hand, I'm certain would cause quite the stir in death. I cannot win a war against Alcaeus if I'm besieged by Neredi and Nakano troops."

"No, you can't," Loralee said smugly, a satisfied smirk on her lips as she looked at the Shah again. Now that they had come to their inevitable conclusion, he was starting to look...uneasy.

Surely you've been preparing for this all your life? Loralee thought.

"Are you asking me to marry you, Shahanshah?" Loralee finally asked.

"I'm asking you to be more than a shield and broodmare. My retinue leaves when the Quorum ends, assassins be damned. I want to see how well you handle yourself in a more dangerous court, away from your father's influence. If you prove yourself capable of handling Madiar, then..." Merikh cleared his throat. "Then yes, I would see you at my side permanently."

"And in your bed," Loralee added, choosing her words deliberately. He had repeated again and again that her conduct was appreciated. Considering her insults, the only conduct she could think of that separated her from other women vying for the throne was sex. She hadn't tried to seduce him, and now she could see why doing so had ended so poorly for other women.

The Shah stiffened almost imperceptibly at the suggestion, his chin raising a little as if to distance himself from her. An oddly uncomfortable look crossed his eyes even as he tried to hide it.

That doesn't bode well, Loralee thought with a sinking feeling. There was more to Merikh putting off succession than simply being busy. Then again, with Mansur as an example of fatherhood, Loralee couldn't blame his reluctance. Even with good parents, even wanting children, Loralee was cautious about having any. There were so many things that could go wrong, even without the added pressure of raising the next shah.

"Yes," Merikh said reluctantly.

"Then may I speak more openly, Shahanshah? As your future wife?"

He nodded.

"You knowingly damaged my reputation this morning. You placed a target on my back. You didn't lie to me—the Ajir don't spread rumors—but I came to you in good faith that my discretion would be reciprocated. I came to fulfill my duty as a good citizen of Shai'Khal, to try and save your life. In return you started rumors that we are *far* more intimate than we are. I understand as khanum my duty will be to protect you and our bloodline. To be obedient to your wishes. But if my reputation must be dragged through the mud for your designs, then I ask to have some agency in it. I'm a better partner than puppet, if you'll respect me enough to cut my strings."

"I am quite certain you'll cut your own strings in Madiar," Merikh said as he stood from the chair.

Loralee stood a moment later, bowing her head respectfully as Merikh left. When the door shut behind him, Loralee let out a deep breath. Her whole body had tensed, leaving her exhausted now that she was alone. The conversation had been a dangerous game. Although Merikh had retreated, Loralee couldn't shake the feeling that, somehow, neither one of them had come out on top.

CHAPTER 13

29th of Tavith, First Harvest, 902 Unified Age
Rajibad, Raudhah Province

Enchanted lamplight bathed the barn, providing just enough pale light to see by in the predawn. Amarante nickered at Loralee as she approached. Grooms had come through earlier, and most of the other horses were still buried in their hay. Amarante knew better and nuzzled Loralee's kaftan pockets for stolen dried dates. Loralee rubbed the mare's jibbah and messed with her forelock before pulling the dates out. They plunked down loudly in Amarante's feed trough. Loralee watched the mare greedily eat, lost in thought. Three days had passed all too quickly. The consequences of her discussion with Merikh had become real this morning as she finished packing her things.

Loralee had come to the Quorum hoping to learn more about the political arena. To see and experience something new, then return home. Only now she wasn't returning home, and Loralee didn't know when she'd see Abadan again. The realization hit with a pang of homesickness. Madiar would be home now, unless she failed whatever tests Merikh decided to throw her way as they planned the royal wedding. Amarante would be the only remnant of the Neredi estate Loralee would have with her until her mother arrived with a few of her possessions. Even so, there was little that mattered that would come with the duqa. Somehow, Loralee doubted her father would let her take her favorite horses with her—other than Amarante—to the royal barns.

When Amarante returned to her hay, Loralee meandered the rest of the Attar barns. Once in front of the barns allocated to the Madiaran horses, Loralee stopped. She had half a mind to go in and get a closer look, but she hesitated. Something felt wrong. Under closer inspection, Loralee saw light reflecting off the middle of the seemingly empty entrance. An almost invisible latticework of ice covered the entryway like a frozen spiderweb. Loralee had no doubt harm would come to anyone whom the Shah deemed unnecessary to enter the barn.

Paranoid. Loralee frowned. She remained there for a moment, resisting the sudden urge to touch the delicate strands as she tilted her head for a better look. She'd never spent much time around magic. It was a relatively rare skill. Even among educated noble sorcerers, few had the strength to keep up such displays out of sight. Most strong enough to do so became scholars, sequestered off in their schools, and every so often returned to deliver the fruits of their efforts to their patron noble house. Enchanted lamps were the extent of what Loralee usually saw, and they required little craftsmanship. At the Neredi estate, the lamps were tended to by their house enchantress, and the woman's skills paled in comparison to the Shah's. The enchantress always looked perpetually exhausted. If such a display caused the Shah any lethargy, he hid it well.

Loralee gave the entrance a wide berth as she walked back toward Amarante's stall. Horses nickered, as there were more people in the barns. The Neredi guards joining her for the journey were readying their horses. Dust motes filled the air and danced in the morning light. The pack horses were left for last, allowing them to enjoy a few extra moments in their stalls before their heavy burdens were loaded.

Loralee took her time tacking up Amarante, carefully grooming every touch of dust off the mare's dapple coat. She double-checked the saddle buckles and smoothed out tassels on the blanket and breast collar. When she couldn't reasonably procrastinate any longer, Loralee led her mare out into the main courtyard.

The sun warmed the white marble of the palace, and Loralee squinted as her eyes adjusted to the light outside the barn. The Shah and his steward were already on their horses, while the Royal and Neredi guards warmed up their mares. Duq Alaziz stood with the Attar family to see off the retinue.

Loralee bowed her head as she approached. She turned back to Amarante and put the reins over the mare's head and behind the saddle horn. Breaking the morning's stoic formality, Loralee turned back and hugged her father. The duq returned it tightly. Alaziz had surprised Loralee with near silence when she'd told him she was leaving with the Shah. Over the past few days, he'd said a few choice words conveying his disappointment. After all, his only child and heir was leaving with the son of a man he despised. The grandson of a man who'd killed Alaziz's father. If Merikh were any man other than the Shah, Alaziz would be expected to seek blood for vengeance, not hand over his daughter and entwine their bloodlines. If it had been up to Alaziz, Loralee was certain she'd remain in Abadan her whole life, primarily taking care of horses and only managing politics when absolutely necessary. It was a quaint fantasy Loralee didn't feel guilty over crushing. At least her mother would be quite proud of her.

"Be careful," Alaziz whispered to Loralee before letting go of her.

She nodded and stepped away, then turned to face Amir Olumide. Loralee bowed her head.

"Thank you, Amir, for your hospitality. You have been a most gracious host."

"We were blessed by your company, Sayida Loralee." Amir Olumide smiled warmly as he spoke before he looked from Loralee to the Shah. "I don't know which gods to entreat to bless your journey home, Shahanshah, but I pray for cool days and warm nights. That jackals stay far from your tents, and that water be fresh and plentiful."

"You have my gratitude, Amir Olumide. I hope to return the hospitality in Madiar soon," the Shah said, his tone characteristically difficult to read.

Amir Olumide laughed. "I certainly hope so."

Loralee turned back to Amarante and mounted the horse gracefully. The mare hadn't moved from where Loralee had left her. There was a long day ahead of them, and Loralee hoped hours in the saddle would quell the nerves and homesickness festering in her mind.

On the road outside of Rajibad, the formality of the group lessened. The Ajir relaxed, and their formation loosened. One of them slipped between the Neredi guards and approached Loralee. The guard bowed her head, moved her reins to her right hand, and placed her left on the center of her chest.

"Sayida, if I may introduce myself? I am Ajir Farhana. If you are ever in need of anything, please feel comfortable speaking with me," Farhana said. Her niqaab veil covered most of her face, but the guard's brown eyes were bright and friendly.

"Thank you, bayan," Loralee said.

Farhana nodded once before moving her mare back closer to the Shah. In the hours that followed, a few other of the Ajir introduced themselves. For the most part, the separate guards kept to themselves. They talked and sang to kill time, though Loralee noticed the Shah stayed quiet. The Ajir steward rode at his side, as did the Ajir captain. Loralee had hoped for an invitation to approach, for the opportunity to get to know Merikh a little better during this journey. But as the sun began to creep back toward the horizon, Loralee abandoned the idea.

As the sky began to burn orange and pink, Loralee was forced to break the silence between her and the Shah. The distance between them had grown, but not because of a conscious effort. The Neredi horses were lagging behind despite the urging of their riders. Loralee had never seen the endurance of the royal horses firsthand and now understood how the Royal Guard could maintain their presence throughout Shai'Khal so easily.

"Shahanshah," Loralee called out as she urged Amarante into a reluctant trot. She pushed through the two lines of guards between her and Merikh and adjusted the veil of her niqaab back as she came alongside the Shah.

"What do you need, Sayida?"

"When do you intend to make camp?" Loralee asked, bowing her head briefly.

Merikh glanced west. "The road should be fine for another hour," Merikh told her, his tone dismissive.

Loralee shook her head and pushed Amarante a little harder to keep up with Merikh's mare. "The Neredi horses won't make it another hour at this pace, Shahanshah," Loralee confessed. She was loath to admit it—Amarante was one of the best horses the Neredis had to offer—but the mare couldn't handle the pace. A sprint? Loralee had no doubt her mare could beat Merikh's. However, if they kept this pace until Madiar, Amarante would be sick within days of their arrival.

To Loralee's surprise, Merikh raised his hand, and the Ajir captain shouted to halt. Merikh looked at Amarante, sidestepped his mare to come close, and placed a hand on Amarante's neck under her mane. Loralee saw a thin layer of ice spread down the mare's neck. It disappeared a moment later, wicking off sweat.

"Why didn't you say so earlier?" the Shah chided before gesturing to the Ajir captain. "Find a safe place to make camp."

A bend in the Kura River provided them with an ideal place to stop far enough off the road not to be harassed by late-night or early-morning travelers. The river provided fresh water to cook and clean with. More importantly, the water had minimal wildlife that the guards could see. They hadn't come across any crocodiles or hippos, and Loralee hoped the horses wouldn't run across either tonight while grazing.

Loralee dismounted and took the other two Neredi horses from her guards. While others prepared the goat-hair tents, Loralee brought the horses to the river for water. As they drank to their heart's content, Loralee watched the camp set up.

Horses were tended to first. The Ajir guards split between those tasked with leading horses to the river and those setting out forage and grain for them. An Ajir earth sorcerer created a makeshift paddock for the horses out of ropes from the packs and stones off the ground. The best patch of grazing was set aside for the royal horses, and a smaller paddock was outlined nearby for the Neredi ones. To merge the horses into one herd on the road was too risky in case of personality clashes among the mares, particularly if one of the mares was unwell. The Shah looked concerned as he groomed his mare.

Something wrong with her? Loralee wondered. She hadn't looked lame.

Merikh gestured for one of the guards and spoke to her quickly. Loralee was too far away to hear what he said, but it wasn't good. The guard nodded grimly and went back to her horse. Despite the sweat from the day's ride, the woman simply put the bridle back on and mounted bareback before taking off from the camp toward the dunes. Loralee pushed it from her mind as she led the horses away from the river.

It had been a long day. She was more tired than she'd expected, and it was easy to just focus on the tasks ahead of her. Loralee untacked the horses and brushed them down gently. When they were clean, she pulled strings of bells from her saddlebags. To each horse, she tied the shortest strings around their legs above their hooves. The longest strands became a collar around each horse's neck. The bells were blessed and supposed to keep djinn away.

Although, Loralee wondered about their efficacy with a necromancer in the camp. Would Merikh's presence dissuade djinns, or call them? The thought wasn't entirely comforting. Pragmatically, the bells made it harder for any horse thieves to slip off with a horse quickly and quietly. With the djinn bells tied, Loralee led the horses to the makeshift paddock and turned them out.

The sky above them gradually turned black while the horizon still glowed faintly. Stars began to flicker overhead as the guards cooked food. With the horses cared for, Loralee joined the circle of guards around the main campfire. She sat on a blanket not far from the Shah and Adrian. The young steward handed Loralee a small bowl of fresh herbs and a flask of water—palate cleansers while the goat cooked over the fire. Fresh food on the road was a nice perk of traveling with an ice sorcerer.

Hoof beats came from the shadows, and a moment later the guard that Merikh had sent out returned. The guard dismounted quickly and approached the campfire.

"Emani?" Merikh asked.

The guard, who turned out to be Farhana, nodded. "A fairly small caravan, Shahanshah. I don't think they saw me. They were heading away from the road and from us. I doubt they'll be too interested in our camp."

The Shah seemed satisfied with that answer, and Loralee would have forgotten about the incident if it weren't for Adrian. He continued to look nervous, *very* nervous. A stark contrast to his seemingly impassive master. Instinctively, Loralee put a hand the hilt of her khanjar, reassured by its presence on her belt.

A few of the guards kept watch on the border of their camp while the rest relaxed around the campfires eating dinner. The Shah remained quiet, not partaking in the conversations around them, and Loralee followed suit. She was exhausted by the day. It'd been a long time since she'd spent that many hours in the saddle, and she was ready for her bedroll. While Umbeah and Tsukarai nobles tended to travel more extravagantly, the Yahidah held to their nomadic roots. A Yahidah noble who couldn't handle a goat-hair tent and a bedroll on a journey like this commanded little respect.

Loralee stretched her legs, about to stand and excuse herself, when Merikh stood. He rose calmly, but the abruptness of it silenced the guards nearby.

"Farhana, you might have misjudged the Emani," Merikh said, his tone still relaxed. "Adrian, illuminate the dunes."

Guards snapped to attention. Curved shamshirs were unsheathed. Small rounded dhal shields paired with katar daggers were quickly put on. Adrian scrambled to his feet, let out a slow breath, and raised his hands toward the fire. It sputtered, then four bolts of flame shot over the camp toward the dunes. Loralee watched the arc of the flames. When they hit the sand, she jumped.

Scattering like scorpions from under a rock were dozens of people. Their weapons and armor glinted in the light. The fires faded quickly, followed by a soft thud. Adrian collapsed on the ground. Loralee rushed to his side and pulled him away from the campfire, as he'd fallen dangerously close to it.

With him out of danger, Loralee stood and reached for her khanjar. Her hand grew cold, and she glanced down at her belt. Ice spread over the sheath and hilt of the dagger under her fingers. It was gone by the time she looked up at the Shah a few feet away from her.

"You won't need it," Merikh assured her as he drew his shamshir. The thin curved blade reflected the firelight. Delicate script in a language foreign to Loralee traced the edge from crossguard to tip.

As the first Emani ran at the camp, the air chilled and shimmered.

Like the webs from the barn, Loralee realized. The ice was nearly invisible at the edge of the firelight. The Emani certainly didn't see it as they approached the camp. Loralee had seen men fall into thorn-tree hunting traps, cut to pieces by the dangerous barbs. The ice was worse. Loralee covered her mouth as her stomach dropped. She'd never heard screams like that. Ice spread through the cuts, turning the skin pale and bloated before darkening to black.

The ice disappeared, and the more cautious Emani hesitated at the edge of the firelight. The ice web had evened the odds a little, but the Emani still outnumbered the guards. The tents were set up in a tight semicircle, funneling the Emani into the line of guards. The Ajir captain hung back, standing near Merikh. As the Emani met the Ajir, it became clear Captain Bashir wasn't staying back to protect the Shah. It was the Shah who kept the Captain safe, and for a good reason. When guards were cut by the Emani's swords or bones broken by clubs, pale-white light emanated from the captain's hands and balmed the wounds. The Ajir were hardly afraid of pain; they had faith in their captain.

When the line broke, spikes of ice shot from the ground in a wall ahead of the Shah and the captain, impaling the Emani who made it through. The ice disappeared quickly, turning into pale-green necrotic fog.

A moment later, the corpses that had fallen to the ground rose to their feet. With a small gesture from Merikh, they turned and headed back to the hole in the guards' line. The confusion the mortoha created allowed injured guards to fall back to be healed while the remaining guards cut down the Emani.

Only one Emani broke through the line and made it to Merikh. He wasn't met with ice or fog. Instead his shamshir was parried by Merikh's blade. The Emani looked proud of himself, as if he had a chance. Loralee had attended enough duels to know an outclassed match when she saw one. The Emani was good, better than she expected. Even so, he never stood a chance.

His shamshir parried twice before he swung too wildly. Merikh's shamshir cut across the Emani's chest, barely grazing the man. Loralee could see only a thin cut from his torn kameez. The Emani stumbled back, his eyes wide in abject horror. The glyphs on Merikh's shamshir glowed green. The blade turned black, as if made of shadow. From the Emani's wound, necrotic fog began to pour. A moment later, it took the form of a man. Loralee's breath caught in her throat.

Is that his soul?

The fog disappeared, and the man collapsed at Merikh's feet. If there were more Emani, they retreated. The guards made quick work of the injured. The mortoha dropped dead and became corpses once more as Merikh stopped controlling them. Guards scrounged anything of worth off the bodies. Emani were outlaws, not given the same rights as others. They wouldn't be returned to family or buried with funeral rites. The guards would pile them onto horses and dump them in the dunes away from camp to keep scavengers at bay.

The race descended from a people trapped in Shai'Khal after the impenetrable mists covered the oceans. They never assimilated into any culture, and their nomadic ways made them easy scapegoats. Loralee doubted it had taken much coin to pay these men and women to attack the Shah's retinue. Likely, each man killed today had known someone killed by Royal Guards for crimes they hadn't committed.

"How is he, Sayida?"

Merikh's words snapped Loralee out of her stupor as he approached. He sounded tired. His steps lacked their usual grace, and he stumbled on the sandy dirt before he reached Loralee and Adrian. Merikh had paid significantly less for a great deal more magic than the Ajir steward had. Loralee shook her head and looked down at Adrian beside her. He hadn't woken.

"I don't know," Loralee admitted as she stepped away from Adrian to make way for Merikh. He crouched down beside the young man and placed his hand on Adrian's chest for a fleeting moment.

"He's simply overdrawn." Merikh shook his head before grabbing Adrian's arm and dragging the younger man to his feet. The steward groaned, muttering something but not waking as Merikh shouldered his weight. A guard jogged over and quickly took Adrian from Merikh, dragging Adrian toward a tent where another healer was tending to the wounded. The ease at which the camp fell into routine unnerved Loralee. She shivered, folding her arms across her chest and rubbing her hands on her biceps.

"Does this happen often, Shahanshah?" Loralee asked as Merikh began to walk away.

He stopped and turned back to her, confusion plain in his eyes as he saw her shock for the first time.

"Only when someone believes they're a more capable shah than I. So yes, Sayida, it happens often. You'd best get used to it." His tone softened a little before one of the Ajir guards approached.

"They're all crawling with tokens of the Pantheon, but I found this," the guard explained quickly. In his hand was a solid black stone amulet in the shape of the Akhenic Sun but with a shamshir carved through the center of it.

"What is it?" Loralee asked, taking a step toward the men. Merikh picked up the amulet and turned it over in his hand, carefully examining it, as if looking for something in particular on it. As if he'd seen one before to compare it to.

"I don't know."

He answered more plainly than Loralee expected. His frown worried her. Merikh pocketed the amulet before he turned away and headed toward the healing tent. Pale-white magic glowed gently in the darkness. Loralee retreated to her tent, closing the privacy curtain behind her. She had no intention of sleeping. Loralee's heart still raced. Her hands were unsteady as she lit the small oil lamp inside the tent.

Normally, she would have gone to Amarante—the mare brought her comfort—but Loralee didn't want to show the weakness she felt. Not when those around her were returning to routine.

You'd best get used to it. But Loralee didn't want to. She'd seen more dead bodies around the Shah in a week than in her lifetime. The thought that this was only the start horrified her. Loralee couldn't imagine growing cold to this. Merikh's indifference made it all the more important she *didn't* grow indifferent to these incidents. After all, Loralee could count on one hand how many times assassins had attempted to kill her father. She certainly had never had any attempts on her own life.

Not yet, at least, Loralee thought with a bitter smile.

"Sayida?" a guard called from the other side of the curtain. When Loralee pulled back the privacy curtain, Farhana stood on the other side. The soldier had tried to wipe the blood off her face, but a few dark smears remained.

"Yes?"

"Captain Bashir asked me to check on you, make sure you were all right," Farhana said. She raised her hand, offering a steaming ceramic cup to Loralee.

"I'm fine, thank you," Loralee lied as she took the cup. It was warm, full to almost the brim of steaming water with lemon slices cut into it.

"Uh-huh. Well, the Shah's recovering. You're welcome by our fires if you need to talk. Everyone's been where you are, Sayida. Seeing walking corpses and souls takes some getting used to."

"The Shah's recovering?" Loralee asked, trying to steer the conversation away from herself or corpses.

"Asleep by now, I imagine. Sorcerers—gotta either give 'em food or a bed after magic like that. Adrian's not gonna wake until tomorrow, though the Shah'll be moving about before anyone else probably." Farhana shrugged.

"You've seen this often?" Loralee asked before taking a sip of the warm water. Farhana nodded.

"I was on the Shah's provincial patrol when he was the Shahzade. A year in the provinces, where he got kicked around a little, and we all got to call him 'Merikh.' His magic knocked him out for a *lot* longer at eighteen years old. I've got plenty of stories if you want to hear them." Farhana waved back toward one of the campfires.

Loralee smiled genuinely but shook her head. "Another time. Oh! The amulet one of the other guards found. The sun—"

"Apologies, Sayida. But the only person with answers about that is the Shah. If even *he* has answers."

Farhana bowed her head before retreating from the tent back to one of the guard fires. Loralee closed the curtain again and sat back down by the lamp. Her hands weren't shaking anymore, and Loralee felt the world returning to normal bit by bit.

As she calmed, exhaustion crept in again. Loralee finished the lemon water quickly. She only hoped sleep would be dreamless and that tomorrow would bring a bloodless day.

CHAPTER 14

3RD OF AYURITH, FIRST HARVEST, 902 UNIFIED AGE
MADIAR, RAUDHAH PROVINCE

The morning after the Emani attack, the Shah roused the guards early. By sunrise, they were already on the road so as to cover as much ground as they could before noonday heat drained their mounts. The pace was undoubtedly slower than the Shah wanted, but if he begrudged their progress, he kept it to himself.

The second day was significantly less eventful, and they only ran into a handful of travelers. Thankfully, no assassins. By the end of the third day, Loralee could see how exhausted Amarante was becoming. They'd reach Madiar tomorrow, and Loralee was excited to let her mare have a few days off. The mare had earned it—they'd never pushed quite this hard before.

Sand dunes burned red with the sunset. With the sky darkening, they could see fires of other camps popping up ahead of them down along the road. The closer they came to Madiar, the more travelers they passed. As they had every night, the retinue camped away from the main road. While the guards began setting up tents and cooking the antelope they'd hunted earlier, Loralee tended to the Neredi horses. They would be parading through Madiar tomorrow, and Loralee wanted them to look as resplendent as possible.

She carefully brushed the dirt from Amarante's coat, prying apart knots in her mane and tail before plaiting them up. The firelight reflected off the nearby sandstone outcropping, providing extra light for Loralee to see by as she finished the last of the finicky plaits.

"Sayida."

Loralee glanced over her shoulder to see Merikh approaching. His mare was already put up.

"Shahanshah?" Loralee turned to face him and bowed her head.

135

"Her leg looks a little swollen," Merikh said, gesturing to Amarante.

Loralee glanced down. *Perhaps a little,* Loralee thought. Certainly nothing concerning. She looked back to the Shah. There was a small jar in his hand, with blue and purple vines painted on the white ceramic. He handed Loralee the jar before running his hand over Amarante's shoulder and down her leg. The mare stomped her leg in irritation, earning a gentle tsk from the Shah, and Loralee saw light reflect off a thin coat of ice.

"Thank you," Loralee said quietly as Merikh worked. He said nothing, and when he was done he straightened up and brushed his hands on his black salwar.

"The ice will wear off in a few minutes, put the camphor on afterward, and she'll feel fine tomorrow."

Loralee nodded. Merikh turned and headed back toward the campfires. It was the most he'd spoken to her all day, as Loralee still didn't ride at his side. The Shah confused her. He'd run her through various tests in Rajibad, but now that they were away from the Quorum, he seemed quite content to simply leave her alone, which made this moment between them odd, as if he'd needed an excuse to see her.

Whether this was another test or not, Loralee couldn't tell. It almost seemed now that he had her, now that the betrothal was public and their wedding more or less confirmed, that he really wasn't sure what to do with her. There was no work for her to do here, and therefore he had nothing to throw at her.

Or perhaps he's trying to let me get comfortable without damaging my reputation again, Loralee thought. It was a kind assumption, and Loralee decided to run with it.

The camphor tingled on Loralee's fingers. Once she'd applied it to Amarante's legs, Loralee wiped the remaining off onto the mare's shoulder. The Shah's saddlebags weren't far, piled with others. Loralee replaced the camphor within it before putting Amarante into the pen with the Neredi horses. As Loralee approached the Shah's fire, she saw flickering light at the edge of camp. When she glanced back to Merikh, she saw a resigned look pass over him.

"Hail, traveler."

The call came from the darkness. A moment later, half a dozen men and women stopped at the edge of the firelight. Their lamps were burning low, and they were heavily laden with their tents and supplies. Loralee assumed they'd seen the fires from the road and thought this was the retinue of a rich merchant. The tents were all a plain brown. The guards hadn't hung the Madiaran standard at the edges of the camp, as they hadn't wanted to draw attention to themselves.

"May we stay at your fire tonight?" a middle-aged man asked, the same voice who had called from the dark before. His kufiyah was pulled away from his face, a gesture of trust. He wore brilliant reds and greens, a thick yellow sash wrapped around his portly waist.

The guards hadn't moved, taking their cue from the Shah as Merikh remained seemingly relaxed at his fire. These people were hardly a threat, and they looked exhausted. Hospitality laws from the Yahidahs' nomadic days still applied in the desert. Those laws demanded fortunate travelers give shelter and safety to the less fortunate, regardless of whether they were paupers or nobles.

The Shah was still dressed as simply as he had been for the Quorum—the black khalat he'd pulled on to stave off the desert night's cold had no ornamentation at all. The signet ring on his hand and the color of his eyes couldn't be easily seen in the firelight. It hardly surprised Loralee that the travelers hadn't realized who Merikh was, though the red achkan coats of the guards should have been a clue.

"Who are you?" Merikh asked, raising a hand and gesturing for the travelers to come into the light.

"Fuad Srour, bayim," the storyteller said. "We're entertainers from Akreh. I'm an ashik, that one"—he pointed back toward one of the women—"can make things disappear without magic, and the rest are the best Baladi dancers to never grace Shah Mansur's court." He gave a self-deprecating smile at the end.

"What brings you from Akreh?" Loralee asked, sitting down at Merikh's fire and reclining back on one of the large pillows on the ground.

"How have you missed the rumors from Rajibad, bayan?" the man asked. "There's to be a royal wedding."

"Is there? Shahanshah, did you know? Congratulations!" Loralee teased, leaning forward from her pillow and looking up at Merikh. The Shah looked less than amused, though his steward looked like he was holding back laughter.

"It had slipped my mind, Sayida," Merikh said, filling the stunned silence as the storyteller gaped at them before falling to his knees. The setar on his back nearly fell over his head. His companions were more composed when they bowed.

"Shahanshah, it is an unparalleled honor." Fuad still looked into the sand on the ground.

"Adrian, see that they're settled," Merikh ordered.

"Thank you, Shahanshah," Fuad said as he stood.

Adrian approached, and the steward guided the entertainers toward one of the guards' fires.

The entertainers brought life—and wine—to the camp. The wine was cheap, but the only one to turn it down when offered was the Shah. Loralee had heard him politely decline it, stating something about wine and necromancy magic not sitting well together. She knew just enough about magic to be certain he was lying. When the meal was finished, instead of retiring to their tents, the ashik storyteller left the guards' fire and approached the Shah's.

"Shahanshah?"

Merikh nodded once for him to continue.

"There's nothing I can offer to repay your hospitality other than my trade. May I?" Fuad gestured to his setar. At first Loralee assumed Merikh would say no. The man took himself entirely too seriously, and Loralee had a difficult time imagining the Shah making time for silly stories. So it surprised Loralee when instead, Merikh nodded.

"Perhaps a tale from Madiar's history, a story the sayida is unfamiliar with?"

Loralee smiled and looked from Merikh to Fuad. "The oasis. I believe there's a story from before the Temple bastardized it?"

"Of course, Sayida."

The strum of the setar quieted the camp, and Fuad had no trouble remembering the story. It was one that Loralee imagined Merikh knew well.

Every so often she checked out of the corner of her eye for his reaction. The man made for a difficult audience.

Perhaps a love story was an ill choice, Loralee thought. Then again, how was she to know? She'd never heard this version.

"Majhiara, nymph sister of the Ocean Goddess
Sailed her days away exploring the Aldruin
Her sails captured the wind
Her beauty caught Vindaram's eye

With oceans tamed
The Air God brought Majhiara to Shai'Khal
To best the sea of sand
But deserts are no place for nymphs
Majhiara could not bear the sun
Houxipil, the mighty Storm God
Took pity upon them
A monsoon overcame the desert
And the lovers sailed the dunes

Mortal farmers cried for sunlight
Akhenios obliged, clearing the skies
Majhiara became bound to the Kura River
To await Vindaram's return from the dunes
Sung upon strong winds

Her beauty entranced another
Skyndar, Chaos incarnate, came to Majhiara
His many eyes leering
Repulsed, Majhiara rejected the god
Skyndar left her undeterred
His desires not easily foiled

Strong winds crested sand dunes
Majhiara saw Vindaram at last!

Shaken by Skyndar's appearance, she called to him
Eagerness overcame prudence
She left the river and raced to her love

But Vindaram was not there
An imp, a shapeshifting creature of Chaos
Had deceived Majhiara's eyes
Her hand touched his
The illusion shattered
Weakened by sun and sand
Majhiara could not escape the imp's grasp
And was dragged deeper into the desert

Near death, Majhiara prayed
For mercy, for revenge
For Vindaram
Skyndar answered, enraged
Turning Majhiara into an oasis

But Majhiara's cries were not unheard
Sisters Meriath and Neharang
Grabbed the hideous imp
And drowned him in the oasis

Cyclones and sandstorms
Shook the world from Vindaram's grief
Skyndar bowed before the Gods Council
Asking forgiveness, finding little
Vindaram stole Skyndar's gift of flight
Unsated, the cataclysm continued

Ikharon, God of the Dead
Built an altar at the oasis
A gateway to Aljemel

A meeting place for Vindaram to see Majhiara
A door closed to Skyndar
Until the sun dies and the world ends."

The storyteller strummed his setar one last time and bowed with a flourish.

"And that, Sayida, is why the White City has such huge walls. For when Vindaram visits Majhiara, he often comes on the edge of a sandstorm," Fuad said.

"What of the oasis?" Loralee asked.

It was Merikh who answered. "The palace was built on the site of the oasis. Ikharon's altar—or Akhenios's, depending on what you believe—was converted to one of the grand fountains."

"I look forward to seeing it," Loralee said, smiling before she looked back to Fuad. "Thank you."

It was a very different tale than the one the Akhenic Temple taught. In that tale, Akhenios slayed an ifrit and marked its grave with water to prevent the fiery creature from ever returning.

"Would you care for another story, Sayida?" Fuad asked.

Loralee shook her head. "If the Shah will excuse me, I fear I must retire for the evening. Sleeps beckons. From the wine and travel, I assure you. Your story was wondrous, if a bit melancholy to tell a bride," Loralee teased lightly.

"I have no doubt, Sayida, if you were to fall to a fate like poor Majhiara, that you would find an equally fitting tribute to your life."

"I have every hope the sayida is more observant and intelligent than Majhiara," Merikh said with a dismissive wave. "You may both retire."

Fuad bowed and retreated back to one of the guards' campfires. Loralee lingered a moment longer.

"Thank you for indulging him. It was a beautiful story," Loralee said quietly.

"If you care for them, you should speak with Grand Vizier Nikias. He may not be an ashik—don't ask him to sing—but he knows more stories than anyone I've ever met and has a knack for telling them. Good night, Sayida."

"Good night, Shahanshah."

The next morning, Loralee woke to the sounds of tents folding. The muffled noise filled her with excitement and dread. They'd reach Madiar today. The Holy City. The seat of power. Her new home.

Or prison. The thought came intrusively, and Loralee forced it from her mind. She shivered as she left her bedroll. The desert night hadn't relented its grip.

Loralee dressed quickly, putting on her pale-blue niqaab, which matched her best sari. Flat luck coins were stitched into her choli blouse. Loralee could feel the cold metal through the fabric on her chest. The gold and silver threads caught the dawn light as she left her tent.

The camp was bustling with activity. Guards were taking down tents, grooming horses, and a few stragglers were finishing up bathing in a makeshift pool of water Loralee assumed was being sustained by the Shah. Merikh was nowhere to be found, still readying himself in the privacy of his tent. It let her steal a glance toward the shirtless male Ajir, and she noted she wasn't the only one to appreciate the view. The steward appeared a little distracted from his duties.

Amarante nickered as Loralee approached; the excitement from the guards had spread to the horses. The gray mare struggled to stand still as Loralee groomed her. The plaits from the night before were time-consuming to remove, but they left the mare's mane in long, clean waves, which made it worth the effort. As far as Loralee was concerned, Amarante was the best-looking mare in the group, and Loralee had every intention of showing her off. The Shah's bay mare was pretty. Her brown coat had a lovely red tinge to it, and her black points had no fade to them. Regardless, the royal mare was plain looking. Amarante looked every bit the part of mount for a khanum. Loralee only wished she had her ceremonial tack with her. They had expected no fanfare in Rajibad, and as such, Loralee had left it in Abadan.

Over Amarante's back, Loralee saw the Shah's tent had been folded and packed. For once, Merikh was easy to spot in the camp. Even he had put a little effort into his appearance this morning. For the first time since they'd met, Merikh actually looked the part of the Shah.

Loralee tried not to stare. His crimson achkan featured stunning golden embroidery. A golden sash was tied across his chest and around his belt.

Even his kufiyah, a plain black cloth, had a golden agal band across to mimic a crown. There was no mistaking him for anyone of lesser station today. Loralee felt woefully underdressed.

The formation changed that morning. Ajir Captain Bashir rode beside Merikh, and Adrian fell back behind Loralee. There were only two lines of guards between her and the Shah. Ajir guard Farhana had taken a liking to Loralee and rode close beside her. It was as they reached a bend in the road that Loralee realized why Farhana had chosen that particular spot. She'd taken it upon herself to become Loralee's personal guide to Madiar and its surrounding landmarks.

"Sayida, over there. Do you see the obelisk?" Farhana asked, pointing south, away from the road. The stone point could barely be seen above the dunes.

"I believe so, yes."

"That's the final resting place of the Madiaran shahs."

"I see."

Loralee had never found tombs of interest. Particularly the tombs of men and women unrelated to her. *At least, currently unrelated,* Loralee wondered if the Royal Tombs might hold greater significance when it came closer to the time she'd buried there. *If* she was buried there. Khanum Aliyah had been transported back to Ramshar to be buried in the Afolayan family crypt. *Well, what was left of her.*

Scaphism was a horrific way to die. Even as a small child, Loralee had understood that the khanum's death had been brutal. The woman had been hung from a cage outside the Hall of Nadlious above a rancid pool of water. Naked and covered in honey, buzzards and insects had eaten her alive over the course of three excruciating days. Then there had been another week of her corpse rotting before Mansur had allowed anyone to move it. By that time, the vultures and insects had left little to bury. Loralee couldn't imagine trying to cope with the loss of a parent in that manner, or growing up watching that level of animosity develop between two people.

Loralee shook the unpleasant thoughts from her head. If they were passing the Royal Tombs, that meant they couldn't be more than a few hours outside of Madiar. Loralee knew the city would be huge. More people lived within its walls than any other city in Shai'Khal. But to actually see it finally?

The very idea of the city took Loralee's breath away.

Madiar was a city unlike anything Loralee had seen before. In the desert heat, its white walls disappeared and reappeared in the haze. Loralee was shocked by how close they had to come before she could be certain the white stone walls weren't a mirage. The city seemed to stretch on forever. Over the grand walls, towers and minarets pierced the clear blue sky. Their bronze domes reflected the light and did little to aid the city's permanence in the haze.

No wonder it's the Holy City. Even as skeptical as Loralee was, she couldn't help the feeling that gods had indeed left their mark on Madiar's walls. The ancient city felt ageless upon approach.

Mounted honor guard lined the road into Madiar, keeping it clear for the retinue. Madiaran banners hung from the lances of the guards, flapping lazily in the slight breeze overhead of the retinue. Bronze sringa horns rang clearly, announcing the Shah's return to the crowds that had gathered along the road.

Inside the city walls, Madiar lost its ethereal quality. Enchanted aqueducts helped to keep the city clean, but in the heat of the day, the Hock District's rancid odor couldn't be avoided. Loralee adjusted her niqaab a little, but the veil hardly helped. Slums were slums, after all. Beggars pressed against the guards, calling to their shah and begging for coin. Loralee glanced over her shoulder and saw Adrian giving alms of coins and food to the guards to distribute. In return, beggars tossed palm fronds, straw, and even worn-out cloth ahead of the retinue to soften the cobblestones' impact on the horses' weary feet.

The farther inside the Hock District they went, the cleaner the city became. Buildings were less crammed together. Loralee could see towers peeking through again. Farhana cleared her throat and gestured to Loralee's right.

"We're almost at the High Temple. You might be able to see a bit of the palace ahead again."

The walls to the Temple District were covered in vines. When they passed, acolytes were scrubbing vandalism off of a cleared section. They stopped and bowed their heads as the retinue went by, but Loralee was certain she heard muttered accusations of Merikh being a djinn's consort and the whelp of the "Mad Jackal."

Once past the Temple District, they rode through the large stone gate into the Mitbah District, and the road became lined with merchant stalls. The scent of spices and perfumes filled the air. Instead of begging for alms, merchants offered wares and tried to force gifts upon the retinue. The bazaar was dizzyingly colorful, selling everything from fruits and grains to huge ornate carpets and animals. Thievery appeared to be a problem, though not by just humans. Loralee looked away and tried hard not to laugh as a man lost a fight with a monkey over a pomegranate. While there was little enough wildlife outside of the city walls—and certainly no monkeys—plenty seemed to have carved a niche within the city itself.

"Sayida." Farhana got her attention again. The guard handed off an ornately and carefully wrapped anarkali dress. Loralee shook her head but took it anyway. *Bribery for the newly favored sayida,* Loralee assumed as she draped the gift along the front of her saddle.

Her presence in the Shah's retinue was far from unnoticed. Loralee guessed if there were entertainers on the road destined for Madiar for the wedding, that news of her betrothal to the Shah had spread throughout Shai'Khal faster than fleas on a rat. Loralee peeked through the cloth wrap around the dress and was unsurprised to see bright crimson fabric. A dress for *after* the marriage. Loralee could only imagine the scandal if she began wearing Madiaran reds before the wedding. It would inflame the rumors of a shahzade in less than nine months, at the minimum. *I'd probably fail one of Merikh's tests too,* Loralee thought.

Outside of the bazaar, the Mitbah District housed and educated the passably wealthy of Madiar. Not the nobles or wealthy merchants, but the educated of either scholarly endeavors or trades. Master smiths rubbed shoulders with philosophers and astronomers. The district was cleaner, but it wasn't until they passed through the massive gate into the Jibbah District that Loralee felt she could finally breathe again.

Here, no one lined the road. The few men and women in the streets bowed their heads but mostly went about their business. A few welcomed the Shah back, but there was nothing awestruck about their tone. After all, the Jibbah District was home to the nobility. These men and women had the opportunity to petition entry into the palace to see Merikh whenever the need arose. To see him like this was hardly rare.

The homes here were larger estates, with small walls protecting their gardens. A large fountain of four horses was placed in the middle of the main square of the Jibbah District. On the street around it were several beautiful white stone buildings—inns and taverns for wealthy visitors to Madiar. Past them, a beautiful vine garden shaded the road that led them up to the golden gates of the Madiar palace.

The gates opened with a small groan, and an awestruck smile grew on Loralee's lips. *Jin was right,* Loralee thought. Rajibad's palace was a poor man's imagining of what an opulent palace would look like on an extreme budget. The Great Prophet had redesigned much of Madiar's palace when he claimed it as home, and the men and women who had come after him had added to his vision.

The palace had a dozen marble towers, each domed and capped in gold. Every line of the palace was soft. The architects had clearly worked with earth sorcerers to sculpt seemingly impossible arched windows and walkways. In one of the nearby windows, Loralee saw the stained glass change colors, the geometric design slowly shifting from squares to crowns. It was either a "welcome home" enchantment for the Shah or a reminder to those inside that their master had returned.

As impressive as the palace was, it could have been a hovel, and Loralee would have still been happy here. Because more important buildings caught her eyes—the barns. They were a city in and of itself. Attached to each of the barns were several paddocks, and aqueducts carried water from the main well to each barn, paddock, and arena. Every stall had doors to turn out, every horse had a herd and a place to run and graze.

"Sayida?"

Loralee glanced back from the barns to Farhana, who had stopped and dismounted. Loralee did the same and followed Farhana. They walked quickly through the main barn and across the yard to a secondary barn behind it.

"Your mare can stay here until she's integrated into the herd," Farhana told her. "Your tack can go in the barn over there, anywhere there's some space."

"Thank you," Loralee said as Farhana bowed then left to care for her own horse. Loralee pulled off Amarante's bridle and tied her by the halter lead to the rail. She untacked the mare quickly, excited to let the mare finally have some rest. Loralee looked forward to having a moment to take the barns in, to finally tour the best breeding barn in the world.

If I'm allowed. The realization hit her hard as she remembered the ice webs from Rajibad. As the most coveted barn in Shai'Khal, it was entirely possible Merikh wouldn't let her near his horses without an escort until after they were married and her loyalty proven. Loralee held back a frustrated sigh. She hoped any restrictions on her freedom would be only temporary. With Amarante groomed, watered, and stalled, Loralee walked back through to the main courtyard where guards were still putting up their horses and servants were hauling the retinue's supplies up to the palace.

"Sayida Loralee?"

An older bald Yahidah man in a brown kaftan gestured her over to him. He bowed his head as she approached. Loralee returned the gesture. The grand vizier's reputation as the Shah's closest confidant had preceded him.

"I am Nikias Soun, grand vizier to the Shah. He asked me to help you settle in," Nikias informed her unnecessarily.

"Thank you."

Loralee glanced past Nikias toward the long flight of stairs that led to the main palace doors. Ornately dressed men and women dogged the Shah's steps as he climbed. If the road had tired him, Loralee couldn't tell.

"How was the ride?" Nikias asked as he turned from the barn toward the stairs.

"It's been a long time since I've made such a trek. It was wonderful," Loralee said as she followed him. It was more or less true. Normally, traveling with her father to deliver horses was a little more entertaining and had fewer assassination attempts. Those journeys were often longer, but the pace was easier. Nikias simply smiled and led her through the dizzying maze of corridors to her room.

It was large, ornately decorated, and truthfully more than what Loralee expected. Massive arched windows let in light through colored glass. Tapestries hung from the walls, depicting ancient royal horses. Loralee recognized one as a depiction of the Great Prophet's warhorse, a gray mare with strange red marks on her shoulders. A cedar coffee table and matching chairs sat in the center of the room atop an ornate rug.

Nikias sat down and gestured for Loralee to do the same. Servants were already in the room unpacking Loralee's bags. One left the clothes on the bed for a moment to pour both the grand vizier and Loralee water.

"Will your guards be staying here or returning to Abadan?" Nikias asked.

Loralee sat down across from him. "They'll return with my father to Abadan after the wedding," Loralee told him.

Ideally, she would have kept them stationed here permanently. Merikh's guards were loyal to him first and foremost, meaning if anything happened between her and Merikh, no one would come to her aid. But her guards were little help against a sorcerer, and they had families and lives in Abadan that Loralee wouldn't tear them from.

"Of course, I'll have space made for them in the barracks for the time being. Now, did the Shah tell you what exactly he expects from you here?" Nikias asked.

Loralee smirked and shook her head. "That would have required the Shah to have spoken with me since we left Rajibad. The man needs an heir, therefore he needs a wife. Beyond that?" Loralee just shrugged.

Nikias nodded, snapped his fingers at the servants, and then pointed to the door. They quickly exited.

"I'm going to be brutally honest with you, Sayida." Nikias hesitated then, and Loralee offered him an encouraging smile.

"I wouldn't have it any other way."

Nikias ran a hand over his bald head. Now that they were alone, he looked exhausted. Trying to run Madiar on his own during Merikh's absence had to have been difficult. Nikias looked much older than Loralee had expected. His reputation made him out to be so much...more than the man who sat in front of her. The man across from her had lines worn into his forehead and around his eyes. He looked grandfatherly. Stern yet fragile. Hardly the force of nature that his reputation made him out to be. Here sat the man who could calm Mansur's rage, who guided Merikh's unflinching justice, and looked as if he could be perhaps blown over by a strong wind.

"The Shah will not make your life easy," Nikias said gently. "He's an exceptionally solitary person. I promise you, he doesn't want you here. If you grew up on the fanciful stories of past shahs sweeping their khanums off their feet with grand gestures and passionate nights...I suggest putting those stories aside. Permanently."

Loralee didn't have expectations of Merikh beyond what she'd already seen. She hadn't yet made up her mind about him. And yet Nikias's frankness couldn't help but make Loralee feel dismayed. After all, who wanted to be told by a stranger how unwanted they were?

"I say this," Nikias continued, "because I want you fully prepared for the task you've put your mind to. You have a great deal to prove, and unfortunately neither you nor the Shah have the luxury of time on your side to become comfortable and acquainted. He's already put off securing succession long enough. Aliyah was pregnant when she married Mansur. *Before* he became shah."

Loralee tried to hide her irritation but failed as she pursed her lips.

"The Shah is lucky to have a servant as dedicated as you are, Vizier."

How did one respond to such a brutal assessment? Everyone knew that Nikias was close to the Shah. Loralee certainly had no intention of becoming pregnant *before* she was khanum. She doubted Merikh had much desire to do so either.

Nikias smiled, attempting to reassure her.

"I admire your father. He kept Mansur on edge, in a good way. If you're anything like the duq, then I think the Shah and his heir will be in good hands."

"Thank you." Loralee felt ridiculous for how often she'd said those simple words since arriving in Madiar, but nothing else felt appropriate. *Perhaps I'm more tired than I thought.*

As if reading her mind, Nikias nodded once and stood. "You should rest, Sayida. I had court canceled today, although I imagine you'll find messengers knocking at your door with invitations soon enough. Everyone wants to get to know the future khanum."

"Except the Shah," Loralee said with a tired smirk. "Thank you, Vizier."

"If you need anything at all, I'm at your disposal." Nikias bowed and left Loralee alone to her thoughts.

CHAPTER 15

16TH OF AYURITH, FIRST HARVEST, 902 UNIFIED AGE
MADIAR, RAUDHAH PROVINCE

After two months of unbearable stagnancy, Sarka was more than ready to leave Madiar. Rain had given way to warmer temperatures and drier days that were quickly becoming intolerable. Even with baths, Sarka was unsure how anyone managed to scrape out a comfortable existence—let alone a prosperous one—in such an inclement place. No wonder the people here were short tempered. The heat left their blood perpetually boiling. Or at least, that's how it left Sarka's.

Maybe it's just politics, she thought.

Ruya, of course, had planted herself firmly in the center of Madiar's political schemes. By now, Sarka was quite certain her companion had broken bread with every important man and woman in Madiar who would see her. Whether they were *converted* was an entirely different matter, one Ruya didn't seem to worry about much. The priestess still acted as if they had all the time in the world to achieve their goals. Death, after all, had a sweet inevitability, but that seemed to lead Ruya to complacency.

How could she not see the dangers of this place? Ruya forgave far too quickly the actions of the people around her. Rabb Khamisi loudly decried them at every turn. Sarka heard how the soldiers spoke in hushed, confused tones about them. While Ruya seemed extremely content in the lavish suite Merikh had given them when they arrived, Sarka was relieved to have her small officer's room in the barracks. She enjoyed the quiet comfort of a disciplined regime, of men and women whose concerns were far more grounded than those with overly imaginative political machinations. The boundaries in war were far easier to delineate, ones allies and enemies shifted slowly, if at all.

151

Unlike politics, where one's allies and enemies might change as quick as lightning. These soldiers were cut from the same cloth as Sarka. She could understand their worries. Sarka had earned a measure of respect from the Royal Guards and tried to reassure the soldiers that Livinja blessed them. That their shah would continue to do right by them. It was hard for Sarka to have her yoke tied to Merikh's.

Ruya's hand bore thin white scars on the palm and the back of her hand. The scars almost went from wrist to knuckles. Ruya was a rather delicately built woman, and the curved blade had done a great deal of damage. The priestess of death simply shrugged off the scarring when Sarka had pointed it out. *"I made a mistake. Now I'll remember not to make it again."*

How did she fail to see how dangerous that was? They were immortal representatives of gods! Merikh should have been the one afraid to cross them, not the other way around. A twenty-four-year-old *boy* should have cowered after the display Ruya had shown him, not tried to cut her hand off!

Sarka had pointed out to Ruya that it wasn't too late to place someone else on the throne. But she might as well have told Ruya she planned on drowning kittens. It would have garnered a similar lecture. Merikh, despite his blatant disrespect, would unfortunately be their prophet shah.

The thought made Sarka want to vomit.

Sarka rubbed her eyes and sighed. She'd been holed up in the archives for weeks now. Between her and Ruya, they'd barely scratched the surface of the ancient tomes contained within. Books made Sarka restless. She didn't mind reading occasionally for enjoyment, but this? Sifting through dreary accounts written by authors who thought far too highly of themselves felt like another punishment from Akhenios.

After a few weeks of picking at it, Ruya had enlisted several additional court scholars to help, but Sarka could see their frustration mounting. They knew what she and Ruya were doing. That they were looking for the Akhenic Key, which may or may not be referred to as such. That it was probably was somewhere in Ydeba, unless Akhenios's Great Prophet had moved it. And that it might be protected by an ancient guardian, but who knew what *that* might be?

Ruya didn't help focus the scholars either, as she happily allowed them to learn anything off topic they encountered, or she spread gossip from her latest chats with nobles. Even these men and women, as removed from politics as they were, were interested in the events of the Rajibad Quorum. Not that Sarka could fault them. Merikh returning with Sayida Loralee and shoring up alliances was rather important. Even without attending, Ruya was happy to speculate with these scholars as to what the repercussions could be.

Focus! Sarka admonished herself with a frown. *There has to be a record of the key somewhere.* It was impossible that Akhenios and Uduak had been able to create the Akhenic Key and keep it completely quiet from everyone.

Uduak. Sarka had forgotten the name until she'd found it in a book. He was usually referred to by his titles, his name only kept in bloodline papers and very old scripts. It amazed Sarka what she'd forgotten in nine hundred years of solitude. Battles she'd fought, places she'd been. Apparently, even the names of people she'd once been close to. Uduak, the Great Prophet of Akhenios, Holy Conqueror and First Blessed Shahanshah of Shai'Khal.

Traitor. Murderer.

Small comfort he was dead. But that begged a more important question: Why? Why had Akhenios let his confidant and representative in Shai'Khal die? Was immortality unattainable outside of the mists without Ikharon's consent? Or had something else happened? Had the creation of the Akhenic Key required sacrifice? Would destroying it demand the same?

By the gods, where is the damn thing? Sarka shut the book in front of her with a frustrated slam. Everyone nearby jumped, the sound earning her glares and dirty looks.

"Sorry," she said, louder than she meant to. Sarka stood and walked the book back to its shelf. Bookcases stretched from floor to the high ceiling, with ladders and walkways to the second-story access for books. Small windows allowed little light in, and reading light was primarily provided by enchanted stone lanterns. Open flames were forbidden. Anyone caught breaking that rule had their eyes put out. As Sarka pushed the book back in place, a chain from the shelf clipped itself onto the book's spine. The bronze ring on Sarka's hand allowed her access through the lock enchantments on the archive's books.

"I think...I think I might have come across something that can help."

One of the scholars raised his hand a little and slowly gestured for Sarka and Ruya to come over to him. The book in front of him wasn't a thick tome; the leather bindings were cracked and dry from dust. It need a good oiling and a little care. Ruya slid down the bench to sit beside the scholar while Sarka walked back from the bookcase. Ruya touched the pages of the journal carefully. There were drawings of maps and creatures, creatures Sarka knew to be banished to the Aldruin islands with their gods.

"This is before Unification," Sarka breathed.

Ruya hesitantly nodded. It was a wonder the journal hadn't fallen completely to pieces. Sarka wondered when the last time this book had been copied and rebound. The scholar flipped back to the front of the journal, where the name of the adventurer had been written.

"Negasi Okafor, Fourth Son of the Waning Moon." The scholar looked up at Ruya and Sarka, a confused look on his face.

"Yasu's priesthood," Ruya explained. "Men and women who followed the Night Goddess. May I?"

The scholar gently handed the journal off to Ruya, who carefully flipped through the pages until she found what she was looking for. Ruya cleared her throat and read from the page.

"They've all gone into hiding. Chinara begged me to go with her. But I can't. I won't hide from them, not from Uduak. I saw his dragon overhead last night. Why he's returned from the front lines, I can only guess. There are rumors of a device Akhenios will use to banish the djinns. Djinns. He calls his own sister one of those creatures!"

Ruya tapped the book gently. "Sarka, that's it. That's the Key. This man must have sought it out!"

"So where is it, then?" Sarka asked, hiding her enthusiasm. "If this man Negasi saw the dragon, it's before they took Raudhah. Before Madiar fell. I killed it in Tanga."

"When?" the scholar asked.

Sarka rubbed her forehead, trying to remember. "I don't know. I can barely remember the fight, let alone details like that." The memory only came to her in flashes, sometimes in dreams as either grand triumphs or horrific nightmares. She bore the scars of the dragon's claws on her leg. Sarka had been lucky not to lose her limb to the creature.

"They'll know when the dragon fell in Ydeba. There might be an Umbeah in the palace who would know off hand. Or a book…" The scholar trailed off as Ruya shook her head. She flipped through another few pages.

"He parted ways with Chinara at the little fort, Kal Natwen. Where is that?" Ruya asked.

"Kal Natwen became Hatai, on the west edge of the Sarafi on the Raudhah-Ydeba border," the scholar explained.

"And then? Where to from there?" Sarka asked. Ruya shrugged and pointed to the last few pages of the book. They were completely faded, impossible to read.

"Southwest. Is there another journal?" Ruya asked, and the scholar stood to consult the bookcase. While he looked, Ruya turned back to the start of the book.

"We probably met him, Negasi, at some point. A Fourth Son would have accompanied Yasu to Madiar occasionally," Ruya said.

"I'm just impressed one of Yasu's people had the guts to try and pursue the Key," Sarka said, gesturing to the journal.

Yasu had been an easy target for Akhenios. As the sun god, it was all too easy to vilify the Moon Goddess. If Akhenios was pure life and good, then Yasu was darkness, death, and everything wrong with the world. A mother of djinn who bestowed her dark gifts upon them. Akhenios claimed that she was the true power behind the false gods. Naturally, that had sat quite ill with the other gods, particularly Ikharon. The god of death had always been among the most powerful of the Pantheon, stronger than Yasu. Yasu's priests and priestesses were hardly the paragon of fighters or resistance. The goddess favored by spies and thieves.

A journal left by one of Belara's people wouldn't have surprised Sarka at all. The Goddess of Vengeance and Wrath would have a banner day once loose from her island prison. Her priesthood had fought hard against Akhenios and Uduak, and her champion had died fighting Onyx Swords. Belara's anger, once free, would scorch at least a few Akhenic temples. Sarka was certain of it.

The scholar returned to the table empty-handed. "If there's another, it's in a different library."

"If there were a number of Waning Moons in Hatai, there might still be some record of where Negasi went after leaving them," Sarka said.

Apparently, that was enough to put a smile on Ruya's face. She hopped up from the bench and walked quickly to the library entrance. A guard was stationed there at all times, and Sarka could hear Ruya asking him for something before she returned to the table. The guard poked his head out the door and barked an order at another guard before returning to his post inside.

Ruya sat down beside Sarka again, a satisfied look on her face.

"I thought it might be time to tell Merikh what we're thinking."

"What *are* we thinking?" Sarka asked, annoyed.

Ruya was impulsive and rarely included Sarka in her planning. *If* she planned anything at all.

"Well," Ruya started, folding her hands in her lap, "you're going after the Key."

"Simple as that, huh?" Sarka asked, her tone resigned as she reached for the journal and began to flip through. She keenly noted that their mission had turned from "we" to just Sarka. *Someone doesn't want to have to hit the road again and sleep in the dirt.*

"Simple as that." Ruya smiled.

It was not simple. Nikias arrived in the library before Merikh did, and when the Shah arrived, he was hounded by messengers. Sarka would have almost felt sorry for him, but it was the first time she'd seen Merikh squirm without someone ending up bloody. Royal weddings, after all, didn't happen every day. Planning one took effort, yet no one seemed to understand how little Merikh wanted to be involved with it. Or how little he cared for the envoy messengers, bearing small gifts from their noble masters, arriving in the city.

Normally, a royal wedding took at least half a year or more to plan. But on the tail of the Rajibad Quorum, with most of the important nobles still present in Raudhah, Merikh had pushed for it to be dealt with quickly. He seemed to be suffering for that decision, and Sarka almost felt guilty for how much she enjoyed it. Almost.

"The other journals could be scattered in libraries all over Shai'Khal by now, *if* any of them were transcribed over the years," Nikias said, "and if this Key is hiding somewhere in Ydeba, you'll need an army to access it. The Katu Mountains will be crawling with Onyx Swords by the time you got there. Plenty of old fortresses and sorcery schools to be reclaimed in the old passes. Duqa Enitan's forces can hole up in those mountains easily and make assailing anything nearby impossible."

"Shahanshah, Albarun Makato—" A messenger bowed. A small envoy entered the library behind him with trays of gifts.

"Out!" Merikh slammed his hand on the table. Shards of ice flew from the impact, and frost laced the table away from his fingertips like veins. "By the gods, bother the sayida with this. She's about to be your khanum; make this her problem. *All* of it. I am not to be bothered with any of this."

Merikh gestured toward the envoys, who were already rapidly retreating from the library. The Makato messenger bowed and backed away, muttering apologies before following his companions out. A thick wall of ice covered the door. Sarka looked away to hide her smirk. The man would pick a fight with the representatives of gods, but a wedding? *That* was overwhelming.

Merikh took a deep breath, then shook his head slowly.

"I am not sending an army with Sarka to find a journal that may or may not be in Ydeba, that may or may not lead to the Key," Merikh said firmly. "I am not wasting soldiers on this, nor risking a confrontation in those mountains."

Sarka begrudgingly nodded. "I don't need an army. I don't *want* an army. It's too many people for something like this. Merikh's right. We don't know if this will lead to the Key or not." Sarka glanced stubbornly at Ruya. Sarka was completely certain that Ruya thought it was a guarantee they'd find the next journal in Hatai and that it'd lead straight to the Key. The high priestess of death was an eternal optimist.

"A handful of scouts, then," Nikias suggested.

"The woman is the champion of war, Vizier, how much help could she possibly need finding a book?" Merikh asked, looking at her pointedly.

"I need a guide, at least," Sarka said. "Someone who can get in the places I can't. I'm going to attract attention regardless of what I do to hide with my aura. But I don't need more than one or two competent people. We can find the journal, and then either return to Madiar to regroup if necessary or pursue the Key directly."

"Take Adrian."

Merikh's words stunned Sarka. The young man was a steward! A man who delivered letters and coffee—or so he had said. Sarka leaned forward, about to protest, when the grand vizier did so instead.

"Shahanshah," Nikias said quietly, "this could be exceptionally dangerous."

"In what way is that different from Adrian's usual errands outside Madiar?" Merikh asked.

Sarka blinked in surprise. *What in Cala do you ask of your steward? What job are you grooming him for?* Sarka shook her head.

"Of course." Nikias cleared his throat, not looking impressed with the situation.

"Your vizier isn't wrong." Sarka looked to Merikh. "I don't know what we're going to encounter if we find the Key. I may not survive handling it, and I can't guarantee the survival of anyone with me."

"I'm sure Ruya can give you and Adrian a beautiful eulogy." Merikh ignored Sarka's glare, his tone cavalier and almost bored.

"Another problematic matter is Sarka disappearing. The champion of war being gone for an indeterminate amount of time on the potential eve of war may be viewed as an ill omen." Nikias looked to Ruya, who shrugged.

"Sarka prefers to stay out of the public eye anyway. Besides, if she leaves around the wedding, who's going to notice? Between Loralee and I, I'm sure we can cause enough of a stir to keep all eyes and tongues quite busy." Ruya winked at Merikh, who looked about to give her another scar.

Is he blushing? No, Sarka realized with disappointment. Merikh looked uncomfortable for but a moment before he regained his composure.

"Then I suppose the wedding will be good for something, at least. I suggest you get ready, Champion," Merikh said as he stood. The wall of ice disappeared from the door. The grand vizier followed Merikh out. Ruya let out a small laugh once they were gone.

"What?" Sarka asked, furrowing her brow.

"I've missed being around the young! They worry about the most adorable things." Ruya pulled the map back to her half of the table. Sarka shook her head. She supposed she couldn't really blame the way Ruya viewed the world. Nine hundred years and only Ikharon and undead for company. Sarka simply tried to be thankful that Ruya was as well-adjusted to the world as she was.

CHAPTER 16

31st of Ayurith, First Harvest, 902 Unified Age

Madiar, Raudhah Province

The room was meant to be comfortable, intimate in spite of its accommodating size. Heavy red curtains accented with gold partitioned the room and covered the arched windows. Sitting pillows covered the floor in circles around hookahs and mats for food. The incense that had burnt earlier in the day had been replaced by the smell of opium, hashish, and musk. Wine and araq was poured freely into the cups of the noblemen present. Servants brought in plenty of food to compensate. Musicians strummed their setars quietly while an ashik regaled them with a myth from before Unification.

The room was alive with drunken laughter. Merikh struggled to pay attention to the ashik. All that was missing were naked women, and the room would have felt much like it had five years ago, when Mansur was alive and frequenting it.

Merikh had forgotten how passionately he *hated* this room. He remembered the first few times he'd come here as a boy. Aliyah had been alive and would drag him here to poke and prod him until he acquiesced to showing off ice magic. Harassed into enchanting little ice creatures to go along with whatever story was being told by the ashik at the time.

After her death, Merikh hadn't come to this room for years. Not until his fifteenth natal anniversary, as Mansur had deemed it worth celebrating. All Merikh remembered from it was waking up naked and sore, wrapped around a whore who hadn't quite moved out of the way fast enough to avoid Merikh's unfortunate stomach purge. After that, he'd kept away from alcohol, hashish, and any woman his father put in front of him. The room was an altar to everything Merikh had abhorred about Mansur. Indulgence, excess, and a gross lack of inhibition.

It's just a room, Merikh tried to convince himself, taking a deep breath and letting it out slowly. But it was hard to push the memories aside, and the night was only beginning.

Merikh had tried to get out of this. He'd had asked Nikias glibly if there was any way to avoid the damned henna night. It had earned him a gentle lecture about tradition, how now more than ever, it was important for him to show respect for the rituals of his ancestors. Traditions that meant men like Nikias and Adrian, common born, couldn't be present while men like Amir Navin and Duq Rashad were.

"Shahanshah?"

An old Yahidah man approached the platform where Merikh sat. His hands were aged and spotted, his back bent even as he stood tall. He carried a leather satchel and a small rest for Merikh's arm. Reluctantly, Merikh gestured for the man to approach.

"My name is Zuhayr. I had the honor of doing your father's henna as well. Are you comfortable? It'll take some time," Zuhayr asked as he placed his tools down carefully beside Merikh.

Comfortable? Not in the least. Merikh didn't say so.

"I'm sure if I need anything, someone will accommodate me. Go on."

Zuhayr nodded before he cleared his throat and gestured at Merikh's red kameez. Reluctantly, Merikh pulled the shirt off and placed it on the pillow next to him. To his great relief, the ashik had the room's attention enough that few noticed. With his back to the wall, the bulk of his scars from Mansur were hidden. Merikh was in no mood to answer questions about them. Not tonight. Probably not ever.

Zuhayr dipped the thin bamboo stick in the henna paste while Merikh removed the signet ring from his left hand and placed it on his right. After a moment's hesitation, Merikh extended his hand to Zuhayr and let the man begin his work.

The temperature plummeted as the bamboo touched Merikh's left hand. He flexed his right hand, forcing the temperature back to a comfortable level. The bamboo didn't hurt in the slightest—if anything, it tickled—but being touched felt confining. The ashik hesitated in his story only a moment before regaining the room's attention again. Amir Navin and Rabb Mahdi, reclined on the lavish pillows, hauled themselves to their feet and came to Merikh's side. His uncles had made no apologies for missing the Quorum when they'd arrived in Madiar two days ago, preferring to gloss over the topic entirely to focus on the wedding.

"Are you all right?" Navin asked, his voice raw from the smoke. He sat down to Merikh's right, out of Zuhayr's way. Mahdi joined Navin and immediately helped himself to the nearby hookah. Navin supposedly looked a great deal like his younger sister had. Lanky, elegant, with a distant coldness that Merikh had clearly inherited. The lankiness was accentuated in Mahdi, who, unlike his older brother, had not aged gracefully. Years spent attached to an opium pipe had dulled his skin and hair, yellowed his teeth, and exhausted his lungs, leaving him even scrawnier than Merikh. Healers had helped as much as they could, but there was only so much they could do against such reckless abuse on his body.

"Perfectly fine, Uncle," Merikh answered.

Noble titles mattered little tonight, unless someone truly stepped out of line. At a henna night, older and married men of the family held the greatest rank. As a young man and the groom, Merikh was expected to defer to almost everyone here.

"You look uncomfortable." Mahdi gestured to another hose on the hookah. "Opium? Fresh from Thraxis."

Merikh shook his head. Of *course* his uncles had brought opium. Probably the hashish too. Any money Navin had been forced to spend on the henna night would undoubtedly be made back tenfold by supplying addicts in Madiar with their intoxicants.

"Please don't move, Shahanshah," Zuhayr asked absentmindedly as he turned Merikh's hand over and began painting a matching design on the palm.

"Apologies," Merikh muttered before carefully looking over to Navin. "I'm fine."

"Nervous for tomorrow?"

"Why would I be?" Merikh deflected the question, but both question and answer had been heard by the room. The answer was met with laughter.

"Well, your new father looks about ready to murder you, so there's that," said Rabb Khaliq, Loralee's older cousin and new heir to Abadan. He raised his glass of wine toward Duq Alaziz. It was good natured, the sort of banter one expected at events like this. Alaziz excused himself from the conversation he'd been having with Duq Hasad and shrugged.

"The man's marrying my daughter. I won't have the chance to hurt him if he crosses her. Loralee's glare could castrate a bull. Good luck."

Alaziz's words were cavalier as he raised his glass and drank. The glare he gave Merikh was anything but. He clearly still believed Merikh would murder his daughter, given time. If anyone else caught the glare, it didn't show in the laughter.

"What *harsh* criticism of such a resplendent woman," Duq Rashad said as he stood from his pillow. He grabbed a decanter of wine and an empty cup, pouring into the glass before walking somewhat unsteadily over to Merikh.

"Now," Rashad said, slurring the word a little as he extended the wineglass, "if you need any advice about tomorrow night—"

"Rashad, you can barely keep a woman around for a single night, let alone a lifetime. I'll take my chances." Merikh took the wine and pretended to drink. He hadn't drunk anything alcoholic in years and had no intention of starting again tonight, if it were at all possible.

Rashad stepped back from the platform, an exaggerated look of offense on his face as he laid his hand on his chest.

"You wound me," Rashad said before laughing and going to grab another glass of wine.

"Ashik, another tale," Merikh ordered, hoping to keep the banter directed at him to a minimum, as the men had quite happily descended on Rashad's promiscuity.

It took three more stories and several rounds of drunken banter between them before Zuhayr finished the henna on Merikh. The intricate design wrapped his arm from index finger to shoulder before covering his collarbone down to his heart. Zuhayr coated the paste with sugar and lemon juice and instructed Merikh to keep the paste on for as long as possible if he wanted it to darken well—and of course he wanted it to darken well. The longer the henna lasted, the more blessed the marriage.

"How long did my father's henna last?" Merikh asked.

Zuhayr didn't answer right away.

"Not long enough," Zuhayr whispered as he packed up his tools.

"I'm sure you've done better this time," Merikh said before gesturing to the hookah nearby. "Partake in whatever you wish, and see the grand vizier for payment."

"Shahanshah, it is an honor. I couldn't possibly accept coin—"

"You have a family to feed, do you not? Surely you eat? The wealthy hardly need charity from the poor. Talk with the vizier."

Zuhayr simply bowed before he left Merikh alone and found an empty place beside a hookah to plant himself. After hours of drinking, the room had quieted down. A handful of noblemen were sleeping off the opium and alcohol on the sitting pillows, while others had pulled out ganjifa cards and were trying their best to still sit upright and keep track of the suits.

With attention away from him, Merikh stretched his legs and stood. Every joint ached after being still for so long. He headed for the small balcony half hidden by one of the thick curtains. Since he couldn't pull the kameez back on without worrying about smearing the paste off, he was glad to have the curtain between his back and the room. The balcony looked out toward the city's south wall, over to the dunes illuminated by moonlight.

"Cold?"

Rashad walked out onto the balcony to join him, two glasses of wine in his hands and a robe draped over his arm. He handed Merikh both glasses, then unfurled the robe.

"One shoulder should keep you more comfortable without cursing impotence on your marriage," Rashad said as he carefully put it over Merikh's right shoulder, covering Merikh's scars without comment. Merikh tried to hand back both wineglasses, but Rashad refused the second one.

"I'll take it back when it's empty."

"I don't drink."

"Great Prophet's cock, I swear I'll pour it down your throat myself. One drink isn't going to kill you, Merikh," Rashad said, leaning against the railing and ignoring the frost on the wineglasses. Merikh shook his head, looked out over the dunes, and then finally took a small sip of wine. It was thick and bitter. Merikh grimaced, and Rashad laughed.

"This is disgusting," Merikh said, shaking his head and resting the glass on the railing.

"Oh, come now! That's one of the finest wines to come out of...wherever!" Rashad said, unable to keep a straight face as he spoke.

"You found this turning to vinegar in my storeroom, didn't you?" Merikh asked, turning to look at Rashad, who shrugged and tried to look innocent. The duq failed miserably and burst out laughing when Merikh shook his head in amused disbelief.

"What? I wasn't going to waste good wine on a man who can't tell the difference between grape juice, vinegar, and the best wine in Shai'Khal!"

"Grape juice is drinkable."

"So's that if you try hard enough." Rashad knocked his glass against Merikh's before downing a large gulp. Merikh tried another small sip.

"Still tastes awful."

"Well, at least it's not Aegalian ale. *That* tastes like horse piss."

"I'm not surprised you know what horse piss tastes like," Merikh said, clearing his throat.

Again, Rashad looked wounded. "Twice in one night! I'm about to take these attacks personally." Both men took another sip of wine. Merikh struggled to down a little more than before.

"You should. I've always hated you."

Merikh was only half joking. Rashad was everything Mansur could have been, if Mansur had known moderation and lacked cruelty. Everything Merikh could have been, if it hadn't been beaten out of him.

"You'd get along great with my little brother. He says the same thing and worships the ground your betrothed walks on."

Rashad finished his wine and put the empty glass down carefully on the tile beside them. He rested his arms on the railing and looked out across the desert. Rashad ran his hand over his cheek, scratching an itch along his stubble-covered jaw.

"You know," Rashad said, "our fathers probably did this, twenty-something years ago."

Merikh glanced back toward the sitting room.

"Only with whores."

"I'm sure Alaziz appreciates not seeing you hip deep in brothel girls the night before you're going to bed his daughter."

"I think he'd appreciate me not bedding his daughter more. I've seen happier men at funerals."

"That an option, not marrying Loralee? Cause I'd happily take her off your hands. The legs on that one…" Rashad joked as he made a lewd gesture with his hands.

Merikh's jaw clenched.

Rashad raised his hands and sobered at the sudden ice on his throat. "I was only playing."

"You touch her, I'll make your cock rot off and feed it to you."

"Can you do that?" Rashad asked, morbidly curious, likely thanks to the wine.

Merikh shrugged his robed shoulder. "I guess we'll see if we find out."

Rashad laughed and shook his head. "Gods help the men who cross you."

The ice disappeared, and Merikh took another sip of his wine. Rashad could have any other woman in Shai'Khal, but Loralee was his. Or rather, would be tomorrow. The thought made a nervous pit in his stomach that Merikh tried foolheartedly to fill with wine. Merikh was hardly why about commitment; he couldn't afford to be as the Shah. But there was nothing about marriage that he felt prepared for, and Merikh *much* preferred making well-informed commitments. It was one thing to have Loralee sitting in on meetings as if she were a new vizier. It was an entirely different matter bringing her to his bed as consort.

Both men glanced back over their shoulders to the room when the sounds of a minor altercation broke out over the card game. It quieted down quickly. Merikh turned back to look out at the dunes.

"You know, I used to hate you too," Rashad said, clearing his throat.

"Used to?" Merikh asked, swirling the wine in his cup. His cavalier attitude hid his interest. Anything said tonight could make for blackmail in the future.

"Mm-hmm, used to. Growing up, I *hated* not knowing if I was really your older brother or not. Figured if I was, all of this"—Rashad gestured toward the palace—"should have been mine. And then Mansur did that to your back, and you've had, what? Four, five attempts on your life over the years?"

"Eight since the Khanum died."

"*Eight.* Gods. Know how many times assassins have come for me?"

Merikh glanced at Rashad, saying nothing.

The duq continued. "None. Well, okay, maybe two. Usually if someone tries to kill me it's because I slept with their wife, but in my defense I *do* check if they're married beforehand. Not my fault if they lie. My point is, everyone who's tried to kill me has done it because I personally slighted them in some way. Not merely for existing. You, on the other hand—"

"Rashad, now you wound me. Give me some credit. I've earned every attempt on my life. You're not the only one with a penchant for irritating people."

Merikh finished his wine, shuddering at the harsh aftertaste before he put it down. His head felt foggy.

"Point is, I couldn't hate you for having a life I don't want. So I stopped."

"Just like that."

"Uh-huh."

"You're full of horse shit, Rashad," Merikh said, smiling, and a short laugh escaped him.

Rashad grinned, straightened from the rail, and clapped his hands once before he turned back to the room. "Done! Hasad, you owe me!" Rashad shouted, pointing to his little brother before turning back to Merikh. "Three good horses said I could make you laugh."

"One of those is mine, you know."

"Whatever you want, little brother," Rashad said with a wink and a cheeky grin. He clapped a hand on Merikh's right shoulder and darted back into the sitting room.

"No one heard it, it doesn't count!" Merikh heard Hasad protest.

"Are you calling me a liar? Go ask him, you dishonorable whelp!"

Merikh shook his head and ran a hand through his hair before leaning against the railing again. Maybe Rashad hadn't lied. Maybe there was a grain of truth somewhere in his narrative beyond bedding married women. It didn't really matter. They were allies, useful to each other for the moment, and that made them as close to friends as Merikh would allow a nobleman. Particularly one with heritage as…ambiguous as Rashad's.

Someone cleared their throat behind Merikh. He straightened up and turned to see Alaziz walking out on the balcony. Unlike Rashad, he came bearing water, and Merikh accepted it without hesitation. They stood on the balcony, saying nothing and staring into the night for a long moment. Jackals prowled the dunes. The pack had found some small animals to hunt in the sand and were happily taking to it.

"Was there something you wanted to say?" Merikh asked finally, finding himself strangely uncomfortable in the silence.

"She loves to dance. I doubt you've learned that by now. She laughs and smiles freely when it's safe to do so. My daughter is very much *alive*," Alaziz said, his stoic tone wavering a little. "Don't…don't take that from her."

"You speak as if you'll never see her again after tomorrow. I don't intend to break her. Loralee can dance, laugh, and smile as much as she likes as long as we have a shahzade and she remains loyal."

Alaziz said nothing. The brief mirth from Rashad had worn off, and Merikh looked at Alaziz.

"All you see is my father. I wonder what you'll see in your grandchild."

"Hopefully, my daughter."

Merikh smiled and raised his glass. "On that, at least, we agree."

The thought of a child scared Merikh. He'd never been around them, and the idea of having one around left him scared, bordering on terrified. It was expected he'd participate in raising his child. Aegalians had it easy—from what Merikh's tutors had taught, the royal family there barely knew each other. Kings slept alone, calling their queens only when they required sex. Their heirs grew up elsewhere, raised by tutors until ready for succession. But even to a man as solitary as Merikh, that sort of family life took things too far. He was far too controlling to allow someone else to shape and mold the future shah. Ancient shahs and khans had once kept many wives, their children raised in their harems and then sent off to finish their studies under scholars. But the practice had fallen rapidly out of favor with the first women rulers of Shai'Khal, leading to the significantly more insular family structure accepted today.

Merikh finished his water, then handed the empty glass back to Alaziz.

"I'm going to retire, if I can make it to the door before someone else stops me. I don't love your daughter. I won't claim to know her well. But I *do* know that if there's an ashik at her henna night, she'll be enchanted by the stories. That she's careful with her horses and treats her mare like a sister. I don't know much about her, Alaziz, but I haven't completely ignored her. Loralee wishes to meet her grandchildren, and I sincerely hope she does."

Alaziz nodded reluctantly and cleared his throat. "Good night."

Merikh bowed his head briefly before entering the sitting room again. He headed first back to his seat to pick up his kameez before heading toward the door. He hesitated for a moment as he passed the hookah that Rashad, Khaliq, and Hasad were sitting around.

"Hasad, you owe him the horses. The best one is mine."

Rashad burst out laughing and slapped his brother's shoulder. "I *told* you."

Hasad, who looked too far gone on opium to particularly care one way or the other, simply nodded. "Loralee can help me pick," he said absentmindedly.

Merikh shrugged. "Make it four horses, Hasad. Give the woman a cut for helping."

"All right." Hasad had no idea what he'd agreed to. The young man wasn't paying the slightest attention.

Rashad cleared his throat. "Okay. Enough of this for one night, Hasad, or you'll give away all of Baba's barn." Rashad pulled the hose away from his brother and wrapped it carefully around the hookah's stem. "Are you trying to leave, Merikh?"

"I'm tired, Rashad. There're rumors of a wedding tomorrow I think I'm supposed to attend." The wine's fogginess hadn't faded, and Merikh worried he'd say something he'd regret in the morning. Or worse, say something any of these men could use against him in the future. To Merikh's surprise, Rashad hauled himself to his feet.

"All right, let me walk you back."

"That's hardly necessary."

"Oh, no, you don't. Someone has to make sure you get back to your room without an assassin getting the better of you or you running off. We all know how skittish you are about women."

Merikh looked dumbfounded. "I'm the *shah*. Where am I supposed to run from a marriage?"

"You know…I don't know. Aegalia? Come on." Rashad stumbled over a pillow but managed to catch himself. Merikh shook his head before glancing to the door. It took a moment for the room to stop moving enough for him to focus his magic on it. The two men left, Rashad struggling with following the straight lines in the marble corridor. When Rashad stumbled over his feet again, Merikh propped him up against a nearby column.

"For a bodyguard, you're terrible. Not sure your flailing would stop anyone."

Rashad grunted. "Come on, who tries to kill anyone on their henna night?"

"I'm sure I've ordered it done."

"And people call *me* a bastard."

Merikh shrugged before helping Rashad straighten up. When Rashad found his feet, the two continued on toward the royal wing. When they reached it, Rashad had sobered up a little and had begun to look a little too satisfied with himself. Merikh, also sobered from the walk, hesitated by the guards at the entrance to the suite. There were souls inside.

"Rashad, what did you do?"

"*I* didn't do anything."

"What did my uncles do?"

"You know, I made a point not to find out *all* the details." Rashad had a self-satisfied smile on his lips.

Merikh ran his right hand over his face while Rashad pushed the door open.

The duq laughed and whistled. "Oh, you're not going to be happy."

No, I imagine not, Merikh thought before entering the room. There were a dangerous number of candles lit through the suite and three half-naked women inside. All of them could have, at first glance, passed for Sayida Loralee.

They had all been resting on the divan and chairs by the coffee table. They stood and bowed when Merikh entered.

"Shahanshah," the three said, almost synchronized.

"Out," Merikh ordered.

"The amir asked us to help with removing the henna paste," the one said.

Merikh pointed to the door.

"I don't care to repeat myself. Take the duq."

Rashad laughed and shook his head. "Make the amir pay you regardless."

Merikh glanced to Rashad, his confusion clear, and Rashad smiled.

"Come on, Merikh, I've had enough of...everything tonight. I'm in no shape to take on a woman, let alone three. It wouldn't do for the duq of Rajibad to be the flaccid laughingstock of brothel girls. I mean, at least, not that way. If you can make a woman laugh, you can get her in your bed eventually. I'd say you should try it, but I worry about your sense of humor."

"You can leave now, reasonably certain there's no one here trying to kill me," Merikh said. "And the guards will prevent me from running off."

Rashad nodded, bowing with mocking flourish before shutting the door behind him and the whores on his way out. The silence that followed was more comforting than Merikh expected. With the flick of his wrist, half the candles were covered in ice. Merikh pulled the robe off his right shoulder and tossed it down on the divan with his kameez. He flexed his left hand. The henna paste had cracked at his joints already, and a few pieces had flaked off. The door to the bathing room opened ahead of him, and once again he covered half the candles in ice.

Were they trying to burn the palace down? Merikh half wondered as he stripped off the rest of his clothes and waded into the bath. It didn't take long to clean the paste off his skin and wash the smell of hookah vapor out of his hair. The wine and evening's events had left him exhausted. Despite the growing anxiety about the wedding, once Merikh was clean, he took to his bed, and sleep found him quickly.

CHAPTER 17

1st of Vindith, First Harvest, 902 Unified Age
Madiar, Raudhah Province

The henna was a rich brown on his skin, having darkened overnight from a reddish tinge to a brown that nearly matched his bay mare. Merikh hadn't left the royal suite yet today, the guards given the order from both Amir Navin and Nikias to keep him there. Nikias was terrified that Merikh would go riding and break his neck. Navin just appreciated not having to keep tabs on where Merikh was at any given point.

Being kept in the royal suite made it far easier to ensure Merikh had no chance of running into anyone from House Neredi this morning. After the end of the henna night, neither bride nor groom's families were allowed to interact until the wedding ceremony itself. Merikh had enjoyed having the day mostly to himself, even though there had been servants in and out all day, moving in Loralee's belongings. The changes in the room made the wedding seem far more real. Amir Navin came to join Merikh for the last hour before the wedding. The servants had all finished, and his uncle helped with the last preparations before the ceremony.

"Is everything in order?" Merikh asked, still looking down at the designs on his hand.

Navin stood nearby and handed Merikh the golden sash to place over his crimson-and-gold achkan. "As far as I know, Duqa Jasira handled everything on their end. The grand vizier has been running around all day making sure the gifts are ready, and he doubled the guard. Temple priests are saying funeral prayers from the minarets in the district, and they've replaced their flags with burnt sackcloth."

Merikh nodded and tied the sash carefully, unsurprised that Alcaeus was taking the wedding poorly. Loralee would be the first khanum of Shai'Khal to be crowned by someone other than an Akhenic priest. Alcaeus could only deride Merikh so much without losing the support of royalist factions. Loralee, on the other hand, was fair game to tear down. Alcaeus could heap all that was wrong with Shai'Khal on her shoulders.

I wonder if she truly understands what she's getting herself into? Merikh thought. Too late if she didn't. Loralee had handled the adjustment to Madiar well. Merikh had begun including her in most of his council meetings whenever her mother could spare her from wedding planning. While traditionally receiving gifts and entertaining out-of-town guests fell to the higher-ranking noble or host, no one had seemed openly offended by Loralee handling them. Loralee was a far more hospitable and approachable host than Merikh.

"Merikh?" Navin said, getting his attention.

Merikh looked up and frowned. "Is that necessary?"

"It's tradition," Navin said sympathetically.

"It's ridiculous," Merikh muttered. Reluctantly, Merikh took the crown from his uncle's outstretched hand.

Merikh had ordered the old crown melted down and remade for the ceremony. While this one was far more to Merikh's taste, it was still frivolous ornamentation as far as he was concerned. It was a straight golden band adorned with garnets and rubies, the Madiaran crest carefully engraved on opposite sides. Between them were the symbols of the nine major gods and goddesses of the Pantheon, including the Akhenic Sun. Merikh doubted the small gesture would be noticed. He held back a frustrated sigh as he placed the crown over the black ghutrah that covered his hair.

"Well, it's almost over," Navin said absentmindedly before handing Merikh his khanjar, the last of the ceremonial attire.

Merikh tied it carefully onto his golden sash. *Over. I wish it were,* Merikh thought. The wedding was the start of an entirely new venture, one Merikh doubted he was prepared for. He'd been less nervous for his coronation, a fact Merikh tried to hide and was certain Navin was oblivious to. Merikh could count on one hand how often he'd seen his uncle since Aliyah's death. Once, when Navin and Mahdi had come to Madiar to retrieve her corpse, and again when they'd ridden to swear fealty to Merikh. The man was a stranger, certainly not the ideal companion for preparing for the ceremony. Navin was only here because tradition demanded it, as he was the closest male relative of the groom. Had Mansur been alive, it would have been his job. The thought made Merikh's stomach turn. It would have been a very different wedding had Mansur decided to follow through with the betrothal agreement before his death.

"Are you ready?" Navin asked, walking toward the door.

Merikh nodded. He would have preferred a moment with Nikias, but the grand vizier had no business here. The door opened ahead of them. On the other side stood Rabb Mahdi and Duq Rashad. Rabb Mahdi looked borderline ill, though Merikh was unsure if that was simply the man's natural look in the harsh light of day or residual effects from the night before. Duq Rashad, on the other hand, grinned and looked overly smug. If he was suffering from the previous night's affair, it didn't show.

"Shahanshah." Rashad bowed his head a little as Merikh passed. Merikh ignored him as they walked. Rashad was far easier to ignore than the pit of nerves that had made its home in Merikh's stomach. He'd been the object of a great deal of attention ever since he was a child. But today, of all days, the idea of having hundreds of eyes on him was horrifying. He'd never felt the urge to melt into the wall so strongly before.

Thank the gods I only have to do this once, Merikh thought as they reached the throne room. The doors opened ahead of him. The hum of conversation died down as Merikh entered, the setar and drum music changing to announce the Shah's arrival.

Red-and-blue banners of Houses Madiaran and Neredi hung from the pillars, garlands of flowers were everywhere, and enchanted lamps bathed the room in gentle light as the sun set behind the city. Barely any light came in from the windows. While there were grand arched windows in the wall behind the throne, there were none positioned where the sun might get directly in a sitting shah's eyes. Partly to buy into the name of the Rising Sun Throne, to bask the shah in the morning's "divine glow." Partly to ensure the shah could always see those before him—and any assassins—clearly.

The red carpet along the aisle covered the necrotic bloodstain left from Mansur's murder and led to the twin seats of the Rising Sun Throne. Even with limited time, Duqa Jasira had pulled together quite the room. It was elaborate and tasteful, no less than what Merikh expected from her reputation. Neredi events were famous thanks to the duqa.

Ruya stood nearby the thrones, grinning from ear to ear as Merikh approached. She'd been overjoyed when Merikh had asked her to crown Loralee as khanum. With Loralee's help, Ruya had pulled the religious overtones from the ceremony and emphasized the old Yahidah traditions. It hadn't changed much, only shortened the ceremony, something Merikh greatly appreciated.

Once Merikh was seated on the throne, Amir Navin and Rabb Mahdi joined the Afolayan family off to the right of the aisle. Duq Rashad remained nearby. His job remained the same from the walk last night—to ensure the event went smoothly, that no attempts on Merikh's life were successful. And, if for some reason Merikh found Loralee not to his liking today, he could pass her off to Rashad instead. Loralee had chosen Amira Jin for the same position, a gesture that showed a certain level of confidence in the fact that she wouldn't change her mind about marrying Merikh, given the amira's marriage and preferences. Of course, it was a ceremonial position—Merikh couldn't recall anyone who'd ever gotten this far into a betrothal to merely pass it off at the last moment. Not without the intention of starting a war.

A herald at the entrance to the throne room rang a bronze bell twice before the Neredi household entered the throne room. Loralee was escorted by the entirety of her family and Amira Jin. Halfway to the throne, Alaziz took Loralee's hand. With Amira Jin behind her, the three approached the throne. If Loralee was nervous, she hid it better than Merikh. She wore the reds of House Madiaran, gold embroidery covered her lehenga skirt and choli blouse. A thin red sari half hid her bare midriff. Henna covered her hands, up her arms, along her neck and up her temple, becoming obscured a little by the golden chain *maathi patti*. In the center of the gold on Loralee's forehead was a large ruby surrounded by garnet stones. She looked every bit the khanum she was about to be.

"On behalf of House Neredi, I thank you for entrusting the preservation of the Madiaran dynasty to our daughter," Alaziz said loudly, though Merikh doubted the sincerity of the man's words. Merikh bowed his head carefully, painfully aware of the gold band around his temple.

"For your sacrifice, the loss of your daughter, and the end of your line, please accept these gifts."

Merikh stood as he gestured toward the door, his tone no more sincere than Alaziz's. It was tradition, but that didn't mean Merikh begrudged losing three of his finest broodmares any less. Grooms led the mares inside the throne room, followed by a line of servants bearing trays of gold, camel milk, honey, and sweet fruits. The mares were wide-eyed and worried, prancing around the grooms. One whinnied for her companions back in the barn.

Alaziz nodded, and the grooms led the mares out quickly. The other gifts were laid out on a long table at the end of the throne room. Duqa Jasira walked to the table and began lighting the candles around the trays, expected to inspect and confirm the gifts were of equal quality of the gift they were giving to Merikh in their daughter.

When the duqa was satisfied, she turned and bowed. Alaziz nodded before placing Loralee's hand in Merikh's. The last time Merikh had taken Loralee's hand, she'd practically squirmed to get away from his cold touch. Now she followed without hesitation. Merikh guided Loralee to her throne on his left before sitting down. Amira Jin stood on the far left, mirroring Rashad's position beside the throne, and Ruya approached to stand in front of Merikh and Loralee.

They repeated ancient vows of fidelity and obedience that no shah or khanum had taken seriously in generations, vows that mirrored the promises they'd already made in Rajibad to each other. The words were the same for men and women, promises to follow where the other led and to lead when the other couldn't. Promises to be truthful and faithful, above all else, to each other. Merikh meant the words he said, but the ceremony was a blur. He was focused on keeping the temperature from reflecting his discomfort.

With oaths taken, Loralee took Merikh's left hand and pulled the plain gold ring from her thumb and placed it on his index finger. Merikh took her hand. A moment later, her ring emerged from the pocket of his achkan coat and fell into his hand. He slipped it carefully on her index finger.

"It's cold," Loralee whispered with a nervous smile, too quiet for even Ruya nearby to hear.

"Apologies," Merikh said just as quietly. He let go of her hand and looked to Ruya. "I have taken this woman to be my wife, and if it pleases my noble court and is favored by the gods, I would have her at my side as khanum."

The room remained silent. Any who would have spoken out against Loralee's crowning hadn't attended—a safer protest than decrying her at her coronation. Ruya nodded and glanced over to the pedestal where the khanum's crown rested. It floated off the pillow and into Ruya's hands.

"Sayida Loralee Madiaran, do you swear your life to the protection of Shai'Khal? To protect and support the Shahanshah, to bear him an heir and to care for the shahzade?" Ruya asked, still beaming.

"I swear," Loralee said, glancing from Ruya to Merikh as she did so.

"Then as Ikharon's high priestess and representative of the Pantheon of Gods, it is my great honor to crown you khanum of Shai'Khal. And hopefully, soon to be the mother of the shahzade," Ruya teased before placing the crown carefully upon Loralee's head.

Merikh bit the inside of his lip but kept his composure. That heir would have to wait until the last possible moment; he could barely cope with the idea of being a husband. He certainly couldn't cope with fatherhood yet.

With Loralee crowned, Merikh took her hand again and stood to present her to the room. She was met with applause and hails. Merikh glanced down to Loralee, who smiled and seemed wrapped up in the moment.

Enjoy it while you can; they'll hate you soon enough, Merikh thought. It wasn't spiteful, simply true. Half of them already did, and they'd remember once the wine and araq wore off. Or once she became pregnant. Loralee would soon learn her newfound power had placed her on an isolating pedestal.

When the newlyweds sat down, the provincial amirs began to approach with gifts. Amir Olumide, with Duqa Emilia and Duq Hasad, were first. Servants brought in a large tray bearing jewels, bolts of cloth, and two ornate bridles.

"I heard my son..." Amir Olumide cleared his throat and gave a pointed look at Duq Hasad. "...also has gifts."

"I do, Shahanshah, and I hope you'll find them fit for your barns," Hasad said before looking back to the doors. Two horses had been brought up, a chestnut mare and a matching stallion. The red stallion pushed through his groom and bit the mare on her withers. The mare promptly squealed and turned, and the room echoed with the thud of her back hooves against the stallion's barrel.

"Let's hope that's not a portent of things to come," Rashad said under his breath, unable to help himself with a small smirk.

"I'm sure they're quite lovely. Thank you, Duq Hasad," Loralee said before waving off the grooms. "Have the stallion looked at," she added quickly. A kick to the ribs like that needed a healer to ensure nothing had broken.

The other gifts from the amirs and the major noble houses were significantly less aggressive or dramatic. Once the presentations were over, servants brought food and more drinks into the hall. The smell of spiced meat filled the room, and Merikh let Loralee help herself to the platter placed between them. His stomach was in knots, and the overwhelming scent was hardly appetizing. Amira Jin and Duq Rashad sat with their families not far from the throne, allowing Merikh and Loralee a bit of privacy as the throne room became loud with the sound of conversation and laughter. The musicians from earlier started again.

"Why did Duq Hasad give us horses?" Loralee asked finally. It was unusual for the child of an amir to give something in addition to their parent.

"He lost a bet with Rashad last night," Merikh explained.

"Ah...probably best if we leave it at that, then." Loralee smiled knowingly. "I'm not sure I want to know what went on at your henna night."

"I assure you, nothing inappropriate, Sa— Loralee." Merikh barely caught himself. It was going to take time to adjust.

Loralee shook her head, smiling gently. "Khanum. Wife. They're titles that will take a little time to adjust to." The nervousness in her voice betrayed the fact she was feeling the weight of those titles, perhaps for the first time.

"You'll do fine." His tone came off less reassuring than he'd meant, but he'd made an attempt, at least. Merikh picked at the platter between them, choosing a piece of spiced naan.

Halfway through the meal, one of the side doors opened, and Nikias emerged. He looked out of breath as he approached the throne and dropped down on his knees in front of Loralee and Merikh.

"Shahanshah, Khanum, a thousand apologies. There is an urgent matter that needs the Shah's attention," Nikias said without looking up, his eyes fixed firmly on the first step of the dais. Merikh glanced at Loralee; a frown was slowly growing on her lips. Undoubtedly, this wouldn't be the last time she would handle the court on her own. Or the last time he'd disappoint her.

Merikh stood, but before he could move, Loralee gently reached over and took his hand. He glanced down to her hand, then to her eyes. *Don't,* was the word written in her dark eyes.

"Apologies, Khanum," Merikh said. He hesitated a moment before his hand cupped her jaw, his fingers entwining in her black hair. He leaned down and kissed her deeply. The court would want to see their cold shah lusting after his bride, after all. Judging from the laughter and cheers that rose from the crowd, he hadn't misjudged them. It made for a good show.

Loralee looked surprised when Merikh pulled away. Undoubtedly, she'd expected something more timid for their first kiss. Well, Loralee wasn't exactly difficult to desire. Rashad wasn't the only one who appreciated her legs. Merikh's hand dropped away from her hair, and he descended the throne.

Nikias rose from his bow and looked to Loralee. "I promise to try to return the Shah to you as quickly as I can."

Nikias hadn't just sworn truthfulness above all else to her. Merikh could see the lie plain as day through the thin veil of simple brownnosing. Merikh followed Nikias out of the room, using the same side exit the grand vizier had entered through.

"You looked about to die up there," Nikias said, frowning.

"That bad?" Merikh asked quickly.

Nikias shook his head. "I doubt many others noticed, but I thought you could use a break. You handled that well." Nikias gestured back toward the throne room. "I probably don't have to rush you back now."

"Thank you."

Merikh felt an unreasonable amount of relief wash over him. He hadn't realized how tense every muscle in his body had become, or how sore he felt. The scars on Merikh's back ached dully.

"Oh, you have *no* idea. I have a gift for you." Nikias smiled. "We have an Onyx Sword below. Scholar turned commander, spent a great deal of time in the Temple Archives. I know Adrian and Sarka left yesterday, but if there's anything this man knows about those journals, you should be able to send a messenger to catch them. I assume you'd rather be handling that than a dance."

Merikh clapped Nikias on the shoulder. "What would I do without you, old man?"

"Probably vomit in front of your bride." Nikias shrugged before following Merikh's lead away from the throne room.

CHAPTER 18

1ST OF VINDITH, FIRST HARVEST, 902 UNIFIED AGE
MADIAR, RAUDHAH PROVINCE

Watching Nikias and Merikh retreat from the throne room nearly made Loralee's jaw drop. Unless Alcaeus had decided at this precise moment to declare open war against the Shah, what could possibly constitute an emergency?

Jin looked livid as she stood from her family table and started to follow Merikh and Nikias. It was her job, after all, to help ensure the wedding went smoothly. Duq Rashad leapt to his feet after her, as if on cue. But unlike the amira, the duq wasn't pursuing the Shah and grand vizier. Instead, he caught the amira's arm and pulled her back toward him. It earned him a venomous glare as the amira shoved his hand off her arm, a glare he ignored as he leaned down and whispered something in Jin's ear. She shook her head, muttered something else back to the duq, then headed back to her family.

Jin shot Loralee a frustrated, sympathetic look, her irritation plain as day. Duq Rashad, on the other hand, smoothed his black ghutrah against his dark-blue khalat and looked positively charming as he approached the throne and bowed.

"Khanum, if it pleases you, might I stand in for the Shah until he returns?" Rashad asked, as was his role.

At least Merikh didn't run off before the vows, Loralee thought. Rashad looked like he was enjoying himself. Loralee nodded. Rashad straightened up and stood at her side on her left, leaving Merikh's throne empty.

"Thank you," Loralee whispered.

Rashad bowed his head ever so slightly. "Hardly fair to ask you to face all this alone. Besides, I'd never leave the most beautiful woman in the room alone for long," Rashad teased quietly.

"Only in the room?" Loralee smiled.

"Apologies. I haven't seen enough of Madiar to judge yet, and I would hate to be unfair."

"Gods forbid." Loralee reached for her previously untouched wine and drank. With Merikh gone, there was an uncomfortable edge to the room. She drummed her fingers against her throne. *Her* throne. The idea was both exciting and terrifying. She'd gone from making suggestions on what horses should be bred in her father's barn to helping hold the reins of an empire. The prospect was a little intimidating.

When Loralee finished her meal and her wine, a servant approached to pour her another glass and take the tray away. A more relaxed tone had settled over the room. Several hookahs were brought out by servants, and the music became louder and more upbeat.

"Duq Rashad, would you join me? Your khanum wishes to dance," Loralee said as she stood.

"Khanum, it would be my pleasure."

He was a better dancer than Loralee assumed Merikh would have been. She doubted her husband could relax enough to enjoy music or movement. After their dance, Loralee left Rashad, grabbing her cousin Khaliq and then Jin, and did her best to distance herself from the duq for the rest of the evening. After all, Loralee knew his reputation and the rumors. He flirted, either harmless or seriously, with any woman within speaking distance. And while he certainly was an amusing companion, Loralee had caught the looks she had earned by dancing with him.

Well, let there be rumors. If Merikh had bothered to stay, there wouldn't be any, she thought before downing a small glass of araq. She put it down on a nearby table before she felt hands on her shoulders. Her father gently steered her to a less populated part of the throne room.

"What in Alhanem is the Shah doing? He should be here with you," Alaziz demanded.

"Baba, don't ask me questions you know I don't have an answer to. Even if I did, you know I wouldn't be able to tell you," Loralee implored. *I wish I knew what he was doing*, Loralee admitted to herself.

Alaziz ran a hand over his chin, rubbing the gray stubble before he shook his head. If he'd intended to speak, he lost his chance, as Khaliq sauntered over and took Loralee's hand.

"Madiaran for an evening and you're already keeping secrets from your poor baba," he interrupted with mock injury before he kissed her new signet ring. He was a few years older than she was, older than Merikh, but his boyish face and light-hearted attitude made him seem much younger. "Come, Uncle, you have much to teach me. I have big shoes to fill, and I haven't the faintest idea who anyone here is," Khaliq said, his bright smile impervious to the glare from Alaziz. It gave Loralee an excuse to walk away and find another glass of wine.

It was a glass she drank far too quickly, considering her company. Loralee knew she ought to be careful. Tying herself to Merikh had permanently bought her many enemies, even as it solidified alliances. But she was the Khanum now! The most powerful woman in Shai'Khal, and she wasn't going to allow Merikh's disappearance to ruin her day. So when Loralee saw Jin pulled into an unfortunate debate with Amir Olumide, Loralee stole Iseul and took to the dance floor again.

Her mood sagged after a few dances when Jin stole back her wife, and Loralee left the dance floor to people-watch. She saw that Nikias had returned at some point. He stood near the door talking hurriedly with an Ajir, though what his role was, she had no idea. The man wore a strange uniform, head to toe in black. Similar to the one Adrian wore, but there was something disconcerting about the man. Loralee was certain she hadn't seen that uniform before. Nikias looked worried and left the room with the man.

If I saw that, so did others. Loralee was hardly the most sober person in the room. Many were falling over drunk, but there were plenty of men and women who had all their wits. A great many nobles had a high tolerance for alcohol.

Rashad approached and interrupted her thoughts. "Khanum." He took her hand and kissed her signet ring, holding her hand just long enough to be too long. "Nikias looks troubled. Should I send someone to put more city guard on watch?"

"Why would you ask?" Loralee said, taking a sip of her wine.

Rashad shrugged but smiled knowingly at her. She loathed it—he knew absolutely nothing. He was being smug, which was not helpful.

"I am simply worried. I mean, we expect the Shah to run from a wedding. But the grand vizier doesn't usually look quite this worried when the Shah tends to other itches."

"Nikias worries what side of the bed the Shah wakes up on and if the sun is too bright on him. Are you trying to make me paranoid, Duq?" Loralee asked, raising a well-sculpted eyebrow. He smirked and shook his head.

"Never! Wouldn't dream of it," Rashad said before grabbing a goblet of wine off a passing servant.

"Is there something else on your mind?" Loralee asked.

"The Khanum shouldn't be drinking by herself on her wedding day. I can't believe the Shah's left you alone this long."

"Especially considering the company he left me with," Loralee teased.

Rashad laughed. "Are you impugning my character? I'm the safest man here for you to be with!"

"Truly?" Loralee had a hard time believing that.

Rashad nodded hurriedly, innocently, as he took half a step closer to Loralee. "Indeed! After all, our bastard would just look like the Shah's child anyway. No one would ever know the difference." He laughed as Loralee slapped his arm.

"I should have you hung for that!"

"Well, if a dying man could have a last request..." Rashad cocked his head a little, and his eyes wandered down her chest.

"Duq Rashad, you're stepping dangerously close to treason," Loralee said firmly.

"Apologies. I'm not serious. Well...I would be if circumstances were different," Rashad said, his tone barely more respectful.

"I wouldn't be."

"How could the Shah possibly be more your type than me?" Rashad asked, gesturing at face. They did look similar. Of course, that was where any potential familial likeness ended.

Loralee smirked. "It might surprise you, but some women actually *like* a man who can keep his cock to himself, except when his wife wants it."

Oh, that did it. Loralee couldn't help but feel a little smug as Rashad fixed an unseen wrinkle in his dark-blue khalat. She'd stung his pride, though he was trying to hide it.

"Utter nonsense, Khanum, that can't be true," Rashad teased, though it lacked the same level of humor as before.

"Mm-hmm. Go chase another woman, Duq Rashad. I'd hate for you to be lonely tonight of all nights."

"Well, if *you* find yourself alone tonight—"

"You must have been looking away when the Shah left, Duq. Judging by that kiss, I doubt I'm going to be alone tonight. And when I'm done with him, neither the Shah nor I will likely be in any shape to leave the royal suite tomorrow."

"Lucky man. Don't break the Shah, Khanum." Rashad didn't sound impressed. He bowed his head before making a quick exit toward a group of Baladi dancers taking a break. Loralee watched him leave before she was distracted by a servant bearing a tray of drinks. She swapped her wine for water and resumed people-watching. Neredi gatherings could last until the early hours of the morning, but Loralee was more than ready to retire already. It was hard to keep her energy and excitement up for a celebration of her marriage when her husband wasn't even here. She waded through the throng of people to find her father and took his arm.

"I'm going to retire for the evening," Loralee said, squeezing his arm gently.

Alaziz looked at her quizzically for a moment before glancing about the room. With Nikias gone and Merikh nowhere to be found, it fell to the bride's parents to host. Duqa Jasira was off dancing with Amir Xolani, and Alaziz was happy to stay out of the way and drink a little.

"Should I have the recession announced?" Alaziz asked, gesturing for a nearby servant.

Loralee shook her head quickly and dismissed the woman. "Please, no," Loralee pleaded, "I don't want to make that walk alone, and I *certainly* don't want to do it with Duq Rashad."

"It's bad enough you spent half the night with him. I can't believe—"

"Baba, I'm going to go find my husband," Loralee interrupted firmly. The last thing she needed was to hear another tirade from her father about the man she'd married.

"Be *careful*, please. You only need to give him an heir. You don't need to indulge anything else. You have your khanjar?" Alaziz asked as he took her hand and squeezed it tightly.

Loralee smiled gently. She knew this was difficult for him to accept. "Stop worrying. Besides, if you're worrying about anyone, you should be worrying about Maman. Please don't let her destroy the palace. I don't want to explain that to Merikh." Loralee kissed her father on the cheek before pulling her hand away and discreetly slipping from the room.

Loralee tried to walk quietly toward the royal suite, although that was made quite impossible by all the golden hoops and bangles around her wrists and ankles. It was exceptionally extravagant, and while part of her enjoyed indulging in such a way, Loralee was looking forward to getting the jewelry off. The golden chotli that ran from the back of her head down the length of her braid made her neck ache.

The guards at the entrance corridor to the royal suite ignored her arrival. Loralee stopped beside them.

"Has the Shah come by?"

"No, Khanum," the guard answered quickly.

Loralee thanked him before walking down the corridor and into the suite. She half expected Merikh to be seated at his desk, poring over paperwork. After all, just because he hadn't passed the guards didn't mean he wasn't here. The suite wasn't appreciably different than it had been the last time Loralee had visited. Nikias had asked her to accompany him on numerous occasions to drop off paperwork with the Shah, and Merikh often met with his viziers within the royal suite. The room wasn't unfamiliar to her, but to be here alone was strange.

Loralee pushed passed the decorum ingrained in her not to touch anything of the Shah's as she walked to Merikh's desk, opened the top drawer, and pulled out a long match. Enchanted by a fire sorcerer, the tip lit up under her touch, and she went about lighting a few candles. There were a *lot* of candles in the room. Loralee barely lit half of them.

Loralee blew out the match and placed it back in Merikh's desk. She wasn't sure if the listlessness that had come over her would have been made better or worse by Merikh being here. Loralee crossed the room to the low coffee table. She poured herself a glass of water from the pitcher on it, took a sip, and then sat down heavily on the nearby divan. For the first time today, she had a moment to herself. She felt nervous as the dizzying pleasure from the wine and araq wore off.

It was ridiculous, she knew that, but she couldn't help it. In the month she'd been in Madiar, Loralee had spent very little time alone with Merikh. In fact, she couldn't think of a single time the two had been completely alone. Not that it was out of the ordinary; most betrothed weren't given even as many opportunities to speak privately as Loralee and Merikh had already stolen. When Loralee had seen Merikh, it had always been in a council meeting of some kind. He'd put her to work almost immediately, and while she appreciated the rapid education she was receiving on how Madiar and Shai'Khal functioned, Loralee didn't feel that she knew much more about Merikh. The man she'd married today was as much a stranger as he had been in Rajibad.

Loralee played with her ring absentmindedly. Merikh had been oddly gentle when he'd placed it on her finger after their vows. *Gods, he was oddly devoted about those too.* Merikh was always serious, but there had been a difference in his tone then. A weight and understanding of the responsibility he was taking on that was heartening to hear. It was a small peek behind his walls, and Loralee hoped that maybe, just maybe, there was a chance this marriage could be reasonably happy.

Her own parents had achieved that. Loralee was certain they even loved each other by now. For a man and woman as opposite as Jasira and Alaziz, they had managed to make it work. Merikh wasn't the monster Alaziz feared, not that Loralee could see. He was obsessively devoted to his work, to the point it made Loralee wonder if there was much else to Merikh than being the Shah. If nothing else, he seemed terrified of letting any walls down and enjoying himself, and that was a problem Loralee was intent on fixing. If he took the vows he'd made seriously, then they had a chance.

The wall opened up behind Loralee, and she nearly spilled her water. She knew there were servant entrances and tunnels throughout the palace, but she hardly knew the network well enough to know where the entrances were and where they led to. She could hear Merikh's riding boots on the stone as he passed the divan without noticing her. The walls he hid behind in public were gone, and he was lost deep in his thoughts. Quite lost apparently, if he hadn't even noticed another soul in the room with him. She wasn't sure if that was a compliment or not. Had he grown used to her soul enough that it didn't register anymore in the same way that Loralee barely noticed his aura? Or was he simply that troubled by whatever had happened?

Merikh stood beside his desk and pulled the khanjar off the golden sash. His crown and ghutrah were tossed on the desk unceremoniously before he untied the small black ribbon keeping his hair back. The red achkan coat and his white kameez were next, carefully folded over the back of his chair.

I didn't know the henna went that far, Loralee thought, a small smile growing on her lips. She settled into the divan. Loralee hadn't seen Merikh shirtless before. Even when she'd seen him in the training yard with the swordmaster, he always had his kameez on. He was thinner than she expected. Considerably so, given the amount of time he spent training with his swordmaster and riding his horses. Magic took its toll, but Loralee wasn't complaining. In the half light of the candles, he looked handsome.

When Merikh's hand went to his belt, Loralee jolted upright. Her words caught in her throat, making more of a strangled squeak than anything coherent. Merikh's modest nature was well known, and Loralee knew he'd already be embarrassed by undressing *this* far without knowing she was here.

A bolt of ice flew at her chest, and at the last possible moment, it disappeared into thin air. Still, there was a small tear in her sari above her heart.

"*Gods*, woman, what are you doing here?" Merikh demanded. He grabbed his kameez and yanked it back on.

Loralee opened her mouth to yell at him but stopped short.

The right side of Merikh's white kameez was dark crimson. He hadn't looked injured, but if Merikh had spent time with a healer, then he wouldn't. But there was no denying that his kameez was covered in blood. Loralee had a dozen questions she wanted to ask, and she wasn't sure where to start. Loralee decided to answer Merikh's first.

"What am I doing here? I *sleep* here now, unless you find that objectionable!" Loralee said as she stood, touching her sari and sticking a finger through the hole.

Merikh frowned and looked away.

Loralee placed her water glass down before walking over to him. "What happened? Is this all yours? What did Nikias need you for? Are you all right?" Loralee blurted out question after question without giving him the chance to answer.

"No, none of it's mine," Merikh said, glancing down to the blood-soaked kameez. "We captured an Onyx Sword Fari commander, an ex-scholar. It's his blood."

"Did...did he attack you? Try to escape?" Loralee asked. She had a sinking feeling as Merikh met her gaze.

"No."

"You were..."

"Torturing a man," Merikh offered.

Loralee resisted the urge to slap him, as he said it with the same sort of innocently helpful tone Rashad used.

"You were *torturing* a man instead of attending our wedding celebration."

Loralee took a step away from him, dumbfounded by the words coming out of her mouth. She wasn't sure where to begin tearing that sentence apart. It didn't surprise her that Merikh participated in torture. There had been rumors all her life that Mansur and Merikh both did so. More rumors that Merikh experimented with his necromancy on criminals, and Loralee hadn't doubted it. He was a necromancer, after all. That sort of magic required corpses, didn't it? But this? Torturing information from an Onyx Sword on their wedding day? Never mind the ramifications if Alcaeus discovering the Crown was behind the disappearance of one of the Faithful.

"Was I needed?" Merikh asked, his tone careful and even.

"Needed?" Loralee repeated, completely flabbergasted. "No, you weren't *needed*. You were expected, wanted. *Missed*, even, but not needed."

"I can't imagine my presence was missed by anyone," Merikh scoffed. He looked openly surprised when he saw Loralee glaring at him. "Oh."

"*'Oh.'* Gods, Merikh, of course you were missed! Do you really think I wanted to spend my wedding with Duq *Rashad*, of all people? He is certainly not you. Did you even think about how it looked? I left discreetly, but what if I'd finished the ceremony with him? Left the throne room on the duq's arm? Who do you think the court would believe fathered the shahzade then, hmm? The man with a hundred bastards or the man who shocked the court by kissing his wife?"

At least was a good kiss, Loralee thought. Not that she was going to ever tell Merikh.

He didn't seem to know what to say. The temperature dropped a little. She could see him searching for the right words, and Loralee folded her arms under her bust. *Try it,* her dark eyes dared him. She almost wanted to see him defend himself, because it was plain as day that Merikh hadn't thought about a damn thing other than getting away from the ceremony. He'd run like a coward at the first opportunity, hiding under the guise of duty.

"I appreciate your discretion."

What's the penalty for slapping the Shah? Loralee bit the inside of her cheek and shook her head. Merikh had kissed her as if he'd wanted her, he'd been gentle and devoted through their vows. Now he'd transformed back into the man who had earned such a callous reputation.

"As I said in Rajibad, I want to live to see my grandchildren. I can't imagine I will if you and the court think I'm sleeping with Duq Rashad," Loralee said.

"Likely not."

Loralee scoffed, looking away from him for a moment. When she looked back, the blood on him caught her attention again, and she let out a disgusted sound.

"Can you please take that off?" Loralee gestured at his chest, a wave of nausea coming over her.

Reluctantly, Merikh acquiesced. He pulled the kameez off and tossed it aside, though he immediately grabbed the achkan coat and pulled it back on. At least the coat wasn't bloody. Loralee took a deep breath and let it out slowly, trying to calm down. The fact that she was arguing with Merikh on their wedding night instead of... Well, honestly she would have preferred almost anything to this. But this, unfortunately, was what Merikh had given her to work with, and she'd try to make the best of it.

"What did you do to the Fari commander? What information did he provide?" Loralee asked after a moment.

"Do you really want to know?"

"You promised me honesty and truth above all else only a few hours ago. You and I don't have the luxury of secrets anymore," Loralee said stubbornly.

Merikh thought about it for a moment. "You start with their feet and their hands. A little goes a long way. The pain is excruciating without being deadly. By the time you finish with the little pieces, you'll have all the information you're going to get. Maybe even a few pieces of truth amongst the lies. Then you dismantle the rest to send a message, and that takes time."

He was trying to shock her. Loralee refused to cower to it.

"And what information did you receive?" Loralee asked. Her words sounded weaker than intended. Torture was reprehensible, a practice falling out of favor with many of the major noble houses. Not with the Madiarans, it seemed.

Merikh ran a hand over his head, pulling his hair away from his eyes and buying himself a moment. He didn't want to share, clearly, but he was struggling to come up with a believable lie. Or perhaps struggling with the idea that he'd vowed *not* to lie to her.

"The amulet from the Emani. He recognized it and says they're coming from Ydeba, but he didn't know who is supplying them. We had him abducted for his knowledge of an obscure copy of the Akhenic Scrolls that catalogs the Great Prophet's last days. The man spoke of a pilgrimage to somewhere in the Katu Mountains, a place that destroys magic."

"Destroys it?" Loralee shook her head, stunned by his words. "How is that even possible?" *Nothing* destroyed magic. It was like water or stone. It could be changed, broken down, but not destroyed completely. Or at least, that was Loralee's limited understanding of it.

"I don't know. It shouldn't be possible. But Duqa Enitan and the Faithful will control the Katu before I can mobilize any meaningful resistance or means to investigate any of it. *If* he wasn't lying."

"*If* being key."

"Yes."

The simplicity of his response made Loralee's blood boil.

"Well, I'm glad you had such an enjoyable evening," Loralee said. "I'm sure the company was far more to your taste. Far easier to feel in control and powerful when you're murdering someone than when you're uncomfortable, and gods forbid anyone make you *uncomfortable*."

She brushed past him, sat down at the desk, and began pulling the golden bangles off her wrists. She dumped them on the desk beside Merikh's crown before unclasping her necklaces.

Merikh let out a frustrated sound as he turned to look at her. "It's not about control or power, the man had—"

"For gods' sake, Merikh, *anyone* could have found out that information. Nikias gave you the opportunity to run away from an uncomfortable situation, and you leapt at the chance. Is he waiting in the wings to save you from me again?" The temperature fell as Loralee called him a coward for the second time since they'd met.

"You are my wife; you vowed to lead when I cannot. As the khanum, celebrations are entirely your purview. I trusted your ability to be discreet and handle the challenges thrown at you tonight with grace and dignity. From what Nikias reported, that trust was not misplaced. You have my gratitude. And the vizier is retired for the night," Merikh said, his tone ending on a softer note.

Loralee reached down and pulled the bangles with their tiny bells off her ankles, taking her time undoing the clasps as she tried to find the words to yell at him again. His tone had stripped away her anger, leaving only frustration and disappointment, even a little sympathy. Merikh wasn't entirely wrong, after all. She'd vowed to compensate for his shortcomings. Anxiety around social events was an unfortunate trait for a shah. She put the bangles inside her slippers before placing them on the floor a few inches away.

Loralee straightened up, pulled the crown carefully off her head, and placed it beside Merikh's. She didn't know what to say to him. Now that her anger had worn off, she simply felt exhausted. She shut her eyes for a moment and sighed as she stood.

"Will you help me?" she asked, gesturing to her hair. "I can't undo it all on my own, and I'm not sleeping on it."

The long gold chotli wasn't the only jewelry wrapped up in her hair. She'd been given ivory pins and turtle-shell clips that Loralee hadn't the foggiest idea how to remove, not without pulling out half her hair or a chunk of her scalp. She had no desire to bring a servant in to do it. Besides, she had to at least try to put Merikh's hands to good use tonight. The man could amputate fingers, surely he wouldn't balk at pulling out a few hairpieces?

Luckily for him, Merikh had enough common sense not to voice any discomfort and simply nodded. Loralee turned her back to him to make it easier. To her surprise, he gently worked the clasps and ties out of her hair without yanking on them. It was relaxing, and the weight of the jewelry off her neck felt wonderful. As Merikh put the last pieces down on the desk, Loralee rubbed her neck.

"Thank you," she said quietly, turning around to look at him. Merikh simply nodded, looking less irritable than before but once more hidden behind his walls.

Gods, I wish the wine had lasted longer, Loralee thought. It was hardly the wedding night she'd imagined growing up, but she pushed the nerves down as she closed the gap between her and Merikh. He flinched as she put her hand on his chest. He hadn't buttoned up the achkan, and his skin was cool under her fingers. Merikh seemed to freeze for a moment, but then he moved her hand off his chest and kissed her. His hands pushed her sari aside and were warm on her waist. They slid to her hips, and he pulled her close. Unthinkingly, Loralee touched his chest again, her hands making their way to his shoulders to push off the achkan.

What the... Loralee hesitated. There was a strange bump, smooth like a scar, but it felt like a thick cord. The temperature plummeted. Merikh stopped kissing her, his hands on her hips gripping her painfully hard. Loralee tried to push away, but he didn't move. His eyes looked far away. Merikh didn't seem to be seeing her at all.

"Let *go!*"

Loralee tried to keep the rising panic out of her voice. She struggled to push away from him as the skin under his hands grew numb. It hurt enough that there'd be bruises come morning.

"Merikh, I'm sorry," Loralee said, unsure of what else to try. Her apology seemed to ground him for a moment. Merikh pushed her away from him, knocking her into the desk as he turned away. Loralee looked down and touched her waist, the skin raw from the cold.

"Vindaram's breath, what happened?" she muttered. She stepped away from the desk, rubbing her back where she'd hit it.

Merikh, now standing off by the chairs and coffee table, didn't answer her. His hands were almost white as he gripped the back of the divan. His chest was heaving. Loralee could hear him breathing, deep and steady for a moment before it quickened, the temperature dropping a few degrees again. Loralee's first instinct was to go to him, try to comfort him and find out exactly what she'd done wrong. But she had enough common sense to know that doing so wouldn't end well for her. It left her feeling useless, like she was intruding on an exceptionally private moment that she had no business being part of yet.

Loralee turned away and left the main area of the suite for the bedroom. She shut the door quietly behind her and then let out a shaky breath as she looked down at her hands. She'd ignored him unthinkingly, and now he was paying a far steeper price for the infraction than she was. Loralee moved her sari out of the way and checked her hips, frowning as she saw dark points where Merikh's fingers had been. She'd have to make sure she wrapped her saris to hide them, or wear long blouses or dresses to hide the bruising.

Loralee had heard plenty of rumors about the beating Mansur had given Merikh. Most claimed he'd used a whip. Some said Mansur had just taken a hunting knife and skinned Merikh's back. Whatever the truth was, Loralee regretted touching him. She'd seen Neredi soldiers, mostly older ones, who reacted poorly to the twang of a bowstring or the smell of blood, who froze at the sound of a sword leaving its sheath.

I handled that poorly, Loralee thought, biting her lip before she crossed the room to her dresser. Her hands were shaking as she opened it and pulled out her muslin nightgown. She changed quickly, laying out her wedding attire on top of the dresser. It'd be kept for another event, such as the first presentation of the future shahzade.

If we get to that point, Loralee thought. No. When. They *had* to. Merikh needed an heir.

Enchanted glass stones lit the bedroom, and Loralee picked up one of her books before standing in front of the bed. Whatever side Merikh normally slept on, she didn't know, and she couldn't tell. She certainly wasn't going back out to ask. There was still a cold touch to the air. Loralee lifted back the blanket and furs before curling up with her book. Her heart was still racing, and her waist still felt cold.

She doubted she'd manage to fall asleep anytime soon.

He felt cold steel around his wrists.

The slosh of a wineskin thrown aside into the sand. The murmur of concerned voices. None would speak out.

Rajiya's perfume. Cinnamon and orange petals. Sweat and dirt. She had run a hand across his shoulders. She cooed something at him. At Mansur?

Pain.

White-hot pain as the whip tore across his back. Again, and again.

He lost his feet. His shoulders cracked loudly when he fell, held up only by the chain attached to the whipping post.

The sharp wet slap of the whip meeting bloodied flesh echoed in his ears.

He could see the spray of his blood on the sand.

And felt nothing but pain.

"He's dead." Merikh barely breathed the words. *He's dead, his body gone. Rajiya's dead. They're dead. I killed them.*

There were voices. Nikias.

"Shahanshah, you're going to kill your son."

Another crack of the whip. Then just black. And pain.

A candle wick popped as it burned. There was a little light to the room. Merikh's back ached. He let go of the back of the divan. When he'd ended up gripping it, Merikh didn't know. The divan was frozen solid to the ground. Ice wrecked the wood and cushions. Frost coated the stone around him. His heart was racing. Merikh glanced down at his wrists, half expecting to see chains. Instead, just the pale thin scars they'd left behind.

The room was freezing. The candles almost burnt out. He didn't know how long he'd been standing there, frozen in a moment.

Loralee. He glanced back toward the desk, then to the bedroom. *We argued, I kissed her, she touched me...* He vaguely recalled pushing her away. Her soul was in the bedroom, and it felt strong. If he'd hurt her, he couldn't have done too much harm. He took several deep breaths until he couldn't hear his heart in his ears anymore, then went to the bedroom.

The enchanted stone still gave off light. Loralee hadn't managed to touch it before falling asleep. She'd curled up with much of the blanket and all the furs to combat the cold of his mood, and a closed book lay in her hand. Merikh glanced at the stone, and the light disappeared from the room. A little still leaked in from under the door and the curtain edges. Just enough to see by as Merikh changed into a pair of night salwar and found a kameez to sleep in. He hesitated for a moment beside the bed.

Loralee was a problem wrapped in a disarming facade. Marrying her made him vulnerable in ways he hadn't been prepared for, couldn't prepare for. And tonight? Perhaps Alaziz was more right to worry than Merikh had thought. He could have killed her if she had tread less carefully. He couldn't afford that. The fallout from *accidentally* murdering the Khanum would be catastrophic. Merikh hadn't expect such a strong reaction. After all, he'd managed to get through the henna night.

Then again, I didn't expect to argue with her. She hadn't been entirely wrong, as much as he loathed to admit it.

Merikh walked quietly to her half of the bed and pried the book from her fingers, putting it down on the nightstand beside the bed. He made it halfway back to his side before he heard the blanket rustle.

"Merikh?"

He cleared his throat in acknowledgment. Loralee pushed off a few of the furs toward his side of the bed.

"I'm sorry, I didn't—"

"You've done nothing wrong," Merikh said bluntly before reluctantly crawling into bed. He was painfully aware of Loralee's presence, wanting nothing more than for the night to be over finally. Loralee said nothing. He felt her shift away from him. Loralee settled, and Merikh imagined she'd find sleep far sooner than he would. His mind was still half in the training yard. Merikh tried to focus on anything else. The blanket smelled faintly of Loralee's perfume, jasmine and lavender.

Nothing like Rajiya's.

CHAPTER 19

2ND OF VINDITH, FIRST HARVEST, 902 UNIFIED AGE
MADIAR, RAUDHAH PROVINCE

Light crept in through the curtains. Sleep's hold began to wane. Merikh took a deep breath and yawned, inhaling the scent of jasmine and lavender. For the moment, the scent didn't seem strange. Neither did the fact that he couldn't move his arm or that he felt a little too warm. He was simply comfortable, and he nearly dozed off again.

Realization jolted Merikh awake when Loralee moved a little and her hair tickled his face. She was tucked against him, her back against his chest. His arm was over her side, and she held it to her chest with a viselike grip. An unhappy, sleepy moan left his wife when Merikh tried to extricate his arm from her. He stopped, not wanting to wake her and get caught like this.

Caught by whom? The thought came unbidden, but it wasn't wrong. There were no other souls nearby, save the guards down the hall. The only witness to them waking up like this would be Loralee.

One witness too many. The idea of being found like this still spooked Merikh. With a thought, he carefully coated his arm with ice. Loralee shivered and let go, replacing his arm with the blanket and curling up tighter. Merikh slipped from the bed. He dressed as quickly and quietly as possible. The last time he'd slept with a woman, Mansur had still been alive and had taken offense. His father had left her raped and flayed body tied to Merikh's bed, a reminder that anything Merikh had was first and foremost Mansur's.

Merikh glanced back at Loralee in his—no, *their*—bed. She looked content. Her hair was a wild mess, her mouth slightly open. The sleeve of her nightgown was bunched at her shoulders, showing off the henna designs down her slender arm.

Thank the gods I woke first. Merikh disliked the thought of their roles reversed, for her to see him in a similar light. To see him so plainly open and vulnerable. He was her husband, but he was still her shah.

Merikh left the bedroom and glanced toward the row of bells near the door. He rang the summons for a servant before sitting down at his desk. It was a few minutes before Merikh felt a soul coming down the hallway. The door opened ahead of the young man.

"Inform Amir Olumide that I intend to test the horses Duq Hasad gave us yesterday, and that his presence would be welcome," Merikh said quietly, trying not to wake Loralee. The attempt was unnecessary, as he heard the door from the bedroom open. Merikh glanced over his shoulder. Loralee hadn't dressed. She'd tried to tame her hair a little with her hands and pulled on a muslin kaftan. Her eyes were still puffy from sleep.

"Please bring coffee and something small to eat," Loralee asked.

The servant bowed before turning to leave the room. He hesitated when he saw the divan.

"Shahanshah, should I have that replaced?"

Merikh nodded, and the servant left.

"Did I wake you?" Merikh asked, not looking at Loralee as he deliberately made himself busy with paperwork on his desk.

"No, I was already waking up when you left. It got cold. We need to talk about last night," Loralee said as she crossed the room. The paperwork rustled as she put her hand down on it.

Merikh shook his head and pulled the papers out from under her fingers. "Someday, perhaps. Not today."

"You woke me up twice last night muttering and freezing the room."

"Would you prefer to sleep somewhere else?" Merikh asked tersely.

Loralee shook her head. "No, I'd rather you talked to me about it," Loralee said earnestly as she turned around to sit on the edge of the desk.

"I'd rather we didn't. Conveniently, I have final say on the matter."

She frowned, hesitating a moment before she touched his hand. Merikh flinched, and she let go immediately. "If you were any other man, you could take as much time as you needed. We don't have that luxury. I know it's a lot to ask—"

"You can't *know*," Merikh muttered under his breath. He doubted Loralee could imagine the barbarism required to brutalize her own kin like he'd suffered.

"But you *can* trust me. If we must buy time, it would be easy to start a rumor that I have a...difficult womb."

Merikh looked at her, unable to hide the mix of surprise and distrust her words stirred. After all, there were already rumors that she was pregnant. To suddenly swing the other way would certainly change her public reputation. It would be a rumor she might never recover from. Not without multiple children, at least. *Gods, that's a horrifying thought.*

"Well, better me than you," Loralee teased before straightening up off the desk.

Merikh ran a hand over his face. Whispers of impotence would start quickly if they didn't lay the blame on Loralee. Those sorts of rumors were as devastating to Shai'Khal's stability as the religious schism.

"Now, more importantly, you're testing the horses without me?" Loralee asked, sounding disappointed.

"Duq Hasad had originally planned on letting you pick the horses, though I imagine Amir Olumide put a firm stop to that," Merikh explained. "I want to make sure he's not throwing us his late-season scraps."

"I could help, if you held off."

"Olumide is a difficult man to read. I don't need your presence complicating matters," Merikh said. "If I bring you, he may bring along the duqa or one of his sons. Too many voices."

"One of those horses is mine, and I want to get a ride in on both of them before you claim one," Loralee told him. The look she gave him was dead serious.

Merikh smirked and nodded. "Naturally."

Loralee nodded once before returning to the bedroom. She was dressed by the time servants returned with coffee, a small tray of fruit and meat, and confirmation from Olumide that of course he'd come. Merikh downed a small cup of coffee quickly, grabbed a handful of dates, and left Loralee in the suite.

By the time Amir Olumide joined Merikh in the barns, Merikh had both the mare and stallion caught and tied at opposite ends of the barn aisle. A soft brush in hand, Merikh carefully groomed and examined the mare for dirt and flaws. Ajir guards were preparing their horses, and two Attar guards accompanied the amir. The older man was dressed in an elaborate blue khalat, the golden thread designs almost garish. His age was just beginning to show, the edges of his beard were turning gray, and lines marked his face. A thin scar ran the length of his beard, apparently earned in a drunken discussion with Mansur when the two had been young. Olumide had given Mansur an almost matching one, and both men had always been happy to retell the story. The details were never the same and left Merikh wondering what the truth actually was.

"Shahanshah," Amir Olumide said, half bowing as he approached Merikh, "what do you think of her?"

Merikh finished brushing her flank before he took a step back.

"Her withers are higher than I'd like."

"Well, they're not *that* high..." the amir said, defending her quickly.

Merikh looked at the amir out of the corner of his eye. "If you were half blind, you'd think she was a camel."

In all honesty, both horses were quite good to look at. Well-built for the most part, probably horses Merikh would have asked for a look at anyway. But he wasn't about to tell the amir that. The royal barns had a reputation to maintain; gift horses were given as much scrutiny as any other. It wasn't considered rude to turn down a horse given from a person of lesser station. But unless both rode poorly, Merikh doubted they'd be returning to Rajibad. The mere fact they were here meant that the amir had intended to try and gain breeding rights to the royal barns. He simply had the misfortune of gamblers for sons.

"Well, I hope you're more impressed with them when you're on their backs. Though I admit, I'm surprised you wanted to ride this early after your wedding night. I don't think Mansur and Aliyah left the suite for a week, and she was pregnant."

"I'm always relieved to hear my actions differ from my father's," Merikh said firmly, his tone clear he was not amused by the line of conversation. He had no desire to lie and make the night into more than what it was, but he certainly wasn't going to tell the truth about it. A ride would clear Merikh's head and give him time to consider Loralee's offer. Or hopefully give him an excuse to forget about it until some other time.

The city was already awake and in a mixed mood. City festivities had been planned for the week, though Merikh had been chagrined to spend much money on it, but the city council had convinced him that celebrating the marriage would give the people something to focus on that wasn't religious.

As Merikh and Olumide rode through Prophet's Way, it was quite clear that religion wasn't far from anyone's minds. Red-and-blue banners hung from the bazaars; auction squares had been taken over by entertainers. Beneath the facade, the religious undertones were strong. Several of the red banners were torn or painted over with Akhenic Suns. Merikh was certain he saw more than a few lewd pictorials and graffiti about the Khanum.

The city was tense, even as it celebrated. That tension was exactly why, even with his guards, Merikh still wore armor for this ride. There were too many nobles in the city—and too many angry religious zealots—for him to ride anywhere without a small manner of protection at least.

Outside the city, the political pressures ceased to exist for an hour. Merikh put the mare through her paces first before switching to the stallion. He had no intention of turning the horses away, but Merikh made enough of a show to make the amir a little nervous. The stallion was more of a handful than Merikh cared for, the horse getting distracted more than a few times by the close proximity of mares but never enough to be dangerous.

"Duq Hasad manages your barn, does he not?" Merikh asked as he turned the horse back toward Madiar.

Olumide nodded quickly, riding beside Merikh. "He does. I've had him spend harvests at the Neredis. I think Duq Alaziz has hopes of stealing my son away."

"You'd be foolish to let him."

Olumide laughed and shook his head. "Perhaps, Shahanshah. You don't see it often. Rashad and Hasad are good brothers most of the time. But...there's tension I fear may end badly for Hasad. Occasionally he likes to think he's got a political bone in his body. He doesn't. I'd hate to see him push Rashad into a corner or end up getting on the wrong side of one of Rashad's more protective mistresses."

"Do you enjoy being the grandfather to an unknowable number of bastards?" Merikh asked.

Olumide shrugged. "The word 'bastard' stopped meaning anything to me a long time ago. Besides, that's Rashad's problem. When he names a successor, there will be angry mistresses and power-hungry children fighting over it. And Rashad doesn't have the means to keep all of them happy—not without bankrupting us."

"An easy problem to solve, Amir."

"Is it, Shahanshah?" Olumide asked, his tone lightly suspicious. After all, Rashad was the only living assumed bastard left of Mansur's, but by no means had he been the only one born.

"We're about to be at war. Surely those mistresses have skills that could be useful outside of Rajibad—repairing horse blankets, tents, tending to wounded soldiers..."

"Whoring."

Merikh shrugged. "A means to build lives for themselves with *other* benefactors. I'm sure Amir Navin can always use fresh hands for the poppy fields."

"I'm sure. But Rashad would simply find new women to amuse himself with."

"I would suggest a wife, but I'm unsure that would change the duq's habits much."

"Probably not," Olumide admitted. "He has a great deal of interest in women and very little interest in marriage."

"Kontess Maliha seems to have a similar view about men and significantly more money," Merikh pointed out.

It was far from the most advantageous political marriage if Rashad ever wanted to make a bid for the throne. The kontess wasn't despised, but she certainly wasn't loved outside of Kuzen. Her support would hinder Rashad. But if Rashad had no intentions toward the crown, then Maliha was ideal. Kontess of her own city already, Merikh had no doubt the woman would turn down the duqa of Rajibad title and remain in Dharipur instead. While in title, the duqa of Rajibad held more weight than a kontess, giving up the reins to a city seemed an unlikely decision for Maliha. As long as legitimate heirs were provided for both of them, neither Maliha nor Rashad would need to spend prolonged periods of time with each other. Their marriage had the potential to strengthen trade ties between the cities, move akhenits from Kuzen to Raudhah. More money for Rashad to keep his mistresses happy with.

"She's not much younger than I am," Olumide pointed out.

Merikh shook his head. "Still young enough to give the duq an heir. You're not that old yet, Amir, and the kontess is still in her thirties."

Reluctantly, Olumide nodded.

"I'll have the Khanum mention it to the kontess," Merikh said before dropping the subject. If they were truly lucky, Rashad's distaste for the proposal would push him into making an imprudent decision. Only one of his mistresses was noble. Even then, she was a merchant sayida—a woman who had bought her title and paid yearly to keep it—hardly appropriate for a duqa. Rashad thinking with his cock was exactly the sort of chaotic distraction Merikh could use to keep the nobles' focus off of more important matters like the future shahzade.

Conversation petered off as they approached Madiar's gates. The tone of the city had changed, and Merikh could smell smoke. It didn't help the Hock's stench. City guards were everywhere. When Merikh looked down one of the side roads, he could see broken merchant stalls and burnt houses, men and women sitting on the ground and healer guards tending to the worst injuries. A riot had broken out.

Curiosity got the better of Merikh. He signaled to the Ajir before heading down the road to personally survey the damage. His guards stayed close, though a few split off to help the city guards move debris from the road and regain order. It was easier said than done as grieving families made demands to find their loved ones.

The guards had lain the dead in an alley. Five adults, four men and a woman, all with injuries that appeared to have been caused by other peasants. Few could afford a proper weapon. Most murders in the Hock were done with small knives or blunt objects. An angry farmer might attack someone with a scythe or an ax, but those were still few and far between.

The dead adults held little interest to Merikh. It was the three dead children who caught his eye. He dismounted the stallion and handed the horse off to one of his guards. Unlike the adults, they weren't bludgeoned. They had been murdered and likely dumped here to incite the riot. Whether they'd been murdered by Onyx Swords or Akhenic Faithful, Merikh didn't care. The message was clearly for him from the Temple.

Their eyes had been cut out. Blood trails covered their little faces and trickled down to their slit throats. Merikh crouched down beside one of the bodies, green fog leaving his fingertips as he touched the dead girl's wrist. Though she'd been dead long enough to go stiff, he could still feel the faintest remnant of magic within her. She'd been innately gifted. Merikh imagined the other two were as well. Common born, they would never have been able to afford the training to become sorcerers and would have likely remained mages. They never would have lived full lives, not if their magic had any strength to it. Without training, mages almost always overextended their magic and killed themselves.

These children would likely have met that fate eventually. But they were young, maybe only three or four. Merikh's ice hadn't manifested until he was five or six, necromancy showing itself a few years later. The chances one of these children had shown magic this young was impossible. While Merikh had no doubt they were killed because of their magic, it hadn't been their auras that had condemned them.

Gold eyes like Merikh's were rare. They only appeared in those with magic and blood ties to the Great Prophet. Ties that proved these children had been pruned from a distant branch of Merikh's family tree. Nine hundred years of bastards meant there were plenty of chances for gold eyes throughout Shai'Khal. Once, gold eyes had been called Akhenios's Blessing, but that name had fallen quickly out of favor when Merikh's necromancy appeared. Eyes like his were met with distrust now. It had undoubtedly cost these children their lives.

Merikh left the corpses and returned to his horse, lost in his thoughts. They'd need a response to this. Murdering children was an impressively low maneuver, and the fact that the Faithful had descended to such levels first? The situation was practically gift wrapped for Merikh. Purging the Priest Council of child murderers had solidified Merikh's moral standard with both peasant and noble alike. While this would make his efforts to end the Akhenic Temple's shadow policy of killing mage children look less successful, it would hurt Alcaeus more than Merikh in the long run.

White-hot pain split his side moments after Merikh settled in the saddle.

A second hit to his shoulder sent Merikh tumbling from the stallion onto the street. His vision went black as he hit the ground, the wind knocked from his lungs. Merikh struggled to get it back. As his vision returned, he saw thick arrow shafts sticking out of his armor on his left side. He tried to sit up but felt hands on him as his guards descended, shields up and blocking out the sun. They were saying something about a healer, arguing over whether to bring him to one or have one brought here.

Merikh couldn't concentrate, his vision blurring, and there was a strange sensation around his wounds.

Venom.

CHAPTER 20

The Oasis Garden within the palace was second only to the royal barns in Loralee's eyes. The fountain was stunning, as if built from opals and glass, painting rainbows on the mosaic tiles of the walkways. Hundreds of flowers lined the paths, cypress and jasmine providing shade from the morning sun. On a clear day, it was breathtakingly beautiful.

Naturally, Maman had complained that the fountain was far too bright, that it was difficult on her eyes, but she'd manage through breakfast *somehow*. The woman was overly dramatic, although no one present was surprised. Jin and Iseul sat together beside Loralee, while Duqa Aminah Afolayan was being bothered by Maman and Loralee's aunt, Sayida Zaida Neredi. The conversation had been light-hearted for breakfast, all dancing around the question Loralee knew *one* of them would inevitably ask.

"So, my dear, is Myeong going to have a playmate in nine months?"

There it is. Loralee had been trying to find a safe way to answer Jin's teasing question all morning. Loralee smiled coyly and took a sip of pear juice.

"One can hope." *If we all pray to Hisahti, and Merikh can learn bear my touch for more than a moment.* Loralee kept her thoughts from her smile.

"Better you than me," Iseul chimed in. Jin had been the one to carry Myeong, and it seemed Iseul had been happy to give that responsibility to her wife.

"Gods be kind, I'm not ready to be a grandmother. I'm not sure I've adjusted to you living *here* yet," Jasira said before looking at Aminah. "They just grow up far too quickly."

"I wouldn't know." The icy tone did nothing to faze Jasira, still smiling and seeming oblivious to it, an act Loralee knew all too well. Before, Jasira would have had to tread carefully around the wife of an amir. Now? Mother of the Khanum, Jasira was close to untouchable.

"*Maman*, that was unkind." Loralee wouldn't have dreamed of scolding her mother in at the Neredi estate. But here? Madiar was her home, and Loralee wouldn't abide her mother behaving quite so comfortably.

"Oh, apologies, Khanum, Duqa. But you have your nephews; I'm sure it's the same. It wasn't long ago that the Shah was a boy riding old mares and playing with wooden swords."

"And still attached to Aliyah's skirts," Aminah said dryly, reclining a little on her divan.

Gods, kill me now. Loralee held back a groan and gestured to a nearby servant.

"Has the Shah returned with Amir Olumide?"

"I'll go find out, Khanum." The man bowed quickly and left. Loralee desperately wanted any excuse to end this breakfast early. Merikh returning with their new horses was exactly the excuse Loralee needed.

"Missing him already?" Sayida Zaida spoke up, trying to help Loralee steer the conversation away from the duqas.

"He took Amir Olumide with him to test horses. I'm curious how it went."

"And you didn't go with him?" Zaida tsked. "I'm disappointed." The older woman smiled, clearly teasing.

"Well, I have to let him think he still has a job to do here, other than sire the shahzade. Can't have a man lose his purpose."

To Loralee's surprise, the garden gate clacked again. The servant had barely left, but he had already returned behind an Ajir guard. The man looked grim. There was blood on his cuirass. Loralee felt her heart stop when he bowed in front of her.

"Khanum, if I may speak to you privately?"

"Spit it out," Jasira snapped. Her expression had changed from toying and politicking to genuine concern. "We've all got eyes. What happened to the Shah?"

"*Out,*" Loralee said before clearing her throat. "Now."

The women rose from their seats quickly and left the garden. Jin walked around the table to squeeze Loralee's shoulder before following the women out. When the gate shut, the guard straightened up and met her gaze.

"He's alive. There was an archer, in the Hock District. When they were returning to the city, the Shah was shot and unhorsed. The amir was shot as well, but the arrow only grazed his arm. The Shah was hit twice: his shoulder and his side. We've brought him to the infirmary."

"Do you have the archer?"

"City guards are looking, and I sent Ajir guards back out. So far, they've found the bow and one of these." The guard handed Loralee a black stone amulet, the same style as the one the Emani had carried. Loralee closed her hand around it, holding it tightly as she stood and smoothed her skirt.

"I expect the archer found, and in a condition to be tried by judges. I don't want to see you until you can report that. Do you understand?" Loralee kept her tone even, trying to choose her words carefully. She'd be judged harshly on how she handled this. If Merikh was in the infirmary, Loralee was confident he'd be fine. Healers would tend to him, and in a matter of hours, he'd be his usual ornery self. The look on the guard's face made her doubt that assumption, and Loralee was glad when he bowed and left. She followed him from the garden, ignored the women milling about by the entrance, and headed quickly for the infirmary.

Loralee saw Olumide immediately upon entering the infirmary, as he sat upon the first bed. A healer beside him tended to the arrow wound on his arm. Nikias and Rashad stood in front of him, speaking quickly in hushed voices. Silk privacy screens partitioned the beds into rooms, and through the screens Loralee could see the silhouettes of four healers around a bed that she assumed was Merikh's.

"Amir, are you all right?" Loralee asked.

Olumide nodded quickly. "Apologies, Khanum, there was nothing anyone could do to stop it. I didn't see anything."

"I'm sure you would have done your very best if you could have." Loralee's tone was distracted as she walked past them.

Nikias joined her as she passed the privacy screen and saw Merikh lying unconscious on the bed. "If you're squeamish, you don't have to be here," Nikias said gently.

"Blood doesn't bother me," Loralee lied. The sight of Merikh's blood made her breath catch, but she watched as the healers methodically clipped the arrows, removed his armor, and took off his clothes to find injuries from the fall. They turned Merikh on his side, pushing the lower arrow through. His body was stiff. Loralee assumed the arrows has been dipped in cobra venom. It paralyzed its victims, and every noble knew its potency against rivals.

With the lower arrow out, the healers laid him back against the bed and began working on digging out the one in his shoulder. Pushing it out had proved impossible, not without going through his shoulder blade. The sound of their tools cutting into his skin made Loralee gag and look away.

"Are you sure you wish to stay?" Nikias asked.

Loralee nodded. She looked back at Merikh while fiddling with the wedding band on her finger. Blood covered Merikh's henna, and Loralee glanced down at the henna on her own hands. It had darkened beautifully; she doubted it would fade for quite a while.

I thought this was supposed to help me have a long and happy marriage?

"I don't think Merikh would want me here," Loralee admitted quietly to Nikias.

The grand vizier scoffed. "He wouldn't want anyone here, but if the worst should happen..." Nikias frowned as he spoke.

"He'll be fine," Loralee reassured Nikias, touching his arm gently. Nikias covered her hand with his and squeezed it gently. When his hand dropped away, so did Loralee's.

"Tell me there's a chance you're pregnant, Khanum," Nikias asked quietly.

Loralee looked back at Merikh and frowned. It was answer enough.

"He's had three attempts on his life so far this year; you two can't dawdle on this. You swore an oath to protect the Madiaran line, Loralee," Nikias said, scolding her gently.

She didn't appreciate it, but Loralee knew it was easier for Nikias to chastise her than to focus on Merikh right now.

"He's going to be *fine*, Nikias," Loralee said firmly. He had to be. Heirless, and on the brink of war? *You can't abandon me now,* Loralee thought.

He had to get through this—his blood relations were pathetic. No one would unite behind Amir Navin. As khanum, Loralee had every right to claim his crown if he died. She was Madiaran now, after all. She could claim his crown, become Shah, and remarry for *her* heir.

But no one would support her on her own. Loralee was an untested sayida. If Merikh died, Loralee doubted even her father would support her claim on the Rising Sun Throne. She could hear Olumide and Rashad talking in hushed whispers a few feet away on the other side of the privacy screen. The threat she'd made in Rajibad still stood. If the two strongest Yahidah houses united, they'd be able to handle the transition of Merikh's death easier.

Stop that, Loralee chided herself. *Merikh will be fine.*

With the arrows out, two healers stood on either side of Merikh's bed, their hands outstretched above him. Warm white light emanated from their fingertips. As the light touched Merikh's skin, he convulsed, and the warm light took on a sickly green hue.

"What in Alhanem..." Loralee muttered, instinctively recoiling.

"Necromancy," Nikias said quietly. "This happens every time he's here. It doesn't coexist well with healing magic. Too much and it'll kill him."

Loralee bit her lip, understanding Nikias's fears now. Particularly as another healer began cleaning the wound before preparing a needle and thread. To have to rely on medicine and surgeries, barbaric methods as likely to kill as to cure? There was something startling about the idea that the Shah relied on the same treatment as those too poor to pay for healing cures.

"Grand vizier?" Rashad spoke up from the other side of the privacy screen, and Nikias excused himself to speak with the duq.

Loralee frowned, folding her arms under her bust and fiddling with her kameez sleeve. She let the men talk. Nikias would tell her anything pertinent. She didn't have enough focus for politics at the moment anyway.

It felt like hours before the healers were done. Black venom oozed out of the arrow wounds and into the air beneath the healer's hands. It hovered for a moment before disappearing. When the stitches were finished, the healers retreated down the hall to recover, exhaustion dogging their steps. A moment later, a different healer approached Loralee and called Nikias over.

"The Shah will recover just fine, but it's going to take a significant amount of patience and time. He shouldn't be riding or doing anything particularly strenuous for at least a few weeks if he expects to heal *properly*. I have enchanted salves that should speed the process, depending on how much he can tolerate. But that still will require him to *take it easy*." The healer placed hard emphasis on his words, but Nikias was already shaking his head. The grand vizier laughed bitterly.

"I can keep him here," the healer continued, looking annoyed.

Nikias shook his head. "Only if you make him into an opium addict. Otherwise, you'll never keep him rested or complacent here." Nikias ran a hand over his bald head and sighed. "Once he wakes, I'll see what I can do to convince him to rest."

"See that you do, Vizier. He wouldn't be the first shah with an addiction, and I have plenty of tinctures to nurse him with."

The healer bowed before walking away. Loralee shook her head. The last thing she could imagine was Merikh in a perpetual poppy fog like Rabb Mahdi. She'd never seen Merikh so much as drink, so part of her believed he'd fight off an addiction on sheer indomitable stubbornness alone.

"I should go, let the nobles know he's all right," Loralee said, turning away from Merikh's bed.

Nikias stopped her with a light hand on her arm. "No, I'll do that. You stay here."

"Don't you think he'd rather see you when he wakes?" Loralee asked, glancing to Merikh.

"Probably. But the duq and amir already left. I guarantee rumors of the Shah's injuries are all over the palace. The nobles will be gathered in the throne room to find out what's going on. Olumide and Rashad are going to control that conversation with my help."

"I'm the Khanum—"

"Who spent more of her wedding celebration at the duq's side than at the Shah's," Nikias said firmly. "Now the Shah is half dead, and an attempt was made on the amir's life as well. You need to stay here as the Shah's dutiful wife until he wakes, then you can come as the bearer of good news."

Loralee wanted to argue. After all, it had been Nikias's fault that she hadn't spent the evening with Merikh. She held her tongue. It didn't matter why she hadn't spent the celebration at Merikh's side; it only matter that she hadn't. Nikias was right. Spun the wrong way, it would be all too easy to lay the blame at her and Rashad's feet. Likely, someone would try.

"Can you be certain that Duq Rashad isn't behind this?" Loralee asked.

Nikias laughed again, the sound cold and mirthless. "I can't be sure *you're* not behind this."

"I'm not. Whoever keeps dropping these is," Loralee said as she took Nikias's hand and placed the amulet on his upturned palm.

"Someone wants credit for killing the Shah, if they ever manage to succeed," Nikias said with a frown. "One of these was found on Alkont Sefu's legate, the one killed in the Quorum..." He trailed off, lost in his thoughts.

"Nikias?"

"It's a strange symbol, don't you think? The Akhenic Sun with a shamshir *through* it. Sefu is Akhenic Faithful, and the servant with the poisoned wine threw suspicion on Duqa Sachiko and the priestesses. The Emani bore Ikharon's sigil and one of these. Now we have an archer with one."

"Sarka and Ruya have no reason to kill Merikh. They have his support. They *need* royal legitimacy."

"I assume these are from fanatics, trying to push war sooner. But fanatics from Pantheon or the Akhenic Temple?"

"If they're from the Temple..."

"Alcaeus might be getting his hands dirtier than I gave him credit for," Nikias said before shaking his head. "Let me deal with this. Keep an eye on the Shah."

Loralee frowned and turned back to Merikh. It was unnerving to see him vulnerable. Under the harsh infirmary light, it was the first good look of Merikh she'd gotten. Muscle seemed stretched reluctantly over bone. It was obvious he didn't eat enough to fuel his magic.

I wonder if force-feeding a man for his own good is a crime? Loralee thought flippantly as she tried to focus on something, anything, other than the event at hand. No one had known Olumide would be out riding with Merikh today, other than herself and a handful of servants and guards. The Ajir wouldn't have fed the information to anyone, but the servants or Attar guards were not above suspicion.

Loralee turned, grabbed a folding chair from the wall nearby, and placed it beside Merikh's bed. She sat down carefully, not trusting the chair, as it creaked. It looked more than a little suspicious that the attack had happened while out with the amir. Particularly following the Emani attack after the Quorum. Yes, Alkont Sefu had been behind the attempt, but it was a leak in the Attar household staff that had allowed for the attempt to happen.

Is Rashad trying to kill you? Loralee thought as she looked at Merikh.

Blame could easily be thrown at numerous people, and it made Loralee's head spin trying to pin it down. Rashad wasn't stupid enough to try and kill Merikh without securing the throne. Alcaeus was the most likely suspect, although Loralee wondered at the logic of it. Alcaeus had no one readily lined up to crown before Loralee would assert her claim. Was he truly vainglorious enough to think the Quorum would allow a half-Aegalian bastard with no royal blood to sit on the Rising Sun Throne? The sun would swap places with the moon long before that happened.

Loralee was lost in her thoughts when Merikh woke. His stirring didn't register at first, but when she glanced at his face and met his bleary-eyed gaze, Loralee nearly fell from her chair.

"Let me get a healer," Loralee said, standing abruptly.

"Wait," Merikh croaked.

Loralee turned back to look at him. He tried to clear his throat, and she saw immediate regret as pain wracked his body. She'd never seen healing like this before. The fact that he was still in pain—seemingly a great deal—was foreign to her.

"I really should get you a healer."

"I don't need a damn healer!" Merikh snapped. He propped himself up on his right elbow, groaning in pain as he did. He was paler than usual.

"Fine, you don't need a healer. I won't get one *if* you lie back down," Loralee offered.

Merikh looked ready to strangle her, clenching his jaw. "I don't need to lie—"

"Great, I'll go get a healer." Loralee folded her arms under her bust, daring him to snap at her again. She was khanum, her oaths promised to protect him. That included protecting him from his own stubbornness.

Merikh relented, lying back down against his pillows. His glare remained. Loralee met it with a satisfied smirk before she sat back down. Worryingly, the room remained warm. Was he too wounded for his magic to react naturally? Her smirk quickly turned to a frown, and she looked away toward the foot of his bed. The healers had covered him in a thin blanket, giving him a small measure of modesty.

"You were shot twice. They had to dig one arrow out of your shoulder. The one on your side almost missed you. The arrows appeared to be dipped in cobra venom. It took quite a toll on the healers to get it out of you." Loralee paused, trying to think of what else he might want to know. "Amir Olumide was grazed, and the healers took good care of him. Nikias is handling the nobility as we speak. You'll recover fully, given time. The healers asked that I ensure you don't do anything...detrimental to your health." *Anything stupid,* she'd almost said, but she thought better of it.

"What better way to convince them I'm *fine* than to get me out of this godsforsaken place?" Merikh countered. He sat up quickly and swung his legs over the bed to face Loralee. The movement sent him teetering for a moment before he steadied himself, and Merikh groaned in pain. Once the pain subsided, realization dawned on Merikh's face.

"Why in Alhanem am I *naked?*" Merikh demanded.

Loralee rolled her eyes. "You're hardly naked. The healers left your underclothes. You can't fault them for being thorough. Let me see if anyone brought you clothes."

Loralee stood, ducked behind the privacy screen, and crossed the hall to the set of drawers recessed into the wall. A servant had indeed left clothes for Merikh.

But as Loralee pulled them out of the drawer, she hesitated. As long as Merikh was naked, he wouldn't try to do anything stupid. Loralee glanced back toward the privacy screen. No, he was behaving like a child, but she could understand why he was self-conscious. If the scar she'd felt last night was anything to go by, then he had good reason to want to hide them. There were a few on his chest, but they'd looked smooth and normal. Still, there were more than Loralee had expected to see on a shah.

Loralee had no doubt Merikh had spent a great deal of time in the infirmary during his life so far, and so she couldn't blame him for feeling uncomfortable here. Loralee picked up the clothes and carried them back to Merikh. She placed them down at the foot of his bed and hesitated. He was favoring his shoulder, and his bandages looked tight enough to hinder movement. Loralee wondered if he was even capable of putting on his kameez.

"Do you want my help?" Loralee asked, her tone gentler than before.

"About as much as I wanted to be shot in the first place," Merikh muttered as he carefully reached for the black salwar.

Loralee tossed her hands in exasperation and sat down on her chair. Merikh stared expectantly for a moment before nodding once toward the privacy screen. Loralee let out a frustrated noise, stood, and walked to the other side of the silk screen.

Happy now? she thought. The man was insufferable!

She could see Merikh's outline through the screen. He stood and managed to pull his salwar on with relative ease before pulling on his riding boots. He sat back down again to pull on his kameez. Merikh seemed to hesitate but tried anyway. When Loralee heard him groan in pain, she walked back around the privacy screen. Merikh didn't notice her until she was standing in front of him.

"I don't need—"

"Respectfully, you're full of horse shit. Hand it over." Loralee extended her hand for the kameez. She squared her shoulders and dared him to argue with her. It was the same look she used around stubborn horses.

Merikh didn't move. She could see him trying to find an excuse behind those golden eyes. The man looked exhausted. It made Loralee all the more determined to make him see reason.

"You're going to rip out your stitches if you do this yourself. Stop being ridiculous. Besides, I'm not going to tell anyone our independent shah needed help to dress," Loralee said.

Merikh finally gave her the shirt.

"Gods forbid anyone find out you *needed* me," she muttered under her breath.

Merikh almost said something, but he seemed to think better of it and simply watched Loralee. The lack of confrontation from him threw her off balance, and she suddenly grew very hesitant to touch him.

Now who's being childish? She took his wrist and carefully guided his arm through the sleeve. He winced as she pulled the kameez over his shoulder, and this time Loralee took extra care not to touch him. The moment Merikh was fully dressed, he stood quickly and brushed past Loralee.

"Merikh," Loralee said, exasperated. She followed him past the privacy screen, just in time to see him falter again. He stumbled and grabbed a nearby screen. Made of nothing more than silk and wood, the screen promptly clattered to the ground. Loralee rushed to Merikh's side and grabbed him. He flinched in spite of Loralee's attempt to be gentle, but it was hard to be gentle when trying to stop a man from falling down. He was breathing heavily and looked even more pale now that he was standing. To Loralee's surprise, he leaned on her for a moment.

"I...may need to lie down," Merikh finally conceded. He tried to push Loralee away, but she gripped his arm tighter.

"I can't help you up if you fall."

Merikh begrudgingly let her guide him back to the bed. He laid down carefully and tried to get comfortable.

"Can I get you anything?" Loralee asked.

"No," he said wearily.

Loralee turned to leave when he grabbed her hand. His hand was warm, the skin rough and calloused. She turned quickly to look at him. Merikh looked about to fall asleep, but he had something to say first.

"Speak with Nikias. There were children. Dead mages, killed by Faithful."

"I'll tell him." Loralee nodded quickly, squeezing Merikh's hand slightly. He let go of her, and his eyes shut. Loralee headed down the hall toward the infirmary door. As she did so, she stopped one of the healers.

"The Shah was awake. Please check on him. He's dressed and might have pulled his stitches," Loralee explained.

The healer's self-restraint was admirable. The woman merely sighed and nodded before heading down the hallway. Undoubtedly, Merikh would be irritated by the healer, but Loralee didn't care. She'd only promised not to send one if Merikh remained lying down. He hadn't.

Loralee almost would have traded places with Merikh when she arrived in the throne room. It was controlled chaos within. Nobles pointed fingers at anyone who had even the slightest cause to harm the Shah. Few noticed the doors open or Loralee enter. She shook her head to prevent the herald from announcing her. Amir Olumide was speaking, and Loralee didn't much care for the words coming out of his mouth.

"...House Attar has been a *loyal* supporter of this shah and the previous two shahs, unlike a great many of those present here today. No one had to ransom our loyalty!"

"No," Loralee interrupted from near the door, "we know how much the Shah appreciates the support of your family, Amir Olumide."

The room fell silent. It felt as if the walls had closed in against her as she spoke. Loralee kept a calm facade, ignoring the men and women around her as she followed the long carpet to the throne. She barely hesitated in front of hers before sitting down. If she let herself think too much on the moment, she knew she'd lose her composure.

"Khanum—" Olumide started.

Loralee raised her hand to stop him. Whatever control of the room Olumide had gained, he'd attacked her house to do it. Who else's loyalty had been "ransomed" quite so profitably?

"You have my gratitude, Amir Olumide, for aiding the guards in returning the Shah to the palace and for taking control of matters here. You must be exhausted from your own brush with death. Duqa Emilia, please see to your husband. A man of his age should be resting after such a taxing experience.

"Now, some of you will be relieved to hear the Shah is resting. He will make a swift recovery. The Shah was already up and moving. While I am certain that no one in this room has anything to do with the attempt today, the Ajir will be speaking with each of you and the retinues brought with you."

Her words went over poorly, met with angry shouts. It would take weeks for the Ajir to speak with everyone, and they all had journeys back to their provinces. They couldn't be held for that long, and Loralee agreed. To hold all of them here would be catastrophic when they'd already been away from their provinces and cities for the Quorum. Loralee raised her hand again. A yell from Nikias quieted the room.

"Anyone who leaves Madiar without the permission of Ajir Captain Bashir or the Shah will be assumed guilty and flayed," Loralee said. "The captain will prioritize those of you who have traveled the farthest and those with the greatest motive. Amir Xolani, the Shah will want you back in Ydeba as quickly as possible. The Attar and Neredi houses both have a great deal to gain if the Madiaran line falls. I expect the retinues to cooperate."

"Who investigates you, Khanum?" Kontess Maliha spoke up, stepping forward from the crowd.

Loralee smiled to hide the flare of indignation. "The Ajir, the grand vizier, and perhaps most importantly, Kontess Maliha, my *husband*. The Shah trusts me. I speak for him on these matters."

Well, that's a reach. Hopefully one that won't hurt me later. Loralee tried to keep the thought from her eyes. She was at least passably convincing, as the kontess didn't fight the point.

Loralee stood.

"I'm returning to the Shah's side. Your prayers and support are, as always, appreciated."

Nikias followed her from the throne room. When the door shut behind them, she felt his hand on her shoulder.

"Are you all right?" he asked.

Loralee nodded hesitantly.

"And the Shah?"

"He could barely stand," Loralee whispered, biting her lip.

"We have a lot of work ahead of us," Nikias told her, running a hand over his bald head.

Loralee nodded. "He told me about last night. Did you get word sent to Adrian?"

"He did?" Nikias couldn't hide his surprise before nodding. "Dispatched a rider last night."

"Good. Thank you."

Loralee continued down the hall with Nikias, passing along the information Merikh had shared with her.

"Even with that, you still want to investigate *every* retinue leaving Madiar?" Nikias asked. "We can narrow it down to just the Faithful, get our people back in their cities. With the Shah infirm, we need the stability in the provinces."

Loralee hesitated. "If Alcaeus thinks we're fumbling in the dark, then perhaps he'll get sloppy."

"There's a fine line between drawing out your enemies and alienating your allies with a plan like this, Khanum."

"I know. I want that archer found. I want to know what that symbol means. The sooner we know, the sooner we can move on Alcaeus."

Nikias bowed his head and excused himself. He had a great deal of work to do, and not enough time to do it. Loralee stopped and watched him retreat, taking the moment alone to collect her thoughts. A moment interrupted when she heard the quick thud of riding boots echoing off the hall behind her. She started walking, but not quickly enough.

"Khanum!"

Loralee bit her lip again, composed herself, and then turned to face Duq Rashad. The man looked flushed and was a little out of breath, as if he'd run from the throne room.

"Duq?"

He bowed quickly. When he straightened up, there was worry written all over his face.

"I apologize, on behalf of my house, for the remarks my father made back in court. There were a great many accusations tossed about, and he sought to protect the Attar name first and foremost."

"One can hardly blame him," Loralee said, trying to keep her suspicions from her tone.

"I...I want to assure you, my family had nothing to do with this. I love my father. I wouldn't see him come to harm. I wish him a long life and quiet death, and I wish the same for the Shah."

"Of course you do, Duq. I'm sure the Shah knows that." Her tone was deliberately unconvinced. Loralee felt no need to reassure Rashad. She turned and began to walk away from him.

"Loralee." Rashad grabbed her arm.

Loralee shoved it off. "You take liberties you haven't earned," she snapped at him. They were certainly far from speaking on a first-name basis. Loralee continued down the hall, and Duq Rashad kept pace.

"Apologies, Khanum. I fear my hands and my tongue have gotten the better of me, and this isn't the first time. I have said some...stupid things between yesterday and the Shah's henna night. But you must understand, I meant no offense. You and the Shah have my unfailing respect and support. My father will attest to my severe lack of ambition."

Loralee stopped walking and glanced up at Rashad. He looked earnest, but that was hardly proof of innocence or honesty. He spoke of loyalty and support, but there was no doubt in Loralee's mind that Rashad would have eagerly taken her back to his bed last night if she'd shown any inclination, loyalty to the Shah be damned. She could only imagine the sorts of things Rashad had said at the henna night. Not to mention at the Quorum, as he'd made a point of showing he'd known of the betrothal before anyone else had. That, in and of itself, made his claim about lacking ambition questionable at best. There was a great deal more to the duq than the disarming smile and charm. She wouldn't let him off so easily.

"I'm glad to hear it, but it doesn't change anything. I want the Attar household spoken to by the Ajir and Nikias. I'm sure there is nothing to find."

"Khanum." Rashad swallowed hard, shifting his weight from foot to foot nervously. "You misunderstand me. I have been careful my whole life, so has my father, to *never* give a Madiaran proper cause for my head. I don't trust the Ajir. Can you tell me, with that renowned Neredi honesty, that you believe the Shah won't use this as a chance to put an end to those bastard rumors?"

Loralee let out a slow breath. *No,* she thought. She didn't know Merikh well enough to guarantee integrity. There was plenty of proof that the Shah was a man who believed ends justified means.

"You have my word, as the Khanum, that whatever results the Ajir find will be examined by myself and the judges. You are not above suspicion, but you are not high on my suspect list. I would hate to see you executed for another person's crime."

Rashad bowed, taking Loralee's hand and kissing the signet ring. "You have my thanks."

He let go of her hand without lingering this time, then retreated back toward the throne room.

Once alone, Loralee ran a hand through her hair. She didn't need that added doubt toward Merikh. He'd been honest last night, at least, but that hadn't bought trust. If he could torture men, Loralee doubted framing one or using an opportune situation to be rid of an irritation would make him lose sleep. Or was this just Rashad getting in her head? A guilty man trying to manipulate her into vouching for his innocence? Normally, she would have sought her father's advice, but he was the last person she could confide in now.

I need my own council, Loralee thought. Until then, she only hoped she could keep innocent men from dying.

CHAPTER 21

3RD OF VINDITH, FIRST HARVEST, 902 UNIFIED AGE
MADIAR, RAUDHAH PROVINCE

Sarka was a quiet travel companion, something Adrian hadn't necessarily minded when they'd traveled from Kasu to Madiar. He could keep his own company well enough, but the silence that fell between them was uncomfortable at the best of times.

They'd left Madiar the afternoon before the wedding day, only speaking when setting up camp or deciding on their route. Both had agreed to avoid people as much as possible, but the Sarafi Desert was treacherous. Shifting sands made travel along anything but the camel roads by day difficult. They navigated by the stars at night. The heat took its toll on everyone save for their pack camel. Even the fire sorceress seemed to struggle under the unrelenting sun and water rationing. There was only so much water they could carry with them, and the horses drank most of it. The two had begrudgingly settled on heading to Soleb.

Soleb was a small trading post and the first guarded well west of Madiar. Two Royal Guard were always stationed there, though patrols passed through often enough that there were usually a dozen guards at any given time. There were a handful of adobe buildings, homes for the few people who lived in Soleb, as well as the inn and bazaar. The town appeared busy with outsiders either heading to or from Madiar around the wedding festivities.

There were more people than Adrian had hoped to see. He could see his disappointment reflected in Sarka's posture. It'd be impossible to hide her aura. Adrian hoped most people wouldn't understand what the feeling meant, just a general disquiet that would earn him and Sarka a little extra space at the inn.

"Can you manage the horses? I'll get a room," Adrian asked as they dismounted.

Sarka nodded, taking the reins from him. Adrian glanced over his shoulder as he walked away, unable to shake the nervous feeling leaving her alone with the horses gave him. Sarka's comfort level with their tack was lacking. He'd often overhead her muttering to herself about it—apparently saddles nine hundred years ago had different buckles and ties. And no stirrups. Adrian still double-checked her saddle every morning to make sure it wouldn't fall off. But she seemed to be managing the horses and camel fine. He'd only be gone for a moment.

The wooden door creaked when Adrian opened it. Smoke from the hearth and the smell of anise from hookahs mixed with the spices of cooked lamb. The scent made his stomach grumble. They'd only eaten dried dates for the morning meal. Adrian was more than willing to share a room with Sarka if it meant they could each have a decent meal. The food had to be at least passable, judging by the low tables surrounded by people.

Adrian waited at the innkeeper's desk. A man rushed by a few times, each time giving Adrian a small nod and reassurance that someone would be able to see him in a moment. Eventually, a woman emerged from the kitchen. She was flushed, sweat glistening on her upper lip. Her hair was frazzled, sticking out from her hijab. Spilled brown sauce of some kind stained the front of her abaya.

"Sorry, what can I do for you?"

"I need a room, if you have one," Adrian asked, glancing over his shoulder.

"Oh, don't be fooled. Half of them are too cheap to pay for a room." The woman raised her voice and pointedly looked behind Adrian at a group nearby. "Some men prefer dirt to a charpai. But never you mind, it'll be a silver akhenit for the night."

"That room had better have two charpai, and I'll give you ten bronze instead," Adrian countered.

"It'll have two, but it's a silver akhenit or you'll be sleeping on the dirt out there. No less." The woman planted her hands on her waist firmly, and Adrian held her gaze. She wasn't about to budge.

"A silver akhenit is extortion," Adrian muttered as he dug into his pockets for one. The silver ones were clipped differently than the bronze, making them easy to find and distinguish.

"Probably, but if everyone in Madiar is making extra off the Shah's wedding, then I ought to too. 'Sides, gotta make money off this lot while people are still willing to part with it."

She handed him a room key, turned the register for him to sign, and then left him at the desk. He signed it "Amon Ziyas." Outside of Madiar, he never signed his name. He put the register back and was about to head out to the inn's barn when Sarka walked through the door.

She was doing her best to hide her hair and fair complexion with her niqaab across her face. Still, her entrance sent a ripple through those present. Conversations quieted, patrons cast her sidelong glances, as they undoubtedly felt the same disquiet Adrian had the first time he'd encountered Sarka. Only most of these travelers wouldn't know to name that unease as a magic aura, simply that there was something off about this woman.

Adrian waved Sarka over and led her to the room that matched the number on the key's tag. They dumped their bags inside by the charpai beds. Sarka began to unpack a few items for their stay while Adrian left her to grab food. It would be impossible for her to eat within the tavern with a veil on. Modest women of the desert knew how to comfortably work around their veils to eat. Sarka would struggle and only draw attention more attention to herself.

There was a new man waiting at the innkeeper's desk when Adrian went back to the front. At first glance, Adrian paid him no heed, but after Adrian sat down at a table, he could feel eyes on him, and he looked back at the desk. The man was dressed plainly, but his cloth looked finer than the average traveler, and he looked cleaner. Another moment of scrutiny, and it clicked in Adrian's mind. They'd worked together before, though Adrian couldn't recall the man's name. He was one of the many discreet messengers employed at the palace.

That doesn't bode well. Adrian frowned.

A man who worked at the inn interrupted Adrian's thoughts as he placed a glass of araq and a glass of water down in front of Adrian.

"Oi, what'd you need? If your lady friend is shy, there are a few of my daughters in the back eating dinner, and she can join them."

"Uh, no. I, uh, just need two of whatever you've got cooking for dinner, and I'll take it back to the room," Adrian said quickly.

The other man nodded and disappeared back into the kitchen. When he did so, the messenger casually approached and sat down with Adrian.

"Mind if I join you?" he asked.

Adrian nodded, and the two men slipping into perfunctory small talk. Anything to make it look like they were simply two travelers getting to know each other. After the food had been dropped off, the man carefully hid a sealed letter on the tray.

"Thanks for the company. Safe travels," Adrian said. As Adrian moved to stand, another one of the tavern patrons abruptly stood from his cushions.

"A round for all, Akhenios be praised!" the man shouted.

"What's the occasion?" another man asked from across the room.

"Good news out of Madiar. Short marriage, dead shah. First step to getting rid of the djinn-worshiping whores in the palace. Akhenios's blessings on the high priest!"

Adrian choked on his araq and looked back to the messenger, who looked more alarmed than Adrian cared to see. A few men with the toasting traveler looked quite pleased with themselves, but they'd misjudged their audience. This close to Madiar, most of the patrons were loyal to the Crown.

"Well, that drink is premature and treasonous. Got half a mind to send for the guards and let them string you up," the man behind the register desk, presumably the innkeeper, said loudly and quite firmly.

The drunk slurred something, and one of his companions dragged him back down to his pillow.

"Premature?" Adrian asked loudly, coughing to clear his throat. "Something happen?"

"So says the rumor mill. The Shah *might* be injured. 'Nother assassination attempt. But certainly not cause enough for worry."

"Well, attempts come and go like the moon's cycles," Adrian said light-heartedly to mask his worry.

The messenger waved the innkeeper over. "What happened?"

The man seemed happy to oblige, sitting down beside Adrian. "Heard the guards talking about it earlier," the innkeeper started, leaning on the table. "Riot broke out in one of the slums; the Shah went to see the grieving. You imagine that? Morning after gettin' married, visiting slums. Never would've seen Mansur doin' that. And someone shot him full of arrows."

Adrian studied a knot in the wood of the tabletop. How much was true and how much was exaggeration, he wouldn't be able to tell from anyone here. Even the guards might not know the full truth of it, and this was a good story. It sounded exactly like something the grand vizier would begin propagating. There was a chance Merikh had gone to the riots, tried to quiet things down, but Adrian had his doubts that it played out exactly as the man said. There was quite the disconnect between the Merikh Adrian knew personally and the Shah. The reforms put in place during Merikh's short reign made him seem far more empathetic to the common folk than he was. Consolidating power was easier with support from the masses.

"Well, healers will have him back in shape quickly. Though"—the messenger leaned back in his chair—"the Shah might use this as a good excuse to stay holed up with the Khanum for longer."

The innkeeper snorted and nodded. "Got a bet going on how long it'll take for an announcement to be made for the shahzade. My money is in a matter of weeks she'll be showing. Why else would she have been brought to Madiar so quickly?"

"I hope you don't have too much money on that bet—you'll lose it. We'll maybe see a shahzade in a year."

Adrian barely listened as the messenger carried the conversation, steering it happily toward the virtues of the new khanum. Adrian was still stuck on the assassination attempt. "Shot full of arrows" meant plenty of healing magic.

How much more can you handle, I wonder? No one missed Adrian when he excused himself and retreated back to the room. Sarka had unpacked the journal from their bag and was reclined on one of the palm charpais.

"What took you so long?" Sarka asked hurriedly, putting the journal down and sitting up.

"News from Madiar. The Shah's been injured, possibly gravely. It's all rumors, but I did get this." Adrian put the tray down and picked up the sealed letter. "There's a messenger downstairs. He left Madiar before the assassination attempt."

"You know, I keep hearing that Merikh's a well-loved Shah. I'd hate to see what you people do to a *hated* one," Sarka said as she helped herself to the lamb and naan.

"He could be dead or dying, and if that's the case, then the Khanum needs her allies back in Madiar—"

"No."

Adrian clenched his jaw as Sarka continued eating, her manner unchanged from before.

"This mission—"

"Hasn't changed. Merikh sent you to help me find the Key. If he dies, his orders still stand, don't they?"

"Unless the Khanum recalls them, and—"

"She won't. Ruya won't let her. Neither will Nikias. This is important, more important than your show of unappreciated loyalty. It's not as if your shah is going to notice. You think Merikh would be anything but irritated if you go back and he's not dead?"

"We should wait and—"

"And what? You expect another letter from the Shah to check in with you? 'Dear Steward, I'm healthy, thanks for worrying.' That doesn't sound like Merikh's style."

"Can I finish a damn sentence?" Adrian snapped.

Sarka bowed her head slightly and gestured for him to continue.

"It won't hurt to wait a few extra days to find out if he's alive or not."

"Rumors say he's alive, right? We'll keep hearing rumors until we get to Hatai. Once we're there, we'll be able to get something closer to the truth. We can't spare the time."

She wasn't wrong, and it infuriated Adrian. Merikh wouldn't be impressed if Adrian returned merely to make sure he wasn't dead. But Adrian remembered as if it were yesterday the last time Merikh had been in the infirmary. He'd fought off death for a month, bedridden and sick. Merikh's necromancy magic fought the healing magic. A fever came and went. The scars under Merikh's bandages took weeks longer than what Adrian had believed normal to form. Nikias had barely left Merikh's side, and Adrian had only left to deliver messages. The longest trip had been to Rajibad, to sit with Amir Olumide and ensure the support of the Attar family. A week away from Madiar, then Adrian had been back, sitting with the grand vizier.

"Adrian?" Sarka interrupted his thoughts, and he nodded.

"Yeah, yeah, we ride for Hatai."

"What's in the letter?"

Adrian glanced down and picked it up. It was closed with red wax, but no seal had been pressed into it. It wasn't addressed to him. These letters never were. It cracked open gently, and Adrian recognized Nikias's writing. The words were gibberish. Adrian crossed the room to his saddlebags and pulled out a small journal. Every mission, he received a new one, a matching one left in Madiar. Glancing between the letter and the book, Adrian began to read.

"Amulets...came from...Ydeba," Adrian muttered.

"Amulets?" Sarka asked, and Adrian ignored her. It was difficult enough finding the translation without Sarka picking at him. There were untranslatable words between the meaningful ones, meant to confuse anyone trying to break the cipher with or without the book.

"The Great Prophet's pilgrimage to...the Katu, brought him to a..." Adrian hesitated and frowned. "To a place that destroys magic."

"What place?" Sarka demanded. She stood and crossed the room to see the paper as if she'd be able to glean something more from it.

"Doesn't say." Adrian crumpled the letter in his palm. With effort, orange flames burned it slowly above his hand. He brushed the ashes off his salwar.

"That sounds like somewhere we need to go. It might be protecting the Key."

"Too bad we don't know where in the Katu. I don't care for the idea of having to look from Membiti to Duak," Adrian said, frowning. The mountain range touched Shai'Khal's north and south coasts and divided Ydeba in half.

"We'll have more answers in Hatai, but at least we have a warning. What could destroy magic?" Adrian asked.

Sarka shrugged, staring off into nothing for a moment.

"There were rumors," she said finally, "that Uduak was working on something that would render the gods' priests and champions obsolete. There was a group of them, Uduak's honor guard. You couldn't get close to them; you'd just faint. Maybe that has something to do with the place mentioned. Maybe not."

Adrian said nothing, allowing them to eat in silence. A question began growing inside of him, and by the time the meal was finished, he couldn't hold it in any longer.

"What did you do for nine hundred years?"

Sarka ignored him and wiped her hands on her salwar before she walked back to her charpai and lay down.

All right, then. Adrian stood up and put their water glasses back on the tray, the clay cups thudding against wood. He glanced at Sarka when she cleared her throat, apparently changing her mind about his question.

"I slept, mostly. I could walk the whole island in a day. At least, I think it was a day. The sun never really made it through the mists, and it wasn't much darker at night. It's not as if I can die, and I don't age. I did watch a few generations of centaurs grow up and die. They have long lives.

"When I didn't sleep, I meditated. When I couldn't do that, I trained. I dueled. Occasionally, shipwrecks brought sailors and I'd get stories, usually from Thalassonian pirates. They'd get stranded, try to build a ship and escape, then get thrown back to our shores by the waves. They grew old and died. But they helped keep us all...hopeful, I suppose."

"Centaurs?" Adrian asked in disbelief.

"Half horse, half man."

"I *know* what they are. You mean to tell me you had centaurs on your island?" *Did you tell Merikh that?* Adrian couldn't believe it. It was one thing to believe in gods and djinn, another to believe in strange animal hybrids.

"Centaurs and a lot more at first. Some of them died off. Akhenios has a lot to answer for," Sarka said. She let out a long breath and closed her eyes.

Conversation over, then, Adrian thought. He gathered up the tray and placed it on the other side of the door. He'd grown up on all manner of stories about fantastical creatures, but he had a hard time believing in them. Djinn, ifrits, and ghuls were no laughing matter. Adrian had seen those with his own eyes, same as mortohas. Occasionally he'd run across rare animals with magic—there was something very disconcerting about seeing a monkey light up a palm leaf to distract a merchant from his wares—but *centaurs*? Impossible.

"So what's your history, Steward?"

Adrian jumped, not expecting the question. He'd thought she'd fallen asleep. Adrian had never met anyone who could fall asleep as fast as Sarka. It seemed as if the moment she put her mind to it, she was out.

"No history. I'm a servant." Adrian shrugged. His response earned a laugh as Sarka opened her eyes.

"Come on, give me some credit. You looked like you were about to tack up your horse and ride back to Madiar *tonight*. I've had lovers less loyal!"

"I owe him a lot, and it's not like that," Adrian clarified quickly, his exasperation plain as he sat down on the charpai to repack his saddle bags. The wicker creaked under his weight.

Sarka rolled over and looked at him expectantly. As soon as Adrian had started taking male lovers, the rumors had started. Rumors that, Adrian noted, were careful never to reach the Shah's prudish ears.

"Come on. I've got almost fifteen hundred years of history for you to pick at. The least you can do is tell me how a servant boy became best friends with a crown prince—or shahzade, or whatever in Alhanem the word you people use is."

"His father abused my mother. Eventually it wasn't enough to hold her life and comfort in his hands. Mansur made sure she knew exactly how tenuous my life was too. That's how I ended up meeting our present shah. Pretty sure I just ended up being a bone to pick between them in their constant power struggle."

"It sounds like you should resent him, then," Sarka pointed out, perhaps fairly. There had been plenty to hold against Merikh over the past decade.

Adrian shook his head. "The Shah made sure I learned how to read, how to write. I...well, we were the only two children in the palace on a regular basis. I think he needed a friend. So I got an education and his trust. All I had to do was help him hobble to the infirmary whenever his tongue got him in trouble with Mansur. Which was often."

Sarka laughed. "I can only imagine."

Adrian shook his head and shifted uncomfortably on his woven bed. In the past few minutes, they'd said more to each other than they had the whole trip thus far.

"What makes you ask? You've been content to be quiet, then we hear the Shah might be gravely wounded, and suddenly you're conversational," Adrian asked.

"I suppose I'm trying to find a reason not to go celebrate."

"He's your ally!" Adrian snapped, trying not to raise his voice.

"He's got Uduak's eyes. You can't imagine how strange it is to see in a Yahidah. That man is a slap in the face to everything we've all suffered through for nine hundred years. Uduak's heirs have built up a godsdamned *dynasty* while I balanced rocks to kill time. Ruya looks at him and sees our savior, as if he's a portent of our bright future." Sarka scoffed and then propped herself up on her elbows to look at Adrian better. "But if I could shape time, I'd go back and stop all of this from happening. In a fair world, your master would never exist."

She reclined back on her bed and shut her eyes. Sarka moved to plant her back firmly against the wall. It was clear she expected her words to be the final statements on the matter.

Unbelievable. Adrian yanked the thin blanket from the foot of the bed and tried to get comfortable. There were plenty of vices in his master, and Adrian could understand many reasons for wanting Merikh dead. But Sarka's were reasons he couldn't fathom. A unified Shai'Khal had benefited thousands, no, millions of people. A few dozen Pantheon priestesses and champions being stuck on an island for a few hundred years was a small price to pay for the protection and stability of the empire.

Just leave it be, he tried to convince himself unsuccessfully. Adrian tossed the blanket aside and left the room. There was a bottle of araq in the tavern calling his name.

CHAPTER 22

7TH OF VINDITH, FIRST HARVEST, 902 UNIFIED AGE
MADIAR, RAUDHAH PROVINCE

Mornings were Ruya's favorite time of day. The slow waking to dawn's light, the reassuring heat of the sun were reminders that she was no longer on Ikharon's island. She spoke with Ikharon in her dreams, told him of all she'd seen in Shai'Khal. Whether they were purely dreams or if Amefi, the goddess of dreams, had enough power to influence and speak through them, Ruya couldn't tell. She could only hope that her dreams were more than what they seemed.

Ruya sat up slowly, stretching languidly and yawning before slipping her legs over the bed. She stood—or tried to. The bed behind her shifted, and large hands grabbed her waist, pulling her back down to the bed.

"You always leave too early, woman. Let me sleep," her companion muttered as he moved closer to her.

Ruya laughed. "You can't sleep alone?"

"Not here. Always need someone to keep me safe. Either a witness or an extra body for the Shah to have to dispose of. You, Priestess, are my well-endowed shield."

"You worry too much. No one thinks you had Merikh or your father shot. Now let go. I'm starving." Ruya batted Rashad's hand away.

The duq let go of her with a reluctant sigh. "You know, they have these people here called 'servants,' and they bring you food. In bed, even. I heard you sorceresses have enough magic that you could hit those summons bells without getting up," Rashad muttered as Ruya got off the bed unhindered.

She leaned down and picked up her clothes off the ground. "Magic shouldn't enable laziness. Besides, I enjoy the bustle of the kitchens. You should join me," Ruya said as she straightened up.

"Eat in the kitchens? With the servants? Next you'll be saying I ought to give them a spot at my table or a drink from my cup." Rashad stifled a yawn as he stretched, then adjusted the blanket over himself. Ruya grabbed his riding boot and tossed it at his chest. The thud was louder than she expected, and Ruya jumped.

"Come on, get up." Ruya stifled her laughter with her hand.

"Gods damn, Ruya!" Rashad snapped, rubbing his chest as he sat up and then tossed the shoe right back at her,. "A priestess ought to know her place. A nobleman doesn't have to take this kind of abuse." His indignation was half-hearted.

Ruya smiled coyly. "You don't *have* to, but then you should probably get out of my bed."

He sighed before rather dramatically tossing off the blanket and hauling himself out of bed.

Ruya laughed again. "Are you this puerile with all your women?"

"Only the old ones," he teased as he crossed the room. Rashad leaned down and kissed her before gathering his clothes.

Ruya shook her head, smiling a little to herself. He was arrogant, and only some of that ego was justified. But he was attentive, and he did try, which was more than she could say about some of her previous lovers.

"You're returning to Rajibad soon, correct? Tomorrow?" Ruya asked as she watched Rashad dress. He shrugged before pulling on his kameez.

"Whenever strikes the Shah's fancy. For *some* reason, Hasad and my mother were already allowed to start back with the horses, alongside Duq Alaziz and the Neredi retinue. My father insists..." Rashad hesitated as he pulled on his salwar. "...that it has nothing to do with the Shah. He's been meeting with Kontess Maliha a great deal. I remain unconvinced."

"I'll speak with Merikh this morning, see if we can get you on your way home."

"You have a meeting?"

"No," Ruya said, shrugging and pulling on a clean abaya, "but that's never stopped me before. Besides, they've had him holed up in the royal suite now for what, almost a week? I'm sure he's itching to see different faces. For some reason, I doubt he's as content in bed as you are."

Rashad walked over to her, placed his hands on her arms, and rubbed them gently, betraying his concern.

"Don't push. He has cause to be irritable."

"Don't do that."

"What?" Rashad took his hands off of her.

Ruya shook her head and smiled. "Not that, that was fine. *Worry.* You'll put lines on that pretty face of yours, and then *what* will you do?" Ruya reached up and patted his cheek before she turned away and headed out of her suite.

The kitchen bustled with life. Ruya's presence went mostly unnoticed; the servants were quite adjusted to her daily morning appearance. The first few days, Ruya had caused quite a disturbance. Servants had tried to look after her or gave her an excessively wide berth. But now? Ruya was met with smiles and happily offered a seat at the staff dining tables. Normally, Ruya was happy to sit for a few hours and speak to anyone who would listen, but today she had no intention of eating breakfast with the servants. Ruya spotted the telltale tray of fruits and eggs, ornately put together and undoubtedly bound for the royal suite. Carefully, she picked her way through the kitchen and sidled up beside the servant.

"Mind if I join you, Gyamfi?" she asked, touching his arm briefly to get his attention.

"I'm just taking this to the royal suite. I'll only be a moment..." he said, misunderstanding her intentions.

Ruya smiled. "Perfect, that's where I'm heading. Surely there's enough there that I can steal a small breakfast."

He glanced down at the try and then back to Ruya. "Undoubtedly. The Shah is eating less than normal..."

"Well, maybe Loralee and I can coax a little extra in him this morning."

Gyamfi regarded her skeptically. Ruya had every intention of plying Merikh with food, though not excessively. The man had survived this long perfectly well. It seemed as if the food issue had been an ongoing clash between him and the kitchen for years. He wasn't about to keel over dead from it today.

Ruya steered the conversation away from Merikh as they walked, instead asking Gyamfi about his sister. The woman was quite sick. Use of the royal healers was a perk of living and working within the palace. A perk extended to the families. Unfortunately for Gyamfi's sister, the healers were quite occupied with guards. The riot and assassination attempt had led to more unrest throughout Madiar's districts, particularly outer Hock. It meant plenty of guards injured, making for long days for the healers. After the Shah, the guards were highest priority.

"If there is anything I can do, please tell me," Ruya said as they reached the royal suite.

Gyamfi nodded, about to knock on the door when Ruya took the tray from him. "I can handle it from here."

Gyamfi bowed and left her at the door. Ruya could feel two souls on the other side. Loralee's was farther away. Ruya wondered if the Khanum was still in bed. Ruya knocked on the door once before trying the knob. It gave easily under her fingers, and no ice formed as she pushed open the door.

A few enchanted lamps compensated for the soft morning light. Merikh sat at his desk, his left arm resting on the smooth wood to stabilize his shoulder. He looked tired. There were dark shadows under his eyes. Ruya smiled to hide her frown. She could feel the healing magic in the ointment under his bandages, which were undoubtedly making him feel ill.

"Since when does breakfast fall under the duties of a priestess?" Merikh asked quietly. He didn't look up from the book he was reading. Loralee's soul hadn't moved, confirming she was still asleep.

"Not a duty. I assumed I'd need an excuse to come visit other than merely being friendly."

Ruya placed the platter down on the coffee table. It still bore the scar from when Merikh had hooked her hand to it with his dagger, but the divan was new. She sat down in one of the chairs and helped herself to a grape.

"I presume you have a more important reason than simply being 'friendly' for intruding this early?"

Ruya shrugged. "Yes, but that can wait until after breakfast. As can your book. How's your side?"

The chill that shuddered through the room might have suggested she'd asked something horribly personal.

"What are you here for, Ruya?"

The chill, or perhaps their voices, caused the soul nearby to stir. Merikh let the question drop as he reached for his sling nearby. Carefully, he slipped it over his arm, wincing as he pulled the back of the sling over his neck. It was on for but a moment before the bedroom door opened and Loralee walked out.

The Khanum looked pitiable. Her dark eyes were swollen from sleep, and the dark circles around them mirrored her husband's. Clearly, neither of them were sleeping well. Loralee had tried to hide it. She'd smoothed her hair and made herself mostly presentable before coming out. But she couldn't hide the weariness on her shoulders, nor the palpable tension between her and Merikh.

"Ruya, what brings you here this morning?" Loralee asked, crossing the room to sit down on the divan across from Ruya.

"I wanted to check in and see how my favorite royal couple is faring."

Ruya's words earned a forced smile from Loralee. The Khanum's eyes betrayed her worries. "The Shah is recovering well," Loralee said, though Ruya doubted her sincerity. Merikh hadn't left the royal suite since the morning he was shot. Loralee and Nikias kept an alternating schedule watching him. That hardly spoke of a man healing well.

"Wonderful!"

Ruya steered the conversation with Loralee to more light-hearted places, every so often trying to engage Merikh in the conversation and failing miserably. The man was desperate to be left alone. Ruya wondered if the constant proximity to Loralee caused as much stress as the healing magic. Anyone who spent even a few minutes around him could see how inherently solitary a person he was. When Loralee stopped picking at the tray, Ruya leaned forward.

"My dear, you look like you could use a break. When was the last time you went to the barns and rode?" Frankly, Ruya couldn't understand the Yahidah fascination with horses, but it was adorable to watch.

"Since before the wedding. Nikias is being worn to the bone right now. I'm not calling on him early." Loralee glanced over her shoulder and shot Merikh a very pointed look. Merikh was lost in the pages of a report and missed Loralee's glare. Ruya reached across the table and took Loralee's hand.

"Go and look after yourself. You're no good to anyone feeling this way. Least of all him." Ruya glanced over at Merikh, who was conspicuously ignoring them.

"He can't be left alone. He's infuriatingly stubborn about taking it easy. I—"

"I'm here, aren't I?" Ruya said. "I have nothing pressing this morning. Only two other people know I'm here. Neither of them are prone to rumors. Go ride. I'm sure I can keep him compliant. I have a little more experience than you do." Ruya winked, and Loralee finally cracked a genuine smile. Ruya leaned back and let go of Loralee's hand.

The Khanum stood and walked back into the bedroom to change into her riding clothes. When Loralee reemerged, she already looked less stressed. Loralee mouthed 'thank you' at Ruya before she left the suite. With the khanum gone, Ruya let out an exaggerated sigh of relief.

"You can take the sling off now. I won't tell anyone."

"What do you want, Ruya?" Merikh demanded, his voice rising just a touch, as his patience had clearly run its course.

"Scribes, if you can spare them. I respectfully kept religion out of the wedding as best I could, and I tried not to proselytize too much to your nobles while they were here. Simply was friendly. But several have left or are leaving soon, and I'd like to send Pantheon scrolls with them."

Papers rustled on his desk, and after a frustrated moment, Merikh yanked the sling off, wincing again as he did so, before finding the correct papers.

"You want copies of these to send with everyone?" he asked, his tone careful as he began to read it.

"Yes. I promise it's nothing you'll disagree with," Ruya assured him. She'd been working on it carefully since Sarka left, consulting one of the scholars in the archives and several of Nikias's lower council of viziers.

"*Your Shahanshah, our Pantheon Prophet*? No." Merikh put the paper down firmly and turned to look at her. "I can't maintain a neutral stance if you're calling me your prophet. I won't allow you to claim my subservience."

"You can't maintain a neutral stance when your khanum was crowned by a Pantheon priestess," Ruya countered.

"She needed to be crowned by *someone*. Alcaeus certainly wouldn't have done so. If *I* had done so, it would have been an intolerable display of ego. Remove this"—Merikh tapped the paper with his finger—"or don't send it."

"I'll change it," Ruya acquiesced as she stood. She picked up the tray from the table and carried it over to Merikh's desk. Carefully, she pushed the clutter out of the way and placed the tray down. She said nothing as she retreated back to the coffee table.

"Is the rest all right?" she asked, waiting for him to finish reading it. When Merikh did, he lay the paper flat on the table before helping himself to a small piece of naan from the tray.

"You may send this, after changing the prophet comment. *But...*"

Ruya smiled a little in spite of the caveat.

"You can't send this unsolicited. For those who've already left, you must send intentions first and only send this with permission. Those remaining here, I expect you to give them the option to take this or leave it. There are royalists who may be willing to listen to you, but I do *not* want you harassing Rabb Boutros or Amir Olumide."

"Olumide's a royalist? Huh," Ruya said, leaning back against her seat. "I thought he was already a Pantheon supporter."

Merikh shook his head. "Not according to my sources."

"Well, mine *might* be more reliable." Ruya smiled and laughed as Merikh's eyes narrowed.

"What have you done?"

"Merely gained a little favor with Rashad. No harm done."

"*Gained a little favor*? Don't tell me you're..."

Ruya nodded innocently. "Sleeping with him? Yes. There's even been *sex.*"

Merikh looked rather adorable when disgusted, though Ruya imagined it was more the discussion of Rashad's love life than the sex itself that bothered the man. Merikh ran his hand over his face.

"Ruya, *stop* having sex with my nobles. You yourself said it months ago—it never ends well when priests and politicians lay together. Stop complicating matters."

"I don't think Rashad's particularly complicated. Some of his tastes perhaps require a little thinking and stretching, but—"

"Ruya!" Merikh snapped at her.

Ruya grinned, unable to keep herself from laughing. "Apologies, Shahanshah. I'll find someone else for an evening diversion. It would be easier, of course, if he wasn't here."

"The man is welcome to leave. The Khanum's investigation cleared the Attars of any wrongdoing days ago."

"Rashad seems to be under the impression he's not allowed to leave until Olumide does. And Olumide seems to be in no hurry to go after his wife, considering the great many meals he's shared with Maliha," Ruya said. She blinked in surprise when Merikh laughed. It was a rare, quiet sound, as if unpracticed. He promptly winced and reflexively grabbed at his left side.

"Perfect."

Ruya didn't press, certain she'd earn another lecture on priests and politics, but it had lightened the mood enough that Merikh began to pick at the tray beside him again, actually seeming interested in it for the first time. She sat in silence for a few moments before boredom got the better of her, and she stood up. There were changes to make, and she wanted to get on them.

"You're leaving?" Merikh sounded surprised as Ruya headed toward the door.

She stopped and smiled wryly. "I can stay if you'd rather?"

"No, by all means, you may leave."

"Your guards will keep you here, won't they? Ordered to protect you and make you rest?"

Merikh simply nodded, his frustration plain.

"You're clearly not dying. Loralee and Nikias are coddling you. I don't feel the need to. Besides, I have work to do. Can't have Rashad running off without a Pantheon scroll," Ruya said with a shrug. She turned and put her hand on the door handle, then hesitated. "You won't do anything...unfortunate? I'd hate to have Loralee upset with me if you *did* do something you shouldn't."

"*Go*, Ruya. I'm buried in papers here. What harm could possibly come to me?"

Ruya smiled mischievously and shrugged. "That entirely depends on how imaginative you can be." The doorknob turned unbidden under her fingers, and Ruya took the hint. She shut the door carefully behind her. As she retreated down the hallway, her steps were dogged by ice. Large spikes were slowly forming, a dangerous field for any other morning well-wishers to cross.

Amarante didn't approve of her time off. The mare needed daily, or almost daily, work. Having spent a week sitting in her stall and paddock meant a ride full of pouting, dourness, and the occasional half buck hop.

By the end of the ride, Loralee had earned a small amount of forgiveness—from her horse, at least. The mare's antics had drawn attention. Loralee could see the barn mistress watching from the rail. Sumiya Nazari, the ornery head trainer of the royal horses, was a woman with a formidable reputation. A woman Loralee had been rather reticent about meeting. She'd hoped the introduction would come from Merikh and her first evaluation ride would be...well, more impressive than today's. Loralee had been determined to make the best of her ride, pretending no one was watching. Easy enough, until it was over.

Loralee dismounted in the arena, rubbed Amarante's gray neck, then loosened the saddle cinch enough to let the mare breathe easier. After drawing the reins over Amarante's head, Loralee led her toward the gate. Sumiya opened it for her, a hard look on the older woman's face. She had to be at least seventy, with deep wrinkles around her lips and eyes.

"That mare needs more work," Sumiya commented as Loralee passed.

"She's had some time off," Loralee explained. "So have I."

The comments earned a disapproving *hmph*. "Well, that explains one of you. She, at least, has an excuse."

Loralee frowned and cleared her throat. "I don't believe we've been introduced—"

"Yeah, yeah, you're the Khanum. If you've got half a brain in your head, you know who I am. Move off it, throw your weight around somewhere else. I don't put up with your husband's shit," Sumiya barked, "and I sure don't have to put up with yours. Where in Alhanem is he, anyway? That little bay stud of his is driving me nuts."

Loralee shook her head in disbelief as the woman walked with her back to the barn. "Injured and recovering. The healers said—"

"*The healers said.* Piss-heads, the lot of them. He got shot in what, the shoulder?" Sumiya asked.

"And the side."

"Pfft, long way from the heart and the head. Not that there's much to hit in either place with that one, but still, the man needs to get back on his horses."

"I think I'll take the word of the healers over the suggestion of a horse trainer when it comes to the Shah's health," Loralee said, her tone cool.

Sumiya just scoffed it off and handed Loralee Amarante's halter. "You need to be here more often. My trainers don't have time to add your horse to their workload, not with those new Attar horses and Merikh's. Especially if he's not showing up here anytime soon."

"I'll do my best. I'd hate to disappoint you," Loralee muttered dryly as she pulled the saddle off.

Sumiya shook her head. "Who gives a piss if you disappoint me? Do right by this little one. She's got promise, and I want a decent line out of her. Your father breeds good horses, and I expect high things from this one if you don't ruin her with disuse."

"Do you talk to the Shah like this?" Loralee snapped, unable to hide her frustration. Merikh had been driving her insane with his inability to rest without pushing his injuries. The Ajir investigation into the assassination attempt was turning up frustratingly little, and Loralee felt more impotent than a new khanum ought to—in her mind, at least. Sumiya's harsh words were pressure Loralee didn't need.

"She does worse," one of the nearby grooms chimed in, undoubtedly seeing the irritation and frustration in Sumiya's newest victim.

"And he'll get worse when he finally drags his lazy, good-for-nothing..." Sumiya kept grumbling as she walked away from Loralee. An older trainer with a young horse acting out had caught Sumiya's eye.

Loralee looked back to Amarante, rolling her eyes before rubbing the mare's forelock. "Worse than Baba. Who'd have thought?" Loralee whispered. She finished taking off Amarante's tack, spending extra time to groom the mare. Loralee needed the time to relax and enjoy the moment. Sumiya's words had rubbed Loralee the wrong way. The last thing she needed was to return to the royal suite in a mood. Undoubtedly, Merikh would already be in one. He'd been left alone with Ruya now for hours. That was just asking for testiness.

With Amarante put away, Loralee returned to the palace and was back to receiving respectful deference from those she passed. As Loralee turned down the hall toward the royal suite, a flustered healer almost walked into her.

"Khanum! Your Majesty." The young woman bowed quickly. "I'm relieved to see you."

"What did he do?" Loralee asked, standing up on her tiptoes to look beyond the woman as if she might find answers there.

"The bandages, they need redoing. More salve and just a general checking in on the Shah's wounds. But...I can't get into the suite. The Shah isn't allowing anyone in."

Married a week, and I'm ready to kill him. Loralee tried to keep her frustration off her face. He wasn't the only one not sleeping well at night. Merikh was hardly a man who suffered alone. Oh, he remained quiet, suffering in silence as one expected of men. But while most of his emotions were held close to the vest, his irritation bled through the room and permeated everything. Loralee extended her hand. Palpable relief washed over the other woman as she handed Loralee her satchel.

"Thank you. There shouldn't be anything you can't handle, but if there is, please send for one of us." The healer bowed again and scurried away quickly, leaving Loralee surprised.

They must be busy if she won't even stay around to help. Loralee pursed her lips. Riots in the Hock District had popped up twice since Merikh's injury. Religious tensions were growing worse by the day. They needed something to try and balm tensions, but Loralee wasn't sure what. Extremist royalists and Pantheon supporters seemed to have an uneasy truce while fights broke out against Akhenic zealots, all stemming from whether or not the assassination attempt had been justified. Or whether Loralee was truly khanum or not. Nikias's intelligence reports were disheartening to read, though Nikias assured her they were usually full of doom and gloom, as Merikh had little care for good news, even at the best of times.

Impassible spikes protruded haphazardly from the frozen slab of ice that covered the corridor to the royal suite. Loralee stood between the two guards stationed at the mouth of the hallway, waiting. Merikh could feel her soul, she knew that. Loralee folded her arms under her bust and waited impatiently.

"How long has all this been here?" she asked, gesturing at the ice.

"Since the high priestess left, Khanum," the guard on her left explained.

Loralee stood in dismayed silence for a moment. "What?" Loralee snapped, her voice more shrill than she'd meant. *Gods damn you, Ruya.*

"The high priestess left...maybe ten minutes after you did. This has been here almost the entire time you've been out."

"Gods..." Loralee muttered in frustration. The last thing Merikh needed to be doing was this! Wasting energy and magic, and on what? A tantrum to prove he was still very much in control? It made the lead healer's offer of keeping Merikh in an opium fog extraordinarily tempting. And Ruya! How dare she! Loralee had every intention of delivering harsh words to the high priestess when this was done.

Goosebumps raised on her arms, and a shiver ran through her as Loralee began to feel the cold. It was another long moment before she noticed a small path, just wide enough for Loralee to walk down. Loralee tread slowly through the path melted for her, afraid of slipping and falling onto one of the many spikes. As she approached the door, it opened and then shut behind her.

Merikh sat at his desk, quill scratching away quickly at a letter. A messenger hawk rested on its perch nearby, preening its feathers. Merikh's left arm was on the armrest, the sling conspicuously hanging over the back of his chair.

"Where's Ruya?" Loralee asked sharply.

Merikh looked up from the letter. "She was here, and then the most novel thing happened—she *left*. I'd forgotten how comforting solitude is."

"I'm sure," Loralee said through gritted teeth. How was it possible to be this insufferable over an injury? Merikh wasn't stupid. He had to know this was all for his own good.

No, maybe he really is just stupid, Loralee thought in irritation. She stood by the door as he finished the letter, sealed it, and affixed it to the hawk. The bird nibbled at his finger for a moment before it alighted from its perch and flew out the open balcony.

"What was that?" Loralee asked.

Merikh frowned and leaned back in his seat. There appeared to be a dark spot on his shirt near his shoulder.

Whatever god might protect you, I hope that's wax and not blood, Loralee thought.

"News from the Royal Guards patrolling Ydeba. An Onyx Sword commander is stirring up trouble, antagonizing guards into fights and burning heretics. What's in the satchel?" he asked, changing the subject and regarding her suspiciously.

"A healer was waiting outside your little ice field, wasting time that could have been spent on the guards who have been injured keeping our city safe. I let her go back to work, which means I have the pleasure of changing your bandages."

"My bandages are fine," Merikh said flippantly as he turned back to the desk and picked up his quill again.

"Oh, really?" Loralee asked.

She crossed the room and poked his shoulder. Merikh groaned in pain and smacked her hand away. He looked about to snap at her when Loralee raised her finger in front of his face. The tip had blood on it.

There is a reason for your sling, Loralee thought. She had no idea what he'd managed to do. For all she knew, he'd gotten up and moved his chair the wrong way to aggravate his injury. The blood seemed to surprise him. Merikh glanced down and saw it leaking through on his white kameez.

"Don't touch me," Merikh ordered.

Loralee snorted in frustration. "Well, that will make this a lot harder."

"I'm not here to make your life easier."

"Obviously." Loralee rolled her eyes as she opened the satchel. She took a deep breath and let it out slowly. "Please don't make this difficult."

Merikh's chair squeaked against the stone floor as he pushed it away from the desk and stood. He took a step away from Loralee then carefully, awkwardly, pulled the kameez off. He winced, and Loralee frowned. A kaftan would have been easier. Ties and buttons wouldn't strain his side or shoulder so much when he dressed and undressed. Of course, Loralee hadn't yet tried to fight that battle with him—there were too many already. This was not the first week of marriage that she had been hoping for.

Loralee took the kameez from Merikh and placed it down on the desk before turning back to examine the bandages. The white bandage was quite red over his shoulder wound, and it yellowed away from it.

"It shouldn't still be bleeding like that," she muttered under her breath. In fact, she didn't think it should have been bleeding at all, but Loralee didn't know. She'd never had to see a wound heal so slowly before. Normally, healers could close wounds like Merikh's in an hour with little to no bruising. The itchiness left over from healing magic usually subsided a few hours after that. For days to go by and the wound to still weep? It made Loralee uneasy.

Merikh said nothing as she undid the bandage clips. Loralee hesitated when it came to unwrapping the bandages. Memories of their wedding night were still fresh. Now that Loralee was close to him, she could see the scar her fingers had touched. It curled over his shoulder from his back, fading into his collarbone. Merikh was tense, his breathing shallow. Combined with his aura, it left Loralee with the same tense feeling she'd had when her cousin Khaliq had given her a "tame" leopard for her fourteenth birthday. She wasn't sure who had the worse bite—the cat or Merikh.

Loralee kept her eyes on the bandage when she unwrapped it. Her fingers only brushed his skin by accident a few times, but each one was met with an irritated flinch or a sharp intake of breath. The temperature in the room dropped a little, but Loralee had become quite accustomed to that over the past week.

I'm trying, she thought as irritation grew in her chest. Most men would have been thrilled to have a beautiful woman doting on them, but Merikh acted as if Loralee's presence was unimaginable torture.

Once the wraps were off, Loralee turned back to the desk. She tried to ignore the breath of relief she heard from Merikh, and she took a deep breath of her own. He hadn't tried to hurt her yet. Not that Loralee felt that should be lauded as an accomplishment. She hadn't set off whatever she had on their wedding night. If that meant she had to listen to a few irritated breaths and sighs of relief, then Loralee supposed she was lucky.

The porcelain salve jar was cool to the touch when Loralee pulled it from the satchel and placed it down on the desk. Beside it, she placed the gauze and bandages she assumed she'd need before turning back to Merikh to assess his injuries. Her jaw almost hit the floor.

"How did you pull your stitches? You're supposed to be taking it easy!" she snapped in wide-eyed disbelief. Somehow, he'd torn the stitches wide open on his shoulder. Blood trickled from the wound almost as freshly as it had the day he'd received it. If he hadn't even *felt* the torn sutures, it meant the opium tinctures and the magic salves were doing their jobs, in spite of Merikh's best efforts to the contrary.

"I have no idea," he said, shrugging his good shoulder while glancing down at the bloody one with an innocent look.

Loralee turned back to the desk and dug through the satchel again to find needle, thread, and a small pair of shears. When she turned back to Merikh, he took half a step away from her and shot her a sidelong glance.

"Do you have any idea what you're doing?" he asked.

Loralee gaped at him for a moment. "I've been sewing since I was a child. I know *exactly* what I'm doing." Well, maybe not *exactly*, but she knew enough to be able to stitch him back together. How hard could it be to tie off a couple knots?

Golden eyes regarded her distrustfully, but Merikh said nothing when Loralee stepped up to him.

"Can you sit down?" she asked. His shoulder was at just the right height to be awkward to stitch. Instead of turning and grabbing the chair, Merikh very carefully leaned to the right and pulled the chair over to him before sitting down slowly.

"Please hold these," Loralee said as she handed him the needle and thread. He took them carefully, avoiding her fingers. Loralee glanced back toward the water basin. His wound needed cleaning to make sure she didn't accidentally snip his skin or miss an old stitch.

"That look hardly inspires," Merikh said warily.

"I just need something to clean the wound with."

Loralee jumped when she felt something cold in her left hand.

"Don't drop it," Merikh said, failing to hide the amusement in his voice or the hint of a lopsided smirk. Loralee raised her hand to see a small block of ice in her palm.

"Don't *do* that."

Her irritation was more forced than she wanted to admit. Loralee bit the inside of her lip and used the ice to wipe away the blood from the edges of the wound. The ice disappeared into thin air when she finished. Loralee glanced up briefly at Merikh before she began clipping off useless stitches. The thin blades were cold, but certainly no colder than the ice had been on his skin a moment ago. Nonetheless, he flinched when the blade slipped between knot and skin.

"Would you rather do this?" she asked, trying not to sound irritated and failing.

Merikh carefully took the shears from her without touching her hand. Loralee bit her lip again, and it was her turn to flinch as he snipped away the stitches. She could just imagine him catching skin and cutting himself. He didn't, however, and once the stitches were clipped, he handed her back the shears.

The next step was far more unpleasant. Loralee moved her hand to do it for him and was batted away. Merikh's jaw clenched as he carefully pulled the threads through his skin, drawing pus along with it. Loralee frowned, admittedly feeling sorry for him. She could imagine the threads felt uncomfortable to pull. With them out, she took back the needle and thread

Merikh had been holding in his left hand. He tensed and barely breathed as she stitched the wound shut. She tried to do it quickly, and when the last stitch was tied and thread cut, Loralee stepped away from him. Relief visibly washed over Merikh. Her pity turned to irritation again. He reacted the same way skittish horses did, and it was quickly becoming tiresome. Horses, at least, had the excuse of a language barrier.

"I need a better look at your side to make sure you didn't pull any of those stitches," Loralee said. She backed away enough for him to stand. Merikh drummed his fingers along the armrest, as if looking for an excuse to remain seated.

Just try it, she thought, her eyes narrowing. Evidently, he couldn't find one and gingerly stood from the chair.

"Thank you."

Loralee took a step to his side as Merikh moved his arm out of the way. The wound curved from his chest to his back, just under his ribs. Loralee stepped behind Merikh to check the last handful of stitches.

In hindsight, Loralee wished she'd had more control over her reaction. Normally, she was far more tactful—or tried to be—when it came to issues of appearance. No one liked to be reminded of their ugliness, and Loralee had met plenty of self-conscious Neredi soldiers. But Loralee hadn't expected to see *this*, and the gasp that left her lips was offensively audible. Loralee covered her mouth immediately and froze in place. Horror and sympathy replaced irritation, as she could understand his skittishness now.

The arrow wounds were nothing. Merikh's back was crisscrossed in uncountable thick, dark cords of scars. Everyone had heard the rumors of Mansur's brutal assault on Merikh. Now the brutality of Mansur's murder felt more justified. To do this to one's own *child*, regardless of age! It made Loralee's stomach turn to think of it.

"Get on with it," Merikh ordered tersely. His cold tone should have warned her away from the subject, but she didn't hear it.

"How..." Loralee gaped for a moment, utterly lost in his scars. *How did you survive this?* If the arrow wounds were anything to go off of, it was a genuine miracle he hadn't died. Without thinking, she reached out and touched the one that curled around his side, just above the arrow wound.

The temperature plummeted. A block of ice hit her chest, knocking her to the ground.

CHAPTER 23

7TH OF VINDITH, FIRST HARVEST, 902 UNIFIED AGE
MADIAR, RAUDHAH PROVINCE

"Merikh? *Merikh!*"

Ice spread over Loralee's chest and anchored her to the ground where she'd fallen. Merikh hadn't moved, as if frozen himself. He wasn't looking at her, or anything as far as Loralee could tell. There was that strange faraway look in his eyes again. Ice was forming in his hands. No, *around* them. Around his wrists, connecting his hands... Manacles?

She yelled his name again, wondering if she'd be better off calling for the guards.

Would they even come? Loralee shivered and tried to push herself up off the cold floor. The ice spread over the stone. She could understand now what happened to the divan. Loralee prayed that Merikh came to his senses before the frost on her kameez burned her skin black.

"Loralee?"

The ice disappeared. The faraway look was gone and replaced with confusion. Merikh had enough presence of mind to walk over to her, extending his left hand and carefully pulling her up off the floor.

"What in Alhanem was that?" Loralee shivered as the room began to warm.

Merikh let go of her hand and walked back to the chair, as if retracing his steps would bring clarity. He looked almost lost, until confusion was quickly replaced with cold anger.

"You just cannot leave it alone, can you? Constant prodding, as if the world is acquiescent to your amusement."

Loralee gaped at him while rage boiled up in her chest.

"How *dare* you! You could have killed me! Twice now," she shouted at him. "And somehow this is *my* fault?"

"If you hadn't pushed—"

"No!" Loralee snapped. "No. I apologize for my lack of tact, but you can't expect me to simply *know* the dangers to avoid when you refuse to tell me!"

Loralee could see Merikh begrudgingly agreed. He sat down heavily at the desk, as if there were a sudden weight on his shoulders. Anger waned, and a distracted look returned to his gold eyes.

"No," he muttered, "I suppose not."

Loralee rubbed her ribs, wincing as she found a sore spot. The impact would leave a bruise. Another one, thanks to her husband.

"I'm not doing this again. I want to know what happened. I want to know how I can help you get through this." She gestured at Merikh. "Because I'm not having a child with you if you might kill me or him for an accidental touch. And I'm quite done getting hurt by you."

"You haven't earned that right."

"Has anyone? *Can* anyone?" Loralee shook her head. "It doesn't matter. I'm your *wife.* You vowed to trust me, and I vowed to protect you. That includes keeping your secrets. But that doesn't mean I have to unnecessarily put myself at risk of death simply because you're uncomfortable letting someone through your walls. I refuse to fumble around in the dark trying to figure out what's safe and what's not. You wouldn't do that to one of your horses! Give me at *least* as much respect as Zahira."

Merikh said nothing. As tempted as Loralee was to fill the silence, she simply waited until Merikh made a move. Eventually, he leaned over to the desk and picked up the white-and-blue ceramic jar. She didn't offer to help as he opened it. A pale-green fog wrapped his finger as he touched the salve, the white cream turning slightly off color before he placed it on his shoulder wound, then his side. Merikh stood when he put the salve back on the desk and picked up the gauze.

"I require your assistance," he said quietly.

Loralee pursed her lips before reluctantly crossing the room. She was careful not to touch his fingers when she took the gauze and bandage roll from him.

"How do I know you won't try to kill me again?"

"I promise I won't."

I don't trust you. Loralee decided against saying it, certain her distrust was easily read in her eyes. She carefully placed the gauze against his skin and wrapped his side. His shoulder took more time to wrap. When she finished, Loralee stepped away and quickly began packing the satchel back up. She heard the door to the bedroom open. When Merikh returned, he had a clean kameez on.

"A kaftan would be easier on your arm," Loralee pointed out. She turned and grabbed the sling off the back of his seat. The gesture earned a grimace from her husband.

"There is a reason for the sling," Loralee said, her frustration mounting. "You need to wear it."

Merikh ignored her and sat down at his desk. He looked tired as he took a deep breath. He was steeling himself for something unpleasant. Merikh's hands gripped the armrests, pressing into the leather as if to remind himself of where he was. He wasn't looking at Loralee when he spoke.

"Her name was Rajiya. My father brought her back to Madiar from Ramshar when I was...twelve? She was only a few years older than I was, but she'd flowered into womanhood quite successfully by then. She basked in my father's attention for *years.* An impressive feat in and of itself, for Mansur's interests and desires changed faster than clouds in a gale. I hated her, naturally, this woman who strutted about the palace as if she were khanum. We both made each other miserable. Or as miserable as we could get away with, considering we both had some level of protection from Mansur.

"I believe she fancied herself a viable khanum. She became pregnant when I was eighteen. Poor woman thought my father would be *happy.* He proceeded to get her drunk and then threw her down a flight of stairs. I knew about the pregnancy. I made a point of being nearby when she told my father. So after he threw her down the stairs and she lay drunk, unconscious, with a very much *alive* child in her belly at the bottom, I offered to put an end to his little problem for a price. I wanted to leave on my patrol. He didn't want me out of his sight for that long. After all, without his close supervision, I might have gotten dangerous ideas in the provinces for a year, or called on you and returned to Madiar with an heir of my own like he did."

Loralee bit her lip as sympathy for Rajiya grew. There were more sides to this story than the one she was hearing. Any woman who depended on the whims of a man like Mansur had her sympathy. The mistress of a shah was a dangerous position to take, one Loralee doubted Rajiya had kept out of anything but enlightened self-interest. Dismissal from Mansur's bed, after all, would likely have meant death.

"He agreed. I aborted her child. Mansur believed I rotted her womb with my magic too, preventing her from getting pregnant again. Instead, I killed his seed. He was too drunk to notice anything."

"That was a kindness," Loralee said quietly.

Merikh laughed. "I was hoping Rajiya would end up pregnant and meet the same messy end my mother did. She either she never strayed from my father, or was far more careful with future pregnancies. It served its purpose either way. There was no longer a bastard to cause problems, and he let me leave for the provinces. What I hadn't counted on was how much a woman can care for her unborn child, even in the earliest stages of pregnancy."

Of course you didn't. Loralee had enough composure not to roll her eyes.

"And I had no idea what lies Mansur had fed her about her baby's death. But when I returned to Madiar, Rajiya had spent the year whispering in Mansur's ear all manner of conspiracies. I think in the end she hated both of us. I'm certain she hoped we'd kill each other. I made the mistake of underestimating those whispers, and I did what I always did. She threw her weight around, and I put her in her place with as much humiliation as possible. A year away from Madiar politics, and I walked blindly into a trap. Nikias warned me to be more careful and patient. I brushed it off until the Ajir came for me."

He waited, undoubtedly for the question he expected Loralee to ask. The one she *did* want to know the answer to: Why had he let them take him? Why hadn't he fought back? Clearly, he could have. Loralee let out a slow breath.

"If you'd tried to defend yourself, it would have been treason," Loralee thought aloud. "Your magic makes you unsympathetic. If you'd killed the Ajir and resisted, you would have had to run. It would have been war if you'd tried to enforce your claim on the throne. Who would have allied themselves with a necromancer shahzade who thought himself above the law? Not with others who might make a claim. Or Mansur could have remarried to try for a legitimate heir."

Merikh nodded once. "At sixteen, you might have been Shai'Khal's khanum and bearing the brunt of Mansur's frustrated impotence."

The thought made her skin crawl. Loralee couldn't remember meeting Mansur as a small girl, but his reputation was enough to make her shudder. The man had tortured his wife to death, thrown his mistress downstairs over a pregnancy, and tortured his own son on the request of that mistress. Loralee didn't care to imagine how short her life could have been, or how painful its end, if Merikh had made different choices that day.

"I doubt my comfort came into your calculations, but you have my thanks nonetheless," Loralee said as she turned and cleared a small space on the desk before she leaned against it. "Your father had the Ajir do that to your back?"

"No, he had them tie me to the whipping post in the training yard. Once a large enough audience gathered and he'd had enough of his wineskin, Mansur did this." Merikh gestured over his shoulder with one hand, the other clenched white against the armrest. "With a nine-tails. From what I've been told, he only stopped when Nikias convinced him I was going to die, and Rajiya agreed the punishment was enough. Mansur assumed I was cowed. I'm certain he believed that right up until the hour he died."

"Nine-tails?" Loralee asked hesitantly.

Merikh smiled bitterly, looking at her for the first time. "A whip favored by Thalassonian pirates and slavers. It's short and easy to use on a ship deck, with multiple lashes attached to a handle. Most have knots at the end. My father's, of course, had iron claws instead. You can see the damage such a whip can do. Even stumbling drunk, Mansur could quite easily do permanent harm in almost no time at all. It's efficient."

Loralee looked away, feeling sick to her stomach at the thought. She'd seen men whipped. Her father had ordered it on more than one occasion for disobedient soldiers and servants. He'd always used a bamboo cane. It left welts and bruises, not scars. Loralee had never seen it break skin. Or seen it used for more than a dozen lashes at a time.

"I'm sorry," Loralee said, though the words seemed hollow. She didn't know what to say.

Merikh shook his head and stood up, crossing the room quickly to the wash basin near the bathing room. There was frost on the pitcher when Merikh poured the water into the basin and scrubbed his hands. Reticently, Loralee straightened up off the desk and picked up the sling from the back of Merikh's chair. He was still scrubbing his hands when Loralee crossed the room to him. An idea came to her.

"I'm going to touch your arm," she said. Loralee gave him a moment's warning before she brushed his elbow. Normally, a touch would have made Merikh flinch. But with warning, he tolerated her touch.

"You need this to heal," Loralee said, presenting the sling to him. "Please. You've used injury to your advantage before, you can do it again regardless of how it stings your pride. Shai'Khal held its breath while you were in the infirmary as the Shahzade. I remember my mother's hushed conversations with nobles in our garden. Now, again, your nobles hold their breath. Duq Rashad came to me, terrified you'd have his head. He can't be the only nervous one. Put your pride aside, rest for a few days, then show these would-be assassins that they have no *idea* what depths of Alhanem you can summon for your justice."

Merikh dried his hands on the nearby towel. Loralee wasn't sure he'd heard a single word she'd said until he turned and carefully took the sling from her. She didn't offer to help as he pulled the sling on and winced; instead she crossed the room back to the satchel and pulled out a small glass vial. The contents were a dark brown, the vial full of opium tincture.

"Don't push it," Merikh told her, a firm edge to his voice. He'd followed her from the wash basin and took the tincture from her carefully. Merikh opened the satchel and placed the vial back inside.

"It'll help with the pain," Loralee pointed out, though her attempt proved futile.

"I spent months on tinctures, then on the pipe. I know well what it does to the mind. I have no desire to cripple mine. The pain is worth the clarity."

Part of her wanted to argue with him. She'd seen plenty of soldiers get better on opium. The healers wouldn't have offered it if they'd thought it hurt. *Then again, I can understand him not wishing to look anything like Rabb Mahdi,* Loralee thought, an unbidden picture of Merikh's sickly uncle coming to mind. She let the matter drop, as another question begged to be answered. Loralee braced herself before she asked.

"What happened to Rajiya?"

"I slit her groin to throat, created a mortoha from her corpse, and paraded her nakedness to court, where Mansur was entertaining petitions. Then, I used a djinn to help me destroy Mansur. You've seen the stain that was left of him once the djinn and mortoha were quite done with his corpse."

Loralee felt sick again. She walked away from Merikh toward the balcony. The doors opened ahead of her, and the breeze from the heat outside was welcome, even if the heat wasn't. The stone railing burned under her hands. She'd argued with her father that perhaps Merikh wasn't as cruel as Mansur, that there was a difference between the men. Now, she felt far less sure.

The back of her neck went cold, but pleasantly so, as a thin strip of ice coated it. Unlike before, this ice didn't feel threatening. The gesture was almost sweet.

"You look pale. If you are going to faint, you should come back inside," Merikh said from inside their suite.

"I'm not prone to doing so."

Merikh didn't belabor the point and left Loralee to her thoughts. She could understand the rivalry between a young man and the woman replacing his mother. She could understand his hatred for what Rajiya had aided in doing to his back. But debasing a corpse like that? It sat ill with Loralee. There were certain taboos one didn't break, even as a necromancer. For him to have trampled right over that for the sake of revenge? Not to mention, he'd rather conspicuously shifted the blame away from his father to the mistress, something Loralee wasn't entirely comfortable with.

The ice disappeared from Loralee's neck when she returned to the cool shade of the room. Merikh was once again reading reports. She felt as if she should say something, but the words escaped her. There was more to the story than what he'd told her; Loralee was certain of it. She *hoped* there was more. Merikh cleared his throat, looked to Loralee, and then extended one of the reports on his desk to her.

"If you need a moment to collect your thoughts, I believe Nikias should be meeting with his viziers at the moment. Labayu Maroun should look at this again. He's the treasury vizier, and these numbers don't look correct."

Loralee took the report from him and unfurled it.

"You're just looking for an excuse to be left alone again," she said.

"Partly, yes. You're not the only one who needs a moment with their thoughts."

The honesty lacked the frustration and irritation Merikh had treated her with for the past week. It was a refreshing change.

"Fine." Loralee rolled up the scroll again. "On the condition you promise me that you'll keep your sling on, and you'll rest. No more work—sit on the divan, read a book, *relax*. Let me handle this."

"The sling, I'll concede."

"That's not a promise." Loralee folded her arms across her chest and waited expectantly.

"I will keep the sling on, you have my word." Merikh spoke with reluctance. Loralee wasn't entirely sure she believed him. But he'd trusted her with his scars. Loralee had to at least try to return the favor.

The large vine-wrapped windows of the council chamber overlooked the main fountain of the palace gardens. A rectangular table sat in the center of the room, with a channel cut into the wood to let a sliding stone ferry paperwork from one side of the table to the other with ease. When Loralee arrived, the vizier council had already begun to disband. She passed off the scroll to the treasury vizier before letting the rest of the men and women filter from the room. Nikias remained seated, organizing the paperwork left with him. When the door shut behind the last vizier, Nikias gestured for Loralee to sit.

"You look like you have a great deal on your mind, Khanum. What can I do to help? I'm surprised to see you here."

Loralee sat down beside the grand vizier, her hands clasped firmly in her lap as she tried to settle on where to begin.

"You warned me when I arrived that Merikh doesn't want me here. Is...is that because of his father, or Rajiya?"

Nikias stopped what he was doing. "Mansur's mistress is an odd name for you to know. How did you come across it? He paraded her around Madiar, but I hadn't thought her important enough to be known in the provinces."

"Merikh told me."

"The Shah spoke to you about Rajiya?" Nikias looked dumbfounded. "How in world did that happen?"

"Vizier, if you speak of this to anyone, I promise it will be the last rumor you manipulate."

"Naturally."

Loralee looked away and fiddled with the ring on her finger. It was made up of four intertwining bands encircling several garnet stones. A Madiaran heirloom, though Loralee wondered if it was perhaps bad luck, considering the lifespans of most of the women who had worn it over the years.

"Merikh spoke to me of his scars. I redid his bandages today and saw the full extent of them on his back. I don't imagine he told me the whole story."

"Most likely not," Nikias said, leaning back in his chair.

"What *is* the whole story, Nikias? I just...he's attacked me twice. On accident!" Loralee added quickly as, to her surprise, Nikias looked furious. "When I touched his scars. He flinches every time I touch him. Did you know he has nightmares? I can always tell the morning after. It's the only time he touches me, and then he holds me as if his life depends on it. Until he wakes, of course, in which case the chasm between us returns."

Nikias ran a hand over his face, the anger from a moment ago replaced with resignation.

"Khanum, Mansur put the Shah in the infirmary for the first time when he was barely able to walk on his own. And I don't think either of us can

imagine the things he's seen looking into Alhanem. As far as your question..."
Nikias let out a slow breath. "I imagine there is a great deal of reticence on the
Shah's behalf regarding how you ended up here. After all, you're yet another
woman put into his life by his father. Even I don't know the extent of how
Rajiya tormented Merikh, but I can assure you based on what I do know that
the humiliation she received in death was fitting."

"You were there?" Loralee leaned forward in her seat.

Nikias nodded. "I'd rather not think about it, if it's all the same to you,
Khanum."

Loralee bit her lip. "Nikias, I know Merikh turned Rajiya into one of
the undead. That he let her and djinns loose to kill Mansur. I just..."

"It seems uneven odds, pitting a mere man against a sorcerer of
Merikh's strength? That it was a grotesque, disrespectful spectacle?"

"Yes," Loralee said, her voice heavy with relief that the grand vizier had
found the words she hadn't.

Nikias shook his head, a bitter look on his face. "You're not wrong. I'll
never forget the screams. But if you're looking for details, I won't give them to
you." Nikias cleared his throat and glanced down at his paperwork. "Is there
any other assistance I can offer?"

"I...I wish someone had informed me of this before I'd married the
Shah."

"Would it have changed your mind?" Nikias asked. His expression and
tone were kind, but Loralee didn't trust it.

"No. But I would have tread more carefully, would have done things
differently. Hopefully avoided all the bruises," Loralee said, her tone a little
more flippant and light-hearted toward the end to try and avoid the
seriousness of her thoughts.

Nikias frowned. "How badly has he hurt you?"

"It's nothing. Just a few bruises."

The look on Nikias's face reminded Loralee of her father. Concern and
anger both equal in the grand vizier's eyes, and this time she didn't doubt his
sincerity.

"Loralee, there are old khanum residences in the garden. If you would
feel safer there, I'll see to having your things moved at once."

Loralee hesitated for a moment, surprising herself as she considered the offer, then shook her head.

"No, thank you. I can't imagine this was easy for Merikh to tell me, and if I turn around and leave because of it, I doubt he'll ever trust me again. I just...I needed someone to talk to. It's been quite the week," Loralee admitted.

Nikias smiled reassuringly before collecting his papers. "Khanum, I'm certain your efforts are not going ignored. While I'm disturbed to hear about your injuries, I assure you that the Shah wouldn't speak to you about the whipping or Rajiya if he didn't believe you trustworthy and an intimate ally. And if you'll permit me to speak on your behalf to the Shah, I can guarantee both that he won't hurt you again and that your efforts will bear fruit."

Loralee fidgeted with her ring. Merikh had sent her to speak with Nikias. Surely he knew his vizier well enough to know this would be the outcome?

"Khanum, if you're worried I'll make things worse, I assure you I'll be subtle."

Loralee smiled politely. "Thank you, Nikias."

The grand vizier stood and bowed deeply.

"I live to serve."

Nikias left Loralee alone, shutting the door quietly behind him. She could hear the garden's many fountains burbling down below and songbirds' repetitive calls to each other. The familiar sounds grounded Loralee, helping to soothe her troubled mind. She'd known there would be challenges within her marriage, but now she felt as if she were wading through a mire, and she was completely unprepared for it.

Nikias's mood didn't need cold temperatures to announce itself. Merikh could feel it the moment the grand vizier walked through the door. The older man's posture was stiff, more upright, his movements quicker. The paperwork in the grand vizier's arms was dumped unceremoniously next to Merikh at his desk, a few of the top sheets sliding off and falling slowly to the ground.

"I take it there's something on your mind, Vizier?" Merikh asked, moving his chair back and turning to look at Nikias.

"Several. I've been debating where to start ever since I left the Khanum."

"She...apprised you of the situation?" Merikh said, choosing his words carefully. Sending her to Nikias immediately after their conversation was...well, Merikh had expected some repercussions from that. But if Merikh were honest with himself, it had been the easiest way to inform Nikias that something had happened. Better for him to hear about it from Loralee than for Merikh to unintentionally gloss over the situation.

"Of what 'situation,' Shahanshah?" Nikias said, playing dumb and becoming stone-faced. It was a tactic that had served him quite well under Mansur and against most nobles. One Merikh had grown up watching Nikias use and was hardly going to play into. Merikh shot Nikias a hard look.

"I'm not in any mood to play games, least of all with you."

"I'm simply being careful. And judging whether you're the man I thought you were, or if all my best intentions were wasted fighting against the inevitable boorish behavior bred into you."

Merikh rubbed his temple, shaking his head. "Nikias, I already have a headache. You're not helping. You wish to speak plainly. Do so. I've been expecting you."

"As you ask," Nikias said. He took a step away from the desk, took a deep breath, then turned to face Merikh again. "I never thought your wife would come to me after being hurt by you. At least, not physically. I know your tongue is cruel, and you forget exactly the depth of suffering it can cause—"

"I never hit—" Merikh said as he began to stand.

"Sit *down!*" Nikias snapped.

Merikh froze halfway out of the chair. Nikias hadn't raised his voice to him in...gods, eight years at least. Not since he was a teenager and the Shahzade. It was the first time Nikias had done so at his own life's peril. Merikh raised his right hand apologetically—his left one was bound by the sling—and sat back down.

"If I may?" Merikh asked.

Nikias nodded.

"I never meant to cause Loralee any harm."

"What a simple way to cast aside any and all responsibility for her bruises. I take it her injuries were her own fault? If only she just hadn't done that one little thing to upset you? Need I go on, or do you hear your father speaking as clearly as I do?"

The temperature dropped. Merikh's hand gripped the armrest rightly.

"I am not Mansur. Loralee touched my scars, and I wasn't here anymore. All I could see, all I could feel, was the day in the yard. When I could get my mind back here... The first time I don't know what happened. This time, my ice had her pinned to the floor. Nikias, I swear, I would never hit her."

Nikias scoffed. "Then you can't hold Mansur culpable for your back. He never hit you, after all, the whip did. Don't you *dare* give me excuses. That woman is already quick to do so and stand by your side despite your best attempts to push her away. I offered her the old khanum's residence. You can guess how she answered."

"She...turned down the offer?" Merikh asked, not meeting Nikias's gaze. There was a pit of shame growing in the center of his chest. She'd offered to sleep elsewhere the first night. Merikh wondered now if he'd chosen poorly by turning it down. That perhaps he'd been too proud, and now she was paying for it.

"She did, because she values the crumb of trust you threw at her today enough to forgive the bruises she had to take to get it. Loralee also seems rather dedicated to the vows she's taken, her duty to Shai'Khal, and by extension, you. Whether Duq Alaziz and Duqa Jasira have done their daughter any good by instilling such strong values in her remains to be seen."

Merikh leaned back into his seat and looked away. "I appreciate you speaking with her," Merikh said, unsure of what else to say. He wasn't his father. Mansur had beaten Aliyah for existing when he was drunk. Merikh had earned plenty of broken bones merely for looking at the man the wrong way. They were unfair injuries... Merikh frowned and ran his free hand over his face.

"Nikias, the results are the same but the place they're coming from are not. I promise. I don't want to hit her. It terrifies me to see how easily I lose myself. Twice in a lifetime would be bad enough. Twice in a week is inexcusable."

The grand vizier nodded. The man said nothing as he walked across the room and sat down at the coffee table. Merikh watched as Nikias poured himself a glass of water. The other man looked back to Merikh expectantly. Merikh took a deep breath and let it out slowly.

"It will not happen again, I promise." *That is going to take a lot of work,* Merikh thought. He'd been completely unable to prevent it from happening the first two times. Then again, Loralee had touched him when she'd approached with the sling. She'd been cautious, spoke softly, and given him warning. Now she knew about the scars, and she seemed to have every intention of avoiding them or giving him warning. Between the two of them, it might be a promise Merikh could keep.

"Good. Personal aspects aside, I hope you realize how close you've come to losing this war before it even started. You're weak right now. If Loralee wrote to her father that you'd hit her, Ruya would be crowning Duq Rashad as Loralee's consort within a month."

"I know."

"If I hear so much as a whisper that you've lost control again, it won't be Loralee writing Alaziz. I would see Rashad on the throne before I see a second Mansur."

"I expect no less of you," Merikh said, "but it won't happen again."

"I know. That's why I'm not writing Alaziz right now."

Merikh scoffed. "Of course."

"Now, if I may make another suggestion? You're not your father. That means I can trust you're not about to make a show of apologizing to the Khanum and mean nothing by it. I imagine both you and Loralee would like to sweep these incidents under the rug. That's fine, as long as you both learned from it. But if I may, I suggest you rest. Once you're able to ride again, then you two should do something nice together. Maybe learn to be friendly, even. That woman isn't your enemy. Don't turn her into one."

Merikh rubbed his temple again. That gnawing headache had only grown in strength. The pain in his arm was gone, but the healing magic that created that temporary relief brought on a whole different set of side effects.

"I appreciate your counsel."

There was silence for a moment as concern grew over Nikias's face. "Are you doing all right?"

Merikh laughed bitterly. "Fantastic. I hit my wife, endangered my birthright and my country, disappointed my mentor, and I did so all by accident. It's quite the list of accomplishments today."

The grand vizier did not miss the dripping sarcasm, nor the shame that it covered. He knew him too well.

One more little mistake and everything I've ever worked for is undone, Merikh thought. He knew he was better than this.

Nikias stood. He walked over to the papers that had fallen on the ground and picked them up carefully. The grand vizier then extended them to Merikh.

"You get to make mistakes. You don't get to repeat them. Make me proud. Now, are you up to looking these over, or should I come back later?" Nikias asked.

Merikh took the papers from him. "Let's get to work."

CHAPTER 24

23rd of Vindith, First Harvest, 902 Unified Age
Hatai, Raudhah Province

Hatai could be smelled before it was seen. The city lay at the edge of the Sarafi Desert, but unlike Madiar or Rajibad, the ruling rabbs of Hatai had never quite figured out a decent sewage system. As host to the Butchers Guild, and as the last bastion of Yahidah culture before Ydeba, the city's animals could be smelled miles away on a bad day.

With a strong west wind and relentless sun, today was not a good day. The city was unremarkable. The Tsukarai cities were clean, even if half of them stank of fish. Most Umbeah cities were religious enough to clean voraciously and pay their sweepers well. Even the corrupt northern cities found a purpose for their refuse so that it didn't build up in the streets as spectacularly as it did in Hatai. Rabb Ghazal had begged for funds from Madiar to clean up his city, but his request fell on deaf ears to no one's surprise.

Adrian envied Sarka, as she had stayed behind to set up camp at a bend in the Hiyashi River. In a city as large as Hatai, the chances of running into someone who could put her aura, the Aegalian sword she carried on her back, and her evasiveness together and realize she was Livinja's champion, was too high.

Immediately upon entering Hatai, Adrian's senses were assaulted by the noxiously sweet cloud of incense coming from the tall burners just behind the gate. Once through the cloud, to his left were several butchers. The foul smell of old and unsold wares seeped underneath the sweet incense. Adrian pulled his kufiyah across his mouth and nose to little avail. He followed the crowd to the bazaar to his first order of business. At one of the stalls, carved discreetly into the wood, was a temple supported by nine pillars. It was an old symbol of the Pantheon that had made a resurgence in friendly cities and with friendly merchants.

"New to Hatai?" the merchant asked as he piled dried orange slices and cinnamon sticks coated in fragrant oils onto a cloth. He folded the cloth and handed the bundle to Adrian, who immediately placed it up to his nose. The citrus scent temporarily blocked out the sewage stink.

"No, just been a long time. I'm looking to meet with a...like-minded scholar or archivist." Adrian cleared his throat and laid his hand on the carving, tapping it with his finger. "Any idea where I might find one?"

"Only public archive's the Temple. So unless you can talk your way around priests or have enough money to grease the rabb's pockets to get into his archives, you'll be chalk out of luck looking at anything firsthand. If you just want to talk to someone, there're a few taverns in the Jasmine District you might want to try. You'll need some better clothes, though."

The merchant looked askance at Adrian's travel-worn clothes. Adrian did have the pull to look at the rabb's archives, but if Merikh had wanted more of his nobles involved, he would have sent word ahead. Discretion was key. Adrian didn't have the money to create a convincing rich alter ego of Amon Ziyas the Scholar. A heavy coin purse always garnered extra attention. Adrian shook his head.

"How much do you know about the, uh, like-minded people here?" Adrian asked as he paid the man.

"Where are you from, stranger?"

"Akreh. It's a little farming town north of Rajibad," Adrian lied easily. The town was his usual go-to. The merchant laughed and nodded knowingly.

"Paranoid country folk. 'Like-minded folk' we call Pantheon supporters. Got plenty of them, even our own high priestess of Amefi." The merchant ducked down behind his table, and Adrian could hear him fishing around for something. When the man emerged again, he handed Adrian a small piece of paper.

"There's where we all meet. If you're quick, you might make the afternoon discussion."

Adrian nodded, thanked the merchant, and found a quiet place away from the bazaar to look over the paper. It had a small map, showing the way to the home where this "high priestess of Amefi" preached. Adrian had his doubts. There were plenty of priests and champions who had begun popping up after Sarka and Ruya had arrived in Shai'Khal, but none had been real.

If Sarka and Ruya are even real. At least this was a start. Adrian had nothing else to go on.

With the map folded back in his pocket and the scented cloth held up to his face, Adrian ventured from the spice market toward the house. He stopped at an inn to leave his gelding, unwilling to drag Majdy through the slums. The ground was wet, with what, he didn't know, but the slop would rot horse hooves given half a chance. Sumiya would murder him if he brought back an injured horse.

The ground squelched beneath Adrian's boots. Even the spice mix couldn't keep out the smell of entrails and excrement. It reminded him all too much of the desmoterion beneath the palace. Adrian tried to push the memories aside, glad when he caught sight of a house with the Pantheon Temple carved into the pediment above the doorway. He scraped the bottom of his boots on a nearby rock before stepping into the unlocked house.

To his surprise, no one stopped him or demanded proof of why he was there. The entryway was empty. Voices could be heard in a nearby room. Adrian followed the sound. The air grew smoky, and Adrian recognized the sound of bubbling and the scent of anise.

At the end of the hallway to Adrian's left was a large room. A crowd of people sat on pillows around several hookahs. They were tucked elbow to elbow, fitting as many people as possible. Each person looked dazed except for the woman standing nearby a makeshift altar. She looked quite clear-headed, not partaking in the hookah's delights. Half Umbeah, half Yahidah, the woman had dark skin, and her black hair fell in ribboned dreadlocks. Golden mabkharas burned frankincense on either side of her. On the altar were several statues of a genderless person in different poses.

"I'm afraid you're late. I'm not sure if there is a place for you," the woman said with a frown, glancing at the hookahs.

"I don't partake. It's fine," Adrian assured her.

She shook her head and straightened up. "No, come with me, we'll find a place for you. I'm sure I have another one I can set up." She approached

Adrian and took his hand, guiding him from the room. Golden bangles on her wrist jingled quietly as she pulled him along with her.

Akhenios, be kind, I don't have time for this, Adrian thought. His head was feeling foggy suddenly, his patience running low.

"How did you learn of us?" she asked, her voice smooth and gentle.

"From a spice merchant near the gate. I had hoped to speak with someone about the Pantheon," Adrian answered.

Alone in the hallway, she stopped them and turned Adrian's hand palm up. "What would you like to know?" she asked, studying his palm.

Great, a palm reader. Merikh doesn't pay me enough for this. Her grip tightened on his hand almost imperceptibly for a moment. *It's bad enough I have to deal with Sarka's shit. I don't need another crazy priestess poking and prodding at every damn thing.*

Then Adrian's eyes went wide with realization. A small flame burst to life in his hand. The woman let go hurriedly.

"Stay out of my head!" he yelled. "How *dare* you." Adrian's hand twitched toward his belt and khanjar.

The woman recoiled from him. She looked about to speak when someone from the hookah room stuck his head out.

"Everything okay?" the man asked.

"Perfectly fine," the priestess said, flashing him a saccharine smile. When the man retreated back into the room, the smile dropped.

"What do you want?" she snapped at Adrian. "You Ajir? Seem mighty friendly with the Shah." She fiddled nervously with one of her bracelets.

"I'm close enough to the Shah that if I wrote to inform him of a telepath in Hatai, you'd be hunted down by Royal Guards until they found you, regardless of how long it takes."

Telepaths were dangerous, the only sorcerers more distrusted than necromancers. They didn't simply read minds—they influenced thoughts, just as she had. A subtle push toward his work and who'd sent him. Telepaths were the only sorcerers confined to the sorcery schools, conscripted into royal service as necessary. And yet, few shahs had ever wanted such a weapon at their side. Those without magic were defenseless against telepathic influence, and even those with magic struggled to keep a good one out of their head. All too easy for a telepath vizier to turn from servant to master.

But the woman across from him wasn't that strong. The fact Adrian had been able to break free of her spoke to that. His magic was weak, his mental control barely enough to function as a sorcerer. Adrian assumed the hookahs were full of hash or opium, something to dull the mind of any sorcerers present to make them all the more susceptible to her influence.

"If?" she repeated hopefully. *"If* you wrote him?"

"I could just drag you in front of Sarka; I don't imagine she appreciates an impostor making them look less credible."

"Or you could get to the point," she demanded brusquely, her hands dropping to her sides, and she finally looked at him.

"Are you the only Pantheon preacher in Hatai?"

She shook her head. "Let me show you." She reached toward him.

"Try it again, and I'll burn you. Who else is here? Anyone *credible?*"

The telepath rolled her eyes. "Who knows? Is your 'champion' credible?" She cleared her throat when Adrian shot her a hard look. "There's the Opal Wings, Circle of Iron, and Waning Moons, all who have their own priests and priestesses preaching. And me, of course."

"The, uh, 'high priestess of Amefi'?"

"Well, who else is? Who's to say I'm not a valid high priestess for our god?"

"Probably Amefi, once they're free." Adrian straightened up from the wall. "You're playing a dangerous game, and if you want to survive, you might want to pick a different con. Or head north."

"I can keep the Swords off my back easily enough, thank you," she said, bristling at his recommendation.

"Suit yourself. Where can I find those factions?"

Adrian left the home with instructions to the three other Pantheon factions, caring little for the first two. Followers of Vindaram or Nadlious would be of little help, but Adrian prayed the Waning Moons might have an old connection remaining to the original priesthood. Something, *anything* to point them in a direction out of Hatai. Otherwise, this would be a frustrating end to a ridiculous mission. Adrian didn't care for going back to Madiar empty-handed.

The telepath's instructions led Adrian through Hatai's slums, past a cheap bazaar, and into slightly better housing. Houses that didn't have quite the same amount of ox blood running in the street. Unlike the telepath's convene, there were no overt Pantheon carvings on any doors or walls. After what felt like hours of searching, Adrian began to wonder if the woman had merely led him astray.

I can still send the Royal Guard after her, at least, he consoled himself. As light began to fade, Adrian turned and headed back down the road. He needed to return to the inn and see if maybe there were other clues left behind in Negasi's journal.

The orange glow from the setting sun cast a shadow on the adobe brick nearby that made Adrian stop dead in his tracks. Cautiously, he approached and ran a finger over the carving revealed by the half-light. Carved into the adobe stairwell was a small crescent moon, the rays from an Akhenic Sun overlapping it. He headed up the stairs to find another symbol like it on the rooftop. Wooden planks led across to another rooftop, and another. A few men and women passed Adrian, though that was hardly odd. Hatai wasn't the only city to have a convoluted rooftop walkway system. Frankly, Adrian was surprised there weren't more people who opted to use it instead of the muck-covered streets below. After a few minutes, and after backtracking twice, Adrian was left on a deserted rooftop with the last crescent-moon carving.

"Well, where in Alhanem do I go now?" he muttered under his breath, running a hand over his eyes. His good luck had run out. Exhaustion plagued him. Weeks in the Sarafi were tough, and a soft bed at the inn called to him. Adrian had just resolved to pick up the search again in the morning when he felt a hand on his shoulder and the sharp point of a knife on the side of his throat.

"Bayim, you're trespassing."

"Completely unintentionally, I promise," Adrian said quickly, raising his hands. While he hadn't worn the kameez with the scorpion emblem for the sake of secrecy, there was always a spare enchantment kept on him in his coin pouch. He could feel it growing cold.

"You looking for something?"

Adrian couldn't tell if the voice was a man or woman, it was muffled by a thick veil, and they were whispering.

"Waning Moons," Adrian admitted. "I need their help."

"And who are you?"

"Amon Ziyas, from Akreh. I have a journal, if you'll let me grab it, from one of the last of the Waning Moons before Unification. I was hoping for some clarification." Adrian gestured carefully toward his side.

The knife point relented, and the hand on his shoulder gave him a small shove away. Adrian happily put space between himself and the other person. Slowly, Adrian turned and began digging through his satchel. The figure now in front of Adrian was covered head to toe in dark brown, making it easy to blend in with the adobe and shadows at first glance. Adrian pulled the journal out carefully, showing it but not handing it over.

"Come on," the figure said as they turned away and hopped off the roof. Reluctantly, Adrian followed to the edge of the roof and was relieved to see a ledge below. He jumped, then hopped off the ledge after the dark figure. They walked through deserted alleys until Adrian felt the telltale aura of powerful magic. He hesitated momentarily as the other person kept walking. The magic wasn't from a person—it didn't have the pulsation that it should have from a life-form. It felt too consistent, too firm for that. An enchantment, then.

Not much I can do about that, Adrian thought as he began following his guide again.

They approached a door, the frame of which was covered in circular glyphs. The same unspeakable language as the glyphs on the Shah's shamshir and scrolls. The person raised their hand and removed their glove, the first hint that Adrian's companion was a man as he placed his ebony hand against the doorframe. The glyphs glowed a faint white before the enchantment temporarily disappeared. The door opened, and Adrian's guide hurried him inside.

Great Prophet, don't let this be the end of my journey, Adrian prayed as the door shut behind him. It would be all too easy to be mugged and left for dead now.

The hallway inside the house was bathed in pale, fluttering white light. Shadows danced across the walls and gave Adrian the distinct impression of impermanence. As if the doors and hallways might shift and move places at any moment. Yasu was the patron goddess of thieves and spies, of light and shadows, and such a place befit her worship.

A door appeared seemingly out of nowhere in front of Adrian. He followed his guide inside. Half a dozen people turned to look as they entered. Adrian shrank back a little. He loathed being outnumbered in a place like this. It was soaked in magic, and he wasn't confident that the scorpion was strong enough to keep him safe. Adrian wasn't a born scrapper either. He knew how to handle his khanjar well enough if pressed. He could probably throw a punch. But he'd never needed to. Hiding and avoiding conflict had always been the safest choice in the palace. After all, anyone who had ever decided to torment him had either been sons of nobles or young guard hopefuls. Adrian never stood a chance. He wouldn't stand much of one here either. He doubted his success when hiding from men and women who worshiped shadows.

"Who is this?" an Umbeah woman asked from across the room. She was sitting at a table with two others playing ganjifa.

"Amon Ziyas of Akreh. Says he's got an artifact from the old Waning Moons, and he wants some questions answered," said the man who'd escorted Adrian. The man crossed the room, removed his veil, and kissed the Umbeah woman. She shooed him away with forced irritation.

Adrian took the moment to pull the journal out again. He pointed to the stamp in the leather cover. It matched the moon carvings he'd found.

"Negasi Okafor was a fourth son of the Waning Moon. He kept this journal during the Unification War. It ends prematurely. I believe there's another one, and I hoped the Waning Moons here in Hatai could help me find it."

"Why?" the Umbeah woman asked.

"He writes about a device used by Akhenios against the Pantheon. I have interested patrons."

"May I?" she asked as she stood and walked over to him. Adrian handed her the book. She flipped through the pages carefully, not reading it but studying the book itself.

"My name is Hadiya. Tell me, how did you acquire this?"

"Bought it from a merchant in Madiar."

"Bought it from a thief more like." Hadiya flipped back to the front and bent the leather cover back a little. In the leather was a small stamp bearing the royal Madiaran seal. She'd known immediately what to look for.

"Does it matter?" Adrian asked warily.

"Maybe. I want to know how someone stole a book from the royal archive without getting caught immediately. I want to know how long it took them to get caught and how far the Royal Guard are behind you."

Adrian bit the inside of his lip. Naturally they were wary people. Adrian couldn't blame them for it. The last thing they needed was the attention of Royal Guards if they were men and women of unsavory means.

"Hadiya, may I speak with you privately?"

She nodded, handing Adrian the journal before leading him from the room. There was a door across the hall that Adrian hadn't noticed before. The room looked as if it were an office at one point, as there was a desk and a few chairs, but it was clearly used most often as a store room; crates and baskets took up most of the space. Hadiya grabbed two chairs, shoving a few crates out of the way to make space. She gestured for Adrian to sit down across from her.

"I need your word you won't say anything to anyone else," Adrian said as he sat down.

Hadiya nodded. "You have it."

"My patrons are Ruya, the high priestess of Ikharon; Sarka, the champion of Livinja; and the Shah."

"Horse shit. Try again."

Adrian dug into his satchel. The scorpion latched on to his finger. When Adrian removed his hand from the satchel, Hadiya inhaled sharply and instinctively pushed her chair back.

"You know, I ran into a few of you Ajir in Ramshar. Not sure if you're better or worse than a regular Red Guard. Least with a Red you know where they stand now that Merikh's the shah. You Ajir, on the other hand...about as trustworthy as a hyena at a kill."

"What brought you from Ramshar?" Adrian asked, genuinely surprised at the move.

Hadiya seemed happy to change the subject, for a coy smile came to her lips. "The Thief Lord willed it, so it happened."

"Now *that* is horse shit," Adrian said with a smile, trying not to roll his eyes. The Thief Lord was a complete fabrication as far as Adrian was concerned. A mythical figurehead all the gangs and nobles in Kuzen seemed to either blame or credit for the goings-on, depending on what saved their skins. Adrian put the scorpion back in the satchel.

"Will you help me? I don't mean you or yours any harm," Adrian insisted.

Hadiya took a deep breath, considering his question for a moment before nodding. "Yes, but on my terms. You leave that journal here for a few days, and I guarantee we'll have something by the third day."

"What will I owe you?" Adrian asked, digging for coins.

Hadiya smiled.

"Oh, more than you have on you, depending on what we find. If the Shah is sending Ajir, then he personally has a stake in this. I want pardons for my people. If you've ever seen the inside of a desmoterion, you'd ask for nothing less for something like this. But for now, I'll take a dozen silver akhenits to help grease palms during my search."

"Even that's more than I have on me," Adrian admitted. He pulled out six silver pieces, leaving two behind.

Hadiya shrugged. "Always figured the Shah was a stingy bastard," Hadiya said as she took the money and the journal from him.

Adrian shrugged. She was right, and more than she knew. Merikh would never pardon her people. Adrian could make honorless promises, though he tried to keep them far and few between. Merikh was rarely informed of any of the Ajir's dealings with the underbelly of society. Easier to give the Shah deniability and keep his hands from getting dirty. As long as Adrian got what he needed, he was happy to let Hadiya believe whatever she wanted to. The journal and coins disappeared into her abaya. Adrian barely saw her hand move before she stood and gestured for him to follow her out the door.

"You can find your way back to your inn on your own?" Hadiya asked.

"I'm sure. I can find my way back here in a few days too."

She smiled and shook her head. "No, we'll find you. Don't come back here. Even that little scorpion won't get you past the door. I don't want to deal with a dead Ajir on my hands."

Adrian nodded, then made his way back down the shadowy hallway to the street. A nearby building had a ladder to the rooftop. Adrian walked the rooftops in the moonlight to find his way back to the inn. At night, the smell of cooking helped stifle some of the day's rot, leaving Hatai decidedly more pleasant. Still, as Adrian looked to the east toward the Sarafi, he felt a pang of homesickness.

Only another month or so, Adrian assured himself.

CHAPTER 25

26TH OF VINDITH, FIRST HARVEST, 902 UNIFIED AGE
HATAI, RAUDHAH PROVINCE

The room at the Jade Jerboa had been Adrian's home for the past three days. He made a point of only leaving when absolutely necessary, preferring the perfumed room to the stink of Hatai. It gave him the perfect opportunity to mend his clothes, consult maps, and most importantly, consult with the other guests. Adrian and Sarka had only run into a handful of travelers along the way to the city, so he'd rarely had time to pick truth out of the rumors they gave him.

But over the last three days, Adrian had spent hours in the teahouse attached to the inn. The perk of a large city were official guards, heralds, and messengers. Men and women Adrian could ply with wine and araq to tell him news from Madiar. He'd spent an afternoon with a rather nervous—and handsy—messenger woman who had informed him that the Shah was healing slowly. That he had yet to make a public appearance after his injury, something that made the legates and nobles nervous. Loralee seemed to be holding the reins relatively well, but that would last only so long before seditious whispers would grow.

All that mattered to Adrian was confirmation that Merikh was alive. The Shah would handle his public image and appearance in due time, well before the Akhenics could use it as a reason to declare war against Loralee. After all, while the Umbeah disliked her, she was well-loved within Raudhah. And an inexperienced leader was always well-tolerated by the crime syndicates in the north.

As comfortable as the room was, and as comforting as the news brought to him had been, by the end of the third day, Adrian was restless. The sun burned gold on the horizon, and Hadiya had yet to make an appearance. He wasn't entirely certain what he'd do if she didn't show.

His nerves weren't warranted. As Adrian began packing up his bags, the latch for the window clicked and was followed by a soft thud. Adrian straightened up as Hadiya gave her kameez one firm tug back in place.

"You," she started firmly, pointing a slender finger at him, "were significantly less careful than I expected from an Ajir. And I, in turn, was less careful than I ought to have been when accepting this from you."

"What are you talking about?" Adrian asked quickly.

"You spoke with that tricky little information whore of Amefi's before finding your way to us. I just assumed you'd found the Moons and followed them, not that you'd been pointed."

"She didn't know I was coming to see you," Adrian clarified.

Hadiya shrugged. "No, but she knew you were interested in the other Pantheon factions. She got the comeuppance a fraud like her deserved, but now we've all got Onyx Swords on our tail."

"How do you know that has anything to do with me? I found that woman through a man in the spice market who wasn't being discreet. *Anyone* could have found her without much effort."

Hadiya scoffed. "It's a little too coincidental for an Ajir to show up and then suddenly all of us start running into problems. Maybe they did just get lucky. You knew she was a telepath, right? Better hope she didn't get anything out of your head. Her body looked pretty worked over, from what I heard."

Shit.

Hadiya saw the look in his eyes and let out a slow breath. "You best get out of Hatai tonight, without drawing any attention to yourself. The gates close in a few hours. Don't be on the wrong side of them."

Hadiya crossed the room and pulled a book from...somewhere. Adrian couldn't tell. The woman seemed to be able to bend light and cast shadows over anything she didn't want him getting a good look at. Hadiya placed it down on his bed.

"This is the only journal of Negasi Okafor we know of. As far as payment"—a letter appeared out of nowhere into her hand—"this will explain everything you need to know. Now, Amon, I sincerely hope to never see you again."

Hadiya disappeared back out the window before Adrian could even pick up the letter on the new journal. The old journal had been conspicuously not returned, though Adrian wasn't surprised by that. The letter had been sealed, but the wax had already been broken before Adrian opened it.

To the servant of our most illustrious Shahanshah,

Please ensure the Shah understands our aid in this matter, as well as our expected payment. Should you require the original Okafor journal back, it's resting safely in Ramshar.

Be certain that if payment falls short, I will have the Shah's uncle convey my displeasure.

TL

Adrian rolled his eyes, burned the note, and brushed the ashes from his palm on his salwar. He could count on one hand how many times the amir had seen the Shah. He knew Amir Navin rarely wrote, preferring to make one of the other city nobles send requests to the Shah. Even so, a letter from the amir would barely garner a second glance from Merikh. Particularly if it spoke of the "Thief Lord." The fact the fictional creation had chosen an Aegalian honorific was something Adrian knew rubbed Merikh the wrong way. If anything, the mere mention of it would have resulted in the letter immediately turning to dust.

Adrian placed the journal in his satchel and headed out from his room. Downstairs on the main floor was the inn's teahouse. Tonight it almost overflowed with people. Careful to avoid sticky fingers, Adrian waded between people toward the inn's main desk and plunked his key down.

"Don't tell me you're leaving without a meal?" the innkeeper, Teka, asked.

"I'm afraid so. Should be on my way."

"Not on an empty stomach. Come on."

Adrian tried protesting, but the larger man clamped his hands down on Adrian's shoulders, steering him toward a table in the corner.

"Come on, Amon, give me a few minutes, and you'll have the best lamb kebab you've ever had," Teka said before heading back toward the kitchen.

Adrian sighed. *It's probably better than anything Sarka's cooking,* he reasoned. What harm could an extra few minutes make? After all, it would seem all the more suspicious to sneak out. Hoping to keep to himself, Adrian pulled the Okafor journal from his satchel. His back was to the corner of the room, making it hard for anyone to peek over his shoulder.

> *The dragon is dead! Rumors abound that Uduak is*
> *soon to join him. Livinja be praised, the tide is turning.*
> *Maybe Chinara won't leave after all. The Flaming Legion is on*
> *its way. Without Uduak, Akhenios's army will flounder.*

Adrian frowned a little before skimming a few pages until he found another entry. It was scrawled quickly, or perhaps angrily.

> *Uduak's alive. Alive and not just denouncing gods*
> *anymore, but magic! His is gone, a pious sacrifice if you*
> *believe the rumors from the Akhenics. Damn him to*
> *Alhanem, I hope djinns take his soul. He has a new brand of*
> *fanatics, the Order of the Onyx Sword, and I don't know what*
> *rumors to believe. They killed Dayo. Not just killed her—these*
> *Onyx Swords stole her magic first. They killed a high*
> *priestess. I don't understand how that's even possible. How*
> *could Vindaram let that happen?*

"Interesting book?"

Adrian jumped and slammed the journal shut. A short woman was making herself comfortable across the table from him. She smiled brightly, her dark eyes clearly expecting an answer.

"I, uh, I hope it will be eventually," Adrian said with a good-natured chuckle to hide his nerves. He didn't want to linger on the journal at all, not with this stranger. He thought the book had been a fairly obvious clue he wasn't looking for company, but this woman seemed bound and determined for his attention.

Adrian tried to see if he could remember her, but he was certain she wasn't one of the "Lotus Flowers" who frequented the teahouse to drum up customers for the brothel down the road. She wasn't dressed scantily; her khalat coat was buttoned up right to her throat. It looked well cared for but road worn. The woman had perhaps come from money once, and she was still trying to keep up the pretense of higher birth. Even if she were a whore, she'd come to the wrong table for a customer. Adrian refrained from sleeping around on missions from the Shah, and she was the wrong gender.

"Is there something you need, bayan?" Adrian asked as Teka arrived with the lamb. As the platter was put down in front of Adrian, he used it as an excuse to hide the journal. When his hands emerged from his satchel, he gestured to his food. Maybe she was just in search of a free meal.

"You simply looked lonely, traveler. Where are you headed?" she asked as she brushed her black hair back behind her ear. It was cut short for a woman, and her gesture allowed gray hairs to betray her age.

"Sujin. You live in Hatai or heading somewhere?" Adrian asked, hoping to move the discussion away from his travels. He only had so many lies to feed this woman, and there was something unsettling about the way she'd come to him. The way she was looking at him felt off. She didn't answer him right away. Instead she shrugged off his question and grabbed a kebab. A disgusted look crossed her face when she bit into the meat. She spat it back onto the plate, right in the middle. Adrian tried to hide his own disgust and disappointment at the ruined meal.

"Traveling, and certainly not here for the food. Everything here tastes like manure. A whole city full of uncivilized creatures. What a blemish."

Adrian said nothing, hoping she'd get the hint and leave as he poked at a kebab not covered in spit.

"So," the woman said, leaning forward and drumming her fingers on the table, "you're off to Sujin, stopped in Hatai. That puts you coming from... Well, you're Yahidah so...Madiar?" Her look was too intent for her question to be anything but serious, even if her tone was friendly.

"Nope," Adrian said. "Where did you come from?"

"Tanga, originally. You can imagine how well-loved a woman of my complexion was there," she said with a self-deprecating laugh. Her skin was fair, somewhere between a full-blooded Tsukarai and Yahidah. Far too pale to be Umbeah. Her hair was nearly as straight as the Tsukarai.

"Tanga? Of all places. Born there or moved?" Adrian asked, leaning forward to fake interest.

She smiled brightly. "Born. Apologies, we've skipped straight through introductions. I'm Dalya of Tanga. And you?"

The pointed question was unavoidable now. Adrian leaned back a little, buying time with a chunk of kebab. The lamb was overcooked and tough but certainly didn't taste of manure. "Amon of Akreh. Same question, then, about your parents. How did they end up in Tanga?" Adrian asked.

She laughed. "You're a rather forward, curious fellow. And perhaps a might bit suspicious, probing as you are. You first, dear. Where in Cala is Akreh, of all places?"

"Middle of nowhere near Rajibad."

"Ah! Not far from Madiar, then. I guessed well enough at the start. You had me worried I'd lost my knack for accents."

"Closer to Rajibad than Madiar," Adrian clarified strongly before he cleared his throat. "I'm sorry, I don't mean to be rude, but I'd hoped for a quiet meal."

"Well, now it's exceeded expectations with a beautiful companion." Dalya winked before she turned and snapped her fingers to get Teka's attention. "Who do I need to kill around here for some araq and food that doesn't taste like wool or shit?"

From across the room, Teka half bowed. He muttered something before quickly retreating from the room. Dalya turned back to Adrian. She planted her elbow firmly on the table, her chin resting in the palm of her hand.

"So, what sends you to Sujin?"

She knew he was lying. Adrian was certain of it the longer she sat with him. She was asking questions Adrian had a feeling she knew the answer to. Or had suspicions about the answers. Knots were forming in his stomach as he realized exactly what he found unsettling about her. Mansur had taught the same interrogation techniques to Merikh. To ask questions that danced around the question one truly wanted to ask, and to never ask a question they didn't already have a suspected answer to. To give their prey enough rope to hang themselves on. Dalya wasn't a simple traveler; there was more to her than that.

I need to run.

"My cousin is getting married to a Tsukarai woman. I'm planning on surprising them with perfume, and I couldn't imagine a better place to find perfume than Hatai. What city would have more skilled perfumers than a city that reeks? Found a man to make a concoction with jasmine that smells like a desert storm. I hear rumors the Khanum wears jasmine. Seems to be the season for it."

The twitch in her pleasant expression at mention of the Khanum confirmed Adrian's fears. It was only a momentary drop of her facade, but it was enough.

He was in trouble.

"I suppose you're right. I'd never thought of it! Who'd you get it from? A woman can never have too many perfume bottles."

Shit.

Teka saved him. The innkeeper placed a tray of naan, hummus, and a pitcher of araq with a pitcher of water and ice between them. He took two glasses off the tray and placed them down in front of Adrian and Dalya. As Teka poured araq into the glass nearest Dalya, Adrian focused on his hand. With a great deal of effort, Adrian made the pitcher slip from Teka's hand and dump its contents into Dalya's lap. Teka began blathering apologies as he pulled a cloth from his apron and tried to help Dalya dry herself.

Dalya shoved his hand away. "You useless son of a goat!" she snarled.

The room went silent. Half a dozen other patrons from all across the room stood suddenly and converged on Teka. One of them threw the innkeeper to the floor. Adrian, seemingly forgotten, stayed frozen to his chair. Teka had been kind to him over the past three days.

Move, now.

Imperative thoughts always seemed to carry Merikh's voice. Adrian leapt to his feet, grabbed his things, and ducked out the door.

He froze in his tracks. At the hitching rail, nine horses were tied. All bore the white-and-yellow diamond sun sigil of Akhenios's Onyx Swords.

How did you find me here? Had she been following Hadiya? Or had Dalya simply gotten lucky? More importantly, where were the others who hadn't been in the tavern? Adrian had only counted seven inside. The two unaccounted for, Adrian guessed, were keeping an eye out here. Adrian hoped their orders were to simply follow him—if they even knew he was the target.

As Adrian passed in front of the horses, he carefully pulled the slip knots on each horse's ties. At the end of the rail, he deliberately stumbled. His flailing arms startled the horses, who, upon finding no resistance from their lines, began to back away from the hitching rail. Adrian hoped it would buy him enough time to get Majdy tacked up before anyone would confront him in the barn.

Adrian made it out of Hatai before he noticed the Onyx Swords following him. The scouts had found their horses and weren't far behind. He left the road quickly, heading south toward the river and Sarka's camp. Two Onyx Swords were out of Adrian's league to handle. The khanjar on Adrian's belt was no competition for their shamshirs. Even if he'd carried a sword, Adrian didn't have a soldier's training. He knew enough to look intimidating to brigands and highwaymen, but against a soldier, he'd do little more than dull their blade. Sarka, on the other hand, could surely handle a mere two Onyx Swords. Adrian had seen her sparring with a few of the guards back in Madiar. She was an impressive sight.

Adrian's tracks in the sand would be easy enough for the Onyx Swords to follow, and Adrian did little to try and hide them. Instead, he pushed Majdy hard enough that he'd have time to explain to Sarka what had happened and to prepare her camp for departure. As the sun dipped beneath the horizon, Adrian could see Sarka's camp and the small fire in front of her low tent. He picked up the pace and felt a small wave of relief at seeing Sarka in front of her fire.

"You're here! Did you find something?" Sarka asked as he approached.

Adrian nodded as he dismounted Majdy. "I did. I have the next journal. But we can talk later. Right now, we have a problem."

Sarka stood from the campfire, a distrustful and resigned look on her face. "What did you do?"

"I may have run afoul of a few Onyx Swords. Two were following me, probably going to be here any moment."

"You brought them here?" Sarka yelled. "Why didn't you lose them?"

"There are more than two of them in their contingent. If I lost them, they'd go back for their Fari commander. I assumed if they followed me out here, you'd..." Adrian drifted off.

Sarka was biting the inside of her cheek and shaking her head. "I'd dispose of them, is that what you're asking for? It'll take longer for the rest of them to follow if they're trying to figure out what set of tracks to follow out of Hatai? Is that what you're saying?"

"Yes."

"I thought you were Akhenic Faithful. Now you're having me kill people to be expedient. Merikh's taught you a few personal lessons, I see."

Sarka glanced at the fire, and the flames went out without smoking. She didn't speak to him again as she took down the tent. Adrian prepped the camel and her horse. He was halfway done when they heard hoofbeats approaching. Calmly, Sarka made for the edge of camp. She spoke loudly enough that Adrian could hear her.

"What can we do for you?"

"Our Fari commander would like to speak with you both."

"Your commander has no jurisdiction here. I don't answer to the Akhenic Temple."

Adrian didn't hear the Swords' response. He looked over his shoulder just in time to see blue-white flames. There was a painful flash of heat, and the Swords' horses squealed in panic as their riders turned into piles of ash. The flames disappeared as quickly as they'd appeared, and the horses tore away from camp. When Sarka turned back to Adrian, her eyes were white. As she approached, they slowly returned to brown.

"That what you wanted?" Sarka asked, returning to tying the last knots around the downed tent.

"How..." Adrian gaped, staring at the spot he imagined the ashes to have landed. In the blink of an eye, those men simply were no more. Sarka let out a small, mirthless laugh.

"I guess Ruya's hard work converting believers to our cause has helped. At my peak, I could do that to *dozens*. At Livinja's side? We'd scorch battlefields if we had to. Soldiers didn't pray to Livinja because they wanted prolonged war or because they loved the bloodshed. They prayed to her for protection. For the hope they'd survive a war with honor or die with it. That we'd *end* that war quickly, with their enemies obliterated. My goddess obliged often. And *those* men"—Sarka gestured back toward the ashes—"they know their history. What it means every time they put on that uniform. I watched countless champions and high priests die at their hands. I remember…" Sarka drifted off a little, and Adrian bit his lip.

"Dayo?"

"What?" Sarka blinked, her confusion plain.

Adrian pulled the journal out of his satchel. "I found the Waning Moons, and they found a new journal. Negasi mentions champions dying, a woman named Dayo. I think she was the champion of—"

"Vindaram," Sarka finished and nodded. "Yeah. She was a friend."

"I'm sorry."

"Not nearly as sorry as Akhenios will be. Vindaram *loved* Dayo, as much as a god can love their champion. When the gods are finally let loose, I guarantee Belara will be the strongest. Everyone wants vengeance. Now let me have a look at that journal and figure out where in this godsforsaken country we're off to next."

Adrian handed her the journal. Sarka tucked it into her belt before mounting her horse while Adrian loaded the tent on their camel. He mounted Majdy, and they headed into the sandstone outcrops of the Sarafi, keeping an eye on the stars and their ears open for horses. With the reins tucked behind the saddle horn and a small flame hovering above her, Sarka pulled the journal out and began reading. She flipped through the pages quickly before she found something worth focusing on.

"*'I spoke with a traveler from Duak today. He took the river north, on his way to Kal Natwen. An Akhenic, but he didn't suspect me, I don't think. I'm ashamed how well I can pass for one of them now. At least they talk to me. He saw Akhenios where the road meets the river, heading toward the Ghul's Teeth.'*"Sarka cleared her throat and looked up from the book to Adrian. "Ghul's Teeth?"

"It's six mountains in southern Katu. There's a pass, but it's supposedly haunted."

"Do you just have Shai'Khal memorized or…"

Adrian smiled a little and shook his head. "My mother was from Ydeba. I have cousins there, though I haven't seen them in years. Ziyadi rests in the shadow of the Ghul's Teeth. It's a good place to start. We can hold to the desert until it hugs the South Osmiti River, then follow it across the grasslands to Ziyadi."

Sarka closed the journal and tucked it into her saddlebag. "Let's hope we can do that without more Onyx Sword harassment."

"No one knows where we're going. I mean, for Akhenios's sake—sorry—we didn't even know. They'll lose us in the desert. Besides, they're Onyx Swords. I know they might have been something worth fearing in your day, but they're glorified temple guards. They're not trackers. So unless Akhenios guides them, we won't see them again." Adrian was trying to be reassuring, even as he felt doubts plaguing him.

Dalya had been no mere temple guard; Adrian was certain of it. He still hadn't shaken the disquiet her presence had caused. The way her guards had snapped to attention spoke of rigorous training. There had been talk of zealots in Ydeba, and Adrian worried these were exactly the sort of people who those rumors spoke of.

Adrian shook his head and tried to push the encounter from his thoughts. They had a long ride tonight, and Adrian didn't want to spend it worrying about what had happened to Teka and the Jade Jerboa.

CHAPTER 26

2ND OF BELITH, DRY SEASON, 902 UNIFIED AGE
MADIAR, RAUDHAH PROVINCE

Dawn light barely crept through the edges of the window curtains. It gave vague shapes to the bedroom furniture, just enough for Merikh to see by as he carefully slid out of bed. The mattress shifted, an irritated moan surfacing from the opposite side of the bed. Loralee clung to the blanket to ward off the morning's chill. Most mornings she slept in later than he did, giving him some peace and privacy before the constant procession of servants, viziers, and nobles that the rising sun would herald.

Merikh stood in front of his dresser for a moment, rubbing his shoulder gingerly. It'd been a month now since the attempt. The wound had closed, and dark bruises had replaced the henna covering his ribs and his shoulder. The healers had finally conceded the sling to be unnecessary, as was his confinement. His swordmaster, Emil, and Sumiya had both been given strict warnings from the healers not to allow him to train or ride. Instructions Sumiya protested yet reluctantly enforced. A month out of the saddle and no training left Merikh feeling more vulnerable than ever. Loralee's presence hardly helped. He had been vulnerable with her. She knew things about him now that only Nikias or Adrian did. It wasn't comforting.

Another soft groan of protest prompted Merikh to hurriedly pull his nightshirt off and get dressed, doing so as quietly and carefully as he could. Even after she'd seen his scars, he wasn't comfortable being around Loralee while shirtless. Loralee tread carefully around him, and as a result, she hadn't set off his memories again. Merikh hadn't put her into a position that she might do so.

That didn't mean she had stopped prodding. In fact, Loralee pushed and prodded his personal space and his walls almost constantly. They were little, innocuous gestures, such as standing close or fleetingly touching his hand. Each time they became less stressful, and as a result he could tolerate her touch without flinching nearly as much. Loralee seemed to have taken him on as her personal project. Merikh wasn't entirely certain whether he found her pursuit flattering or infuriating. He liked his walls where they were. His solitary existence had suited him perfectly comfortably before Loralee had appeared. Now, she stirred all manner of emotions and desires that he'd quite happily confined and ignored.

And yet, how could she not? Even Merikh had eyes. Loralee had…impeccable conformation. But he'd seen the deleterious effect Rajiya had on Mansur. Merikh refused to give Loralee the same pull over him simply because she had the eyes of Kamadhi and the hips of Hisahti.

Of course, that didn't mean Loralee had to be miserable—the opposite, in fact. Nikias's conversation had only reiterated the importance of Loralee's happiness. The Khanum had put in an exceptional effort in performing her duties. It was only fair that Merikh tried to make doing so less of a chore for her. Particularly if he wanted to keep Duq Alaziz and Amira Jin happy and their armies at home.

After Merikh was dressed, he turned back to the bed. Loralee was quite happily clinging to sleep, curled up tightly with her blankets against the morning chill.

"Loralee," Merikh said. It solicited no response. He sat down on the bed near her before he touched her shoulder gently. The touch earned him an irritated whine. He couldn't blame her. Normally, Merikh rose hours before she did. Today was no exception. He didn't need her awake for long, but he'd promised Nikias that he wouldn't leave this message in a note.

"Loralee, I need to speak with you for a moment." His voice was groggy, and he stifled a yawn with his hand.

"No, you don't," Loralee murmured sleepily, burying her face in her pillow stubbornly.

Merikh gave her shoulder another gentle squeeze. She acquiesced after a moment, sighing before rolling over.

"How early is it?" Loralee asked, squinting at him sleepily.

"A little before dawn."

Merikh's words were met with an unhappy groan. Loralee shut her eyes again. "What is it?"

"I spoke with the healers, and I had Nikias speak with Sumiya. I've arranged for us to take the mare herd out to the Kura this morning. Your company is requested." Required, in truth, but "requested" gave the illusion of politeness.

Loralee sat up in bed slowly, her brow furrowed in sleepy confusion. "What? No, you're not riding yet. The healers are still—"

"We've come to an arrangement."

Loralee looked at him skeptically, brushing her wild morning hair out of her eyes. "What arrangement? Forgive me if I speak to them on my own," Loralee said, her mistrust very obvious without her masks.

"I will only walk Zahira," Merikh said, his distaste for the painfully slow gait obvious. "Either you or a healer will inspect my wounds afterward to ensure nothing has torn open. It's not my favorite arrangement, but it gets me back on a horse. That, and the people of Madiar have yet to see their shah and khanum together. It is long overdue."

The Khanum didn't seemed convinced. Loralee frowned as she leaned forward, and to Merikh's surprise, she touched his face. He flinched away instinctively.

"Huh, not dreaming. Okay. We're not leaving now, are we?"

"No, I have a matter to attend to first."

"Thank the gods." Loralee flopped onto her pillow and pulled her blanket back over herself.

Once her eyes were shut, Merikh couldn't help but shake his head, and a small smile cracked his facade. He envied her ability to sleep. It eluded Merikh until exhaustion forced sleep upon him. The slightest morning light always drove it away quickly. Merikh straightened up off the bed. To his surprise, Loralee reached out from under the covers and caught his hand.

"Thank you," she said, her words muffled by her pillow.

Merikh gave her hand a small squeeze before pulling away and turning to the door. A black khalat hung from a hook beside it, and Merikh pulled the coat on. He crossed the room and passed the divan, heading to one of the servant entrances. While most mornings he would have waited for coffee here and seen to paperwork left over from the previous night, there was a far more pressing issue requiring the delicate shadows of dawn.

Flickering torchlight lit the desmoterion below the palace. The circuitous passageway from the royal suite to the desmoterion led into a large chamber. The ceilings were low, the walls covered in shelves and hooks. The far side of the room had a set of double doors. Nearby was a desk. The grand vizier sat at it with two steaming cups of coffee. Two guards dressed in all black stood by the doors. Grotesque masks covered their faces. It was a tad theatrical, but it was effective. The masks inspired terror in those living within the desmoterion. They brought comfort to the men and women who wore them. It was a face they could remove before they hugged their wives, husbands, and children. Not all of them took pleasure in their work. Many simply viewed it as a grim necessity to continue the Madiaran rule. Others were scholars hoping to discover something new that might help healers or necromancers with their work.

Merikh crossed the room and picked up the full cup of coffee off of Nikias's desk. He took a small sip, and the cup thudded against the desk when he put it down. The sound echoed off the room's walls.

"I spoke with the Khanum, as I promised. By midmorning, I imagine she'll be much more appreciative of the gesture," Merikh said, running a finger over the rim of the cup absentmindedly.

"Oh? I'd assumed she'd enjoy going out with the herd," Nikias said, frowning.

Merikh shook his head. "I'm sure she will, but in the morning Loralee prefers sleep above all else—even horses."

"Ah, well, Khanum's privilege, I suppose. Though I do remember a certain shahzade who used to enjoy languishing all hours of the morning in his bed," Nikias said before clearing his throat. He dunked his glass pen in the inkwell before making a note of the date on the paper.

"I have no idea what you are talking about," Merikh said innocently, looking away from Nikias. The large double doors opened, and two guards dragged a Yahidah man inside. The man's ankles were badly mangled. Hobbling was the initiation ritual for new residents of the palace desmoterion.

Escaping was far harder when one's only option was to crawl. Particularly when the halls were haunted just frequently enough by mortoha and ghuls to make crawling to freedom extremely tenuous, even when a guard patrol wasn't immediately present.

"Do we know his name?" Merikh asked.

"Hasn't given one that I find reliable," Nikias said as the guards strapped the man down onto the table in the center of the room. It didn't matter. Merikh had little faith they'd find anything of value from the man. After all, the man was already humming to himself and tapping his knuckles on the wood. The man was either mad, trained, or both.

"A candle, Nikias?" Merikh asked with an outstretched hand.

Nikias opened the desk drawer and pulled one out, lighting the wick with another already-lit candle on the writing desk before handing it over. Merikh crossed the room to the table and glanced at a stool underneath it. The stool slid quietly out. Ice coated the seat and became an impromptu candlestick. While there were plenty of tools hanging from the walls to inflict unimaginable amounts of pain and discomfort, Merikh preferred simple solutions for simple problems. The man before him would serve as a message. A very particular one.

The man switched from simply humming to muttering a worship song quietly. It would protect him about as much as the pendant hanging from his neck would—it bore the Akhenic Sun with a shamshir through it.

"You should have spent more time practicing your aim than your prayers," Merikh said as ice formed around a small spot on the metal pendant chain. The metal snapped with almost no effort when Merikh picked up the pendant.

"I shouldn't have been impatient, but we all have our vices, don't we? I thought I had an opportunity. Guess I didn't."

There was a slight tremor in the man's voice. It betrayed the fear lying beneath the surface.

"Clearly not. I would have thought the high inquisitor capable of finding a patient assassin in Madiar," Merikh said, his tone conversational as he turned the pendant over in his hands and watched the man's reaction. The assassin laughed, the sound echoing off the walls almost maniacally.

"The high inquisitor couldn't find sand in a desert."

On that we agree, Merikh thought. High Inquisitor Adunbi Bah had been promoted after the Priest Council purge, but what exactly the position of high inquisitor entailed seemed quite open for interpretation. High inquisitors of old had been pillars of the Akhenic faith. Adunbi appeared to be little more than a figurehead for the Onyx Swords, not a competent commander. A sentiment the assassin seemed to share, though whether this was genuine deprecation or an effort to throw suspicion away from the high inquisitor, Merikh wasn't certain.

Behind him, Nikias wrote down answers and observations. The assassin wouldn't survive this encounter, but everything he said would be compared with notes from the previous Fari commander and others who had been tortured before him. Reports from spies throughout Shai'Khal would be checked for any similarities to his answers.

"That's an odd sentiment for an Onyx Sword to keep," Merikh said.

The assassin looked as if a foul smell had just passed over him but said nothing. Merikh placed the pendant in the pocket of his khalat before moving the stool underneath the assassin's bare feet. The flame wasn't strong, but it didn't take much for concentrated heat to burn skin. It would become painful well before it blistered.

"Who hired you?" Merikh asked. He loathed to ask the question so plainly, but he didn't know enough about the Ydeban fanatics to ask about them without betraying how little he knew. General ignorance instead of specific ignorance was the better feint. Merikh had no doubt the assassination attempt was from the Akhenic Faithful. Pantheon fanatics had nothing to truly gain if an assassination attempt succeeded. It would only weaken their position.

The assassin tried to jerk his feet away from the heat unsuccessfully. "I *volunteered.* And others will follow me."

Ice coated the bottom of the assassin's feet, granting temporary relief that the man would soon learn to loathe.

"You volunteered on behalf of whom?" Merikh's tone remained conversational.

"All the Faithful. If the high priest finds himself bound, we're here to unbind him. If the high inquisitor won't protect the Temple, we will."

"I see you intended on staying in Madiar to fulfill that purpose." Merikh found it far too convenient that this man had stayed in Madiar. He had a death wish, one that Merikh would happily grant. No one who left one of these amulets before had survived. The servant had been executed. The Emani attackers decimated. The man before Merikh must have expected to die, yet he had run from the guards. Why had he come out of hiding and allowed himself to be caught?

"I was hoping for a shot at your whores. Just couldn't decide if I wanted the Yahidah or Tsukarai and whether to use my arrows or cock. Too late now, I guess. Although I might feel more cooperative with the sayida's tits in my face."

The ice disappeared from the man's feet; the rawness left behind by the cold would burn all the more painfully in a moment. Merikh pulled the pendant back out of his pocket and held it out in plain view for the assassin to see.

"A shamshir through the sun. I thought it sacrilegious at first, but my scholars found it in our old history books. The pendants of the first Onyx Swords, Akhenios's closest men."

"*The Sanctified Sun keeps Yasuan djinns at bay*, so we try."

Merikh smirked. "You count yourself worthy of such a task?"

The assassin shrugged, then groaned in pain as he twitched against his restraints. Merikh lifted his left hand, a showy gesture toward the man's feet. Green fog emanated from Merikh's fingertips, guiding the tortured man's eyes to his feet. They were red and raw until the fog touched them. Then the skin began to darken, and his toes and feet began to swell and blacken. It only took a moment before the necrosis completely covered his toes and slowly crawled down the man's feet. The fog disappeared, but the man's pained cries did not. Merikh waited patiently for the panicking man to calm down enough to let the Shah be heard.

"Aegalians call it 'frostbite.'" The word seemed exceptionally appropriate, though it felt a little odd on Merikh's tongue. "If your feet aren't amputated, the rot will kill you slowly. How many volunteers will replace you?"

The assassin inhaled sharply. "I don't know the high inquisitor's mind! She has many of us, and we will do what's necessary to save Shai'Khal!"

She? Merikh hung on the slipped word. Now he had both a name for the group trying to kill him and a title for the new player. A gender would narrow down their search a little too.

"Where?"

Merikh didn't receive an answer. The man was stubbornly humming again. Merikh took the stool and moved the candle to underneath the assassin's hand. The flame crackled and grazed the tortured man's hand before ice covered it.

By the time the assassin's hands matched his feet, Merikh had most of the answers he had been looking for. After a point, the man had simply burst into old songs, some of war and others of Akhenios. Songs that no longer echoed in the chamber once the assassin's tongue matched his hands.

"Have him removed and dumped at the Temple gates discreetly. Leave the pendant on him," Merikh ordered the Ajir guards. They bowed and began to unstrap the man from the table. Once the guards had left, Merikh finished his coffee and turned to Nikias.

"What do you know of the 'Sanctified Suns'?"

"Nothing," Nikias said honestly. "I've never heard the name before. But if he's quoting the Scrolls, then they're likely referenced in an ancient tome or two. I'll have a vizier look into it."

"Good. If they're the Ydeban fanatics I keep hearing about, then we finally have a name for them. Even if not, I want to know everything we can about them. I've received word about a Fari commander stirring up trouble in Ydeba. I wonder if that commander may be connected to this high inquisitor."

"Onyx Swords working with these Akhenic fanatics?" Nikias shook his head thoughtfully. "Not sure if that's a bigger problem to you or Alcaeus."

"Somehow, I doubt Alcaeus will consider handling these fanatics with a joint force," Merikh said with a smirk.

Nikias simply sighed and finished up his notes. "I'll send you anything pertinent once I've finished going over these," Nikias said, picking up the paperwork as he stood. "I'm sure I'll have these ready for you by the afternoon."

"Is there anyone else?" Merikh asked, looking toward the double doors that led to the cells.

Nikias shook his head. "Not for you. You and the Khanum have the hearts and minds of the common people to win."

Merikh nodded before leaving the room. Even with this bloodless torture, he had every desire to wash up and put on clean clothes that didn't smell of death.

Loralee's soul was still within the suite. When the door opened, Merikh saw her glance over the divan toward him before returning to breakfast. She said nothing, but even across the room, Merikh could feel her distaste. Between her stiff posture and narrowed eyes, that brief look had said it all. The morning was not going to go as smoothly as he had hoped. He tossed aside the black khalat to be washed before changing into a new salwar kameez. When he emerged from their bedroom, Loralee was still sitting at the divan.

"Who died?" she asked as Merikh crossed the room to scrub his hands in the wash basin.

"The would-be assassin."

"You caught him?" Loralee's voice rose in surprise. "I had ordered the Ajir to bring him in for a fair trial."

Merikh dried his hands and hung the towel again carefully before he turned to look at her. "Yes, you did. My orders outrank yours. I was unwilling to provide that man a platform for continued insurgency."

"Did he say who hired him?"

"Not entirely."

Loralee took a deep breath, smoothed an unseen wrinkle from her riding salwar, and refused to meet his gaze when she spoke again.

"I'm not comfortable with this. I wasn't on our wedding night, and I haven't been any time since. While I appreciate you haven't hidden this from me, it's not right. Surely there are better ways or other men who can do this for you."

"I will not ask the Ajir to commit acts I am unwilling to do myself. They have faith in that leadership. The moment I break that covenant is the moment I can no longer trust they'll always put their life on the line for mine. Regarding your discomfort…" Merikh hesitated for a moment, suddenly unable to find the words he wanted. "I wouldn't have you comfortable nor part of what happens below. But those men and women wouldn't waste a moment in committing unspeakable acts upon you. The man this morning said as much."

It wasn't the answer she wanted. Loralee took in a deep breath, as if steeling herself for an unpleasant answer to a reticent question.

"Do you enjoy it?" she asked.

Merikh blinked in surprise. It wasn't the question he'd expected, and it wasn't one he'd ever considered.

"Does it matter?"

"I wouldn't ask if it didn't." Loralee looked at him again, worry clear in her dark eyes.

"Do I enjoy it? What 'it' are you referring to?" He didn't give her a chance to answer the question. "If you mean the intrigue, finding the pieces they don't want me to find, yes. I enjoy the puzzle. If you mean the discovery of how the body works, of how my magic interacts with it, and the renewed realization that I have *much* left to learn, then yes to that as well. If you're asking if I find pleasure in their pain the way my father did…" Merikh's tone grew acerbic. "The answer is no. I don't care if they suffer or how they do so. I want answers. Sometimes they give those answers in life. Other times in death. Can you live with that?"

His words were met with a short, bitter laugh as Loralee stood.

"What choice do I have? If I asked you to stop, you wouldn't. You're the Shah. As you said, you outrank me."

Merikh said nothing, certain anything he said would either be false or would upset her or both. Loralee took a deep breath, let it out slowly, and walked to her mirror. She carefully twisted her braid and pinned it tight to the nape of her neck. With her hair pulled up, he could see the chain kusari underneath her kameez. It was thin armor that would do little against arrows, but if she were pulled from her horse, it would stop a khanjar or shamshir cut. Loralee grabbed the crimson-and-gold scarf off the nearby stand, folded it in half, and placed the crease along her forehead before pinning it under her chin. Once wrapped firmly around her head, she pinned the veil across, leaving only her eyes and the heavy kohl accenting them visible.

"You might not want your kufiyah," she said. "The people should see their shah. And please put on some armor; the Ajir will worry. I'll meet you at the barn."

Loralee's tone was unexpectedly and impressively cold. As she headed for the door, Merikh met her. When she turned to move around him, Merikh reluctantly caught her arm.

"Loralee..." He let go of her arm. "I...don't mean to upset you."

Her expression softened a little as she glanced down at her arm where his hand had been, surprised by his touch.

"It's one matter to know the Shah tortures men and women. It's another to know your husband, the man who sleeps at your side and will father your child, brutalizes them."

What a beautifully naive world Alaziz raised you in, Merikh thought. The duq had done her no favors by hoping to find a way to avoid the marriage instead of preparing her for it.

"I am what I am. I assure you, it isn't without reason. What I did today made Shai'Khal safer for you. Safer for our child."

Merikh saw her head tilt ever so slightly at the word *child.* Merikh usually referred to their future progeny as the shahzade. He'd chosen the word deliberately. Judging by how her eyes softened, his choice had paid off. Merikh stepped out of her way in case she still chose to leave. He crossed the room to grab his cuirass. Loralee waited silently by the door until Merikh was dressed to leave. The two walked in silence to the barn with a comfortable distance between them. Or at least, comfortable for Merikh.

The guards were ready with their horses, warming up while Merikh and Loralee saw to theirs. Sumiya, to Merikh's surprise, was nowhere to be found—busy with young horses, likely—and it left him unassailed as he saw to grooming Zahira. The bay mare hadn't forgiven him for neglecting her, though by the time she was saddled, her mood seemed far more amenable. His side twinged with pain as he mounted, an ardent reminder that all wasn't well yet with his wounds. But settled in the saddle, Merikh couldn't help the small smile that cracked his masks. It had been far too long.

The Kura was the lifeblood of Madiar. It flooded every monsoon. The large aquifer that lay under the city was all that allowed for Madiar to survive on the edge of the desert. Farms lay on the floodplain, and at one point they'd been enough to support the capital. But with its growth, the farms on the riverbank now did little more than cater to the rich. The rest of Madiar relied on trade for food and necessities, most of which came through Rajibad. The route to the river was always packed with merchants. Taking the royal horses out shut down commerce for a few hours, but the sight of it always brought happy crowds and made for equally happy horses. Today, the crowds were tempered by twice as many Royal Guards than what normally accompanied the herd. Ajir Captain Bashir was taking no chances today.

The herd of mares and foals were simple to control; the mares themselves easily followed the road and didn't push on the riders. Only the boldest foals snuck past the guards and stable hands to duck down alleys and sniff at the crowds, but they were quickly turned back by their mother's calls. Normally, Merikh's focus would have been entirely on the herd. But today, foals slipped past him. The pain in his side and shoulder ached with every step Zahira took. He coated the worst of his injuries in a thin layer of ice to numb the pain, helping his focus. Loralee, however, was a distraction he found impossible to ignore.

Peasants strained to touch Loralee's outstretched hand, to receive a smile and good wishes from their khanum. Merikh overheard Captain Bashir scolding her gently, repeatedly, telling her that she could be easily unhorsed by allowing such close interaction. It was a worry Loralee clearly didn't share, as she brushed hands with another veiled woman before dropping a few coins to the children who stepped forward from the crowd.

Behind the pommel of Loralee's saddle lay a flower a peasant must have given her. Merikh couldn't fathom the ease with which she interacted with the poor. There was a deep-seated empathy to the way she acted, which was undoubtedly a breath of fresh air for these people compared to their last khanum. Aliyah had always been distant. An untouchable beauty, to be looked at and admired from afar or else the illusion would shatter. Loralee was far more grounded. Of course, Abadan was a much kinder city to its nobles than Madiar or Ramshar.

Something darted in from of Zahira. Merikh pulled back gently on the reins.

"Whoa," he breathed. The mare stopped firmly. Merikh assumed it was a foal, until the guards fell upon him in a circle with shamshirs drawn. Zahira sidestepped, and Merikh could see a terrified child standing in front of his horse holding...flowers. Merikh moved his reins into his right hand, glanced at the guards, and gestured for them to back off. If even *he* didn't use children for assassinations, Merikh doubted that the Temple would. Alcaeus surely didn't have the stomach for it. The boy looked barely four years old.

"What's your name?" Merikh asked, his tone firm but gentle, the same he'd used for Zahira.

The child mumbled something Merikh couldn't make out before he raised his hands as high as he could and presented Merikh with the wildflowers.

"Forthekhanum," the boy mumbled. The flowers were too low for Merikh to reach comfortably. He moved the mare to line up with the boy a little better before leaning down to take them. Merikh winced as hot pain stabbed his side in a glaring reminder that he probably shouldn't be moving like this.

As soon as the flowers left the boy's tiny hands, he ran back to his mother on the side of the road. She held her son's hand protectively, the boy clinging to the brown folds of her chador and excitedly yammering about what he'd managed. Once Merikh settled back straight in the saddle, he bowed his head briefly toward the mother before urging Zahira forward. He cut behind the herd to Loralee. Her mood toward him seemed to have improved, as her eyes smiled as Merikh rode alongside her. The smile turned to surprise when Merikh offered her the flowers.

"Thank you."

Loralee placed them carefully behind the pommel with her other flowers. The gesture was received warmly by those watching, met with awws, smiles, and a short spattering of applause. Merikh hid the disdain from his eyes. He understood the need for the common people to glimpse of the lives of their leaders, to identify with them in these little moments. For Merikh, it felt far too much like being on display. His life wasn't a show, not meant for entertaining the common mob.

Loralee, on the other hand, looked satisfied with the crowd's reaction. She smiled brightly, the gesture clearly visible in her eyes despite the veil. The people fawned over their new khanum and this human side she brought out in their cold shah.

The crowds didn't follow when they left the city. The guards and grooms fanned out wider, and the herd took to their newfound freedom. Mares spread out and occasionally played with their foals. A few of the older mares knew where they were going, having taken the trip many times, and helped keep a few of the younger mares and foals in line. It was an important task closer to the river. The Kura had begun to narrow and dry out, pressing its inhabitants into closer and crankier proximity. The guards kept a sharp eye, but Merikh felt no strong souls nearby. No one wanted to lose a foal to crocodiles or have an unfortunate altercation with a group of hippos.

Zahira carefully picked her way along the riverbank, finding an appropriately gentle slope to traverse into the Kura. Muddy water splashed onto Merikh's salwar and boots, soaking into his saddle blanket. As Zahira's knees began to buckle and the mare gave all-too-serious thought to lying down in the cold water, Merikh's heel prodded her sharply in her ribs. She sprang out toward the other side of the river, and Merikh heard Loralee's laugh over the splashing.

"Is this better than paperwork?" she asked, riding Amarante across the river back to his side. Whatever lingering irritations she might have been harboring at the beginning of the day were forgotten or buried.

Begrudgingly, Merikh nodded. "Only just."

His lackluster enthusiasm was met with rolled eyes. The ends of Loralee's reins slipped beneath the Kura's cloudy surface, and when she snapped them back up, Loralee splashed water on him and Zahira. The unexpected water made Merikh jump, and a few drops managed to find the nape of his neck and slide down his skin before his magic evaporated it. Merikh shot Loralee a look. She returned it playfully, innocently.

"Are you sure you want to start that with an *ice* sorcerer?"

She laughed before her eyes went wide, and she shrieked. A small ice cube had formed under her kameez along her back. It slid down along her spine and then disappeared.

"That's *not* fair!" she exclaimed with forced irritation.

Merikh shrugged. He tried to keep a straight face and failed completely. Despite the mountain of paperwork on his desk, the information from the assassin, and the looming threat of war, Merikh was genuinely pleased with how the morning had turned out. Nikias's suggestion had been a good one, as they usually were.

They let the horses play in the water for a short while before turning them back toward the city. The midday sun was burning down, making the road hot on the horses' hooves and everyone antsy. Crowds thinned, opting to move inside for midday meals and the cool of shaded buildings. Those who remained to welcome the retinue back into the city had thrown down palm leaves for the horses to walk on. Again, Loralee spoke with those who had come to see the retinue, this time allowing a few of the men and women to walk with them for a time. Horses parted as Captain Bashir rode to Merikh's side, his irritation plain.

"The Khanum is going to get herself killed, Shahanshah," Bashir said, trying to temper his frustration with respect. "This isn't Abadan, and she's not a Neredi anymore."

"Are you implying my city doesn't love their khanum?" Merikh asked dryly before nodding. "She'll figure that out soon enough, without dying. Keep her safe, in spite of herself. You have my permission to do whatever is necessary to keep her alive."

Bashir nodded, though Merikh was certain he heard the captain mumble something under his breath as he rode off toward Loralee. She looked less than enthused when Bashir rode between her and the man she'd been speaking to, and then remained between her and the commoners until they passed through the Jibbah District Gate. The captain only left her completely alone once they entered the palace complex. The mares and foals were herded back into their pastures by the grooms.

Gingerly, Merikh dismounted Zahira. The whole left side of his torso hurt, making it difficult to untack the mare and groom her, but he did so unassisted. Once Zahira was put up in her pasture, Merikh headed from the barn to the royal suite, followed closely by Loralee.

"How are you feeling?" she asked.

"Fine."

Merikh tried to let his arm relax and swing normally, but his shoulder ached from the ride. Loralee dropped the subject, and the remainder of the walk was silent until they reached the suite. Once inside, Loralee crossed the room to Merikh's desk and opened a drawer. From it, she pulled the blue-and-white jar of healing salve and then turned to look at him.

"Fine or not, I remember you saying something this morning about promising the healers you'd let me look at you," Loralee said. The implication that most men wouldn't be so reluctant to let their wives close was left unsaid. Merikh knew how much his desire for space wounded Loralee's pride. The kameez hid Merikh's wince as he pulled the shirt over his head and then tossed it on the nearby divan.

"It looks worse than it feels, I imagine."

Merikh glanced down at the dark bruises. The scars hadn't split open. As far as Merikh was concerned, he was fine. Loralee frowned and walked over to him, lifting the lid off the jar. Before she placed any of the salve on him, she hesitated and met his gaze.

"I'm going to touch your side," she said before reaching out and carefully placing the salve on his fresh scar. The sound of her voice kept him from hearing the whip crack. Her tone was never condescending, even when she was frustrated. She was putting in the best effort she could, to be both khanum and wife in the only way she'd ever been taught.

The salve itched, burning coldly as the healing magic reacted faintly against the necromancy. Loralee was careful, barely touching the bruises as she tended them before she closed the jar. She walked back to the desk. Merikh pulled his kameez back on, his shoulder hurting far less as he did so.

"Thank you for arranging the ride out today. It was nice," Loralee said as she opened the desk drawer. She was right. It had been nice, and it was the first time in months that Merikh had felt relaxed. The first time in a long time that Loralee had looked happy.

Merikh crossed the room, took her arm, and turned her away from the desk. Her crimson-and-gold veil was still pinned across her face. Merikh carefully unpinned the delicate clasp. The veil fell aside as he tipped her chin up and kissed her. It had been far too long since he'd done so. Merikh could feel Loralee's surprise before her hands found his hips, pulling him against her.

But even as Merikh began to pull the hem of her kameez up, his magic forced his mind to wander away from Loralee's soft curves. A familiar soul approached. Merikh pulled away to breathe, to focus. When Loralee leaned up to kiss him again, her hand reaching into his hair to pull him back to her, Merikh shook his head. He glanced back to the door, and it opened a crack. Merikh missed the exasperated glare Loralee shot him as he stepped away from her.

Nikias knocked on the doorframe as he entered the suite. The mood immediately darkened with worry. Nikias carried a thick package just barely small enough to be carried by bird.

"Shahanshah, Khanum." Nikias bowed his head before shutting the door behind him. "Word from Hatai."

The grand vizier was oblivious to the encounter he'd interrupted. Merikh ran a hand over his hair to try and tame whatever Loralee had unsettled. The Khanum, meanwhile, fixed her kameez back down over the few inches of exposed skin.

"Adrian?" Merikh asked.

Nikias shook his head. "Not directly, at least."

Nikias handed Merikh the letter. It felt heavy in his hand and was tainted with death. Merikh flipped it over. A wild dog was pressed into the dark-brown wax—House Boutros. The seal yielded easily when pressed, cracking and crumbling onto the desk. The paper unfolded quickly on its own, and Merikh dropped it on the desk instinctively.

A Sarafi scorpion, large and venomous, lay dead inside the package. A pin fashioned to look like a dagger impaled a black Sanctified Sun amulet into the yellow body. Around it, the letter was coated in what appeared to be dust, but as Merikh reached for the letter again, he knew better. He opened the middle drawer of his desk and pulled a small vial from it. With a glance, the scorpion was lifted gently from the paper and put onto the desk. Merikh picked up the paper and carefully folded it to pour the dust into the vial. Once finished, Merikh placed it down flat against the desk to let Loralee read it over his shoulder.

To Our Most Exalted Shahanshah,

Firstly, allow me to convey my heartfelt relief at news of your swift recovery. Your loyal servants in Hatai hope any future assassins have equally poor aim.

Secondly, I humbly beg for assistance for my city. Rumors abound that we recently were visited by an Ajir agent, and that rumor set the Onyx Swords passing through Hatai into an unfortunate frenzy. One particular contingent of Swords set fire to houses and an inn within the Palm District. Enclosed are the ashes from the encounter, as well as the amulet and scorpion my guards found pinned to a hitching post with an unsavory carving addressed to you. I believe any additional Ajir or Royal Guards may exacerbate the situation, but I cannot afford the akhenits to compensate my current guards for their time as it is, much less to keep the peace in troubled times.

As of writing this plea, I have also implored Amir Xolani and eagerly await responses from both your great houses.

Your humblest servant,
Ghazal Boutros, Rabb of Hatai

Whether Loralee or Nikias had finished reading, Merikh didn't consider when he tossed it aside.

"That man has been begging for funds since before I could walk. Any excuse to try and tease a trickle from royal coffers. Now this? Writing to an amir not his own for funds?"

Merikh scoffed. It was a bold move, one Merikh couldn't ignore. For all his talk of loyalty, Rabb Ghazal would quickly swear fealty to whoever sent him akhenits to handle his problems. He would force a conflict between Xolani and Olumide over the Raudhah-Ydeban border for sewage money. Loralee reached past him and picked up the letter, reading it over again quietly.

"Akhenits or not, Shahanshah, this is troubling news," Nikias said, gesturing to the scorpion. "Adrian's being careless if an Onyx Sword could find him."

"These aren't ordinary Swords, you know that," Merikh said. He froze the stinger on the Sarafi scorpion before he pried the amulet off of it. Even dead, the stinger could cause harm. The venom within it could kill an elephant within minutes.

"He shouldn't be drawing the kind of attention that gets houses and inns razed," Nikias chided, earning him a cold look.

Adrian had made mistakes, Merikh agreed. But Nikias had never cared for the Ajir steward, and he had always been unnecessarily hard on the young man. It was true, Adrian didn't have the sort of training the Ajir guards did. But he had an earnestness that helped people open up to him. That quality couldn't be taught, and Merikh needed that in his steward.

"Hatai isn't a stronghold of the Faithful," Loralee said as she finished the letter. "This is brazen, especially leaving that amulet for you. They want a confrontation and a reaction. Your Ajir are welcome to travel anywhere in Shai'Khal. It shouldn't *matter* how careful or careless Adrian is." Her words weren't spoken naïvely. It was clear that behind her dark eyes she was planning out a response.

Merikh nodded, flipping the amulet over in his hand a few times as he thought. "Alcaeus has condemned the riots in the Hock District thus far, correct?" Merikh asked.

Nikias nodded. "Unequivocally. He doesn't want a citizens war if he can avoid it. He's hoping you'll put the Faithful down brutally and give him cause for a truly righteous holy war. A cause he can sway the undecided nobles with."

"These fanatics will destroy any alliances he might have or attempt to attain with Yahidah houses. Hatai may be half Umbeah, but it's still a Yahidah city," Loralee said quickly. "And Amir Olumide won't tolerate Amir Xolani interfering in Raudhah."

"If we're distracted by a border war, that only strengthens Alcaeus's Umbeah ties," Merikh said. "Hopefully Xolani will choose correctly. Nikias, make sure Olumide is informed about Hatai. He can chide Ghazal for stirring up unnecessary troubles."

The amulet fell on the desk with a firm thud as Merikh picked up the vial again. Green fog left his fingertips, wrapping around the vial and stirring the ashes within. The remains made it easier to call back souls of the deceased. Merikh could feel one in particular making a desperate crawl for the land of the living. A ghost in denial of its death, happy to search out its body.

A child formed in the fog a few feet away from the desk, and both Loralee and Nikias jumped.

"Where's Maman?" the ghost asked, its voice thin and airy. Made from fog, it was nearly impossible to tell if the child was a boy or girl in life.

"Dead," Merikh said plainly.

The child shook its head adamantly. *"No! She was just talking with those people in the other room! But different people than usual. These ones weren't here for Amefi. Whatever Amefi is."*

"Who were they?"

The child shrugged and began to meander the royal suite. The ghost's hand was outstretched, as if running along a tabletop as it walked through the back of the divan.

"What did they look like?"

"A bunch of soldiers."

"Did they wear a sun on their chest?"

Merikh's question earned him an eerie laugh from the child, one that he could see sent a shiver down Loralee's spine.

"No silly, the sun is in the sky!"

"Did they carry one of these?" Merikh picked up the amulet, and a small trail of fog left his fingertips and forced the ghost to turn back toward the desk, a gesture that upset the soul.

"I don't KNOW!" The ghost opened its mouth wide and screamed. The unearthly sound was one Merikh had learned to ignore years ago, although a quick glance toward Nikias and Loralee showed them not to be immune. The blood had drained from their faces. Merikh held back a frustrated sigh, the magic disappearing and the ghost with it.

"I will write a condemnation of the actions of these Onyx Swords," Merikh said. "In addition, I will invite Alcaeus to join us and the Royal Guard in an effort to prevent further attacks. Nikias, have scribes available to make copies to send to the provinces."

"Of course, Shahanshah," Nikias said, bowing his head.

"If I may?" Loralee asked before Merikh could speak again. "I'd like to speak with Ruya. While you support a military response, let me handle the religious one. Ruya and I can arrange a vigil for the dead. We can invite Alcaeus to join us."

The name dripped with a personal distaste, more than Merikh expected from Loralee. He nodded.

"Speak with Captain Bashir before you do so. He'll find you a safe and appropriate location. Asking for his input may help put him in a more charitable mood after this morning," Merikh said with a smirk.

Loralee scoffed. "I was never in any danger."

"The captain believes differently."

Loralee rolled her eyes. She then turned to Nikias. "Will you walk with me, Vizier?" Loralee asked.

Nikias bowed his head once more. "Of course, Khanum."

Once the door shut behind them, Merikh ran a hand through his hair and looked down at the dead scorpion on his desk. The brief relaxation this morning's ride had brought was gone. Once more, the world intruded, and Merikh couldn't help but worry. Adrian was usually discreet. To have such an occurrence happen when Adrian might still be in Hatai? It was too close for comfort. If he'd been caught, then everything they'd planned was simply lost.

Adrian, don't do anything reckless, Merikh thought.

CHAPTER 27

8TH OF BELITH, DRY SEASON, 902 UNIFIED AGE
ZIYADI, YDEBA PROVINCE

Adrian couldn't shake the feeling they were being followed. They'd kept off the main roads, skirting the Sarafi as much as possible, then only crossing into the Katu Savanna when it became absolutely necessary. Crossing the grasslands left Adrian looking over his shoulder more so than in the desert. At least in the Sarafi, sandstone crags hid their fires from attention. On the savanna, fires were visible for miles—both theirs and other travelers'. Of the campfires they could see dotting the horizon at night, Adrian imagined each of them to be Onyx Swords. The encounter had been too close for comfort. Even with Sarka's aid, Adrian hoped not to have another. He hadn't become the Ajir steward to watch people die.

Flat savannas gave way to gentle hills midway through the morning. Clouds threatened to storm over the mountains, the Dry Season coming late or perhaps not at all to Ydeba.

Akhenios, hold off the rain. The last thing we need are flooded passes, Adrian prayed, keenly aware of the irony. He had the distinct impression that these prayers were likely to remain unanswered at best, actively countermanded at worst. *Well, maybe Livinja can do something about the weather,* Adrian thought with a mirthless smile behind his veil.

As he had in Hatai, Adrian had left Sarka on the outskirts of Ziyadi. It was a small village. Like most of its size, anyone unusual was quickly noticed and gossiped about. Adrian, with his pack camel and decent gelding, was eye-catching enough without having a vexing woman at his side. Besides, Adrian was already pushing his luck.

Ikbal Charmichi, Adrian's cousin, was a devout man Adrian hadn't seen in ten years. The last time was when Adrian's mother had managed to get leave from the former Ajir steward and had brought Adrian to Ziyadi. His few missions on the Shah's behalf had always taken him to more major cities within Ydeba. Adrian had never plucked up the courage to see his family. Why doing so made him nervous, Adrian couldn't quite put his finger on. Ikbal had treated him fairly and kindly even ten years ago. Adrian hoped that Ikbal's courtesy would have only grown since then.

Ziyadi hadn't changed much since Adrian had been a boy. It was too small for a proper wall. The only fortifications were a half-hearted ditch dug and then forgotten about. Most of the buildings were stone or adobe—only the wealthiest citizens could afford to buy good lumber from the forests far to the west or north. The village magistrate's home was easy to spot, with a grand wooden fence protecting it. The only other wooden structure in town was the auction stage in the bazaar square, in the middle of Ziyadi. One look at the stage made a lump form in Adrian's throat.

Hanging from it were four white-and-yellow Akhenic banners and two dead women. Wooden signs hung from their necks with "HERETIC" carved into it. Adrian glanced discreetly at the stage as he passed. Black amulets were tied to the ropes around the bound hands of each woman.

May the Great Prophet guide your souls to Aljemel, Adrian looked down at his horse. These were not the Onyx Swords Adrian had grown up seeing at the temple. Those men and women had always protected the poor, protected priests bestowing alms. Nothing like this.

Adrian's stomach dropped when he passed the stage and saw a contingent of Onyx Swords trying to provoke several guards. Adrian recognized the orange uniforms. They were Amir Xolani Iherjirika's men. Oval shields and long spears made them stand out from the crowd. They felt his gaze and returned it suspiciously, but their presence gave Adrian some relief. Perhaps the Shah's law still held some sway here.

"Go back to the desert!"

A stone thudded against Majdy's flank. The horse leapt forward, nearly tossing Adrian from the saddle. The camel, slow to respond, almost wrenched Adrian's arm from its socket as he tried to hold on to the lead rope and get control over Majdy. Other shouts rose from the crowd. The amir's provincial guards were quick to action.

Unfortunately, so were the Onyx Swords.

"Go on, about your business!" the Iherjirika guard captain shouted at the villagers as the guards approached Adrian. The Onyx Swords joined them. Adrian was all they needed to push the balance of power within the village. In this struggle, every inch of ground and every town, regardless of size, mattered.

"What's your business in Ziyadi?" an Onyx Sword soldier asked Adrian.

"I don't answer to you," Adrian said firmly before looking to the guard captain. "I have family here."

"Oh? Where are you visiting from?" the Onyx Sword asked again, placing his hand on the bit of Majdy's bridle.

"*Stop* pestering the man." The guard captain did nothing to hide his irritation. It was met with a sneer from the other soldier.

"I'm merely making conversation."

"Not your business, not your place."

"Do you really want to start that here?" The Onyx Sword's words brought a sinking feeling through Adrian's chest. Restlessness spread through the crowd. The amir's guards had a level of respect brought on by their uniforms, but it wouldn't keep Adrian safe if pushed.

"Adrian?"

A Yahidah man approached through the crowd. He was older than Adrian by a few years, and those years had been good to him. His brown kaftan stretched over a well-fed belly. He was only a few inches taller than Adrian, shorter than most of the Umbeah around them. He had a warm, boisterous presence that seemed to put everyone at ease.

"Ikbal?" Adrian said tentatively before dismounting his horse. The other man nodded, a surprised look on his face that gave way to a bright smile. He strode up to Adrian and pulled him into a rib-crushing hug.

"Akhenios be kind, what are they feeding you? You're skin and bones!"

"I promise I'm not," Adrian said dryly, not wanting to talk about his employment with Onyx Swords around. Ikbal didn't press the issue. Instead, he glanced at the Onyx Sword captain.

"Are you finished? The boy needs a decent meal, and Imani will be overjoyed for the company."

"Of course." The Onyx Sword gave the captain a smug look that was met with a glare. Adrian didn't care whose permission he was given as long as it got him out of the square. Ikbal took Adrian's camel's rope. Adrian led Majdy beside his cousin.

"How's Aunt Haniaa?" Ikbal asked as they left the bazaar, glancing to Adrian. "I'm surprised she's not with you."

"She, uh, she died eight years ago. Sleeping sickness."

Adrian had been twelve at the time when the disease had swept through Madiar. The city had shut down, merchants rerouted to Rajibad, and the Royal Guards were the only ones permitted to transport goods into the city. Adrian remembered the constant black smoke from funeral pyres. Those who caught the disease and didn't die right away were dragged from the city if found, left to die outside its walls if they were too poor to afford the services of a healer. The Temple's healers had been overrun trying to look after the sick.

The palace had remained the last bastion of good health in Madiar, but it, too, eventually succumbed. The grooms had been hit especially hard, taking up most of the healers' time and still not always surviving. It hadn't taken long for even the palace workers to receive the same treatment as the poor—quick removal. Mansur had locked himself away, terrified of the disease. When Adrian had found his mother weak, feverish, her neck swollen, he'd gone to the only person he'd trusted to keep his secret.

"She's going to die," Merikh said, standing against the wall and barely looking at Maman. At sixteen, he towered over Adrian, a lanky dark specter in his black scholar kaftan. The Shahzade held part of his ghutrah across his mouth and nose, but it did nothing to hide his indifference.

"Can't the healers do anything? Please..." Adrian pleaded.

"Four grooms died this morning. The healers are tired. I'll be surprised if one or two of them don't succumb to exhaustion or this"—he gestured at Maman—"before long."

"But you can stop her from dying."

Adrian had never forgotten the look Merikh had given him: one of long-suffering pity. The sort of look one gave the barn cats when they fell off a bale of feed while stalking a mouse.

"No, Adrian. I can't stop her from dying, not without prolonging her suffering."

"But you can do something!"

"Yes...I can end it painlessly."

Ikbal looked away from Adrian, muttering a prayer under his breath before he apologized for not knowing. Adrian simply shook his head and let the quiet engulf them as they walked.

"Are you still at the, uh...well, you know..." Ikbal asked, breaking the silence.

Adrian appreciated his caution and nodded. "It's good work."

"Well, it's work."

"You're not a Royalist then?" Adrian asked, his heart sinking.

Ikbal frowned and smoothed his kaftan, briefly touching the plain Akhenic pendant that rested on his chest. "I don't know. The Shah is a long way from here, and Amir Xolani's guards are only as decent as they must be to us Yahidah. The Swords...well, I don't like any of it. I just want it all out of Ziyadi, if there must be war."

"Have you thought about leaving Ziyadi? Heading east? Or north, even. Kaitan will be neutral territory."

Ikbal sighed and shook his head. "It's not that easy."

Adrian nodded, letting the subject drop as they approached a small adobe house. It was one of many in a row, with a small plot of land for a garden and a communal barn nearby. Ikbal helped Adrian untack the camel and gelding before helping Adrian haul his bags inside. The door creaked a little as they entered. The air smelled earthy, of barley wine and cooking mutton.

"You brew?" Adrian asked.

Ikbal shook his head. "Imani brews, I sell it. Sometimes I get lucky and merchants'll be passing through. I had to borrow an ox and cart from Afram last time to take it down to Duak a few months ago," Ikbal said before clearing his throat. "Mani!"

There was grumbling from the far side of the house. A curtain pulled across a doorframe and a short Yahidah woman waddled through. Her frame was small, and her pregnant belly looked ready to burst at any moment.

Adrian held back a sigh. *No wonder it's complicated.* He regretted coming now. He'd never involved family in the Shah's affairs before; he shouldn't have done so now. Adrian bowed his head a little to hide his mixed feelings as Ikbal made a quick introduction to his wife, Imani.

"Well, we're happy to have an extra person to fetch the midwife if necessary," Imani joked before gesturing to the cushions on the floor near the low coffee table. "Food should be done soon. Ikbal can make chai if you'd like it. Or maybe pour some wine?" Imani asked before crossing the room and getting comfortable. Ikbal didn't seem bothered at all to have her hostessing duties pushed off on him instead.

"Barley wine sounds lovely. I don't get to drink it in Madiar," Adrian said, deliberately omitting that most of the barley brought into Madiar was for horse feed, not brewing. But after time on the road, anything different from what he'd packed was a welcome change.

"How long are you here?" Imani asked, gesturing for Adrian to come and sit. He did so, buying himself time to answer.

"I'm...afraid I'm not here entirely on personal matters. I'm here following the Shah's orders. I don't know how long that might require me to stay in the area. I need to leave in the morning, but I might be back in the evening. I don't know."

Imani looked confused, glancing toward the kitchen and Ikbal. "But you're a servant. I thought in the kitchens?"

Ikbal cleared his throat. "No, he *used* to work the kitchens, Mani. Now he runs the place."

"I don't run the place," Adrian corrected quickly. "I do what I'm told. Sometimes I get to pass orders down, sometimes not. Most of the time that means I handle events within the palace. Sometimes that means I handle the Shah's more delicate affairs outside of Madiar."

"And what could possibly be of interest to the Shah in Ziyadi?" Imani asked, shifting her weight a little on the cushion and touching her belly absentmindedly.

"There's something in the Ghul's Teeth I need to find. If I can rest for the night, I can leave in the morning. I don't want to inconvenience anyone."

"Ghul's Teeth? There's nothing there but ghosts and djinn."

Ikbal scoffed. "Well, then there's plenty of interest for the Shah."

Adrian frowned. Ikbal brought him a cup of dark-brown barley wine, and Adrian took a long drink. It was bitter but not as strong as the araq he was used to.

"I can sleep elsewhere, if that would be easier. The Swords don't seem to take kindly to newcomers, and I wouldn't want to bring trouble to you. If my position in the palace makes you uncomfortable, then I can leave. But it's been a long time since I've been through here, and my map is old. If you can point me in the direction of anything interesting, I'd be in your debt."

"There isn't an inn, and you don't have a tent on that camel," Ikbal said. "I won't have you sleeping on a bedroll under the stars. It gets cold out there."

"I have a companion with the tent," Adrian offered reluctantly.

"Why didn't he join you here? There's room for one more. It wouldn't have offended us at all if..." Ikbal trailed off.

"If I brought her here, you'd have Onyx Swords at your door. I'm trying to not draw attention, if I can," Adrian explained. Ikbal looked away and swore under his breath, making it clear he understood the unsaid. Sarka had been missing from the public eye now for a significant amount of time for her little "pilgrimage." There was bound to be talk among the provinces.

"If I were a righteous man, a truly righteous man, I'd walk out that door and fetch the Sword captain. Adrian...you brought this right to our doorstep. Into my home!"

"I can leave," Adrian said as he began to stand. Imani tsked and gestured at him to sit back down. Reluctantly, he did so.

"Ikbal, stop blustering. Upsets my girl."

"Thank you," said Adrian.

Imani touched her stomach. "As far as interesting places near the Ghul's Teeth, you're on your own, Adrian. But if you're going through the C'ezaji Pass, the old Neveh ruins were converted to a fort for the Onyx Swords. And their Fari commander is *not* kind. If you enter Kal Neveh, you won't be returning to Madiar."

The room fell into a tense silence. Ikbal pulled goat kebabs from the tandoor oven and laid them down on earthen trays, splitting them to make enough for three people. He placed the tray down between them before sitting down carefully beside Imani, then absentmindedly touched her belly before kissing her cheek.

Adrian smiled a little. Fatherhood would always be out of the question for Adrian; he knew that. Even adopting an orphan was out of the question as long as he was the Ajir steward, a position he'd hold until Merikh saw fit to retire him—something Adrian doubted would happen—or the next shah decided to. After all, Adrian wholeheartedly expected to outlive Merikh. Shahs had short life expectancies of late.

"So you believe in them, then, hmm?" Ikbal pressed, breaking the silence.

Adrian took a long sip of the barley wine.

"I believe in Akhenios. I don't know if He's alone, or if there are more. I don't...I don't really think it matters, honestly. One god, a dozen gods. Doesn't change who I believe in."

"The high priest says the Shah denounced Akhenios personally."

Adrian ran a hand over his face. "Yeah...well, between us and the walls, the Shah might have run his mouth a little. He doesn't necessarily believe what he said. I can't speak for him and what he believes, but the Shah says Akhenios is part of the Pantheon. Akhenic worship will remain legal alongside the Pantheon. You can trust that."

Ikbal choked on his wine and coughed loudly to clear his throat. "I'd trust a rat in our grain stores more than a nobleman's promise."

"And how many noblemen do you know?" Imani interrupted, shooting her husband a knowing smile. Ikbal struggled to find an answer, and Adrian continued.

"The Shah tries to do what's best for the country, from what we can see in Madiar," Adrian explained. "But yes, politics get in the way of the best-laid plans. The high priest isn't helping anyone by trying to paint the Shah or the champions as villains. Nobody wants war."

Ikbal frowned and shook his head. "No one in *Madiar* wants war. Maybe no one in Kuzen or Kaitan wants war. But here in Ydeba? Duqa Enitan has been beating war drums since she blossomed into womanhood. They want independence west of the Katu, at minimum. I don't think the Shah can hold the empire together without the high priest. I'm no politician, but you split apart the heart and soul of an empire, then what holds it together? The blood of the Great Prophet means nothing if the Shah worships Ikharon. If it means nothing, then who cares about a Madiaran shah? What makes him better than the amir? At least Amir Xolani knows the province, sees his people. It's been years since the Shah bothered to come west."

"I'll mention that people miss him here when I get home," Adrian said with a shrug.

Ikbal grumbled something under his breath that Adrian was glad he couldn't understand.

"Ikbal, I don't disagree. I grew up with the Shah, so I know better than most what a tyrant Mansur was, and of course the Shah isn't entirely unlike his father. But I would take a good man with no soul over a terrible man with one. He can be brutal, but he's not a bad man."

"I don't particularly care how good or bad the man in the palace is when his troops come bearing down on Ydeba."

Imani let out a frustrated sigh and waved her hands dismissively at both men. "If you're going to argue politics, you can both go away. Now, Adrian, is the Shah the only man in your life, or have you found someone else special?"

Adrian coughed, choking on his wine. It had been years since someone had cracked a joke like that, at both his and Merikh's expense. No one in Madiar would have dared. Most people didn't tempt fate to joke about the Shah's love life before the Khanum had appeared, and definitely not now.

"I, uh, one of the servants, we had something before I left, maybe. We'll see if that's still the case in a month or two when I get back to Madiar."

Conversation moved on to Imani's pregnancy, brewing, the refreshingly mundane. Topics that were hardly matters of life and death on a grand scale. Nothing that would destabilize Shai'Khal. Just the plain, simple, humble topics of concern for the common man, and Adrian drank it in. It lacked the bitterness that talking with Sarka always ended on, the trailing off after ranting about the unfair prison she'd spent nine hundred years wallowing on. It had been too long since Adrian had had a conversation that didn't revolve immediately around the palace.

For the first time in a long time, Adrian felt truly relaxed. Even at home in the palace, there was always a certain tension. Summons bells could ring at any moment, bringing work or bad news. To be free of it completely brought peace, a feeling that wouldn't last, but for the moment, Adrian was happy.

That happiness waned as the evening wore on. Eventually Imani and Ikbal retreated to their bedroom, leaving Adrian to sleep on the divan. They left an oil lamp for him, and with its light, Adrian pulled out the Waning Moons journal. He'd done his best to read it while they'd ridden from Hatai, but there was only so much he could read while riding. At night they'd kept the campfire light to a bare minimum—anything to keep any pursuing Onyx Swords away from their camp. The leather creaked gently as Adrian opened the journal. He placed the silk ribbon bookmark aside.

> *Neveh has become a sanctuary of sorts. Akhenios comes here often, poring through the archives. His guards keep everyone away. What could possibly be here that a god would find of use? But he leaves the school itself alone, and there are lots of us here who believe in the Pantheon. I don't understand it. Everywhere else they purge us from cities, but here? Here we're safe. It doesn't make sense.*

> *One of the scholars is keeping me here, quietly. The uniform makes it easy to blend in, and I've spent my days poring over books too. If I can find what Akhenios is looking for first, maybe I can bring it to Yasu. Maybe save them.*

The entries often ended abruptly, as if Negasi were interrupted while writing them. The next entry was dated a few days later.

> *The earth sorcerers built statues. Maybe memorials for the devata? Two dragons, one from stone and the other from gold. Massive dragons, but they're unfinished. There are mounts for jewels along the back and*

Adrian flipped the page, but the next entry bore a new date and a crude sketch of the dragon statue at the mouth of a cave. Stairs were carved into the mountain. The dragon ran the length of the entrance, and maybe there was a door? The sketch was difficult to interpret.

This! This is the place where the guards keep going to. Why? It looks like a temple, perhaps. They keep bringing supplies as if they've made camp inside. Uduak is nowhere to be found. I think he's back sieging Madiar. Never liked the Raudhah shah, but gods keep Burhan and let him hold out. No one is taking that desert city. Uduak's going to die from the heat before anyone breaches those walls. Vindaram's oasis will hold for those inside, Ikharon's holding the Temple, and Livinja is leading the defense. What sort of hold does Uduak think he can gain?

Negasi's lack of focus frustrated Adrian. The man's mind wandered from thought to thought without care. *He must've assumed no one would read this,* Adrian thought. The next entry was barely legible, dated weeks later.

Was he right? They're gone. I can't feel Yasu when I pray. My magic is practically gone. Madiar's "liberated." Rumors say Kuzen is going to surrender. A unified Shai'Khal. No more fighting, no more wars, and no more scrapping for power with other priesthoods.

Were...were they djinn? Were they keeping us from fighting amongst ourselves for their own power, like Akhenios said? How could he banish gods if they were all gods like him? I don't know what to believe anymore. Was everything I ever believed in a lie?

I'm going to that temple. I'm going to find out.

"Me too," Adrian breathed. He skimmed the next few pages. They contained Negasi's doubts, a few personal lamentations, but nothing more about the temple. The picture was enough. If it was along the C'ezaji Pass, even off the trail a little, they'd find it. Adrian assumed there would have to be residual magic of some kind that Sarka could follow. There had to be.

Or maybe there will be nothing there because these gods don't exist, Adrian thought. *Or they really are djinn, and Merikh is going to let loose the end of the world.*

There was something unsurprising about the thought.

CHAPTER 28

9th of Belith, Dry Season, 902 Unified Age
Ziyadi, Ydeba Province

By the time dawn began to warm the Katu peaks, Adrian had eyes on Sarka's tent. She'd camped along the mountainside, not too far from the outskirts of Ziyadi and Ikbal's home. Adrian stopped several yards away, clearing his throat before whistling loudly.

Every evening, Sarka laid small fire traps at the periphery of their camp. Adrian had no doubt she'd done the same last night. He didn't feel the need to test Merikh's ice scorpion against a champion's fire. The sound roused Sarka from her bedroll. With a dismissive wave of her hand, Adrian felt a shudder down his spine as her enchantments lost their magic.

"Morning," Adrian said as he dismounted. It was met with a tired grunt as Sarka dug through her saddlebag for food. She ate quickly while Adrian groomed her horse and tacked it up.

"Any idea where we're off to?" Sarka asked.

Adrian shrugged. "Only one pass through the Ghul's, though there's a fort we need to avoid. I assume it's best we head for the most haunted place and go from there." Adrian led Sarka's horse to her before going back to his and pulling out the journal. He opened it to the page with the temple drawing and showed it to her. "I think that's what we're looking for."

She stifled a yawn while nodding. Sarka packed her bedroll onto her mare and mounted up quickly. The saddle only gave a little.

You're welcome, Adrian thought with irritation. No groom tacked up horses, not even for the Shah! The fact he'd now done so almost daily for a month was insulting. Adrian pushed the feeling down as he mounted his own horse and waved Sarka over to follow him. He'd lead until they reached the mountains. From there, he hoped Sarka's magic would show them the way.

They passed close to Ikbal's home, skirting the edge of Ziyadi until they hit the mouth of the C'ezaji Pass. The trail looked well-traveled, as it was the only riding pass through the southern mountains. The Dragonwater River passed through not far from here, but it was only passable during certain seasons. Even then, the boats often needed to be portaged through low spots. Most merchants stuck to ships. Even with the mists, it was relatively safe to skirt the shoreline.

The mountain air had a brisk chill to it, energizing the horses and the night animals still wandering. Stones scattered down from the mountain ridges, a telltale sign that goats and cats were making their rounds higher up. The riders kept a sharp ear for the sound of horse hooves. Adrian wished they had Ruya or Merikh with them—a necromancer able to feel souls ahead on the trail would mean no surprise encounters with Onyx Sword patrols. The trail had more offshoots than Adrian expected, whether they were from goats or secret trails of the Swords, he couldn't tell. They did offer places to get off the main pass if necessary.

Adrian picked through Negasi's journal again, just in case there was something he was missing. Sarka took point. Majdy followed Sarka's mare with little input from Adrian, and when the man did finally look up from the journal, his heart wavered for a moment. They'd left the main trail some time ago. There was a sheer drop to his left.

"Uh, Sarka?"

She didn't say anything.

"Any idea where we are?" Adrian asked as he put the journal back in his saddlebag.

"I don't know, honestly. The trail is pretty straightforward, so it'll be easy to follow back. I just...can't shake this feeling. My stomach is in knots. I assume that's a good sign that the Key is nearby," Sarka said, glancing over her shoulder. Her brown eyes betrayed how nervous she had become. She looked tense, and her mare fed off the energy. The normally calm and collected horse held her head up high, her ears pointed forward and her neck rigid.

Don't bolt. Adrian glanced down at the cliff's edge. It was a long, fatal fall if either of them left the path. Nerves began to make butterflies in Adrian's stomach. After another bend in the trail, Adrian couldn't shake the feeling that one of them wasn't making it back to Madiar.

"There, do you see it?" Sarka asked. She pointed down the trail, toward what might have been stairs at one time. They led up to a cave entrance that didn't seem to have any special ornamentation.

"Are you sure?" Adrian asked.

"I'll be more sure when we encounter a dragon."

Adrian couldn't quite tell from her tone if she meant the dragon statues from the journal or an *actual* dragon. Adrian pushed the latter thought aside—if there were a real dragon in these mountains, someone would have seen it over the past nine hundred years.

The twisting mountain path seemed to take hours to navigate, the sun nearing its zenith by the time the pair dismounted. Centuries of neglect had worn the stairs into almost nothing. Boulders had fallen and taken out large chunks from the stairs. There was no way even the most sure-footed horse could navigate them.

Adrian dismounted and pulled his saddlebags off Majdy. Sarka followed his lead after a moment and laid hers on the ground nearby. They left the halter ropes dangling loosely from their horses, giving them the illusion of being ground tied. Adrian didn't trust the horses not to hurt themselves if hobbled, and there was nothing to tie them to. Even if they wandered a little, Adrian was confident he could find Majdy, at least. The gelding rarely went far without him.

Sarka clambered up the stairs ahead of Adrian, causing small rock slides in her wake. He waited until she was at the top before he ascended. As he picked his way up the ruined stairs, he slipped and scraped his knees on the rocks.

"Careful," Sarka said, unnecessarily reproaching him as she unpinned her niqaab veil.

Adrian shot the rocks in front of him a withering glare before he finished the climb. At the top, he brushed the dirt off his salwar.

"I found the dragon." Sarka pointed just inside the entrance to the cave.

Adrian squinted into the dark, and a moment later, his eyes adjusted. It looked like gold, but Adrian doubted it. Nine hundred years seemed an awful long time for a golden statue to be left alone by looters. The statue ran the entirety of the archway. Its tail rested on the ground on the right side of the entrance, rose up along the ceiling, and then its head rested on the ground on the other side, mouth agape toward the entrance. Horns, twisted like a kudu's, protruded from its head. Large tendril whiskers ran along the nose to mid-jaw. It had a lion's mane with taloned feet like a great eagle. The eyes and scales of the back were made from smooth black stones with white flecks spattered through them. Sunlight reflecting off the eyes gave Adrian an unsettling feeling of being watched.

"Wow," Adrian breathed. The drawing hadn't done the statue justice.

Sarka snorted derisively before raising her hand. A fireball ignited and hovered above the two of them, illuminating the path inside. Adrian stepped over the remnants of an old door, passed the dragon, and grabbed a torch off the wall. He barely noticed the dull twinge of a headache that began as he crossed the threshold.

"Adrian—" Sarka gasped.

He turned quickly and saw her fall to her knees. The flame extinguished. Adrian rushed to her side. Her face was deathly pale, and her clothes felt cold when he put his hands on her shoulders.

"What happened?" Adrian asked, stunned. She'd been fine a moment ago.

"I...I don't know. I can't feel my magic. *I can't feel my magic.*" The panic rose in her voice, and she grabbed Adrian. He helped her to her unsteady feet.

"We should leave," Adrian said without thinking, trying to walk her back out of the temple.

Sarka planted her feet as best she could. "*No!* We haven't learned anything yet!"

"I'm pretty sure we found the right place, and anything that can make you lose touch with your magic seems bad."

Sarka shook her head and pulled away from him. "I can do this," she pleaded.

The look in her eyes scared him. Sarka was indomitable, aloof, and brash. A force of nature in and of herself. Now, she looked like nothing more than a worn-out and tired woman. What little fire she had left inside, Adrian didn't have the heart to put out.

"Fine."

He dug around in his pocket for flint. As soon as he felt Sarka could stand on her own without falling, he let go of her and picked up his dropped torch. It took a few tries, but the ancient kindling burst into flame. The warm light didn't help Sarka's complexion, as the champion looked prone to collapsing. Adrian offered her his arm, but Sarka pushed it away. She grabbed another torch off the wall and lit it from Adrian's, then proceeded ahead of him down the hall.

The main corridor led farther down into the mountain. Minor cave-ins partially blocked off parts of the halls, slowing their progress. Ornate carvings of Akhenic Suns and dragons were still clearly carved into the walls. Some of the doors were still intact, and Adrian pushed one open. He jumped when he saw desiccated corpses lying on stone beds carved from the mountain.

No wonder the mountains are haunted, Adrian thought.

"I think we're in the right place," Adrian said quietly as he returned from the room.

Sarka leaned against the far wall and nodded.

"What I don't understand," Adrian continued, "is why there's anyone dead here. They lived here, why'd they die here? Why didn't anyone remove them?"

"Your little scorpion friend can't summon souls?" The champion gestured at Adrian's pockets.

He shook his head. "It's just ice, and I left it in my saddlebag," Adrian said. A lucky decision—he doubted it would have survived past the dragon.

They headed farther down the hall, finding more rooms with dead soldiers. There was a kitchen and storeroom as well, though the storeroom had been picked clean.

"This doesn't make sense," Adrian said as they left the storeroom. "Why leave the corpses? Why leave their armor, the amulets? Why leave the dragon and the gemstones on it? *Someone* had to have found this temple over the last nine hundred years. Why hasn't it been destroyed?"

"We knew what to look for. Maybe we were lucky. Or maybe we're going to find the corpses of unfortunate adventurers who failed to loot this place further. I don't know." Sarka's nonchalant tone made Adrian scoff.

"Don't tell me you think this is normal?"

"No, it's not normal. But those Swords probably starved to death here on Uduak's orders. Or maybe on Themba's—he was the first high priest after the Great Prophet, wasn't he? Maybe this place hasn't been abandoned as long as I've been gone. Who knows? It doesn't matter. We're not going to be here long enough to find out." Sarka's words grew feverish, and Adrian could see sweat beading on her forehead despite the cold air inside the mountain.

The passageway began to narrow as they pressed on, the air growing heavier and damp. Carvings along the wall grew fewer, and Adrian deliberately slowed his pace. If the Key was as valuable as everyone thought, there would be traps to catch anyone who made it past the guards alive. Even after slowing down, Adrian found Sarka struggling to keep up.

Stones crunched under Adrian's feet, and he stopped dead. He grabbed Sarka's sleeve when she, oblivious, began to walk past him.

"Don't," Adrian said firmly, giving her a small push backward before lowering his torch a little. "Shale."

The dark flat stone covered the ground in front of them. It would have been nothing to clear it if Adrian could use his magic. Without it? The rock made Adrian nervous. It was difficult to walk on, slippery, and it all too easily hid traps. And to top it off...

Adrian pulled Sarka back a few steps and threw his torch into the middle of the shale. The oil-covered stone burst into flame.

"That's a new trick," Sarka said, raising her hand quickly to shield her eyes from the sudden light. Adrian pulled his kufiyah across his face again, and Sarka pinned up her veil as the smoke thickened.

"Yeah, maybe there's a way around or something left over in one of the rooms that we can use to clear this once it's burned out. I don't want to slip into a spike trap."

Sarka followed Adrian back to the rooms. As they receded, the champion began to look stronger. When they stood outside the closest room, Adrian stopped.

"You should stay here."

"No. We've been over this. Stop it," Sarka ordered. She brushed past him into the room.

Adrian followed and helped her snap the legs off of an old wooden table. It was rotted, nearly falling apart in his hands, but it would have to do. They waited inside the room for the thick smoke to clear. It made Adrian's eyes water, burning his throat. When they walked back to the shale, a massive spiked iron ball was swinging gently from the ceiling.

"Must have burned through the trigger rope," Adrian muttered as he walked to the edge. Slowly, carefully, he began pushing the shale to one side. After a few feet, one of the stones fell into a spike pit.

And that's why we're taking it slow, Adrian thought. He tried not to look at the white bones in the bottom of the pit.

"You know, for a steward, you have a rather surprising skill set," Sarka commented. "Spying, circumventing traps, delivering letters, fetching coffee. Is there any task you *don't* jump to do when Merikh asks?"

"He's the Shah," Adrian said as he worked on a path around the pit. "Everyone jumps when he says to."

"Grooms stick to horses, soldiers stick to guarding and fighting, nobles play their games. You seem to do a bit of everything. Why? How'd you get so much trust when you're, what, twenty? Younger than Merikh, I think. He doesn't seem like a man who has much time for contemporaries, let alone juveniles."

"Can't this wait?" Adrian asked tersely. "I'd like not to die. And I think the Shah appreciates my dedication to that particular task."

"Apologies." Sarka raised her hands defensively before she followed Adrian with her torch. He worked in silence as they crossed the shale.

On the other side, he straightened up and glanced at Sarka. What he saw didn't inspire confidence. She looked sickly pale and was sweating profusely, despite the cold. Adrian opened his mouth to speak and was silenced by Sarka's glare, as if she'd read his mind.

All right, fine.

They continued to follow the narrowing path, Adrian carefully leading the way through in case of additional traps. Normally, he used his limited telekinesis to search for mechanisms. Anything that would move and potentially trigger something nasty. Without that ability, he tread carefully. They were down to one torch, and he didn't want to lose their light on another set of shale. Or to the water dripping down from small cracks in the ceiling. Both Adrian and Sarka slipped more times than they cared to, as the floor sloped sharply.

At the base on the left side were more spikes. Once again, Adrian tried to ignore the bones. It looked like remains of people who had been impaled in the leg, unable to free themselves from the trap.

Sarka, on the other hand, carefully walked up to it and pulled something from its hand. "Adrian...look at this."

Reluctantly, Adrian turned. There was a leather-bound book crumbling in Sarka's hand, bearing the Yasuan moon. She handed Adrian the torch, and he leaned over her shoulder to look as she carefully opened it. The journal was dated several years after the one in Adrian's saddlebag.

I'm going to die here. With nothing to show for it.

For no reason. Yasu forgive me. Akhenios forgive me.

Chinara...I'm sorry.

His plea to Yasu was scratched out almost beyond reading. Adrian glanced at the ground. There was a glass vial not far from what looked like a worn leather satchel. Negasi had been an archivist until the end; keeping the journal must have given him some sort of comfort. Sarka placed the journal back down on the ground, and Adrian bowed his head respectfully as she muttered a prayer.

"Come on," Adrian said after she finished, skirting around the spikes that had impaled their ancient compatriot.

The cave leveled out and was easier to walk for a short while. Then Adrian froze. There was another dragon. Time had been unkind to this one. Tendrils were missing; a claw lay broken on the ground. Maybe it was the torchlight, but it looked far more menacing than the first. Adrian shivered. His headache returned, stronger than before.

A sickening thud came from behind him. Adrian spun around. Sarka was limp on the ground. Blood trickled from a gash on her head.

"Sarka!"

Adrian crouched down beside her. He held his hand in front of her mouth, relieved when he felt breath. *Stupid, stubborn woman!* He had to get her away from the statue. Adrian bit his lip. Could he even carry her? Dragging her out would be impossible while carrying the torch, and he couldn't navigate the slope or the shale pit traps without light. No, he'd have to carry her and hope he could make it up the slippery incline without killing either one of them on Negasi's spikes.

Akhenios... Adrian cut off the prayer with a bitter smile. It seemed wrong to pray to the god he was actively countermanding for help in that task. *Livinja, if you exist, some help would be appreciated.*

Adrian placed the torch on the ground and carefully grabbed Sarka. He groaned, his muscles aching as he pulled her limp body across his shoulders. He grabbed the torch in one hand and used the wall to help himself stand. Pain sharply spasmed across his back as Adrian carefully picked a path away from the stone dragon. As he reached the slope, the light reflecting off the wet, slick stones showed him a better path. Undoubtedly it had been carved for the former guards to patrol.

Once past the shale, Adrian laid Sarka down on the ground, propping her up against the wall. He turned to go back and hesitated. They only had one torch now, what would happen if she woke up in the dark? She wouldn't know which way to the entrance. If she tried to cross the shale, she'd likely end up in a spike pit. If she somehow made it past the shale, she'd die on the same slope as Negasi. Sarka was a liability Adrian couldn't afford. He could get farther on his own if he didn't have to worry about her. Adrian looked back down at her and frowned.

"How do I get you out of here?" he muttered. The dragons were a problem. If he took Sarka past the golden one again, would it kill her? Was the other dragon stronger, or was whatever magic these dragons somehow possessed cumulative? Adrian let out an angry shout and kicked a rock across the hall. He couldn't leave her here, yet he didn't know enough to ensure he wouldn't kill her if he left. His stomach turned to knots, and a lump grew in his throat. If he left her here, if he pushed farther into the dark reaches of the temple, would he find the Key? If he destroyed it, would it end the effects of the dragons?

Or would he simply find another task he was ill-equipped to handle? If there were traps around the Key and he got injured or killed, who would get Sarka out of here? Adrian felt small again, painfully useless.

What would you do? Adrian thought. Not to Akhenios or the Great Prophet. Not to Livinja. To Merikh. Usually, at this sort of juncture, Adrian went to his master for answers. The most dangerous of his missions had always occurred at Merikh's side. Adrian took in a measured breath and let it out slowly. *You wouldn't have sent me if you didn't think I could find my way back home. I have all the tools I need to get there again. Think!* No answers came to him. Adrian leaned back against the wall and slid down to sit beside Sarka.

"You know, *you're* the one who's supposed to be making the life-and-death decisions," Adrian muttered. The mission had now gone horribly awry, and all he wanted to do was sink into the wall and disappear. He'd done that sort of trick plenty of times in the palace whenever he'd been tormented by the children of visiting nobles.

Adrian leapt to his feet. Tunnels. Of course! The servant corridors weren't the only ones in the palace. There were plenty that allowed discreet passage out of the palace into Madiar itself, built for royals to have private rendezvous. Others led out of the city entirely, in case the palace fell to invaders. There had to be a way out of the temple in case of cave-ins, if nothing else. Adrian just hoped the cave-in exit hadn't succumbed to age or deliberate destruction. He headed back toward the entrance, stopping in each of the rooms and searching them for hidden access points in the walls. Tapestries had been eaten away by moths and insects, valances hinting at their locations. Those were the first places Adrian checked.

But after six rooms and no luck, Adrian's enthusiasm had been replaced by sore muscles and scrapes. He'd fruitlessly given a few good shoves to unsuspecting walls and relics. And *this* door was proving uncooperative too. Adrian gave it a final, frustrated shove and was sent tumbling through the doorframe. He brushed himself off, cursing under his breath as he found his torch a few feet away, sitting in front of another broken door, this one leading into a tunnel with a strong draft and the smell of fresh mountain air.

They had a way out.

Adrian ran back to Sarka. With renewed vigor, he hauled her over his shoulders and carried her down the hall to the tunnel. It was dark, and the air was thick. Cobwebs covered the tunnel, and Adrian tried to ignore the skittering sounds and little shadows moving away from the light. At the end of the tunnel, Adrian clawed at the wall to find a cobweb-covered handle. Worryingly, when Adrian grabbed the handle and pushed it back into the recess, nothing happened.

Shit, what now?

The mechanism groaned, and sunlight assaulted Adrian's eyes. He carefully maneuvered Sarka through the door before it shut behind them. The door opened onto a cliff's edge, no more than ten feet across, before it narrowed.

"Sarka?" Adrian shook his shoulders a little but didn't manage to rouse her. If he was lucky, he could maybe get the horses through. Adrian put Sarka on the ground and began carefully winding his way along the mountain toward the horses. After nine hundred years, whatever trail the Onyx Swords had cleared or made was gone.

By the time Adrian found the horses and found a route back to Sarka that was safe for them, the sun was setting behind the Ghul's Teeth. Sarka hadn't moved from where Adrian had left her. When he took her hand, it still felt cold and clammy. She was limp as Adrian hauled her onto her horse. He tied her carefully to the saddle. Adrian did his best to tie her niqaab, hiding her hair as much as he could. The last thing they needed was to be discovered on their way back into Ziyadi.

The moon was high in the sky, and the stars danced brightly in and out of cloud cover as Ziyadi came into view. Most houses were dark, only a few streetlamps were lit, and Adrian assumed the brightest building was the tavern. The late hour gave Adrian a measure of privacy, and he took the back roads and alleys to ensure it.

He tied the horses outside the Charmichi home and pulled Sarka off the saddle. She groaned at the rough treatment, and Adrian nearly dropped her in surprise. Sarka hadn't made a peep since they'd left the temple. Adrian hoped this boded well.

Ikbal answered the knock at the door. Adrian scrambled inside, nearly knocking over Ikbal in his hurry.

"What in Alhanem happened to her?" Ikbal demanded. "Is that the—"

"Sarka. Her name is Sarka, and I don't rightfully know."

Ikbal stifled a yawn as he closed the door behind them. Adrian carried Sarka into the living room and laid her down on the divan. Adrian pulled off Sarka's boots and placed them beside the pillows as quietly as he could, not wishing to wake Imani. He carefully pulled off Sarka's kaftan, then placed it over her like a blanket. Adrian disentangled her niqaab, letting her fiery hair cascade over the pillow in a rat's nest of dirt and cobwebs.

"Will you watch her for me tomorrow?" Adrian asked as he straightened up.

"What? No! Where do you think you're going?" Ikbal looked about to burst.

"I have to go back there and—"

"And what? End up like her?"

"Whatever hurt her didn't affect me as far as I can tell. I don't think it can. I should be just fine," Adrian insisted.

"And if not? Who's gonna help *you* get home?"

Adrian was surprised by Ikbal's concern, and it left him stuttering. "I-I can't have a lot of people around with the work I do."

"You need better work," Ikbal scoffed. He reluctantly nodded. "I'll keep an eye on her. You need to rest too, otherwise I'm not letting you leave later."

Adrian gave his cousin a weary smile. "Can you take care of the horses, then? And, uh, be careful—they're the Shah's; they're worth more than my life."

Ikbal sighed and nodded. As he walked out of his house, Ikbal muttered under his breath. Adrian imagined the words weren't exactly fit for polite company and most likely were complaints about the Shah. But at the moment, Adrian couldn't have cared less. His bedroll and comfortable pillows called to him. Sleep sounded perfect to his aching muscles.

◈

What Adrian missed when he noticed the brightly lit tavern were the horses tied to the hitching post. Seven horses, with matching Akhenic Suns on their blankets. Five riders inside, two left outside to watch the town.

One saw a suspicious rider with an unconscious companion ride into town. In the light of Ikbal's doorstep, the scout saw a flash of red hair before they disappeared inside.

CHAPTER 29

10TH OF BELITH, DRY SEASON, 902 UNIFIED AGE
ZIYADI, YDEBA PROVINCE

"Adrian, get up!"

Adrian groggily shoved away the hand violently shaking his shoulder.

"What?" Adrian snapped, scrambling to find his feet. He felt as if he'd only just shut his eyes. A glance toward the windows told him he wasn't entirely wrong. It was still quite dark outside.

"You weren't careful. I *told* you to be careful! Someone saw you come back with her." Ikbal pointed at Sarka. "And the Swords found out. Only reason I got a heads-up is Imani's sister works at the tavern. The Fari commander went back to Kal Neveh for reinforcements, and they'll be back in Ziyadi any moment now."

Adrian bolted for his saddlebags, the ones Ikbal had brought in sometime while he'd been sleeping.

"Help me get her out of here," Adrian ordered, digging through the bag quickly. "Is there time to tack up horses and go?"

Adrian paused to look up at his cousin. Ikbal shook his head, the color draining from his face. Adrian returned to rummaging around in his bag.

Where is it? He knew he had it! When his hand touched black silk, instant relief displaced panic. It was bitterly cold, and Adrian shoved it in his pocket before returning to Sarka's side.

"Sarka?" Adrian shook her shoulders, but she didn't wake. He draped her arm over his shoulder and pulled her up. Ikbal took her other arm and followed Adrian out the back door. Outside, they could hear riders approaching from the main road.

"Go back inside, see to Imani." Adrian didn't have to tell Ikbal twice. The man immediately let go of Sarka and ran back inside. Alone, Adrian pulled

333

Sarka behind the communal barn and unceremoniously dumped her behind a wooden post. He pulled the black silk handkerchief from his pocket and unwrapped the ice scorpion.

I hope this doesn't kill you, Adrian thought. Powerful opposing magics could be unpredictable when forced to interact.

"Protect her," Adrian whispered, holding the scorpion in his hand. It leapt off, landed on Sarka's shoulder, and then changed. A thin web of ice began to cover Sarka. It would have to do. There wasn't time to ready the horses and get out of Ziyadi, not with Sarka like this. Adrian only hoped the Iherjirika guards were still present from earlier and willing to help him.

There was shouting from Ikbal's home. Adrian desperately wanted to flee, but there was nowhere to go. Before courage failed him, Adrian walked back to the house and in through the back door. Imani had been dragged from the bed. Ikbal stood near her with blood trickling from his nose. Most of the Swords who stood in their home were just soldiers, so the Fari commander stood out. She was short, her dark hair cropped around her face, and equally dark eyes gleamed in the lamplight. Her uniform was impeccable, though it was not one Adrian had ever seen. The Akhenic Sun had a shamshir through it. Even if he hadn't recognized her eyes, her smile unnerved him now just as it had in Hatai. A wolfish smile that looked more ready to strip flesh from bone than convey any sort of emotion. An odd look to see on a woman, even a soldier.

"You're a long way from Sujin, Amon."

"I don't know what you mean," Adrian said, trying not to look like he recognized the woman from Hatai. Dalya's smile turned coy before she glanced up to her guards and gestured toward the door Adrian had come from.

"Where's your friend? I'd very much like to have a few words with her, particularly in her current state."

How do you know? Adrian tried to hide his surprise and fear. No one had been around last night. The streets had been deserted, and Sarka had kept herself covered every time she'd been outside. *Did I pull her niqaab off her hair, or was it already coming loose?* The question froze Adrian. He didn't know the answer.

"I came alone," Adrian lied.

Dalya laughed. "Come now, that's just rude. Just because she's a Lily doesn't mean she's not *human*, though I suppose an argument could be made..."

"He's my cousin," Ikbal said, his words thick from his broken nose. "He came to stay with us, and he came on his own."

Dalya snapped her fingers, an excited look on her face. "Is this the cousin marrying the Tsukarai? Well, isn't *this* a convoluted mess?" Dalya pointed toward Imani's pregnant belly. Adrian knew there was no lie he could spin to get himself out of this web he'd made. He opted for silence, biting his lip when an Onyx Sword began picking through Adrian's saddlebag. The journal with the Waning Moons symbol stamped into the leather was inside. It was only a matter of time before the Sword would find it. But when the man straightened up, what was in his hand surprised Adrian. It was the journal, of course, but there was an empty, scrunched up coin purse as well.

Shit. Adrian had thought he'd left that coin purse back in Madiar. He didn't usually bring it along with him, for obvious reasons. Embroidered on the side was the Madiaran royal crest. The Sword handed both the journal and pouch to Dalya, who put the book under her arm and examined the embroidery carefully.

"Amon, Amon, you poor misguided soul. You're a *long* way from the palace."

"Still the Empire of Shai'Khal, isn't it?" Adrian asked.

Dalya carefully pocketed the coin purse. "Not if I can help it."

Why do you care? She wasn't Umbeah. If anything she looked at least half Tsukarai, maybe part Aegalian and some Yahidah in her somewhere. She was too pale, her hair far too straight to be Umbeah. No one would thank her for aiding Ydeban independence.

Dalya rounded on Ikbal and Imani. "You knew you were harboring an agent of the Shah's?" she demanded.

"I'm a servant! Nothing more. Not any sort of 'agent,'" Adrian clarified quickly. "They didn't do anythi—" The hand of a nearby Sword slammed into his jaw, interrupting him.

"You'll have plenty of time to talk later," Dalya ordered, not looking at him. "Be a good lad and know your place. If you're a servant, you should be well-practiced at keeping your tongue behind your teeth."

"He's my cousin, he's family. The Great Prophet teaches us to welcome family into your home, not to turn anyone away, no matter how prodigal," Ikbal said hurriedly.

If he can out-argue a Sword, he might have half a chance, Adrian thought.

"The Great Prophet wrote those words *after* Unification. *After* he purged his enemies from Shai'Khal. They hardly apply now when our enemies take shape in those closest to us. Context matters, dear. And you're harboring an apostate and a heretic at best."

In the blink of an eye, Dalya pulled her katar from its sheath and plunged the dagger through Ikbal's neck. Adrian froze, unable to move in spite of Imani's screams. He'd seen men die. He'd seen men die more violently. Never with so little warning, though. Adrian couldn't tear his eyes away. Imani was frantically trying to stop the bleeding with her hands, but even with a healer, the wound would have been difficult to fix. Without one, Ikbal quickly grew pale; his eyes became distant.

"Shh now. Stop screaming. It won't bring him back. How far along are you?" Dalya demanded, prodding Imani's shoulder. Imani didn't answer. Two of the Onyx Swords pulled her away from Ikbal's bleeding body.

"How far along?" Dalya asked again.

"I...the midwife thinks not long now," Imani answered, choking back tears.

Adrian couldn't keep quiet any longer. "She didn't know anything about my employment. I swear to Akhenios and the Great Prophet—"

"*You* don't get to swear by anything," Dalya interrupted, raising her voice. For the first time, she sounded something other than amused.

Adrian stepped forward, and the closest Sword yanked him back. The next moments were a blur as Adrian struggled against the hands on him.

A garbled, throttled cry filled the air.

Crimson blood splattered all over the wall.

Dalya's blade had slit Imani's throat.

The blade turned downward. Tearing cloth filled the silence. Blood pooled on the ground as Dalya cut open Imani's womb.

When Imani went mercifully quiet, a new wail filled the house.

"Guess the midwife was right. Go find a wet nurse, then get this thing on its way to Duak's temple. Might be a half-decent Sword or acolyte one day."

One of the Swords took the crying baby from Dalya and left the home. Dalya wiped her dagger off on a clean patch of Imani's abaya before she straightened up and rounded on Adrian.

"Anything you'd like to clarify?"

Adrian shook his head, not trusting himself to open his mouth without vomiting. He could hear footsteps of soldiers returning from behind the house. Adrian had no doubt they'd found Sarka.

"There's a chunk of ice by the barn, maybe looks like it's covering someone," the Sword explained.

Dalya let out a bored sigh. "Well, it can't sit there indefinitely. Even Merikh's not that strong. Go melt it, then take her back to Neveh."

The Swords left the house. Dalya looked at the one holding Adrian.

"Hobble and bind him, then torch the house. I'd rather play with him where I have all my toys."

Fear broke him. Adrian made a run for the door. He made it all of one stride before a Sword knocked him on the ground. Adrian cried out when burning pain shot up from his ankle. One of the guards had stepped on it, *hard*. Now his foot was bent at an odd angle. He didn't try to stand, only tried to steady his breathing.

Don't break the other one. Akhenios be kind, don't break my other one. Adrian had seen the men down below the palace. All of them hobbled, both ankles broken. They couldn't do more than crawl.

"I won't. I won't run again," Adrian said quickly, trying to get his rapid breathing under control. He didn't want to end up like the men below.

"Good," the soldier said, his tone absentminded as he hauled Adrian upright. The Sword tied Adrian's hands with cloth from Ikbal's home. Adrian leaned against the soldier as he was dragged from the house. The horizon was just beginning to warm from black to blue; the stars were still half covered in clouds.

These might be the last stars I see.

It was dark and cold. Why was it cold? Sarka took a deep breath—or attempted to. Something covered her tightly, bound her in place. She tried to move her limbs. Anything more than the slightest wiggle of a finger or toe was met with icy resistance.

Why can't I move? She needed to get out! Her breathing grew shallow, panicked. *Calm down.* She could hear Livinja's voice in her mind. The goddess had always been patient with Sarka's fears. But why couldn't she move? Why was it all so damn cold? Sarka slowed her breathing, focused her thoughts, and tried calling on her magic. She needed light...but her magic was unresponsive. *Why is it taking so long?*

The temple. Was she still in the temple? She was given her answer when she saw torches on the other side of...ice? There were four points of flickering flame outside her icy coffin. In the light, she could see buildings behind them. Back in Ziyadi? But how? The last thing Sarka recalled was talking to Adrian about Negasi. Now she was here.

There was shouting. Sarka focused her magic again. Ice was easy enough to melt through, but Sarka stopped suddenly, letting go of what little magic she'd focused. This wasn't just ice. Not if this was from Adrian. If he'd dragged her from the temple, if he'd left her here covered in ice, then she was willing to bet that this magic came from Merikh. Sarka had seen the little scorpion Adrian carried. It reeked of ice and death. Merikh's ice magic was something Sarka could normally manage in a heartbeat. Her flames would simply melt it before it could cause any harm. But necromancy? That could kill her without Ruya's aid.

Damn it, Adrian. What am I supposed to do? Sarka couldn't move. She felt panic threatening to overwhelm her again. She *needed* out of this. The temple had been bad enough with the narrowing passage burrowing into the mountain. At least there she had been able to breathe comfortably. There, nothing had pressed against her. Now, the ice threatened her. Her magic, what little she could feel, reeled against the threat.

Torches grew closer. Sarka could see the soldiers on the other side had made up their minds to at least try something to remove the ice. *Livinja, let them be Swords.* Sarka didn't want to see the Iherjirika guards fall prey to whatever happened when the ice was disturbed. If it was anything like the enchantment from Kasu, it wouldn't be pretty.

Shards of ice exploded as one of the figures touched her frozen coffin, burying into each of the soldiers' exposed skin. As soon as she was free, Sarka bolted upright and drew her sword. It wasn't necessary. The ice took on a faint green tone, the frozen skin quickly turning black. Gangrene spread quickly, into their mouths and into their lungs. Each of the four soldiers collapsed, gasping, coughing up dark liquid. Sarka wrinkled her nose in disgust. It was overkill, and a horrible way to die.

Sarka approached the dead and felt relief when she saw the Akhenic Sun stamped into their leather cuirasses. She lingered only long enough to find boots that fit her, as she noticed hers were missing for some reason. As was her coat, but she wasn't about to scavenge a coat from one of these men. Sarka would rather die than be seen in Akhenios's colors.

If there were four of them here, then there were others. They weren't far from a fort. She needed to get her bearings and find Adrian. The fact he hadn't used the scorpion to protect both of them boded ill. Adrian had left her propped up against a building that smelled of grass and manure, likely the barn he'd kept their horses and camel in. Did that mean his cousin's home was nearby? And what was his name? Ik-something? Shared family name at least, Charmichi. If Sarka had to ask around, she'd be able to find the right place.

But then the building off to her right burst into flames, and Sarka assumed she wouldn't have to guess. She skirted the barn wall, sticking to the long shadows of dawn. There were easily a dozen Onyx Swords around the burning house. Neighbors began to pour from their homes. Sarka looked to the dancing flames, took a deep slow breath, and focused on the fire. Even if she couldn't ignite flames of her own right now, perhaps she could still influence them. Something was better than nothing, at least.

After a moment, she felt her magic connect with the fire. She felt the flames, and she pushed to make them stronger. They exploded with a loud *pop* out from the door toward the Swords, sending a startled wave through the crowd. Sarka had her sword, her magic, a target, and a handful of questions. Those dozen Swords were going to give her answers.

Flames leapt from the house, burning a trail around the Onyx Sword soldiers and separating them from the onlooking crowd. While keeping an eye open for any other Swords, Sarka left the safety of the barn's shadows and walked straight for the flames. They danced over her skin without burning her or her clothes. She stood at the edge of the flames encircling the Swords, her own blade drawn.

"My name is Sarka. I am the champion of Livinja and grand general of the Flaming Legion. If you answer my questions and lay down your arms, you will leave here unharmed."

It pained her to offer clemency to men and women who willingly bore the symbol of a traitor. Men and women who, by now, couldn't possibly be ignorant of the origins of their order, what they stood for, then and now. They wanted her dead. They wanted her goddess to remain imprisoned for eternity without any true guidance from Akhenios. They weren't ill-educated in Sarka's eyes; they were willfully ignorant. Unlike Ruya, Sarka had a hard time forgiving that. All she needed was for one of them to break. The rest of them she hoped would give her reason to fight. The sword in her hand had gone too long without use.

One of the soldiers stepped forward toward the flames, his shamshir drawn.

"We are Sanctified, and the speaker for djinns doesn't scare us."

It had been a long time since her straight blade had met a curved shamshir, but the champion had greater reach and centuries of pent-up rage. The Onyx Sword didn't see her blade coming when he stepped forward. Two more shifted their posture, their weight moving back to let them lunge forward. That was as close as they got before their blood met the dirt beneath their fallen feet.

Three dead, nine to go. Their odds weren't as unfavorable as they appeared—in the small confines of the fiery circle, even if she weren't a champion, the Swords would have simply gotten in each other's way if they all tried to overwhelm her. As it was, she could see they were spooked. If the first had been the most faithful among them, then to see him fall with two others left a leadership gap.

"I came here with a young man, a Yahidah. He came to town..." *Gods, what day is it even?* Sarka had no idea how long she'd been unconscious, if it had been only hours or days.

One of the Swords looked ready to surrender, to offer more information.

"The Fari commander took him back to Kal Neveh—" Before he could finish, the curved edge of his companion's shamshir slit his throat.

Flames exploded around them in Sarka's rage, the Swords turning to ash before they could scream. The heat on Sarka's skin rid her of the lingering chill from Merikh's ice. Whatever had made her lose her magic still held some sway, and she felt far more exhausted now than she knew she should be. The flames died around her, and Sarka wearily looked around at the townsfolk.

"Where is Kal Neveh?"

They weren't far from Ziyadi when the mountain road ended in a rock wall. Wooden scaffolding spoke of renovations to rebuild the derelict, and a large wooden gate and guard house were temporary structures until the stone could be purchased for permanent ones. Kal Neveh was undergoing massive reconstruction.

When Adrian passed through the gate, his heart sank. The yard had dozens of wooden buildings. There were barns, blacksmiths, what looked like a temporary armory... Adrian swallowed hard. If he somehow managed to escape the fort itself, Adrian knew he'd never make it back to the gate. He'd never make it far enough to steal a horse.

Adrian was pulled from the horse in front of the fortress itself. Kal Neveh was built directly into the mountain. Part of the fort looked quite standard, with obvious brick and stonework. Other parts looked as if the mountain's rock face had been left completely alone, save for an odd window cut out. The guard prodded a limping Adrian forward into the fort. They headed down stone steps into the basement.

At the bottom, an unfortunately familiar scent filled the air. It had easily been almost ten years since the last time he'd been in the palace desmoterion. But the smell was not one Adrian would ever forget. The guard prodded him past storerooms that had been converted into prison cells. A frightening number of people were held within them.

Adrian's escort pushed open the doors at the end of the hall. Inside, the large storeroom had been converted into an interrogation chamber. Adrian numbly recognized a great many of the tools that hung from hooks or were laying on shelves. There was a single chair in the room, but no table. Adrian understood why when the guard replaced the cloth binding his hand with shackles. A hook hung from the middle of the ceiling. The guard pulled it down and attached it to Adrian's manacles. It forced Adrian's hands above his head.

"You're awfully quiet," the guard said as he stepped away from Adrian. "Most of your kind start sniveling about what connections they have and how much nicer my life might get if I just helped you escape."

Adrian looked at the guard. "What connections?"

The guard laughed. "Ah, so you're one of those. She loves it when you play dumb."

The guard turned and walked away, shutting the door behind him. Adrian couldn't tell if he'd been sarcastic or not. He tried to find a neutral part of the room to look at, something not covered in dried blood or showcasing an implement of torture. It didn't matter if he played dumb or not. There was only so much Dalya could pry from him anyway—Merikh only shared so much. All Adrian had to try to do was prevent her from discovering how close he was to Merikh.

Torture, as Merikh had instructed him once, was as much about extracting information as it was leaving a message. If Dalya thought she was leaving a personal message to Merikh by torturing his steward, Adrian assumed his torment would be all the worse. If Sarka didn't save him, Adrian hoped he'd manage to seem unimportant enough to die without prolonged...toying.

The door opened again, and Dalya walked in alone. She shut it behind her, crossed the room briskly, and sat down in the chair before Adrian. In one hand she held the Waning Moons journal. In the other, the coin purse. On her belt were several knives and what looked like a pair of shears. Adrian swallowed hard, trying to hide his fear and failing.

"I'm going to make this quite simple for you. First." She held up one finger. "I won't lie to you. I swear on my honor as an Onyx Sword and on my oath to the Great Prophet. Anything I promise you will come to pass. Second, I don't trust you. You're going to have to earn back that trust. Once that happens, we can have a productive conversation. Do you understand?"

Adrian nodded. "Yes."

"Good. I'm going to cut pieces off you whenever I don't believe what you've told me. I will allow you relief whenever I *do* believe you. Tell me believable things, and you might even survive this."

I've heard similar words in a far more familiar voice. It was a lie then, and it's a lie now, Adrian thought. A tremor of fear shuddered through Adrian.

"What do you want me to say?"

"Well, a real name would be lovely."

He hesitated. Ikbal and Imani were already dead, as was his mother. Who else was he protecting by not giving his name? Did it matter, in the end, how hard he tried to resist? It took too long for him to come up with an answer.

Dalya stood up. Pain exploded across his cheek. At first, Adrian thought she'd simply backhanded him. His eye hurt and his cheek stung. Then he felt something drip onto his salwar. When he glanced down, he saw blood. Adrian's tongue touched the inside of his cheek, and the wrongness of it made him shudder. She hadn't simply slapped him. Dalya had a sharp ring that had sliced up his cheek.

"Adrian. Adrian Charmichi." He spoke carefully, trying not to move his cheek, whimpering in pain when the movement was too much.

Dalya let out a sympathetic little sound. "My dear little Adrian, you're not built for this. You should have been an acolyte, hmm? You believe in Akhenios after all?"

Adrian nodded. Dalya hadn't sat back down. Instead, she stood in front of him and made a show of removing her ring.

"You believe in the Great Prophet?"

Adrian nodded again as Dalya put her ring in a pouch on her belt. She then closed the gap between them, standing uncomfortably close. Adrian pulled at the manacles as his weight shifted back onto his heels.

"And his divine blood?"

He began to nod again but stopped almost immediately when he realized what exactly she was asking him. Dalya laughed and placed her hand on his chest.

"Oh, no, please be honest. It's *refreshing*. You believe that djinn-worshiping horse fucker on the throne is Shai'Khal's salvation. *Please* enlighten me about how that's supposed to work."

Her hand slid down along his chest to his belt. Adrian clenched his teeth and instinctively tried to arch away from her hand. "I don't know that it needs saving."

"Of course," she purred. Dalya tilted her head a little, and Adrian glanced away from her as she undid his belt, her hand groping at him. Of all the tortures he'd imagined would be thrown at him, this was not one he'd expected. "I'm sure they're just misunderstood, these cultists. Minding their own business. That's why one advises the Shah and the other... Well, just what *is* she up to?"

"I don't know," Adrian answered through gritted teeth. Her hand dropped away from his crotch, and Adrian's relief quickly turned to dread as he saw her hand go to her belt.

"No, no, no, dear, you were so promising!" Dalya's singsong voice grew excited.

Adrian couldn't pull any farther away from her than he already was. Her hand grabbed his jaw, and Adrian tried to jerk his head away but was shocked at her grip. Her other hand held a razor-sharp dagger. He barely felt anything at first, just an odd tug followed by a soft *plop* on the ground. Then came the searing pain. Dalya stepped away from him. She wiped the blood off her dagger. Adrian made the mistake of looking down. Panic rose in his chest. His left ear was on the ground. Adrian dry-heaved and looked away.

"You know, I would have thought one of the Shah's men might have a better stomach for such things."

Adrian shot her as potent a glare as he could muster, though it was short-lived as Dalya stepped close again. He wouldn't tell her about the Key. He *couldn't.* If the Key fell into the wrong hands, Merikh's support would sputter out. If Alcaeus was proven correct, then Merikh would fall. The Shah trusted him to keep this secret. He was Ajir. He was *worthwhile*, damn it!

"I can't tell you what I don't know."

"Is your master going to care for your sacrifice and suffering?"

"I...don't know." Adrian didn't realize he'd given his thoughts breath until he felt Dalya's hand tracing his thigh to his groin. He pulled away and tried to ignore the smirk on the woman's face.

"There isn't a reason for you to suffer, Adrian. I'm going to enjoy myself either way. You might as well do so too."

Adrian squirmed away from her, and Dalya laughed.

"I flipped through the journal before coming in here. An old djinn worshiper leading you to a lost Akhenic temple, hmm? To find something that explains why those 'Pantheon gods' no longer walk the world? You naïve fool." Dalya tsked, and her hand dropped away from him. "They are *djinns*, Adrian. You want to help let loose djinns upon the world? Have you ever seen one? A ghul or an ifrit? I have. I've seen what they do to the possessed. Unspeakable things that make *me* look kind. I will not let you or any other cultist let those abominations loose in Shai'Khal."

Adrian *had* seen an ifrit once, in the palace desmoterion. One of Merikh's tutors had been trying to...Adrian wasn't sure what. Teach Merikh some sort of necromancy lesson? All Adrian remembered was the circle of glyphs, a sudden coldness, and then lightning-blue eyes. He'd passed out at that point, and Merikh had filled in the gaps.

"I asked you a question, Adrian. What are you looking for?"

"I don't *know.*"

Dalya sighed. Her hand around his cock squeezed painfully hard before she let go. She pulled the shears off her belt. Adrian pulled away frantically, almost relieved when she reached up for his hand. Still, Dalya wasn't the tallest woman, and Adrian could make it impossible for her to easily reach his hand. For a brief moment, he saw frustration in Dalya's eyes. It was quickly replaced by dark satisfaction.

"It's your choice what you keep, Adrian." Her free hand ran down his chest as they both looked down at his open salwar.

"No, no—" Adrian panicked. He barely noticed when she caught his fingers in her hand until the coldness of the shears touched his skin. His screams echoed off the walls. He tried to yank his hand away again, only stopping when he felt the slick wetness of the blades on his next finger.

"I'll do it again if you don't stop lying. I *know* what you are. The telepath in Hatai screamed everything she could about you. She wanted to save her daughter. I burned that disgusting district to the ground, and Akhenios willing, that fire took the rest of Hatai with it. I know you, Adrian Charmichi. I know the bitch you've got hidden under the ice is Sarka. And that ice means you're Ajir. You're going to tell me about the journal, and the temple, or I'm going to start removing more than fingers. But not before I call in one of my men to fuck you bloody."

Adrian gritted his teeth. She sounded both excited and frustrated. She wanted the information. She wanted him to suffer. Her nature was at odds with her needs.

"I don't know... No, no, please, I can—"

The shears snapped shut, and another finger fell to the ground. Dalya put the shears back on her belt and grabbed a cloth off it instead. She tied it over his fingers.

"You can what?"

Adrian panted heavily, trying to focus through the pain.

"I'm not Ajir, not *yet*. I'm too young," Adrian lied. His lie was interrupted as Dalya slid her hand into his salwar and cupped him.

"Not *too* young by the feel of it." She winked at him, her tone suddenly conversational and light-hearted. As if she hadn't just cut off his fingers.

"I help run the household. I deliver *letters*, I fetch coffee. I don't know anything valuable."

"You know enough that you were sent here with Sarka."

"The Shah wanted someone to keep an eye on her while she followed this trail of nonsense. I was the lowest-ranking person and got stuck with the job." His words were thick as he tried to keep his cheek still.

"Really? Nonsense?" Dalya cocked her head slightly. "Do better, dear. Why would you protect nonsense so hard? Has it been worth losing so much over?"

She removed her hand from inside his salwar and grabbed the shears again. Dalya yanked away the cloth despite Adrian trying to grab it with his remaining fingers. He wasn't losing another one! Adrian panicked, and in his desperation forgot about his broken ankle. He tried to put weight on it, to kick her with his stronger leg. Instead, he lost his balance. The pain in his ankle almost eclipsed the pain of losing another finger.

I wish I'd never left home. I never should have become Ajir. I should have turned it down. I saved your life once, damn it! You promised—you promised!—I'd never see the inside of another desmoterion.

Nausea became worse. Sweat mingled with blood. The torture chamber seemed to be getting hotter, though Adrian didn't know if that was in his head or not. Dalya asked him a question, but she was hard to hear. She'd moved closer to his left side now. All he could hear was the sound of his heart beating. A draft sent a chill over Adrian. The pressure on his arm from Dalya disappeared as a sudden blaze of flames flashed in front of Adrian. The Fari commander was sent tumbling away from him, her kameez on fire. Dalya hit the wall and fell limply to the ground, the shears now embedded in her inner thigh.

Sarka stood at the entrance to the torture chamber. Her hair wild, eyes white, and body wreathed in flame. She looked every bit the djinn Akhenics feared.

CHAPTER 30

Sarka ran forward, careful of the blood on the ground. Adrian was barely recognizable from his injuries.

"I've got you," Sarka said as she focused on the manacles. A little telekinesis snapped the locking mechanism, and Sarka supported Adrian, who clearly favored one of his ankles. His hands were shaking as he brought them to the ties of his salwar. Sarka bit her lip as she saw the missing fingers.

You deranged bitch, Sarka thought as she realized Adrian was trying to tie his salwar closed.

"I'm sorry," Adrian muttered.

"Don't be. I've got you. This is going to hurt, but it'll stop the bleeding," Sarka said, barely giving him warning before flames danced over his hand. He cried in pain, but the look he gave her didn't seem to begrudge it. Sarka glanced toward Adrian's assailant. Judging by the flames, smoke, and the blood pooling from around her thigh, the Fari commander had minutes to live.

So do we if we don't get moving, Sarka thought. She'd set most of Kal Neveh on fire to get in, and even though Sarka was impervious to flames, the smoke could kill her as easily as it would Adrian.

Sarka shouldered most of Adrian's slight frame and helped him hobble from the room. She retraced their way back through the burning fortress. The thick black smoke choked her lungs and clouded her vision. Sarka followed the vague human silhouettes of others escaping the fortress. It felt like an eternity before they found the door and cold morning air hit Sarka's lungs. She coughed, then winced in sympathy as she heard Adrian do the same. Only his sounded far more pained. The yard was in chaos as soldiers tried to put out the fires.

"Horses," Adrian rasped.

"Yeah, I have them out there." Sarka gestured with her free hand toward the gate. "Just hang on a bit longer."

Two Swords tried to stop them passing through the gate. A look from Sarka turned them into piles of ashes. Her head felt as if someone had taken a club to it, from both magic and the smoke around them.

Once outside the fort, the horses were thankfully not far. Just far enough off the road to Ziyadi that no one had noticed them. Awkwardly, Sarka helped Adrian into his saddle and put his reins to his left hand. She kept the lead from his gelding when she mounted her own, unwilling to give Adrian full control of his horse in case he lost his reins. His right hand was useless.

They followed the road north, toward the Membiti-Buhet fork. For the majority of the day, they stuck to the road and only left it when Sarka feared an Onyx Sword patrol. She kept one eye on the sky, watching as the sun hit its zenith and slowly began its descent. Sarka half expected to see messenger birds speeding through the sky to alert Onyx Sword garrisons of their passage. If Sarka had managed to save their supplies and camel, they would have left the road, headed straight east for the Sarafi, and followed along the route they'd used from Hatai. But cutting across the savanna was too dangerous this close to Ziyadi—visibility was too far. The foothills of the mountains at least provided them with some shelter and a better chance of hunting or scavenging food.

When the sun set, they rode off the path to the nearest tall hill. On the far side of its peak, Sarka dismounted. Adrian waited, and she pulled him off carefully. His ankle had swollen in his boot; she could see the ties were stretched. She didn't let her eyes linger, instead setting herself to the task at hand.

A small flame appeared in front of her, just barely enough to see by to undo the tack. She placed the saddles and blankets down carefully, laying the bridles nearby before hobbling the horses. Sarka dug a handful of dried dates out of her saddlebag and offered them to Adrian. He'd propped himself up against one of the saddles and pulled his gelding's saddle blanket over himself for warmth. He shook his head before turning away from Sarka and making as if he was trying to sleep. She doubted he'd find any, but she left him to it and walked up the hill a ways to keep watch.

Small pinpricks of light checkered the lowlands around them. Most stayed close to the road. Sarka wondered how many of them were Onyx Swords and not travelers stuck between cities. For the moment at least, she couldn't see movement. The night was calm.

Sarka walked the hill, placing small enchanted traps around its base. They'd set off a small fire, enough to warn them if Swords were incoming. Sarka hoped their luck would improve. She could handle a few dozen again, if she had to, but not a garrison. Her body still ached from the day's exertion, her throat sore and her head pounding dully.

Where's Dayo when you need her? Sarka thought with a bitter smile. Dayo had fought at Sarka's side during the Unification War. The champion of Vindaram had kept smoke away from Sarka and in her enemies' eyes. Dayo had been the perfect ally, right up until she died.

When Sarka finished, she made her way back to camp. The horses were grazing contentedly, and for a moment, Sarka thought Adrian asleep. Then she saw the shaking, heard the catching of breath of a strangled sob. It wasn't the first time Sarka wished she were a healer, and it wouldn't be the last. Adrian wasn't a soldier. He was unassuming, happy to hide in the shadows of greater men. Protected by them. If he'd ever had to see darkness like that before, it had always been from a safe distance. Merikh had put a great deal of faith in Adrian, but at the end of the day, Adrian had barely outgrown boyhood.

I should have pushed for someone else. A soldier, Sarka thought. Then again, if she had, they might never have found the second journal. She would be wandering Hatai hoping for a clue to drop in her lap without him.

"Thank you for saving me from the temple," Sarka said quietly, sitting down beside her saddle and her mare's blanket a few feet away from Adrian. He said nothing, and Sarka let out a slow breath. She'd never been good at this. Nine hundred years with few companions only made it more difficult.

"What happened to your cousin?" she asked. Sarka didn't necessarily expect a response, but she appreciated when Adrian rolled over onto his back. He was cradling his injured arm. At some point while she'd been setting traps, he'd dug through the saddlebags and found something to cover it with.

"They're dead because of me. I screwed everything up." Adrian's words were slow, a little slurred together as he tried hard not to move his mouth much.

"You did everything you thought was right. You did everything you could. It's not your fault." Sarka tried to be convincing, but it didn't work. All it earned her was a glare she could feel in the darkness.

"My best wasn't good enough. And now it'll never be good enough. What am I supposed to do with half a hand? How many crippled Ajir have you seen?"

None. But Sarka wasn't about to say it.

"Yeah." Adrian scoffed. "There isn't the space for useless people in the palace. I'm going to lose my work, my home, everything."

"Come on, Adrian, Merikh trusts you, and surely that'll count for something," Sarka pointed out. "A home in the Jibbah District, maybe? And you've got plenty of connections to leverage. Give yourself some credit." Her words were met with a short, bitter laugh.

"*Connections to leverage* because the Shah trusts me. You're right. I won't just lose my home and work, the Shah'll finish the job himself to make sure I'm not a fount of information to support my lifestyle."

Livinja, this would be much easier if I didn't think he was right, Sarka thought. Adrian already knew her opinions about Merikh. She hadn't exactly been quiet about them, and perhaps a month of whispering in Adrian's ears about what a truly terrible master his friend was had undercut any credibility she had in trying to convince him that Merikh would honor the sacrifices given.

"Adrian, you saved my life. I don't know if Merikh will thank you for that or not. But I swear as Livinja's champion, I will use every ounce of my strength to keep you safe. You would be safe if I hadn't been stubborn, and I refuse to let you keep paying the price for something that was not your fault."

She could feel his skepticism in the dark, and she heard him turn away from her and get comfortable on his side again. Or as comfortable as one could get using a saddle for a pillow.

"Don't make promises you can't keep, Champion."

"I don't." *Ikharon take me if I do.*

CHAPTER 31

12th of Belith, Dry Season, 902 Unified Age
Madiar, Raudhah Province

"Mawla? The sanctum is nearly full."

The acolyte looked nervous standing in the doorway of Alcaeus's chamber.

"Good, thank you," Alcaeus said, distracted as he straightened his kaftan. Alcaeus reached for the nearby ghutrah and placed the long scarf over his head. Alcaeus took a deep, deliberate breath. No one enjoyed presiding over memorial ceremonies.

"Did my invitation receive any response?" Alcaeus asked. A messenger had come from the palace inviting Alcaeus to the vigil that Loralee and Ruya were holding for the dead from Hatai's riot. An invitation that, unsurprisingly, he had turned down. Instead, he sent the royal messenger back to the palace with an invitation to the Shah, to have Merikh join Alcaeus here today instead.

Alcaeus was hardly surprised when the acolyte shook her head. The invitation had been a purely political move, after all. Alcaeus had lost all hope of being able to sway Merikh back to the light after his renunciation of Akhenios in private. The renouncement, combined with Merikh's marriage and a khanum "crowned" by that priestess? The Shah could claim neutrality all he liked, but it was quite clear where his priorities and loyalties lay.

It doesn't matter, Alcaeus thought, *not in the end.* The Shah had false priestesses and djinn. He had Akhenios. Alcaeus looked over to the acolyte and gestured for her to head out of the room. He followed her to the main sanctum as the last of the stragglers filtered in from outside. The acolyte left Alcaeus at the entrance, heading toward the minarets to silence the criers. Any remaining stragglers would have to enter the main sanctum quietly.

Incense of myrrh perfumed the main sanctum as Alcaeus entered. He washed his hands and bare feet in the ablution fountain near the door. The sound of water splashing began to silence those within the sanctum. Alcaeus took a candle from an acolyte. The vigil would be a purification ceremony, born of fire and water and prayer.

"We are here to pray for the souls of the Faithful lost in Hatai, for the salvation of misguided souls, and for wisdom to grace and continue to grace our Onyx Swords and priesthood," Alcaeus said as he approached the altar with his candle.

One of the Priest Council, Pedhani Priestess Maysa, joined Alcaeus at the altar. Upon it were numerous sticks of incense as well as a large basin of water from the ablution fountain. Alcaeus lit one of the incense sticks, watching and waiting for ashes to fall into the wooden base.

"The Great Prophet purified himself before every great battle of Unification for protection, and after for the souls lost. Through purification, we shed the blemishes from our souls and offer more pleasing prayers to Akhenios. Following the Great Prophet's footsteps, we pray for those in Hatai. For those who died defending Akhenios. For those who died without knowing salvation. We pray Akhenios might take pity on their souls and welcome them to Aljemel."

Alcaeus took the ashes from the incense and rubbed them over his hands. Some were still painfully hot. Alcaeus tried to hide his flinching.

"As always, we pray for the end of djinnic influence over our country. For the wisdom to see false prophets for what they are, and the humility to admit failure..."

There was a very quiet murmur through the normally silent congregation, though Alcaeus imagined what he had left to say would silence their sounds of agreement.

"...and keep the hearts and minds of the Faithful open to their prodigal neighbors, to encourage and accept them kindly back into the Temple. To keep ego and arrogance removed from our souls as best we can. The Great Prophet himself charges us to welcome the misguided into our arms and homes, to show them Akhenios's truth."

Maysa gently took Alcaeus's hands in hers and scrubbed the ashes off his skin, rinsing the grime into the basin of holy water. Once his hands were clean, she handed him a white towel to dry them with before she lit another piece of incense. Her prayers were quiet, for Akhenios only.

When she finished, her hands coated in ashes, Alcaeus washed hers clean before turning toward the Akhenic Faithful. He gestured toward the altar, an open invitation for anyone who wished to purify and pray. Acolytes and priests created lines, and the poorest citizens of Madiar were, as always, first to the altar, as guided by the Scrolls. Poor men had less sunlight to spend. The rich could afford to do their dealings by candlelight.

When the parishioners had emptied from the main sanctum, Alcaeus remained at the altar to wait for the last pieces of incense to burn. He mixed the ashes into the dirty water before he picked up the basin. Water in the desert was too precious to go to waste. Within the Akhenic Scrolls, the Great Prophet had outlined exactly what uses sinful water could have.

The water sloshed in the basin, threatening to spill onto Alcaeus's gray kaftan as he carried it from the sanctum. At the entrance to the garden, Alcaeus put the basin down and pulled on a pair of sandals. The stone paths that led to the fruit trees were burning hot. Alcaeus picked his way through the path until he found the oldest tree in the garden and poured the basin out at its roots. The old date tree had purified a great deal of water over the years, and its fruits had fed plenty of Madiar's poorest. It was living proof that goodness and truth sprung forth and won the day over sin and decay.

"Mawla?"

Alcaeus shook the last few drips of the basin out on the tree before turning to see who'd addressed him. An acolyte stood a little way down the path and bore a thick letter.

"Thank you," Alcaeus said, taking the letter from the boy and giving him the basin in exchange. The letter was heavy, with a strange lump inside it. Alcaeus carried it to the cool privacy of his office. The wax seal bore the Akhenic Sun with two swords below it, a symbol only an Onyx Sword Fari Commander would have.

Alcaeus sat down at his desk and cracked the letter open. As he unfolded it, a pendant fell heavily onto his desk. It was a silver Akhenic Sun with a strange onyx stone set in the middle. Overlaid on it in silver was half a shamshir, to look as if it was impaling the sun. Alcaeus bit his lip. Rabb Khamisi, Duqa Enitan's legate, had told him about the pendants that appeared around the Shah whenever an assassination attempt happened of late. Was this meant as a warning? Alcaeus placed the pendant down on his desk, the light from a sunbeam dancing off of the silver brightly.

To Akhenios's Most Blessed, High Priest Alcaeus,

The penmanship was poor, as though whoever had written it had tried at first to make it legible and then had given up halfway through.

I take full responsibility for the events of Hatai and Ziyadi. In fact, I take credit for doing what was needed to be done when no one else would act. I have followed the path Akhenios has set before me, and I believe I can no longer follow that path from Kal Neveh. As such, I've sent this bird ahead of my arrival in Madiar bearing a gift.

"Well, that's bold," Alcaeus muttered under his breath as he kept reading.

Be careful who you wear this pendant around. You'll soon find out who among your priests and Swords can be trusted. I certainly have.
Akhenios's faithful servant,
Dalya Maki
Fari Commander of Kal Neveh
High Inquisitor of the Sanctified Suns

Alcaeus let out a slow breath and put the letter down near the pendant. A shadow crossed the window briefly, followed by a soft *thud* against the ground. Alcaeus picked up the pendant and crossed the room to the window. On the ground a few feet below lay a dead raven, though it didn't look like it had hit the temple or been attacked by anything. Alcaeus receded back from the casement, shaking his head. He wasn't a terribly superstitious man, but that was hardly a good omen. Alcaeus turned the pendant over in his hand before placing it back down on the table and picking up the letter again.

Her words made his heart sink. The pendant confirmed his fears. Merikh had crippled him with the Priest Council purge. He'd struggled for years to keep the Temple on a uniform message, trying to avoid this *exact* sort of thing. Zealots, driven by their own purpose. And he'd failed.

How many innocent people have been killed for this? There was a vizier who had been poisoned months ago. Amir Olumide had nearly fallen to an assassin who, according to Rabb Khamisi, was rumored to be connected to the first attack. Now Hatai? Even worse, what did she mean by events in Ziyadi? What had this woman done?

Akhenios, I don't have the heart for this. What were the Faithful coming to? It had been one thing to *say* he'd do anything to save the Akhenic Temple; it was another to do it. Alcaeus put the letter back down, picked up the pendant, and left the office. It was a short walk through tapestry-lined halls to the high inquisitor's office. The door was ajar enough for Alcaeus to see the man's riding boots on his desk. Alcaeus woke the other man from his nap with a knock on the door.

"Mawla! Apologies." High Inquisitor Adunbi quickly scrambled to his feet.

"What do you know of Kal Neveh?" Alcaeus asked, not hiding his irritation. Adunbi hadn't attended the vigil for Hatai, and he certainly had work he could have been doing instead of napping.

"It's, uh, it's an outpost in the Katu. I think it's fairly new, under Inquisitor Kwesi's jurisdiction in Tanga." Adunbi sat back down in his chair behind his desk and rummaged through a drawer until he pulled out a map. He smoothed it down on the desk as Alcaeus approached.

"That's close to the Southern Pass. A rather important fort," Alcaeus said.

"If we're moving troops... Are we moving troops?"

"Are you?" Alcaeus demanded. "If it's a new fort, you signed off on it. Are you moving Onyx Swords east?"

Adunbi stammered for a moment before he began digging through his drawers again. "All of the inquisitors have the right to proselytize and set up temples wherever there are people."

"Funny, I thought this was the Madiar temple, not Kal Madiar. If Kal Neveh is a temple, where is its city? What other forts have popped up along the Katu that you haven't kept me apprised of? What sort of control do you even *have* over your Swords?" Alcaeus was shouting by the end, drawing a small crowd.

"Apologies, Mawla. I appear to be negligent in my duties." Adunbi's tone betrayed his irritation. "But my inquisitors are doing exactly what they've always done, under every other high inquisitor. If you expect different reports, then you'll have them. You need only ask."

Doing what they've always done, except that was peacetime. Now is the deep breath before diving into battle. Alcaeus wanted to shake the other man but doubted it would do any good.

"I want your signature on every new fort, and I want an accurate counting of our Swords by the end of the month. I'd prefer it by the end of the week, but I don't expect any numbers you may have to be accurate."

"As you ask, Mawla."

Alcaeus nodded and left the room. The crowd in the hallway quickly scattered back to their prayers and studies as Alcaeus found his way to the inner sanctum. He'd meant to ask Adunbi about the pendant but hadn't the heart to do so in front of an audience. He needed to calm down first, then perhaps he'd consult the Temple Archives instead. He had a strange feeling he'd seen the symbol before, but he couldn't place it.

After washing in the ablution fountain, Alcaeus approached the statue of Akhenios. It was as cold as ever when Alcaeus gently touched its base.

Send me something, Akhenios. Strike down the priestesses, send me a Faithful Madiaran bastard, anything. As usual, the statue was silent. Its inaction lacked the comfort Alcaeus wanted. He placed the pendant at the foot of the statue before he took a few steps back and kneeled down on a prayer mat. Meditation and supplication would balm his anger. Perhaps even provide the divine inspiration he desperately needed.

CHAPTER 32

The olive-tree table took up most of the room. Carved into the tabletop was a map of Shai'Khal in exquisite detail. Every major city in Shai'Khal was marked, along with major topographical points. The rivers bore enchantments to showcase which were impassable during the Monsoon Season, and there were points along the Sarafi's edge that marked areas prone to sandstorms during the Dry Season. Small tokens covered the table's surface, symbols of the various noble houses and the Akhenic Temple.

To the west of the Katu, the territory was void of royal allies. Half a province already sworn to a power they deemed higher than the Shah, just skirting the line to war. No official declaration had come from Duqa Enitan yet, nor from Alcaeus, but after Hatai, it was inevitably close. War breathed down Merikh's neck, yet no one wanted to make the first move. His hands were bound; the Temple had yet to move openly against him. Without Duqa Enitan moving troops, without Alcaeus declaring a holy war, Merikh had to keep the peace if he meant to claim the higher moral ground. Keeping the high ground would matter in the eyes of history, if nothing else.

The north, at least, was quiet. Though how long it would remain so, Merikh didn't trust. Amir Navin would keep a hold over the houses bound to him by marriage and blood. The rest of the north claimed to be allies or at least neutral. The only thing more rampant than poppy in the north was corruption; fealty from one of those nobles came and went faster than the air it was spoken on.

No wonder Mansur preferred it. If funds hadn't been diverted for immediate gratification, Mansur would have built a northern palace in Ramshar. Merikh doubted there would be any sudden religious conversions from the northern nobles. How much coin the Akhenic Faithful peasantry could raise, however, was an unknown Merikh didn't care for. In the northwest, if

Amira Jin couldn't keep that promised neutrality, Merikh didn't favor Madiar's defensibility. If forces came down the Kura, if Abadan and Rajibad fell, there was nothing to prevent a siege from starving out Madiar.

"How many ships do we have?" Merikh asked. There were twelve men and women in the war room with Merikh: ten Sardar generals, Ajir Captain Bashir, and a vizier scribe in the corner. One of the Sardar generals flipped through a stack of papers on the corner of the table before pulling out a report with an exaggerated flourish.

"Fifty-one. Eighteen that will remain loyal to you. Scouts say there are likely seventeen ships that will fly Akhenic banners as soon as war's declared. Amira Jin has six ships of her own, and there's another ten who aren't reliable as either for or against us. So that leaves sixteen vessels that can keep pirates off trade routes or be commandeered by either side. Duqa Enitan has Nabi's shipyard. Arashti's shipyards won't be reliable for us. Baruna Masih has committed to staying *out* of this, if possible. Not a northern problem in her mind."

The baruna would undoubtedly sell them ships, but Merikh shuddered to think at the cost she'd charge for them. Nothing in life was free, even for a shah.

"I want Nabi's shipyard burned, sooner rather than later. We need reinforcements in Ogot. It's our only port in Ydeba," Merikh said, gesturing to the port on the table. "I want Duqa Sachiko's forces bolstered, and I want Luma under our control."

Ogot and Luma were parallel cities on opposite sides of Ydeba, Luma in the north and Ogot in the south. If he could hold both ports, he had a staging point for holding the coast.

The scribe took down hurried notes. Sardar General Harith Aritza, a wizened Yahidah commander, cleared his throat. The man was old enough to retire, but Merikh valued his counsel. The Sardar general had been an Ajir when he'd led Merikh's year-long patrol as a teenager. Merikh was more than willing to trust his life to the man once again.

"Al Haraf and Metif should be easily defended. All but one of their ships can be moved to Ogot." The Sardar general moved the ships from the desert ports to Ogot as he spoke. "As far as Luma, Sayida Aret won't take kindly to troop movements. If we move ships before war is declared, I fear we'll have them burned in port."

"Then leave them in Shira. We can move them slowly, and the alkont won't be able to say no to patrols," Merikh said.

"Won't that violate the neutrality terms you negotiated with the amira? If you break it, there may be others driven to Duqa Enitan's side," Harith pointed out.

Merikh gave a small shrug. "Alkont Rinji owes me for his sister's happiness. Why else do you think I pushed for marital reforms? I hardly care about same-gender marriages. I wanted an amira and alkont in my pocket. He'll keep quiet. Besides, if Rabb Swaran decides to send all his ships to protect a shipment to a merchant in Shira, and those ships just happen to stay in port until the war starts, that's hardly a violation."

"Amira Jin has the largest fleet of ships in Shai'Khal. Manipulating her brother-in-law is a risky proposition when she's Faithful."

"Her closest childhood friend is my wife. The amira's anger can be balmed easily," Merikh said firmly. Amira Jin had looked for a means to avoid fighting. She wouldn't look for cause to join it. Merikh was certain he could rely on that. Harith frowned but didn't argue. Merikh looked back to the table and continued.

"I want Duqa Enitan's only option to be through the Katu," he instructed. "If she wants to march on my cities, she'll have to brave mountain passes. Have trade embargoes on Bayaba, Nabi, and Duak ready. Make the duqa decide what gets priority in those passes—supplies or soldiers."

"That puts all the pressure on Amir Xolani, Shahanshah," Harith said, gesturing toward Membiti and the Katu.

"My garrisons can handle it, Aritza," Sardar General Opeyemi Sastre's tone was cool, the woman the lone Umbeah in the room. Normally she stayed with her garrison in Membiti, but Merikh had recalled his generals for this one last consultation. Messengers and birds could easily be intercepted or killed. Here at least his generals would know exactly what he expected of them before they left.

"Your loyalty isn't in question, Opeyemi," Harith said, "but your people are ardently religious. There are more Onyx Swords in Ydeba than anywhere else. If we push the amir too hard, if the civilian costs grow too high, his hand might be forced to betrayal."

"If that's the case, I'll bring the Shah the amir's head on my shield." Opeyemi glanced to Merikh, the beads in her dreadlocks rattling.

He ignored the general's posturing. Merikh had no doubt of Opeyemi's abilities. The woman had proven herself against Emani and rogue Umbeah chieftains and tribes time and time again. But Harith wasn't wrong. Amir Xolani was caught in a bloody trap with few ways out. His life, his family, could easily hang in the balance. Membiti couldn't fall, not at any cost. They needed the amir's support or Ydeba would be lost. Merikh ran his hand over his jaw, staring at the map.

Opeyemi continued. "If you can afford troops from Kal Mahar's desmoterion, we can reinforce Ogot and Buhet. Kabatwe should be safe on Lake Osmiti if we have Luma's port shut down. My garrison is already stretched thin. If Rajibad or Abadan can afford troops, then we can protect Membiti."

"Not Rajibad," Harith said quickly. "Keep the amir's men as a bulwark for Madiar. We need safe trade from Rajibad. Never mind threats coming down the Kura. If we move too many troops to reinforce cities, we'll have Akhenic zealots popping up away from Ydeba. This isn't simply a power-hungry duqa seeking Ydeban independence. You have enemies all over the country within temples. Just because there aren't armies in the north rallied against you, doesn't mean there won't be uprisings."

"We're working on that," Bashir spoke up from beside Merikh. "The grand vizier and I have been trying to find leaders in the Akhenic community that fall outside of the temple structure, and we have been putting a quiet end to them when possible. Reputation smearing is slow work, but it at least doesn't create martyrs."

Silence followed. Merikh knew what needed to be done, who needed to be sent. Two months ago he wouldn't have hesitated. Now? He was surprised by his own reticence, the underlying worry that Loralee wouldn't approve.

"The Neredi cavalry is the best in the country. If we send Duq Alaziz to Ydeba, they can prevent any siege weaponry or forces coming from the south. Amir Xolani can focus on holding the northern pass."

Another of the Sardar generals looked uncomfortable, shifting from foot to foot. "If Amir Navin changes his mind, the Mureadi Grasslands are easy for northern armies to cross. We'd be better off keeping the cavalry between us and enemies. The Sarafi will wear down any forces from the west."

"I cannot leave everything as is, worrying that war might come from the north," said Merikh. "What makes you think my uncle will move against Madiar? He's terrified of me. He didn't lift a finger to save his own *sister*. He's not going to risk spilling blood over faith, *if* he worships anything other than gold. Worst he'll do is manufacture an opium crisis to drive up prices. My coffers can handle it."

One hopes. Merikh kept the thought to himself. Mansur had nearly emptied the royal coffers by the time Merikh had killed him. Four years of trimming fat and raising taxes had slowly begun to refill them. But wars were expensive. Unpaid soldiers were easily swayed from their posts.

"That's fine defensively. We need to take, at minimum, six cities," Opeyemi said, placing tokens on Tanga, Nabi, Bayaba, Sek, Duak, and Luma, "if we want to deal with the traitorous noble families. Ideally, if we could take Tanga first, that cuts the head off the snake, but short of a miracle, that won't happen. Sek is buried in the mountains. Easy to siege if there aren't any tunnels out of the city. If there are, it'll be nearly impossible to take without a great deal of sorcerers.

"I think the priority should be to take Nabi. If we have to burn the shipyards, then we do so, but I'd rather take the city and keep the yards if possible. Then we have a staging point for taking Duak and Tanga. Otherwise, we need a safe beach to land on and set up a fort, something I don't think the duqa will give us time for. If we can't get a beachhead, we're fighting with the duqa in the mountain passes, a situation I think we can all agree should be avoided at all costs."

"Kontess Dalal has offered Metif's troops. Start moving them south," Merikh said. "I will speak with Amir Xolani. He might be able to convince his sister to remain away from the offensive and keep her forces simply defending Duak instead of pursuing our fleet. If not, I'll push Kontess Rehema in Buhet to sacrifice troops to take the C'ezaji Pass and have troops from Ogot meet them there to siege the city."

For the first time, Merikh regretted the lack of a shahzade. Now that the khanum title was taken, eyes moved to the future. To the *next* khanum or khan. It would be easier to barter off that title with a baby on Loralee's lap.

There was a murmur of agreement through the generals before Captain Bashir spoke up.

"What about Madiar?" Bashir asked carefully. "We've been restricting districts, increasing guards on patrols, and trying to minimize and frustrate movements of Onyx Swords coming into the city and those already here. The more we prepare for the inevitable, the sooner it'll happen."

Merikh had already seen the fruits of Bashir's efforts. More merchant petitions in court demanding the restrictions and searches at the city gates be returned to normal. Getting into the city was much harder now, and took far longer. Once within the city, guard patrols had effectively shut down certain thoroughfares. They only allowed a certain number of people through along any one road. Necessary barricades and restrictions to ensure the city could withstand an internal uprising. But the measures were certainly making the law-abiding citizenry frustrated.

"Burn the temple," one of the Sardar generals said flippantly before a supplicatory raising of his hands. "I'm not serious," he clarified.

It hardly quelled the glares. Despite the looks, Merikh didn't entirely disagree with the general. The temple couldn't be razed, but it couldn't be left as an Akhenic stronghold. Alcaeus had to be forced out. Madiar had room for only one ruler, and Merikh would see the city burn before he left his throne to Alcaeus.

"Once an official declaration of war has been made, Alcaeus will be given the chance to leave the city with his priests and Swords. They'll be given safe passage to Ydeba." Merikh raised his hand to quell inevitable protests. "He won't accept it. In that case, Madiar will fall into martial law. The Mitbah District homes that back onto the Temple District will be evacuated, the Kelle Bazaar shut down."

"That bazaar caters to the city nobles, and your kitchens, almost exclusively," Bashir pointed out.

"Then it is a good thing I am a man of simple tastes. The rest of the palace and nobles can learn to follow suit. Worry more about the ire raised by relocating the people," Merikh said with a frown.

These moves would make him unpopular, more so than he was already becoming. After all, it would be all too easy for Alcaeus to point out there were no plans to move the poorest in the Hock District away from the fighting. There were too many of them; it would already be difficult to find a place for the displaced from the Mitbah.

Well, I can live with being despised, Merikh thought.

"Anything else?" Merikh asked. There was a murmur of "no" through the generals. Merikh took a deep breath, letting it out slowly as he looked over the table.

"Then I regret to inform this council that I do not feel adequately informed nor prepared. Press your scouts, your contacts, for greater information. Bashir, I want more work done here in Madiar to destroy Alcaeus's reputation. He's been sitting on a pedestal too long. Find me *something.*"

His words were met with affirmations. Merikh flicked over one of the Akhenic Sun tokens over by Madiar before he turned and left the room. They were holding back; Merikh was certain. He'd seen his father lose his temper repeatedly in council meetings at the generals, and Merikh knew old habits died hard. Most of the Sardar generals serving Merikh had served his father. Only a few had reacted poorly to Merikh's succession and had needed removal. That meant most of these men and women were used to a shah whose temper was prone to erupting at any bad news and reaching impulsive solutions. Merikh would admit it had been a long time since he'd visited the provinces, particularly west. He'd never won a war—his battles were all small skirmishes against highwaymen or Emani. He'd studied his forefathers' wars but not as thoroughly as his generals had. Unlike his father, Merikh had no desire to try to prove himself smarter than his subordinates. He merely had to trust them, something far easier said than done.

Amir Xolani would hate their plan. Duq Alaziz would undoubtedly take issue with it as well. The duq would have preferred staying in Abadan and protecting the Mureadi Grasslands, or perhaps sending reinforcements to

Madiar to allow the Royal Guard to reinforce Membiti. But Merikh wouldn't be a captive in his own city by Neredi guards, men more loyal to the whims of the Khanum than the Shah.

Not that Loralee is prone to whims, thank the gods, Merikh thought as he walked out of the barracks. The sun blinded him for a moment as he stepped into the training yard. The barracks neighbored the barns, and the large training arenas separated them. The main arena was busy. Several riders worked lines and circles, carefully avoiding each other. In the far corner, two spahi riders practiced with heavy leather-bound shamshirs to knock targets off posts. Merikh recognized the horses: two six-year-old bay stallions. There were five years of groundwork put into the royal horses before a rider's seat ever touched their saddles. Another five of riding instruction before they were put into a real work scenario with their partners.

If we can afford the time. Merikh looked away from them as he walked to the opposite arena fence.

Loralee had returned from the vigil and gotten to work immediately, riding her allotment of horses. She had Merikh's bay stallion, Iksandar, out. For how long, Merikh couldn't tell. The horse looked exceptionally fresh despite the sweat gleaming off his dark shoulders. Fourteen and still acting like a yearling half the time—this ride was no exception.

Absentmindedly, Merikh rubbed his shoulder. He hadn't ridden since the trip out to the Kura. The healers certainly weren't allowing him to ride his more challenging horses. They were still worried about his recovery. It had been Nikias's idea to have Loralee exercise Merikh's horses, and so far she hadn't been unseated, despite Iksandar's best attempts.

Loralee found a comfortable circle and asked for a canter. Her request was met with an indignant squeal before the stallion dropped his head and bucked twice. His fit over, Iksandar picked up into a canter. Merikh tsked under his breath.

"He's an idiot. I don't know why you keep him," a gruff voice muttered behind Merikh. He didn't have to look to know Sumiya approached.

"Yes, you do," Merikh told her as he leaned on the arena fence.

Loralee slowed the horse back to a stop before asking again. It was less explosive this time, but hardly perfect, as Iksandar kicked up his heels again. Merikh shifted his weight unconsciously.

"Well, if you can do better, go do better," Sumiya scoffed, waving a hand at the horse and rider.

"I can't at the moment," Merikh admittedly half-heartedly.

"Then shut up and let her do it. You're being loud." Sumiya gestured at all of him with a sour look on her weathered face. She joined him leaning against the rail. She was easily two feet shorter than him—one of the arena rails was set nearly at her eye level—making her slouch to see Loralee work.

"How come you're not dead yet, Sumi?"

"Ask your horses. They're doing a piss-poor job of sending me to Aljemel," Sumiya told him with a snort.

Merikh shook his head, the faintest touch of a smile on his face as he glanced down at the old woman. Sumiya was the only woman Merikh could remember standing up to his father and winning, the only person whose opinion could defeat Mansur's—at least in the barns. She didn't take any nonsense from Merikh either. Even if she often irritated him, even if her advice had to be deciphered through an uncouth tongue, Merikh appreciated her wisdom.

Loralee asked for the canter again, and her rein slapped Iksandar's flank when he threatened to kick up. Another indignant squeal left the stallion's throat before he cantered off politely. Loralee stopped him, rubbed his flank with her hand, then asked again. Iksandar gave it half a thought before picking himself up politely and taking the canter.

"What do you think?" Merikh asked, his tone serious.

"I told you, Iksandar is an idiot, and you have half a dozen stallions with a better brain. He's lucky his foals take after their dams."

"About the Khanum. Iksandar is a one-rider horse, you *know* he wouldn't dream of pulling those moves with me."

"That's why the healers won't let you near him, hmm?" Sumiya rolled her eyes before taking a deep breath. She let it out slowly and got lost in her thoughts for a while.

"Your father was a terrible shah," she said. "But if he'd been born a groom, he'd have been my replacement. Never met anyone with a better eye for flesh, horse or otherwise. Could look at a weanling and just *know* what it'd be good for. Picked the best pairs for perfect foals, better than I can, or you."

"Then the Khanum will produce the perfect shahzade," Merikh interrupted snidely. It earned him a hard jab in the ribs from Sumiya's thumb. Thankfully she stood on his right and not his left.

"Don't interrupt when you ask my advice, or I'll stop giving it," Sumiya scolded firmly. "Yes, she probably will. She's pretty and smart like your mother was, and you turned out not half bad. But she's got a good head on her shoulders, good seat and good hands. Proper horsewoman, *unlike* your mother." Sumiya looked away from Merikh and spat in the dirt. He couldn't help but laugh—it was the worst insult Sumiya could think of, being poor with horses.

"Then in your mind, I ought to trust her," Merikh said quietly, more to himself than Sumiya as he looked back toward Loralee. He didn't see Sumiya step up onto the lowest railing of the arena fence. Even with the added inches, she barely managed to slap the back of his head.

"If you're asking me, then you're an idiot, and Akhenios help Shai'Khal."

"I'm going to hang you from a tower by your ankles, old woman," Merikh snapped at her, rubbing the back of his head.

Sumiya scoffed before walking away from the arena. She knew a false threat when she saw one. Merikh couldn't afford to lose her counsel.

Merikh caught Loralee's eye, and with two fingers, waved her over to the fence. She stopped a few feet away. Iksandar lowered his head to scratch an itch on his leg, the stallion letting out a happy groan as he did so.

"He's a handful," Loralee said carefully, as if unsure whether she'd ridden well enough to earn another ride on such a horse or if Merikh was about to admonish her.

"You did fine."

They stood in silence for a moment, Loralee waiting patiently for him to say something. She was slowly growing more comfortable in the silences between them, no longer looking as if the emptiness would strangle her.

"I have a matter to discuss with you, about the Neredi cavalry," Merikh informed her.

She nodded, taking her feet out of her stirrups.

Merikh shook his head. "No, finish here. It can wait until you're done with him. How was the vigil?"

"Protested, but there were more attendees than protestors, so it certainly could have been worse. What do you need my father's men for?" Loralee asked, not distracted for long.

"Defending Membiti," Merikh answered honestly.

Loralee frowned only for the briefest of moments before hiding her displeasure at the thought. "We'll be done soon."

Merikh left her to ride, heading inside and back to the royal suite. He had enough letters to write to keep him occupied until he could speak with Loralee.

Waiting outside the royal suite was a servant from the aviary. Even without being able to feel the man's soul, Merikh would have known he was there—his clothes reeked of bird excrement. The servant bowed deeply, holding out a letter in front of him.

"Shahanshah, this just arrived."

Merikh took the letter and dismissed the man before the door opened ahead of him. The orange seal bore the oxen horns of House Iherjirika. Between the two horns were the crossed spears of the amir. News from Xolani hardly boded well. Merikh sat down at his desk before cracking open the seal.

Shahanshah,

> *I humbly request permission to prosecute Onyx Swords in Ydeba. While I understand this task falls to the Temple, I cannot allow these acts to continue. I formally request a royal warrant upon Dalya Maki, Fari Commander of the Onyx Swords in Kal Neveh. My scouts came upon the village of Ziyadi razed to the ground, credit openly taken by these rogue Swords, the "Sanctified Suns." If High Priest Alcaeus cannot control his men, then I implore you to allow me to do so.*
>
> *Your humble servant,*

Xolani Iherjirika, Amir of Ydeba

Xolani knew Merikh well enough to get to the point, dispensing with perfunctory flattery. The amir would have the royal warrant written today. A village burned, Swords openly taking credit? Burning out a district in Hatai that was notorious for cultists was one thing. Burning down an entire village? That was something else entirely. If they played it right, it would be something they could easily spin against Alcaeus. Merikh didn't imagine such an act had been sanctioned by the man, but the high priest had a short temper, though he was far too righteous to do something like this. Still, without Adrian here, Merikh didn't have ears in the temple that he trusted to relay accurate information, and he needed to know what Alcaeus was doing.

The bottom drawer of Merikh's desk opened. It was nearly bursting with scrolls, some yellowed and browned with age, while others were a crisp white. Merikh rummaged through the drawer before pulling out a scroll with a green seal. He shut the drawer with his foot as he cracked the wax. Drawn in the center of the scroll was a raven with intricate glyphs encircling it.

Merikh stood and carried the scroll out to the balcony, hesitating for a moment. He didn't much care for the side effects of these enchantments. The headache could last for days and left him painfully sensitive to light. But he saw few other timely options. Merikh let go of the scroll, and it hovered in front of him. He raised his right hand above the parchment. The black glyphs began to glow green.

His world went black. Ink shot off the parchment into a raven flying above the palace. Its eyes changed from black to pale green. Merikh could feel the wind beneath the raven's wings, and the world grew more vibrant. Soul displacement was a strange experience, as was flying. The headache set in, and while normally it started out as a dull, subtle ache, this one was far sharper. The healing enchantments in the salves for his injuries made necromancy more difficult. No matter. If all went well, he wouldn't need this body for long.

The bird was hungry, flying toward the Kelle Bazaar. That would have to wait. Once Merikh gained his bearings, he turned the bird toward the Temple. Its minarets glistened in the sun. Below, the Prophet's Shade was busy. A long line of people walked under the old olive branches. More were milling about within the courtyard by the fountains.

Carefully, Merikh landed in one of the olive trees. Human voices were more difficult to decipher through a bird. It was hard to keep the raven focused when it tried to watch for predators and look for food. But Merikh managed to hear a little bit of the conversation.

"I can't believe the high priest said that. How can he expect us to accept cultists back into the Temple? They're cultists! They'll never repent."

"I don't know…"

"Have you ever met one? Sanctimonious zealots. As if they've suddenly come upon some grand truth!"

"I went to the cultist vigil this morning. The priestess—"

The second man was immediately talked over by the first, reamed out for admitting to doing something so outlandish and dangerous. Merikh took the raven from fountain to fountain, trying to find anyone more important than the two he'd overheard before he brought the bird close to the temple walls. Alcaeus's office would have a window; Merikh had no doubt of that. After a few minutes of searching, Merikh felt Alcaeus's soul.

The window was open, and Merikh intended on having the bird land on its sill. He could see Alcaeus poring over a letter, a pendant nearby. But as he got close to the window, the headache worsened as if he'd been struck by an ax to the head. It was the last thing Merikh remembered before the world went black.

CHAPTER 33

Iksandar was not a horse to ride when distracted, and Merikh's interruption had left Loralee very much so. She knew her reaction was foolish, the sudden realization that yes, her father would be required to fight for the Shah. Naïvely, Loralee had hoped that her family would remain in Abadan, or at least in Raudhah. A relatively safe place, not sent straight into the fire.

Was it punishment? Her father always skirted dangerously close to the line between respectful and offensive. His personal opinion of Merikh was painfully low and obvious. Was this Merikh's way of removing her father, placing her cousin Khaliq as duq and hoping a younger man would cow easier to his wishes?

The stallion snorted at a nearby mare, and Loralee reprimanded him sharply. Well-behaved stallions could ignore mares, but it took a great deal of training and constant vigilance to make sure that training never lapsed. Loralee's mind was no longer in the saddle with her. She walked him through two more cooldown circles before she dismounted and led him to the barn. His manners were much improved on the ground, and he waited patiently for Loralee to finish up before she turned him back out in the paddock he shared with one of the Ajir's geldings. Loralee watched them play for a moment before hanging up Iksandar's halter and heading back inside the palace.

"Loralee!"

She had barely made it past the vestibule before Ruya bounded over, a bright smile on the high priestess's face.

"Do you have a moment? I know I've taken a great deal of your time already today, but I hoped we could regroup after this morning. I thought it went well, and having the Khanum at services certainly helps."

"I'm about to meet with the Shah," Loralee told her.

As usual, Ruya was unfazed.

"Perfect, I need to talk with Merikh too. Unless it's one of *those* meetings," Ruya teased, making a small lewd gesture with her hands.

Loralee couldn't help but shake her head and smile tiredly. Merikh's moods and desires were still as unpredictable as ever. He had yet to find the time to do much more than kiss her. Most nights, Loralee barely woke when he finally passed out on the bed. Loralee highly doubted that would change until she did something—and she wasn't going to push him while he was injured.

"I very much doubt it—"

"Perfect, then we can save some time and have words together," Ruya said before walking away from Loralee toward the royal suite.

"Ruya," Loralee started before sighing and giving up. There was little point arguing with the priestess. Whatever Ruya wanted to speak with Merikh about could be done first and done quickly. It would give her more time to prepare for whatever plan Merikh and his council had created for her father's men. Ruya surprised Loralee by letting them walk in silence toward the suite. As they turned down the corridor, Ruya hesitated. Her jaw dropped a little, and she cocked her head slightly in confusion. Loralee stopped and turned to look at her.

"What is it?"

"It's the strangest thing. I can feel Merikh's aura, but...there's no soul in that room. Well, no *human* soul," Ruya said, her tone confused, seemingly amused instead of worried.

"What on Cala are you talking about?" Loralee demanded before hurrying the last few steps to the door. It didn't open ahead of her as it usually did when Merikh was inside. She pushed the door open and looked immediately to her left. Merikh stood at the balcony. At first, Loralee felt relief. He was fine, though he was unusually still, even for him.

"Guar—"

"No, no, Loralee, don't trouble the guards. He's fine," Ruya said, shutting the door behind them. "He's using some very dangerous magic, but he's fine. Come on."

Ruya crossed the room and gestured for Loralee to follow. In front of Merikh, a scroll levitated. On it was a very panicked *moving* illustration of a bird.

"What in Alhanem..." Loralee muttered under her breath, resisting the urge to touch the paper. She twitched when she looked up to Merikh's face and saw his eyes were pale green and unblinking.

"Soul displacement. I believe your husband is flying. That poor bird is never going to be the same after being locked in ink. Better that than Merikh's body. I had a novice once who didn't displace properly, and he ended up in the body of an ostrich and the ostrich's soul in his body. Poor man never lived down the embarrassment."

"I imagine so," Loralee said, barely listening as she struggled with the idea of Merikh moving his *soul* into another creature. Before she had time to adjust, the scroll fell to the ground, and Merikh stumbled back as if pushed. Loralee caught him before he could fall and barely stepped out of the way in time as he vomited on the stone floor. His eyes were gold when he met her gaze. Merikh looked disoriented, blinking quickly and squinting at her.

"Loralee?" he barely managed to breathe her name. "The bed..."

"Ruya, help me!" Loralee snapped. Even as lanky as Merikh was, Loralee couldn't move him by herself when he went limp.

Ruya simply used her magic to help haul Merikh into the bedroom, leaving him on his side in case he was sick again. When they left the room, Loralee headed straight for the bells. First, pulling the one for Nikias, then reaching for the healers. She stopped when Ruya tsked.

"Loralee, he's *fine*. He overextended; it happens. He's ambitious, and that's a difficult scroll. He'll be back to normal after a little nap."

"Stop telling me he's fine," Loralee snapped. "Merikh doesn't overextend. He's too careful for that."

"My dear, there isn't another explanation. He overextended, and while it's worrisome that he's so sick from it, he'll be fine. I can feel his soul isn't troubled; it isn't weak. He's—"

Loralee glared at Ruya, and the priestess reconsidered her choice of words.

"—going to be a little cranky when he wakes, I'm sure. But he doesn't need a healer."

Loralee paced from the door to the divan, waiting for Nikias to arrive. Ruya crossed the room and sat down in one of the chairs by the coffee table.

"Have you heard from Sarka or Adrian?" Ruya asked, changing the subject.

Loralee shook her head, only half listening as Ruya tried to initiate conversation. Ruya was wrong; this wasn't simple overextension. She'd seen that before, seen when Adrian had pushed too hard. He'd passed out, but he hadn't been sick. He'd merely fainted. What happened to Merikh just now was different. Loralee just didn't know enough to tell the extent. Ruya wouldn't be able to convince her to be so cavalier about it. She could understand his disorientation. Loralee imagined it was rather confusing switching bodies. But that didn't seem like that was all that was wrong.

Ruya sighed, stood up, and walked into Loralee's path. The priestess took Loralee's hands.

"Sorcerers are human. We make mistakes, we push ourselves too hard. Is it so strange to think Merikh would push himself?" Ruya asked. "Trust me, soul displacement is *tough*. It's exhausting. The whole time you're fighting with the instincts of a creature you don't understand. Keeping an eye out for dangers you didn't have to before. He's still recovering from his wounds. You can see the pain he carries with him when he walks and moves. I doubt he remembers this when he does his magic. Proud men rarely remember their limitations. Why are you so worried?"

Ruya's hands were warm and squeezed Loralee's hands in a reassuring, motherly way. Loralee bit her lip, searching for an answer. Maybe Ruya was right.

"I...I've seen him like this far more often than I ever expected to. His reputation as shah... Well, he's a sorcerer with *two* specialties. He always seemed...invincible."

"We either put our leaders on pedestals or in gutters; there are few places in between. They're either godlike or scum. We expect nothing else from them," Ruya said gently. "Now you've discovered he's a fallible, breakable human with all the virtues and vices that come with that. He made a mistake, and he will recover from it. No amount of worry now will pull him through. Besides, Nikias will be here soon, and he worries enough about Merikh for all of Shai'Khal."

Ruya let go of Loralee's hands and walked back to her seat. A breeze shifted from the open balcony, and Loralee wrinkled her nose from the vomit. She crossed the room again to the bells, summoning a servant before she walked to the bathing room and grabbed a towel. As she walked over to the vomit on the floor, she glanced back to Ruya.

"After nine hundred years, how far off the pedestal did Ikharon fall?" Loralee asked, glancing at the vomit before she reticently began cleaning it off the floor.

"Ikharon's a god. There's a difference. Of course, nine hundred years with rakshasas, mortohas, and other undead make you appreciate the living all the more," Ruya said, leaning back into the chair.

Loralee shook her head as she carefully took the dirty towel back to the bathing room and shut it behind the door. It helped the smell. "Rakshasas? You're not serious," Loralee said, sitting down on the chaise. They were dangerous creatures of legend, undead monsters who fed off of blood. Hideous creatures that according to legend, could hide themselves among men with powerful illusions.

Ruya nodded energetically. "They're Ikharon's favorites! Not that he has favorites, of course." Ruya winked. "I may be high priestess, but Kyran is practically Ikharon's son." Her tone grew wistful, and Loralee hesitated to ask.

Curiosity got the better of her.

"Kyran?"

"Eldest of the rakshasas. He's quite charming when he's well-fed. He was already ancient when I became high priestess, and I've been at Ikharon's side for thirteen hundred years. He scared the life out of me when I was first in the temple, but most of the time he'd keep up the illusion of looking like a man. But *gods*, the first time he dropped the facade around me, my heart nearly stopped. Not a sight you want to see. They're horrifically pale, and the teeth... The stories of blood drinking don't fully prepare you for what they are. But when you get past that, when he's decided you're a decent enough human to remain a companion...he's a gentleman. I miss him."

"Is he on the island, or did he die during Unification?" Loralee asked, unable to keep herself from hoping it was the latter.

"On the island still, though like most of his kind, he's starving. There aren't enough sailors shipwrecking, and they can't stave off their hunger long enough to create a human population on the island."

Loralee stared at Ruya, unable to comprehend the ease with which Ruya was talking about *farming people*.

"Are...are there many of them? And they'll...be set free with Ikharon when the Key is destroyed?" Loralee asked carefully.

Ruya smiled, trying to be reassuring, it seemed. "Don't worry. You'll have protection from anything on the islands. The allies of the Pantheon will be graciously rewarded for their part. The enemies? Well, I don't think Kyran will be starving anymore."

Ruya's attitude left Loralee speechless. Even after the Pantheon had begun its resurgence, Loralee hadn't really put much faith in it. Even now, she had a hard time believing in the gods. Faith had always been a struggle for her. She hadn't considered that there would be other creatures on the island with the gods. Now, the realization had slapped her in the face. There were monsters, as terrifying as any djinn, that they would be letting loose upon their country. Rakshasas weren't even the worst of it. What if rocs existed? Dragons? Creatures that could level whole *cities* with a breath? Loralee blamed the faint smell of bile for her sudden light-headedness.

A knock on the door bought Loralee's focus back to the here and now. Nikias entered the room, a servant behind him.

"Khanum?" Nikias asked, bowing his head a little. The servant kept his eyes firmly on the ground.

"The Shah wore himself out with magic. There's a dirty towel in the bathing room that needs washing. A spot on the floor there"—Loralee pointed to it—"will need cleaning once we've left the room."

The servant nodded and quickly attended to removing the towel. As the door shut behind him, Nikias crossed the room to the bedroom and looked in.

"He vomited? What was he doing? He's *never* gotten sick from his magic before." Nikias sounded spooked, and Loralee appreciated having someone else taking the situation seriously.

"Soul displacement. He's fine," Ruya said. This time, she sounded tired of having to repeat herself.

"I thought it was strange as well," Loralee said as she joined Nikias at the bedroom door. "He looked confused before he passed out."

Nikias frowned, then walked away from the bedroom. He grabbed the ebony chair from Merikh's desk and carried it into the bedroom. It thudded gently against the rug on Merikh's side of the bed.

"I'm getting tired of having to do this," Nikias muttered, barely loud enough for Loralee to hear. He looked exhausted.

"You've been here all his life?" Loralee asked gently, unsure of the answer. She couldn't recall another grand vizier.

Nikias nodded. "I started the day he was born, though I don't think Mansur planned it that way. I don't think he planned it at all, really. One of his viziers was a friend of my father's and told him I was good with mathematics. I arrived, was summoned to the royal suite, and Mansur was here. Drunk, of course, with then-Duq Olumide and Duqa Emilia. Asked me maybe three questions before having me pour myself some wine and celebrate the news of a baby boy. I've been here through every illness, every beating, every broken bone, every assassination attempt. I'm worried I'm going to outlive another shah."

"He'll outlive us all from sheer stubbornness, I'm sure," Loralee said, glad when it earned a smile.

"How long has he been like this?" Nikias asked.

"I summoned you here right after we found him."

"It could be hours before he wakes, then," Nikias said. He leaned over the bed to grab a pillow, putting it between himself and the back of the stiff chair. "Would you bring me some of the paperwork off his desk?"

Loralee nodded, turning back to the royal suite. Ruya caught her eye, and Loralee held back a frustrated sound.

"Ruya, I'm afraid your meeting with the Shah is going to have to wait. Will you excuse us? I'll send for you once he is available," Loralee said, her tone firm.

Ruya opened her mouth to protest, then reconsidered it. "Of course, dear, I'll come back whenever Merikh's ready."

The door shut quietly behind Ruya. Loralee let herself breathe for a moment before crossing to Merikh's desk. On it was a letter from Amir Xolani that Merikh had clearly been reading before he'd used the scroll. Loralee bit the inside of her cheek. Hatai, now Ziyadi? They needed to push back or else they'd appear weak. War had already come to Ydeba, only no one was willing to call it that yet.

Is that where Sarka is? Did war simply follow its champion? Loralee picked up another pile of papers, carried them to the bedroom, and handed them off to Nikias.

"Have you seen this?" she asked, pointing to the amir's letter. Nikias shook his head, frowning as he read the letter.

"I think you and the high priestess may be very busy with vigils in the future, Khanum."

"I believe so," Loralee said with a frown before leaving the bedroom. She moved paperwork from Merikh's desk to the coffee table. Shai'Khal didn't stop moving simply because its shah slept.

There were souls nearby.

One in the royal suite proper.

One here in the room.

Nikias?

The headache still throbbed dully. It was a faint shadow of the pain from earlier. Slowly, Merikh eased open his eyes. The bedroom wasn't bright—the curtains were closed. The only source of light came from the slightly ajar door. Merikh heard papers rustle.

"What in Alhanem were you thinking?" Nikias snapped, putting paperwork down on the nightstand nearby. He was angry. No, that wasn't the emotion. Nikias's eyes were wide from worry, the deep wrinkles of his frown were tight in disappointment. The blood hadn't risen up his neck for fury.

"I was thinking," Merikh said as he rolled over from his side to his back, "how convenient it would be to have a spy in the temple. So I became one." His voice croaked, his mouth dry and the taste of vomit still on his tongue.

"That's what you have Ajir for! You don't have to do everything on your own. You have people for that! Did you even think about what would happen if you hurt yourself? You scared me half to death, and Loralee—"

"The Khanum will live, I'm sure," Merikh scoffed, sitting up and swinging his legs over the bed. He instantly regretted doing so, as his vision swam, tunneling for a moment before the black receded.

"That's not the point, and you know it! She was the one who found you."

Merikh focused on Nikias's voice, then on Nikias as the room steadied. "Water?" Merikh asked.

Nikias leaned over to the nightstand and poured water from the pitcher into the small cup beside it. He handed Merikh the cup, and ice frosted it as Merikh gulped down the water. The cold hit like a punch to the gut, but it helped ease his headache.

"I didn't intend to worry you," Merikh said. "You know that. You taught me self-reliance."

"I tried to teach you respect for your underlings, not to put yourself in dangerous situations for their sake. You're their shah. Your father's memory is still fresh enough that your requests look reasonable. Don't try to say you're a poor student. I spoke with more of your tutors than Mansur did, and I know that's not true," Nikias said, pointing his finger at Merikh when the younger man was about to interrupt to make light of the situation.

Fine, old man. Merikh half-heartedly glared at Nikias. The grand vizier stepped out of line often. Ordinarily, Merikh would have reminded him so. But usually when Nikias overstepped, he didn't look so worried or scared.

"I will refrain from personally spying on the Temple in the future," Merikh promised. "Otherwise you'll kill yourself worrying before you meet the Shahzade."

Nikias's eyes grew a little brighter. "Oh? When might that be?"

"Gods only know, but it'll keep you around for a while." Merikh's smirk turned into a small smile as Nikias's shook his head and chuckled. Both men sobered quickly, and Merikh took another sip of water.

"Loralee's outside?" Merikh asked.

Nikias nodded.

"I suppose she deserves an apology?"

"Only if you don't want her to poison you, but to each his own. Neredi women have a temper. I'm sure you've seen it."

"Not as often as I expected. She's patient. And she's been kind, if not infuriatingly aware of..." Merikh drifted off and gestured over his shoulder toward his back.

"How *awful*, Shahanshah." Nikias rolled his eyes as he stood and headed out of the bedroom into the suite proper.

Merikh stood to follow him, his feet unsteady. His vision tunneled and blurred again for a moment before the world came back into focus. Merikh's stomach didn't agree with standing, but he wasn't about to remain bedridden.

Loralee sat on the divan, papers strewn over the coffee table. Nikias sat across from her, and after a moment's hesitation, Merikh sat down beside her. She moved, almost imperceptibly, away from him. Her posture was stiff, and she refused to look at him.

"How was Iksandar?" Merikh asked.

"Fine." Her tone was acerbic.

"Nikias said you found me when I..."

"Was catatonic? Yes. Right before you were sick on the floor and collapsed in my arms."

Merikh grimaced. He didn't remember anything between the temple and waking up.

"That shouldn't have happened. Nikias, we need more spies in the temple. If we can buy a priest, an acolyte, I don't care about the cost, but the Ajir need a man inside. Alcaeus has something that protects him from magic."

"What are you talking about?" Loralee asked, sounding as if Merikh was rambling nonsense. He had a hard time believing what he was saying.

"I can't remember what happened. I had the raven, overheard a few parishioners complaining, then went to find Alcaeus. I found him, and then I woke up in bed. He was...reading a letter? Or there was a...something on his desk. I don't know."

"Is it some sort of...healing enchantment? Is that possible?" Loralee asked, her irritation replaced with concerned curiosity.

Merikh shook his head. "No. It wouldn't force me from the body. Another necromancer could have done it, but it doesn't feel right. I don't remember feeling an aura."

"Alcaeus wouldn't use a necromancer," Nikias said quickly, shaking his head. "One of the Priest Council just put out an essay on the evils of necromancy. They wouldn't turn around and then hire one to protect the high priest. Who aside from a necromancer is going to know the sorts of things you can do?"

"I don't know, and that lack of knowledge is going to get me killed. So we return to needing better intelligence in the temple, regardless of cost," Merikh ordered.

"What of the amir's letter?" Nikias asked.

"He'll have his warrant," Loralee answered. "I've already sent word to Sardar General Opeyemi to help handle it. That Fari commander needs a stretched neck."

"And the Sanctified Suns?" Nikias asked again.

"The monarchy acknowledges the legality of the Onyx Swords. The Sanctified Suns are an illegal mercenary group, to be arrested and executed if their crimes warrant it," Merikh said.

Nikias nodded before standing. "Is there anything else, Shahanshah? Khanum?"

"Ginger tea and something light to eat," Merikh asked.

Nikias bowed his head before excusing himself from the room. Loralee quickly returned to the paperwork in front of her as soon as they were alone.

"In Rajibad, you told me you were a far more valuable partner than puppet," Merikh said, then hesitated. Loralee was making a show of ignoring him. "You've proven that."

"Have I?" Loralee said. Her tone had regained its acidity. Loralee picked up the glass pen from nearby, dipped it in the inkwell, and began making notes on the papers in front of her.

"If I didn't trust you, you wouldn't still be here," Merikh said. It was true. If he hadn't trusted her, he would have arranged for an accident with her horses by now.

"How reassuring."

"Loralee—"

She turned to look at him. The hurt and the worry in her eyes left Merikh unsure of what to say. It continued to surprise him whenever she looked genuinely concerned. Loralee scoffed, shaking her head.

"Merikh, you scared me. And it's not the first time, either. What am I supposed to do if you die?"

"I'm not going to die, Loralee."

"Really? You're going to stop being reckless, then?"

Merikh ran a hand over his head, pulling his black hair back out of his eyes. "Loralee, I couldn't imagine what happened today *happening*. I cannot plan for every single contingency or scenario. I would be paralyzed with indecision."

"There are a few contingencies you can plan for. If you're going to perform dangerous magic, you could at least wait until I'm here to keep an eye on you. If nothing else, I could have had a bucket for you to vomit in."

Merikh grimaced, running his tongue over his teeth unconsciously. *Where is that damn tea?* His stomach hadn't fully settled yet.

"I am *not* going to ask your permission before using my magic," Merikh told her firmly.

It was the wrong thing to say. Loralee threw the pen on the table, shattering the delicate tip in her anger. She didn't seem to notice it when she stood.

"Damn it, Merikh! I'm not telling you to ask permission. I'm asking you to be careful! To let me help you without kicking and screaming! Gods, I think you'd try to run Shai'Khal all by yourself if there wasn't already a vizier council. Hisahti be kind, if you could figure out a means of having an heir without me, you probably would! What was the point of my vows if you won't let me fulfill them?"

"Honestly, I didn't expect you'd take them quite so seriously," Merikh said flippantly.

Loralee's eyes went wide, and she wrung her hands as if trying to keep herself from slapping him. She certainly looked ready to murder him as she tried to find words.

"Why are you trying so hard to make me hate you?" she asked, finally settling on the impossible question. "Every time you do anything to make me think that maybe, just maybe, we could be passably happy, you slap me in the face with callous indifference. Do you want to end up like your father?"

Merikh didn't hear her anything she said beyond "happy," which was lucky, as he didn't take kindly to comparisons to Mansur. Instead, he simply stared at her with an unabashedly dumbfounded look on his face. Merikh shook his head and laughed, which he immediately regretted, as his headache throbbed. He leaned forward, pressing his iced fingertips to his temple and closed eyes in a vain hope it would help the pain.

"I'm glad you find that amusing," Loralee snapped.

Merikh shook his head. "No, I..." He couldn't find the words without sounding like he was belittling her, and it wasn't his intention. "I never thought about us being happy. You actually have a hope or a plan for us. At least, some personal expectation that we're going to end up similar to your parents. I always just hoped to avoid uxoricide. Happiness never crossed my mind."

Merikh expected Loralee to snap at him again, to lose that hot-headed temper of hers. Instead, he heard her sigh. When he looked at her, Loralee's posture had softened, and he loathed the pitying look on her face.

"Of course I plan to be happy. I don't want to be miserable all my life. I would see you part of that. You have every means at your disposal to *be* content, if you wanted to be. If you stopped getting in your own way for a moment, that would help a great deal."

Loralee sat back down on the divan. A moment later, a servant knocked on the door and brought in tea and fruit. Heat radiated from the teapot, and ice covered the handle when Merikh picked it up to pour. The smell of ginger laced with honey and lemon wafted gently through the steam, and his stomach already felt more settled. Merikh placed the pot down and handed one of the cups to Loralee. She took it from him carefully and blew once before she took a sip.

"I apologize for frightening you," Merikh said before he took a sip of tea.

Loralee put her cup down. "Don't do it again."

"What, apologize?" Merikh said with a deliberate smirk. Loralee glared at him. "I will do better to consider those more personally affected by my choices regarding my health."

Loralee nodded and looking slightly mollified. She turned back to the paperwork and brushed the shattered pieces of glass toward the center of the table. She then pulled a scroll from the pile of papers.

"A first step to that might be telling me what you plan to do after we set the gods free," Loralee said as she pulled out a large scroll from under the pile. "And what you're doing with this?"

It was an old schematic from the archive of the High Temple, one long outdated. He'd found it the other night in the archive and brought it here for further study, and to keep it from other prying eyes. Ruya still had access to the archive, and she spent a great deal of time talking with the scholars, undoubtedly after the same thing Merikh was.

"Did Ruya say something?" Merikh asked, curious at what now spurred on Loralee's first question.

"Rakshasas. There are *monsters* on those islands with the gods. We aren't simply letting loose gods; we're giving truth to myths. There might be creatures in those mists who can level cities with a breath. Destructive forces that could destabilize the empire."

"Rakshasas...are those the ones who disembowel and wear their victim's innards as a turban or the ones who drink blood at night? I can never keep them straight," Merikh said cavalierly.

"Don't mock me." Loralee glared at him, and Merikh shook his head.

"I'm not. I tried to raise the former creature against Mansur when I was a boy. Ended up with a bloody mess of a corpse on the ground, an unhappy ifrit, and a broken arm after Mansur discovered me. At the time I simply thought the creatures never existed, not that they were merely banished to places I couldn't find."

Loralee gaped at him as Merikh leaned forward and put his tea back down on the coffee table. He placed his hand down on the temple schematics and tapped his finger on the inner sanctum.

"When Ruya and Sarka arrived here, Ruya shared her memories with me. There are monsters in the mists, of that I have no doubt. The myths show us humans are little more than fodder for most of them. I do not intend our people to become second-class citizens in their own country, terrified of creatures in the night. I will not see monuments destroyed to the gales caused by rocs. Ruya claims the gods and their priesthoods will protect the world from their creatures, but looking at the old myths, you can see how *well* they did so. Now, each of the gods have relics, tokens that amplify their powers."

Merikh stopped and glanced over the divan toward his desk. A book unburied itself from another stack of papers and flew over to Merikh's hand. The magic didn't make his headache worse—a small relief, as Merikh hadn't given it a second thought before doing so.

"At every turn, Ruya has been surprised by my magic. She has made mistakes because of it."

Merikh opened the book, moving a thin leather bookmark out of the way before he handed it to Loralee. "In her memories, I found where she left Ikharon's grimoire—the High Temple of Madiar."

"'*The Grimoire is said to be the key to immortality, the scale on which life and death are balanced,'*" Loralee read. She looked up to Merikh. "This is dangerous."

"Exceptionally so, in the wrong hands. I'm not convinced Ruya's are the right ones. Alcaeus is sitting on a weapon that will change the tides of this war, once we get it. With it, we can *choose* whether to release their gods or not. If we release them, at least we'd have a bargaining chip of our own then. And there are others—Livinja's shield, Belara's pendant, relics I doubt made it into the mists."

"If Ruya left it in the temple," Loralee said quickly, "then she must have left it guarded. Her magic was fueled by Ikharon. The enchantments will kill you if you try to take this. It's too dangerous." She put the bookmark back in place and closed the book. "Promise me you won't go after it."

"Do you trust me?"

Merikh knew the answer. It was written all over her face and spoken repeatedly through their argument. No, she certainly didn't trust him. Not his personal judgment, not with magic. Loralee let out a slow breath and looked away.

"I have no desire to die, Loralee," Merikh reassured her. "There is much I'd like to see accomplished first, and whether you believe me or not, I know my limits. Displays like this, where Ruya sees my weaknesses, only makes her more complacent. If the grimoire is too dangerous, I will see it destroyed."

"You'd put yourself directly in confrontation with the god of *death*!"

"Right now I am in direct confrontation with the god of the sun, yet I haven't been burned to ashes. The gods owe me a favor; Ruya left that open-ended. The grimoire is my assurance that the gods follow through on their promises."

"Does Nikias know?" Loralee asked.

Merikh shook his head. "No. I doubt he'd approve."

"For good reason," Loralee said.

Merikh stiffened, despite trying to hide his mistrust and frustration. Loralee had grown close to Nikias. While Merikh appreciated his wife and vizier getting along, he didn't appreciate the coalition they seemed to have formed against him.

Loralee saw his walls return and shook her head. Hesitantly, she reached forward and gently took Merikh's hand. "Not reasons I share. I want our empire and its people safe. If that requires maneuvering Ruya out of the way and holding the grimoire ransom...then so be it. Just...don't make me a widow."

Merikh squeezed her hand then pulled away from her. "I won't."

He had no intention of being killed by a book.

CHAPTER 34

16TH OF BELITH, DRY SEASON, 902 UNIFIED AGE
BUHET, YDEBA PROVINCE

Buhet's wooden gates loomed, wide open yet uninviting. Sarka wondered again if it was worth the risk.

You didn't save him to watch him die, Sarka chided herself. Adrian's wounds had taken a turn for the worse a few days ago, and Sarka doubted he'd make it across the Sarafi alive. Hatai was only another three days away, on the right side of the Ydeba-Raudhah border. Sarka glanced at Adrian, confirming her worries. He was pale, and sweat beaded his brow and soaked his kufiyah. He wouldn't make it another three days. He was barely able to sit upright in the saddle as it was. Dalya hadn't kept clean knives, perhaps intentionally.

The gate guards were too busy inspecting a merchant's cart to notice them as they rode into the city. Unlike Hatai, Buhet didn't announce its presence on the wind. The city was a waypoint for many travelers from Luma, Kabatwe, and even Membiti on their way south to Ogot or Duak.

The main road was spotted with many adobe inns. Even as accustomed to travelers as Buhet was, both Sarka and Adrian were given a wide berth. They stood out like sore thumbs with their Yahidah clothing and horses. More importantly, Adrian clearly looked unwell. No one wanted to be sick, nor did they want to inspect closer to find out whether what Adrian had was something they could become sick from.

Sarka followed signposts from the main road and hospitality district toward the bazaar. Keeping Adrian close, Sarka found a merchant selling hunting supplies and headed for him. Without their camel, Sarka had been forced to hunt down a few dik-diks for food, skinning the small deer for furs and keeping the bones to sell. The merchant regarded her with some suspicion, as Sarka didn't dare remove her veil. Niceties be damned, they were in Umbeah country, and she didn't fancy another encounter with Onyx Swords anytime soon. Sarka unloaded the furs and bones onto the wooden table. The merchant eyed them carefully and inspected the small brown deer pelts. After a moment, he carefully began counting out several bronze akhenits and one silver.

"Thanks," Sarka grumbled. "Can you point me toward a healer?"

He pointed down the road behind her. "Mosi treats the poor for cheap. Otherwise, there's a butcher and a surgeon down toward the gate who might help you."

Sarka nodded, pocketing the coins. She turned and led the horses down the road toward where the man had pointed. It was easy to spot the healer's building. Above the door was a wooden sign bearing a crescent moon inside a sun, a lizard superimposed atop it. The tail had been cut off and rested below the sun and moon. A symbol of Ayurlyse, the goddess of healing, with the Akhenic Sun added.

They've probably forgotten what that symbol truly means, Sarka thought as she tied the horses to the hitching post out front. She hesitated, wondering if there was a safer place to hitch them, but she didn't see one. Surely it was taboo to steal horses from in front of a healer? Once the horses were tied, she went to Adrian's side and helped him from his horse. Careful not to jar him too much, Sarka pulled him from the saddle and helped him up the wooden step.

The door creaked, and bells hanging from the door handle chimed obnoxiously. Dried herbs hung from the ceiling. Shelves and cabinets lined the walls, full of various poultices, vials, and jars of ointments and supplies. Beyond the front desk, a curtain closed off a room. As the curtain parted, a tall Umbeah man walked out. He frowned and crossed the room quickly to take Adrian from Sarka.

"Are you injured too?" he asked, his words thick with an ill-educated Ydeban accent.

Sarka shook her head.

"Good. Name's Mosi, if you need it. Whatever you're paying with, toss it there." He gestured with his free hand toward a bowl on the desk before he disappeared with Adrian behind the curtain. Sarka walked over to the desk and dropped most of their remaining coins in the small ceramic bowl. She still needed to buy supplies to cross the Sarafi. They'd need a tent, or else their skin would be stripped off in the first sandstorm they encountered.

Sarka followed Mosi behind the curtain. He had laid Adrian down on a charpai and was quietly asking the younger man if he was comfortable and asking where he hurt.

Everywhere, I imagine, Sarka thought. She didn't need to be a healer to know Adrian wasn't in good shape. The fever, the sweat, that was enough to show something had gotten into his blood. And his hand, below where she'd burned it to stop the bleeding, had begun to turn black. After a moment, Mosi straightened up and walked away from Adrian to Sarka.

"What happened?" Mosi asked.

"Tortured, without magic."

Mosi frowned. "Akhenios be kind. They did a number on him. Who did this? I have to tell the guards."

"I've left enough compensation that you won't have to," Sarka told him firmly.

"It's not a question of money. The boy deserves justice," Mosi said.

"Believe me, he'll have it. Either by his master's hands or mine."

Mosi didn't argue with her again. He walked back to Adrian. Mosi raised his hands over Adrian's chest, and a white orb formed under his fingers. The orb began to spread over Adrian's body. After a moment, Sarka could see Adrian beginning to doze, and she smiled a little. Healing magic felt like slipping into a warm bath, soothing every ache. It was relaxing, if not a little itchy when all was said and done at the end. Having healing magic work alongside the body's normal responses was exhausting.

The orb disappeared before Adrian could fall asleep completely. Mosi stood up and walked back to Sarka. He looked worried and tired, and beads of sweat dappled his forehead. Mosi ran a hand over the thin braids of his hair.

"There's only so much I can do right now. Another day, two, I might be able to set everything right. Except for that hand." Mosi gestured to it. "There's nothing I can do for it. It's dead. The closest necromancer I know of is a week west, holed up in some old qasbah in the Katu. By the time he gets here, even he won't be able to stop the rot from killing your friend. I'll have to cut it off."

"We need to leave Buhet today. Whatever you can do to make him roadworthy, do it," Sarka ordered, crossing her arms.

Mosi left the room with a grim look in his eyes.

"What'd he say?" Adrian asked groggily.

Sarka ignored him, instead looking toward the curtain as Mosi came back through it with a bone saw.

"No! No, don't you dare!" Adrian shot up straight from the bed, shaking.

"It's dead. I'm sorry," Mosi said and gestured to Adrian's hand.

"Sarka, please!" Adrian begged.

Sarka met his gaze but said nothing. Instead, she stepped forward and grabbed Adrian's arm. She planted it firmly on the stone table beside the cot.

"Adrian, you're going to die if you keep a dead limb. We're *helping* you."

Sarka's words fell on deaf ears as Adrian fought them. Mosi shoved a wooden rod bound in leather into Adrian's mouth. The Ajir steward passed out moments after the first pull of the saw blade against his arm. When the hand dropped away, white light wrapped the stump to close the wound.

Bells rang.

Sarka let go of Adrian, the young man still unconscious, and walked over to the curtain. She glanced through a small hole in the dark-gray fabric and held back a curse. There were four men wearing tan uniforms with black sashes. Two had spears and shields like the Ydeban guards, the other two had shamshirs and khanjars. Buhet guards from the kontess.

Sarka looked back to Mosi. He'd grabbed bandages from a nearby shelf and was wrapping Adrian's stump. Sarka moved away silently from the curtain as the guards approached. One of them pulled back the curtain and stepped into the room.

"Mosi, helping thieves again?" the guard chided.

"Always." Mosi didn't look up from bandaging Adrian, his tone distracted. It was clear he hadn't heard the question.

"He's not a thief," Sarka said. The guard looked over and saw her for the first time. Sarka tried to discreetly check that her veil was still in place.

"So those are your horses, then?" the guard asked.

"Yes, they are."

"Really? You breed them or buy them?" the guard asked, his hand resting on his shamshir. Unlike Mosi, his accent spoke of a decent education. Well-bred, not someone raised in the slums or lower classes.

"Neither, I borrowed them with permission. I don't see what the point of this questioning is, since I guarantee those horses don't match the description of any reported stolen here."

"No, you're right, they don't match any stolen horse descriptions. Mostly because I haven't seen horses that fine from anything but Neredi or Madiaran lines. You don't see those out here."

Sarka held back a sigh. As much as she would have preferred to remain anonymous, Sarka didn't see a means to do so now. They'd be discovered either way, and Sarka disliked the idea of being arrested as a horse thief. She reached up and unpinned her veil, drawing it away from her face before pulling the scarf off her hair.

"No shit," Sarka said. "Who d'you think I borrowed them from? Merikh gave them to me for the trip, along with his servant. Now, I'd like to see the kontess, and I'd like you to get your hand off your sword." Sarka ran her hand through her hair.

The guard cursed and shook his head before he looked at Mosi. "You always have the most *interesting* clients," the guard muttered. He snapped the curtain back and pointed to one of the other guards. "Go get an escort. We're the lucky bastards who found the champion of Livinja. And she wants to see the kontess."

There was a murmur of doubt through the guard's companions that was silenced when Sarka emerged. There were probably only a handful of red-haired women in all of Shai'Khal, and Sarka very much doubted those few tried to impersonate her. Who in their right mind would want to be called the champion of war in unfriendly Ydeba, after all?

Adrian was still unconscious when the guards returned with their escort. Mosi gave them a stretcher to pull behind Adrian's horse. None of the guards particularly leapt at the idea of helping Sarka. They stuck to a protective formation, their tall shields almost hiding Sarka from view. She'd retied her niqaab, her veil in front of her face again. Whether or not her face would start a riot or simply earn them rocks or dead fruit thrown at them, Sarka didn't want to find out.

Metal gates to the kontess's estate opened ahead of them, and their escort winnowed back down to the four guards originally in Mosi's shop.

"Take him to the healer. See if anything can be done by someone competent," the guard from earlier ordered before he gestured to Sarka. "The kontess awaits."

Now more than ever, Sarka wished she remembered the kontess's allegiance. She was certain that the kontess of Buhet had been at the Quorum, and that she did in fact support the Shah. But there was quite the gap between those who supported the Shah and the Pantheon and those who were rather offended by the Shah's support of her gods. The guard led her through the main door of the manor, down a hall to the left wing. The manor was on top of the hill the city was built around, and the left wing had the best view of the gate and the southern road.

Word had either traveled quickly or Sarka had terrible timing. Neither would have surprised her. The Buhet court was in full swung, the city's nobles and viziers present. The guard bowed as they approached the simple throne where the kontess sat, gray and imposing. If Sarka had less of a spine, she would have found the kontess intimidating. The alkont stood half a step to the left and behind the kontess, a scrutinizing look in his dark eyes. For all the complications of Shai'Khal's political system, inheritance at least seemed simple. Eldest child, regardless of gender, inherited titles. Everyone maneuvered to marry their younger children up. Sarka only hoped that whoever the alkont's older sibling was, it wasn't one of the Akhenic Faithful nobles.

"Kontess Rehema," the guard said, bowing. "May I present Sarka, the champion of Livinja."

Sarka didn't bow. She didn't bow for Merikh, and she certainly wouldn't bow for a kontess. Her loyalty was sworn, undying and unchanging, to Livinja.

"Champion."

The word dropped coldly from the kontess's lips. The Umbeah noblewoman drummed her fingers on her armrests, the gold bangles on her wrists tinkling quietly as she did so. The wrinkles around her eyes exaggerated their narrowing. The kontess looked at Sarka in much the same way one might look at a stray dog.

Be nice, Sarka reminded herself. There was no point in making enemies here. They had enough armies set against them as it was. Not to mention, she and Adrian were at the mercy of this woman. She didn't want to see Adrian suffer more.

"Kontess Rehema, my companion is being escorted as we speak to your healers, and you have my thanks for his care," Sarka said. She missed having Ruya here; the other woman was much better at playing politics and smoothing over ruffled feathers.

"Indeed," Kontess Rehema scoffed. "It will be far better than the care he received in the outer districts. Now, why have you come here unannounced? Why does the Shah send you here without intentions or regards?"

Which offends you more, my presence or being seemingly snubbed by Merikh? Sarka took a deep breath.

"It was never my intention to come to Buhet—"

"So my city is below notice of both the Shah and Livinja? Where is your destination, then?" Rehema demanded.

Sarka bit her tongue. She hated being interrupted, particularly when it was clear the old noblewoman was searching for cause to be offended.

"We're on our way back to Madiar. I've been performing a pilgrimage to old shrines of Livinja's. My companion was tortured when he ran afoul of Onyx Swords to the south. I would like to return him to his master's care as soon as I can."

"His master?" Rehema asked.

Sarka realized she hadn't made Adrian's position clear. "The man in your care is Adrian Charmichi, Merikh's Ajir steward." Sarka realized the moment she'd said Merikh's name she'd made a mistake. The kontess looked appalled, as if Sarka had just slapped her with a dead rat.

"The Shahanshah's steward," Sarka corrected. The title felt strange on her tongue, wrong to say. She'd never had to supplicate to anyone other than

Livinja in nine hundred years. "Apologies, I'm weary from the road and forget myself." Well, it sounded like what Ruya would have said, even if she hadn't managed to make it sound sincere.

"Apologies? Show some respect! Our Shah is a son of the Great Prophet," Kontess Rehema snapped before she stood.

"Walk with me," the kontess ordered, leaving no room for protest as she walked past Sarka.

The champion could hear the other woman muttering about titles and the importance of knowing one's place as Rehema walked by. Sarka tried not to roll her eyes. She understood hierarchy better than half these politicians. The chain of command was important, vitally so to an army. But excessive amounts of kissing a commander's feet or ass made for weakness. As far as Sarka was concerned, all of these fleeting mortals and their titles could pound sand. Sarka was the grand general of the Flaming Legion, the champion of Livinja. She contended with gods. She outranked a mere *shah*. Before banishment, all of Shai'Khal's noble leaders had bowed before champions. It was unheard of for a champion or high priest to supplicate before a mortal. Once the gods were free, these people would be reminded of their place.

The two walked alone to a council room, and Kontess Rehema gestured for Sarka to follow her inside. Sarka sat down at the table across from the kontess and cleared her throat.

"Kontess, as I said, as soon as Adrian is ready for travel, we'll be out of your city," Sarka assured her.

"You said yourself that you're weary from the road. You need rest, and the steward will need time to recover if the injuries reported to me were even half true," Rehema told her firmly, still palpably irritated. "It will be quite impossible to keep your presence here unassuming, and should you leave without a proper escort, the Onyx Swords will kill you. I have no desire to be the object of the Shah's displeasure if one of his Ajir dies due to my negligence."

"That isn't necessary. It won't happen. I assure—"

"Your assurances mean nothing to me, Champion. I don't believe in your god or your heresies. Whatever poison has been whispered in the Shah's ear, I can only hope High Priest Alcaeus will be able to remove it before much more damage is done, either by your false priestess or the whore sullying the

Khanum's crown." Rehema's diatribe made Sarka bite her tongue, and she forced herself to stop the heat in her palms from bursting into flames.

"Your hospitality is appreciated," Sarka said through gritted teeth. "May I impose on you for a bird? I'd like to send word to the false priestess, congratulations to the whore, and a report to Merikh."

Two can play at this game. Sarka had no intention of referring to Merikh as anything other than his name for the remainder of her stay here.

"Tomorrow, my servants will help you compose your letter." Rehema stood, walked back to the door, and opened it. She snapped her fingers twice, and a servant appeared. "Find this one a room," Rehema ordered before the old noblewoman walked back toward court.

Sarka hid her frustration until the servant escorted her to a bedroom. It was small, only containing a desk, chair, and bed. More than what she'd had on the road, but Sarka knew a cage when she saw one. She could easily break free, burn the place down without so much as a second thought, much like she had Kal Neveh. Undoubtedly, she'd return to Madiar without any support, and Merikh would want her head. In all likelihood, so would Ruya.

Sarka pushed the thought from her mind and flopped down on the bed. She couldn't live with herself if she massacred all those innocent people out of a burning rage at the kontess. Pragmatically, the kontess was only doing what she believed to be right, as misguided as it was. But after nine hundred years in a cage, feeling one closing in on her again made it hard to breathe.

Patience, Sarka reminded herself.

CHAPTER 35

17th of Belith, Dry Season, 902 Unified Age
Madiar, Raudhah Province

Petitions were a necessary evil of ruling a country. Perhaps more necessary than ever with the unease throughout Madiar. It was the time the poor were given a chance to speak with Merikh directly, though few truly took advantage of the opportunity. Most were turned away by the lower viziers before their petitions ever made it to the throne room. Nitpicky requests that would waste Merikh's time were usually thinned out and sent away with a few akhenits for their trouble—a means of giving alms to the poor without having to filter it through the temple.

Of those who managed to get their requests past the viziers, most were so overwhelmed by the grandeur of the palace and throne room that they lost their courage and left before presenting their petition. The man in front of Merikh today seemed to be barely holding his composure as he walked the long carpet from the entrance toward the throne. He fell to his knees when the guards stopped him before the throne, then threw his hands to the ground. His turban touched the rug, and the man began muttering into the floor. His fingers were pushed deep into the rug, as if he were trying to bury himself in the stitching and protect himself from any ire his request might invoke. Nikias, standing to Merikh's left, cleared his throat to get the man's attention.

"You may rise. Speak up," Nikias instructed.

The old commoner touched his turban as he rose as if to soothe his nerves. He stared at the dais beneath the Rising Sun Throne. As he spoke again, Merikh strained to parse out his words, resisting the urge to lean forward.

The man was a shepherd. His skin looked like dried leather, and it was clear the man had little formal education. His words were slurred together, and the few words Merikh could make out clearly were lowborn slang that was foreign and incomprehensible to him. The longer Merikh stayed silent, the more the shepherd seemed to stumble over himself, trying to explain his problem. Merikh raised his hand off the armrest, silencing the shepherd before gesturing to Nikias. The vizier leaned over.

"I can't understand a word he's said," Merikh whispered, hiding his irritation.

He'd only ever shown that irritation once. As a teenager, he'd mocked an uneducated man during petitions, demanding he return after learning to speak properly. It was one of the few times Nikias had ever looked openly livid at Merikh and one of the last times Nikias had ever pulled him aside for a lecture. A lecture that had promised if Merikh couldn't pretend to have even a little respect for the people whose livelihoods made sure he had food to eat, Nikias would personally see to it that instead of a military patrol, he'd be stuck working on farms for a year for his provincial education. The threat had worked.

"I believe he's complaining that the northern fields toward the Kura are overrun by wild dogs. He's lost some of his herd, and he's hoping for compensation," Nikias clarified.

Merikh nodded at the clarification. Suddenly the repeated references to "spid wildigs" made much more sense. Merikh cleared his throat, and Nikias straightened up.

"A vizier will return with you to your fields for the purpose of calculating your compensation. With that compensation, increase your herd and hire hunters to remove the dogs. Bring one of the pelts back to the palace as proof the matter has been dealt with," Merikh ordered.

The shepherd struggled over Merikh's words, though the overall meaning was understood. The shepherd bowed almost to the floor again while he mumbled thanks and retreated from the room. The doors opened, but instead of allowing in another peasant, a servant from the aviary approached. In his hands were two letters. Both sealed in tan wax, though only one bore the monkey sigil of House Sall.

This never bodes well. Merikh had received more letters in the last month from his Ydeban nobles than he had in almost four years. Merikh cracked open the letter from Kontess Rehema and kept his reaction from his face as he read ill tidings.

"Shahanshah?" Nikias asked. "Should I send for the next petition?"

"No," Merikh said, not looking up from the letter. "Have them return tomorrow. Those too poor to find lodgings nearby, have them put up in empty servant quarters. Fetch Ruya and the Khanum, then join me in the council chamber."

Merikh stood and gestured toward the door at the back of the throne room. Nikias bowed his head before he set to his tasks. The council chamber door opened ahead of Merikh, and he sat down at the head of the long table. He placed Kontess Rehema's letter down on the table in front of him before cracking open the other one.

Merikh,

The kontess won't let us leave. Apparently we're "guests." If that's the case, your people have a strange sense of hospitality.

Adrian was caught and tortured by Swords. He'll recover, but he's missing his right hand. Even if Rehema lets us leave, neither Adrian nor I can return to that place.

The rest of the letter used the codex sent with Adrian, turning to unreadable gibberish without Nikias's cipher. Merikh tossed it down on the table. He still had no solid information about what Alcaeus had in the Temple that had so forcefully rebuked Merikh's magic. The Onyx Sword Merikh had tortured on his wedding night had spoken of a device that could destroy magic, but they hadn't known anything certain about it or if it even existed in the Katu. Merikh feared worse news was coded within Sarka's letter.

What did the Swords now know because of Adrian? Adrian had plenty of dangerous missions behind him. Perhaps none that had ever put him in harm's way in quite this fashion, but Adrian was a careful young man. Cautious, he didn't tend to make deadly mistakes.

Well, it puts an end to his travels. A replacement would have to be found and trained, not a task Merikh was excited to start. There were other Ajir, of course, but none Merikh trusted quite like Adrian. Merikh could already hear Nikias's admonishments. The grand vizier had never supported Adrian's elevation to steward, a servant boy without the breeding or training to be Ajir in the first place. But Adrian had the necessary intangible, that fierce unpurchaseable loyalty that had kept him lapping up every small scrap of attention Merikh had ever dropped for him. Now Adrian had lost his hand for those scraps. *How much did you tell the Swords?*

Three souls approached the door. Ruya's aura announced her presence well before she'd reached the throne room, let alone the council chamber. The door opened ahead of them. Loralee had come from the barns; there was a stray piece of hay on her riding skirt's hem. The plaits in her hair were coming loose, framing her face in soft black waves. Loralee sat down to his right, Nikias and Ruya sitting down opposite. Merikh handed Loralee Kontess Rehema's letter. The one from Sarka slid across the table to Nikias with only a thought.

"I trust you can translate?" Merikh asked.

Nikias nodded and pulled a small leather notebook from the inside pockets of his kaftan.

"Kontess Rehema...I don't recall her from the wedding. She was at the Quorum?" Loralee asked as she read the letter.

"She was. She abstained from our wedding to protest. Officially, she dislikes the elevation of a sayida to khanum and supported Duqa Adanna for the throne instead. Unofficially"—Merikh cleared his throat—"she was an ardent follower of my father. I doubt she understands you were his choice. All she remembers is that your father was barely this side of being a traitor."

"How offensive it is that you'd prefer the daughter of a disloyal Yahidah over a proven loyal Umbeah." Loralee scoffed. "The woman isn't fond of you, then?"

"On the contrary, Kontess Rehema is a Royalist. You are a corrupting influence holding sway over me," Merikh said with a small smile. The idea of Loralee corrupting *him* was quaint, a sentiment Loralee shared, considering her smirk.

Nikias cleared his throat before he closed the book and looked up. "They found the Key, or at least they're both quite certain they found it."

Ruya lit up, practically bouncing in her seat. "And? It's not destroyed; I would have felt it. What happened?"

"And nothing," Nikias said. "It's in the C'ezaji Pass. The defenses around it stole Sarka's magic temporarily and made her faint. Adrian retreated with her back to Ziyadi. There, Onyx Swords captured Adrian. Sarka burned Kal Neveh to save him, and our favorite rogue Fari commander razed Ziyadi in response. I believe our champion of war lost the first fight. Now she's retreated to Buhet and upset Kontess Rehema."

Merikh leaned back into his chair, frowned, and drummed his fingers on the armrest.

"Change the warrant. I want that Fari commander tried in Madiar. I want her head rotting on the north gate."

Now they'd have to skirt convincingly around the question of what Sarka was doing in the Katu. Amir Xolani wouldn't be impressed that a champion was wandering his province without him knowing, especially since she was the cause of these new problems. If the Onyx Swords had any idea that the temple was in the pass—or that there was anything of interest to the Crown there—it'd be impossible to attain quietly.

"Kontess Rehema is loyal, if crotchety," Merikh said after a moment. "Sarka and Adrian will be safe for now. The kontess has no intention of allowing them to leave without a royal escort, for their safety and more likely for the safety of her guards. Word has already been sent to Duq Alaziz?"

Loralee nodded. "He's rallying our...*his* riders, organizing supplies. They should be ready to move out within a matter of weeks."

"Good. Nikias, there must be a Royal Guard patrol arriving in Buhet within the next month. Have word sent for Adrian to join them and recall back to Madiar. Sarka will remain in Ydeba to aid Amir Xolani's leadership."

Ruya fidgeted in her seat. "What about the Key? Protections or not, it still needs to be destroyed."

Nikias scoffed. "Protections? Pray tell, Priestess, do you mean the armies of rebel Umbeah and Onyx Swords or the destructive magic? We need an entirely new approach. The subtle one Sarka proposed failed."

The one Sarka and I proposed, you mean. Merikh kept the thought to himself.

"You're sending troops, are you not? You'll have to do what you originally suggested, Nikias. Take and destroy the Key by force," Ruya said, unperturbed by the vizier's irritation.

Loralee leaned forward, picking up Kontess Rehema's letter again and rereading it.

"Might I make a more palatable suggestion?" Loralee asked after a moment. "We do already have troops moving to the area—"

"*Neredi* troops," Nikias interrupted. "And we've already established how thrilled Kontess Rehema will be to see more power in the hands of the duq."

"Nikias, the Khanum was speaking," Merikh admonished gently.

Nikias bowed his head stiffly, surprised, before gesturing for Loralee to continue.

"The grand vizier is right. The kontess will be displeased to see my father or my cousin with their troops. Therefore, don't send either of them. We need a representative of the Shah to smooth over relations in Ydeba. The royalists already want to see the Shah remain in power, regardless of racial and religious tensions. I know my father's men; they will follow my orders. The Umbeah need to see that even if I am a cultist, I have the Shah and Shai'Khal's best interests at heart.

"*And,*" Loralee said firmly, as protests were barely contained by Nikias shaking his head, "the only people who know of the Key are sitting at this table or already failed to destroy the Key. Only two of us here have no magic. Only one of us is able-bodied enough to handle whatever tasks may be thrown at them after a month on the road. What will offend Kontess Rehema more after all this—an apology from the Shah for the incident from a servant or heartfelt appreciation from the royal family? If Ruya accompanies me, then we've removed the 'undue influence' of the Pantheon from the Shah's immediate vicinity, and they won't be able to argue any longer that Merikh's choices are being swayed by beautiful women at his side."

In one fell swoop, Loralee had opened up *months* of opportunity for Merikh to study the grimoire without Ruya's intervention.

Trust me, Loralee's dark eyes implored, *I'm on your side.* It was obvious for Merikh to read.

"Apologies, Khanum, but that's far too dangerous," Nikias said dismissively, still shaking his head. "There would be assassins dogging your every step, some of whom would be more than mere peasant zealots."

"Were those not the same arguments made by Mansur? Reasons why his precious son shouldn't be allowed to follow generations of tradition for his patrol?" Merikh pointed out.

Nikias looked stunned, unable to speak for a moment. Undoubtedly, he'd expected Merikh to support his protest. After all, the vizier wasn't wrong.

"I-I...yes, I suppose they were. But we are on the verge of war now. We weren't back then."

"Of course, Vizier. The country will be at war, Madiar included. What better hope do we have to destroy the Key and begin earning the love of the Umbeah? They believe themselves neglected at best. Loralee can arrive in Buhet to thank the kontess and be met there by Amir Xolani and Duqa Adanna. They can share a few meals, be friendly. Perhaps the Khanum will win over the future amira of Ydeba, securing alliances." Merikh looked from Nikias to Loralee. If he had to make nice with Duq Rashad, then she could do the same with her closest rival.

"How soon would we be leaving to join the Neredi troops?" Ruya asked, breaking her uncharacteristic silence. She seemed cautious. The idea of being sent from Madiar hadn't factored into her plans, it seemed.

"A month, if not sooner, given the estimate from the duq," Loralee answered.

"Will you be able to remove the priest from the Temple in that time?" Ruya asked Merikh pointedly. "I'd rather not leave Madiar until we can establish a proper Pantheon temple, and if I'm here when the Temple falls, then there must be someone for those here to turn to with their faith."

"I will speak with the Ajir and Sardar generals, and we will see," Merikh said. "I cannot plan a winning strategy for a war around your preferences, Ruya."

"Naturally. I would simply like to be considered. My gods are, after all, the reason you're at war."

She was trying to dodge around the grimoire, perhaps hoping that Merikh had forgotten seeing it or never realized its worth. Dancing around mentioning that there was something of great value to her, to Ikharon, hidden deep within the Temple.

"Raudhah is loyal to me, and I am loyal to your gods. Ydeba is where the greatest challenge to your gods will come from, and what better place, then, for you and Sarka to be? I've made up my mind. Nikias, I need that new warrant for the Fari commander, and Duq Alaziz needs to be informed of this council's decision. Ruya, you are dismissed."

Merikh lifted his hand and gestured to the opening door. Loralee didn't need to be asked to stay. She remained seated as the other two stood. Both appeared to be debating protests. As soon as the door shut, the murmur of an unhappy priestess could be heard.

"I didn't expect you to agree with me so easily," Loralee admitted carefully, trying to hide the twinge of disappointment his agreement had created. Undoubtedly, she had hoped Merikh would have required more convincing to send his wife away.

"I dislike your suggestion. I believe it dangerous, and you are not likely to return from it. However, I am at a loss for trusted options. You raised a few good points. Ydeba should know their khanum; perhaps learn to appreciate her. I would feel more comfortable if I were joining you, but we can't abandon Madiar to Nikias's guidance now."

Merikh and Loralee could perhaps travel within Raudhah together, but to both be in the same hostile political environment? It might just be enough for the Faithful to put aside their dislike for sorcerers long enough to hire a contingent to approach the problem with a scorched-earth policy.

"You've managed to survive your assassins. There's no reason that an Ajir bodyguard won't be able to protect me. The Neredi cavalry will have every desire to keep me safe. Sarka will be at my side in Buhet. I can't imagine anyone able to harm me with her around."

"I'm certain Adrian believed the same right up until Dalya was torturing him. I prefer keeping the monopoly on scars in this relationship."

Loralee bit her lip. "I do too. But we all make sacrifices for our country. Your back, Adrian's injuries, potentially my life."

"Your life, my dynasty. I have no intention of remarrying. You made a promise to protect the Madiaran line. I expect it fulfilled."

Loralee's posture changed, a coy half smile belying her amusement. "Is that your way of saying you'll miss me and I ought to be careful? That, dare I say it, my husband is maybe even *fond* of me? Appreciative, even?"

"Well, that might be going too far," he said with a smirk. Merikh found his out, a means to squirm away from the conversation without having to agree with her that yes, she was right.

"I don't think so," Loralee teased. "I think you might actually have some *feelings* peeking out from behind those walls, Shahanshah. There might be a human in there somewhere."

Admittedly, he couldn't help but smile and shake his head. She was getting to him, finding ways to make him relax. Saying things that a month ago would have simply given him more reason to hide behind his walls. A reason to keep her at arm's length, to push her away. But Loralee had wormed her way behind those walls, and Merikh didn't find himself begrudging it.

"Human or not, I have work to do, and so do you," Merikh said as he pushed the chair back and stood.

Loralee stood, but she merely turned around, hitched her skirt up comfortably, and sat back down on the table. She snatched up the letters from Sarka and Kontess Rehema when Merikh reached for them. Her coy smile hadn't disappeared; she wasn't done toying with him yet.

"You have letters to write? A personalized acknowledgment to the dear kontess?" Loralee asked, holding the letters out of reach.

"It would be appropriate." The irritation was more a put-on than Merikh would ever admit.

"And my duties?"

"I want you training with my swordmaster. You need to know how to take care of yourself in case someone does slip past your Ajir," Merikh told her before he stepped around Loralee's chair and held out his hand for the letters. He could have easily focused his magic on them and pulled them from her grip, but she hadn't earned that rudeness.

"Because you'll miss me if I die?" Loralee teased, moving the letters as far away as she could without losing her balance.

"Loralee..."

"Yes?"

Merikh forced a frustrated sigh, and he reached across Loralee for the letters. She handed them to him easily before she put her hand on his arm, straightened up as far as she could, and kissed him. Her other hand pulled at the front of his kameez, keeping him close.

"I will miss your stubbornness," Loralee said when she pulled away.

The letters fell back onto the desk. Merikh's hand went to her thigh as he leaned forward to kiss her again. Loralee let out a surprised sound; undoubtedly he'd caught her off guard. Merikh's hands dropped away, and he took a step back. That coy smile had been replaced with a wary desire; she clearly didn't trust Merikh to continue pursuing her after a kiss like that. They'd always been interrupted before, after all. Or rather, he'd always *allowed* them to be interrupted. The room was private. There were no souls left in the throne room or nearby. And *gods*, part of him desperately wanted her. It'd been years since he'd been with a woman, and she lay beside him every night. She knew not to touch his back, to keep her hands to herself more or less. It was safe.

But there were letters to write, a country to run, and the need to do tomorrow's work today, as the petitions would displace it. Merikh straightened up and brushed Loralee's cheek with his hand.

"I may miss you."

"May?" The coyness returned as she shook her head. "You can do better than 'may.'"

Loralee let go of his kameez. She reached behind herself and undid the low clasps of her choli. The small golden blouse was tossed carelessly on the desk. A month of marriage, and this was the first time Merikh had actually seen her topless. Loralee mistook his silence, giving him a look *daring* him to excuse himself. Merikh didn't notice. His eyes were drawn to her breasts.

"Work can wait," Loralee said as she undid the ties of his salwar, her warm hand sliding inside.

Merikh pulled her close and kissed her, his free hand tracing her thigh as he pulled up her skirt. For once, his hands weren't cold on her skin. It fleetingly crossed Merikh's mind to take her back to the royal suite. To a comfortable bed, instead of the table now pressed against Loralee's back. But he didn't want to lose the moment, and from the urgency with which Loralee's pressed against him, she didn't seem to mind. Instead, Merikh lost himself in satisfying the ache and desire that Loralee had carefully teased. He took her hands in one of his, careful to prevent Loralee from touching his scars while he memorized her soft curves.

With a shudder and a breath, it was over. Merikh pulled away from Loralee and retied his salwar. He helped Loralee off the table once she'd placed her blouse back on. She leaned on him for a moment before looking up at him.

"You'll miss me," she said quietly, a satisfied smirk on her lips. Merikh shook his head and placed his hand on the bare small of her back, rubbing it gently.

"You may be right."

CHAPTER 36

20TH OF BELITH, DRY SEASON, 902 UNIFIED AGE
BUHET, YDEBA PROVINCE

Adrian stood at the infirmary entrance. His left hand was pressed against the door, partly to keep it open and partly to distract him from the pain radiating from his right wrist up through his shoulder.

"It still *hurts*," Adrian insisted.

The healer in front of him didn't hide her glare or her exasperation. "Bayim, there is nothing more I can do for it. The stump is healed. I already gave you some opium tincture, and I'm not giving you more. We don't *have* more to spare on you. Madiar might have nice access to the amir's poppy fields, but we do *not*." The healer ducked under Adrian's arm and began walking down the corridor. The lightning pain down his right arm relaxed a little, replaced by a persistent ache.

"You understand who I work for?"

The words made Adrian wince. They were out of his mouth before he could help himself. He *hated* invoking the Shah's title for something like this.

"I do," the healer answered as she turned around, regarding him coldly. "But *my* employer is here. If the Shah himself arrives, then he can request the opium for you, and I'll happily give it to him. Until then, the kontess wants the opium left for our soldiers. In case you've forgotten, they're the ones keeping you safe."

Safe. Adrian scoffed. He wasn't safe in an Umbeah stronghold. He hadn't been safe since he left Madiar. He'd simply been deluded enough to believe he was untouchable. The people here resented him. As far as they were concerned, he was a Yahidah apostate. There wasn't much worse. If the healer knew the reason why Adrian had been captured by Onyx Swords in the first place, he doubted she would have given him what little tincture she had.

Adrian watched as she turned and receded down the hallway. This time he kept his thoughts to himself. His frustration was instead taken out against the ebony door under his hand as it banged loudly against the wall.

Or at least, Adrian hoped it had. His hearing was softened now. Everything on his left sounded as if a pillow were snuggly stuffed over it. Mosi had closed over his ear when he healed it, causing permanent disability.

At least the man can fix an ankle, Adrian thought. It was a small mercy he no longer limped, but he still felt lopsided. He couldn't look in a mirror without seeing what he'd lost. Even with the opium tincture, the pain never truly went away. It ached constantly on the good days. On the bad, the lightning pain didn't stop, and it was all Adrian could think of. At night, the pain kept him awake. If it didn't, then the memories did. He could feel Dalya's hands on him in the dark, could hear her voice. *I know you,* the whisper said, sending a chill down Adrian's spine.

It could be worse, the little voice in Adrian's head reminded him. Ikbal and Imani had paid a far higher price for his crimes. Imani's screams haunted him. And what of the baby?

The stump of his wrist bumped into someone as Adrian rounded the corridor. A string of expletives filled the air as Adrian cradled his arm. The bone was close to the skin, and white-hot pain shot down his arm when it was jarred.

"Apologies! Are you all right?" the servant asked. The older woman seemed to be genuinely concerned.

Adrian shook his arm out of habit, as if shaking the pain from his phantom hand would solve anything. "Yeah, fine," Adrian said before he looked properly at the woman. There was a letter in her hand, crisp white paper folded tightly and sealed with red wax.

Red wax.

There were twin rearing horses facing a crown.

The Akhenic Sun was conspicuously absent from the Madiaran royal crest now.

"The Shah sends word?" Adrian's heart caught in his throat, hoping beyond hope that Merikh had sent him *something*, anything to make the loss of appendages and lives better.

"For the kontess," she said with a frown and a nod.

"I can deliver it," Adrian said. He extended his right hand...his right wrist, then brought it back to his side and reached with his left arm. The woman shrank away, holding the letter tight to her chest.

"No, thank you."

"I've carried far more sensitive letters on the Shah's behalf before," Adrian said, trying to reassure her, only to have it earn him another distrustful look as she walked around him. Without thinking, Adrian followed her.

"That may be, bayim, but I don't know you. I don't know that you really *are* the Ajir steward. You didn't come to us wearing anything official. All I know is that the letter is addressed to the kontess; she's the only person I'm leaving it with. If you'll excuse me..." She stopped walking and gestured back down the hallway from where they'd come.

Adrian shrugged. "I'm here on the Shah's authority. I'll escort you."

Not that I can do much else, Adrian thought. He wanted to see what Merikh had written, and in Madiar, she would have had to answer to him. There was nothing she could say short of calling the guards to prevent him from walking with her. Reluctantly, the woman nodded, and silence fell between them as they walked the halls of Sall Manor.

The manor had been built from granite quarried from either Sek or Membiti, the stone darker than the white marble of the Madiar palace. It gave the manor a more oppressive feeling. Windows were glassless, shuttered only by wood. There was a fake sense of opulence, as if the manor were trying to compete with the wealthier Ydeba cities and failing. Without mines or quarries, Buhet relied on trade. The town was built on the backs of fishermen and farmers, not artisans. It showed in the clunky architecture. The manor had as much bluster as the nobles residing within it.

Sunlight hurt Adrian's eyes as the servant woman opened the door ahead of them, leading to a creekside garden. Gravel crunched under their boots as they followed the path to a vine-covered gazebo. A fountain on the far side gurgled loudly, though Adrian couldn't see it as they approached. He lost all interest in looking for it when he saw Sarka inside the gazebo with Kontess Rehema. At the entrance, both Adrian and the servant woman bowed.

"What is it?" Kontess Rehema asked brusquely.

"I have a letter from the Shah," the woman said as she straightened up.

Adrian did the same, glancing from the servant woman to Sarka. The champion looked determined, a look he saw on her face often now. She trained with the Sall spearmen and seemed to be taking their retreat from Kal Neveh to heart. He buried the sudden flare of resentment and looked to the kontess.

"It took the two of you to deliver it, Makeda?" Kontess Rehema asked, extending her hand. Makeda approached quickly and shook her head.

"He insisted on coming along."

"I did," Adrian admitted. "If there's word from the Shah, I'd like to hear it."

"I see. Affairs in Madiar must have become dire indeed if a mere steward is privileged to know all of the Shah's correspondence." Kontess Rehema dismissed her servant with a wave but allowed Adrian to stay. Not in the gazebo, of course, but in the heat of the midday sun. It was only a moment before the kontess finished reading, scoffed, and then dangled the letter toward Adrian.

"Perhaps you can read this and parse out a hidden message for me, Steward."

He sent it coded? Adrian couldn't help the elation in his chest. If that was coded, it meant new orders. It meant he still had a purpose. Adrian tried not to show his eagerness as he stepped within the cool shadows of the gazebo and took the letter.

> *Kontess Rehema Sall,*
>
> > *You have my sincere gratitude for the care shown to my steward and the continued hospitality shown toward the champion. The Khanum will arrive before the end of the Dry Season with reparations for the inconvenience their presence has caused.*
> >
> *Merikh Madiaran*
> *Shahanshah of Shai'Khal*

The words were plain on the paper, the curved script written carefully and clearly from Merikh's own hand. Adrian had seen Merikh's writing plenty of times to know these words hadn't been rushed. They had been thought over and likely rewritten at least once before Merikh had decided upon them. There was no code, nothing Adrian could interpret differently from these words than what the kontess had read.

You expect me to sit here and wait for two months? The elation had disappeared, leaving Adrian's throat dry. He pushed the letter back to the kontess. "I appreciate the care of your healers, Kontess," Adrian said when he'd found the words.

The kontess scoffed.

"My healers, my food, until the Second Harvest? One would have thought the delicate balance of supplies through Dry Season would have meant more to a desert shah!"

"He sends reparations that will more than compensate. We don't use that much." Sarka didn't hide the disdain in her voice as she leaned back in her chair. "What more could you want?"

"Reparations." The kontess snorted. "Brought on the backs of Royal Guards, I imagine. With the so-called Khanum. I tire of your company. You may both leave."

Kontess Rehema dropped the letter, snapped her fingers, and then pointed back toward the manor. Adrian bowed before he headed back down the gravel path. He didn't wait for Sarka—he'd been actively avoiding talking to her and had no plans to change that. Sarka, on the other hand, seemed tired of being ignored. The taller woman caught up quickly. She walked beside him into the manor, and once inside, she tapped his shoulder. He glanced at her, and Sarka pulled a letter from the pocket of her khalat.

"I received this yesterday. It's a little wordier. Come with me."

Without hesitation, Adrian followed her back to the privacy of her quarters. They were cramped, as the bed took up most of the room. Adrian sat down on it as Sarka closed the door. When she turned around, she hesitated for a moment.

"How are you feeling?" Sarka asked.

"Impatient," Adrian answered. He lifted his left hand for the letter. She frowned, hesitating for a moment before she handed it to him. Adrian smoothed the letter down on the bed.

"Don't get your hopes up," she said carefully.

Sarka,

> *In the future, refrain from starting wars without my consent, particularly if you plan on losing the first engagements. A mere Fari*

commander of a ceremonial guard should not have greater gains than the champion of war. If this is the aid I can expect from Livinja, then I would prefer you to advise the Akhenic Temple.

The Khanum will be joining you with troops and provisions. I expect her to be returned to Madiar in better condition than the steward and horses I've entrusted to your care. Should there be troops to spare, a Royal Guard patrol will return Adrian to Madiar. If you're capable, prevent Adrian from losing any more body parts while he's under your protection. Perhaps leave him in the care of the kontess's competent guards.

Merikh Madiaran

Shahanshah of Shai'Khal

"He wants you back in Madiar," Sarka said as she realized Adrian had finished the letter.

"I don't know what I expected," he whispered, his voice trembling. *Something* more. Something perhaps less acerbic, with a hint of worry about Adrian's well-being. Something written for him personally. Condolences from a friend for his loss. The thought made Adrian smirk bitterly.

In all the years I've known him, what could possibly make me think he'd ever actually show a little compassion when someone might witness it? Since Merikh's whipping, he'd grown much colder. *I would have thought you of all people would know what I'm going through. That you'd tell me what to do next.*

"I'm sorry." Sarka shrugged apologetically, interrupting and redirecting his thoughts as she pulled the chair from her desk and sat down.

"Yeah, well…that doesn't really do much for me, does it?" Adrian glanced down at his hands…hand. The healers had given him a leather cover for the stump, soft lambskin like the kontess's riding gloves. It was hot and itchy with prolonged wear, but at least it saved Adrian from looking at the pale wrinkled skin drawn taut over bone. A nub that ended far too soon.

"I wish we could have fixed it. It was dead. I can't fix that; healers can't fix it. The nearest necromancer was weeks away, *if* he'd even have come," Sarka said, her tone hesitant.

Adrian knew deep down she'd done her best. Necromancers were notoriously reclusive. Adrian remembered how much Nikias had struggled to find one willing to answer the Shah's summons to tutor Merikh. The few who did all had been strange men and women.

"You would have lost the rest of your arm," Sarka continued, filling the silence. "The bad blood could have killed you outright if you hadn't lost the hand. I wish I hadn't been as stubborn at the Temple. It won't happen again. You would have thought nine hundred years might have taught me some patience." She was trying to lighten the mood a little, but her words only sparked anger.

"I'm glad I was a valuable *lesson* for you," Adrian said as he stood. Restlessness took him. He needed to move, to pace or to wander. To do something other than merely sit here. He needed a distraction from the pain radiating a few inches away from his wrist. How a missing hand could still hurt so much, Adrian didn't understand. Neither did the healers. But it *did*.

"What can I do to help you?" Sarka asked.

"Get me home."

"Merikh's handling that, even if you don't like it. I don't know patrol schedules. Rehema certainly won't help me with that."

"Opium tincture, then. The healers are hoarding it for the soldiers. Personally, I think it's a load of horse shit. They just don't like Yahidahs. What they gave me wouldn't have even taken the edge off of this." Adrian gestured to the scar on his cheek. He watched as Sarka leaned almost imperceptibly back into her chair, her lips pursing a little and her hand twitching toward her dagger. She tended to fidget with the small tassel on the end of the hilt when she needed to think.

"Not sure they're going to like an Aegalian cultist much more, but I'm a soldier, at least," Sarka said reluctantly before standing. She pulled the door open, and Adrian scrambled off the bed to follow her. They didn't speak as they walked, and when she reached the infirmary, Adrian hung back. He didn't expect her to receive any, let alone actually give it to him. So when she returned a few minutes later and freely handed him three small vials of brown liquid, Adrian stood in dumbfounded stupor.

"I've seen what losing limbs does to soldiers," she said. "Merikh should never have thrown you into this life without training you in how to handle it. If you're anything like I worry you are, you're thinking of upending one of these and chasing it down with a large mug of pito. Don't. I have a better idea."

Sarka put her hand on his shoulder. Adrian flinched and shoved her hand off, a sickening pit in his stomach growing the second she put her hand on him. There was a strange pressure on him from his chest down to his groin.

"Don't touch me," Adrian snapped at her. He didn't notice how shallow his breathing became.

Sarka frowned and took a step away from him. "Apologies. Just...let's go somewhere you're more comfortable," Sarka said as she gestured down the hall.

Reluctantly, Adrian acquiesced. He followed Sarka back to his quarters, surprised at her choice of location. There wasn't much room here, and he really didn't want to be alone with her. His quarters were larger than hers, at least.

Sarka shut the door and gestured for him to sit on the bed as she grabbed the chair from his desk. She turned it around and sat down, her arms resting over the back.

"What are you doing?" Adrian asked cautiously, squeezing the vials in his hands gently.

"Drink half of one, then chase it with this." Sarka pulled a flask off her hip and tossed it to him. It landed on the bed beside him. Adrian put the vials down and picked it up. He popped the cork off. To his disappointment, the liquid had no scent. Water.

"I'm here to make sure you don't do anything stupid. Plus, that tincture should knock you on your ass. Or it'll send your mind funny places that you probably shouldn't wander alone. So I'm here."

Adrian didn't want Sarka here. But he didn't want to be alone either. If she'd asked who he wanted, Adrian would have been hard-pressed to find an answer. Her tone had been firm enough that he knew asking her to leave would simply be ignored.

All right, fine. Adrian acquiesced, closing the cork on the flask and picking up one of the bottles. It was sealed tightly. Adrian groped at the cap uselessly with his left hand. The glass vial slipped from his hand and bounced on the bed.

"A little help, maybe?" Adrian snapped.

Sarka didn't move, her look remained impassive. "No. Come on. I know you can do this. Slow down. Use your mind—literally. You have fire magic. You have telekinesis. I shouldn't have to help you open a bottle."

The answer was so simple. An embarrassed heat came to Adrian's cheeks. He avoided using his magic most of the time. It wore him out too easily, and he couldn't afford that in a strange and dangerous place. The fact that Sarka came to that answer so quickly shamed him. Adrian picked up the vial again and focused his magic on the glass. Small orange flames flickered around the neck of the vial for a moment before they disappeared. As it cooled, Adrian focused on the cork. It popped out from the vial and fell on his knee.

"*Half,*" Sarka reminded him firmly.

Adrian barely heard her as he brought the warm vial to his lips. The brown liquid was bitter; they'd done nothing to help the taste of it as it flowed over his tongue. The healers in Madiar took the edge off with honey. The glass was being tugged away from his hand—Sarka's magic reminding him to pull it away when it reached the halfway point.

Reluctantly, he put the vial down and used his magic to put the cork back in. Adrian swept up the other vials and put them in Sarka's outstretched hand. It didn't surprise him how little she trusted him. He then chugged half the water from her flask, then tossed it aside. He leaned back against the wall beside his bed.

"I know what this stuff does," Adrian said absentmindedly. "I've seen Mer— I've seen people on it before. I'm probably just going to sleep."

He'd had to hold his tongue. Adrian's frustration and anger at his master didn't negate their friendship, nor the trust Merikh had in him. He wasn't about to tempt Sarka with stories of Merikh on opium tincture after the whipping. Those were stories Nikias and Adrian would take to their graves. Half the time, the tinctures put Merikh to sleep. The other half, it became impossible to keep Merikh in bed. The lack of pain had brought on strange ideas that he *had* to get written down before he lost them—odd enchantments that usually didn't work once the opium cleared, wandering essays about whatever had caught the then-Shahzade's fancy. It'd made Merikh even more paranoid too, although that had been easy enough to handle. More unsettling had been the intermittent bouts of euphoria.

It had been an odd month after the whipping.

"Yeah, well, you probably haven't had a concentration like this before," Sarka said. "So that's what I'm here for." She cleared her throat, then placed the vials inside her pocket. The flask moved from the bed into her hand, and she tied it back to her belt.

"Don't trust me not to drink more?" Adrian asked, deciding to put the unsaid out in the open.

"Nope," Sarka admittedly candidly. "If you get up and start pacing or acting wild, I want everything in a safe place. I don't want to see them get broken and wasted. I doubt the healers will give me more for a long time."

"I don't need you here if you're just doing it out of guilt. I've got enough false friends born from obligations or hoping for advancement without needing another one."

"Oh, come off it, Adrian. We're not friends," Sarka teased before her smile faded a little. "I'm not here out of guilt, and I sure as hell don't want to curry favor with Merikh. He can... What's one of your colloquialisms?"

"Walk behind a mare in heat? I think that's the one you're looking for."

"What in Alhanem is that supposed to mean anyway?" Sarka asked.

Adrian shrugged. "It's a stupid place to be. You're probably going to get kicked. Seems like a thing you'd wish on him."

"You know, I don't want him dead," Sarka clarified. "I just...wish he'd learn his place."

Adrian burst out laughing, shaking his head and rubbing his eyes with his hands...*hand*. He bumped his wrist against his eye and winced.

"Yeah, you and Mansur both. If Merikh is sure of anything, it's his own damn superiority. So if you're hoping for a little humility, you're never going to see it." The brutal cynicism of his statement surprised Adrian. Usually he tried to cushion his words when speaking about a superior—particularly a man he considered a friend.

"Well, the gods will knock a little into him. Livinja doesn't have much time for anyone who can't respect command. Nadlious won't approve of him much either, considering the way he toys around with the law." Sarka's tone grew a touch bitter, still sour about the scorpion in Kasu, apparently.

"What are they like? Your gods, I mean." Adrian asked. He leaned forward, his head swimming as he did so. The tincture's effects were starting to show. Sarka looked away from him toward the wall, a small smile growing on her lips as she thought.

"They're all different. Livinja is what you'd hope for in a goddess of war—tactical, calm, honorable. The best war is a short war that leaves plenty of heroics for the bards to sing about."

"Bards?" Adrian interrupted. The Aegalian word was strange to him.

"A storyteller? Someone who sings and plays music?"

"Oh, an ashik."

Sarka nodded before she continued. "Right. Plenty for the ashiks to sing about and plenty of soldiers who get to go home to their families. A good commander keeps the loss of life to a minimum. Sacrifices are made only to prevent greater losses. She values the sacrifices made for her, and her troops love her for that."

"And how does she pick a side in a war?" Adrian asked. "Surely both sides would pray to the goddess of war. So how does she pick the winner?" It was an earnest question, one that bothered Adrian when it came to gods and war. Or anything, really, that required a god to favor one side or person over another.

"Righteousness of the cause, what the other gods support, it depends every time. Livinja takes my advice into account if she needs it. Prayers are prayers, and she doesn't want to see casualties. Livinja might very well bless both sides with swift victories and merciful surrenders, depending on what will save lives."

"That sounds remarkably political."

"Politics was invented by the gods."

Adrian smiled lopsidedly as he leaned back against the wall. Or at least, that had been the plan. He found himself instead leaning sideways, his head landing on the pillow. His eyelids were growing heavy.

"Politics is a load of horse shit."

"Probably, but I'm not sure where we'd be without it."

Adrian sank into the pillow. He rolled his shoulders into the blanket. As he realized he could no longer feel pain in his limbs—missing or real—he let out a long, slow breath.

"Home."

CHAPTER 37

16TH OF LIVITH, DRY SEASON, 902 UNIFIED AGE
MADIAR, RAUDHAH PROVINCE

Forty-seven thousand one hundred and thirty-three. High Inquisitor Adunbi had given Alcaeus the report this morning with the last known numbers on how many Onyx Swords were currently on the Temple payroll.

Duqa Enitan had promised almost ten times as many troops from her allies. Numbers that looked quite impressive on paper, written in neat rows explaining how many were foot soldiers, how many were cavalry, how many were sorcerers, and where. Of course, there was the not-so-minor detail that Merikh had seven armies pledged to him compared to their six, the best cavalry in the world, and the Royal Guard itself, which stood sixty thousand men strong at any given time.

Well, we have mountains and peasants on our side, at least. The geography would destroy Merikh's advantage trying to cross the Katu. Then again, the grand crusade that Duqa Enitan seemed to envision would struggle to get any footing on the savanna or desert.

At least, it would if each side fought honorably. If they stayed on battlefields, away from peasants and only fought soldier to soldier... Alcaeus sighed heavily. That choice had already been taken away. Commoners rioted in Madiar any time a Royal Guard even appeared to slight one of the Faithful. Cultists fought against any attempts at conversion.

We both have armies of untrained soldiers who won't listen to leadership. Alcaeus wondered who was better at balming the masses, him or Merikh? *Maybe I should get married, even the odds,* Alcaeus thought with a small self-deprecating smile. If only it were that easy. Besides, there were enough women in his life causing trouble.

Dalya Maki had sent word two days ago of her impending arrival in Madiar and a request for aid entering the city. At first instinct, Alcaeus had almost denied her request. The Royal Guard had a warrant out for her, and from what Alcaeus had heard, it was more than justified. Merikh wanted her head on a spike. Alcaeus was tempted to give it to him. But Dalya was an Onyx Sword, regardless of her flights of fancy and brutality. If she asked for sanctuary in the Temple, it was the least he could grant her. Much of her first letter had appeared to be gibberish, and Alcaeus wanted his questions answered.

The pendant had made several of the priests and acolytes sick. As long as it had been at the foot of the statue, no one had been able to light the nearby candles or keep them lit with magic. Alcaeus had removed it and hidden in his desk drawer. Even there, it made meeting with certain acolytes and priests difficult. He wanted to know more about the stone. Until he had those answers, the Fari commander's head would remain firmly attached to her neck.

"Mawla?"

An acolyte knocked on the doorframe, the young man warily eyeing Alcaeus's desk.

"Yes?"

"High Inquisitor Adunbi has returned. He's with the Fari commander. You may wish to hurry. I think the high inquisitor might explode."

They could hear shouting as they approached the main antechamber. The high inquisitor was maroon-faced with veins bulging when Alcaeus arrived. Whatever had been said, it would have ended the Fari commander's career if the inquisitor were the one deciding that.

"Keep it down, Inquisitor! You're within the temple," Alcaeus chided as he approached.

The Onyx Swords each bowed their heads briefly. On the left stood a small woman who was impervious to Adunbi's shouting. A nasty-looking burn scarred her right cheek up past her eye, receding her hairline around her ear. It almost masked the wrinkles starting around her eyes, where age was starting to take its toll.

"Apologies, Mawla, but the Fari commander seems to be under the mistaken impression that there will be no consequences for her insubordination, the reckless endangerment of her troops, or the loss of civilian lives."

"On the contrary, I expect a promotion," Dalya said, unabashedly brazen and with a smile on her lips. It was unnerving. Her words sent the high inquisitor back into sputtering anger.

Alcaeus raised his hand and quieted Adunbi.

"I'll have words with the commander before we decide the appropriate course of action." Alcaeus tried to sound reassuring, but Adunbi still looked put off. The man didn't care to have Alcaeus inserting himself into this, but it was far too political a matter to let a man as lazy as Adunbi have full control.

Alcaeus gestured for Dalya to follow him down the hallway to the nearby atrium. The walk was slow, as Dalya periodically stopped and studied the tapestries on the wall and spent a little too long staring at a statue.

"I've never been to Madiar before," she said by way of explanation when the atrium door shut behind them. "It's not what I expected."

"How so?"

"I expected more from the High Temple. You can barely see its minarets from outside the city. The palace domes, on the other hand, you can see for *miles*."

"The High Temple was never meant to compete with the egos of nobles in that way. Akhenits were spent on alms for the poor and food for the needy, not in competition with the rich and powerful," Alcaeus said as he sat down on the bench.

"Inspiring."

The words dripped with sarcasm as Dalya plopped herself down across from Alcaeus. She leaned back and rested her feet on the fountain.

Alcaeus took a deep breath, steadying himself. "I'm going to hand you over to the judges for trial unless you can give me a valid reason not to. I've seen the warrant from the Shah. I've heard the rumors you tortured the Shah's personal steward—"

"Really?" She looked far too proud of herself at the realization. "I knew he was Ajir, never dreamed he was that important."

"Even if you didn't, the deaths in Hatai and Ziyadi more than warrant a secular punishment."

"Oh, for pity's sake, it's *war*, Mawla."

"Not officially, not yet. If I can…" Alcaeus trailed off as Dalya rolled her eyes.

"If you can what? I'm trying to *help* you, since you and that sand puffer Adunbi seem to be flailing about without any real course of action. Might be different here in the big city, sitting in the necromancer's shadow, but out in the rest of Shai'Khal, it's already war. It's been war for years since those cultist whores showed up on our shores and started their onslaught against Akhenios. My men have been dying for the Great Prophet."

"And what men are those? 'Sanctified Suns'?"

Dalya puffed herself up proudly and pulled a pendant out from underneath her road-worn khalat. It matched the one she'd sent Alcaeus.

"Yes."

"That's sedition."

"I don't particularly care, if I'm honest. I follow Akhenios. I follow you so long as your feet are on the right path. But the high inquisitor out there"—Dalya pointed with her thumb toward the door—"should have retired a decade ago. The Onyx Swords are weak, ceremonial guards at best. Of course, they'll all willingly die for you and Akhenios. But my men? They'll kill for you. And most of the time, they're rather efficient at it."

"Most of the time. When you sent me the pendant, I wondered where I'd seen the design before. It was etched in a stone pendant around the neck of a servant tried for the murder of a vizier. For the attempted murder of the Shah."

"You know, in his defense, it's *very* hard to parse out what's true about the Shah's eccentricities and what's not. Who could have known that Mansur's baby boy doesn't drink? Next you'll be telling me the corpse-fucking rumor is false."

"I didn't realize that *was* a rumor," Alcaeus admitted, thrown off by her words. Merikh was a famous prude, at least in Madiar.

Dalya shrugged. "Again, I do what I can to help our cause in Ydeba. No one there knows whether that rumor or the dozens of ones we've started are false or not."

Alcaeus shook his head, speechless for a moment.

Dalya laughed. "See, this is why you're not going to hand me over to Merikh, or the judges, or strip me of my command. You, the necromancer, Adunbi, you're all playing with a small set of rules. No one's officially made their intentions of war known, therefore let's all just try to play nicely and ignore the fire. You're forgetting that the empire is *already* on fire. You might as well fan the flames and let it burn. Our faith came out of the ashes once before, and it's time for rebirth from ashes again."

You prayed for Akhenios to send you help. The thought came unbidden and disturbed Alcaeus to his foundation. This woman, hungry for blood, was not what he'd meant when he'd implored Akhenios.

"Look." Dalya leaned forward and pulled her legs off the fountain. They swung idly under the bench, the toe of her boot barely scraping the ground. "The only thing that really matters is why I came here. The warrant doesn't matter. I die, one of my men replaces me. We'll continue our mission, and it's more important now than ever. Do you know our history, the Onyx Swords? We were made by Akhenios to protect Him, to guard His temples. Well, I think I found the First Temple. I think I found the *reason* we're the Onyx Swords. Why the Great Prophet was able to cleanse the land of magic's corruption. I have the means to do so again."

Dalya settled in, as if preparing to tell quite the tale but was waiting for permission to speak. No, that wasn't quite it. She had that smug touch to her lips, the way a parent might force their child to say "please" in just the right inflection before handing them a sweet mint.

"Go on."

She cracked her fingers, then her neck before she nodded.

"Hatai's slums burned because I found a telepath. She told me about an Ajir roaming the city looking for Pantheon supporters. She showed me how to find those supporters, and they all were preying on the ignorant slum dwellers. So I set the place ablaze to purge it, but not before running into a bright young man in an inn. A man reading a book and matching the telepath's description exactly. He couldn't leave fast enough when he realized what I was. The men I sent after him died. We found ash prints where their trail ended.

"We followed them south to Ziyadi, and I returned to Kal Neveh when we lost them. I left scouts to find out where they were off to next. When my scouts found them, they were returning from the Katu. The Ajir, Adrian, had an unconscious Sarka attached to her saddle. I found this in his bag."

Dalya pulled a journal from her satchel and tossed it to Alcaeus. He didn't open it, instead waiting for her to continue.

"It speaks of a temple, with something inside that Akhenios wanted to keep safe from djinn. They found it. More importantly, *I* found it. I've left forty good men to guard it. More than enough, since none of the passes to it are wide enough for more than three horsemen. Curiosity got the better of me, and while I haven't thoroughly searched the temple, that's where the stone in your pendant came from. Where mine did."

Dalya grew suddenly very serious. She moved up to the edge of her bench seat, planted her feet on the floor, and her eyes met Alcaeus's. She held his gaze unblinkingly.

"I took mages up to it. Whatever these stones are, they're what made Sarka faint. They destroy magic, if only temporarily. Prolonged exposure, though, that *kills*. I have what it takes to destroy the blasphemous whelp sitting on Mansur's throne, the cultists who advise him, the sorcerers in his legions. We can bring Shai'Khal back to a glorious age where we depend on *ourselves* again, not on crutches built of magic."

A knock on the door bought Alcaeus time to think. When it opened, two Onyx Swords escorted in a woman clad in a red, a silver scorpion on her chest. Dalya's posture lost its seriousness, an amused smile on her lips. Her hand absentmindedly—Akhenios be kind, Alcaeus *hoped* it was an absentminded gesture—went to her dagger.

"Mawla, I have a warrant for that woman's arrest," the Ajir said, her tone defensive.

"Come take me, dear," Dalya taunted. She was poised, ready to strike at the slightest provocation. The Ajir, on the other hand, simply looked exasperated. Dalya wouldn't receive the fight she was baiting the woman for.

"Disciplining Onyx Swords is a Temple matter," Alcaeus said. "Therefore, the commander's crimes will be dealt with internally." His words didn't surprise the soldier. The Ajir stepped toward Alcaeus as she pulled a letter from her achkan.

"Then your presence is required in court tomorrow afternoon."

"That will be all. Shoo," Dalya said and gestured toward the door. The wave was summarily ignored until Alcaeus mirrored the sentiment. He opened the letter, cracking the red seal as the door shut. Alcaeus smiled bitterly as he recognized the script. Nikias had written it. Merikh had simply read it and signed the summons.

"Are you going?" Dalya asked.

Alcaeus took a breath and let it out slowly. "I believe ignoring this would only make me look unreasonable. I can't afford to have cultists spreading rumors that I'm a stubborn pig, can I?"

Dalya shrugged. "I think going is a great idea. As long as you're wearing one of my pendants, that is. See for yourself what it can do against someone powerful. And if it does all that I promise, then I want a permanent post here in Madiar. I want to move my men into the city, and I want to get rid of that incompetent man you have as inquisitor."

"One thing at a time. Let's see if your pendants do all you promise."

CHAPTER 38

17th of Livith, Dry Season, 902 Unified Age
Madiar, Raudhah Province

"You shouldn't have come," Khamisi muttered under his breath. The legate had joined Alcaeus at the stable to escort the high priest to the throne room. The Onyx Swords who had accompanied Alcaeus to the palace remained at the stable, ready to leave the moment Alcaeus returned.

"Maybe not, but I'm here now."

Alcaeus raised his hand to his chest and touched the pendant under his kaftan. It was insanity, coming to the palace wearing a pendant that did what Dalya claimed. He didn't entirely believe her. When seated at the base of Akhenios's statue, the pendant had never caused the level of disruption to the sorcerer priests and acolytes that she described. If it did anything to Merikh, it might make him uncomfortable.

That, at least, is something I'm happy to do.

"Well, the grand vizier looks like the horse that snuck into grain stores: entirely too pleased with himself. Whatever you think you're doing here, I hope you're flexible."

"Palm trees bend in a breeze, but their roots never move. I'm happy to be as flexible as necessary without compromising my soul."

Khamisi nodded, unconvinced. Alcaeus didn't have time to allay his fears. Guards opened the large olive-wood doors to the throne room. Inside, the room was packed with people. City nobles, the legates, important merchants, all lined the aisle to the Rising Sun Throne. There was little sunlight from the grand arched windows. The sun had hit its zenith outside, leaving the room in cold shadows. The rug felt uneven under Alcaeus's sandals, a groove worn into the middle from petitioners. He could feel the exact moment where most petitioners stopped and bowed, as he almost stumbled at the sudden thickness.

426

Khamisi stayed a few feet behind him, but Alcaeus could feel the animosity from the legate. He didn't have to look to know Khamisi was ready to draw his sword the moment he felt Alcaeus was threatened.

Don't get me imprisoned with your protection.

Alcaeus steeled himself to the task at hand. His gaze briefly moved to the throne itself. The Rising Sun Throne was named as such for the carved half sun that connected the Shah and Khanum's seats. The delicate rays looked more like imposing golden thorns to Alcaeus. Once, there had been a matching throne for the Temple, the thrones made for the Great Prophet's sons. Centuries ago, one of Alcaeus's predecessors had deemed it inappropriate for even a high priest to sit on a throne, and it had been destroyed. Now, seeing Merikh and Loralee sitting upon this one, Alcaeus couldn't help but wonder if the Rising Sun Throne had outlived its truth. If it had turned into something blasphemous and distasteful.

"Shahanshah." Alcaeus bowed his head briefly. "I must insist that it's beyond inappropriate for a sayida to sit in the khanum's place of honor."

Plainly dressed in the Madiaran reds and golds, no crown on Merikh's head, he was coldly stoic and unreadable. Loralee sat at his side, a beautiful adornment for the Shah. She was decidedly more transparent with her thoughts. Her lips were tight, as if smelling something distasteful.

"Equally inappropriate to address the Khanum as a sayida," Merikh said, "but that's hardly why you've been summoned here. You're harboring a traitor and mass murderer in the Temple. I expect her to be handed over."

"Discipline of the Onyx Swords is entirely up to the high inquisitor. The Fari commander has asked for and been granted sanctuary. Your warrant meddles in religious affairs."

"How are you planning in disciplining the commander?"

"That is yet to be determined. We've hardly had the time to investigate thoroughly—"

"You have had plenty of time since Hatai's slums burned," Merikh interrupted. The Shah leaned forward ever so slightly, and Alcaeus fought the urge to step back. He'd never grown accustomed to the strange aura surrounding Merikh, the pressing feeling that he'd forgotten something and ought to *run*. The fingers on Merikh's left hand raised a little off the armrest as if summoning something. That little flick was for show; Alcaeus knew that. Sorcerers of Merikh's level didn't have to move to manipulate the flow of magic through them. But nothing came, and a brief flicker of confusion crossed Merikh's face before he continued. "There were children among the dead. It seems that the Priest Council purge did little to teach the Akhenic Temple moral decency."

"Can you truly preach about moral decency sitting there, when you used djinn to acquire it?"

They stood merely feet away from the dark stain on the floor, hidden by the rug. That was all that was left of Mansur. Merikh smirked, as if amused by that minor detail, before he stood. Loralee glanced up to him warily, although she remained seated.

"Come with me," Merikh said as he stepped down from the throne and gestured for Alcaeus to follow.

So you don't want to give me a public audience after all. That didn't truly surprise Alcaeus. Whatever magical theatrics Merikh had planned on happening weren't working. He was having to improvise now. It served neither of them to stand and squabble, and neither could concede anything in public, not safely. Maybe, just maybe, if Alcaeus had Merikh off balance, they could make some real progress. Alcaeus followed a half step behind Merikh to the council room door, almost walking into him when Merikh stopped rather suddenly.

The door didn't open.

It took Alcaeus a moment to realize that was the problem. The pendant was indeed hindering Merikh's magic, and his instinct to open the door with telekinesis left Merikh stunned.

You've probably never used a doorknob before, Alcaeus thought, smiling in amused disbelief as he stepped around Merikh. Fortunately for the Shah, Alcaeus was rather adept with doors. He could even close them.

"Not feeling well?" Alcaeus asked, sitting down at the long council table across from Merikh.

"Are you going to pray for my health?"

"I do, often. Both your physical and spiritual health, though it appears Akhenios's response might be 'no' on both fronts."

"If only you could speak with him more directly," Merikh said before he settled into his seat. He looked uncomfortable, maybe even a bit pale. "You're losing the sympathy of the people, with women like the Fari commander in your ranks. Burning villages and slums? That's not the Akhenic Temple most people want to see. You have fewer sworn men to your cause. If you lose the support of the people, you lose the war. It's not too late to create a united front against these Akhenic fanatics."

"You mean the Faithful. Fari Commander Dalya's methods are brutal, yes, but everything she's done, she's done to protect the Faithful from assault. An assault you've personally backed, considering you gave your steward to that so-called champion of Livinja. Your people burned an Onyx Sword fort to the ground—"

"Come now, Alcaeus, don't try to put burning a fort on the same level as burning a *village*. If your Swords don't understand death is a common discharge from service, then they shouldn't be soldiers. The cobbler in Ziyadi probably didn't expect to be burned alive. I doubt Adrian expected to lose a hand after an encounter with your Fari commander. *Adrian*, of all people, Alcaeus. You've met him. He's Faithful."

Merikh had him there. Alcaeus conceded the point and looked away from the younger man. Adrian was a good man, but Alcaeus had warned him. If all he lost was his hand to this war, then Adrian would be lucky. Alcaeus still hoped to save his soul, even if Dalya had made that harder.

"What would you give me for an alliance against these so-called Akhenic fanatics?" Alcaeus asked.

"I'll have the Pantheon return your lost temples, including Kasu. In exchange for Pantheon access to the High Temple. They will build their own temples elsewhere, but the High Temple once held statues of the entire Pantheon and can do so again. You would remain high priest of Akhenios for as long as your god wishes you to. You would acknowledge Loralee as the Khanum, and any children from her as legitimate..."

Children? Akhenios be kind, let them die in childbirth.

"...and you'll hand over the Fari commander for trial."

"Those aren't concessions," Alcaeus pointed out.

"No, they are not."

"Then I can't agree. But I'll make exchanges with you." Alcaeus paused for a moment before he raised his hand and began counting off fingers. "Dalya for Ruya and Sarka. Duqa Adanna for Sayida Loralee. Your marriage may be lawful, but no khanum of Shai'Khal has ever been crowned by anyone other than an Akhenic priest. If you are truly attached to the sayida, then I won't begrudge you keeping her as a mistress, but the marriage must be annulled and Duqa Adanna made khanum."

"Is that all?" Merikh said, his tone one Alcaeus had heard older boys humor their younger siblings with.

"No. You'll give the Onyx Swords royal aid to convert cultists back to Akhenios," Alcaeus said firmly.

Merikh shook his head. "Alcaeus, at best you have six armies. Your Onyx Swords are ceremonial guards who barely know which end of a spear to use. Soon enough, I'll have *gods* on my side. Until then, I have magic. Your people—"

"Magic doesn't matter," Alcaeus interrupted, pulling the pendant out from under his kaftan impulsively. He placed it on the table and pushed it toward Merikh. The other man always had impeccable posture, but now he stiffened uncomfortably as his golden eyes took in the shamshir-pierced sun. That moment of realization turned from stiffness to laughter. Laughter! The sound made goosebumps rise on his skin.

Merikh shook his head. "I didn't believe you had it in you. I assumed the Temple was behind the attacks, but I didn't think you personally had the stomach for them. Not in that way. So many men have died for you."

More than the vizier? Alcaeus tried to hide his surprise. He'd only known of two attempts. Had there been more?

"I thought you cared more about casualties than that." Merikh reached forward for the pendant. His hand was inches away when time seemed to slow for a moment. A shadow formed around the pendant, and in the blink of an eye, it lashed out at Merikh's chest like a whip. The Shah hit the back of his chair before he collapsed forward limply. The thud seemed to resonate around the room, and only when the room fell silent again did Alcaeus dare to breathe.

That wasn't what he'd expected. Honestly, he wasn't sure *what* he'd been expecting. Nothing that violent.

I am a god-damned fool, Alcaeus thought as he scrambled away from the table. He hadn't taken Dalya seriously. Alcaeus hadn't thought anything would truly happen. Now he'd attacked Merikh in his own damn palace. There were a thousand guards between him and the safety of the temple.

Alcaeus swept up the pendant in his hand, then made for the door. He tried to act normal as he opened and shut the door behind him. Those who had come hoping to witness the exchange between Alcaeus and Merikh had begun milling about the throne room, and Alcaeus's exit was barely acknowledged at first. He didn't give anyone time to ask questions as he picked his way through the crowd to Khamisi.

"You need to get me out of here. *Now!*" Alcaeus whispered.

The legate gestured for Alcaeus to follow him. Onyx Swords waited in the barns. If they could get to them and then get out of the palace gates, then they were safe.

"Dare I ask?" Khamisi said as sun hit their faces.

Alcaeus took a deep breath, hoping this wasn't the last free air he was going to breathe.

"The Fari commander came bearing a weapon that she claimed would change the outcome of this war. I didn't believe her, and I think I just accidentally used it on the Shah. He might still be alive, but I don't know. I didn't dare to check."

Khamisi stumbled on the last stair down to the barn, barely catching himself before falling. "You did *what?*"

"I'm sorry. I don't think you'll be welcome back in the palace after this. A room will be prepared for you in the temple, if you'll have it."

"If we make it there with our heads," Khamisi grumbled as they met the Onyx Swords at the barn. One of the Swords, sensing urgency from Alcaeus, dismounted and offered Khamisi his horse and followed them from the barn on foot. Or he would have, had he made it past the palace gate closing behind the riders.

Royal Guards descended on the barn but thought twice about pursuing Alcaeus in the streets. Arresting Alcaeus in the privacy of the palace was one thing. To make an attempt, even in the Jibbah District, was asking for peasant interference at best. At worst, Madiar Faithful zealots would burn the city to the ground in retaliation.

High Inquisitor Adunbi and Fari Commander Dalya were waiting at the temple steps when Alcaeus returned. Dalya paced in the sort of way Alcaeus had seen dogs or horses pace at gates waiting to be let loose.

"Is he dead?" Dalya blurted out as Alcaeus dismounted.

"I don't know."

"But he *is* injured?" Her stare was intense, unrelenting, and Alcaeus was certain the only thing keeping her from shaking him for answers was the thin line of propriety she wasn't willing to cross.

"To some degree, yes."

Dalya laughed. "Then we have work to do." She turned toward the doors.

Adunbi looked livid. "*We* have work to do. *You* can retire to the barracks," Adunbi snapped.

Alcaeus let out an irritated sound. "Both of you, stop. I'm going to collect my thoughts, and I will call on you later." He left which "you" he was referring to up to each of their interpretations. Alcaeus breezed past them into the cool of the temple antechamber and straight to the inner sanctum. His knees hurt when he fell into prostration in front of Akhenios's statue. He pressed his palms deeply into the prayer mat to stop them from shaking.

The stone had done exactly what Dalya had promised. She'd arrived on the heels of a prayer asking for something to turn the tide of this war. But Alcaeus couldn't shake the feeling that he was entering into an agreement with djinns himself.

Merikh had never been so cold in his life. What little strength he might have had was lost to shivering.

"I think he's waking."

The voice belonged to a woman. Merikh assumed it was Loralee, but trying to focus on it simply made his head throb. He felt as if a horse were stepping on his temple, shifting its weight on and off. There was a hand on his shoulder. He could feel that now as the cold started to wane. Pale sunlight began to draw the world into focus. He could see the council chamber again. Nikias and Loralee were with him, along with one of the Ajir.

"Get out," Merikh muttered weakly. It was an instinctive thing to say, but no one heeded him.

"What happened?" Loralee demanded gently. It was her hand on his shoulder, holding him up against the back of the chair.

What happened indeed? Alcaeus had been here, they'd been speaking, and then—

"Alcaeus! The stone!" Merikh tried to stand, and Loralee pushed him back down. "Damn it, woman, it's important!" He tried to claw her hand off of him, but Merikh barely found the strength to lean forward against her. His hand merely rested on hers.

"Alcaeus fled the palace before we understood the situation. The Ajir captured one of his Swords and is currently interrogating the man. But Alcaeus has returned to the temple, alongside Rabb Khamisi."

"Coward."

Khamisi's responsibilities were *here*, to answer for Duqa Enitan's disobedience. *What does it matter now?* Merikh conceded to himself. Alcaeus had tried to kill him. If he didn't feel so weak, Merikh would have laughed. He'd never expected a move that bold from Alcaeus. He wouldn't make that mistake again.

The door opened, interrupting Merikh's thoughts as a healer walked in. He smirked and shook his head.

"Your presence is unnecessary."

He'd stopped shivering, his strength slowly returning and his mind clearing of the fog the stone had left behind. Merikh squeezed Loralee's hand on his shoulder and pulled it off of him gently. He didn't need her to sit up anymore. Merikh glanced at the door, focused on it to try and open it.

The door still remained closed. A flash of panic came over him.

"What's wrong?" Nikias asked.

"Get them out of here." Merikh gestured to the Ajir and the healer, who both stubbornly remained still.

"Am I still the Shah?" Merikh snapped.

Reluctantly, both men left. They shut the door behind them. Merikh realized he couldn't tell if they stood on the other side or not.

He couldn't even feel Loralee or Nikias beside him.

"I can't…I can't feel my magic. It's the same as what happened with the raven at the temple, only worse."

He tried to keep his fear from showing, but the concerned looks on both Loralee and Nikias's faces made it clear he'd failed.

"How is that possible?" Loralee asked, glancing to Nikias.

The grand vizier simply shook his head. "It's not."

"It *is*," Merikh snapped defensively. He couldn't shake the feeling of being a boy and having to explain something for the umpteenth time to Mansur.

Nikias raised his hands apologetically. "I didn't mean it like that, Shahanshah. It's not *supposed* to be possible."

"Your lack of knowledge is going to get me killed, Vizier," Merikh chastised Nikias, who bowed his head.

"I'll look into it."

Nikias hurried from the room, the door shutting behind him entirely without magic. Loralee folded her arms across her chest, rubbing them with her hands as if trying to keep warm. As if doing so might fix the problem.

"It came back before, though, after the raven," Loralee said, biting her lip.

"It did, and it will again. I can…just barely feel it on the edges." He was feeling less hollow, even if he still couldn't feel Loralee's soul. At least he could focus on cup nearby and make it wobble.

Instinctively, Loralee put her hand down on the cup and stopped it. "Are you sure you're better?" Her worries hadn't let her connect the wobbling cup and Merikh's magic.

He nodded before raising his hand. A moment later, a small puddle of water formed in his palm and began to slowly freeze. "Bit by bit."

The water evaporated, and Merikh shook the last few droplets off his hand. A few landed on Loralee's sari.

"I can't imagine how that felt." Loralee seemed to stop short, as if deciding against puzzling it out aloud.

"It's not the same as when I overextend. That feels like my magic is smothering me. To have it disappear completely feels as if I'm trying to breathe and there's simply no air."

"You need to be more careful. I've *told* you to be more careful," Loralee said, beginning to pace. "You could have died today, and where would that have left us? The empire?"

"I will be."

He was too tired to argue with her. Objectively she wasn't wrong. But who would have imagined a direct strike from Alcaeus? Such things were unheard of. Opposing leaders met at the negotiating table in every war. Rarely did it end with one leader trying to murder the other openly. Merikh had thought Alcaeus far too honorable—and spineless—for such actions.

"Can you stand?"

Merikh looked up at Loralee and blinked. She'd broken his thoughts, and he wasn't sure why she was trying to get him moving. His limbs still felt as if they were weighed down.

"The rumors will have started already. If we don't get you out there sooner rather than later, then reports of your death will become *extraordinarily* exaggerated. Worse, if your brief magical inability becomes part of that rumor, it will look a lot like divine judgment. We can't afford that."

"Divine judgment." Merikh scoffed. "By what right does a god have to judge?" He grabbed the armrest of the chair and pushed himself to his feet. He stood unsteadily for a moment before he found his strength.

"Do you know what you're going to say?" Loralee asked.

Merikh smirked. "Say? No. Show them? Yes. Alcaeus managed to get the opening move at my expense, but I can do better. He got lucky."

Loralee walked half a step behind Merikh out of the council room. The throne room was half empty. The Akhenic Faithful and those leaning that way had disappeared once the cry went out to shut the gates. They had vainly hoped to somehow beat the message runners. They *would* be allowed to leave—especially now that Merikh was, in fact, alive—once the Ajir were certain none of them had anything to do with Alcaeus's attack.

I should have gone with Merikh into the room, Loralee thought. Her khanjar was attached to her belt. Alcaeus could have had a lovely tour of the infirmary. There was little point dwelling on the past, though, so Loralee turned her thoughts quickly to Merikh in the here and now.

He walked with every stepped dogged by lethargy. He looked run down, weak, even. A mere man, not a shah. The room was silent as they walked, all eyes on Merikh when he stopped at a point in the long carpet they all knew. The long rug only partially covered the stain. Even seeing a small part of the black stain made Loralee uncomfortable.

When Merikh crouched down and carefully pulled the rug back, Loralee instinctively retreated a few steps. Green fog began to emanate from Merikh's fingertips. It thickened as it touched the ground. After a moment, the fog completed a circle around the stain. Strange glyphs that resembled the ones from the raven scroll ran along the outside rim of the circle.

"It would seem a history lesson is in order," Merikh said, his voice stronger than it had been inside the council room. Merikh placed his palm in the center of the stain.

The room went cold. Not the sort of cold that happened when Merikh grew irritable. The sort of cold that cut to Loralee's bones and made them feel brittle. Her joints ached when she brought her hands to her bare arms. Even when she rubbed her skin, she couldn't make them warm. It was only after that realization that Loralee came to another one: the room was dark, as if the sun were setting.

Run. Every fiber of her being was telling her to do so. Her feet, however, were firmly planted in place. Even if she'd truly wanted to move, Loralee felt as if something was keeping her here. Fog began to spiral up from the center of the circle.

At first, Loralee wasn't sure what the form was. Slowly, as it finished taking shape, she could see it was a man. Unlike the ghost of the child burned in Hatai, this man looked more solid. Even though he was made from fog, there was a faint brown tinge to his skin, crimson and gold to his elaborate achkan.

Realization hit Loralee like a kick to the gut when she looked at what was left of the man's face.

Mansur. There wasn't much familial resemblance. The soul was a big man, broad shouldered, and looked as if he could snap a man in half without breaking a sweat. His eyes—no, his *eye,* as half his face looked as if a beast had torn it off—seemed to have a brown tint, much darker than Merikh's golden eyes.

Merikh rose. The room abruptly became bright again, and the soul-crushing chill left the room. The soul turned and faced Merikh. When Mansur recognized his son, he rushed the edge of the circle. The soul appeared to be screaming, but unlike the ghost, no sound came out.

Small mercy, Loralee thought.

Merikh raised a finger. The gesture seemed to get Mansur's attention. Merikh pointed down to the edge of the circle in a clear message. There were boundaries. Loralee glanced about the room, relieved to see that her discomfort was shared in the faces of the men and women around her. Every hair on Loralee's neck was raised, and that desire to run was beginning to come back.

"This man kept close ties to the Akhenic Temple, both with Idowu and Alcaeus," Merikh said, his hand raised to gesture at his father. "He aided in murdering *children,* at your last high priest's behest. He prayed at the temple, then returned here to terrorize your families. His actions were known by the Temple, but they simply never cared to depose him, as Mansur tithed nicely."

The soul had settled into his circle. Mansur paced the line, prodding it with his toe and pulling his leg back when it disappeared into the fog.

Gods, Merikh, I hope you know what you're doing, Loralee thought.

"Mansur was selfish, undisciplined, and allowed anyone to whisper ideas into his mind if it could be bent to hedonistic purpose—priest or whore alike."

The next few words, Loralee didn't catch. Mansur's attention had turned back to Merikh briefly. Then, upon the mention of "whore," the soul snapped around to face Loralee with eerie expedience. She'd been told often, once womanhood had started to widen her hips and her breasts had appeared overnight, that she looked like her mother. There was more familial resemblance between her and Jasira than Merikh and Mansur.

Mansur could see it. The sick little twitch of his lip into a smirk made Loralee's skin crawl. Every woman knew that leer; it didn't matter that Mansur only had one eye. It sent a shudder down Loralee's spine, as well as the desire to bury herself under as many layers of shapeless clothes as possible—not that doing so had ever stopped those sorts of men.

Focus. Mansur is dead.

"More than a few of us bear scars from his temper. Perhaps I do not have to remind any of you of that." Merikh hesitated in his speech when he looked at Loralee. Now she saw a different twitch, and Mansur's soul fell to his knees, contorting in pain. Merikh offered Loralee his hand, and she took it without hesitation. He guided her to his right, to the far side of the circle with him now between her and Mansur. He let go of her hand when he began to speak again.

"Alcaeus does not seek to work with your rightful shah. He does not see the need for compromise. When Mansur stopped seeking what was best for our country, you all rallied to my cause. Since then, you have *all* reaped the rewards of it. Now, Alcaeus seeks to depose me. Not because of any wrongs that I have done against our people or our country, but because I will not allow the Temple to dictate government policies. Who do you think Alcaeus will place on the throne, should he succeed? If not himself directly, then a puppet dangling from his strings. Would you see a half-Aegalian bastard sitting on Shai'Khal's throne? A man who would undo every reform I've put in place? Do you think any of you would survive that undoing unscathed?"

Merikh looked back to Mansur. With a flick of his wrist, the fog dissipated, and Mansur's soul returned to Alhanem. This time, there was only a brief flash of cold, the darkness the sort felt when the sun passed behind a cloud. With the toe of his riding boot, Merikh rolled the edge of the rug back over the stain.

"We all saw the door. Is there something that stops magic? How could you hope to defeat Alcaeus, then?" a merchant sayida spoke up from the crowd of nobles.

Loralee tried discreetly to find who spoke up to no success. She expected Merikh to spin that as some sort of test. Instead, Merikh bowed his head ever so slightly, a smirk on his lips. He then looked to Ruya, who stood at the edge of the crowd. The priestess looked uncomfortable with the display. Perhaps the arguably cavalier way Merikh had simply opened a portal to Alhanem in the throne room had left her with cause for concern.

"I believe it's time for a miracle."

CHAPTER 39

18th of Livith, Dry Season, 902 Unified Age
Madiar, Raudhah Province

Captain Bashir was unimpressed with the details of the morning's event. Merikh had spent the previous afternoon with Ruya and Captain Bashir planning it out. Normally, they would have taken weeks to plan such a spectacle, to organize soldiers and invite appropriate nobles. But they needed to get ahead of the rumors that stemmed from yesterday's incident. Word spread quickly. Merikh was already certain that exaggerations would speak of his death or his permanent handicap. Well, they'd put those rumors to a far more permanent grave today.

The barns were organized chaos as soldiers prepared horses. Merikh shifted his weight a little in the saddle. Zahira stretched her neck down and rubbed her ear on her leg impatiently. Captain Bashir barked orders at his soldiers as they mounted and found formation. This was risky—Merikh understood that. They didn't have time to properly ensure the streets would be safe. Not with so little time to organize soldiers. Something could have been overlooked. The retinue could easily be mobbed with rioters or met with impromptu peasant blockades. Then there was always a possibility of Alcaeus's stone.

Loralee mounted Amarante and rode up beside Merikh. Both the Shah and Khanum wore leather breastplates stamped with the Madiaran House crest, and Merikh wore kusari mail under his black kaftan. The Royal Guards with them were in their full dress uniforms with kusaris under their red achkan coats. Ruya, of course, waved off any sort of protection. She insisted on a simple brown choli and skirt, a black sari embroidered with gold and silver wrapped around her. Muted yet ornate, perfect for the show ahead of them.

Merikh loathed playing the performer. Abhorred cavalier use of magic. His distaste was apparent.

"Look a little more impressed once the people can see you. It'll be worth it," Loralee assured him.

Merikh said nothing back. She was right, of course, but he'd be damned if he admitted that.

The Jibbah District was nearly empty as they rode from the palace. The sun crested the eastern dunes and began to warm the morning air. Legates had been instructed to be within the Westhock Bazaar, along with their scribes. Whether the rest of the city's nobility could be roused from their beds, Merikh didn't know. It didn't matter. It wasn't a display for them.

Crowds began to gather and push their way toward the Westhock Bazaar. The guards kept a tight formation around Merikh and Loralee, a few of the horses nipping at the peasants who came too close. With the crowds growing, Merikh took the reins in one hand and focused on his magic. A moment later, the crowd began to exclaim in awe as the air filled with a gentle flurry of thick white snowflakes.

"How did you learn to do this?" Loralee asked, gathering the reins in one hand and catching a few delicate flakes in the other. Her wide-eyed smile was reflected in the crowd around them. Most of those present had never experienced anything like snow. The flakes melted slowly in Loralee's hand, and she brushed them off on Amarante's shoulder.

"The Katu Mountains, during the Monsoon Season. A few of the mountains always have snow," Merikh told her. It had been years ago, on his royal patrol as the Shahzade. Snow was harder to create than ice and hardly practical. It was the mere challenge of it that had caught Merikh's attention, and he'd been determined to master it. Now, the little crystalline structures took little effort.

By the time they reached the Westhock Bazaar and the auction stage they were using for their display, snow drifts had begun to form on the ground. Untouched piles remained white, while others were becoming brown from the dirt around them. Guards kept a watchful eye on the crowd, looking for anywhere the snow didn't fall, which would reveal Alcaeus's stone. Children were running around kicking up snow. A few realized it could be packed together like mud balls and began slinging them at each other.

The auction stage was small and empty. Guards surrounded it, preventing anyone from getting too close. Merikh only hoped they would be enough to stop the stage from being mobbed. Merikh dismounted Zahira behind the stage and handed the reins to Loralee. She remained on Amarante and took the reins for Ruya's horse as well. The high priestess followed Merikh up the stairs. With a wave of his hand, the snow on the stage disappeared.

"Anything you'd like to say?" Ruya asked.

Merikh shook his head. "I don't want anything lost in speeches."

"Very well." Ruya smiled with her usual effervescence and walked to the edge of the stage. She scanned the crowd before she leaned down and tapped a guard on his shoulder. Ruya pointed to a woman close by. The guard escorted her to the stage. Snow hardened into steps, allowing the woman to climb up.

The woman was clearly poor, if not by the shoddy quality of her clothes then by the smell that preceded her on the breeze. Her abaya was dirt-stained, her veil pulled aside. She wasn't old. Perhaps a little older than Merikh, but he couldn't tell. Dirt and sunspots aged her. She walked with a limp and cradled a bundle in her arms. Her eyes were swollen and red, her cheeks stained with tears. Ruya held the woman's elbow gently and led her toward Merikh. The woman fell to her knees and choked back a sob.

"Please," was all she managed to say as she held the bundle above her head.

Ruya took it from her gently and handed it to Merikh. He pulled the cloth back, unsurprised by the dead golden eyes staring back at him. The skin was pale, blotchy from blood pooling, but the baby hadn't been dead for long, maybe a day. A thin white foam had dried on its lips.

Probably drowned, Merikh thought. It wasn't necessarily a cruel fate. The woman obviously couldn't afford the education necessary for the child to become a sorcerer. Many mothers drowned, suffocated, or abandoned their mage babies, and most city guards turned a blind eye to it. Mages without the formal training to become sorcerers inevitably wreaked havoc and had to be imprisoned or killed. It was not a happy life. But this mother didn't look like a mother who had drowned her own child. Merikh was inclined to lay the blame at the feet of an Onyx Sword.

Ruya put a hand on Merikh's shoulder. The world stopped spinning quickly this time after her dizzying touch. Her magic flowed through him, but unlike before, there was no vision, just an intoxicating sense of power unlike anything he'd ever known. Merikh held the bundle in the crook of his right arm and raised his left hand above it. Pale fog left his fingertips, wrapping a shroud around the child. The shape of the fog, its target, Merikh controlled that. But it was Ruya who reached into Aljemel.

The world paled around him, becoming dull as Aljemel's warmth called to his soul. It was a dangerous place for a living soul to be seduced by. It would have been easy to slip away from this world to the next without an anchor, a memory of life or desire strong enough to tie him to the world of the living. But Merikh had a war to win. Spite was as good a reason to live as any.

Ruya found the soul she searched for, the one that belonged to the baby's body. Through Merikh, she called the soul back. At the soul's touch, the baby's bodily decay reversed. Completely, not the simple reanimation Merikh was used to. This was different. The body wasn't going to turn into a mortoha like Merikh's experiments. There was no perversion here; this child would live without the control or supervision of a necromancer. A true reversal of death. It had been one thing to plan these miracles with Ruya. It was something else entirely to see it firsthand. Her magic was unlike any necromancy Merikh had ever practiced, anything he had ever heard of.

How?

The fog disappeared. Ruya's hand dropped from his shoulder, and an unhappy shriek left the baby's mouth. Its skin returned to a warm brown, its golden eyes looked up at Merikh with the innocent anguish only a hungry baby could muster, not the howling snarl of a mortoha. The mother stayed kneeling in stunned silence before her child's cry pulled her to her feet. She carefully took the baby from Merikh, and he deciphered a "thank you" from her happy sobs. He bowed his head briefly before Ruya stepped around him and helped the woman back down the snowy stairs. It was an uncanny feeling, to hear an entire bazaar struck dumb in silence save for a crying baby.

The moment didn't last.

People jostled to see the baby and its mother. Some quickly decried it as blasphemy and an abomination, but the guards made quick work of removing the Akhenic supporters from the crowd. Ruya beamed as she found the next person to pull in front of Merikh. To be in front of a crowd again—a crowd with people undoubtedly praying to her god—was clearly what she lived for. The next person she chose was a blind man and was much older. Older than Nikias.

What are you doing? Merikh thought.

"His eyes." Ruya leaned close as she whispered to him, touching touched his shoulder.

Merikh turned his head a little and met the man's cloudy, vacant gaze. *What can I possibly do about that?*

Despite his misgivings, Merikh called on his magic. Fog covered the man's face. Ruya took control of it and guided it through the man's eyes. Merikh couldn't understand how. As with the corpse, she reversed the decay old age and disease had forced upon the man. If this was what Ikharon made possible, it made Merikh's talents look like child's play.

When the fog disappeared, the man blinked and rubbed his eyes. Eyes that had once been cloudy and dead were bright with life. The old man stared openly at Merikh, his mouth agape for a long moment before he fell to his knees, blabbering praises. Merikh barely stopped himself from recoiling as the man's gnarled hands grabbed the hem of Merikh's kaftan. The old man kissed the hem.

"Gods bless you, Shahanshah. Long may you reign."

If everyone was going to be this grateful, it would be a very trying day. The man stood after a moment and walked by himself down the stairs. Before Ruya could snatch another person from the crowd, Merikh shot her a look. *How?* It was met with a smile.

"Faith," Ruya said simply before she looked to the crowd once again. That was an answer for a child, unsatisfying yet unfortunately final. For now.

It was hours before exhaustion became too great for Merikh to continue. Ruya seemed unflappable, but Merikh could feel her powers weakening too. A few more "miracles," and he'd be getting carried off the stage.

Ruya wouldn't be far behind him. After a young girl who had died two days ago from illness walked off the stage, Merikh touched Ruya's arm before she could grab another from the crowd. He shook his head.

"Enough. I need to rest."

Ruya nodded, and Merikh turned away from the front of the stage. As the crowd realized it was over, an uproar emerged. People clamored against the guards, calling out for their or their loved one's turn. Merikh ignored them, descending the stairs behind the stage. Loralee handed him Zahira's reins, concern in her eyes. He barely noticed her as he mounted up, surprised instead by how hard it was to do so. Every motion felt like he was slogging through waist-deep mud.

"Are you all right?" Loralee asked.

He nodded and glanced back toward the stage. He expected to see Ruya behind him. Instead, the guards had parted a little, and Ruya sat on the edge of the stage. He couldn't see, but judging from the faces of those in front of Ruya, Merikh imagined she was touching hands and talking. Proselytizing. He'd done what he'd had to—shown his strength and awed the crowd. Ruya could do the rest.

"Keep her safe," Merikh ordered the closest guard.

Captain Bashir began to organize his men. The mounted Ajir guards escorted Merikh and Loralee carefully through the crowd. The horses didn't give way for people. After one man had his foot stepped on and was pushed aside by a guard's horse, the crowd gave a little room. A few commoners still pressed on the guards, offering coin or goods to try and earn just *one* more miracle. Merikh ignored them.

As soon as they passed from the Westhock Bazaar, they were given greater breathing room. Merikh stopped the snow. It began to melt quickly in the heat. Ending the constant drain of magic gave Merikh a little more energy, but it still took a great deal of effort to sit upright in the saddle. He barely noticed as they passed through the Mitbah and Jibbah Districts.

When the palace gates closed behind the retinue, it felt like a breath of fresh air. Merikh dismounted Zahira quickly and nearly fell as his ankles wobbled unsteadily. He needed to rest, eat, restore the energy he'd lost. First things first, though. Merikh led Zahira to the barn.

"Shahanshah, I can take her," one of the grooms offered.

Merikh waved the girl off. Tired as he was, Zahira came first.

CHAPTER 40

19TH OF LIVITH, DRY SEASON 902, UNIFIED AGE
MADIAR, RAUDHAH PROVINCE

Mansur's ghost brought memories to the surface that Nikias had hoped to leave good and buried for the rest of his life. Merikh had made a point of ordering Adrian away from the throne room that day, and there was a part of Nikias that would be eternally jealous of that consideration.

I saved his life, Nikias rationalized. Merikh had needed him there, otherwise Mansur would have been dead and Merikh not far behind. Or worse, they'd have ended the day with a shah possessed by a djinn. But he'd had nightmares for weeks of the mortoha Merikh had created from Rajiya and nightmares for months punctuated by Mansur's screams. Worse had been his attempt to not to look at Merikh any differently afterward, when Nikias no longer saw the quiet young boy trying his hardest to perfect just one more enchantment before bed.

"You are brooding, Nikias."

"Apologies, Shahanshah. I haven't been sleeping well, and I fear it's caught up with me," Nikias said as he stifled a yawn.

Merikh gestured toward the silver coffee carafe on the table between them. "Take whatever you need."

He didn't want any more coffee, but there was a flicker of concern in those golden eyes. A touch of a frown that forced Nikias to humor Merikh's worries and pour himself a small cup. It was always too bitter for his tastes, and the amount of honey he needed to add always made Merikh look at him askance. The Shah, as a small boy, had earnestly asked him once if there was enough honey in Shai'Khal to supplement his habit.

"You don't believe in giving Alcaeus a means out of the city?" Merikh asked, misjudging Nikias's worry as something far more tangible and present.

Nikias shook his head before taking a sip of coffee, grimacing as he put it down. "I think no matter what you do, you're going to be wrong. Offer him a means to leave, and you look weak. Burn the High Temple with him in it, and you look monstrous. You've turned both weakness and monstrosities to your advantage, but fewer shows of force make me happy."

"You look positively *thrilled*," Merikh said as he leaned forward and took the lid off of the honey jar sitting next to the carafe. When Nikias didn't take the hint, Merikh picked up the nearby spoon and heaped a generous amount of the pale syrup into Nikias's coffee.

"What does the Khanum think? She's rather conspicuously absent this morning," Nikias commented.

"She's training with Emil."

The touch of a frown from earlier became unmasked and plain.

"It's not going well?"

"No, she's doing well," Merikh said reluctantly, running a hand over his hair and pulling it out of his eyes. "I would simply prefer someone *else* handle the situation in Ydeba."

"Like yourself?"

Merikh scoffed, though it was plain he meant *yes*.

"Adrian is there to help her speak for you. Send one of my viziers along with her. In spite of the dangers, it's a fairly safe mission to get her more accustomed to ruling. Half the noble families in Ydeba are going to be replaced by the time this war is over. If she angers one of them with a mistake, it'll be undone within a few years. As far as the Key destruction, the Khanum will do what she deems best once she's there, whether that's to attend to it personally or send someone else to do so in her stead. She's given you no reason to mistrust her judgment, correct?"

"Not yet. But it is dangerous."

"And that's why she's training with Emil." Nikias picked up his coffee and took a sip before continuing. "If you're truly worried, then send someone else. If you want to keep her at your side, no one will fault you for it. She's been good for you. Personally I like seeing this side of you."

"What, me worrying? You see that plenty."

"*Genuine* concern for another person."

Merikh shifted uncomfortably in his seat on the divan. "Loralee is a means to an end, Nikias. Nothing more."

Nikias shot him a skeptical look. He'd seen the little changes between Merikh and Loralee, the small glances when Merikh didn't think anyone was looking—not to mention the way Merikh had put himself between Loralee and the mere *soul* of his father. It was the only reason Nikias put any stock in the rumor that Merikh and Loralee had put one of the council rooms to a more...*intimate* use a few weeks ago. Nikias let the subject drop and instead took another sip of his coffee. He feigned a grimace.

"Too much honey."

"Horse shit." Merikh rolled his eyes before standing up, a smirk replacing his frown. "That's half what you usually put."

Merikh crossed the room to his desk, one of the drawers opening ahead of him. Merikh seemed no worse for wear after the encounter with Alcaeus, but Nikias could swear he saw a little reticence in how Merikh used his magic now.

Or maybe I'm just worrying and seeing things. That was always a possibility. Nikias looked down into his coffee, swirling the liquid in the cup.

"All right, what is it?"

Nikias twitched when he saw Merikh was seated again and a letter hovering in front of Nikias's face. Nikias placed his coffee down and took the letter.

"Your father has a rather disquieting affect."

Merikh leaned back in his seat and let out a frustrated noise. "Well, that *was* the point, I simply didn't expect *you* to be the most unnerved. I had thought you'd left the room."

Nikias shook his head. "One of the merchant rabbs stopped me with a few questions. He looked worried enough at the flight of the Akhenics for me not to brush him off. I can still recognize an Alhanem portal when it opens. I wasn't about to leave until it was all over. I wasn't sure what your plan was at first. It seems to have worked well. A great many people were disquieted by Mansur, although next time you might not want the Khanum so close by. She looked rather unnerved, too."

"There won't be a next time," Merikh said. His tone was irritated, but not at Nikias. "I refuse to give him another respite from whatever torments are being inflicted upon him. Especially since he hasn't learned anything yet." Merikh shook his head in disbelief. "I didn't expect him to eye Loralee like that."

Nikias shrugged.

"In spite of the discomfort it caused both of you, it was still heartening to see your protective side with her. Your *means to an end*."

His teasing was met with an exasperated breath. Merikh had never grown out of the boyish need to pretend to be aloof to everything. But even if Merikh wouldn't admit it to himself, Nikias knew there were feelings for Loralee forming that went beyond merely being friendly and protective.

"The letter is the declaration for Alcaeus," Merikh said, changing the subject. "I meet with the Sardar generals after court to ensure we have the men in Madiar to keep control until we're ready to move on the temple. I worry about a peasant uprising. The palace gates aren't much of a match for a hundred-thousand-strong mob."

"I'll see what I can do to prevent one. If Alcaeus is amenable to talking."

"Be careful," Merikh said, his tone earnest. "Keep an Ajir with you at all times."

"I have no magic. Alcaeus isn't going to sully the temple with my blood." Nikias stood and bowed before heading to the now-open door.

Dust mingled with heat haze, the city overcome in a gritty sweat. Guards were hard at work dividing districts, shutting down the Kelle Bazaar, and moving merchants. At least now, coasting on the goodwill Merikh had earned from the "Miracles of Westhock," Nikias hoped the blame for this would fall on Alcaeus. Nikias and Bashir had instructed the city's criers to tell how Alcaeus had attacked the Shah with a weapon, though they left the details minimal and certainly mentioned nothing of magic.

At the Temple District Gate, the Onyx Swords forced Nikias and his Ajir guards to dismount. Four of them remained with the horses while one joined Nikias to walk through the Prophet's Shade. It was quiet, a place of holy contemplation, though Nikias could feel the contempt of the Faithful walking with him. While they were under the shadows of the trees, no one bothered him. That peace gave way when the unrelenting sun hit Nikias's riding boots and he was met by Swords and Faithful. Men and women spat on the ground before him, sneering ill-mannered words that Nikias let slide off him. He'd been in hostile situations before, and while this was not ideal, it could be far worse.

Nikias wiped sweat from his brow with the back of his sleeve as he walked up the temple steps. The portico shade was keenly appreciated, and Nikias paused for a moment. It had been a long time since he'd come to the temple. Religious attendance had been waning for years. Nikias could remember whispered conversations in his youth about how to draw parishioners back to temples.

Starting a religious war is one way to scare everyone back to Akhenios, I suppose. Nikias took a deep breath before he pushed the heavy temple door open. The service was between prayers, and the temple wasn't full. One of the Priest Council approached, a tall Tsukarai woman dressed in a simple black abaya.

"Vizier, how may I help you?" Her tone was cloyingly pleasant.

"I have a declaration to deliver personally to the high priest."

"Of course." She smiled before she bowed her head and gestured for Nikias to follow. Half a step behind him, Nikias could practically feel the Ajir with him stiffen uncomfortably. Guards were always paranoid. Nikias would have preferred to leave the man outside, particularly since there was nothing for the guard to worry about as they walked the temple's halls. All the same, Nikias didn't want to hear Merikh's lecture if he left the guard behind. Their escort stopped in front of a pale wooden door and knocked. She opened the door a crack and stuck her head inside. When she withdrew out into the hallway, she opened the door wide.

"The high priest will see you."

The room was dark, the windows shuttered in an attempt to keep out the heat. Alcaeus sat at his desk and gestured for Nikias to sit down across from him.

"Thank you, Maysa," Alcaeus said before looking to Nikias. "What can I do for you, Nikias? I imagine the Shah would send a different assassin, if he had that in mind. So you bear...a warrant for arrest?"

"No," Nikias said as he put the letter down on the desk. He'd written the first few drafts of this letter, but Merikh had rewritten it once and put his signature to that copy. There were details and specifics that were a mystery to Nikias, questions that plagued him and almost made him ask Alcaeus for details when the priest picked up the letter.

Alcaeus forced a laugh and put the letter down after reading it.

"You know, it's easy to forget that the Shah has a flair for the dramatic. *'Banished forthwith from Shai'Khal'* to whatever island in the mists I might find, just like his so-called gods."

"Better than death," Nikias pointed out half-heartedly.

"Only a fool views banishment better than death, Nikias. For all your faults, idiocy is not among them. The Shah not only seeks to banish me but all Onyx Sword inquisitors, as well as Dalya Maki."

"You've all betrayed Shai'Khal. What more could you hope for?"

"Conversion, apologies, *reason*. But we're long past the time for that, I see. You may leave, unless you'd like to seek sanctuary here and renounce your master?" Alcaeus hardly sounded hopeful, but the offer appeared genuine. Nikias shook his head, pushed his seat back, and stood. He was admittedly shocked by how quickly Alcaeus wanted him gone.

"Is there anything you would have me tell the Shah?"

"You may tell him I eagerly await the repudiation of his beliefs and abdication from the throne."

Nikias shook his head and gestured for the Ajir to get the door. There was nothing more to say. Merikh and Alcaeus had now observed the niceties required before they openly began trying to murder each other. But Alcaeus's request for abdication worried Nikias. There was only one man who the Yahidah might rally behind other than Merikh, certainly no Umbeah.

We need to hurry along Duq Rashad's marriage and find someone suitable for Duqa Adanna, Nikias thought as he walked back toward the temple doors. Removing Duq Rashad as a threat, however remote a possibility of him trying for the throne, was important, but Duqa Adanna was still a problem. The future amira was well-loved, and if they weren't careful, they'd find her crowned Shahbanu of Ydeba. *Who knows how well Loralee will handle her.*

Nikias's stomach roiled, interrupting his thoughts and reminding him that these scenarios were best dealt with on a fuller stomach and perhaps left to his own viziers to solve.

"Are you all right, bayim?" the guard asked as they walked toward the Prophet's Shade.

Nikias nodded.

"Went better than it could have, honestly."

"If you say so, Vizier."

They walked in respectful silence back to the gate, though the world was far from quiet. They could hear shouting outside of the district walls, and as they arrived at the gate, Nikias could see grim determination on the faces of the guards he'd left with the horses.

"Our welcome is more than worn out," the one guard announced as he handed Nikias the chestnut mare.

"Can you get us back to the palace?" Nikias asked. The nod he received in answer wasn't reassuring. Nikias frowned as he mounted the horse. After gathering the reins, he dug through his pocket until his fingers went numb. The scorpion latched on to his hand as Nikias pulled it out, light reflecting painfully off of the ice.

"After you," Nikias said, gesturing to the guards. The riders surrounded Nikias and began to push through the angry mob. There was little peasants could do to frighten war horses, as the mares were quick to bite or kick anyone who came too close. Nikias had seen the broken bones and bruises on careless grooms. The cries of the bitten were enough to give a few of the angry onlookers pause. It didn't stop the thrown stones, the angry shouts, or the mob from pressing in on them whenever the road narrowed. The mob slowed their progress.

To Nikias's grim realization, they were being herded. He could see it in the Ajir as they tried to find a way out of the mob. To wider roads, away from the buildings, *anywhere* away from where they were being forced to go. The horses could only push the crowd away so far, particularly as they had to cater to the weakest rider in the group. Nikias knew he'd fall from his mare if she tried to jump and clear more room. Ahead, tall buildings lined the road. Ropes for drying clothes were stretched over the road. A perfect place for archers to rain arrows down on them without being seen. Nikias raised the scorpion in his hand.

"Come on, you useless creature," Nikias muttered. "Give us some shelter."

If they could make it past the first buildings, the road opened up. Nikias was quite certain they'd be able to push the horses through the mob. The scorpion leapt from Nikias's hand into the air above them, losing its shape and turning into a thick square sheet of ice large enough to cover the riders. Sunlight reflected off it painfully, and Nikias hoped it blinded more than just him.

His heart sank when the ice simply vanished. It didn't melt or shatter, it was simply *gone.* It was followed almost immediately by the sickening thud of arrows hitting leather and horse flesh. His horse panicked, throwing Nikias down hard onto the cobblestone road. Searing pain pierced his chest, and when Nikias craned to look, he could see arrow shafts sticking out of his chest and legs. The Ajir didn't look much better; two of their horses had been knocked off their feet, and the other horses had fled. The mob had descended as soon as the arrows stopped. The Ajir left alive after the arrows were bludgeoned to death by whatever the mob had on them.

Nikias doubted it was good fortune that let him crawl away from the dead, finding the strength to make it to the nearby wall to prop himself up on. He looked back at the ground, at the trail of crimson that he'd left behind in the dirt. *There's a chance, if I get to a healer,* Nikias thought. But the only healer he knew of was miles away in the palace or back inside the Temple District.

Thoughts of a healer disappeared when a woman walked over to him, turned around, and slid down the wall to sit beside him.

"The ice is a handy little trick. Killed a half dozen of my men last time I saw it used. Amazing what a little stone can do, hmm?" she yapped away as the world began to blur a little.

"Might I presume...that you're Fari Commander Maki, then?" Nikias asked as he slowly looked over to her.

She smiled and bowed her head. "*Inquisitor* Dalya Maki, at your service, Grand Vizier. Though, really, it's more *you* at my service."

"And what," Nikias said, then hesitated, looking for the right word through his mental fog, "exactly do you want?"

"Just stay sitting up, rather like that. Maybe look up a little at the sky. It'll make my life easier, and then I don't have to worry about mangling that jaw of yours. I need you recognizable, dear." Her bare hand patted his cheek before she stood up and stretched languidly.

Nikias smiled bitterly, then looked up at the sky. The sun was high in the cloudless blue. Other than the heat, it wasn't a bad last day.

Coffee had been pleasant this morning. Merikh had learned all that Nikias could teach him by now anyway. Besides, Merikh had Loralee now. He'd be all right.

I hope your blade is sharp.

Post-petition mingling was unusually tedious. It was an event that lent itself to people-watching. The city's nobles pestered each other and the legates from the greater noble houses. The legates in turn solved or made petty squabbles, and every so often a dagger would be drawn and the guards would have to interfere—or not, depending on how well the defender could stand on their own.

Merikh was left blissfully alone, save for the occasional brave soul who tried to ply Merikh for a new answer to an old petition. Normally those people were fended off by Nikias, but the grand vizier was still conspicuously absent. Loralee did her best to compensate, as her novelty had yet to wear out among the nobles. She garnered more attention than Merikh cared for, if he was being honest. There were a few too many young men who dogged her steps, though Loralee put each firmly in their place. Castration would do so more completely, but most of the young men were allies or sons of allies. And perhaps Merikh was feeling a *tad* possessive.

All sense of normalcy disappeared when the throne room doors crashed open. Nobles parted, allowing the newcomer to walk to Merikh unhindered. The room was quiet save for the guard's footsteps, a pace that slowed the closer he came. Not that Merikh could blame him. The parcel in his hands had an all too familiar aura of death. The guard bowed deeply in front of Merikh and didn't rise as he extended the parcel.

"Shahanshah," he said quietly. Blood darkened the golden cuffs of the guard's sleeve.

"How many dead?" Merikh asked quietly, surprised at his voice. He was normally soft-spoken, but he'd barely been able to breathe his question.

"All of them, Shahanshah. Captain Bashir has men already looking—"

"Clear the room," Merikh said, finding his voice again as he carefully took the parcel from the guard. *"Now."*

The guard rose, gestured to the other guards, then pointed to the door. The nobles near Merikh, any that had a lick of common sense, were already following his instruction. The room had begun to chill. Loralee maneuvered her way through the crowd to him.

"Merikh?" she said quietly, touching his elbow.

"Get out!"

He couldn't remember the last time anyone in the room had heard him yell. The sound practically echoed and quickly cleared the room. The raw anger and hurt had been there for all to hear, and Loralee reluctantly turned away from him. The temperature continued to plummet. When the door shut behind Loralee and the last guards, ice coated the doors and windows.

Finally alone, Merikh reluctantly drew open the sack and gently raised Nikias's head out. There wasn't much blood dripping from it now, but the last few drops stained Merikh's white sleeve. The back of Nikias's head rested in Merikh's palm. The lack of hair made it impossible to hold any other way than respectfully.

Merikh felt sick, staring into the dark eyes of his mentor. He'd been a small boy the last time a corpse had made him nauseous. Now, he leaned against a nearby column and slid down to the floor, his knees weak. The expression was calm, despite the lifeless eyes. Whoever had beheaded him had done so quickly. Merikh doubted the speed had been for anything other than efficiency. Certainly not mercy.

Green fog left Merikh's fingertips, wrapping Nikias's skull, and the room cooled as Merikh searched for Nikias's ghost. He wasn't sure if he was disappointed or relieved when he couldn't find it. Nikias was dead, his soul moved on. Better still, moved on to Aljemel. If the man had to be dead, at least he could enjoy eternal paradise.

Ruya could bring him back.

The thought came unbidden, and it disturbed Merikh how long it tempted him. But what could Merikh offer Nikias that Aljemel could not? Nikias had suffered through enough worry and pain. Merikh could only offer more. The right thing to do, as much as Merikh loathed it, was to leave him be.

The realization hit Merikh harder than the lashes had. His hands shook, and Merikh had to steady himself not to drop Nikias's head on the ground. *So this is grief,* he thought. He'd never felt this before. Aliyah in death had been sickening to see as a child. Scaphism was an ugly way to die, but Merikh hadn't seen it firsthand. Mansur had been merciful enough to hurry him from the trial before Aliyah had been sentenced. He'd only seen Aliyah's ghost—a nightmare in and of itself. Nikias had helped him banish it. It had been inappropriate, but Nikias had always come when Merikh had called as a boy, regardless of the hour. Nikias had always been the safe one to call on, the one who wouldn't immediately report back to either Mansur or Aliyah or the Ajir steward.

Merikh was certain Nikias had always wanted to be a father, to have a family of his own. That would have been impossible under Mansur. Any distraction from his duties—particularly female ones—would have been disposed of in as degrading a method as possible.

Perhaps being involved in my life was his own petty revenge, Merikh thought with a small smile. Nikias had been the master of passive-aggressive jabs, little things Mansur never picked up on. Up until the end, Merikh was quite certain Mansur had thought Nikias was *his* loyal dog.

At least he survived working for Mansur.

The thought came unbidden and was most unwelcome. The war had barely begun, and he'd already lost his grand vizier. His steward was maimed potentially beyond usefulness, *and* he was sending away the Khanum. *Sometimes you have to sacrifice pieces to win the game.* It had been a lesson

Nikias had taught Merikh as a boy learning to play shatranj. Merikh had always tried to survive the game with as many pieces as possible, a strategy Nikias repeatedly destroyed. Merikh could remember sitting at the table, fuming at Nikias's handful of tokens that had cornered his shah.

Clearly, Merikh had since learned his lesson well.

Merikh took a deep breath and let it out slowly. The nausea from seeing Nikias like this had passed, replaced with a strange hollowness. It felt oddly like the attack from the stone. A part of him was missing, inaccessible. The permanence of holding Nikias's head in his hand, the weight of it, was surreal. Merikh had counted on having years, decades, even, of advice from Nikias. A small flare of panic shot up as Merikh realized how much he'd been counting on fatherly advice from Nikias regarding the future shahzade. Merikh didn't know the first thing about children. Didn't know the first thing about being a father.

Alcaeus sought to cripple him with this blow, more so than anything else. The thought turned grief to cold anger. Merikh let Nikias's head roll off his hand as stood. He could lock away this emotion just like any other, build walls to keep it hidden and buried. He was the *Shah.* He couldn't afford these emotional distractions.

Means to an end. If this is the price of victory, I'll pay it gladly. Wallowing in grief did no one any good, and the thought of it disgusted Merikh. He left the head on the ground and crossed the room, ice beginning to disappear from the windows and doors despite the continued cold. Merikh hesitated for a moment at the door. He could feel Loralee, a handful of guards, and a spattering of nobles on the other side still waiting for him. Merikh firmly put down the small part of him that wanted to leave the throne room through one of the servant exits. The door opened ahead of Merikh, and he met those on the other side with cold composure.

"Where is the grand vizier's body?" Merikh asked, his words measured and careful.

"A thousand apologies, Shahanshah. We weren't able to recover it," the guard said, bowing deeply again.

Merikh nodded. "Have the head disposed of quietly. No need to make a spectacle of this," Merikh said before he stepped forward, expecting the small crowd to part. Most did. Loralee, naturally, didn't. She looked upset, but her cheeks weren't tear-stained. The Khanum hadn't fallen apart yet. It was a small mercy Merikh appreciated. He'd never seen her cry before. He wasn't sure he wanted to find out how to handle it with an audience.

"What about a funeral?" Loralee asked, her tone as shaken as she looked. Merikh looked at her, deliberately confused. It was more difficult to do than it should have been.

"He's a glorified servant. I believe he may have had a cousin in the north. If they wish to have a memorial for him, they are welcome to. I have a war to win and a replacement to find. If you're feeling *sentimental...*" The word dripped with mockery. "Then, Khanum, do whatever you want."

Merikh left her standing in the hall with the nobles. He had nothing more to say on it, nothing more he trusted himself to say on it. Nikias was one less person to have to worry or care about. One less person to protect, one less vulnerability. Or at least, that's what Merikh was working hard to convince himself of.

Grief, and the guilt that came with it, was far harder to lock away than he thought.

CHAPTER 41

"Stop."

The guard froze, his hand inches above Nikias's head. The sack the head had been wrapped in lay a few feet away, and Loralee forced herself to stare at that instead.

"Please cover him," Loralee ordered as she hesitantly approached the guard.

He nodded and leaned over to grab the cloth. He wrapped Nikias's head in it as he picked it up.

"Apologies, Khanum. I didn't think anyone would be in he—"

"Just stop, please."

She was trying *desperately* to be strong. Loralee had never seen a head without a body before, and for it to be Nikias? Nikias, of all men! He had always been honest with Loralee, the only person here she truly trusted to be straight with her at all times. He'd been invaluable when Merikh had been injured, and their many conversations and shared frustrations had made them closer than Loralee had expected.

Now a guard held Nikias's head, his body missing. Her eyes threatened tears, and she brushed them back with a quick touch of her hand.

"Please consult with Ruya. I want his body—whatever of it we may end up with—taken care of appropriately."

The guard nodded. As he stepped forward, Loralee put her hand on his shoulder.

"I don't mean for you to do what the Shah asked. Notify Nikias's family, of course. But we *will* see to burying him. Nikias has served his empire and two shahs well. He deserves more than what the Shah ordered."

"As you ask, Khanum."

The man bowed, and Loralee let him pass. She stood alone in the throne room for a long moment, staring at the spot on the ground where Nikias's head had been. There was a smear on the stone where blood and...whatever else had been left. The sight of it nearly made her sick, and she turned away from it quickly.

She couldn't stay here any longer, but she had no stomach to face those outside the hall. To see those who had borne witness to Merikh's selfish display. Part of her wanted to run to the barn, to Amarante, and bury her face in the mare's soft mane. Instead, Loralee latched on to the flash of anger felt at the thought of her husband. The man was a godsdamned disrespectful and callous fool. She had every intention of making that opinion known. It was easier to be angry at Merikh than upset over Nikias.

To Loralee's surprise, the door to the royal suite opened ahead of her. Merikh was alone in the room, sitting at his desk and flitting through paperwork. That didn't surprise her at all, and she felt rage rising in her chest again as she looked at him. He hadn't glanced at her yet. Undoubtedly, he could feel her seething and was deciding what to do about it. She didn't plan on giving him time to sort it out.

"A glorified *servant?* What does that make me, your glorified whore?" Loralee snapped.

"What are you talking about?" Merikh asked, glancing up briefly from his paperwork.

"Nikias! Your grand vizier! The man who, by most accounts, raised you! Or did you forget him when you picked up those damn papers?" Loralee shouted, gesturing at the table. "How *dare* you! Did he really mean so little to you?"

The room grew cold. Loralee didn't notice, and she wouldn't have cared in the slightest if she had. Merikh pushed his seat away from the desk and stood to look at her.

"Loralee, you're treading into dangerous territory, and I suggest you calm down."

"*Calm down?* Gods forbid one of us isn't a callous prick! The least you could do is take care of a funeral yourself, but *no*, of course not. Gods forbid you actually show anyone you have a heart—if you have one!"

Her tongue had run away with her, further than she meant to let it. Loralee bit her lip when she realized what she'd said.

"I'm sorry," she said, covering her mouth briefly with one hand. The room was quite cold, the water in the pitcher on the table had frozen solid.

"Sorry for what? Hurting my *feelings*? You're hardly capable of inflicting such injury, Loralee, if it were possible at all."

The moment Loralee realized she'd crossed the room was when her palm hit the side of Merikh's face. Nearly complete silence followed, save for the reverberation of the slap off the walls. Her stomach sank as she stood there, her eyes wide as she stared at the side of Merikh's face. He hadn't moved when her hand fell away, his jaw clenched and eyes firmly away from Loralee. His olive skin was taking on a red tinge underneath his cheekbone.

At least I'm capable of something, she couldn't help but think. He'd just sounded so *smug*. Loralee hadn't been able to stop herself. If this was the last thing she did with her life, at least she'd know it had stung.

"If you were a glorified whore, I would kill you in the slowest, most painful way I know how for this. Do that again and I will."

She took the threat seriously. Loralee didn't dare move when Merikh walked away from her toward the balcony. When the doors opened ahead of Merikh, the warm draft forced Loralee to realize just how cold the room itself had gotten. She shivered.

"Merikh...I didn't think..."

He laughed mirthlessly and turned to look at her.

"No, of course you didn't. You're a hot-headed Neredi woman. Your mouth and your hands run away with you. Why would you ever need to keep your opinions to yourself? You have all the answers and see the world so *clearly*, don't you?" Merikh gestured at the city behind him.

"No! But in this case, yes! Nikias deserves better from you, he gave you everything—"

"Tell me, Loralee, how often have you encountered death? How many friends have you lost? What funerals have you planned?"

He took the bluster out of her words. Merikh stared at her, demanding an answer. She struggled to find one.

"My stillborn brother, and my grandmaman," Loralee said quietly. The mocking look from Merikh made her want to slap him again.

"In that case, you're quite the authority on grief."

Loralee threw her hands up in the air. "Fine, Merikh. You're right. You win that contest. You've lost the most people. You've got all the answers and know exactly what you should be doing now. Let's simply toss Nikias's ashes over the wall and be done with him. Gods, why even bother with that? The war hounds would probably love to have a new toy. Pragmatically, why should we waste something as trivial as *respect* on Nikias?"

Loralee turned away and walked to the door. The doorknob was cold beneath her fingers. When she tried to yanked the door open, it only opened a fraction of an inch before slamming shut again.

"You've made your point."

She assumed Merikh's magic had shut the door and jumped a foot when she looked up and saw him standing beside her with his hand on it. The image of Nikias's head being gnawed on by dogs had seemingly hit its mark.

"Good," Loralee said stubbornly, folding her arms across her stomach. "I told the guard to consult Ruya about funeral preparations. He can have a proper send-off before his cousin arrives to take his ashes."

"I expected no less of you."

"You...excuse me?"

Merikh pointed to his desk. The letter he had been working on flew into his hand.

"You should put your anger to more productive use," he said as he handed the paper to her.

She expected it to be a list of the current vizier council, the men and women most capable of replacing Nikias. Instead, it was a draft of a letter to Amir Olumide. A call to arms for the Attars to mobilize troops, an outline for preparations to hit back hard against the Akhenic Temple, and a paragraph that had been scratched out and rewritten—and still needed another rewrite— about Nikias's death. A rather personal note, at that.

"I...this is what you wanted to tell me when you asked me to calm down?" Loralee asked quietly.

"It was. I admit, the conversation rapidly got out of hand."

"I'm sorry I slapped you, I just…the way you left Nikias! You just…you were so cavalier about it all. As if Nikias didn't matter."

"I made a mistake. But Alcaeus seeks to break me. He has now made an attempt on almost everything I hold dear. I will not give him the satisfaction of seeing me as anything *but* cavalier. You, on the other hand, the people love because of your empathy. Leaving him…" Merikh hesitated, and for the first time since he'd threatened her, Loralee saw real emotion cross his face. "That will have worked best to maintain our reputations, if perhaps a little too well. I didn't expect this level of vitriol when you came here. I…had no idea he meant so much to you."

"Nikias was the first honest person, first *completely* honest person, I met in Madiar," Loralee said before she tentatively reached for Merikh's hand. "And even if he didn't matter to me, he mattered to you."

Merikh stiffened when she spoke and touched him, looking incredibly uncomfortable. He gently moved his hand out of hers and took back the letter. Loralee pushed down the sudden pang of hurt his gesture caused. She hadn't realized the comfort she needed, and now she knew it wouldn't come from him.

I did just hit him. The realization struck with guilt. She was probably the first person to strike him since the last time Mansur had done so.

"I…cannot handle the funerary arrangements," Merikh said, clearing his throat and pulling Loralee from her thoughts. "Those duties fall entirely on your shoulders, and Ruya's. Amir Olumide, I imagine, will wish to attend. Therefore, arrangements should give him time enough to arrive in Madiar with his men."

"Of course. Is there anything else I can do?"

Merikh seemed to carefully consider her request. He looked tired now, his perfect posture weighed down in his shoulders. She'd misjudged his reaction. Now, Loralee didn't know how to handle him.

"Would you like me to leave?" she asked. Loralee reached for the doorknob.

Merikh sighed and shook his head ever so slightly. He reached over and gently pulled her hand off the knob. "No."

"Is…is there anything I can do to help you?" She hoped it was clear that she didn't mean the funeral arrangements.

"Just...stop prodding," Merikh said as he let go of her hand. He turned away and walked back to his desk. Loralee stood by the door for a long moment as Merikh picked up his pen once more. She looked away and felt tears threatening once more as she looked at the coffee table. She'd had plenty of lunches and coffees there with Nikias. The silence was suffocating. Worse, the sound of the pen on paper reminded her all too much of Nikias taking notes in a meeting.

"Merikh." Her voice nearly cracked as she brushed away tears. "I can't grieve like you do. I can't do this alone."

Now that he wasn't disgusted, Loralee hoped...she didn't know what she hoped. She needed something other than indifference from her husband, and the *worst* part was knowing he couldn't provide it. Merikh let go of the pen and turned to look at her warily.

He doesn't have the faintest clue, Loralee realized. And right now, she couldn't teach him how to read her. How to know when to come and simply hold her. Right now, she couldn't bring herself to have to beg her husband for an ounce of comfort. Loralee shook her head and closed her eyes. She took a deep breath, and when she opened her eyes Loralee started walking to the bedroom. She hesitated when Merikh rose from his chair.

"I don't know what you need," he admitted quietly. To his credit, Merikh sounded concerned.

"I know," Loralee said, feeling exhausted. Surprising herself, Loralee turned and walked to him. She placed her hands on his chest, ignoring the instinctive flinch, and then rested her head against his shoulder. Merikh's collarbone protruded uncomfortably against her. It took him a moment to place a hand on Loralee's back. His stiffness, the fact she knew he was uncomfortable, ruined any comfort she could draw from the moment. Being held by him like this simply felt...hollow. If anything, it made her feel worse. Loralee pulled away from him, brushing the last tears away from her eyes. She'd left damp spots on his white kameez.

"You have a letter to finish," she said, gesturing to the desk. "And I have a funeral to plan."

Merikh simply nodded, smart enough not to show his relief at she stepped away from him. Loralee leaned past him and opened up the desk drawer. Maybe Merikh was right, and burying herself in her work would bring the comfort and closure she desperately wanted.

CHAPTER 42

23RD OF LIVITH, DRY SEASON, 902 UNIFIED AGE
MADIAR, RAUDHAH PROVINCE

Something kept tickling Loralee's shoulder, slowly waking her. She groaned into her pillow, burying her face into it—or trying to. Merikh's shoulder was rather unyielding. It took another moment to realize the annoying touch on her shoulder came from Merikh toying with her hair. Loralee moved just enough to reach her hand across and take his.

"That tickles," she murmured before getting comfortable again. It was cold outside of the blanket, though Loralee assumed that had more to do with the cold desert nights than her husband's mood. He'd been awake half the night at least, restless in bed. After waking up for the fourth time, Loralee had gotten up and pulled off her nightgown to put his mind and body to work on a far more pleasurable task. It had allowed both of them to sleep better. Or at least, Merikh hadn't woken her up until now, and it felt like it had been hours.

"Apologies," Merikh said, his voice distracted.

To Loralee's dismay, his realization of her wakefulness seemed to signal that it was time to get up. As Merikh slid out from under her, she groaned and replaced his warm torso with his equally warm pillow. The nearby dresser opened, and clothes met Merikh halfway. He was still half dressed from the night. Loralee routinely ended up naked, but Merikh never stripped more than was necessary. He was still overly self-conscious about his scars, though Loralee supposed it was safest that way. If wearing his kameez meant Merikh didn't try to kill her in the middle of sex, Loralee was happy to never see him shirtless again.

"How early is it?" Loralee asked, curling up with the warm blanket he'd left behind.

"Predawn still, I believe. You have to meet with Ruya."

She stifled her groan. Merikh didn't need to remind her. She'd been dreading this for four days.

"Are you meeting the amir? I'm worried about you alone today," Loralee said as she sat up. She drew the blanket up to keep warm. If she stayed lying down, she knew she'd fall back asleep.

"Stop worrying. I will be with Olumide until you and Ruya are ready."

Merikh finished dressing, head to toe in ashen gray. He sat down on the bed to pull on his riding boots, and Loralee reached out to touch his arm.

"Are you sure you're all right?"

The irritated half glare he gave her made her drop the subject. He wasn't okay, and her constant pestering was only going to make him snap at her.

Maybe the amir will be able to help him a little, Loralee thought. Amir Olumide had arrived yesterday with his personal guard. The rest of the Attar troops would be arriving in a few days with Hasad. Duq Rashad was busy in Dharipur, apparently negotiating marriage terms with the kontess.

Merikh stood, and the door to the bedroom opened ahead of him when he left. A moment later, the blankets yanked away from Loralee and bunched at the foot of the bed.

"That's not fair!" she gasped as she clawed one of the furs. Goosebumps covered her skin.

"Get up," Merikh said with a hint of amusement from somewhere in the suite.

Loralee grumbled under her breath as she did so. She walked around the piles of her night clothes and undergarments before she pulled open her drawers. Her shapeless abaya matched Merikh's gray clothes, and she grabbed the matching headscarf. Merikh was gone from the room by the time Loralee was dressed. She crossed the room, poured herself some water, and grabbed a few slices of dried mango before leaving to meet Ruya.

The Night Garden still bloomed. The sun hadn't colored the horizon yet, even as the stars began to wane. Delicate pale flowers still opened toward the sky, though they'd twist closed before dawn.

In the center of the garden stood a tall gazebo built from metal and glass, shimmering in the enchanted blue light. Eight Ajir stood guard, one at each entrance. They wore their ceremonial uniforms, but the golden sashes had been replaced by somber gray ones. Inside the gazebo was a long table, a silver urn, and a sandstone ossuary that had been enchanted to preserve Nikias's head. Alcaeus hadn't deigned to return the body, and there were rumors the Onyx Swords were dragging it through the streets in the Hock District in celebration. The thought made Loralee sick.

"Loralee."

A gentle hand touched Loralee's shoulder. She turned to see Ruya standing behind her.

"I'm glad you're here," the priestess of death said. A servant stood a few feet away from Ruya, carrying two satchels and a bucket of water.

"Of course," Loralee said, trying to hide her reservations. Ruya smiled gently before she entered the gazebo. Loralee followed her, the servant entering last and depositing the satchels and water bucket on the ground beside the table.

"You may leave. Thank you," Loralee said, dismissing the servant.

He bowed, hesitating only for a moment to pay his respects before turning and leaving. Nikias had been one of the longest-lasting members of the palace staff. Only Sumiya and a handful of archivists had been here longer. All of the servants had known Nikias in one way or another. Loralee expected most of the staff had come by the gazebo to pay their respects over the next four days.

Ruya opened the satchels and placed their contents on the table. First the four towels, then the bushels of dried herbs and flowers. Ruya picked up the plants and sent eight of the bushels flying from her hands to rest above each of the entrances. There were small bells hidden inside that gently rang as the bushels moved. Ruya brushed the rest of the herbs and flowers off the table into the bucket. She stirred it with her hand.

"I believe your traditions would dictate entreating Akhenios to protect and guide Nikias's soul to Aljemel, but his soul is already quite gone from here," Ruya explained. "Pantheon beliefs honor the deceased and protect the body from djinnic interference or corruption. I will make sure no djinnic influence wreaks havoc with his soul. But I can't claim to have known Nikias well. If you want to talk…"

"I'm fine to work in silence," Loralee said, taking a step closer to the table.

She couldn't claim to have known Nikias well either. But Loralee was the closest person Nikias had to a female relative; it made Loralee the only one who could attend to him now. Merikh was required by tradition to host mourners. His morning meal was to be attended by Olumide and anyone else who sought to pass along condolences or be consoled. Normally, the meal was hosted by the closest male relative, but they'd had difficulty finding Nikias's cousin.

Loralee took in a deep breath before she pushed the lid off the ossuary. The ice lining inside shimmered from the pale-green fog that had preserved the head. Ruya pulled Nikias's remains out and placed his head gently on the table. She handed Loralee a towel, then picked up the bucket and placed it on the table between them.

Loralee had only ever helped prepare one other body for burial: her grandmaman. Even then, she'd been young enough that she'd only sat nearby and waited for everything to be done. Loralee submerged the towel in the water, letting it soak for a moment before wringing it out. She hesitated, then placed the towel delicately against Nikias's forehead. Normally, Ruya would have been attending to other parts of the body. Instead, she remained here as Loralee's support.

By the time Nikias's head was perfectly ceremonially cleansed, the horizon had turned orange and the Night Garden blooms were closing. Ruya took the dirty towels from Loralee and gently placed them in one of the satchels. They still had use for the next matter Ruya had to attend to. But first, Ruya picked up Nikias and placed him back in the ossuary. The ice and necromancy fog had disappeared. Ruya pulled a scroll from the other satchel and placed it inside. She quickly put the lid back on, her hand pressing firmly down on the top. A moment later, the stone cracked; Loralee could feel the heat from it. When Ruya lifted the lid, the head had been reduced to ash.

"Loralee, you should leave. I can attend to the rest."

Undoubtedly, Ruya was trying to spare Loralee seeing the unceremonious transfer of ashes from the ossuary into the urn. Loralee nodded silent thanks before she turned and left the garden. She'd join Merikh, and once Ruya had the last preparations made, they'd leave for the tomb.

It was a cold walk back inside the palace.

Morning light broke over the dunes and glinted off the armor of the funeral procession. Every precaution was being taken today, and the road was lined with barricades and gates to minimize access to anyone outside of the procession. Loralee was certain today would not go by peacefully. Whether there would be rioting or an outright attack from the Temple, Loralee wasn't sure.

What she was certain of, was that Alcaeus had already given his people license to run wild and disrespect the rules of war. She hardly expected them to respect customs of decency. Loralee had returned to the royal suite after the cleansing ceremony to put on her kusari armor; Merikh had done the same before they'd arrived at the barns, only his armor was far more visible. The Madiaran House cuirass covered his chest, and a pauldron and vambrace protected his riding arm. He looked more prepared for a fight than a funeral.

Amir Olumide, along with a small contingent of the city nobles and the vizier council, rode behind Loralee and Merikh. Some servants from the palace followed along the procession, paying respects. Ponied alongside Merikh's horse was a stunning gray mare, one of the oldest war mares in the royal herd. She wore an empty saddle with full saddlebags. The towels they'd used to cleanse Nikias were draped over her shoulders. They'd been stained with blood, from what, Loralee wasn't sure.

Probably a goat, Loralee couldn't help but glibly think. It should have been blood of the deceased, had Nikias's body been returned with his head. Ruya had made do with what she had.

The great sandstone tomb of the Madiaran shahs rose suddenly from the dunes east of Madiar, outlined harshly by the rising sun. Soldiers, dressed the same as the ones who'd guarded the gazebo, protected the tomb's entrance. Servants had come by yesterday with incense and dried herbs to try and air out the tomb.

As they reached the entrance, Merikh stopped Zahira and the war mare, then dismounted. Loralee followed suit, dismounting Amarante before taking Zahira from him. Merikh took the war mare and tied her to the stone rail beside the tomb. The mare stood still for a moment before stretching out her neck and giving herself a satisfied shake. The braids of her mane whipped loudly along her neck.

Merikh moved to her saddlebags, untying the flap before pulling out a small bell from inside. Carefully, he tied it to one of the mare's braids. His hand hesitated for a moment near the bloody shroud before he walked back to Loralee and took Zahira from her. At first glance, Merikh looked like his usual stoic self, but Loralee could see behind his walls better now. There was a subtle change to his walk and an almost imperceptible slouch through his neck and shoulders. He was exhausted, and he was hurting. Nikias had been far more than merely the grand vizier. Whatever void was left behind from that would be impossible to fill. Death always left empty places within the heart, even one as small and cold as Merikh's.

Merikh took Amarante from Loralee as she walked up to the war mare. There were dozens of small bells inside her saddlebag. Loralee tried not to jingle all of them as she pulled one out. Not everyone would do so, but there was an expectation that the mare's braids would be full of the bells before the urn was put to rest.

It would be.

After Loralee returned to Amarante, the rest of the procession began to take their moments of reverence. When no one was left to approach the horse, Merikh handed Zahira back to Loralee and walked with Ruya to the mare. Ruya pulled the shroud off of the mare's neck. The blood had stained the mare's shoulders a rusty brown. Ruya gently pulled the urn from the saddlebags and wrapped it in the shroud. She then turned to Merikh, hesitating before she handed it to him. He showed equal hesitation in taking the urn before he trudged off into the tomb itself.

Loralee bit her lip, unsure if she was expected to follow. Judging from the silence and the lack of sidelong glances, she assumed holding Zahira was fine. Merikh wouldn't want her inside anyway. If he had any last words for Nikias, they were certainly too private for her to hear. Besides, in the contemplative silence outside the tomb, Loralee could get lost in her own thoughts. And her worries.

We all lose our parents someday, Loralee thought. Nikias's wisdom had been invaluable for both Loralee and Merikh, but eventually they would have lost it. She only wished it had been after she'd returned from Ydeba. Perhaps after the birth of the shahzade.

Sex was a mixed blessing. Nikias had been, albeit gently, haranguing her to get pregnant ever since Merikh's injury. Now that Merikh had recovered, now that he seemed to trust her enough to *let* her get close enough to have sex, pregnancy was inevitably on the horizon. Loralee worried now more than ever about Merikh's capabilities as a father without Nikias around to prod him. Or perhaps to temper him. That fell on her shoulders now. Loralee wasn't sure she was ready for that full responsibility. She had every intention of ensuring Merikh had a more active role in parenting their child than simply being the man who fathered it. But who knew how ingrained the lessons he had been taught by Mansur were? Would she be escorting their child to the infirmary after an altercation with Merikh? The thought turned Loralee's stomach.

Zahira broke Loralee's thoughts by rubbing her itchy head on Loralee's arm. Loralee smiled a little in spite of herself and pushed the mare off of her gently, using her fingernails to scratch the mare's forehead instead.

There, that better? Horses, at least, were simple. If nothing else, Loralee would always have those to keep her sane when Merikh rubbed her the wrong way.

Merikh returned from the tomb, magic shutting the stone behind him. He walked to the war mare first, undoing the breast collar and cinch before pulling the saddle off of her. He untied her before he slipped the halter off. Merikh turned the mare away from the wall. With a small wave of his hand, Merikh sent the mare off. She was free to wander the dunes to find the wild desert horses or to follow the horses back to the barn and remain retired there. A memorial horse was sacred. She would never be worked or bred again by man.

The mare trotted a few feet away and dropped down in the sand to roll, bells jingling loudly. Merikh watched her for a moment before he came over to Loralee and took Zahira. When he mounted his horse, Loralee and the rest of the riders present followed suit. As the procession left the tomb, Loralee could hear the sound of bells faintly following behind them.

Morning in Madiar bustled with life. An apprehensive air rested over the city as they rode through the Hock District. The city waited with dread for the next fight, the next riot, the next clash of Royal Guards and Onyx Swords. It waited for the inevitable retribution from Merikh for Nikias. Whatever Merikh had planned, Loralee had every confidence it would be planned quietly and executed with the greatest of care. She only hoped the innocent people caught in the wake of his cold fury would survive.

The procession slowed. Loralee looked back to see guards moving to surround Ruya more tightly. On the other side of the barricade, Loralee heard shouting. Stones flew over, one of which hit Ruya's gelding squarely on his forehead. The little horse spooked, jumping sideways before he caught himself. He nearly sent Ruya tumbling to the ground. The priestess wasn't much of a rider.

"Shahanshah, we need to keep you moving," Captain Bashir said to Merikh, who nodded.

Loralee urged Amarante forward quickly, her stomach turning in knots. Something like this was exactly what Loralee had feared happening. She wanted to be back within the palace gates as quickly as possible.

A ceramic ball rolled onto the road from behind the barricade. Loralee would have ignored it if it weren't for Captain Bashir. After all, it looked like a perfume jar. But Captain Bashir yanked his horse around and shouted, *"Back!"*

A column of ice rose before them just as the jar exploded, shards embedding themselves almost all the way through the ice. Amarante was spooked sideways, almost pushing Loralee into the barricade. On the other side of the makeshift wall, Loralee could hear fighting.

Another jar rolled under the barricade. When Amarante launched herself forward, Loralee let her run. They were obvious targets on the main road, stuck between barricades with nowhere to go except back toward the Sunrise Gate or pressing forward to the Mitbah Gate. Behind them, Loralee could hear the sickening *pop* of ceramic jars exploding. Men and horses screamed.

When she could no longer hear them, Loralee pulled Amarante to a stop. She turned and tried to get the mare to focus again. The horse was unprepared for this level of chaos. The guards who had kept up with them, their horses remained as calm as ever. They'd been trained for this since birth, almost like their riders.

"Where is the Shah?" Loralee demanded the moment she noticed Merikh wasn't here with her.

"Stayed back with Captain Bashir, Khanum. We need to get you back to the palace."

Other city nobles caught up to them. A few of them and their horses were bloody. Their numbers had thinned. Loralee hoped that it meant many had stayed behind with Merikh, not that they lay dead on the ground. The handful of servants who had followed to pay respects caught up on foot, but few stopped with their khanum. Loralee couldn't blame them. The Ajir were going to protect her first and foremost, then the nobles. The servants were their lowest priority.

"Keep them moving," Loralee ordered, gesturing to the nobles.

"Khanum, you can't remain here," the guard insisted.

"Get them out of here," Loralee ordered again. She was reluctant to leave without knowing Merikh was alive, and now that she'd managed to calm Amarante down, she didn't want to ride into another trap. The guards could scout ahead and rouse more while protecting the city's nobility.

The barricade exploded.

Her ears rang as she hit the ground. Amarante tore off down the road. Loralee gasped for breath, trying to get the wind back into her lungs.

Get up! Loralee struggled to her feet, her head spinning. Her ribs protested angrily.

A beam from the barricade had knocked the guard off his horse, pinning him to the ground. Blood pooled around him. His eyes were wide and growing more distant by the second.

"Khanum," he breathed as he raised a hand toward the gap. Rioters carefully climbed through the debris. Loralee didn't have her dhal shield, but her shamshir was on her hip. She drew the curved sword quickly, not wishing to leave the dying guard.

You're outnumbered and outmatched, Loralee thought as she tried to hold down her fear. The commoners didn't have swords—none of them could afford them—but Emil hadn't yet taught her how to defend best against a club or an ax.

I'm not ready for this, she thought, her eyes going wide. She was no soldier.

The decision was made for her when a man ran at her, wooden club raised high with a wild yell. Her training took over. The shamshir rattled in her hand as she deflected the blow. Without thinking, Loralee slashed at his chest. The man, unsteady from her parry, tripped forward, and her blade bit high. It cut across his chest and sliced the side of his neck.

Loralee jumped when her right arm was yanked roughly. An Ajir guard grabbed her and pulled her out of his way. He finished off the man who'd attacked her. The guard then turned and shoved Loralee back toward his horse, and she didn't have to be told again. Sheathing her sword, she quickly mounted the mare. The horse didn't stop until the Mitbah Gate, where Ajir reinforcements were pouring through. A noblewoman held Amarante's reins, the mare calmer now with the group. Loralee dismounted and traded horses, sending the Ajir horse back with the guards heading into the fray.

The ride back to the palace was a blur. The Mitbah District lacked the same unrest as the Hock, and the barricades disappeared from alongside the road before the Jibbah Gate. Her guards still kept a tight formation around her until they reached the palace gate, leaving her once she was inside to return to the Shah.

"Are you all right, Khanum?" one of the palace guards asked, his tone worried as he stared at Loralee.

"I'm fine," Loralee lied, though she was unable to hide the wince when she dismounted. "My ribs, they're sore from a fall. I'll see a healer when I'm done here." She had to care for Amarante before the adrenaline wore off and she found out just how badly her ribs were hurt.

It was the wrong answer. A groom immediately snatched Amarante's reins from her, and the guards ignored her protests as they herded her into the palace. In hindsight, she wouldn't blame them. Undoubtedly they were all afraid of how the Shah would react if he'd returned from burying Nikias to find Loralee injured. But in the moment, Loralee felt frustratingly like a child.

Inside the infirmary, nobles, guards, and servants alike were being treated for injuries. There were bloody towels everywhere. Healers were working quickly to close wounds, some by hand, some by magic. One came to her quickly and pushed Loralee down onto a bed.

"Where are you hurt?" she asked brusquely, inspecting Loralee quickly.

"Only my ribs, I think."

Loralee didn't feel anything other than sore muscles anywhere else. The healer seemed to concur. Warm light left the healer's fingertips and wrapped around Loralee's chest. It tickled a little, itching as she felt the odd sensation of her cracked rib bone healing quickly but relatively painlessly.

"Bathe with salts, lavender, and rosewater. Your muscles will be fine, Khanum. Out," the healer ordered before she turned on her heel and moved on to the next bed.

With the healer gone, Loralee hurried from the bed and out the door. In the heat of the moment, she walked out and expected to see Nikias standing on the other side, wringing his hands and waiting to be apprised of what had happened. She felt a pang of loss when he wasn't there. Loralee walked slowly to the royal suite, stopping a servant along the way.

"When the Shah returns, I wish to be informed immediately."

The man nodded and hurried off to whatever other duties he was charged with.

Loralee shut the door to the royal suite behind her gently. She leaned against it, looking off toward the balcony. She could see smoke through the glass. Just how much of the city was burning, she couldn't tell. Was it isolated to the broken barricade? Or had more of the Hock District joined the fight?

Loralee straightened up from the door, intending to cross the room to the balcony for a better look, but a strong ache down her backside reminded her that the healer had ordered a bath. Reluctantly, she gingerly walked to the bathing room. Enchantments on the spigot drew warm water into the recessed marble bath. Loralee pulled two small pouches from a nearby set of drawers and emptied the contents into the water. Pale salts mixed with purple lavender sprigs. She then poured a generous amount of rosewater from a ceramic jug near the spigot. As the bath filled and steam rose off the water, Loralee began to undress. She untied the shamshir from her waist and placed it on the drawers. It clattered as she put it down, her hands shaking.

The crossguard was covered in blood.

So were her hands.

Loralee looked down and for the first time saw the red on her gray abaya. Her sleeve was stained dark crimson, the spray continuing across her chest.

I killed a man.

The realization hit Loralee hard, and she scrambled out of her clothes. She tossed them away from her, the kusari armor clattering to the ground. The water almost burned her as she slid into it. Loralee grabbed the pale-orange luffa from the side of the bath. The coarse sponge was harsh on her skin as Loralee began to frantically scrub the blood off of her.

It suddenly made sense why Merikh obsessively washed his hands.

CHAPTER 43

The second explosion startled Zahira, but she barely moved from where Merikh had planted her. She'd survived a year in the provinces with him during his Shahzade patrol. The mare had seen worse, had been prepared for far worse. It didn't surprise Merikh to see Amarante run. Loralee was of no use to him here. The sooner she returned to the palace the better. Her mare would get her to safety.

Ice protected Merikh from the next two blasts. By the third, he found his magic difficult to call upon. It failed to protect most of his guards from the blast. By the fourth grenade, Merikh felt a sickening emptiness where his magic ought to have been. Ruya fainted from her horse, and Merikh barely kept his stomach from emptying on the ground nearby as rioters poured through the breach in the barricade. Someone in the plain-dressed crowd was an Onyx Sword bearing Alcaeus's stone.

Merikh didn't bother to draw his shamshir, the enchanted blade too dangerous for him to use. Merikh didn't want to find out how the enchantment would react to the stone. His khanjar was useless from horseback. Yet Merikh gave no thought to running like Loralee. His pride wouldn't allow it. Zahira would have to be enough. The mare's ears pinned flat against her skull as a man ran at them. Zahira turned around to show the man her back feet. Her hooves met his head with skull-cracking ferocity.

The man crumpled to the ground.

Another grenade exploded, but this time it felled more rioters than guards. In the chaos, another group of Onyx Swords or rioters slipped past Merikh's guards. Zahira tensed. Merikh sat deep in the saddle as the mare drew up her forelegs, leaned back, and launched herself into the air, kicking out with her back feet. She nearly slipped when her hooves hit the cobblestones beneath them. She recovered quickly, and at Merikh's urging, broke through the startled line of men in front of them.

Ice formed around Merikh's hand. Whoever had the stone had retreated, or perhaps it had been destroyed. Either way, Merikh didn't care. Raising his left hand, he blocked the gap in the barricade with a wall of ice. Of the dead nearby, Merikh focused on a handful of the cut-down peasants. Green fog wrapped around their bodies before they clamored to their feet, snarling and pursuing their former allies. As more guards arrived, the assailants either fled or became a meal for the undead mortoha.

"Are you all right, Shahanshah?" Captain Bashir asked, leading his horse. At some point in the fight, the captain had been forced from his mare.

Merikh nodded. "There were Onyx Swords with Alcaeus's stone," Merikh explained.

Bashir frowned. "Explains the priestess, then," Bashir said, gesturing back toward where his men had pulled Ruya to safety. The priestess was slowly waking.

We need a solution to that stone, Merikh thought. He relied heavily on his magic to fight. He'd never had a reason not to before. Another shamshir would need to be made for him, and Merikh needed more training with Emil. Everything he'd practiced for years all involved using his magic in one way or another. It gave him an edge. Without it, he was vulnerable. Merikh didn't care for the thought.

"Shahanshah?" Another guard approached, and Merikh nodded for him to continue. "The Khanum, she made it safely to the palace, but I've heard conflicting reports. She may have been injured along the way. Another part of the barricade broke."

Merikh held his tongue, tempted to ask what in Alhanem the man was good for if he couldn't get a reliable report or keep the Khanum safe. But he knew better than to snap. The Ajir were beyond reliable. If Loralee had been hurt, there had been nothing the Ajir could have done to prevent it.

"Thank you," Merikh said instead, turning Zahira down the road toward the palace. The Ajir guards followed him, while the rest of the Royal Guards began to clear the road and recover the dead.

The barns were organized chaos when Merikh arrived. Guards looked after their horses while healers tended to the injured animals. Merikh brought Zahira around to her stall. He removed her tack quickly before checking her over for cuts and injuries. Her legs undoubtedly hurt after the jump. They felt warmer than they should.

"What in Alhanem are you doing here?"

Merikh looked up and saw Sumiya glowering from outside Zahira's stall, salve in one hand and wraps in the other.

"She needs care," Merikh answered, admittedly dumbfounded by the head trainer's question. She'd never before asked him a question with such an obvious answer.

"Get out," Sumiya grumbled, swinging open the stall door. "You have injured men, and your wife was covered in blood when she got here. You have bigger problems than Zahira's legs. She looks fine." Sumiya prodded Merikh out of the way.

"She has a few cuts and scrapes from—"

"They *all* do," Sumiya's tone softened a little, and she glanced up at Merikh. "Your mare isn't going to be offended you've left her with me." The woman dug around in her pocket before pulling out a honey mint. "Particularly if she's bribed."

Zahira immediately craned her neck to look at him expectantly, her delicate ears perked forward. Merikh took the mint reluctantly before he stepped around Sumiya and let Zahira greedily take the treat from him.

"Thank you."

"Why are you still here yammering?" Sumiya wasn't a woman to appreciate societal niceties. They made her more uncomfortable than they made Merikh. He left without another word, his walk to the infirmary unhindered. The door opened ahead of him, and Merikh picked his way through the bustle to find a healer he could speak with. It barely took a moment, the healer undoubtedly assuming he was injured.

"I am fine," Merikh said, loudly and clearly to make sure no one misheard. "Now, I was told the Khanum was injured."

"A couple of cracked ribs. She was sent back to the royal suite to tend to her sore muscles and relax."

"Casualties?"

"Only the ones you would have seen on the road. Everyone brought to us has survived so far."

The healer gestured back toward the infirmary beds before she led Merikh to the injured soldiers recovering. He spent a moment with each, thanking them for their service and finding out the specifics of their injuries. His life depended on the Ajir. While he had been friendlier with the Ajir as the Shahzade, Merikh made sure each of the men and women who protected him understood his gratitude. Whatever he could do to inspire their exceptional loyalty, he did. A moment here in the infirmary with each of them before going to see Loralee might mean the difference between guards willing to lay down their lives to protect his or not.

Once his rounds were completed, Merikh left the infirmary and walked back to the royal suite. It was the first time since Loralee woke up this morning that he'd had a moment to himself. He found it plagued with doubt. Alcaeus had now repeatedly hit him. Merikh had been lenient, patient with the Faithful within Madiar. The gesture was hardly appreciated.

Let them have their moment. Merikh steadied himself. The higher they climbed, the better they felt, the harder they'd fall. The better an example they'd make to the rest of Shai'Khal. Madiar was *his* city. Before long, the Faithful of the empire would remember that.

As Merikh passed the guards at the entrance hallway to the suite, he was surprised to see a servant pacing outside the door. The man bowed deeply as Merikh approached.

"Yes?" Merikh asked.

"Apologies, Shahanshah, the Khanum asked to be apprised the moment you returned, but I haven't managed to locate her. I thought she was inside, but no one—"

"That will be all. I will inform her you tried." Merikh dismissed the man as the door opened. He could feel Loralee within the room, simply not within the main area. She'd been ordered to tend to her muscles, so Merikh wasn't surprised she didn't answer the door. Her soul was in the bathing room.

Merikh left her there as he carefully undid the buckles and ties of his armor. He pulled the metal and leather pieces off, carefully placing them down in the armoire before depositing his shamshir beside it. When none of the noise drew a response from the bathing room, Merikh crossed the room to the door reluctantly. Despite everything, he still found it violating a boundary to walk in on her bathing. Neither had much in the way of privacy anymore, and privacy was something sacred to him. But he hadn't felt Loralee's soul move, and if the servant had been trying to rouse her...

"Loralee?" Merikh said, brushing his knuckles against the wooden door. When Loralee neither moved nor responded, Merikh dropped his hand, and the door opened for him.

The bathwater had a faint pink tinge to it. The air smelled sweetly of lavender and roses. Merikh stopped by Loralee's bloody abaya, crouching down and touching it briefly before he straightened up and walked to the drawers. He picked up the bloody shamshir hilt and drew the sword a few inches out of its sheath. The blade dragged stubbornly against the leather, dried blood flaking off.

You need to take better care of your weapons, Merikh thought. He'd leave that critique for later, the thought lost when he looked to Loralee. Her black hair was pooled around her shoulders, the water rippling around her. Small chunks of orange luffa had drifted away from Loralee, even as she still scrubbed at her hands with the chunk that was left. As Merikh stepped closer to the bath edge, he could see how painfully raw her hands looked. There were pinpricks of blood on the backs of her hands.

"Loralee, *stop,*" Merikh ordered. His words fell on deaf ears. She hadn't so much as looked up since he'd entered the room.

Merikh pulled off his riding boots and tossed the socks inside them before walking down two of the steps into the bath beside Loralee. The water was cold on his bare feet, soaking up from the hem of his gray salwar. Merikh leaned over and pulled the sponge pieces from Loralee's hands. Loralee jumped, as if finally seeing him, and splashed water all over his kameez.

"Vindaram's breath! I didn't even hear you! The servants were supposed to tell me when you returned."

"They tried."

She blinked at him, absolutely stunned. Merikh tossed the luffa pieces away from the bath and took her hand.

"There's leftover salve left in my desk that you can use on your hands," he said before he pulled her up from sitting and moved her toward the bath steps. Merikh glanced over to the towels. One flew into his right hand. With Loralee out of the bath, he wrapped the towel gently around her shoulders.

"What happened?" he asked, gesturing to the bloody clothes on the ground.

Loralee was shivering, though Merikh wasn't sure if it was shock or the cold from the water. He didn't wait for an answer from her. Merikh led her out of the bathing room back into the main suite. He carefully pushed her down onto the divan, leaving her there as he walked to the desk to find the salve.

"The barricade exploded. It killed one of the Ajir, and...a man tried to kill me. I...I think I killed him."

"Better him than you," Merikh said as he dug through the various drawers. The salve jar had ended up kicked to the back of the right-middle drawer. Without knowing exactly where it was, he couldn't summon it with magic.

"I can't be sure he was trying to kill me or that he would have given the chance! Gods, Merikh, he might have had a spouse, *children*."

"Or he might have been a lonely fanatic bent on doing whatever he could to end the Madiaran line and destroy the cultist whore wearing the khanum's crown. Personally, I prefer my hypothetical over yours."

Salve in hand, Merikh walked back to Loralee's side and handed it to her.

"I don't *care*! Either way, a man is dead because of me. Directly because of me. His blood is on my hands."

"No, that's your own blood now," Merikh said, unable to help himself as he sat down beside her. "Use that."

He suddenly felt a great deal of empathy for what Loralee had struggled with when she'd been ministering to him. Loralee glanced down at the jar, her looked dazed, as if she was trying to puzzle out what he'd handed to her. Then, slowly, she unscrewed the lid. Merikh took a deep breath and ran his hand over his face before trying to find the words that might help her even a little.

"You simply defended yourself, Loralee. You are *my* wife, eventually the mother of the shahzade, the guarantor of a dynasty's continuance. Your life matters to Shai'Khal more than a peasant's, regardless of whether he has family or not."

"How do you do that?" Loralee asked, not looking at him. "Justify *killing* someone so quickly?"

"I was not raised to view lives equally. I speak, Shai'Khal listens. I can level cities or have entire new forests planted with a handful of words. That peasant probably couldn't have talked his way into a free cup of wine. I will not lose sleep over the loss of that man when the alternative was to lose you. You may do more good or ill in one lifetime than that man could over several. Your life is worth his several times over."

Loralee continued to rub the salve into her hands. She appeared reluctant to believe him. When the scrapes left from the luffa were healed, Loralee screwed the lid back on and put the container down on the table in front of them. She wrapped the towel around her naked body tighter.

"So, a grandiose ego is what helps you sleep at night," she said with a shiver and a reluctant smile.

Merikh shrugged. "If it works, it works."

Of course, it hadn't last night. The knowing look she shot him clearly stated as much. Loralee sighed, and to Merikh's surprise, she leaned against him. Instinctively, Merikh tensed. She had seemed disappointed with him the last time she'd sought comfort from him like this. He wasn't sure what she wanted from him, or *how* she wanted it. Merikh could see the lack of affection was difficult for her. He saw the little twitches when she wanted to take his hand, or when she had to restrain herself from sitting close and leaning on him. But unlike last time, she seemed fine telling him what she wanted. Loralee took his arm and moved it over her shoulders as she pulled her feet up onto the divan.

"Don't be stupid," she muttered. "This didn't kill you last time; it won't kill you now."

Merikh didn't argue. Instead, he rubbed her bare shoulder before his fingers absentmindedly began playing with the wet ends of her hair.

"You understand, in Ydeba, you'll likely have to kill again?" he asked. "Or order someone dead? The Ajir will do their best to protect you, and without me there as a distraction, they will do a better job. But they're only human. Assassins may find ways to get past them."

Loralee said nothing. Merikh wasn't sure if she was deliberately ignoring him or simply didn't want to think about it. She'd probably never seen anything growing up in Abadan like she had here in Madiar over the past week. Despite the small gap in years between them, moments like this made Merikh feel old and Loralee seem quite young.

"I can send someone else, off the vizier council, if you'd prefer to stay," Merikh offered, surprising himself a little. Surprising Loralee, too, it seemed, as she craned her head to look at him.

"No, I can handle that still."

Good. Merikh didn't much care for telling another person about the Key. Too many people already knew about the temple in the Katu as it was.

"You're going after Alcaeus and the grimoire soon?" Loralee asked.

"As soon as Ruya is out of the city, once the Attar troops are here. Olumide is eager to bury Alcaeus. He's never cared for an Aegalian leading the Temple."

"You've ordered Alcaeus exiled?"

Merikh nodded. "I thought it fitting. He's not going to surrender to an execution or banishment. At least one of them is passably poetic. I rather like the idea of him adrift on the Aldruin until washing ashore on some deserted island."

"And here I thought you were too stuffy for that sort of thing," Loralee said with a tired smile before she straightened up off of him. Her hair left a wet spot on his chest.

"Are you all right? You're not hurt?" Loralee asked.

"Zahira took care of me. You should dress," Merikh said as he stood. "I need you to check on Amarante and Zahira while I confer with Bashir and the Sardar generals."

Loralee would be fine. Seeing the horses would do her good, and Merikh had a great deal more to plan. The Akhenic Faithful were emboldened by their successes. Merikh was certain they believed him complacent in all this. Perhaps even cowed.

Mansur had made the same mistake.

CHAPTER 44

25th of Livith, Dry Season, 902 Unified Age
Madiar, Raudhah Province

A knock on the door woke Ruya. The servant bringing breakfast had been deliberately loud, as Ruya had instructed the night before. She didn't want to be late this morning of all mornings. Excitement was mixed with dread for this journey. It wouldn't be easy, as there were plenty of dangers, but if all went well, Ikharon would be free within a few months. Nine hundred years of waiting was almost over. Ruya looked forward to being in contact with her god again. The years without any had been incredibly difficult.

"You 'ave to leave?" Salome asked. The servant woman had almost jumped out of bed when the other servant had knocked.

"You can have breakfast with me first," Ruya said as she got up and dressed.

Salome nodded, though she took decidedly longer to rise from the bed. Scars on her back and her arms betrayed her run-ins with less-pleasant bedfellows over the years, but most of them had been courtesy of the last shah. They'd faded over time, some now hidden by rolls and wrinkles brought on by aging. Salome's old broken bones, even those mended with healing magic, tended to ache in the morning. Ruya walked over to the tray on the table nearby, picked it up, and brought it back to the bed.

"Another one of my lovers pointed out that breakfast is, in fact, consumable in bed. Though he had an overfondness for spending the entire day there," Ruya said as she sat down, crossing her legs and helping herself to a salted piece of smoked lamb.

"Do I know that lover?" Salome asked. The woman rarely engaged in bouts of jealousy, so the question seemed earnest.

Ruya smiled and nodded. "Duq Rashad Attar."

"Oh, Ruya, I thought you had standards!" Salome said as she tossed a piece of dried fruit at Ruya. "That man makes my skin crawl, ever since he was a teen. 'Not a Mansur bastard,' my ass."

"You're aging yourself, dear."

"As if this doesn't." Salome gestured at the faint streaks of silver starting to streak her hair.

"I like them," Ruya said as she reached across the bed and brushed a few hairs back behind Salome's ear. Ruya had no trouble finding beauty in the marks left behind on the body from a life well lived.

"Yeah, that's why you don't have any."

Fair point. Ruya indulged in a youthful glow brought on by her magic. Ikharon gave her immortality. Ruya's magic gave her youth. She rarely aged, and she usually reversed it rather quickly. Ruya shrugged and stood up to get water. When she returned, Salome had dressed and was wrapping food into a cloth to shove in her pockets.

"You don't have to rush," Ruya told her, a little crestfallen.

Salome shook her head. "You need to go. You don't want to keep the Shah or Khanum waiting."

"They'll wait for me."

Salome rolled her eyes and stuffed the cloth into her pocket. "Not happily, and while I enjoy the palace when it's cool, I don't like slipping on random patches of ice."

"Royals! So touchy!" Ruya smiled as she walked Salome to the door. The priestess stopped and pulled the servant woman into a tight hug. "Look after yourself, please."

Salome snorted in amusement. "Shouldn't I be saying that to you?" she asked.

"I'm going to be fine."

Ruya had every confidence that Loralee would fulfill her duties and the Key would be destroyed. What she didn't have faith in was Merikh keeping his end of the bargain. With Nikias dead, if Merikh attempted to break into the catacombs and take the grimoire, Madiar and Shai'Khal would quickly become leaderless. Even if the vizier council still answered to Loralee, she would only be able to do so much from afar. Amir Olumide was likely to take over. While Ruya knew she could sway Rashad to her purposes, his father was another matter entirely.

Salome interrupted Ruya's thoughts with a quick kiss goodbye. Ruya watched the door close before she walked back to her bed and flopped down by the food. She was happy to indulge in her last comforts. A month on horseback sounded awful enough in and of itself, but a month on horseback through the Sarafi sounded unbearable.

Ruya had one stop to make before the barns, one the Royal Guards assigned to her were not happy to be making this early. Ruya was not going to leave Madiar without one last prayer at Ikharon's temple. The Jibbah District was nearly deserted, and the only men and women out in the streets were the servants from the noble houses readying for the day.

One of the city nobles had donated a part of his estate to Pantheon worship. He'd repurposed the garden house and erected a statue of Ikharon inside. One of the side rooms had been given to Salim Basara, a homeless man from the Hock District who Ruya had named an acolyte of Ikharon. The man who, alongside Merikh, would keep Ikharon's name alive in Madiar while she was gone.

Gods, guide their choices, Ruya prayed as she approached the temple. It was simply built, a large adobe rectangle covered in green vines with vibrant purple flowers. It wasn't much, but it was more than Ikharon had on his island. Salim had come through earlier and lit candles around Ikharon's statue, giving the sanctum a warm glow. It was still predawn outside, the starlight not illuminating much of anything.

"We'll wait outside," the Royal Guard told Ruya before exiting.

"Thank you," she said quickly before she approached Ikharon's statue. It didn't look much like him. The sculptor had done his best with the description Ruya had given him. He looked thicker than Ikharon was supposed to. More substantial. The real god of death looked as if he were on death's door at first glance, old and worn.

"Maybe it's just the island's effect on you," Ruya said quietly. "You'll be back to normal soon, I hope."

She bent down in front of the statue. From a pocket of her kaftan, she pulled a letter for Salim. The man wasn't very well educated. Ruya had simplified her words a great deal to make sure he'd understand. A firm, supportive letter to remind him that he was *her* representative. That in her absence, he spoke for her, and that meant he spoke for Ikharon. To that end, he needed to be careful with his words.

Ruya's letter encouraged him not to be intimidated by Merikh. Easier said than done when putting a formerly homeless peasant in the same league as the Shah. But Salim was wilier than Merikh would give him credit for, and that might be all the edge Salim needed.

Hopefully he won't need to meet with Merikh at all before I come back.

Ruya doubted the world would be that perfect. But he'd do his best. Salim was meant to speak to those Merikh wouldn't have the stomach to. She'd seen the looks Merikh had tried to hide at Westhock, the way his stomach clearly turned at the smells of the poor. It was easy to forget that the people there, covered in muck, didn't live that way because they chose to. Who wouldn't prefer perfumed baths and fresh clothes? Ruya had certainly, unashamedly, taken to them again. Those accoutrements hardly made her superior. They didn't make Merikh any better either.

That said, she would miss them dearly on the road.

The morning sun had risen just enough to glint off the golden palace gates when Ruya returned. Her guards seemed happy to leave her and return to their more pressing duties. Ruya entered the barn alone, her things already stacked at the entrance alongside someone else's.

"You're staring. Make yourself useful and grab my tack, will you?" Ruya heard Loralee say from far inside the barn.

When her eyes adjusted to the dark, she saw Merikh walk away from Amarante's stall toward the tack room. A moment later, he returned with Amarante's things.

It was a strange thing to see, the contrast between the Yahidah and Tsukarai nobles. She'd spent years in the Kaitan and Kuzen provinces, met a great number of lower-ranking Tsukarai nobles, and had spent a great deal of time with Duqa Sachiko. None of them would have been caught dead in a dusty tack room or in a stall. But here were the two most powerful people in Shai'Khal, horse manure ground into their boots and dust on their hands. Even with their perfumed baths, they both always faintly smelled of horse or leather. The barn, it seemed, was a great equalizer of the Yahidah.

Ruya found her way to her horse, admittedly only able to truly remember his stall. The brown gelding was handsome, she supposed. His coat was rich, the color of roasted coffee beans. He had no white markings whatsoever, and there were easily a dozen other horses that looked like him. The grooms had thought to let Ruya catch her gelding out in the pasture, only to be horrified when she'd brought back what was apparently a notoriously unruly horse. Instead, she was given little Qaphi, who was as docile as they came. He barely flitted an ear her way when she opened his stall door, his head firmly buried in his hay.

"Let's get your head up," she said as she fumbled with his halter. Naturally the gelding ignored her. The more she prodded him to pay attention, the more adamant he became about his food.

"You should be glad Sumiya isn't here," Merikh said.

Ruya's pathetic attempts had apparently caught his attention. He entered the stall and took the halter from Ruya.

"That woman terrifies me," Ruya said, only half joking.

"As she should. Come on, Qaphi." Merikh stuck his finger into the hay. Judging by the way Qaphi's head shot out of the hay, his eyes wide and indignant, Ruya imagined Merikh had poked Qaphi right in one of his flared nostrils. Merikh slipped the halter over the gelding's tiny ears, then handed the lead line to Ruya.

"Thank you," she said with a bright smile. It felt more forced than normal. Ever since Loralee had pushed for Ruya to accompany her to Ydeba, Ruya had been unable to shake the feeling that the Madiaran couple was simply trying to be rid of her. There was only one reason Ruya could think of, or at least only one that made any manner of sense.

"Merikh?" she said, catching his attention as he turned his back to leave the stall. He turned to face her once the stall was closed behind him.

"I am *not* a groom." His voice was terse, as he seemed to assume Ruya needed more help tacking up. Ruya expected he'd much prefer spending these last few moments with Loralee instead.

"You understand the High Temple here must be preserved, yes? I have appointed an acolyte who can attend to it in my absence. There are dangers within that you aren't prepared for. That the gods won't thank you for disturbing."

Merikh bowed his head, a gesture Ruya hardly found comforting in its disdain.

"I live to serve."

"I mean it. You'll kill yourself."

"I have a war to win and a country to run," Merikh said. "I can hardly afford flights of fancy that might interrupt the smooth course of either. You should spend more time worrying about where you're going. I expect you to return my wife in the same fashion I've given her to your cause. Unlike Sarka did with Adrian."

Merikh walked away. The air between them hung discontent. His magic had grown more powerful in direct correlation with the Pantheon's strength, just as Ruya's had. Magic was slowly returning to its old might in the world. It made Ruya worry that men like Merikh would begin to try and see how deep their access to those wells of power were. How far they could now push themselves.

He's not a fool. Of all the things Merikh was, he wasn't as foolish as most young men his age. *Maybe that's what scares me.*

A groom helped Ruya saddle Qaphi and pack her things onto him. When Ruya led him from the stall, the sun was almost above the horizon. The cold of the night before was ebbing away. The guards escorting them warmed up their horses and readied to leave. The groom held on to Qaphi's reins as Ruya carefully turned the stirrup for her foot, and she hauled herself clumsily into the saddle. She settled in just in time to see Loralee mount Amarante, though she did so far more gracefully. Merikh stood beside her, the sunlight reflecting off ice scorpion in his hand.

"That won't help in the temple," Loralee pointed out quietly.

"There is a great deal between here and there that this *will* help," Merikh insisted as he placed it in her saddlebag.

Loralee leaned down and kissed him. The couple looked more comfortable than Ruya expected. The gesture was both surprising and heartening to see. She doubted anyone had actually *seen* any affection between Merikh and Loralee since their wedding.

"Be careful," Merikh said as Loralee straightened up.

She nodded and gave Merikh a small smile. "Shahanshah, I promise she won't come to harm," said one of the Ajir guards, a woman maybe ten years older than Merikh by the name of Farhana.

There were no more parting words. The captain led the group away from the barns and main gate. He took them to one of the discreet passageways from the palace that was large enough for the horses to pass through without dismounting. A small mercy, as Ruya's legs always ached most getting on and off these animals.

The passageway was well lit with enchanted light, though being in such an enclosed space made even the war horses nervous. It was a long walk through the musty passage before they reached the exit. The sandstone gates groaned as the levers opened them and sand poured in from the dunes outside the city walls. The winds had shifted, half burying the exit since its last use. There was just enough space for the horses to clamor through if their riders hugged close to their necks.

On the other side, not far from where they'd exited, Ruya could see riders on the horizon. A banner hung lazily from the lead rider's pole, wrapping the dark wood in pale blue and silver. Ruya looked over to Loralee.

"Are you ready?" Ruya asked.

Loralee smiled, not at all as tired or nervous as Ruya had expected her to look. "Yes."

The word was spoken quickly, without reservation.

Good, at least one of us is.

CHAPTER 45

27TH OF LIVITH, DRY SEASON, 902 UNIFIED AGE
MADIAR, RAUDHAH PROVINCE

Duq Hasad stood nervously beside Merikh. He was trying desperately to mirror the calmness of the noblemen around him, but Hasad's fingers betrayed him. Out of the corner of his eye, Merikh could see the young duq restlessly drumming his fingers on his shamshir hilt. It was amplifying the shuddering of his right knee as his heel tapped the ground. If he could keep still, the young duq would have almost looked impressive. Amir Olumide was currently giving a stirring speech to the troops, punctuated by Sardar General Harith as necessary. All but a handful of the men and women before them had seen combat before. The duq, on the other hand, had never seen much more than the occasional scuffle with Emani highwaymen.

"Put your hands behind your back. Push them down," Merikh whispered to Hasad. The duq let go of the shamshir hilt immediately and folded his hands behind his back. At least there, he could fiddle with his fingers as much as he liked and no one would be able to see it. Pushing them down forced him to press into his feet, stabilizing his heels and stopping the shaking; it puffed up the young man's chest enough to almost exude confidence.

"Apologies, Shahanshah. Thank you," Duq Hasad breathed.

The amir's speech ended in cheers, though the soldiers sobered rather quickly as they began attending to their duties. The captains of each contingent approached Merikh, each man bowing deeply before taking turns leaving satchels at his feet. Death tokens from their soldiers. Gifts and letters meant for their families, should the men and women die. Most of the soldiers would get them back. A handful, Merikh would see personally delivered. At least, Merikh hoped it would be only a handful.

"Are you ready, Hasad?" Amir Olumide asked as they watched the soldiers. Some were in charge of the horses pulling the battering ram, while

495

others would carry the ladders to take the temple wall. The rest had the uncomplicated but unpleasant task of ensuring those tasked with taking the temple weren't flanked by Onyx Swords or peasants.

"Of course, Amir," Duq Hasad answered quickly, betraying his nerves.

Olumide laughed and clapped his son on the back. "It's his first taste of war," Olumide said as he looked at Merikh. "Might be a little steadier on his feet once we're done."

"I'm sure," Merikh said, watching as Hasad seemed to grow paler by the second. Somehow, Merikh doubted Hasad would come out of today with anything remotely similar to bloodlust. Perhaps some grim determination, if he managed to quell his fears at all. Hasad would hardly turn into a strong commander.

"I look forward to speaking with you both in the temple," Merikh said. Both the amir and duq bowed and headed to their tacked-up horses. Merikh waited a moment, listening to the palace gates opening and the sound of horses and men marching into the street. While he was allowing Olumide to take command of the situation, Merikh had no desire to be absent. Alcaeus's stone was a problem, but how much of one Merikh didn't know. It meant none of his sorcerers had been pulled from the ranks. If they fell, it gave Merikh a warning to retreat.

The Ajir gathered around Merikh as he walked to the barn. Zahira was tacked up in all her finery. Leather and metal armor covered her face, neck, chest, and flank. She was adorned in brilliant crimson and gold. Merikh's armor was subdued in comparison. If all went well, he wouldn't need much of it. Merikh mounted Zahira, and the Ajir mounted their horses. They rode with him to follow the Royal and Attar guards toward the temple.

The districts were silent as the guards passed. The last time Merikh had ridden through the streets with a large contingent of guards had been for his year-long patrol as Shahzade. Then, the road had been lined from the Jibbah to the Hock Districts with well-wishers. Now, the nobles in the Jibbah District stayed in their homes. Anyone in the Mitbah District bowed their heads and hurried away. No one was under any illusions as to what was about to happen.

Merikh gathered his reins in one hand and raised the other. Ice formed in delicate ribbons around his hand before it turned into snow. From the cloudless sky, snow began to fall, melting and evaporating the instant it hit the ground in the Dry Season's heat. It would help keep his soldiers cool and once again give Merikh notice if Alcaeus's stone was nearby.

The walls of the Temple District were thin. There were no ramparts, no walkways for the Onyx Swords to hold and defend from. There was one main gate, but a second smaller one on the far side of the district fed into the Hock. A large contingent of Merikh's soldiers were positioned there, knowing the fighting would undoubtedly spill over into the impoverished district.

Merikh doubted the Faithful masses would take kindly to a direct attack on the temple. The soldiers on the far side were there to curtail any escaping Onyx Swords or Alcaeus. They weren't expected to take the district. But if by some miracle they managed to safely enter it, they had orders to open the front gate. Merikh expected the battering ram to make quicker work of it than the soldiers. It would be followed by a shield wall, a phalanx of spearmen to break whatever wall of Onyx Swords would be met on the other side. Beyond that, the soldiers would split into several groups to gain control of the main garden while the ram would be moved to the temple itself and repeat the maneuver if required. The time for sanctuary was long gone, and if the gods took issue with Merikh's tactics... Well, until Livinja was free to provide suggestions, the gods could pound sand.

Merikh couldn't see much from the back of the column, as was undoubtedly Olumide's point. But he could hear the moment the leopard-headed battering ram hit the Temple District's gate. Steel met wood with a thundering crack. Soldiers shouted to each other, encouragement and rhythm for those swinging the ram. Merikh looked toward the wall. He felt none of the strangeness from the stones. As arrows began to fly over the wall toward the red-and-blue guards, Merikh turned the snow above them into a canopy of ice.

"Are you sure that's safe?" Captain Bashir asked.

"It is, Captain."

The gate shuddered again. The Onyx Swords on the other side of the wall couldn't see where their arrows landed. Couldn't see that their arrows had yet to take out any of their foes. The Royal Guard returned their volleys not with arrows but sulfur grenades. The smoke began to fill the air inside the Temple District. It was as much a detriment to them as the Onyx Swords, but the smoke would dissipate fairly thoroughly by the time Royal and Attar guards were past the gate. Or at least, that was Olumide's theory.

It didn't take long for the gate to crack loudly, followed by the sound of steel spears piercing flesh or knocking against shields. Screams resonated in the air. Merikh could feel his necromancy magic stirring as souls were rapidly torn from their bodies and sent to the afterlife. He rode forward toward the gate, drawing on his magic and raising the corpses nearby. They turned quickly on the Onyx Swords.

Everyone in the temple had been holding their breath for the past two days, ever since Neredi soldiers had been spotted on the horizon. Rumors said that the Khanum had left Madiar, but who knew whether those were true. The Attar troops bolstering the Royal Guards hadn't boded well when they'd arrived either, leaving everyone in a state of concern or dread.

Or at least, *almost* everyone. Dalya was almost prancing everywhere she walked, pushing the Onyx Swords hard in training and terrorizing the acolytes to more ardent prayers. Adunbi was ready to have her hung or handed over to Merikh, and there were moments Alcaeus was almost willing to let him. Most times, though, Alcaeus simply ordered her to the archives or barracks, anywhere that kept her out of Adunbi's way.

For every acolyte she terrorized, Dalya seemed to inspire three or four peasants. The recent upheaval the Hock District was entirely her doing. Nikias had been her idea. Alcaeus had spent the morning after Nikias had left in inner sanctum praying at Akhenios's feet. The old vizier had been a good man. Alcaeus had made her promise to execute him quickly. Nikias didn't deserve to suffer, and as far as Alcaeus heard, he hadn't. The only one who was meant to suffer was Merikh. And he had, judging from the rumors.

The doors to the inner sanctum banged open loudly. Alcaeus jumped to his feet from the prayer mat. Dalya strode toward him, an irritating grin on her face. She'd never *dared* to be this impudent before!

"You're not allowed in here, Inquisitor."

"Well, Akhenios is going to have to forgive me, Mawla, because you and I are taking a little walk."

"Excuse me?"

"I mean, you *could* stay. But I just saw a few semaphores getting set up on nearby rooftops, and there's some yelling. Pretty sure the Shah is about to rain Alhanem down on us."

"The walls will—"

"Have you *looked* at your walls?" Dalya asked, rolling her eyes. The district walls weren't built nearly as thick as the outer city walls.

"They can't use magic to take them. You've set your people with the stones around them, haven't you?"

"Nope, because I know a losing fight when I see one, and fuck if I'm losing men and stones in the first real confrontation with the necromancer. He's got us outnumbered handily. Even with the training I've put into Adunbi's guards, they're no match for even the shittiest Royal or Attar guard. Adunbi can have his mighty last stand. My Sanctified Suns are getting out of here. Unless you wish to be a martyr, I suggest you come with me."

Alcaeus stared dumbfounded for a moment, unsure if he'd actually heard any of what Dalya had said. He blinked at her, then gaped, searching for words. His silence was met with a frustrated groan from the older woman. As devoted as she seemed to be to Akhenios, the chain of command often eluded her when it came to making plans and following through with them.

"There are Royal Guards and Attar infantry," Dalya said, her words slow and deliberate as if speaking to a moronic child. "In the city. They are going to descend on the temple with the only goal being to take it for the Pantheon. If you die, we lose. The palace complex is built to withstand a fight. This place? Not so much. They will blow a hole in the wall or the gate. If we all stay, we'll put up a valiant fight that someone might even put to song. But we'll all die. Or, we can leave some useless peacocks like Adunbi to fight and die like martyrs to protect their temple. You barely escape the Pantheon horde, and the Faithful will rally to their high priest. Then we come back with Duqa Enitan's troops to retake the temple and destroy the cultists who have defiled her. What more do I need to say?"

"How...how long have you been planning this?" Alcaeus asked, shaking his head in disbelief. "There are relics we need to save, need to move with us—"

"Nothing that we don't have a greater version of in Tanga. Besides, anything I thought important I already had removed before we killed Nikias."

"On whose authority?" Alcaeus demanded.

Dalya rolled her eyes before she grabbed his sandals from nearby the ablution fountain. She tossed them at his feet. "Akhenios's. Mine. I'm going to save the Faith, if you'll let me and keep everyone else out of my way. Are you coming?"

Alcaeus scrambled to pull on his sandals before he followed Dalya from the inner sanctum. Within the main halls of the temple, it was eerily quiet. That ended when they turned down one of the outer hallways near a window. He could hear shouting, Onyx Sword commanders rallying troops and scrambling defenses. There was a clattering of metal, the shouting of orders, and then the shuddering sound of a battering ram meeting the main gate.

"How are we getting out of here?" Alcaeus barely breathed as he stopped beside the window.

There was a strange flurry of white ice falling to the ground outside that turned to water when it hit the heat of the stone walkways. The same cold omen from the so-called "Miracles of Westhock." Dalya grabbed his arm roughly and pulled him away.

"I swear to Akhenios, what *were* you doing without me? What do you think I was doing when you forced me to sit in the archives out of Adunbi's way?"

Dalya dragged him down the hallway, past his office, and out one of the back doors of the temple. They hurried across the garden path to an old gardening shed that no one had used in years. It was overgrown with vines, most of which were dying in the Dry Season's heat. Dalya pushed open the door and shoved Alcaeus inside.

One of her Sanctified Suns stood over a trap door.

"You really think all of your predecessors were good family men who never needed a discreet way to wet their cocks?" Dalya asked as she shut the door behind them. "Let's go."

Dalya brushed past Alcaeus and climbed the ladder down into the tunnel quickly. After a moment's hesitation, Alcaeus followed her. Dalya had the only torch. The smoke mingling with the dust kicked up by their shoes made it difficult to see. He wasn't a fan of tight spaces. The more he thought of how old the dirt passage they were walking through was, the more he had to fight panic in his chest. Roots pulled at his black ghutrah. Small clods of dirt worked their way between his feet and his sandals, but he didn't dare stop. Minutes ago, he'd been in prayer and reflection. Now he'd abandoned the temple and was running away beneath it. He was trusting a woman—whose sanity was perhaps questionable—to have taken care of organizing everything he'd need to go wherever she was sneaking him away to. Reality had yet to sink in.

The tunnel grew lighter, and Alcaeus saw a ladder. Dalya reached it first, handing the torch up to someone above before she climbed up. Alcaeus followed her quickly, relieved to be back out in the open. Without thinking, he took a deep breath, then promptly coughed. The air was thick, stinking of perfume, sweat, and seed. Cheap curtains were hung over ropes for makeshift walls, not that they muffled the sounds of the patrons on the other side at all. His dumbstruck moment made Dalya laugh.

"Ah, Mawla, a man from outside of the world. Come on, someone else can educate you later. We have to go."

"Where?" Alcaeus demanded as he brushed aside a thin purple curtain to follow Dalya. A group of men and women were waiting near the door. All were dressed plainly, but all wore pendants that matched Dalya's. All were armed to the teeth.

"Tanga, eventually."

"Is Rabb Khamisi joining us?" Alcaeus asked, realizing the legate wasn't with them.

Dalya shrugged. "I've sent men for him, but I've ordered my Suns to place escape as their highest priority. I don't have the time to train replacements if they die. Rabb Khamisi is more expendable than any one of them. He's only a legate."

"Rabb Khamisi has been devoted to our cause, and a great help."

"Then I sincerely hope he finds his way to the garden shed before Merikh makes it through the gate," Dalya said. She gestured to Alcaeus's ghutrah. "You should cover your face. I can't make any promises about what we're going to encounter out there. Do you have a dagger?"

"Of course not," Alcaeus said, mortified at the suggestion. A priest with a knife! The world was not that far gone.

Alcaeus pulled a pin out of his pocket and tied the ghutrah across his face. His blue eyes were still quite plain to see, if anyone looked. Dalya took a scarf from one of her Sanctified Suns and covered her face. Even behind her veil, he could see the wolfish pleasure when she opened the door to the chaos outside. The attack on the temple had galvanized the Faithful in Madiar to riot. Alcaeus recognized the Hock District as they stepped out of the brothel. He could hear explosions, shouts, and screams. The air had the faint smell of sulfur.

Smoke grenades, Alcaeus realized. Dalya grabbed Alcaeus's arm and pulled him down an alley.

"Whatever you do, stay close to me," she ordered.

This is too easy, Merikh thought. He saw Amir Olumide and Duq Hasad splitting off into the Temple District to gain control. The doors to the temple itself were flung open, not barricaded. Merikh let out a frustrated noise.

"Alcaeus is gone."

"Are you certain, Shahanshah?" Captain Bashir asked with a frown.

"The defense has fallen all too easily. They found a way out that we didn't."

Merikh pushed Zahira forward through the soldiers. Sardar General Harith led the main column and was startled by Merikh's approach.

"Shahanshah?"

"Get your men out to the gates, through the Hock. Alcaeus isn't here. The stones aren't here. Find him before he finds a means out of the city. I want his head."

Harith nodded once before barking out orders to his men to regroup. Spikes of ice shot from the ground around Merikh in a protective half wall as he surveyed the battle around him. If it could be called that. The Royal and Attar guards were barely fighting anymore. Most of the Onyx Swords had surrendered and were being disarmed. A few decided to martyr themselves on Royal Guard spears. Duq Hasad dismounted and was fighting an older-looking soldier.

Merikh smiled slightly. The young duq had found the biggest prize on the field. High Inquisitor Adunbi Bah. To Merikh's surprise, despite the duq's nerves, he was holding his own quite well. But the inquisitor was better. If left alone, Merikh doubted Hasad was long for this world. With a thought, ice formed under the inquisitor's kameez along his skin. A thousand pinpricks of ice shot into his spine just as Hasad swung his sword. The shamshir connected and cut through the leather armor. Merikh let go of the ice as Adunbi fell to his knees in pain. The high inquisitor dropped his sword in surrender.

Amir Olumide beamed with pride as he rode over to his son. The high inquisitor was captured. Royal Guards were walking out of the temple with the priests and priestesses who had been unable—or perhaps unwilling—to flee. Among them was Rabb Khamisi. The legate appeared to have surrendered quite peacefully. His kaftan was undamaged, and there was no blood on him. Undoubtedly, he hoped to be held for ransom or treated as a bargaining chip.

Merikh had no intention of letting him off so comfortably.

"Is the temple clear?" Merikh asked the guard at the head of the prisoners.

"It is, Shahanshah."

The ice disappeared from around Merikh. He glanced toward the mortoha wandering the yard. Merikh could hear fighting going on in the Hock District, the smoke from sulfur grenades filling the sky. With a thought, Merikh sent the mortoha out into the district. Without Merikh's supervision, the creatures would turn on anyone they saw. They were easy enough to kill; his guards would do so. But Merikh impressed upon the creatures the two strongest desires for their hunger—the yellow kaftans of the Onyx Swords and blue eyes.

Alcaeus hadn't realized how convoluted the Hock had become. Last time he'd ridden through it had been before the Royal Guard put barricades up everywhere. To Alcaeus's dismay, even Dalya looked frustrated.

"My map was outdated, apparently," she muttered through gritted teeth as they encountered yet another barricade. "We need to get near the Sunset Gate."

Dalya prodded the barricade with the back end of her katar dagger, as if trying to test whether she could easily climb it or perhaps break it.

"Inquisitor."

It was one of the Sanctified Suns. Dalya and Alcaeus turned around to see crimson guards standing at the mouth of the road. At the use of Dalya's title, the Royal Guards seemed to stand a little taller, then readied their swords and shields. Dalya muttered something under her breath as she stepped in front of Alcaeus.

"Push them back. You know where to go," Dalya ordered loudly. "Defend the faith! Purify yourselves in their blood."

Alcaeus felt his heart sink as the Royal Guards approached. He knew they trained harder than the average guard, particularly in Madiar. Most were trained from childhood. But Dalya's Sanctified Suns hardly shied away from them. Instead, as swords met shields, Alcaeus was shocked to see Dalya's men holding their ground. They even managed to push back on the Royal Guards. Dalya had no patience for his gawking and grabbed his arm. There was a narrow gap in the Royal Guards near the wall. Dalya pulled her shamshir, put herself between Alcaeus and the Royal Guards, and cut down the guard who saw them trying to get past.

Once behind the guards, Dalya grabbed Alcaeus again and shoved him ahead of her.

"My men will find us. Run," she said as she sheathed her sword.

They took off down the road, now able to hide in the chaos. Dalya directed their path, slowing back to a walk once they were far enough from her men. Alcaeus's lungs burned. The sulfur and smoke was carried on the breeze. Alcaeus couldn't tell if it was from the temple or the districts.

"This is insane," Alcaeus said hesitantly as they encountered another barricade.

"And it's just getting started, Mawla," Dalya said with a smile. "This is war, and this is all long overdue. You should feel honored that Merikh's willing to tear apart his beloved city to find you."

"We're never getting out of here," Alcaeus breathed.

Dalya rolled her eyes. "I have a man waiting to transport us out of the city. Paid good money for it, too. I'm not wasting it. Or giving the necromancer the pleasure of watching us die. Besides, I think I recognize this area."

Dalya waved for him to follow, and they walked down a poor road. Alcaeus glanced behind them and cursed under his breath when he saw Royal Guards. Dalya looked over her shoulder casually, then walked up to the nearest door. The houses were all adobe mud, the doors flimsily attached. The door Dalya chose yielded easily with one solid shove. Alcaeus followed her inside. Dalya grabbed the nearest object, a large clay vase, and propped it up against the door. The guards hadn't appeared to be following them; their posture hadn't shown knowing intention. Dalya had her hand on her shamshir just in case. Alcaeus, on the other hand, took a moment to study the room and realized they weren't alone.

"Apologies," Alcaeus whispered. The adobe home was simply one large room with a cooking oven in the corner. Near it was a woman huddled on the ground, a fearful child under each arm. Dalya shushed him unnecessarily, then realized what he saw.

"Stay quiet," Dalya hissed.

Alcaeus unpinned his ghutrah and approached them slowly.

"Do you know who I am?" he asked gently.

The woman nodded quickly, then gestured toward the hearth. Above it was an Akhenic Sun affixed to the wall. A makeshift altar sat beside the hearth. The statue of Akhenios that should have been on the hearth was instead clutched tightly in the hands of the young girl clinging to her mother. The young boy relaxed a little upon seeing Alcaeus's face.

"Mawla, we need to leave," Dalya said. She crossed the room to the back door.

"Inquisitor, stop. We can wait a moment."

Dalya let out a frustrated growl. Alcaeus raised his hand.

"Make time. You're lost, we don't know where the barricades are." Alcaeus sat down on the floor in front of the woman. "What's your name?'

"M-Mirza Amin," the woman whispered. "What's going on out there?"

"Mirza, the Shah attacked the temple. The city is in chaos. Don't leave your house. Where's your husband?" Alcaeus asked.

She shook her head. "I don't have one."

"Okay, good. You have no reason to leave here, then, correct?" Alcaeus asked. She nodded, and he smiled. "Can you explain to my inquisitor how best to get to the Sunset Gate from here?"

"Oh!" the boy exclaimed. Dalya shot him a venomous look, and he shied a little. "The rooftops."

"Lovely. We'll get shot in the gut by one of Merikh's archers. Try again," Dalya said harshly. Alcaeus shot her a look, and Dalya sighed heavily. She left the door and walked toward Mirza.

"How do we get out of here?"

It took longer than Alcaeus had wanted for Dalya to memorize the directions. She paced the room, repeating the turns and the landmarks back to Mirza. Once Dalya was certain she knew where she was going, she headed to the door. Alcaeus stood from the floor and placed a hand on Mirza's head.

"Blessings of the Great Prophet be upon you and your children. May his shield protect you from harm, may the light of Aljemel guide your way through the coming darkness."

"Mawla, we have a problem. Maybe a major problem."

For the first time, Dalya sounded unnerved. Alcaeus smiled reassuringly at Mirza before he joined Dalya. She'd moved to the window and drawn back the curtain just a touch. Alcaeus looked out and froze.

"But the stones—"

"You know, I haven't had the chance to see what sort of scale they act on," Dalya whispered. "We know they'll take down a sorcerer. I just don't know if they'll take down their creations without the necromancer being nearby. And I don't see our golden-eyed boy out there, do you?" She was right, Alcaeus couldn't see Merikh.

What he could see was a horde of mortoha shambling down the road. They let the curtain fall back into place. The window had no glass, the door was flimsy. They could hear the ungodly sounds of mortoha shrieking and rushing after prey, followed by soul-chilling screams.

"Being eaten alive isn't high on my list of ways to die," Dalya muttered again. "If they catch wind of us in here, they'll fall against the door until they make it through. Or one might get smart and crawl in through the window."

The blood had drained from Mirza's face. She held her children close, and Alcaeus could see the younger one crying quietly.

"Don't worry," Alcaeus said quietly with a reassuring smile. "Inquisitor Dalya is one of the best in Shai'Khal. She'll get us through this."

"Well, isn't that sweet of you, Mawla." Dalya smiled, then gestured to the boy. "I need your help."

The boy rose from his mother's side and approached Dalya warily. She stood by the door, and he could undoubtedly hear the creatures outside. Dalya crouched down to his level, pulled her pendant off, and placed it over his head.

"How old are you?" she asked.

"I don't know," he said plainly.

Dalya shrugged. To Alcaeus, it looked like the boy was under ten. Dalya smiled, stood up, and placed her hand on the boy's shoulder.

"Dalya…"

Alcaeus warned too late. Dalya opened the door and shoved the boy outside. She slammed the door behind him. His fists beat against the door. Mirza leapt to her feet, and Dalya drew her shamshir.

"Patience, please. Your son is probably fine. And if he's not, then save your grief and point your anger at the man controlling the beasts out there."

Alcaeus walked up to Dalya, honestly a little surprised when he wasn't met by her shamshir. He shoved her out of his way and opened the door. The young boy clambered inside and immediately threw off the pendant. As Alcaeus shut the door, he saw the pile of corpses that had descended on the boy. The pendant had broken the curse—the corpses were lying there unmoving.

"You had no idea he would live!" Alcaeus snapped at Dalya.

She smiled. "You blessed him, Mawla. Akhenios blessed those pendants. Of course he lived. And so will we." Dalya leaned down and picked up the pendant. Alcaeus gaped at her in silence for a moment.

"If you leave us, those things will come here, won't they? We'll die," Mirza said.

"No, you'll be fine. They'll follow us and then die," Dalya said. Her tone was unconvincing.

Alcaeus looked at Dalya as he crossed the room back to Mirza. He took her hand as he pulled the pendant off his neck and placed it in her palm.

"Mawla!" Dalya exclaimed. "Those are limited. We—"

"Be silent, Inquisitor. Your one stone will be plenty enough for us. Mirza, be careful who sees this," Alcaeus said.

Mirza gripped the pendant in her hand tightly. Alcaeus heard Dalya swear under her breath before she shoved open the door.

"Come on, Mawla, we have to leave." Her tone lacked all of the amusement and innocence from before. Now she was simply irritated. Alcaeus bowed his head to Mirza, placed his hand on her shoulder briefly, then followed Dalya out into the horde.

Alcaeus's skin crawled as the mortoha came rushing at them in a hideous torrent of flailing limbs and inhuman snarls. Alcaeus had seen illustrations of these creatures before in books, but these creatures had none of the decay those pictures had shown. These men and women were...fresh. They looked human still, save for the mortal blows and strangely twisted limbs. A few bore the yellow kaftans of the Onyx Swords. The temple had fallen.

A hand reached out and snagged Alcaeus's sleeve. The weight of the corpse as it lost the curse tore Alcaeus's sleeve, and he tripped. Dalya caught him before he fell into the hungry arms of a mortoha rushing toward him.

"Keep close, Mawla," Dalya said, grabbing his hand as the mortoha collapsed, unmoving, in front of them. "I don't know what the range is."

Alcaeus nodded. His hands were shaking, his feet unsteady as he walked with her. The horde followed, and they left a trail of dead corpses in their wake. Dalya navigated them through the corpses that fell ahead of them. Alcaeus tried not to think about what he was stepping on or over, his heart pounding.

The mortoha suddenly thinned, inhuman cries screeching from their mouths. Alcaeus craned to see, and his heart stopped. There was a group of men and women fighting, likely Faithful against cultists or Royalists. The horde overwhelmed them. Alcaeus froze in place at the screams. The sound of flesh and cloth tearing underscored the cries of pain.

"Dalya, we can help—"

"I swear to Akhenios, Mawla, you don't have a lick of common sense." Dalya pulled him down a different road, away from the distracted horde, following Mirza's instructions.

"I'm supposed to help people," Alcaeus said numbly, "not get them killed."

Dalya turned and grabbed the front of Alcaeus's kameez. She gave him a short, frustrated shake.

"You are supposed to *lead*. We" —she gestured herself and then back down the road toward the horde and its victims—"are supposed to die for you. But I refuse to let my life be simply thrown away for no fucking reason. Remember those people. Mirza and her brats. Merikh will pay for his crimes. Now will you let me save your life or not?"

Alcaeus nodded.

"Good."

Dalya let go of him and began walking down the road. Alcaeus followed her silently, relieved as they encountered no barricades or Royal Guards. Luck, it seemed, was finally on their side. They turned down an alley, and at the end stood a tall man. Beside him was a pair of donkeys attached to a wagon. If Dalya had been looking for an inconspicuous exit, this man was not it. Everything about him screamed thief or criminal of some sort. He was the tallest Yahidah Alcaeus had ever seen, with shaggy black and gray hair. An eyepatch covered one eye, and a long scar traced down from eye to chin. He was dressed in a shade of green just barely too bright to be House Afolayan. The wagon was painted to match him, and a tawny pigeon was painted on the side. Whoever he was, he had a bone to pick with the Afolayans. As they approached, the man bowed with a flourish.

"Lovely to see you again, Inquisitor. I presume this is the high priest?"

Alcaeus nodded before he asked, "Who are you?"

"Bishan Choundhry, at your service. Are you ready?"

"For what?" Alcaeus eyed the wagon suspiciously.

"Your inquisitor has paid me barely enough to get you out of Madiar. This"—he patted the wagon—"is your carriage."

Alcaeus approached the wagon. As he did so, the smell of rot hit him hard. He covered his mouth, pressing the ghutrah against his nose as best he could and tried not to breathe. Dalya stepped up to the wagon and wrinkled her nose in disgust.

"You're going to ferry the high priest out of Madiar in a refuse wagon?"

Bishan smiled brightly before he kicked the pigeon on the side of the wagon. A false bottom popped down from the wagon, big enough for three people to lie down on.

"It rises up so you can't be seen, but you won't get any of the, uh, *juices* on you."

Dalya glared at Bishan, seeming to consider whether such transport was worth it or if she just wanted to add Bishan's bowels to the refuse. Alcaeus chose for her. He carefully slid on his stomach into the compartment. He heard Dalya mumble something to Bishan before she slid in beside him. They heard Bishan kick again, and the compartment slowly rose into the wagon. The smell made Alcaeus want to vomit. He barely managed to hold it in as the donkeys began to move and the wagon rocked back and forth. The smell was bad, but the wet squelching sound above them was even more unbearable.

The wagon stopped.

"Bayim, what's this? The gate is closed, by order of the Shah," Alcaeus heard someone say, presumably a guard.

"I'm paid to remove this, see?" Bishan said. Alcaeus thought he heard rustling papers. "Got the permits to get this out regardless."

"No one is leaving until I get word from the palace to open this gate."

"All right, but I've got more of this shit to move. I'll dump it here and fetch another load. Might as well put this time to good use if I can't leave the city."

Alcaeus couldn't hear what the guard said back, but a moment later he heard the groaning of stone gates. *Thank the Great Prophet,* Alcaeus prayed silently. He had no desire to be stuck in this wagon while Bishan took loads back and forth if he'd ended up following through on that promise. Alcaeus had to give the smuggler credit. No one wanted this to hang around the city and bake in the heat. As much as Alcaeus felt like he was going to be sick, at least he wasn't going to die.

The wagon stopped again. This time, they heard Bishan kick the pigeon. The platform dropped quickly, and Alcaeus scrambled out from under it. Dalya crawled out the other side, closest to Bishan. The older man smiled disarmingly before he gestured back behind the wagon down the road. In the distance, Alcaeus could see the shimmering walls of the white city, the plumes of black and yellow smoke billowing from her.

"Pity, she's a beautiful city," Bishan lamented.

Alcaeus felt his heart sink. Madiar *was* a beautiful city. He'd spent most of his life within her walls. It pained him to see his city turned into a beacon of depravity.

"She'll be restored to her former glory again soon enough," Alcaeus promised, mostly to himself. His words made Bishan laugh before he walked over to Dalya for his payment.

"You'll go back for my men. They have the rest of it," Dalya explained when Bishan pointed out the purse was light. He nodded before he bowed his head to Alcaeus and then headed back to his cart. As the cart began to rattle off down the road, Dalya began walking toward a fork in the path. Alcaeus followed her, and half a mile down the road, they found a dozen horses tied and a Sanctified Sun guarding them.

"Soleb is three days from here, give or take, depending on how hard we can push and how many Royal Guard we have on our tail. Ready?" Dalya asked, handing Alcaeus his horse. He nodded.

"To Soleb."

CHAPTER 46

Merikh rode Zahira to the stairs of the temple, then dismounted. She could have easily handled the stairs, but Merikh decided against making his reputation as a blasphemous heretic any worse. It had been years since Merikh had entered the temple. The last time, he'd followed Mansur. They'd stopped at the ablution fountain and then gone in front of the altar. They'd bowed in supplication before a god Mansur feared and Merikh had never been certain existed. Ruya's memories had given him proof of a powerful being. Perhaps divinity.

But today, Merikh passed the ablution fountain without cleansing. Without removing his shoes, he approached the altar. Merikh hesitated for a moment in front of the large statue of Akhenios before he walked around the altar. There was a small door in the wall behind it that led to the inner sanctum. He pushed it open with no resistance, holding his magic at the ready in case the guards had been wrong about clearing the entire temple. They hadn't.

The inner sanctum was small. There was another ablution fountain, prayer mats, and a large statue of Akhenios in the center. Unlike the main sanctum, there were rows of bookcases along the east wall. Long sticks of incense were stored beside the altar. It was clearly a place of quiet contemplation, a holy place meant for the high priest and few others. Even a Faithful shah wouldn't have been welcome here.

Merikh approached the back wall, remembering clearly where Ruya had gone in her memory. There had been stairs leading down into the catacombs. Now there was a tapestry of the Great Prophet over solid alabaster. Merikh tore the tapestry down, the wooden rod clattering dully to the floor. He ran his hand over the stone. Water flowed over the cracks, seeping in. When it rapidly froze, the stone cracked. A little green fog wore the pieces to dust.

A chill shuddered down Merikh's spine, much the same as when he'd first felt Ruya and Sarka's auras. In the darkness before him, there was exceptional danger. The draft of centuries-old air passed over Merikh, a smell of sickeningly sweet rot. Ruya had warned him about this.

It will kill you. He heard her voice in his head.

Merikh turned away back to the altar. He grabbed a candlestick from it and used one of the nearby matches to light it. An orb of ice hung above it, just outside of the heat column, refracting the light and illuminating the dark stairwell as Merikh approached. It was covered in cobwebs. Spiders and scorpions scurried away from the light. With a thought, Merikh cleared the cobwebs to the side before descending into the catacombs.

The air was thick. As Merikh reached the bottom of the stairs, an unnatural draft flickered the candlelight. The magic here was heavy, oppressive, and full of a dread that Merikh knew well. Blighted necromantic magic festered upon the catacombs. The stone might have been white at one point, but black veins of necrotic rot covered the stone like vines or cobwebs. The barrier between Alhanem and Cala was thin here. Merikh stayed in the middle of the path, glad the ceiling was just high enough that he didn't need to crouch. He was careful not to touch the rot. His footfalls echoed in the cramped hall. It would be only a matter of time before whatever guardians Ruya had put in place here would find him. Merikh kept his shamshir in its sheath. Pale fog wrapped Merikh's hand instead. The sword would be of no use in such close quarters.

Ghostly whispers began to tug at his mind.

Leave.

It's not safe here.

A ghostly wail interrupted the begging.

Leave us, Merikh.

These weren't ghosts, Merikh realized. They were djinnic whispers, the temptations that whispered at one's mind when they opened portals to Alhanem. The barrier between the living and the dead was *very* thin here.

Go home. Go back to the warmth of daylight above, of the palace. Back to the pleasures of the living. Leave.

Merikh continued through the catacombs.

Go back to Loralee. Leave now and you'll see her again. Think of the softness of her skin, how good her body feels—

Merikh smirked. Of all the things to appeal to, his base desires would do them little good. They weren't wrong—he had every desire to see Loralee again—but she was miles away, and his ambition was a greater hunger. Loralee had bought him this opportunity; Merikh wasn't going to waste it. He pressed on, working harder to quiet the voices in his mind and push them away.

The voices were silenced. Then, deafening screams filled the catacombs. Angry ghosts appeared all around him in pale pale-green fog. They clawed at him, but Merikh had been banishing ghosts since he was a small boy. The first time, he'd needed a scroll to help him focus the spell. Now, Merikh brushed the fog off his shoulders and simply refocused it around the ghosts. They were bound here by Ruya's will, and that manifested itself as rune down the corridor from him. Ice shattered the lines, and the first guardians disappeared. They had been here to spook away the skittish or drive them insane. That and to ensure the second guardians would wake. No one used ghosts and djinnic whispers as their only line of defense. In the quiet left behind, Merikh could hear the next guardians coming.

There was the telltale sound of useless limbs dragging across stone. Unearthly guttural snarls of mortoha echoed off the walls. Sounds that set off the instinct to run. An instinct Merikh had learned to quiet but not disregard. Merikh had no desire to meet a horde of them in such close quarters. Human teeth, after all, were not particularly efficient when it came to killing. With all the blight around him, Merikh couldn't feel the difference between the rot on the wall and the mortoha approaching. Merikh focused on the ground behind him. Ice formed into an ice scorpion the size of a dog. It followed a few feet behind him, keeping Merikh safe from a mortoha ambush. At the very least, it would warn him about the first wave.

He didn't have to wait long for the ice scorpion to explode behind him. Merikh threw a wall of ice up where the scorpion had been. Pale-green fog leapt from his fingertips and through the wall toward the creatures behind him. Their snarls were muffled by the ice. As was the thud of the corpses as the curse dissipated.

In the darkness ahead of Merikh, he began to make out the shambling forms of desiccated mortoha. These dried, rotten remains of venerated priests and priestess bore little resemblance to the freshly dead mortoha Merikh occasionally discovered in the desmoterion or personally created. But their bite was no less dangerous, their bony hands resembling claws better than the fresh ones. Even to a necromancer, the cursed bite could still kill.

Ice shards wrapped in necrotic fog shot through the horde scrambling toward him. Merikh drew spikes from the ground, encasing the mortohas as fog drew out the curse and left the sinuous sacks of bones calm. Merikh hesitated for a moment. He bent down and picked up a loose fragment of stone and tossed it. The stone bounced off the ground in the center of the seemingly dead horde. No reaction. Merikh never crossed through a mass of corpses unless he was confident one wasn't going to grab him. He carefully found his way through the corpses, emerging on the other side of the hallway in time for another horde to find him. Necrotic ice spikes tore through them. He tested for movement again and saw none. Merikh continued down the hall, through the dead.

A hand caught his foot. Teeth closed on Merikh's boot as he fell into a pile of rotted bones. Ice shot from Merikh's hand and shattered the skull. Ice coated his limbs as he felt another hand reaching. He'd missed the movements of the bodies that had been split in half and missed by the necrotic fog. Fog exploded from his hands along the ground, turning the remaining mortoha crawling at him to dust. Merikh scrambled to his feet and carefully checked his leg, his heart pounding in his chest. Fog was readied at his fingertips to draw out the curse, if necessary. How powerful Ruya's curse might be, Merikh didn't know.

It will kill you, echoed in his mind once again.

A deep sigh of relief left Merikh as he saw his boot was still perfectly intact. Broken teeth were embedded in the leather, but none had pierced it. Luck was on his side, if only for the moment. He heard no more shuffling, no more snarls as he walked through the catacombs. Past the bend in the hall was a large room. Green fog poured out of it in gentle waves, but it bore no rot. The wrongness of the crypt that once pressed upon Merikh the need to leave had changed. Now there was a gentle push on the edges of his mind to go forward.

A seductive pull toward the large ossuary in the center. Merikh approached it cautiously. He placed the candle on the ground and put a wall of ice over the entrance to the room. If there were more mortoha, he didn't want them to ambush him while he dealt with whatever protections Ruya had put in place here.

Long fingers brushed dust from the top of the ossuary. Merikh ran his hands along the edge, finding the best spot to push the stone slab free. After a moment of exertion, it fell rapidly to the ground on the other side. He flinched at the painful echo. If there were any other creatures left that hadn't known he was here, they certainly would now. Merikh leaned over the ossuary to look inside.

The grimoire had deep symbols carved into black leather. A heavy lock clasped it shut, and the power from it took Merikh's breath away. Not even Ruya or Sarka's auras matched this. The book was on an entirely different level than anything Merikh had ever encountered before. For a fleeting moment, he wondered if he'd bitten off more than he could chew. But it didn't matter anymore. The unanswered what-ifs would haunt him for the rest of his days if he left now. Merikh reached down and carefully picked the book up with both hands.

His cries echoed off the crypt's walls. Merikh's knees gave out. He collapsed beside the ossuary, the book firm in his hands as he rapidly aged. He was all too familiar with this curse. Merikh's black hair turned gray, his hands became veined and spotted.

No! Merikh pushed back against the curse with every ounce of strength and magic he had. He refused to be brought down by a book. He'd made a promise he intended to keep.

The world went black.

"He's a problematic soul."

The world was still dark, the pain still excruciating. But the words rang clear with the distinct feeling that he was in a memory. Merikh didn't recognize the man's voice.

"Pull it from the cycle, then, if he worries you so." Another voice, but this time Merikh recognized it. Ruya.

"I've tried for nothing more than what you've already achieved! Be merciful!" Another male voice. His words were terrified. Full of panic, desperation, and pain. That voice Merikh was certain he knew, but it confused him most.

How had his *father* spoken to Ruya? What cycle were they talking about? What had Mansur done? His voice was...thinner. It wasn't as deep as Merikh remembered it. There was something off about it, unfamiliar yet familiar. Of course, if he'd been tortured, that would account for it.

Merikh fought against the curse. He wanted answers, damn it! How had his father managed to do anything that might somehow garner the attention of Ruya and the other man? Mansur had been dead by the time Ruya and Sarka had landed on Shai'Khal's shores, hadn't he? Had they arrived earlier than Nikias had discovered? Just how long had they been undermining the Akhenic faith?

The world around Merikh began to feel warm. Comfortable, even. Merikh began to instinctively relax...

No! He tried to focus on the crypt around him. The catacombs were cold. There was stone beneath his feet. Faint candlelight. And he was *not* comfortable. In fact, there was supposed to be excruciating amounts of pain. Merikh refused to pass to Aljemel, if that was indeed his soul's final resting place.

A moment later, the memory or delusion faded. Light ebbed into his vision again. Everything was out of focus. He lay on the ground, his legs too weak to hold him. As he slowly felt strength return to his limbs, Merikh stretched out one hand to grip the ossuary; the other clutched the grimoire to his chest. He climbed to his feet as the world began to come back into focus. His hair turned black, his back ached less, and his hands grew young and strong again. As he straightened up, Merikh froze. The ice blocking the entrance was gone. And before him stood the last guardian.

It was the largest striped hyena Merikh had ever laid eyes on. It was easily the size of a small horse or donkey. Its face was nearly as large as that of the black bears he'd seen in the north. A long mane of hair stretched from its crown down to its tail. Large bat-like ears were perked forward, and dark-green eyes stared intelligently, warily, into his. The creature walked slowly toward

Merikh, closing the gap between them, sniffing the air. Merikh stumbled back a step as if knocked back by wind. There was no breeze. Just the creature's mind pushing against his. It wasn't truly telepathic, but the animal was clearly powerful. It pushed its feelings onto Merikh. She was confused, afraid, wary, and desperately lonely.

You're safe, Merikh tried to impress upon her. The striped hyena cocked her head to the side, her lips curling into a soundless warning. As she stood in the pool of light from the candle, the fur nearly shimmered. The black stripes almost absorbed the light, whereas the pale white was nearly opalescent. She was no ordinary hyena, clearly, but Merikh let out a surprised breath as realization hit him. She wasn't just some magical monstrosity either. No, he recalled the small statues of Ikharon that had begun popping up around Madiar. Statues of a tall man with a snake coiled around his arm and a hyena lying at his feet. The creature before Merikh was Ikharon's devata. The god of death's devoted protector. His pet.

His spy.

And she'd been left behind for nearly a thousand years to protect the one thing Ikharon held dearest. Merikh raised his hand off the ossuary. The gesture earned him a short, warbled growl.

"It's been far too long," Merikh said cryptically, his tone calm and holding the same warmth he spoke to Zahira with. Far too long since this creature had seen daylight. If the creature were intelligent enough to understand human speech, then Merikh hoped the familiarity might cause her to confuse him for Ikharon, or perhaps one of his old priests. As long as it worked, Merikh didn't care what the creature thought.

The hyena took another step closer and rubbed its head under Merikh's outstretched hand. He let out a small sigh of relief and rubbed his hand behind the hyena's ears and down her neck. Merikh then walked past her, picked up the candle, and headed toward the archway.

"Are you coming?" he asked, glancing back toward her. The devata cast one last long look at the ossuary, then looked toward the grimoire in Merikh's hand. She followed alongside him as they walked back through the crypt. Her presence seemed to be enough to avoid any more creatures that might emerge from the darkness.

The hyena hesitated at the base of the stairs. She'd spent nine hundred years in the dark. The light would be harsh on her eyes. Merikh put the candle down, afraid to let go of the grimoire around all this necrotic rot. He pulled out his khanjar. Using the curved blade, he cut off a section of his kameez sleeve. The crimson fabric was long enough to wrap over the hyena's eyes, thick enough to give her an appreciable amount of shade from the light. Merikh snuffed out the candle, leaving it behind as he placed a hand on the hyena's shoulder and helped guide the creature up the stairs.

The inner sanctum was still empty when Merikh emerged, but as he left it to enter the main sanctum, the world around them froze. The soldiers all looked varying levels of spooked at the massive hyena walking alongside their shah. The astute would have seen mortoha teeth still stuck in the ankle of his boot and the book under his arm. Merikh ignored them, guiding the hyena with him outside of the sanctum. The nerves and worry from the creature were amplified, pressing on him for reassurance. The calm confidence it was met with was reassurance enough.

As they left the temple, the devata shied away from the light for a moment. Merikh almost didn't notice, as at the same time Zahira let out a squeal and spooked sideways away from the stairs. His hand dropped away from the hyena, and he took the stairs quickly but calmly toward his horse.

"Easy, mare," Merikh reassured her as he placed his hand on her rein, then along her neck. "You're fine."

The warhorse begged to differ, her eyes wide and white. There was the loud sound of the creature shaking, and the devata pawed the blindfold off her face. It blinked, almost sleepily, before squinting and walking toward Merikh. As it made it to the bottom of the stairs, Zahira let out another squeal, this time out of protectiveness, not fear. The mare pushed Merikh aside as she turned, her back hooves flying toward the hyena's skull.

A sharp correction burst from Merikh's lips as he smacked the mare's flank, and both horse and hyena sulked to opposite sides of the Shah. The hyena stayed a respectful distance from Zahira when Merikh mounted his horse, though the mare kept tensing as if wanting to kick the creature and then thinking better of it.

"What in Alhanem is that?" Amir Olumide exclaimed as Merikh rode to him and Duq Hasad.

"Ikharon's devata," Merikh answered, as if it were as plain as day. He ignored the looks around him and pulled the grimoire from under his arm. He could hear fighting throughout the Hock District.

Surely there is something within these pages that might be of use? Merikh thought as he opened the grimoire. As if by his intention, the book fell open to the perfect page. Merikh glanced over it quickly. There were spells, different enchantments, and—perhaps most usefully—notes from Ikharon himself. The grimoire wasn't merely a spell book. It contained the thoughts and conclusions of the god of death. And what Merikh found on the page he opened almost made him giddy.

"Will you join me, Amir Olumide?" Merikh asked, his tone almost improperly pleasant given the dead bodies strewn about the temple yard.

"Of course, Shahanshah," Amir Olumide said. "Duq, oversee the proper treatment of the prisoners. Help the Sardar general."

Merikh signaled for the Ajir, who formed up around him and the devata unquestioningly. They passed the Royal Guards holding the Temple District Gate and headed toward the sound of swords and screams.

The Hock District burned. Attar and Royal Guards were fighting hard at the Mitbah Gate when Merikh arrived. His arrival brought renewed vigor to his guards, which made them all the more confused when Merikh rode forward through them. The brazen action and the massive hyena at his side pushed back the attacking Onyx Swords and Faithful. The fighting stopped for a moment.

"If you wish to survive, then you should flee. Clemency will be granted to those who drop their weapons."

The devata caught sight of an Onyx Sword uniform and snapped its jaws toward the man, a strange snarl coming from deep within its throat. A stone whizzed past Merikh's ear. He glanced down at the grimoire and then back to the crowd. He focused his magic and narrowed in on the feeling of the souls around him.

Fog appeared before Zahira and washed over the men and women who were rushing at him. Their bodies hit the fog, then the ground. Their corpses were bones before they were within five feet of the warhorse, their souls ripped from them into the fog. Each time the fog overwhelmed more of the attackers, Merikh expected to feel more fatigued. But instead, the fog grew stronger, and so did Merikh. He felt alive when he should have felt exhausted.

He felt more powerful than he ever had before.

With a thought, Merikh made the fog disappear. The corpses rose to their feet as mortoha. The creatures rushed their former allies. Hail wrapped in pale-green fog burst from the sky. Screams filled the air as the icy stones hit people. It began to cover the ground like snow.

Merikh exhaled, letting go of his magic—except for the mortoha. He allowed those to join the ranks of the others hunting down Onyx Swords. Now and only now did Merikh become conscious of a slight weariness. The sort of sluggishness one felt after overeating.

"Shahanshah…" Olumide barely dared to breathe the word. Doing so snapped Merikh back to reality.

For the first time, he saw the true extent of his magic. It hadn't simply affected the people in front of him. The nearby buildings were buckling under their weight. The stone and wooden supports were rotted and cracked, turning to dust. Whatever the fog had touched, it died. The people hit by the necrotic hail had turned to piles of dust, already being blown away by the wind. Merikh glanced to his right and saw necrotic rot beginning to form on the nearest walls and on the cobblestones near Zahira's feet. The Mitbah Gate would be scarred with the same black corruption of the temple catacombs.

Another building collapsed farther down the road. More screams.

Merikh shook his head, unable to stop the smile and laugh as realization dawned on him. This was what Ruya had feared. Who needed favors from gods when he could take this? He had his payment now. Merikh turned Zahira back to the gate, stopping beside Amir Olumide. The older man was pale, his hands shaking on the reins. The amir watched over Merikh's shoulder as more buildings buckled.

"Amir, if you will? We have work to do."

A great deal of it.

EPILOGUE

The scrying stone turned black as Ikharon stepped away from it, the image of Merikh holding the grimoire fading.

"Is that as bad as I think it is?" Kyran asked, sitting on the ground nearby. The rakshasas picked gristle out of his fangs, all that remained of the last sailor to have shipwrecked on their island.

"It's no matter," Ikharon lied.

You should have left Sarka to attend to the Key, Ruya, Ikharon lamented. He'd been afraid of something like this. There was a reason the Akhenic Key was failing *now*, of all times. He hadn't recognized it at first. Nine hundred years had clouded his mind, but it was clearing.

Ikharon frowned.

"How do you feel, Kyran?"

"Stronger." The rakshasas stood up and wiped his bloody hands on the makeshift temple's wall.

"Did your brothers and sisters destroy that boat?" Ikharon asked.

Kyran shook his head. "Not yet."

"Don't. You'll need something to get you to Shai'Khal's shores. You have a shah to curtail."

523

APPENDICES

THE CAST

PERSPECTIVE

Merikh Madiaran: Shahanshah of Shai'Khal. Born to Shah Mansur and Khanum Aliyah (both deceased)
Loralee Neredi: Sayida of Abadan
Adrian Charmichi: Ajir Steward to Shah Merikh Madiaran.
Alcaeus Tawfeek: High Priest of Akhenios.
Sarka: Grand General of the Flaming Legion, Champion of Livinja.
Ruya: High Priestess of the Order of the Pale Eye, in service to Ikharon.

MINOR CHARACTERS

Navin Afolayan: Amir of Kuzen Province. Uncle to Shah Merikh Madiaran
Mahdi Afolayan: Rabb of Rohara. Uncle to Shah Merikh Madiaran.
Olumide Attar: Amir of Raudhah Province
Emilia Attar: Duqa of Rajibad
Rashad Attar: Duq of Rajibad, heir to Amir Olumide Attar
Hasad Attar: Duq of Rajibad
Adunbi Bah: High Inquisitor of the Onyx Swords
Salim Basara: Acolyte of the Order of the Pale Eye
Enitan Bhengani: Duqa of Tanga
Munashe Bhengani: Sayida of Tanga, heir to Duqa Enitan Bhenghani
Sachiko Himoto: Duqa of Kasu
Xolani Iherjirika: Amir of Ydeba Province
Adanna Iherjirika: Duqa of Ydeba, heir to Amir Xolani Iherjirika
Dalya Maki: Fari-Commander of the Onyx Swords, High Inquisitor of the Sanctified Suns
Jin Nakano: Amira of Kaitan Province
Alaziz Neredi: Duq of Abadan
Jasira Neredi: Duqa of Abadan
Rehema Sall: Kontess of Buhet

Khamisi Saqqaf: Legate to Duqa Enitan Bhengani, Rabb.
Nikias Soun: Grand Vizier to Shah Merikh Madiaran.
Maliha Zabat: Kontess of Dharipur

THE AKHENIC FAITH

Akhenios: God of the Akhenic faith, and the Sun God of the Pantheon.

PANTHEON GODS

Amanicus: genderless God of Logos
Amefi: genderless Goddess of Dreams
Ayurlyse: Goddess of Healing
Belara: Goddess of Wrath and Vengeance
Danai: Goddess Patron of Animals
Du'aniq: God of Peace
Hisahti: Goddess of Fertility and Childbirth
Houxipil: God of Storms
Ikharon: God of Death
Kamadhi: Goddess of Love
Kei: God of Luck
Keracelia: Goddess of Art and Imagination
Livinja: Goddess of War
Meriath: Goddess of the Ocean
Muraten: God of Wine and Pleasure
Nadlious: God of Justice and Order
Neharang: Goddess of Oasis and Rivers
Siorbos: God of Plants and the Harvest
Skyndar: genderless God of Chaos
Symin: God of Wealth
Vindaram: God of Air
Wesswa: God of Family
Yasu: Goddess of the Moon and Night

GLOSSARY

RACES

Yahidah: the ruling race of Shai'Khal. They are desert-folk with brown skin, generally black or brown hair with dark eyes.

<u>Tsukarai</u>: primarily from the north and coastal regions of Shai'Khal, their skin is fairer than the other races of Shai'Khal. They usually have straight, black hair.

<u>Umbeah</u>: the Umbeah are the tall, dark-skinned people of the western regions of Shai'Khal. They tend to have black hair, which will often be plaited or in dreadlocks.

<u>Emani</u>: they are the ostracized and stigmatized nomads of Shai'Khal. Not originally native to Shai'Khal, they have traits from each race.

<u>Aegalian</u>: the pale race from across the Aldruin.

<u>FACTIONS</u>

<u>Akhenic Faithful</u>: followers of god Akhenios who follow the teachings of the Akhenic Temple.

> <u>Priest Council</u>: the highest ranking priests of the Akhenic Temple who provide council to the High Priest.
>
> <u>The Order of the Onyx Swords</u>: the Akhenic Temple Guards who protect temples and help keep the peace in outlying villages. A primarily ceremonial position in big cities such as Madiar.
>
> > <u>The Sanctified Suns</u>: a fanatical offshoot of the Onyx Swords
>
> <u>Royalists</u>: a faction of the Akhenic Faithful who believe in a prophecy that another Great Prophet will come from the first Great Prophet's descendants, the Madiarans

<u>Royal Guard</u>: Shai'Khal's standing army, paid by the shah. During peacetime they keep roads clear of bandits, collect taxes, and help the provincial amirs' guards to keep the peace. Also known as the Red Guard because of their crimson uniforms

> <u>Ajir</u>: a subset of the Royal Guard, they trusted elite servants and guards of the shah. They are men and women with exceptional training and undying loyalty to the Madiaran family. Their uniforms always bear a silver scorpion on their breast.

<u>The Circle of Iron</u>: the priesthood of the god Nadlious

<u>The Flaming Legion</u>: the priesthood of the goddess Livinja

<u>The Opal Wings</u>: the priesthood of the god Vindaram

<u>The Order of the Pale Eye</u>: the priesthood of the god Ikharon

<u>The Waning Moons</u>: the priesthood of the goddess Yasu

<u>POLITICAL TITLES</u>

(In order of political power)

<u>Shahanshah</u>: the ruling monarch of Shai'Khal

<u>Khanum</u>: the consort of shah

<u>Shahzade</u>: the heir of the shah

<u>Amir/Amira</u>: the provincial governors, as well as the title given to the other children of the shah

<u>Duq/Duqa</u>: the spouses of amirs/amiras; governors of the cities Abadan, Kasu, Nashika, and Tanga

<u>Alkont/Alkontess</u>: governors of the cities Nabi, Shira, Metif, Al Haraf, Dharipur, Buhet, Kaidaku, and their spouses.

<u>Albarun/Baruna</u>: governors of the cities Bayaba, Chima, Agrah, Arashti, Dracton, Duak, Kabatwe, and their spouses.

<u>Rabb/Sayida</u>: governors of the cities Sek, Ogot, Luma, Sujin, Chamichi, Hatai, An Sheifa, Sayla, Rohara, Balaghi, and their spouses. The title granted to the children of Duqs, Alkonts, Albaruns, and Rabbs.

<u>Merchant Rabb/Sayida</u>: wealthy citizens who purchase their noble titles and renew them periodically. These titles do not pass along to spouses or children upon death.

<u>NOBLE HOUSES OF IMPORT</u>

<u>Madiaran</u>: the ruling house of Shai'Khal since the Unification War. Their colors are red and gold. The house sigil is two rearing horses facing each other, a crown and Akhenic Sun between them. They rule from the capital city of Madiar.

<u>Afolayan</u>: the family's important members are Amir Navin and his wife, Duqa Aminah. They govern Kuzen Province on behalf of the shah while residing in Ramshar. Their color is dark green. Their sigil is a perched tawny colored hawk.

<u>Attar</u>: the family consists of Amir Olumide, his wife Duqa Emilia, and their two sons Duq Rashad and Duq Hasad. They govern Raudhah Province on behalf of the shah while residing in Rajibad. Their colors are dark blue; their sigil is a snarling leopard in profile.

<u>Bhengani</u>: the important family members are Duqa Enitan and her daughter, Sayida Munashe. Duqa Enitan is supposed to govern the city of Tanga on behalf of the shah and Amir Xolani but is an ardent supporter of Ydeban independence. The Bhengani house color is purple. Their sigil is a white crocodile.

<u>Himoto</u>: the family's matriarch is Duqa Sachiko. She governs the city of Kasu on behalf of the shah and Amir Navin. Their color is white. Their sigil is a black crab.

<u>Iherjirika</u>: the family rules Ydeba Province on behalf of the shah while residing in Membiti. The important family members are Amir Xolani, and his daughter

and heir Duqa Adanna. Their color is orange; their sigil is two spears crossed between bull horns.

<u>Nakano</u>: the family's important members are Amira Jin, Duqa Iseul, and their young daughter Duqa Myeong. They rule Kaitan Province from the city of Inaza on behalf of the shah. Their color is black. Their sigil is a silver, white, and blue fish leaping out of water. House Nakano and House Neredi are both allies and good friends, particularly Amira Jin and Sayida Loralee.

<u>Neredi</u>: the family consists of Duq Alaziz, Duqa Jasira, and their daughter Sayida Loralee. They rule the city of Abadan on behalf of Amir Olumide and the shah. Their color is pale blue. Their sigil is an antelope mid-leap.

<u>MISCELLANEOUS</u>

A

<u>Achkan</u>: a knee length jacket

<u>Agal</u>: a banded accessory which keeps a ghutrah on the wearer's head

<u>Akhenit</u>: the coin currency of Shai'Khal. It comes in copper, silver, and gold denominations, with each type clipped differently.

<u>Anarkali Suit</u>: a floor length dress

<u>Araq</u>: an alcoholic anise drink, usually served two parts alcohol and one part water, into a frozen cup

<u>Ashik</u>: a professional storyteller

B

<u>Baladi</u>: a dance focused on hip movements, with little use of the arms performed to folk music

<u>Bayan</u>: a respectful title with which to address a woman

<u>Bayim</u>: a respectful title with which to address a man

C

<u>Chador</u>: a full body length cloak worn by women

<u>Charpai</u>: a woven, elevated bed

<u>Choli</u>: a blouse which leaves the midriff bare

<u>Chotli</u>: an ornate golden chain that covers braided wedding hair for women

D

<u>Desmoterion</u>: a prison

<u>Devata</u>: the animal companion of a Pantheon God, they double as spies for their god

<u>Dhal</u>: A small to medium sized round shield

G

<u>Ganjifa</u>: a card game

<u>Ghul</u>: the least powerful class of djinn
<u>Ghutrah</u>: a cloth headcover for men
H

<u>Hakama</u>: a seven pleated style of trousers
<u>Haori</u>: a thigh length kimono-style jacket
I

<u>Ifrit</u>: a powerful djinn, generally with blue eyes. It is a creature of fire.
K

<u>Kaftan</u>: a robe worn by men or women. Some styles are used as an overcoat
<u>Kameez</u>: a long tunic
<u>Katana</u>: a slightly curved, single-edged sword
<u>Katar</u>: a push dagger with an H-shaped hand grip
<u>Khalat</u>: a long coat
<u>Khanjar</u>: a curved dagger
<u>Kufiyah</u>: a cloth headcover for men long enough to tie across the face to protect the wearer from sun and sand.
<u>Kujaree</u>: mid-level priest of the Akhenic Faith
<u>Kusari</u>: chain armor
L

<u>Lily</u>: often used as a slur against anyone with overly pale skin hinting at Aegalian heritage.
<u>Lotus Flowers</u>: a name for prostitutes
M

<u>Mabkhara</u>: an incense burner varying in size from small enough to fit on a coffee table to obelisks.
<u>Maman</u>: an affectionate term for 'mother'
<u>Matagi</u>: large dogs bred for hunting bear and boar, they have curly tails and thick coats
<u>Mawla</u>: The respectful title given to religious figures, particularly the High Priest of Akhenios.
<u>Mortoha</u>: undead creatures made by necromancy with a ravenous hunger for flesh
N

<u>Naginata</u>: a pole weapon with a long blade on the end
<u>Niqaab</u>: a headcover with a veil for women
P

<u>Pito</u>: a watered down type of beer generally consumed by the poor.
Q

Qasbah: a fortress
Quorum: an assembly of the most powerful people in Shai'Khal to make important political decisions, such as name the next Shah or begin a war.
R

Rakshasas: an immortal creature associated with Ikharon. They drink blood and can change shape from their monstrous form into one that passes as human.
Rising Sun Throne: the seat of power in Shai'Khal.
S

Salwar: a loose fitting trouser worn by men and women.
Sardar: the highest Shai'Khal military rank
Sari: a long, draping cloth wrapped around a woman in many different styles usually leaving the midriff bare.
Setar: a three string musical instrument
Shahbanu: the title for a woman shah instead of 'Shahanshah'
Shai'Khal Calendar: There are four seasons within the Shai'Khal calendar
> Monsoon Months: Skyth, Du'ith, Amanith
> First Harvest: Tavith, Ayurith, Vindith
> Dry Season: Belith, Livith, Nadith
> Second Harvest: Kerith, Hisith, Amith

Shamshir: a sword with a thin, curved blade (more exaggerated towards the tip than a katana) used primarily by the Yahidah and cavalry officers.
Shatranj: a boardgame played by two players.
Spahi: a cavalry officer
Sringa: a long curved horn made in either an 'S' or 'C' shape.

ACKNOWLEDGEMENTS

"This would be a great book, if you actually wrote it."

I'm paraphrasing, but that was one of the greatest criticisms given by my husband, Rob Stanton, when he read the first half of my original manuscript. Conventional advice is never hand off your book to your family for beta reading. I am forever grateful that Rob is a partner not afraid of telling me hard truths in the most hilarious way possible. You can blame him for the length of this book, but you can credit him for the fleshed-out characters and proper story. I didn't think I could do it. Thank you, Rob, for pushing me out of my comfort zone. And for doing the dishes.

Thank you to Noelle and Tristan Riley, and to Chris Dickey, for always being incredible sounding boards for ideas. Thank you to Noelle for finding all the little (and sometimes not-so-little) grammar abominations within the second draft. Perhaps most importantly, thank you Noelle for enabling my coffee addiction.

Pikko's House, in particular Crystal Watanabe, did an excellent editing job. The dark little plot issues that I couldn't figure out how to fix were easily illuminated by Crystal. Plus, there were cookies. Delicious Hawaiian cookies. Thank you. Any grammar errors found within this book are entirely my fault and should be congratulated for sticking around.

I worked with several amazing artists on the road to publication. Tarmo Juhola did the beautiful main website art, and Randy Hagmann drew the various black & white line arts. Last, but far from least, Nele Diel designed and painted our cover art. These incredible artists have brought Shai'Khal to life.

To Chip Bradford, Alexa Adams, and the mysterious EarlySpark for their patronage. It means so much to have your support. Having a reliable income while working on *The Gods Chronicle* projects has helped give me peace of mind.

Thank you to Mom and Dad for always fostering my creativity. I may have been nervous to share with you what I wrote at first, but your support has meant the world to me.

Without Kasey Leath, I would have given up on writing a decade ago. She renewed my passion for the art and kept stoking it with *just one more post*.

ABOUT THE AUTHOR

L.J. Stanton grew up in Alberta, Canada. She moved to the United States and now lives in Orange County, California with her husband. Together they have two dogs, Boo the Shiba Inu, and Chekov the service dog.

If you loved Merikh, Loralee, Nikias, and others, short stories are released periodically on Patreon at www.patreon.com/ljstanton . Current stories include the death of Merikh's mother, and Loralee discovering the betrothal.

Sign up for our monthly newsletter *The Household* at www.swordandboard.gg